# THE WILD IRISES

## S. J. Richfield

To Evin,

With best wishes,
Sheila Richfield

**The Wild Irises**
Copyright © S. J. Richfield 2015

ISBN: 978-1-326-40436-9

PublishNation, London
www.publishnation.co.uk

*To Adrian, for his tireless encouragement, reading and listening.*

*To my lovely daughters and their families:*
*Pippa, Mark and Freddie*
*Charlie, Dan and Leah*

# THE SOURCE

## Chapter 1

The truth about Great-Aunt Silvie was one of my family's best-kept secrets - her life was one of concealment and she departed this world in silence. She slipped away without disturbing the peace of the night but as she released her last breath, round her arose a white flame surrounded by an aura of gold - fire and light – which in seconds dispersed, leaving a dark blue after-image.

Earlier that day, while the priest heard her confession, I had wandered through the gardens of Castle Rise, the nursing home in which she had lived for more than thirty years. I'd watched as pale pink cherry blossom quivered against the azure sky of a cold spring afternoon and thought how I had grown to admire Silvie, not only her intelligence, erudition and spirited nature but her determination not to be rendered invisible by the Armsted's tendency to redact those people or events they regarded as unsatisfactory.

I held her hand as she was anointed with oil and saw how her face cleared. The anxious expression she had worn all day had disappeared and she lay back to rest, white haired, pale, against the fresh linen of her bed, her rosary of olive wood and silver twined through her thin, gnarled fingers.

When the priest left, she slept peacefully for several hours until something unseen and unheard startled her awake. Her grey eyes searched mine, clear and piercing, 'I've forgiven them all,' she said and laughed softly, a low sound in her chest - no more than the whisper of water running underground.

I leant forward to kiss her cool forehead. Touching the rosary caught fast in her hands, I knelt with my head on my arms, feeling the small mound of her wasted legs beneath the bedcover - *how useless those limbs had been, how unable to support her.*

In a short while, one of the nurses looked in, disturbing the quietness and stillness of the room.

'She's gone...' I said, but I had no tears, only a dry, hollowed-out sensation.

'Should I call anyone?' she asked.

I shook my head. Through the window, I could see dawn breaking - tender pink and yellow in a dove grey sky - it was too soon for the prosaic rites of death to begin.

The sun rose, warming the garden. From Silvie's window was visible the fountain soaring from its round stone basin, its plume of water flying upward catching the soft sunlight. Silvie had once written, *the secrets of our being are like water – they emerge from an underground source, become a spring and then flow outward to become a river or an ocean.* Her words had inspired me. Her philosophy, filled with energy and hope, had been an antidote to the belief in chaos and fragmentation which I had inherited from my parents and which seemed to have shaped my existence, whether I ascribed to it or not.

Silvie's wheelchair, usually folded by the bookcase, had been taken away. The room and the remaining things that had once belonged to her seemed diminished by her passing. Opposite her bed, hung a painting by her father, Bernard Armsted, a landscape of Clave Valley on Littern Island, where in spring, wild blue irises grew in such profusion they flowed down the hillside like a brook. A place of such loveliness, Silvie had said - that not even her father had been able to do it justice.

I lifted the painting down from the wall, there was a note taped to the frame at the back, giving her final instructions. *Iris - Don't stay in Esterlea for my funeral – go home to your family.* Silvie had been nothing if not direct.

She had first written to me at a time when I had lost all faith in my life and belief in myself. I'd longed for love, a safe home for my children, the freedom to work and be happy, but found instead I was alone and steeped in regrets. Silvie's faith, her trust, had poured out to me – somehow, she had known a small gesture can change a life forever. She had encouraged me to return to Littern - against all instinct – when for me the serenity of the island had been shattered by tragedy and Marisands, the family home, had become a place of mourning.

The task she presented had set me on a journey. Seeking the truth of my mother's death, I examined correspondence, books, paintings, photographs and diaries, listened to hearsay and uncovered threads of connection woven into an intricate web of lies.

Often, I felt lost, as if standing between two mirrors, where images streamed backwards and forwards and with each step I took expecting to move into the future - I found I had retreated into the past.

Silvie was confident the facts, however painful, would be liberating. She had come to believe that the family's long-cherished secrets exerted a powerful and destructive influence, that unsolved mysteries should be brought into the light, where they could no longer do harm.

In her note, Silvie had asked that her ashes should be scattered in Clave Valley - the willow tree on the hillside had special meaning for her.

We had loved one another in a simple way, overcoming the many years which divided us in age. So when I returned to the island, I would cross Littern in the footsteps of her father. My walk would mark the end of our story, just as Bernard's had marked the beginning. His encounter with the island was the source of all that ensued, of the hidden things which had determined the lives of succeeding generations – intruding not only on Silvie's existence, but on mine.

*

In April 1898, my great-grandfather, Bernard Armsted, ran away from his home in the Potteries, hoping to escape the career his father had chosen for him as manager of *Parfit China and Glass*. As the only son, he would be the inheritor of the family business - his father pointed out that Bernard had a duty – an argument backed up with threats of cutting him off financially, if he persisted with his lunatic idea of becoming a painter.

Bernard had read of the beauty of the West Country landscape and over the next few weeks, he walked south, arriving in Devon in May, when wild flowers jewelled the banks and gorse blossom swathed the landscape with gold.

From Bideford, he made his way to Safford Bridge, a small market town renowned for the crocuses which lined its river banks in spring and for St. Safan's Priory, founded in the thirteenth century by an order of Augustinian monks. In a further nine miles, his ramblings took him to the picturesque seaside resort of Narescombe, with its steep wooded hills, horseshoe harbour and seafront hotel. From there, rather than retracing his steps, locals suggested he take a route through the hamlet of Osford and continue his journey towards Bude by joining a track which wound its way westward along the coastline.

An inexperienced walker, heavy in build, Bernard had set out wearing a pair of tough leather boots he'd scarcely broken in. The idea of avoiding an arduous climb appealed to him, especially when a short level hike would bring him to a farmhouse where he could spend a day or two at little expense, allowing the blisters on his feet to heal.

After a morning exploring the narrow streets of Narescombe, he left the main square of the town by Osford Lane and before long encountered a band of gypsies, who offered him – as a fellow traveller - a lift on one of their horse-drawn carts. They were making their way to an area of common land, where they would spend the summer and seek work on the surrounding farmland.

The lane ran the length of a broad peninsula, Palk's Reach. Passing beneath an archway of trees, the road was rough and rutted, but in less than an hour they left Osford with its scattering of low white cottages and Bernard reckoned the jolting of his body as the cart rattled along was less painful than if he had been forced to make his way on foot.

The overarching trees grew less dense and the road descended into a deep hollow before rising once more and entering a further wooded stretch of land. Bernard asked to alight from the gypsies' cart when he spotted the house, Whitcroft, a single dwelling, isolated from the rest of the hamlet. From there, a left turn along a clearly marked footpath brought him to his destination, Yew Tree Farm, where he would seek food, rest and hospitality.

That night, Bernard was the only guest at the Farm. He was served dinner in the front parlour, overlooking the gully in the road across which the gypsies had continued towards their camp.

While he ate, he gazed out of the window and became aware of an unexpected phenomenon. A current of water flowed rapidly into the gully, until in a few minutes, the road had become impassable and the body of land where the gypsies had gone was cut off from the peninsula by an expanse of open sea.

The farmer's wife explained that for centuries Littern had been a tidal island, though no-one seemed to know when it had broken free from the mainland. Some said the fracture had been caused by a violent storm or an act of God, others claimed that the natural reshaping of the coastline meant the sea had encroached, separating farms from their fields and making it necessary to know the time of high tide in order to cross the causeway safely.

Browsing through the farmhouse bookshelves, Bernard discovered a slim volume entitled *The Legends and History of Littern Island*. Cheap paper and the fuzziness of the photographs didn't do justice to the writer's determination to achieve accuracy on the subjects of geography, topography and social history, but fascinated by what he had learned, Bernard decided to borrow the booklet. In the morning he would explore the island, which had, by now, exerted a firm grip on his imagination.

Though he came from a family of bluff Midlanders, Bernard was at heart a romantic. Littern Island was a place of natural beauty with fern-covered hills, marshes, mudflats, wide sandy beaches, cliffs, rocks and an abundance of wildlife - but his interest lay in the hidden places, Clave Valley, where the wild blue iris grew and the holy well associated

4

with the legend of St. Thrif, said to have been beheaded in the island's woods.

Touched by the plight of a vulnerable woman, Bernard read and re-read the legend. Thrif, an orphan, had been put into service in the house of a nobleman only to be taken advantage of by his eldest son. A pious girl, who before her misfortune had only one desire - to enter a convent - Thrif was deeply ashamed at finding herself pregnant and escaped from the nobleman's house, setting out on a pilgrimage in the belief she could expiate her sins. As she journeyed, she prayed she would find a community of nuns who might take pity on her and permit her to be of service to them in some humble way.

Discovering her absence and fearing disgrace for his son, the nobleman sent three men of his household to pursue and kill her. Spurring their horses on, they caught up with Thrif after a shepherd informed them he had seen a lone woman making her way towards the woodlands beyond Narescombe.

Thrif had crossed the gully at Osford, having learned of a convent in a position of great seclusion on the island. Hurrying along the narrow track, hoof beats pounding behind her, she took refuge among the trees. In her haste and panic, she disturbed the scrubby bushes that bordered the road and left a remnant of cloth from her skirt, snagged on a thorn.

As they drew near, her stumbling progress through the woods was heard by the men, whose senses were sharpened by the excitement of the chase. Before she could take cover, Thrif tripped on a branch in the undergrowth and fell to the ground, where she lay gasping for breath among the brambles and bracken.

She had lost the will or strength to crawl into hiding and waited in terror for the death blow to be struck. Certain her life was to be ended, she cried aloud in prayer, and at that moment, the Virgin Mary appeared to her, dressed not in her traditional blue clothing, but in a pure white robe.

Thrif raised her face towards the vision. Taking his opportunity, the foremost of the men struck off her head, deaf to his companions' warnings of the dangers of desecrating the church land on which the girl had taken sanctuary.

Where Thrif's blood ran into the earth, a fountain of water with healing powers sprung up and her head was miraculously restored. White hellebores flowered in the glade where she had been wounded and were to become her emblem. Her special patronage was for sufferers of mental distress, who found relief from drinking at the well, reputed to have its strongest powers in July, which would become the month of her feast-day.

The author of *The Legends and History* didn't flinch from the moral and spiritual dimensions of the island, but made it clear there could be no certainty St. Thrif had ever lived or that her legend contained more than a grain of truth. What could be established was that an abandoned property on the island, known as The Retreat, had once been a convent - and perched on the cliffs above Whitcroft Cove, near a row of ruined fishermen's cottages, stood a stone hut believed to be a hermitage or oratory.

Thrif's unborn child hadn't survived and it was said she had spent the remainder of her life there, living in prayerful isolation and encouraging good works in the local community. In a niche above the oratory door stood the weather-beaten statue of a woman with shorn hair, holding her head under her arm. This was revered by local people as a figure of the saint and over the years a cult had developed around sightings of The White Virgin in Thrifswell Woods.

The next morning, armed with the rough sketch map at the front of the booklet, Bernard embarked on a search for the holy well and Clave Valley. Littern Island was served by a single road, with paths and dirt tracks leading off to give access to Osford Chapel, the marshland between Hagdon Hills and the beaches at Whitcroft Cove and Morrow Bay.

When she handed him his packed lunch, the farmer's wife warned him to avoid the treacherous marshes and to pay close attention to the times of the tides. She mentioned a recent incident of drowning and described how powerful currents could sweep an inexperienced swimmer far out to sea where no-one would hear their cries for help.

On a warm, bright morning, alive with birdsong and buzzing with the hum of insects, such dangers were furthest from Bernard's mind. As he made the climb up Holtleigh Hill towards the highest point on the island, he noted ancient beech trees, a number of fine oaks and the yellow lichen and fresh green moss growing on stones and branches. The roadside was studded with a profusion of pink and white Campion flowers, mauve periwinkles, golden yellow dandelions and buttercups and he could hear the gentle whispering of the sea as it broke on the distant shore.

Bernard reached a disused farmhouse, its name, Lyncross, marked clearly on the gatepost. The lane was at its summit and he could look down on the marshlands nestled between two cup-shaped hillocks and a white building, perhaps the convent of which the booklet had spoken. Against the skyline, on the seaward hill, was a circular stone tower reputed to have been used by wreckers. His map was marked with a cross below the foot of the tower showing the way into Clave Valley, though from his vantage point, Bernard could see no sign of the narrow fold of land it suggested was there. To the south, the hillsides consisted of unbroken meadowland, while to the north they dissolved into rough grass and dunes, giving tantalising glimpses of a beach with unblemished white sands.

The iron gates of Lyncross had been padlocked and as the drive made a sharp curve, little of the farmhouse could be seen through the trees, except a small corner of its grey stone walls and slate roof. Bernard walked the perimeter of the garden, following the high laurel hedge that marked its borders. Finding no place where he could easily trespass, he gave up and continued a further half mile along the lane until he found a clearing where he could force his way into the woods, beating down brambles and nettles that blocked his way with a stout stick he had picked up from the ground.

Littern Island was a place where it was difficult to get lost, but which offered many places to hide and he might never have found the holy well if he hadn't heard the thrumming sound of wings and seen a flash of white as a heron took off through the tree tops, suggesting a body of water must be nearby.

Bernard trod down a path towards a small glade where a standing stone marked the source of the well. Into a moss covered basin, pure, clear water bubbled up from beneath the earth - water reputed by pilgrims to cure disturbances of the mind. The spring rippled down through a rocky channel to form a wide pool so tranquil its surface mirrored a perfect image of the green leaves and ragged patches of blue sky overhead.

Bernard knelt to wash his face and met his own reflection: a ruddy-faced young man, eyes narrowed by the fleshiness of his cheeks, brown haired and with a thin moustache sprouting on his upper lip. He drank long and deep from the well, scooping the cool water into his cupped hands. Then he rested on a rock ledge above the pool, while he ate his sandwiches, entranced by silvery music like that of a flute, floating above the crystal notes of the tumbling stream.

The sketch Bernard made that afternoon would become his first painting of the island, *St. Thrif's Holy Well*. Later in life, when his story had become apocryphal, he would claim his visit to Littern had marked the onset of his artistic career. In his work, he had managed to capture the spirit of place – the striking contrasts of the white bird and the dark woods, the still pool and the trees trembling above the water in the sea breeze.

The sun was at its height as Bernard returned to the lane. Keeping the tower in his sights, he began the long descent to the sea. At first, the trees cast a dappled shade, protecting him from the worst of the scorching heat, but as he drew close to the rim of the bay - his skin burned and his eyes ached with the blinding glare from the arc of white sand.

Where it drew level with The Retreat, the lane petered out. According to the farmer's wife, the building had become a home for orphaned children, run by the Church – yet not a single sound of children playing escaped from its open windows or disturbed its empty gardens.

With the tower looming above him, Bernard followed a narrow path, not much more than a sheep-track, towards the marshes. Consulting his map, he scrambled over the lower slopes of Hagdon Hills searching for Clave Valley. His feet suffered several soakings as he found himself mired in boggy ground, so he climbed the hill to the tower and finding the metal door open, ascended the winding steps to the roof, from where he had an unbroken view of the entire island.

When he turned to the south-west, he caught sight of a broad ribbon of purplish-blue flowers sweeping towards the marshes in long drifts. He hurried down the tower steps, slipping and sliding across the face of the hill, as if afraid the valley might elude him. His earlier explorations hadn't taken him far enough into the hills, so he continued until he met with a scrubby knoll of wind-sculptured trees. Dropping onto his hands and knees, Bernard crawled through the low brush, until at last he discovered a place where he could squeeze out into the open air -

Standing upright, he beheld a vision, dusky blue irises covering the grassy slopes in glorious profusion. The peace, the sequestered nature of the valley spoke to him. *The Legends and History* had suggested it had once been part of the extensive lands belonging to the convent, possibly the site of the nuns' Garden of Remembrance.

Bernard sat in the shade of a willow tree, high on the hillside – he couldn't possess the scene - but he hoped through the medium of his art to be able to capture it. Later, packing away his pad of paper and his pencils, he realised if he lingered in that mysterious place much longer he would almost certainly miss the tide. The shortest route back to the causeway was to retrace his steps and follow the stream down from the pool in Thrifswell Woods to where it ran out across the beach, a distance he reckoned of about three-quarters of a mile.

Arriving at the shore, his clothing torn and covered with leaves and twigs, he turned towards Osford, striding along the sands. Steep cliffs rose above him and he scanned the landscape for signs of the oratory, described in the booklet as perched on a rocky plateau above Whitcroft Cove.

He had soon reached the cove, only to be confronted by a jagged pyramid of rock, too daunting to climb and lapped by the incoming tide. When he glanced behind him, it was to find that the beach he had just traversed had been reduced to no more than a narrow strip of sea-weed draped rocks. Bernard pulled off his boots, rolled up his trouser legs and waded round the base of the pyramid - his heart racing as he discovered that the cove through which he had hoped to pass was now churning with white-crested, rolling waves.

From where he stood, up to his thighs in water, he could make out steps built into the cliff and about half way up, a rough stone hut, with a niche above the door. With his boots and haversack hoisted high above his head, he forged his way towards the foot of the steps and climbed to safety. Secure on the plateau, by the oratory door, he stared up at the statue of St. Thrif with her shorn head held under her arm and offered a prayer of thanks – grateful that he hadn't drowned.

Facing the sea, he surveyed the coast of the island. The woodland stretched like a spine from Palk's Reach as far as Morrow Bay offering some protection to a place exposed to westerly gales and the battering of the Atlantic.

Above him on the cliff top, white flowers grew within a small copse of silver birches suggesting there might once have been a garden – a single gravestone leant precariously over the cliff edge – was it possible St. Thrif had been buried there?

To Bernard, Littern appeared a haven of tranquillity pounded by the elements - a contradiction which struck him as sublime. Yet like many wanderers who make their way to the island, that night, he would find himself stranded, forced to remain with the birds and animals which made their home in an enchanted place largely unknown to the rest of mankind.

*

A cold night on a hard wooden bench in the oratory didn't cure Bernard of his intrigue with the place, but only confirmed that the island with its mixture of earthiness and mystery would compel his return.

His desire wouldn't be fulfilled until thirteen years later, when in 1911 he brought his young bride, Yvette Moreau, to live there. They had met while living in Paris and he had fallen in love with her petite figure and dark good looks, offset by a delicious hint of Gallic wit and vivacity.

Yvette had grown up in a small town on the west coast of Brittany. She yearned for the sea, the grey stone, the blues and greens of the Finistere landscape to be rediscovered in England and eager to please the woman he loved, Bernard had enquired about Lyncross, the empty farmhouse he'd encountered on his memorable walk across Littern.

By the time of his marriage, Bernard was successful as a painter and though his father disapproved both of his wife and his profession, he had inherited money from an uncle. With his new-found wealth, Bernard planned to make certain improvements to the island's landscape, such as opening the way to Clave Valley. In addition to Lyncross, he intended to purchase The Retreat - the orphanage was for sale – and he would run it as a lodge for artists, birdwatchers and naturalists who visited the island. Having taken over the island's property, he earned the title locally "King of Littern" and whether that epithet was intended by his neighbours as mocking or affectionate, Bernard enjoyed modest celebrity as monarch of his tiny kingdom.

My mother said that though he was gruff and stern in old age, as a young man, Bernard had been kind-hearted and generous. In many ways, he was the quintessential Englishman of his time – patriotic and proud, whiskered and well-upholstered - not averse to conspicuous displays of wealth, such as the fine French piano he bought Yvette as a wedding gift.

He also had a strong sense of duty, understanding and practising the art of philanthropy. According to family lore, during his negotiations for the purchase of The Retreat, it had come to Bernard's attention that two or three of the orphaned children had failed to find homes. One of them, a baby girl, had crippled legs, but her pale face and enormous grey eyes had captivated him. He couldn't forget the child and troubled by his conscience, determined to adopt her. Yvette, so far, had failed to bless them with offspring and when she saw the helpless infant, he was certain she would agree to his proposal.

The girl, named Silvie, proved to be sickly. Doctors advised that the child would never walk and Yvette, repelled by her obvious imperfections, had taken the news badly. Of a more sanguine nature than his wife, Bernard refused to relent. With love and good nursing Silvie could lead a happy existence in the peaceful atmosphere of the island, and God willing, she would soon have brothers and sisters to provide her with suitable companionship.

Bernard's reputation as a landscape painter continued to grow and Yvette's miniatures were prized among local wealthy families and dignitaries. Despite his father's misgivings, Bernard would contribute three designs to the family business, successfully saving *Parfit China and Glass* from financial disaster by bringing their products in line with modern taste. *Wildflowers, Marshlands* and *Seaspray* - all inspired by Littern – would remain the most popular lines until the firm closed its doors, for the last time, in the early 1960's. But before long, Bernard became aware he had overestimated his talent as an entrepreneur and after a brief period The Retreat was sold back to the Church, who would make use of it as a home for unmarried mothers.

Yvette and Bernard went on to have two healthy daughters, though they produced no son. Yvette had proved not to be a good breeder. The birth of Alice drained her strength and Flora, though she would become a gifted portraitist, was said to be fey, or "not quite right" by those who observed her sensitive nature.

Despite her eccentricities, it was Flora, rather than Alice, who Bernard trusted. Alice was a prim, upright child inclined to absolute belief in her moral duty, which included informing her mother of her father's intentions, when they failed to meet with her approval. Quiet and biddable, Flora was to accompany her father to London, where he would purchase books and seek a suitable tutor for Silvie, who had a keen, enquiring mind. Silvie's physical disadvantages meant she didn't attend school and was unlikely to marry. A good education, he reasoned, would bring her pleasure and occupy empty hours when the more active members of the household were busy.

Silvie's relationship with her father and Flora had quickly matured into affection; she had a warm, open nature and seemed eager to overcome the apparent indifference with which she had been treated during the early part of her life. Her father's faith in her intelligence and her capacity to learn had strengthened the bond between them and as Yvette was unable to cope, apart from her most intimate needs, it was Bernard who looked after her. When she became too tall for him to carry any distance on his back, he created a special chair for Silvie, a basket lined with plump cushions and set on wheels, which he used to take her about the island, pulling her along the lane, so he could show her the hidden places, such as Thrifswell Woods, the holy well and Clave Valley.

The years passed and Alice grew resentful of the repeated favours shown to her sisters, particularly her invalid "sister", who stole all her father's attention. Always studious, Alice became a teacher of history and French at the local convent school, where she was known as "the demon dictator", while, Flora, dreamy and impractical, attracted what in her sister's view, was undeserved notice from a following of naive young men.

Bernard's trips away from the island had continued. Silvie was an avid reader and her thirst for new books was difficult to assuage - Flora, he claimed, derived benefit from visiting galleries, where he had the opportunity to expand her knowledge and appreciation of art.

He was naturally expected to act as Flora's chaperone on their trips to London. So it was surprising when he couldn't account for how she had managed to find herself alone in the company of a man long enough for them to fall in love and resolve to marry - an arrangement, which if disgrace was to be avoided, would prove to be essential.

Silent, at first, on the subject of her embarrassing situation, Flora then offered a tale, which the family dismissed as gibberish, an unlikely story about the grandson of a Russian émigré, who she had met at an exhibition in London. The Armsteds preferred to concoct their own explanation - Flora must have been taken advantage of while out for a walk - gypsies camped on the island in summer - tramps took shelter under the island's hedges or in the caves which pitted the cliffs near the oratory. Given her natural modesty, it was supposed she had been too shocked and ashamed to confide in either her mother or her sisters. She suffered from overwhelming feelings of sympathy and might have taken pity on some poor man in need of comfort - the sort of comfort which in her ignorance of the possible consequences had landed her in serious trouble.

Bernard, normally protective of the family's honour, attempted no recourse for his daughter's condition, neither did he send her away. He withdrew, as Flora was required to do, from any society beyond the island and remained on Littern with his wife, to whom his shrinking from the outside world made little difference – by then, she rarely ventured beyond the gates of Lyncross. His restrained response to Flora's dilemma would soon demonstrate his wisdom, as in the nick of time she produced the living, breathing presence of Alexander Martin, the man she had met in London. Saved from embarrassment, the family breathed a sigh of relief. Hasty arrangements were made and the couple were married at All Souls Church, Narescombe - four months before my mother, Juliet, was born.

To begin with, the newly-weds lived at Lyncross, until Flora confided in Silvie that Yvette had no patience with Alexander or the new baby. For their mother, home was no longer the place of respite she needed to keep her attacks of anxiety at bay; some resolution was needed.

Silvie spoke to her father and realising that his own happiness depended on the well-being of his womenfolk, Bernard decided to build a house on the island for Flora and to renovate one of the fishermen's cottages near the oratory for Alice. He was old-fashioned, though not unfeeling and despite his strenuous efforts on her behalf, Alice had shown no sign of getting married, seeming to prefer the company of her colleague and friend at school, Edith Pearson, to the eligible young men he presented to her.

Flora's new home, Marisands, was a white walled, slate–roofed house with a studio designed by M.J. Butler, the "architect of light". Clear north light poured down through high windows, unfiltered by the woodland that sheltered the rest of the garden. In the branches of a beech tree nearby was The Robin's Nest – it was to be a playhouse for Juliet where she could occupy herself, leaving Flora free to concentrate on her painting.

The long T-shaped garden of Marisands was divided by a rose covered pergola. Behind it, stood Thrift Cottage - named for the pink sea-thrift, which lined the nearby pathway leading down to the cove. Alice felt once again, Bernard had openly favoured Flora. She described the cottage as little better than a peasant's hovel and wrote in a letter to Edith, "for once I am going to rebel". Her rebellion would be a small one. She refused to share the facilities of Marisands and insisted her father should equip Thrift Cottage so she could enjoy complete independence. Rather than find herself beholden to her sister, she preferred to make her meals in the tiny kitchen Bernard installed and to bathe in a tin bath in front of the fire, while the sound of the sea crashing against the shore, as if against the foundations of her home, upset her normally unshakeable nerves.

The two houses had been intended by Bernard to provide his daughters with a sense of permanence and security, but when Yvette died in 1952, he found Littern's many associations with his wife melancholy and decided to leave the island for Dulwich, where his mother's family had long-standing connections.

Bernard's reign as King of Littern was over. Now in his early seventies, he could no longer be expected to care for Silvie. Though Flora seemed unlikely to be a competent nurse, her husband, Alexander, was a down-to-earth man, a carpenter, and Juliet, at twelve, didn't require much looking after. With modifications to Marisands, and with help from Alice, Alexander was sure they could manage. Silvie would provide Flora with female company, when his trade took him, as it frequently did, over to the mainland.

The work at Marisands was soon completed - widening doorways and adapting a ground floor room – and within months, Bernard had left the island and Silvie moved in with her sister. Lyncross was bought by a Dr. Edgar Piran and his wife, who were in need of a large property to accommodate their five children and their ward, James Millford, whose family - farmers in Kenya - had with their two youngest children been slaughtered during a native uprising.

Questioned by Alice about their new neighbours, Bernard remarked that though there was Irish blood in their background, the Pirans appeared respectable. Given the relative proximity of Lyncross to Marisands and the seclusion of Littern, he was certain that the lives of the two families would in the future - to their mutual benefit - become inextricably entwined.

# Chapter 2

Flora's portraits of my mother show her pale face framed by u.
brown hair, her heavy fringe accentuating the largeness of her clear
grey eyes. She had been gifted by the fairies, Flora declared, having
brains, beauty and a natural ability to break down resistance in those
who tried to prevent her from having her own way.

Yet, three years after the Pirans' arrival on the island, Juliet had
faced a serious disappointment. During the last war, her father,
Alexander, against his natural inclinations, had been required to join the
army. Introspective and gentle, he had been unsuited to the life of a
soldier, being overwhelmed by fear and revulsion at his own actions
and those of his fellow men. His painful memories had refused to
subside and the result was a breakdown. Whereas he had once longed to
desert the army, he now deserted his family, taking off from Littern as
suddenly and mysteriously as he had first appeared.

With Alexander gone, Flora became more unhinged and Alice
grasped the opportunity to move into Marisands - she'd had enough of
living rough in a cottage which was "not much bigger than a dolls'
house". According to her, Silvie was suffering gross neglect and as
Flora was incapable of exerting discipline, Juliet was becoming nothing
better than an extremely spoiled child.

Determined to cure Juliet's tendency to brood on her father's
absence, Alice confiscated her most prized possession, a carved wooden
box given to her by Alexander. Inside, she had kept the small figure he
had fashioned of the White Virgin, and his rosary, which was made of
smooth, black glass beads, mottled with points of light, like stars in a
night sky.

Juliet was lonely, but contact with the Piran children was
discouraged by Alice. There were too many boys in the family and the
daughter, Beatrix, could have been male, as she imitated her brothers'
exploits in a way utterly devoid of the graces of femininity. The
family's belief, that in the hierarchy of the island, a Piran might be
equal to an Armsted was reprehensible - as her father had done - Alice
took pride in the family name and Bernard's former status as King of
Littern had made a powerful and lasting impression.

Timing their journeys according to the tides, Juliet cycled to school
and home again with Alice. Alice had also taken charge of Silvie's care,

ile Flora filled her life with painting, arousing her sister's anger. "I have to do everything," she said.

Despite Alice's displeasure, the new arrangement of accommodation at Marisands continued and if not exactly happy, suited everyone, until, in time Bernard's health had begun to fail. Rather than employ a stranger, he insisted Alice should to move to Dulwich and nurse him into his old age.

Many reasonable arguments were put forward, but Flora was determined to stay on the island with Silvie. Alice thought caring for an invalid and the upkeep of a house were beyond anything Flora could manage - she chided her sister - she had been favoured by her father, yet was unwilling to help now he had become sick and frail. When she could find a chance to speak, Silvie reminded Alice that she could assist Flora – the fact she was in a wheelchair didn't mean she couldn't dust, iron and do simple cooking. If she was unconvinced, Alice became resigned, she would go to London as her father required, leaving the two of them to sink into unutterable chaos at Marisands.

As my mother grew up, she made acceptable progress at school in those subjects which interested her and developed a passion for classical ballet. With Alice gone, the rules had relaxed and Juliet befriended the Piran boys, Antony and Tom. With James Millford, the Piran's ward, she belonged to a dance and drama group in Narescombe, which encouraged their shared ambition to achieve a future career on the London stage.

Juliet's newfound friendships meant greater contact between the two families and though she missed her husband, Flora developed a fondness for Edgar Piran with his Irish charm and twinkling, dark-blue eyes. Reclusive, diffident, she expressed her feelings only through concern for his wife's fragile health and an interest in their robust, adventurous children. A little in love with Edgar herself, Silvie had allowed her no misconceptions - Edgar was devoted to his wife, a woman whose charm and elegance was beyond anything either of them could hope to attain.

Flora must have sensed change was coming. She wouldn't be able to confine her daughter to the island forever and she began to paint Juliet in locations all over Littern, until capturing her likeness on canvas had become an obsession and she directed all her attention towards images of my mother, paying little heed to the activities of the actual young woman.

At the age of seventeen, Juliet announced her intention to go to London and attend ballet school in fulfilment of her childhood dreams. She was tall, slender and long-limbed - she knew she had a gift. When she danced, she moved with fluid grace - when she was still, she was perfectly poised. She was also strong-willed and refused to settle until arrangements were made for her to attend auditions and in due time she was accepted by the establishment of her choice. Though distraught at the prospect of losing her, Flora understood her ambition and as Silvie had pointed out, Juliet's friends, Antony and James, would be moving to London that year and it was understandable if a lively young woman thought she might be bored on Littern, with no-one for company but her disabled aunt and her delicate mother.

Given Juliet's determination, it seemed inexplicable, when in the spring, only months before her life as a dancer was due to commence, she suddenly changed her mind. She told Flora she would prefer to study painting, though what hadn't altered was her desire to live in London, where Antony and James, like older brothers, would look out for her welfare.

The news of her altered plans reached Dulwich, where Bernard offered lodgings at his home, Wren House, and said he would exert his influence with the head of the art faculty at the local college, where Juliet proposed to test her vocation. Arrangements were quickly made - Juliet would be a late-comer, joining the Fine Art course after the Easter holidays. Bernard had found the college eager to agree, when the proposal was backed up by the donation of a large painting of the South Downs - a permanent gift - to be hung in a prominent position in their main foyer.

*

Juliet left the seclusion of her life on the island, recording in her diary that she felt as if she were a wild flower transplanted from its natural environment. In London, she had entered a world where a wave of social and sexual revolution was gathering momentum.

She would always maintain that my father, Willem Muys, fell in love with her at first sight. A student in his life drawing class, he'd told her she was the loveliest creature in the room, more beautiful than the models with their white, jellyfish bodies. A Dutchman, William, spoke with a rolling, guttural accent - he had straw blonde hair and pale blue eyes, a striking contrast to the dark loveliness my mother had inherited from Yvette. Her chestnut hair tumbled about her shoulders and framed her pale oval face, bringing out flecks of gold in her clear, grey eyes. If William was all ice, she was all fire, his coolness acting as a foil to her warmth and passion.

17

Flora had become increasingly detached from the realities of life and it fell to Alice and Bernard to raise questions about William. He was not only much older than Juliet - and her teacher - but was estranged from his family and had a reputation as a womaniser. He was a pacifist and Bernard, who in World War I had served in France as a war artist, found his resistance to the idea of defending his country weak-minded and effete. If that wasn't sufficient to make him an unsuitable choice, the man painted in a style so bizarre, that in Bernard's view his work could – and perhaps should - have landed him in a lunatic asylum.

Given the history of Flora's marriage, Bernard may have harboured fears that with Juliet it might prove to be a case of "like mother, like daughter". A fear found to be justified, when before she had completed the first term of her studies, Juliet confessed to her pregnancy and later, when asked, claimed to be in no doubt that William Muys was the father of her child.

Alice had taken charge of the situation and though she was a woman of strict moral rectitude, rather than remonstrating with my mother, acted in a way which seemed entirely reasonable. William had lost his job and in the natural course of events Juliet's condition would soon become obvious. It made sense to send them to Littern - the obscurity of the island meant it was the perfect place for their situation to be concealed, and they could take care of Silvie. Alice believed that the newly-weds' relationship wouldn't be enhanced by having Flora living in Thrift Cottage at the foot of Marisands' garden, as had been proposed, so without further consideration of her sister's feelings, Flora was instructed to move out of her home and to join her and Bernard, in Dulwich.

Alice's carefully conceived plan demonstrated ingenuity - and a dash of spite towards her sister – but she had underestimated Flora's love for Juliet and for the island. Flora resolved that if she couldn't live out the remainder of her life on Littern, she would make sure her daughter could. She asked Bernard if she might make a gift of Marisands to Juliet, an encouragement to my father not to renege on his promise of marriage, and a decision which was to result in Alice and Flora not speaking to one another for over five years.

My parents arrived on the island in August, during a violent summer storm. Sheet lightning filled the sky, rain lashed down, the wind snatched at the trees and howled round the roof and chimneys of Marisands. William, shocked and exhilarated by the ferocity of the weather, stood in Whitcroft Cove captivated by savagery, as waves hurled in from the Atlantic Ocean and thrashed the cliffs and rocks without mercy.

A Frisian, an islander by birth, he had experienced no qualms at the idea of moving to such a sequestered place. Marisands stood at the head of a large garden, it was comfortably furnished and equipped with an excellent studio, and in case further inducement was needed, Bernard was willing to pay him an allowance, until he could establish his career as a painter -

As Alice remarked, '...What more could he want? Only a greater fool than William could possibly have refused...'

William might have replied he would have preferred not to have the encumbrance of Silvie - but freed by Bernard's financial assistance from the need to find paid employment, he began to work earnestly on his paintings. Life had presented him with an opportunity to pursue his own interests and like a cuckoo in the nest he showed no remorse for Flora's eviction from her home or studio.

William soon settled, but Juliet's joy was to be tarnished as she became aware of the movements of Geraldine Ottley, an ex-colleague of her husband's from the art college in London. At the time they had moved to Littern, Geraldine had resigned her job and was now renting Whitcroft, the cottage which stood alone at the edge of the gully, across the causeway from the island. It had taken less than a month for Geraldine to appear at Marisands on the pretext of visiting William, and only slightly longer for Juliet to understand that though not living on the island, she intended to make her presence felt as a close neighbour.

My mother's response was to turn to Lyncross. The grey stone house stood like a stronghold on Holtleigh Hill - it reminded her of a fortress and seemed to offer shelter and safety. In the Pirans, she found a loving family to support and protect her and throughout the summer of her return, Juliet joined them on expeditions to Narescombe and Safford Bridge, for picnics on the beach and walks on the marshes as far as Beckhead Cliffs, where grey seals could be found swimming - and in fine weather there were views of an islet off the west coast, populated by puffins.

For Juliet, that autumn would be one of poignancy. Antony was to leave home for university in October, he would be studying Divinity, and James intended to take up his place at RADA. For months, they had looked forward to spending time in London together. Now she would be stranded on Littern with an unsympathetic husband and the prospect of a small child to look after, as well as her aunt. She envied her friends' freedom, their ability to shape their own destinies - as the year closed in, she busied herself preparing for her baby's arrival, but she could foresee a time when living on the island might cause her to feel just as

19

abandoned as when Alexander had left her in doubt of his love and uncertain about her future.

Noticing her low spirits, Edgar Piran encouraged Juliet to look forward to her confinement, if he observed any discrepancy in the date of her marriage and the expected arrival of her child, accustomed to the vagaries of human nature, he didn't mention it. Edgar was of the opinion that the process of childbirth went more easily for women who had taken plenty of exercise during pregnancy, a theory which would prove correct, when during the early hours of a snowy morning in December I entered the world in Silvie's bedroom at Marisands, without undue difficulty.

When she saw me, the midwife, a solid, red-haired Irish girl said, 'What a little moon-face.'

I had inherited my mother's milky complexion, my pale face surrounded by a thick halo of dark hair.

'I'm going to call her Thrif, after the island's saint,' Juliet said.

The midwife smiled at Silvie, who had come to see the new baby, 'What's wrong with Lucy? Today's her feast day,' she suggested and looked with pity on my mother. Sometimes the shock of giving birth for the first time turned a woman's head. 'Wait and ask your man,' she recommended, 'when he turns up, he's sure to have an opinion.'

Using Silvie's presence as an excuse, William had absented himself from the house, cycling through the wintry night to fetch Geraldine, who he thought could help Juliet until she was strong enough to resume her duties as a housewife. The evening's icy showers had become a blizzard and as my mother cradled me in her arms, she lay watching the snow drift thickly against the frame of the window.

The midwife was also anxious about the weather, but seeing my mother had no-one except an invalid to assist her, said, 'I'll wait with you - William has no choice but to come back before the tide turns.'

'It's already turned,' Silvie informed her, sharp-tongued, 'if you want to leave Littern tonight, you'd better go now...'

The midwife was young and inexperienced. She replied that she didn't want to be trapped overnight, but neither could she find peace of mind about leaving her charge alone in a remote place with a new baby and a woman in a wheelchair.

'Perhaps you would bring us tea...' Juliet said and the girl went to the kitchen.

While she was out of the room, my mother told Silvie, 'This is how it will be – me alone with the child and her father in the arms of his lover...'

Days passed, my mother moved upstairs and the temperature dropped so low that frost ferns grew across the inside of the bedroom window. My parents quarrelled about my name, as they would later quarrel about everything. William condemned "Thrif" as ridiculous, a name which would mark me out for teasing. Why not Frith, he argued, of which Thrif was almost certainly a bastardisation? Frith had connotations of peace and tranquillity; it wouldn't evoke thoughts of the saint's bloody martyrdom or of the White Virgin, a bland Christian substitute for the moon goddess, whose statue stood in the niche above the door of the oratory.

When my mother declined his suggestion, he offered Agnes, pronounced in the Dutch way – *Achness* - as if someone had sneezed. Juliet said, if it came to that, she would prefer Lucy or Luus - but my father took exception and countered with Isabel, which Juliet thought too formal.

Finally, when I was three weeks old, they settled on Iris. Juliet with the help of James had been compiling notebooks of the flowers that grew on the island. At the edge of the marshes, they had discovered Clave Valley with its dark blue irises - it was one of my mother's favourite places – and William had agreed, "Iris would do".

Then, as subtly and invisibly as the wind changing direction, their squabbles shifted towards the thornier and more pressing subject of Geraldine Ottley. Juliet had hoped Kathleen Piran would be her companion during the first days after my birth, but according to William, Geraldine was running the house quite adequately.

Silvie advised my mother not to complain and Juliet, noticing how Geraldine was able to predict William's moods and forestall his demands, resolved rather than resenting the older woman's presence in her home, to learn how better to please her husband.

Juliet's diary records how less than a month had passed before she felt she had learned more than sufficient from Geraldine. She employed what she hoped were tactful means of relieving the woman of her responsibilities, but rather than seeming glad to be free of the domesticity she claimed to loathe, *it was harder to get rid of Geraldine than to prise a limpet from a stone in one of the island's rock pools.*

*

I was a child who was the image of her mother, but as I grew up, my brown hair developed deep red lights and my pale complexion was found to be readily given to blushing. Juliet, a natural story teller, described the treasures of Marisands to me as landmarks of our family history. The walls were hung with Bernard's paintings of the island, Yvette's miniatures and Flora's portraits of the family, including *The Mirror Portrait,* depicting three generations of Armsted women. In the hall, was an icon of Jesus and a silver holy water stoup by the front door - they had belonged to my grandfather, Alexander Martin.

Silvie's bedroom was in a small chamber at the back of the house. To make space for her, Yvette's piano had been moved into the living room, with her collection of faience china. The mirrors in Silvie's room were of old glass and in them I saw my reflection – shimmering - as if immersed in rippling green water. If Silvie was absent, the room became unnaturally silent – a silence as profound as death – and after a few moments alone, I would run to Juliet, begging for reassurance.

My imagination was riddled with strange fears – the dread of dying, of stepping into one of the many fairy rings on Littern and becoming invisible. Known to my mother as "little moon face" (the midwife's nickname had stuck); to the Pirans as "little shadow" and to my father as *muyskens,* "little mouse" – so much smallness suggested it would be unremarkable if I should grow tinier and tinier, until finally, I disappeared.

Our lives were governed by William's demands and I began to fear my father. He was an admirer of *Art Brut*, "the art of madness" and bitterly regretted his training, which he complained had ruined any chance of spontaneity. Yet, despite his preferred style of painting, he was a man of self-discipline and rigid routine, disappearing into the studio after breakfast and reappearing only in the evening, when he expected my mother to have a meal ready for him on the table.

If his work had gone well, my father returned to the house quietly, a smile softening his eyes. When frustrated, he would come in, white-faced, and kick the front door behind him, slamming it shut with a violent crash that made the windows rattle. On those days, after supper, he would closet himself in the spare bedroom and pore over the volumes of art he had discovered at Marisands, seeking inspiration from their pages and often not emerging until the early hours of the following morning.

As William became more disheartened with his work, his resentment of Silvie grew. He ordered her not to play the piano when he was in the house. He thought she should move out of Marisands either to live in the downstairs of Thrift Cottage, or better still with Bernard, Flora and Alice in Dulwich.

Tired of his ill-temper, Juliet spent much of her time at Lyncross, causing my father to regard the Pirans with increasing displeasure. Among the younger children, he claimed he had never encountered such unruly, noisy behaviour - you might find them anywhere, hiding behind a bush or hanging from a tree, poised to leap out at you.

Kindly, attentive and scrupulous as a doctor, Edgar had grown up in the countryside of south-west Ireland and believed it essential to a happy, healthy childhood that children should be allowed to run free. If Kathleen, from a family of Dublin academics, dissented from his view, she submitted to it. As a scientist, her husband respected order and pattern - yet there was something in the man that tended towards a subversion of those principles and she loved him for it. The core of her life was seeing her children develop strength and self-confidence - her fulfilment was in her intelligent, good-looking brood, with their peat-black hair and dark blue eyes – so like their father.

When we went to Lyncross - I was in paradise. I didn't have to creep about to avoid disturbing William or sit still and silent for hours while he painted me, in monstrous and unrecognisable forms that gave me nightmares. While with the Pirans, I didn't need to endure listening to his criticisms of Juliet - the vindictive, cruel words with which he set out to destroy her character.

Lyncross was a house of certainties. The rules, though frequently broken, were fair and enforced with gentle remonstrations from Kathleen and severe threats from Edgar, threats which he rarely carried out. At Marisands, demands shifted and reshaped themselves from day to day like the island's sand dunes. William was distant, cold and untouchable, the warmth and hospitality of the Pirans had been a revelation and each night, when I knelt at my bedside, I prayed fervently that Juliet and I might always be made welcome in their home and that my father would never prevent us from visiting them.

Under pressure from William, Silvie had moved into Thrift Cottage. She didn't complain, but my mother was incensed – William was selfish and inconsiderate - her aunt couldn't possibly manage – his action was no more than a calculated ruse to force her to leave Littern. The more Juliet railed against his unkindness the more autocratic my father became. He didn't want Silvie spending time in the garden – he didn't want to see her moving about when he was working – he didn't want "that woman" having anything to do with his impressionable young daughter.

Though life at Marisands was disquieting, when the time came to begin school, I didn't want to go and asked to be taught at home as Silvie had been. I'd been brought up to be bi-lingual and could read quite well in English and French. My mother had kept a diary since childhood and as soon as I was able, encouraged me to write simply about life on the island.

23

As the prospect of school loomed closer, I questioned Juliet endlessly, shocked to discover that Patrick, Nicholas, and Beatrix Piran attended St. Safan's, in Safford Bridge, where their parents paid what William termed ridiculous, unnecessary and extortionate fees to have their children brainwashed. The Pirans, he explained were not only Catholics but members of the bourgeoisie...

'...While we must behave like left-wing intellectuals, even at the age of five?' my mother asked him.

Regardless of my protests and my father's objections, I began my education at the local convent, St. Mary's, Fernley, where Alice had once taught and where my mother had been a pupil. The school was housed in a pretty Georgian building of yellow sandstone, covered in ivy and Virginia creeper. A wisteria framed the entrance and a chestnut tree stood on the front lawn, the ground beneath it strewn with spiky green cases, which by the end of autumn had split open to reveal gleaming red-brown conkers inside.

Light flooded into the interior of the school through its tall sash windows. The walls, painted the delicate colours of sugared almonds, displayed rows of the pupils' art. In the hallway, stood tables of craftwork, shells, pressed flowers, brightly coloured leaves, and twigs dusted with pale green algae – the kind of natural history specimens I collected at home.

The Anglican nuns who ran the school belonged to the Order of St. Stephen, and though strict weren't unduly authoritarian. My form mistress, Sister Odelia, had been a school friend of my mother's and any difficulties I experienced were to lie not with the teachers or with my lessons, but with the local people, who had made Juliet and William the subject of their tittle-tattle.

Tales about what might go on at Marisands ran rife, there were whispers of pagan rites, people dancing naked in the rain or under the moonlight - engaging in forms of debauchery, which were beyond my understanding and were never clearly defined.

Finding I was excluded from the society of children whose families were more respectable, I made friends with another outcast, Breda Reynolds, a mouse-haired girl, whose appearance was made distinctive by the fact of her having one blue eye and one brown.

Breda compensated for her lack of intellect by appearing *bold*, something even the benign nuns of St. Mary's found exasperating. Anxious not be singled out, I wasn't blind to the truth that because she attracted disapproval, the nuns didn't notice me. Breda's family was poor - she was a charity case - a fact some of the older Sisters were unwilling to forget. In return for her services as a decoy, I became

24

fiercely protective and insisted Juliet take us for a weekly Friday afternoon tea at the Blue Mountain Cafe in Narescombe.

St. Mary's practised an "auntie" system, where an older girl looked after a younger one. My auntie, Kelda Sullivan, was fifteen and prominent in the Senior School for her freckled face, wild tawny hair and her outstanding ability as a musician. The nuns reminded us often of their expectations that as an adult, Kelda was likely to become something of a musical "star".

As the distinct separation of one part of my life from another was comfortable, I was keen to preserve it. My problem with Kelda was that she knew the Pirans and came to the island, a trespasser on my territory. I didn't want to share the pleasures of Lyncross or the difficulties at Marisands with anyone and certainly not with a girl who was inclined to gossip and might provide further ammunition for the rumour-mongers, as she observed the inconsistencies of our lives.

Geraldine Ottley was constantly at our house - she would appear as if she had as much right to be at Marisands as Juliet or me. We would arrive home to find her working in the studio with my father, where increasingly we were forbidden entry. Her visits were often a precursor to the onset of my mother's headaches, a malaise which was becoming an unpleasant and regular feature of our lives and which infuriated my father.

\*

Following my fifth birthday, my mother took me to Dulwich. Alice had written to say Bernard's health was deteriorating and Juliet thought we should visit. While she was in London, Kathleen would look after Silvie and Juliet would consult a specialist about her headaches, now so severe she frequently took to bed for days, anything to escape the insistent nausea and pain.

We left the island on a bone-chilling December day, Edgar Piran drove us to Safford Bridge station and William, resolutely cheerful about our departure, hung about in the lane, watching until we had disappeared round the first sharp corner and begun the steep descent towards the causeway.

That William was no good with children, must have struck my mother early in their marriage. She seemed exhausted by her efforts to keep me quiet, to care for Silvie and run the house. She struggled to suppress my natural curiosity about the long hours my father spent incarcerated in the studio, without ever producing much to show for it. She must have looked forward to a time of respite, while I was excited

25

by the prospect of seeing life beyond the island - of staying in London at Wren House - a red-brick, Edwardian villa with sharply pointed gables and beautiful gardens.

My mother had warned me that, 'If Flora and Alice could build a wall down the centre of the house to divide it – they would.'

In the front garden, where Alice was responsible, there were well kept lawns and neatly clipped shrubs. At the back, in Flora's garden, the flowerbeds flowed in elegant curves, winding their way like a brook through the trees and grass. And when we arrived, I noticed at once, how Alice was tall and straight and Flora bent over as if suffering from a condition which led her always to be staring at the floor.

If I found Alice severe and Flora otherworldly, I was terrified of Bernard, who was confined in a room on a half landing, where the curtains were always closed and an unpleasant odour emanated from the bed. I was taken to meet him and he reached out with a claw-like hand to touch me. He spoke and his voice was like a bear growling, "How do you like my island, Iris?" he asked, meaning Littern. Overwhelmed, I dived behind Juliet's skirts.

Like Marisands, Wren House was cluttered with heavy oak furniture, but while at home the decor reflected all the colours of the island, the rooms in Dulwich had been painted in dull shades of cream and green and every available space was crammed with books and bookcases. My mother and Alice did the chores and Flora read to me, or when frowned at by her sister for sitting doing nothing, took me for walks in the park, where she told stories about the fairies that lived in the trees. To my grandmother, the whole of nature was charged with lively, mischievous spirits.

One day, we went by underground train into town, where Flora showed me Buckingham Palace and Big Ben, so Juliet could attend her appointment with the specialist, without the distraction of a child. Before returning to Wren House for tea, we ate roast chestnuts from a paper bag, warming ourselves by the red hot brazier. From Trafalgar Square, we watched the sun go down on a frosty afternoon, staining the sky with amethyst, ruby and amber, transforming the dark city skyline into something dramatic and mysterious.

We had been in Dulwich for about ten days when Juliet explained she was to have an operation. She had phoned Kathleen, who assured her she would continue to care for Silvie, so she wrote to William suggesting if he was managing, she might stay in London until she had completely recovered.

She waited anxiously for my father's reply, but he answered promptly and encouraged her to remain with her family. He mentioned that the sculptress, Shirley Fredericks, a mutual friend, might visit Marisands for a few days - she hoped to find inspiration for her work from the sea and rocks and in the driftwood that washed up on the shore in Whitcroft Cove.

With the prospect of Juliet's operation in view, the atmosphere at Wren House altered. Flora, always vague, became prone to make little mistakes and was more easily upset than usual. Alice supervised us with close attention and grew in authority, explaining she didn't want me afflicted with the faults which enfeebled the women of our family - faults which stemmed from sentimentality coupled with a lack of self-discipline.

I was too young to be told the details, but my mother's operation didn't go well and we were delayed from returning to the island, until the beginning of May. While we remained in Dulwich, Alice took charge of my education, nursed both my mother and Bernard, managed the house and continued to teach at St. Catherine's School. Confused and upset by her daughter's illness, Flora worried my mother with her over-anxious care. As Juliet was to remark later, if there was any benefit derived from the situation, it was only that Alice and Flora had been forced by circumstances to speak to one another and their long-held, silent antipathy had begun to thaw.

We returned to Devon to find Marisands in disorder. William had let things go and Geraldine, by her own admission, hadn't the inclinations or habits of a suburban housewife and could only hold back domestic chaos in short bursts of activity. When my mother complained there had been two women to help, William was quick to point out that Shirley, as a guest, could hardly have been expected to don an apron or wield a duster - she had come to the island to focus on her sculpture.

In uncultivated parts of the garden, the grass had grown so tall I vanished between waves of pale green stems which rose high above my head, blotting out the sky. My mother sketched me, wearing William's Panama hat, appearing through the fronds of grass, like an intrepid explorer in Africa. When she had restored order, she painted a watercolour of the garden, placing her easel outside the kitchen window, opposite the rose-covered pergola, through which she could see Thrift Cottage, the studio and the edge of the white flower borders, belonging to the oratory.

Not long after our return, Edgar and Kathleen had confronted my mother. They were angry, not only at the length of time Kathleen - a sick woman - had been expected to care for Silvie, but because it was obvious Thrift Cottage was entirely unsuitable for an invalid. If Juliet couldn't influence William for the better, Silvie should leave the island

27

- with her permission, they had already made a few enquiries. She had told them she might prefer to return to Sussex, where she had been placed in an orphanage shortly after her birth and they had found a nursing home, called Castle Rise, at Esterlea, a small holiday resort close to the sea.

Juliet made sure Silvie was content with their plans, but her mind was focussed on other things. Our absence had left her and my father awkward with one another and before the summer was out, any question as to the nature of William's relationship with Shirley had been answered, not with great drama, but in a slow, steady emergence of the truth, as inexorable as the rising of the tide.

My mother, perhaps, was naive rather than foolish. Her apparent failure to comprehend that William and Shirley were conducting an affair was due less to an inability to notice what was taking place under her nose, than that in her childhood she had known genuine love and freedom - not the travesty of those values practised by my father.

The fact that Shirley was engaged in a bizarre *ménage a trois* with William and Geraldine must have left her feeling that her marriage was being assaulted on every side. In her diary, she wrote *...they are not happy - their moods are like the waves of the sea, churning between agony and ecstasy...* and what became clear was that from the moment of her enlightenment, my mother's emotions and frame of mind were also uncertain. Her sense of betrayal poured out and was inscribed on the pages of her journal - a deadly dance between regret, anger and depression.

*

Juliet retreated to Lyncross with such frequency and for such long periods of time, it was as if she no longer cared what William thought. In return, my father became more outspoken in his hostility towards the Pirans.

I overheard him in heated conversation with Edgar - William had consistently refused to contribute to the upkeep of the private road that served Littern and Edgar called him a shirker. When my father retorted that he was nothing more than a sanctimonious hypocrite, they had almost come to blows.

The Piran offspring had been dubbed by William "the Barbarians". The extent of their freedom was evidence to him that they were uncultured and uncared for. Yet, what I envied at Lyncross wasn't the children's independence, but the way each member of the family had a sense of being essential to the pattern of Edgar and Kathleen's lives.

They belonged without question, despite the usual jealousies and arguments. Any anxiety they caused, seemed only to strengthen their bonds.

In fine weather, the Pirans trooped down to Morrow Bay. They wound their way along the narrow lane, carrying blankets, balls, bats, striped sunshades and windbreaks and I went with the younger members of the family, the twins - Patrick and Nicholas - and Beatrix. Sometimes, Antony or Tom would take us to explore the marshes or Thrifswell Woods and the holy well, where we could swim in the calm, clear pool. While we were occupied, James and my mother tramped all over the island, searching for unusual insects, birds and flowers.

At first, I missed the comfort of Juliet's presence, but it wasn't long before I learned not to make a fuss when I fell over, walked through stinging nettles or cut my foot on the sharp edge of a rock or shell. Patrick had shown me how to wash cuts and grazes clean in the pool or the sea, how to soothe nettle rash by rubbing it with a dock leaf. The Pirans had no time for scaredy cats or cry-babies and my fear of their three enormous dogs, Irish Wolfhounds, was ignored. William claimed the dogs were an affectation. Edgar insisted they were the only Irish thing about him since his exile to England. He seemed oblivious to the truth that his Irish heritage was as intrinsic to his existence as breathing.

The rhythm of the seasons, including the seasons of the Church, were for Edgar imbued with deep significance. He tried to research any rites which had been carried out on St. Thrif's feast day, but could find no record of practices used by local people to pay homage to the White Virgin or to St. Thrif.

Further enquiries proved fruitless and he determined that if he couldn't revive a tradition, he would devise a suitable alternative. One day over supper, he described the idea of the Clootie Well, which existed both in Scotland and Ireland. He suggested that the glade where the holy well stood should be decorated in honour of the extraordinary events which had once taken place there.

The word "Clootie" he explained, referred either to strips of rag dipped in the well and tied to nearby trees to procure healing or to pieces of fine cloth given to pay homage to the indwelling spirit of the spring. According to legend, hadn't the fugitive, Thrif, torn her skirt on a bush, leaving a scrap of material snagged on a thorn? And didn't that occurrence - if nothing else - make the concept more than entirely appropriate?

Antony was nominated to organise the event on the first fine evening around St. Thrif's day. He was the one the others looked up to – except for James who referred to him as "the sainted brother" - and it was hoped he might gain the co-operation of the rest of the family in preparing for the party which would take place in the garden at Lyncross after the ceremony.

Much of July that year was sultry and stormy. So it was towards the end of the month when on a clear, warm evening we formed a procession, carrying our votive offerings down Holtleigh Hill to the gap in the line of trees, where Bernard had once forged his way into the woods. The boys and Edgar wore white shirts and Antony suggested that Juliet and I should wear white dresses, as Kathleen and Beatrix would do. The effect was intended to be one of holiness and purity, though James had remarked that we looked like a chapter of Druids.

As we followed the narrow path, the undergrowth rustled and cracked beneath our feet. Reaching the glade, we walked round the well without speaking, treading down the broad palmate leaves of the hellebores, passing the marker stone three times, before stopping and forming a circle. As the youngest, I stepped forward and left a shell as a gift. Patrick had shown me how if I held a shell to my ear, I could hear the sound of the sea, the gathering place of the earth's many waters. Next, I tied a white felt bird onto an ash sapling and then stood back and watched as the others left flowers, religious texts or holy medals by the well, before fixing a scarf, a ribbon, a piece of lace, a glove, a sock and a bandage into the branches of the overhanging trees.

A gentle breeze blew, swishing the canopy of leaves, their whispering indistinguishable from the shushing sound of the sea breaking on the shore in Morrow Bay. Gulls flew overhead with their searing cries - robins and blackbirds sang. From the depths of the woods, a nightingale was heard, its notes ringing out as the sun floated down to hang, suspended on the horizon.

Antony said a prayer. He encouraged compassion for the unfortunate, protection of the weak and gratitude for the value of simple human kindness. Littern he reminded us was a special place - a place of enclosure and sanctuary - a place where the veil between man and God had been lifted.

However touching his words, they would soon be forgotten - our progress back to Lyncross was noisy and peppered with disagreements. My father had dismissed the concept of the Clootie Well as superstitious rubbish and wanted nothing to do with the Piran's party. Strolling between Antony and James – my mother laughingly recounted his vitriolic outburst at the suggestion he might like to participate in our home-grown religious rites.

Overhearing, Edgar remarked that Juliet was poised between the devil and an angel. James was rebellious and unpredictable, a fierce, damaged person – while Antony, experienced a pull towards God, as irresistible as the moon tugging the tides.

Kathleen didn't reply. The walk had tired her and she leaned heavily on Edgar and Tom, struggling to catch her breath as she climbed the hill, refusing, between gasps of air, their offer to fetch the car. As his mother's health failed, there had developed closeness between Tom and his father. Tom was training to be a doctor and Edgar's overt pride in his achievements had in Nicholas's words, "recently been identified as a primary cause of chronic nausea". Nicholas's own response was to develop a brooding insularity, which he expressed through his interests in nature and photography – interests he shared, if at all - only with Patrick, his twin brother.

I hung back, dawdling. Nicholas and Beatrix were sparking off one another like flint striking stone. Beatrix argued that the closeness between the twins was *unnatural* – a word with particular emphasis in the Catholic lexicon. She told him that when she went to Mass, she thanked God that he and Patrick hadn't been born identical, a sentiment with which – she claimed - the rest of the family agreed. Furious, Nicholas side-stepped suddenly, almost knocking her over – Beatrix, he retorted, was bitter and eaten up with jealousy. She talked too much and bored everyone with her unsolicited opinions - thank God, unlike her - he and Patrick had little need of words to communicate with each other -

But the twins weren't alike. Apparently courteous, Nicholas demolished people with his sarcasm and barbed tongue, while Patrick, outwardly reserved, was invariably peace-loving and kind. His readiness to point out things of interest – magpies with their white-tipped flashing wings, young gulls, hares, hawks and baby rabbits with their clean white scuts - had awoken a childish devotion in me and I pursued him with relentless questioning:

*Why did the tide come in at a different time every day?*

*How did the moon change size? Why was the harvest moon a different colour?*

*Why were there so many hares on Littern?*

*And why did rabbits on the mainland suffer from myxomatosis while those on the island didn't..?*

Patrick began to explain it might be because the island's rabbits were physically isolated - the sea had protected them from disease.

But Nicholas interrupted, 'Actually, the myxomatosis virus is an unwanted pestilence imported from France...'

Beatrix laughed - a single harsh sound, 'Iris the virus,' she chanted, 'why don't you go away and leave us alone? Patrick's tired of his little shadow...' Then as if she'd forgotten the accusations made earlier against her brothers, 'You should never come between twins - Pa says they've been together since the beginning of time.'

I stared down at the road. Day dreams for me were not just a surface-light exploration of fantasies. They encapsulated my deepest desires, such as my longing to become part of the Piran family, as James had done - James who showed little honour, yet was still valued. Though he was frequently a cause of concern for Kathleen and Edgar, his passion for the flora and fauna of the island had been indulged until Lyncross was overburdened with cases of stuffed animals, drawers of birds' eggs and wall-mounted frames containing rows of moths and butterflies.

Beatrix, I knew, had regarded me as her enemy since I'd made the mistake of calling her Trixie; shortening her name was a form of torment practised regularly by her brothers. Then Edgar had criticised her for her rough and tumble ways - couldn't she be more feminine? "Like Iris?"James had asked, before stirring up further bad feeling by adding that Beatrix was too clever and that her father's sharply contrasted good looks sat badly on a girl. When she had criticised him in return, he had slapped her and no-one had bothered to reprimand him.

I lagged further behind as we reached the top of Holtleigh Hill and stopped to catch a last view of the island before darkness, hoping I might glimpse Clave Valley, a place which meant so much to my mother, a place to which she had refused to tell me the way. There was a huge moon that night, the rim touched with blood-red - I stood on tiptoe and jumped as high as I could, trying in the bright moonlight to make out the secret fold in the hills,.

'Want a bunk up?' Patrick called out. He had turned back, noticing I was no longer following on his heels.

I shook my head.

'Why not climb on a rock then?' he asked and gave me his hand while I clambered onto a large boulder. When I was steady on my feet, he stepped up beside me - he and Nicholas had grown that summer and were now nearly full-grown men.

'Don't mind Nick, he's in a bad mood,' Patrick said.

'So is everybody, especially Beatrix...'

'Antony's prayer was rather long,' he suggested with a grin, 'I don't think Pa intended the occasion to be taken quite so seriously.'

'*I* think he did...' I objected. For me the ceremony had been something unsullied, like a nun's marriage to Christ, or a first communion – rituals known to me only by hearsay.

Patrick smiled, and pointed beyond the marshes. 'If you look over there you can see a glow from the gypsies' campfires.'

All summer, I'd been pleading to be taken to the common land, curious about the gypsies with their carts and vans, horses, dogs and scruffy children, all living on the stony clearing. For most of the year, nothing flourished there except thistles and weeds, but Juliet said, in July and August, the wildflowers came out, transforming the field into a shimmering sheet of gold.

'What do you think they're cooking – sausages and bacon?' Patrick asked. 'Could we go now, please? I'm starving.'

I didn't want to go and remained perched on the rock, staring at the moonlit hills and sea.

'Do you know where the wild irises grow? Has James told you?'

'I think that's James's special secret.'

'He's told my mother...' I said.

'If you don't come soon, Pa will send the dogs out to find you,' he teased, knowing how much the prospect would terrify me.

'Why do wolfhounds have to be so big?' I asked.

'If you were going to tackle a wolf wouldn't you want to be big – not a little squirt like Iris Muys?'

Jumping down from the rock onto the thick grass, I landed awkwardly and Patrick caught my arm to prevent me stumbling.

'Are there wolves on the island?'

'Not the sort you mean.'

'What sort, then?'

'The sort that eats little girls who ask too many questions...'

We ambled towards Lyncross, which at night appeared stern and foreboding, enclosed by its high laurel hedge, the windows protected by dark green shutters. In the sunshine, its stones sparkled and the place became the perfect backdrop for swathes of daffodils, hellebores and tulips in spring, and in summer for the mass of white lilies that lined the drive. Now, as we turned towards the house, it was as if all light had been gathered into the garden - pouring down from the moon, spilling out from the French doors onto the lawns, where bulrush torches had been lodged in the earth, a bonfire lit, and small lanterns twinkled among the shrubs and trees.

Sitting cross-legged on a rug spread out on the grass, Antony played the guitar and sang folk songs. I helped myself to a plate of food from the kitchen and then lay down in front of him to listen. Owls hooted in the woods. Every now and then someone would break into a snatch of a different song, causing a wave of laughter. Nearby, Tom leant against a tree, his girlfriend, Nina beside him, her head resting on his shoulder.

As they began to kiss and to murmur to one another, I left feeling embarrassed and went in search of my mother.

Juliet was nowhere to be found, so I went to Kathleen who was reclining on a lounger near the house, with Edgar hovering round her anxiously, fetching strawberries, a glass of wine and then a cardigan when she said she felt cold.

'Sit by me, Iris,' she said.

Edgar had gone to fetch a blanket. Slender and willowy, Kathleen often complained she couldn't get warm. I settled on the lounger beside her, but before Edgar returned, angry voices were heard from the house, shouting between him and James.

'James can be very difficult,' Kathleen said and sighed. 'I'm afraid your mother encourages him.'

My mother slipped out into the garden through the French doors. Stepping into the shadows, she braided her loose hair into the neat plait she had been wearing when we left home earlier that afternoon.

Seeing her, Antony stopped playing and called us to gather round the fire, where Nicholas, he said, would tell blood-chilling tales of the exploits of the island's wreckers. The wreckers shone lights from the stone tower to lure ships onto the rocks. The caves in the cliffs were the place where smugglers had stashed their loot, loot now guarded by ghosts. The sands of Morrow Bay were pure white, being made of the crushed bones of murdered sailors and their children and wives...

I shivered, feeling frightened and sensed tension in Kathleen.

'If you can't sit still, you'd better go to your mother,' she said.

Juliet was with James - his face white in the moonlight, his auburn hair untidy and ruffled. Upset by images of smugglers, ghosts and bones, I reached for Juliet's hand, but she shook me off.

'We'll be leaving soon,' she said. But at least an hour would pass before we set out for Marisands.

James offered to walk us home, but Juliet advised he had better not. Kathleen had retired to bed early - she had swept past us without saying goodnight. Her silent withdrawal sent an unmistakeable message – my mother's relationship with the Pirans was no longer the close friendship it had once been – something had begun to go wrong.

# Chapter 3

By September, Silvie had left the island. Her image faded into the half-light of childhood memory, until all that remained was a sense of the silent movement of her wheelchair and a faint scent, sweet and elusive – *Devon Violets* – which had lingered on the air when she was near. We'd had little opportunity to know one another. I had been made shy by the enigma of what lay beneath the blankets and voluminous clothes which concealed her legs - she had respected William's request that she have little contact with me.

Later that autumn, my mother began to swell up. I remarked on it to Patrick, who laughed in disbelief at my ignorance, 'Your mother's having a baby,' he said, 'don't you know anything?'

The baby, my sister, was stillborn in April the following year and for once, my parents didn't argue, keeping their feelings to themselves. Afterwards, my mother stopped attending the church in Narescombe. She spent hours in the music room, playing mournful tunes on Yvette's piano or she went to the outhouse, her chisel tap-tapping, chipping away at blocks of white stone, creating strange forms, twisted and crumpled like discarded scraps of paper.

The oratory garden was planted with white trees and flowers: silver birch and cherry - white crocus, roses, irises and the chalice shaped hellebores associated with St. Thrif. When he built Marisands, Bernard had removed the gravestone, which he'd found on the cliff top to among the silver birches. Juliet called it "the ghost-garden". Some of the statues she had placed there were like pantomime ghosts - figures draped in billowing white sheets - but others were skeletal, as if constructed of thin, bleached bones.

As a child, I thought the oratory garden dull, until one moonlit night, Juliet showed me how the white flowers floated in the darkness like constellations of stars and how the white irises were like moths with spectral wings, circling the moon's reflection in the still water of the pond. She told me Flora had restored the garden. Bernard had been in favour of having the white plants taken away and replaced with more colourful flowers, but my grandmother had insisted the garden should be left intact. She had harboured the fear that her father in his well-intentioned, blustering way had built a house where a church had once stood and had desecrated holy ground.

Dreading divine reprisal, Flora developed a horror of Juliet escaping the garden onto the oratory steps, where she might fall to her death in Whitcroft Cove. Her fears had wriggled their way into Juliet's consciousness and were passed in turn to me. The resounding boom of the sea breaking against the jagged rocks at the foot of the cliffs could be heard as far as Marisands and the gate that led to the oratory steps was always kept shut with two stout padlocks.

It was only after my sister's death that Juliet said she would take me to the oratory. Holding tightly onto her hand, I stepped out onto the cliff top. From above, the rough stone hut appeared like the barnacled hull of a boat, the rugged face of its walls broken only by a tiny window and by the niche over the door, which held the headless statue of St. Thrif, with her shorn hair.

The steep stone steps, which had been built into the cliff-side, were treacherous and I clung to the handrail, trying not to slip as I resisted the urge to look down the vertiginous slope to the pyramid of rock rising from the shore below, as black and as ominous as a shark's fin.

We had reached the plateau on which the oratory stood and Juliet forced me to face the sea. She grasped my chin so that I had to peer down at the roiling waves as they sifted and spat out pebbles at the water's edge with a harsh grating sound.

'That's what you have to fear...' she said.

And I was afraid, as much of her intensity as of the terror of tumbling down the steps onto the rocks or into the thrashing water. The sea struck the land - the land trembled - and I trembled, until we stepped into the interior of the oratory. The walls were lined with shells from the island's bays, softly iridescent, their delicate shades of pink, cream and mauve arranged into swirling patterns with motifs of fish, angels, trees and birds. As my eyes adjusted to the darkness, I saw the stone hut was only a facade; the back of the oratory had been hollowed out of the cliff face as rain and wind-borne sand had once worn out a broad shallow cave.

We sat together on the long wooden bench and Juliet related the story of how Bernard had chanced upon Littern and had slept there when he had been stranded on the island for the night. Her voice echoed, her words were reflected back to us and then melted away, fading, fading, fading...

We lit candles for my sister and left them burning on the altar. As we scaled the precipitous steps back to the cliff top, their flickering light was still visible through the salt-encrusted panes of the oratory window.

Re-locking the gate, Juliet forbade me to go to there alone. When she mentioned our exploits to my father, for once he agreed with her –

his atheism had become so aggressive that the oratory held no interest for him, its purpose as a place of prayer lay entirely beyond his comprehension.

*

William and Juliet's marriage had never been made for mutual comfort and tensions at Marisands grew palpable – until the atmosphere was unpredictable and as charged as lightning.

My father complained about everything. Silvie's room, now a music room once more, was wasted space. The dining room was dank and uninviting. The excess of windows in the sitting room made it too cold in winter and too hot in summer and the studio was no better...

One evening, I heard my parents quarrelling in the kitchen, directly beneath my bedroom. I crept downstairs and hid in the hall. The kitchen door had been left ajar and through the crack I saw my mother hurl an Armsted plate at my father's head. She threw it with a deft, graceful flick of her wrist - he deflected it with a quick agile movement, so it crashed onto the tiled floor.

'There aren't many of those left,' he warned.

Our collection of Bernard's distinctive designs had been steadily diminishing -the wall behind the green enamelled stove was pitted and scarred by the missiles of my mother's rage. The plate was followed in its trajectory by a stream of words, peppered with French, which infuriated my father - he regarded my mother's lapses into a language he couldn't understand as the epitome of bad manners.

They were arguing about Geraldine Ottley - *la blatte* – the cockroach - an expression of distaste which required little translation even for my father. William wanted Shirley Fredericks to stay at Marisands that summer and my mother had refused. Didn't she have enough to put up with, giving house room to Geraldine? Not to mention the students my father had picked in a pub in Narescombe, who now hung about in the house, smoking, drinking coffee and expecting her to cook meals for them.

William called the students "Disciples" - Juliet called them "Detritus". Words flew from her in sparks of anger. Shirley, she suggested, could stay in Thrift Cottage. It had been good enough for Silvie and would be good enough for her. William argued the cottage had always been primitive and was now unfit to be used as anything but a store room. My mother said she couldn't care less – she demanded instead that he explain Shirley's plans to set up a studio in Narescombe, *why here - why now?*

Juliet's red-hot fury alarmed me less than my father's rage. Cold, hard words slithered from his mouth – accusations about money, my schooling, James Millford, the Pirans...

'You dare to accuse me?' my mother asked.

William's hand flicked out and slapped her face - she buckled forward and was sick on the floor.

A few days later, I was made to help my mother prepare Thrift Cottage for William's guest. Since Silvie had left, my father had been using it as an annexe to the studio, a place to store blank canvases, stocks of paint and other equipment. We carried those things to the house, traipsing across the garden with each load and then arranging them in the spare room. In the upstairs of the cottage were Flora's religious artefacts, which William had removed from Marisands: statues of the saints, crucifixes and paintings of the sacred heart, which were taken to be stowed in the cellar beneath the larder floor, where my father said, he hoped never to catch sight of them again.

Towards the end of the holidays, Shirley Fredericks arrived on the island in her red sports car. She had been invited by William to stay in Thrift Cottage for as long as she liked. The throaty sound of her car engine reached the house long before she did, the fluctuations in volume marking her progress along the winding lane from the causeway to the oak tree, where she turned into the drive.

Under the shade of the trees in the oratory garden, Juliet had laid out a salad lunch on a trestle table covered with a red and white chequered cloth, weighed down at the corners with stones. White daisies, delphiniums and roses were in flower and her white statues stood dotted across the lawn, their images reflected in the surface of the pond, between the water lilies.

The meal was an unaccustomed feast, William was frugal with money, but there were platters of hard boiled eggs, ham and tinned salmon to go with the salad and huge hunks of home-made bread – to follow there was apple tart and strawberries with cream.

When lunch was finished, the adults talked and drank wine. Unlike Geraldine with her clipped, upper class accent, Shirley had a sinuous, well-modulated voice, she made my father laugh, but at jokes so private no-one else could join in.

She teased Juliet, nagging her about the fact she didn't wear make-up and did nothing interesting with her hair, and William didn't defend her - he seemed to agree. Both Geraldine and Juliet were sending him what my school-friend, Breda, would have called "dagger looks with knobs on". Geraldine sat forward in her deckchair watching Shirley's every move. Shirley was tall and statuesque, with a mane of blonde hair while Geraldine was dumpy, her short, coarse hair and tanned skin a study in brown.

After a while, William and Shirley disappeared to the studio and stayed there together for a very long time. Tired of sitting still, I offered to help clear up, but Juliet was irritable and as I seemed to be in the way, I climbed up into The Robin's Nest, lonely and bored.

The Pirans weren't welcome at Marisands and I brooded over the fact they must be on the beach playing and running free, while I had to stay at home on my best behaviour. It was late in the afternoon before Juliet shouted up to me - William had suggested we have a picnic at Morrow Bay - the last picnic of summer. I clambered down the rope ladder and jumped onto the lawn, only to be told by William that if the Pirans were on the beach, I was to ignore them.

My mother had made an uneasy peace with Kathleen and Edgar and during Shirley's stay had delivered me to Lyncross each day so she could return home to discuss sculpture and take Shirley to interesting places round the island. Under the watchful eye of Antony, Patrick had been teaching me to swim in the pool in Thrifswell Woods. The Piran boys were all powerful swimmers and when we went to Morrow Bay, they raced each other across a turbulent stretch of water. Since Beatrix now swam part of the way, I was desperate to join them. I hated being left at the shore's edge, watching until they appeared on the dark outcrop of rocks, from where they waved back across a vast expanse of sea.

My father took a firm hand in the arrangements for our picnic. Juliet, Geraldine and I were to cycle to the bay - he wanted to ride in Shirley's sports car and there was only room for two people. Alice's old bicycle was found beneath a tarpaulin in one of the sheds. Geraldine mentioned it was unmanageable and heavy, but Juliet didn't offer her own lighter bike in exchange. She hung her wicker basket from the handlebars and when everything was agreed, led the way as we set off behind Shirley's red car.

We skimmed along the lane between grey stone walls draped with pink valerian and sea thrift, until at the top of Holtleigh Hill, we drew level with Lyncross. Juliet pulled over onto the grass verge - she needed to call at the Piran's house - Geraldine could take me to the bay, where she would catch up with us later.

The wrought iron gates to Lyncross had been left wide open and instead of doing as Juliet asked, Geraldine propped her bike against the gate post and strode up the drive. My mother's expression was one of unhappiness and concern – my face and neck burned with shame as I followed my mother, hoping the Pirans wouldn't be at home.

Usually we walked round to the back of the house, calling out as we let ourselves into the kitchen, but the dogs had been left loose and were barking and growling.

'Stay there,' Juliet ordered, as she approached the front door.

I wanted to be close to my mother, not wait with Geraldine, who had strayed into the garden. I was afraid if Edgar saw us, he would be angry at the unwelcome intrusion into his home.

The garden spread out in broad terraces of velvet lawns. Geraldine stood near the shrubbery, staring back at the square, stone-built house, her eyes narrowed as she shaded them from the sun with her hand. From an upstairs window, the sound of dance music drifted out into the warm afternoon and my mother hammered on the front door, as if frantic to be heard.

Eventually, James answered, the sunlight catching the copper lights in his hair. Behind him, stood my auntie from school, Kelda Sullivan with her tawny curls loose and her cheeks daubed with the thick make-up she used to hide her freckles. In the shadows, with her blanched face and halo of hair, she appeared like a dark angel.

Geraldine strolled back across the grass, Kelda had vanished and James and Juliet were speaking in low, urgent voices. I could hear only snatches of their conversation, until my mother took her leave, shouting to James, 'See you down at the bay...'

As we remounted our bicycles, Juliet remarked, 'All holiday, Kelda's hung round James like a bad smell.'

Geraldine didn't reply and the atmosphere was of a false, heavy calm, like the lull between two storms. No-one spoke as we free-wheeled down the last few hundred yards to where the trees thinned out as they met the sand dunes and the shining sea came into view.

We left our bikes leaning against the wall. Edgar's black Rover was parked there with Shirley's red sports car tucked in behind. The sun was fierce and the breeze hardly cooled my skin. Geraldine's cropped brown curls were moist with sweat and lay flat against her head. Riding behind her, I had noticed her rear view was broad, how with her thickset calves, her feet had pumped the pedals of the heavy bike without strain. From a sleeveless shirt and shorts, her pink, sunburnt limbs emerged plump as a sow's and with a child's instinct, I loathed her.

The white sands of Morrow Bay were dazzling against the turquoise sea, sharp as a crescent moon against a twilight sky. William had spread out a tartan rug on the beach, and emptied the colourful assortment of bags into which we'd packed picnic food. That morning, Shirley had roared off in her sports car to buy wine in Narescombe, and Geraldine had made Spanakopita, supposedly exotic, but which looked to me like sick in a pie and smelt like it. I imagined describing its awfulness to Breda, when I returned to school.

James had arrived with Kelda, but they stayed together at the top of the sands, lounging in the shade of the trees. Across the beach towards the old quay, the Pirans were encamped. Edgar and Kathleen were at the heart of their family, seated on a blanket with a vast picnic hamper beside them. Nina was there, distinctive, with her straight blonde hair gleaming among the dark heads of the Pirans.

Edgar wore a print shirt in every garish shade of blue and orange, which my father remarked was "as much a violation of good taste as having a large family". Kathleen, her light brown hair swept up into a French pleat, looked fragile in a gauzy summer dress, as restrained as Edgar was loud - serene - though recently there had been fears she was suffering from an illness so serious, it was spoken of only in whispers.

Juliet had waved to Kathleen when my father wasn't looking, but once they had eaten tea, the Piran children were too intent on their games of French cricket and shuttlecock to notice me. I was distracted by Shirley, who exuded sophistication, though my mother said her attractions were cheap and could be bought in a bottle, a reference to her dyed blonde hair. Shirley had lived in the south of France and dressed in a way I had considered chic. "Mutton dressed as lamb", Juliet said when I commented on it and since then I'd kept my thoughts to myself, though I was certain Shirley's pleasing appearance had an influence on my father's being unnaturally good-humoured when in her company.

William announced he would take Shirley and Geraldine for a walk. From the marshes, they would climb the hill to the stone tower, a notable landmark with its macabre history and outstanding views.

Juliet sat sewing for a while, though she had a headache and said the brilliant light and relentless heat were making it worse. When she felt unable continue darning and mending, she moved into the shadow of a clump of rocks and lay resting on a towel, white faced and rigid with pain - her dark plaited hair coiling across the pale sand.

I couldn't interest her in listening to descriptions of my new prowess in swimming or my detailed knowledge of where the rip tides ran. I considered swimming on my own, but suspected in the breaking waves I would make a few ungainly strokes before sinking below the surface like a stone. So while Juliet dozed, I wandered down to the water's edge and crouched in the shallows, moving my arms as if doing the breaststroke, but keeping my feet planted firmly on the sea-bed.

My mother slept and I played listlessly with a bucket and spade, gathering seashells, and calculating how close I dared move towards the

Pirans without breaking my word to my father. I used my spade to dig deep channels in the beach, but the tide was ebbing and my efforts to make the sea flow through them were useless. I counted waves and enjoyed the strange sensation as my feet were sucked gently into the soft sand. *Was there another world below this one, a world of dead sailors and their children and wives?*

There was no-one to answer my question and as Juliet didn't wake, a mood of dissatisfaction took hold of me. I hated my swim suit patterned in an ugly yellow-brown like camouflage. The sun sent down piercing rays that reflected off the water and made my eyes hurt. The beach usually so welcoming, stretched out its arms far away from me as gulls circled above, looping through a meaningless spiral of arcs.

The sea with its pale turquoise blue lapped my bare calves turning them an unearthly green. Closing my eyes, I listened to the rhythmic shushing of the breaking water until I felt dizzy and had to sit down. Wriggling my legs into the warm, wet sand, I picked at the stones and shells I'd collected, rinsing them in my bucket, letting them dry and then rinsing them again to bring out the depth of their colours.

When I could think of nothing else to do, I ran back to my mother and took out the book I'd tucked into her basket before we left home. Wrapping a towel round my shoulders, I leant against the rocks and read while Juliet continued to sleep in the afternoon sun.

I had almost finished my book when my mother woke - she checked her watch - two hours had passed and William hadn't yet returned from the tower.

'I'm going after them,' she said.

Despite my father's wishes expressed so vehemently earlier in the day, Juliet picked up our belongings and we filed across the beach to ask Kathleen if she would look after me. William, my mother suspected, had forgotten the time.

'Where has your father gone?' Kathleen asked.

I shrugged in reply, close to tears because William had drawn attention to us in the wrong way.

'Cry baby,' Beatrix hissed. But just as Kathleen had said nothing about my rudeness to her, now she ignored Beatrix's meanness.

'Have you eaten at all?' Edgar asked. He was surveying the beach, woods and marshes with a pair of field glasses. 'No one can solve mysteries on an empty stomach.'

Kathleen opened their picnic hamper and offered me a slice of chicken pie and a rosy apple. I'd barely picked at the Spanakopita Geraldine had provided and was hungry, so I tucked in and after a cup of lemonade began to feel better.

When I'd finished Beatrix asked, 'Would you like to play?'

Like her father, she had a shock of black curly hair and a penetrating gaze. A tomboy, she wasn't usually interested in me, frustrated by my inability to hit a ball, catch or run fast. But I knew if I didn't distract myself, fears about Juliet and my father would build until I cried, and then Beatrix would call me a sissy.

I joined in a few rounds of "piggy-in–the-middle" with her and the twins, trying not to mind when I was given privileged treatment on account of my age and diminutive size. When we'd grown tired of the game, I followed Patrick to the rock pools by the pier and borrowed his fishing net to catch the tiny silver fish that darted among the red and green fronds of seaweed.

Putting my hand in the water, I allowed the fish to nibble my fingers. The twins had learned from James the names and habits of the flora and fauna of the island - and Patrick seemed eager to share his knowledge. I concentrated, wanting to remember everything he said, though I knew he wouldn't mind if I didn't. The family's sharp intellect and cutting wit were softened in him. Like the others, he managed the outward things, catching crabs, dislodging limpets and was a strong swimmer, but if at fourteen years old, he was fed-up minding a little girl, he gave no indication.

Together, we poked at the red jelly mounds of sea anemones and popped pods of seaweed, but I knew he was watching and listening for the tide to turn. On the island, the only time that mattered was that of the cycles and rhythms of the sea and all summer he had made me practise sensing the moment when the tide had changed from ebb to flow or back again. So far, I'd heard and felt nothing and had come to the conclusion he was teasing. Now I didn't want to hear, because then he and his brothers would swim out to the rocks and I would be left on the beach with nothing to do.

Patrick tugged playfully at my plaited hair. He said it was time to go and we headed across the beach towards his family, me trailing after him, dragging my feet.

'Come on slow coach,' he said.

Patrick was always scruffy - his t-shirt full of holes, his shorts torn. He walked backwards away from me smiling broadly - his eyes sparkling like the play of sunlight on water – his was a smile that meant I couldn't help smiling too.

Kathleen and Edgar had returned to Lyncross for what Edgar called their siesta and Antony, Tom and Nina, had been left in charge. I'd heard Edgar giving his orders, "watch Iris, not a hair on her head is to come to harm" and had glowed inwardly at being cared for by a man more loving towards me than my own father.

The disappearance of their parents was the signal for the Piran children to undertake activities of which they would disapprove - paddling round the foot of the quay - or jumping off the pier, where a chain of underwater rocks made diving hazardous.

I lay on the blanket as Nicholas, Patrick and Tom ran to the edge of the beach. They waded through the waves and then plunged into the clean, blue water, striking out to the west, where the sea was calm.

Antony offered to row Beatrix towards the rocks in their wooden boat, *The Silver Arrow* – I wished he had invited me. Far in the distance, I caught sight of Juliet hurrying along the footpath that led away from the tower. She was staring ahead of her to where James, at the edge of the beach, was lurking alone by the woods. Kelda had disappeared.

Though James was my mother's friend, I was glad he had chosen to stay apart - he was the one who pushed things too far. Nicholas said he had stolen the birds' eggs he kept in drawers at Lyncross. He liked a fight and was a bully. Edgar's sons grumbled at his unfairness, at the excuses he made for James – that he had "been through a lot" appeared to provide endless justification of his behaviour. Now, James was smoking, something we all knew was expressly against Edgar's wishes. When he'd set off for the tower, William had stopped to speak to James and he must have borrowed cigarettes - both Geraldine and my father were heavy smokers.

I hardly knew Nina - we were both shy and sun-bathed together on the blanket making no attempt at conversation. Occasionally, I craned my neck to check Juliet's progress as she approached along the path, skirting the garden wall of The Retreat, just beyond the pier. I'd intended to show her what I'd caught in my bucket at the rock pools, but feeling fretful and restless I emptied the contents back into the sea, aimlessly scooping up water and tipping it out again. Nina lay back, propped on her elbows, eyes half closed, her face turned to the sun, though her fair skin was already red and peeling.

Juliet's slight figure was moving at speed along the lane, her bright pink sundress conspicuous against the bleached grasses of the marshlands. Soon she would turn towards the beach and make her way through the sand dunes – *But where was my father? Where were Shirley and Geraldine?*

I threw my bucket into a ridge of seaweed, releasing its stale cabbage smell into the air. As my mother drew nearer, I could see she was no longer carrying her basket, she must have left it somewhere. I paddled further out towards the rocks and began to practise what Patrick had taught me, how to float on my front like a starfish, my face in the water. When I ran out of breath, I rolled over onto my back and saw Antony had handed the oars of *The Silver Arrow* to Beatrix who was messing about so that they drifted aimlessly round in circles.

Out to sea, Tom, Nicholas and Patrick were clambering onto the rocks and I decided to explore how much further I could wade towards them. The beach shelved gently at first and as the tide was only just coming in, I thought I could cover some distance without getting out of my depth.

Juliet drew closer and I plunged on through the waves, not caring where I was going, not bothering to wonder why she was now rushing towards the water's edge, her gaze fixed on me.

The last time I glanced round, she was surging through the sea, her dress billowing round her in the water. I squinted up at her - shocked at her appearance – her face wore a rigid expression, her long plait had vanished and what was left of her hair stuck out in ragged wedges at the sides of her face.

'Mummy...' I cried. She didn't slow down.

As she reached my side, she caught hold of my left hand and grabbing me roughly, jerked my arm up and forward. She grasped my wrist so tightly, I had no choice but to follow her and my other hand flew out as she quickened her pace and I lost my balance.

'Come with me,' she said, her voice harsh, her breath emerging in rapid gasps.

*Was she was angry with me for paddling out so far?* Juliet's punishments were usually lenient, but perhaps this time I had been really bad and she intended to teach me a lesson.

She lunged forward in a straight line with the rocks, though they should never be approached in that way and Edgar had warned us repeatedly to avoid those areas of water where the surface was always turbulent.

I cried out again, but it was as if my mother couldn't hear me above the roar of the sea, as if she mistook my voice for a seagull's cry. She started to swim, dragging me out of my depth, compelling me to attempt with my free arm the newly acquired swimming strokes Patrick had taught me, strokes that were not much more than a doggy paddle.

We were far from the beach and I clung to her until, with a violent jerk, her arm was torn from me – my hand had slipped on her wet skin and I couldn't hold on. A wave struck my side and hurled me round to face the shore. Nina jumped to her feet and signalled furiously to Antony, who was tying the boat to the pier. With a sickening sensation,

I was sucked down and when I bobbed to the surface again, James was running down the beach pointing and shouting. A breaking wave slapped my body, thrusting me round again - there were dark figures on the top of the rocks and I saw the arc of his body as Patrick dived into the sea.

Beneath the water, booming sounds filled my ears until all other noises were muffled and remote. I surfaced, gulping in saltwater and gasping for breath. I spotted Juliet far ahead of me – but then sank again with a roaring in my ears and a flash of bright green where sunlight struck the surface of sea and blinded me.

My arms thrashed - my lungs were bursting. The more I struggled, the less strength I had to force my head above the water to take a breath - until at last, surrendering, I drifted down beneath the waves, dead to all noise and movement, floating into a haze of light, the diffuse red-gold cloud filling my vision.

All fear and panic had gone. But then, water rushed past my ears as I was hoisted up to the surface by an arm looped round my throat. My face broke through the waves and I drew in draughts of air and cried out, searching for my mother.

On the shore, I collapsed as if the sea had spewed me out. Patrick stood over me, pale and breathless, bent forward, his hands on his knees. Tom crouched down by my side and asked if I was all right - I nodded - unable to speak, my mouth and throat full of the choking salt-taste of the sea.

Beatrix sprinted up the beach to where Edgar and Kathleen had arrived with fresh supplies of cake and flasks of tea. The dogs were with them and spun round their legs in frantic circles, barking loudly.

I retched and tried not to be sick. Patrick and Tom were transfixed by something out by the clump of black rocks. James yelled to Edgar and Kathleen - Beatrix was crying. In the water, Nicholas's dark head was just visible above the waves as he swam to shore without Antony or my mother.

Edgar dropped the picnic basket. It spilled open sending a flask rolling down the rake of the beach.

Patrick shouted, 'I'm going in again,' but Edgar gripped his arm to restrain him.

'Get that child away from here,' he said, 'and tell your mother to go home and call for help.'

I flinched at his anger, but did as I was told, hot tears coursing down my cheeks.

Edgar, Nicholas and Tom were in the sea and swimming towards the rocks. Patrick clasped my hand, constantly swinging round to watch his father and his brothers. Gripping his fingers tightly, I asked, *were Juliet and Antony hidden behind the rocky outcrop – were they still there in the water?*

Kathleen pushed me into the car with Nina and Beatrix while James and Patrick raced up the lane ahead of us. No-one had seen William and his friends and no-one knew where Kelda had gone.

All the way up Holtleigh Hill, Kathleen drove in lurching fits and starts. She asked, 'What happened?'

Beatrix said, 'Iris walked into the sea where she knows she shouldn't go and Juliet went after her.'

Dazed and confused, too shaken to contradict her, I heard Nina start to speak, but she seemed to think better of it and fell silent. I was no longer sure – had Juliet pulled me after her or was Beatrix right and my mother had run into the sea to save me?

Kathleen crashed the gears on the car and then as she turned awkwardly into the drive of Lyncross, gouged a deep scar into one of the gate posts.

Her face white and pinched, she looked lost, distant – but once inside the house, she handed me a towel and a hot drink, before shutting herself into Edgar's study, where her sobbing could be heard through the closed door.

James had called the coastguard, Beatrix had disappeared to her room, and the boys hung round in the garden kicking at the trees or each other, tense, alert, waiting for their father to return with news.

I crawled under the kitchen table wrapped in the towel and curled up in the darkness. Around me, everything appeared the same, the shabby, comfortable interior, the dark heavy furnishings, James's cases of moths and butterflies, the stuffed birds - yet everything had changed. Edgar had been angry - and I didn't understand what had happened in the sea.

Soon, I heard a police car or ambulance roaring along the lane, its bell clanging and clapped my hands over my ears. Much later, Edgar, Nicholas and Tom came back to the house and went straight to Kathleen. From the study, I heard the telephone being used and crept further under the table, dry eyed, not making a sound.

By the time Edgar found me, I'd fallen into an exhausted sleep.

When I woke, Juliet, instead of being a vivid presence had become a figure that dwelt in the shadows - a figment of my imagination - someone who I would never see, hear or touch again - from now on, she would visit me only in dreams.

# Chapter 4

All hope is lost when the words relating a death are spoken, and it was Edgar Piran, not my father, who explained how Juliet had drowned and Antony had been thrown against the rocks, injuring his back, as he tried to save her.

Edgar had taken me into the study, where Flora's portrait of Kathleen hung over the fireplace. Dressed in white against a sombre background, she had a powerful presence, full of light and energy. I felt insubstantial, scared and alone.

He said, 'Whatever happens we have to believe God forgives us – without that, life would be intolerable...'

I hung my head. His words were painful because I was certain God would never forgive me for what I had done. I was sensitised by the atmosphere of blame and distress, the rapid comings and goings, the angry outbursts, tears and empty phrases, which more than anything meant something terrible had happened. When my father came to Lyncross to collect me, there was no comfort in the prospect of going home.

The next day, there was a terrible row. Edgar, with Antony in hospital in fear of his life, was incensed with William and had driven to Marisands to reproach him. William sent me to my room, but as I sat at the top of the stairs, Edgar's stricken voice rang through the house, 'If you'd been on the beach, none of this would have happened - because of you - my children risked their lives and I may lose my son.'

William could have pointed out that he had already lost his wife, but he seemed to say nothing as Edgar continued, shouting that Juliet had become irresponsible, corrupt, a bad influence on his family with her lax morals – no doubt the result of living with him.

When Edgar had gone, William referred to him as a self-righteous old goat, but later that evening, told Geraldine, 'The Piran boy may never walk again - they say it's nearly killed his mother.'

Afraid I too might die of grief, I remembered stories I'd heard at school, stories from the Bible. Jesus had raised Lazarus from the dead - he might raise Juliet. He had ordered people to stand up and walk - perhaps he would command Antony to walk again and Kathleen would recover.

Then, around my mother's death, there grew a circle of silence. Juliet was not to be spoken of at home, she felt like a mother who had belonged to another child and my world shifted, becoming dangerous and unsteady.

Between disbelief and sadness, I couldn't be reconciled to life without her and the silence of those around me crept slowly inside, until my voice became locked in my throat and it was more terrifying to relinquish a soundless existence than to endure the angry attempts of adults to cajole me into speaking.

On the day of Juliet's funeral my father left me at Marisands with Geraldine. We stood by the oak tree at the gateway to the house and watched the hearse drive slowly down the lane. I stared at the red and cream flowers on my mother's coffin, until the hearse turned the corner and disappeared. I bit hard on my lip and then tasted salt on my tongue - I'd drawn blood.

Geraldine ordered me back into the house, her manner abrupt as she told me to stay in my room. I sat on the cold lino floor and didn't move, clenching my fists, digging my nails hard into my palms until my father came home from Safford Bridge and released me.

He stormed up the stairs, his face grey and angry. James Millford had turned up the funeral, 'I could have bloody killed him,' he said to Geraldine, 'it was the final humiliation.' When he realised I'd heard him, William lost his temper, 'Get out! I'm sick of seeing your little moon face everywhere I turn.'

I escaped into the garden and up into The Robin's Nest, determined to stay there all night if William didn't calm down. Inside the tree house, I curled into a tight ball, in the semi-darkness. Shrinking back against the wooden walls, I lay on a heap of sacking, my arms wrapped round my knees, making myself as tiny as possible. Since Juliet had died, at the pit of my stomach was a constant ache, an unhealed wound, and as I pulled the sacking over my head, a cry escaped me, a thread of sound no more than a whimper.

When no-one came to find me, I thought would run away and never come back.

Cold and hungry, I climbed down the ladder and left the garden through the gate by Thrift Cottage, turning down the stony path to the cove. The tide had turned, so I hurried along the sands towards Morrow Bay, past the darkest part of the woods, to where the stream from the holy well flowed over the beach. If I followed the water upstream, it would bring me out in the lane, beyond Lyncross. My bare legs were scratched and bleeding as I stumbled against fallen branches and rocks in the undergrowth. My heart quickened at every unfamiliar sound as birds and animals scurried about beneath the bushes.

By the holy well, I cupped my hands and drank the cold, clear water as it bubbled up from under the earth into the stone basin. I slithered down the bank to the edge of the pool and washed the blood from my legs, drying the cuts and grazes with the sleeve of my blouse. Over the summer, we had worn a track with our feet, from the lane to the pool. I found it easily and soon the grey wall that bordered the lane came into view - using my arms to lever myself up, keeping my body low, I scrambled over the top before jumping down onto the road on the other side.

I wanted to find Clave Valley, which my mother had loved - I might feel close to her there. Walking steadily downhill towards the Bay, I noticed a car parked at the side of the lane, near The Retreat – sun-bleached, turquoise blue – just like the car that belonged to James. Though The Retreat had been empty for as long as I could remember, sometimes James and the others went into the overgrown garden to share a bottle of wine. James liked to smoke there and had once set the long grass on fire.

I clambered up a grassy bank onto the sheep track that led across the marshes, before scurrying up the side of Hagdon Hill until I reached the tower. The door stood lodged open and I wriggled inside. Neglected for years, the tower had become unsafe. The stone flags on the floor had been lifted by tree roots - grass and nettles grew up through the cracks. Careful not to stumble, I picked my way to the foot of the winding stairs and began to climb.

There was a noise above me, from high in the building - then a bird flew out through a gap in the broken masonry, soaring up into the darkening sky with thrumming wings. The staircase narrowed as it reached the top - I squeezed my way through the space that opened onto the tower roof – then dropped down to crawl on my hands and knees.

'What the hell are you doing?'

I jumped to my feet – James was on the roof, cigarette in hand, the scent of the smoke like freshly cut hay.

I still wasn't speaking, and stared at him, silent, not sure whether to run away – afraid if I did I might fall.

'You shouldn't be here – go home, Iris.'

Usually, James ignored me - I was beneath his notice, an irrelevance. His longed for career on the London stage had so far come to nothing - he worked for a lowly Repertory company in Safford Bridge, but his manner was no less arrogant.

'I don't know what you expected to see – the light's going.' He threw his cigarette onto the floor and ground it out with his heel. 'I'll drive you as far as Lyncross, if you want – but you'd better make sure

Pa Piran doesn't see you, his temper is decidedly volatile. He never wants to clap eyes on you or your family again.'

James's pale face and glittering eyes were frightening, but it was a long way back to Marisands along the lane and the tide would be coming in, making the beach impassable.

I nodded - I would go with him.

'Get a move on then...'

I slid down onto the stairs, in my haste missing my step and grazing my forehead against the tower wall.

'For God's sake...'

He waited impatiently on the path while I slid down the hill. His cigarette made a glowing point of red ahead of me in the dusky light - as he walked rapidly towards his car, I scampered behind him, trying to keep up.

'When we get to the top of Holtleigh Hill, hide,' he said.

He revved the car engine hard and pulled away onto the lane, speeding up the hill in minutes - I crouched down in the well beneath the passenger seat –

'Damn it – don't move,' he said.

The car came to an abrupt halt and I was thrown forward. James opened the window and whistled softly - I heard voices.

'You can get out in a minute,' he whispered, 'Edgar's been repairing the gash in the gate-post - I'm waiting for Patrick to clear up...'

When everything was quiet, he reached over and opened the passenger door, 'Hop out and make yourself scarce.'

Creeping forward in shadow of the laurel hedge, I dropped onto all fours, crawling along the grass verge and then lowering myself onto my tummy. Edgar and Tom were walking up the drive towards the house, leaving Patrick alone.

'Could you take this little wraith home?' James hissed at him, 'If your father catches her, there'll be all hell to pay.'

Patrick had gathered their tools into a cement-splattered bucket - he started to brush away the mess on the drive with a moth-eaten broom.

'Leave that to me,' James said, 'I'll tell them you've gone for a walk, which is true isn't it? I'm sure they'll believe me.'

Patrick seemed nervous – he glanced over his shoulder towards the front door as if worried his father would find him with me.

'Drop her off by Marisands' gate - she shouldn't be wandering about in the dark, not on her own...'

Patrick moved the bucket off the drive and leant the broom against the gatepost, out of James's way.

'Come on then...' he said, but I knew he didn't want the bother of taking me home. 'What were you doing?'

I shrugged in reply.

He grabbed my hand and pulled me along. 'You'll have to speak sometime, though it hardly matters as we're not allowed to talk to you.'

Unseen in the dark, I blinked away tears; it was unlike Patrick to scold.

He said, 'Antony is the person I most admire in the world - none of us wants God to take him away.'

I felt the warmth of his body, inhaled the clean scent of his breath as he spoke, but when I looked at his face, his eyes were glimmering, as if seen through water, and I knew he was crying.

'One day, perhaps you'll understand...' he told me when we had reached the blackthorn hedge that marked the border of Marisands, 'I'll watch you to the gate.'

I didn't move and he tugged his hand from my grasp, leaving mine to drop limply by my side.

'I have to be with my family, Iris, I can't be with you.'

Rooted to the spot, I fixed my gaze on his tall figure. I searched his eyes for an indication that we had once been friends – that we might be friends again in the future.

He backed away from me, up the hill. 'It's no good crying,' he said, his voice breaking, 'it isn't going to help...'

The front door had been left off the latch and I crept in, not sure what to do. Standing in the hall, I could hear my father in the living room making strange noises, 'Oh God, Oh God...' he moaned, my father who dismissed God's existence as immaterial.

Not daring to disturb him, I stole upstairs to my room. Shivering, I huddled beneath the blankets. Had I become an outcast, hated and despised like Breda?

Stranded in my bed, surrounded by a sea of blue lino – I wondered if I placed my foot on the floor, would I sink into the watery world where my mother had gone - a world where past, present and future had floated apart so far, it seemed impossible they could drift back together and collide.

A few days earlier, my father and I had picked white flowers from the oratory garden and we'd scattered them onto the sea from the pier at Morrow Bay - in memory of Juliet. They had been blown away by the wind or swallowed by the waves, as if my mother was nowhere, and I too was nowhere – as if we had both disappeared, inseparable from the melancholy that now shrouded Littern Island like an impenetrable fog.

*

After the October half term, I was sent back to St. Mary's School, still refusing to speak, still torn between my inner life of fears and memories and the outward necessities of eating, drinking, and doing lessons.

My father was considering teaching at the art college in Safford Bridge. He'd bought a car so he could travel from the island more easily, but as the weeks passed, he did nothing about finding a job. Instead, he spent hours in the studio, staring at the ghostly white statues in the oratory garden, as if being among my mother's work might relieve the state of despair in which he now found himself.

Then one night, early in the New Year, William had come to my bedroom and told me to get dressed in my warmest clothes. I pulled on a thick jumper, skirt and socks, as he began emptying the cupboards and drawers and filling my suitcase. He removed the pillows and eiderdown from my bed and when I was ready, carried them downstairs.

My father had never behaved like this before and I scented danger. In the kitchen he made a sandwich of bread and margarine and a cup of cocoa, explaining we were going on a long journey and needed to leave soon to catch the tide.

Bewildered, I settled onto the backseat of the car, forming a nest within my bedding. An owl hooted from the nearby trees and I stared out at the black sky and full moon, which Juliet had once described as a goddess among her attendants, the tiny twinkling stars.

The tyres of the car crunched softly on the gravel of the drive, and then whispered against the damp surface of the road. The moon became a great ball bouncing within the frame of the windscreen as we rushed along Osford Lane. When we reached the causeway, my father crossed so fast that water lying in our path splashed up against the car windows - we were going, he said, *de Overkant* - over to the other side.

We reached Dulwich, in the grey hours of early morning. My father said, 'This isn't a punishment, Iris, it's for your own good, when I see you, I see your mother.'

I was remembering the visit I'd made to Wren House with Juliet and the nightmare figure in the bedroom on the half landing - my great-grandfather, Bernard - confined to a room where the curtains were never opened, where I had been overwhelmed by the acrid smell emanating from his person as he reached out to touch me.

Alice came to the door, tall, straight, austere - she must have heard the car pull up in the road.

'Look at you...' she exclaimed as we walked up the path.

I wasn't sure if she meant me or my father. William was as I'd always known him, passably tidy, fair hair combed, clean-shaven, hands and fingernails spattered with paint. I wore the blue coat Flora had sent as a birthday gift when I was six. Juliet had stood me in front of the mirror and brushed my long, brown hair over my shoulders into a fan shape, "Where did you get those lovely eyes?" she'd teased, "From the fairies that live in the woods?"

As we went inside the house, Alice pointed out we were late and sounded disapproving. She was a woman whose life was orderly and disciplined and she expected those qualities to be demonstrated by others. She had set out food in the dining room; triangles of bread and butter had been heaped onto flowery plates. Seeing them, my stomach turned, but before the ordeal of breakfast, I was to carry my case upstairs to see where I'd be sleeping.

Part way, we passed the bedroom in which Bernard had lain bedridden. Alice opened the door and I waited, eyes searching the gloom. Breathing in air impregnated with the odour of urine - my attention locked on the figure in the bed which drew me with the fascination of an object of horror. I froze, seeing eyes that glinted dangerously from a face whose features I couldn't distinguish. Alice pushed me forward and I braced myself for Bernard's unwanted kiss - dry and whiskery - for the hand clawing mine - but then she snapped on the light and the room was empty. Bernard had died, months earlier, and no-one had told me.

Alice removed blankets from an ottoman and I followed her up a short flight of stairs to the attic room, where she unfolded them across the foot of the bed. When Juliet and I had visited Wren house, I'd been given a cot-bed beside my mother, now I would be sleeping alone. I wondered where my father was going to spend the night and whether, if I asked politely, I might be allowed to share his room.

I placed my leather suitcase beside the chest of drawers and Alice beckoned me to the window. In the pearl-grey light of dawn, she showed me the view across Dulwich – red tiled roofs, brick walls and a patchwork of small gardens, so different from the green world of Littern.

Over the bed, was a drawing of St. James's Park, which she told me William had made – simple and conventional - it was nothing like the canvases in his studio at home, where his paintings were composed of images arranged in an unsettling juxtaposition, driven by a rationale impossible for a seven year old to comprehend.

'I'm sure you'll be comfortable here,' Alice said.

The room was as plain as a nun's cell, with its faded curtains and bedspread. The only ornaments were statuettes of the saints – Francis, Antony and Theresa, "the little flower". A small rug, the colour of mud, was set by the bedside on the board floor, but the most striking thing in the room was the bitter cold.

'Shall we eat? Why don't you take off your overcoat?' Alice asked but I refused to be parted from the blue coat. On the stairs, she said, 'You must be quiet, Flora has to rest - she's resting now.'

While we had been in my bedroom, William had carried the remainder of my belongings in from the car and had piled them in the hall beside a tall bookcase.

Alice invited us to go into the dining room for breakfast and my father seemed hungry, tucking into a plate of bread and ham. I wouldn't eat and couldn't drink the glass of milk Alice offered, so she removed me to the kitchen. On the green Formica table was set out a jar of clean water, a new paintbrush, a tin of watercolours and a painting book.

'I expect you like to draw and paint.'

I nodded - certain I would disappoint – my father was unmistakeably let down by the pictures I made for him at school.

'I need to talk to William,' she said. Though Alice was a teacher, she seemed ill at ease with a child.

The kitchen and the dining room doors were left open and without moving from my chair, I could hear every word of their conversation.

'I'm sure this is the right thing,' Alice remarked, keeping her voice low.

'Are you?' my father's tone was abrupt, his Dutch accent strong - when he was upset, his reaction was to strike out.

'I've made arrangements with St. Catherine's, I'm sure she'll improve, the school has an excellent reputation for dealing with difficult girls...'

William said, 'Geraldine can't cope and neither can I. Perhaps you'll be good for her.'

'I thought I was an old maid, not good for anything,' Alice replied tartly.

William cleared his throat, 'I'm sorry,' he said.

'You should be - and if you're not sorry in this world, you will be in the next.'

My father's chair squeaked as he stood up. He was leaving and my chest filled with the pressure that usually preceded a bout of weeping. I pressed my fists into my eyes, determined not to cry, though I was shocked at William's indifference and by the way that in my father's

55

company, Alice grew harsh, outspoken until the atmosphere between them crackled with antipathy.

William appeared at the door - the painting things remained untouched, spread out on the kitchen table.

'You're to stay with Aunt Alice and your grandmother,' he said.

I met his eyes, my mind full of questions.

'While you're a child, you'll do what I decide is best for you.'

I wanted to know if I would see him again, but if I spoke, the scream I was holding in would escape and tear through the house, disturbing Flora resting in her room.

My ears throbbed with an insistent drumming, so that I heard nothing else as Alice showed William out of the house.

The front door closed and Flora came downstairs, wrapped in a fuzzy brown cardigan. With her grey-brown hair and small round figure she bore a resemblance to a field mouse or a little garden bird, one of the wrens after which the house had been named.

Alice began to fuss. When the food was put away and she had washed up, she said, 'It's time I was going - Flora will look after you.' She fetched her hat, tweed coat and a leather briefcase from the hall and left for work.

'She's gone now,' Flora said soothingly, her relief as palpable as mine. She asked in a gentle murmur, 'What shall we do, Iris? Shall we read?'

I nodded my agreement and she smiled in her diffident way – without difficulty, we had established common ground.

In the sitting room, she put a match to the fire and we huddled together on the sofa with a pile of books, savouring passages from one story after another. We read Kipling. My favourite of the *Just-so Stories* was *The Crab that Played with the Sea,* which told about the creation of the tides. There were pictures of the beach and the ocean, which living on an island had been such a vital part of my life.

Almost imperceptibly, time began to slip by – first minutes and hours, then days, until in the following weeks, what had seemed impossible became a probability - that I could become accustomed to a new way of life in London.

Flora and I grew close. Until I started at St. Catherine's School, we would attend Mass at the Anglo-Catholic church each morning - I didn't mind - all that was required of me was to sit quietly beside her and observe the rituals. The drama of the liturgy, the smoky aroma of candles and incense drowned out unwelcome thoughts about how my existence had changed since I had lost my mother.

'Lit candles are silent prayers, Flora told me. 'Their flames carry small sparks of light up to heaven. In your life, there will be many instances of darkness and light - but you must always look for the light...'

It was during this period of limbo that Flora suggested we go to Esterlea to see Silvie at Castle Rise, the nursing home where she now lived. Alice, she informed me, would very much prefer not to know what we were doing. She touched her finger to my lips, but as I was still refusing to speak the warning and the gesture were unnecessary.

I'd made Silvie a drawing of Marisands and eager to show everything, had included Thrift Cottage, the studio and the oratory. When I handed the picture to her, rather shyly, Silvie thanked me in her rich, sonorous voice and informed me that the family name, Armsted, was derived from the Old French "ermite", meaning hermit and the Old English "stede" meaning place. Perhaps one day I would go back to the island, 'We were meant to live there...' she said.

Silvie's room faced a formal garden. There was a fountain shaped like an enormous fish with water spouting out of its mouth - and like Alice's garden at the front of Wren House, the flower beds were neat and squared off – kept in order by tiny little hedges – I wondered if they had been clipped by one of the pixies Flora claimed took up residence in people's potting sheds.

While we had tea, Flora sat in the armchair and I sat at Silvie's desk and looked anywhere except at her – I hadn't outgrown my fear of what lay concealed beneath the thick rug covering Silvie's legs.

Above the fireplace was a seascape I recognised as Morrow Bay – Silvie had made it from memory. Opposite her bed was a picture in oils of Clave Valley, *The Wild Irises*, painted by Bernard in 1899. The dusky, purplish flowers, Silvie said, were Iris *Patefaciens*, unique to the island.

Flora and Silvie spoke in guarded terms about my mother and the effect of her death on me. Since leaving Littern, I had become more nervous and fearful and had developed a dread of water falling on my face, making a fuss about washing, especially washing my hair. Alice believed that in the summer I should be taken to the beach and forced to swim - no-one should be afraid of water or of the sea. My grandmother shook her head and Silvie agreed that insisted upon too soon, the plan might be a form of mental cruelty – Alice should show more understanding, more sympathy.

While they talked, I closed my eyes so tightly, my eyelids ached. Imagining entering the water, my heart pounded - seeing myself stepping into rippling waves I felt sick. Forcing my eyes open, I focussed on every detail of my smooth, pink hands comparing them to Silvie's - with their gnarled veins and thick nails - using those contrasting images to beat down memories of Juliet's drowning, which afflicted me, sleeping and waking, in a never-ending series of nightmares.

Noticing my distress, Silvie recommended an ice-cream parlour we might visit when we left her – 'Do you like ice cream?'

I nodded, though I felt ill.

'And do you like reading poetry?' she asked. She wheeled her chair to the bookcase and took down a small volume bound in soft green leather, tooled with blue and red flowers – the pages edged with shiny gold, like a bible.

'S. F. Messenger's *English Poetry*,' she said.

She turned the pages and found a poem by Shelley, and read from the fourth verse - lines which she told me described irises like those in Clave Valley, like those in the painting opposite her bed.

Placing the marker at the page, she smiled. 'This is for you – would you like it?'

I nodded again - Juliet had read me poetry.

Silvie laughed. 'How extraordinary and how lovely to see your dear, little solemn face once more - so utterly transparent – no-one could fail to trust you...'

Leaving the stuffy atmosphere of the nursing home, we followed Silvie's directions to a small cafe that overlooked the sea. The quiet gentility of Esterlea felt very different from the wildness and freedom of Littern, where summers had been spent running barefoot, living in faded shorts and tee-shirts, skin turning a deep nut-brown. I thought of the people who lived there and missed them. Alice refused to mention the Pirans or to disclose what had happened to Antony, though she admitted she knew.

Her discovery that Flora and I had visited Silvie would result in a scene that reduced my grandmother to such helpless sobbing. I wept with her. Alice said that as an adult, Flora could do as she liked, but in future, her underhand plots were never to include me.

I associated Alice with the more unpleasant aspects of my life, like visits to the specialist in London, which were meant to cure my obstinate silence, but in practice meant an hour of being plied with questions, while I sat with my lips pressed tightly closed, fidgeting in the seat, until it was time to go home.

Alice had her own peculiar set of fears - of colds, draughts, damp and digestive irregularities. She had a cabinet in the bathroom filled with home remedies and my requirement for having olive oil in my ears, taking castor oil or syrup of figs, or having chapped skin rubbed with camphor ice didn't abate throughout the winter. Otherwise, if she expressed her feelings at all, it was through her love of music - she ran a music appreciation club at the school, to which I would be obliged to belong.

If Alice demonstrated duty, moral rectitude and the virtue of self-discipline, Flora taught me compassion. She was uncertain and ill-defined, just like me. Childlike in her innocence and her suffering, she absorbed everything into her other-worldly existence, where she wove tales of saints, fairies and angels, as if there was no discernible difference between the pagan supernatural and the Christian.

When we wandered among the trees in the park she would still always ask, 'Do you see the fairies?'

And I believed I could see them: shimmering iridescent lights settling on twiggy branches or emerging from the heart of a bush or flower. Together, we trod carefully round fairy rings – neither of us wanted to disappear into the unknown realm of the little people, who lived beneath the earth.

It was also through Flora, I discovered that the artistic genes of the Armsted family had, after all, left some imprint on me. I learned to make pen and ink sketches like those my mother had drawn in her diaries and illustrated stories I'd invented about Littern, renamed *Seabright Island.* Flora understood, instinctively, my need to attempt to make peace with all that happened at Marisands.

When I began my new school, I found Alice had registered me as Iris Armsted instead of Iris Muys. There had been no discussion - as if Alice believed my identity could be changed overnight - as if I had become her child. We travelled by bus to St. Catherine's together. Alice smart in her best tweed coat and leather gloves, clutching my hand possessively as I sat beside her, resplendent in the school's elaborate uniform of broad brimmed felt hat and dark blue cloak.

St. Catherine's was a sister school to St. Mary's and also run by the Order of St. Stephen. Their motto "Sacrifice and Service" was emphasised more in London than it had been in Fernley and was known by pupils, with a typical schoolgirl mixture of black humour and naivety, as "the SS code". With few exceptions, the nuns of my new school were sticklers for rule keeping. Their ethos was that suffering and self-sacrifice were the true paths to God, and the story of the stoning of St. Stephen was venerated as a model of devout behaviour, which even as children, we should strive to emulate in the face of adversity.

Fortunately, Sister Miriam, my class teacher was young and a rebel and had the grace and humour to counsel us that Service and Sacrifice didn't need to be taken too literally- *not yet* – there would be time enough for being martyred, when we had grown up and married.

I had been at the school for two weeks, when I was introduced to Verena Plaschy, a Swiss girl, a boarder, who had been appointed as my auntie. Unlike Kelda, she was close to me in age. Sister Miriam explained Verena was – like me - an only child whose mother had died. That we were both in a similar predicament didn't guarantee we would get along, but Verena was down to earth and practical, a counterbalance to my unsteadiness and I would come to rely on her common sense and ability to interpret the complex, unspoken rules that governed life at the school.

When we met, Verena was performing her duties as ink monitor. Everything about her was immaculate, her uniform, her neat honey-coloured hair, her faultless English, without the trace of an accent. Not a drop of the grainy blue-black ink, with its remarkable staining properties, had spattered onto her dress or fingers, a feat which impressed me.

She invited me to check the pens which had been left out on each pupil's desk for inspection – I was to examine them and discard any nibs which had become bent or splayed. At eight years old, Verena had an innate understanding of people and refused to be put off by taking charge of a timid seven year old, one who appeared to have taken a vow of silence.

Not long after our meeting, I began to talk to her, abandoning the habit of remaining mute, which had become both a discipline and a penance. As we confided in one another, we discovered that what we had in common was less our circumstances than a perception of guilt, drawn from a belief we were responsible for the death of our mothers - Verena's mother had died giving birth to her.

She described Geneva and her father, who was a psychiatrist. I explained about Littern, Marisands and the Pirans. Verena was curious, full of questions and we fell into the custom of speaking French, her native tongue. More fluent than our contemporaries and most of the nuns, it became our secret language, until two years later we were joined in friendship by Rose Ingram - a devout Roman Catholic, with a mop of brown curls and a complete inability to master foreign languages.

Rose and Verena were both made welcome at Wren House and if they were puzzled by the tension between Alice's strictness and Flora's eccentricities they were too polite to mention it.

There was never any question of my returning to Littern and any feelings about the island, Marisands and the friends I'd left behind had gradually changed – I never wanted to go back. I continued to have dreams about Juliet whispering "come with me" and the dragging sensation as the sea sucked me down beneath its surface. And though I tried to forget them, the details remained as clear as the water in St. Thrif's Well, as sharp as the cold winter moon which had followed us, when I left the island in the middle of the night, with my father.

Alice had told me Kathleen Piran wanted no further communication between our families. To her edict, William had added that I should have no contact with my old school, not even with Breda, and having given her word, Alice intended to see that their wishes were carried out to the last letter.

I enquired occasionally about my mother, but couldn't bear to see Flora reduced to a tremulous state at the mention of Juliet's name. Flora's nerves had never been strong and having already lost her husband, the misfortune of losing her daughter had caused her to withdraw further into her private world.

As Alice proclaimed, 'In the Armsted family, we don't deal well with love or loss.'

It sounded like a curse, but Alice began dispensing moral advice before breakfast, "curiosity killed the cat", was a favourite response to any enquiries. Flora, despite her misalignment with the world, was tender, loving and attentive and so for her sake I suppressed both my desire for information and a growing rebelliousness against Alice's dictatorial manner.

I hadn't been sure what to expect from my father. He travelled to London and visited art galleries and exhibitions, but didn't come to Dulwich to visit us. Alice and Flora agreed on one thing - that my father was no good - they appeared to believe *he* was as responsible for my mother's death as I had been, though neither of them would reveal how or why.

Despite her contempt for William, Alice believed in filial duty and once a year we met him for lunch, a meal during which he was uncomfortable and I was bored. Nothing happened except stilted conversation from my great aunt on the subject of my progress - or otherwise - at school and at home – a subject which didn't appear to interest him.

William didn't send gifts at Christmas - a festival in which he had no faith - but he did for a while remember my birthday and when I was nine sent a heavy parcel, which arrived at Wren House, while I was at school.

Excited at the prospect of receiving a gift, I wanted to open it at once, but Alice insisted I must wait - it could be unwrapped only under her careful supervision.

Our evening routine was invariable - homework, meal, washing up, reading, bath and bed, but after we'd cleared the dishes that night, the parcel was placed on the kitchen table ready for inspection.

I undid the string and broke the blob of red sealing wax, under Alice's scrutiny. When I peeled back the shiny brown wrapping paper from the object inside – it contained the carved wooden box in which my mother had kept her personal treasures as a child.

On the lid of the box were carvings of two trees, their branches entwined - by the lock was the symbol of crossed keys. An envelope contained a brief note from my father, "I thought you should have the enclosed..." and with it was a hand-decorated card made by Juliet, on which she had written a quote from Arnaud Brisbois, an artist she had admired:

*Life is composed of fragments of experience shaped as much by imagination as by memory. When we examine those pieces we should try not to force them into any prejudged form, but allow them to arrange themselves into their own pattern.*

*If we are patient, the motif or theme of our life or work will suggest itself as quietly as a diffident guest and reveal the meaning of those fragments so that they catch the light like brightly coloured pieces in a stained glass window or the tesserae of a mosaic.*

The meaning of the words was beyond my comprehension, but they were written in Juliet's hand, on a card she had touched and I was overwhelmed. It was as if she had spoken to me from beyond the grave.

I read the card aloud and Flora stopped putting crockery away on the kitchen shelves and stood by me at the table. When I had replaced the card in the envelope, she explained there was a trick to opening the box, a little lever hidden underneath in a tiny compartment – she would show me.

Her hands trembled as she found the catch that released the lock allowing the lid to spring open.

'This box should be put away,' she said, 'it belongs at Marisands...'

I couldn't think why I should put the box away when I'd only just received it, Flora had strange ideas sometimes. Lifting the lid, the scent of tuberose drifted out into the air and I remembered my mother wearing it.

A green fabric bag with a drawstring top was folded inside the box. The bag held my mother's rosary in a leather pouch, the beads made of smooth black glass, mottled and spotted with specks of white like stars.

With the rosary, was the painted figure of the White Virgin carved by Alexander, and a faded photograph of Juliet, wearing a boat-necked top, her single dark plait of hair brought forward across her shoulder.

Clipped to the photograph, I found yellowed newspaper cuttings from the *Narescombe Courier*, with detailed reports of my mother's drowning.

'Those are hardly suitable for a child,' Alice said.

'Hardly suitable,' Flora repeated, often when she spoke she was Alice's little echo.

'Put them away,' Alice ordered, 'you can have these things when you're grown up.'

Instead of pushing the box towards her as she wanted, I put my hand in again. At the bottom, was a long, heavy shape wrapped in green tissue. Placing the object on the table, I peeled back the delicate paper, layer by layer. There, inside, was my mother's severed plait – her braid of hair curled into a question mark, as if it represented everything that troubled me – as if it could voice all my doubts about what had happened to Juliet.

Before anyone could speak, Alice snatched the hair away, wrapping the green tissue round it as if trying to contain a dangerous animal.

I didn't want the plait of hair, didn't want to touch it, the thought repelled me, but afraid she would steal my other treasures, I scooped them into my arms and ran upstairs to my bedroom.

When neither Alice nor Flora followed, I laid my new possessions on the bedspread and examined them carefully. The black glass of Juliet's rosary was so silky, the beads felt soft and cool to the touch. They were strung on a silver chain with a medal of Jesus and an enamel heart with a tiny round window containing a picture of Mary, dressed all in white.

Afraid Alice or Flora would disturb me, I pushed the rosary under my pillow, the next day, I would ask Rose, who knew the practices of the Roman Catholic faith how I should use it. The figure of the White Virgin, I hid at the back of a drawer of clothes - the newspaper clippings, I placed unread, in the envelope which had contained my father's note.

I knew I would want to look at my mother's photograph often, so I slipped it into my diary. Alice had told me a personal diary was something no honourable person would ever open without the owner's permission.

The photograph would offer me something I had lost when Juliet had drowned - a measure of how much I could, if I chose, resemble my mother. I recognised my own face in hers, pale and heavily framed by dark hair. My clear, grey eyes searched the image for some expression which might reveal my character to be like hers.

Each morning, since I'd been at Wren House, Flora had woven my hair into two long pigtails, but from that day, I styled my hair as Juliet had done - tied back but loose round my face and falling in a single heavy plait that draped forwards across my shoulder.

Though I couldn't have Juliet back, I could *be* her. By resembling my mother, I could have her with me forever.

The secret of Juliet's after-life was not to be in heaven, as I had been taught, but within me, where I would keep it buried in the darkness, like a tender, precious seed.

# Chapter 5

If I had understood how complex a person Juliet was or how convoluted the last years of her brief life, I might have hesitated to make the decision to adopt her identity and not only because to do so meant abandoning mine.

Though my father's gift might be considered unsuitable for a child, the contents of the carved wooden box became the way in which I created small rituals to express my love for my mother and to keep her memory alive - in a sense - it contained the whole world of my childhood and its most significant events.

From Rose, I had learned how to use the rosary beads and in times of distress prayed to the White Virgin and believed that she helped me. I envied Rose some of the arcane practices of the Roman Catholic Church, which I thought might offer expiation for the unrelieved guilt I felt regarding my mother's drowning.

On the anniversary of Juliet's death, I would read the newspaper accounts of what had happened and the need to relive those events, for a while, remained a painful but necessary experience – to forget, I felt would be a terrible betrayal.

Pressed for information, Alice had finally told me that Antony Piran had survived his injuries and made a partial recovery, news which allowed me to put certain fears at rest. But I was no longer part of the life of Littern and like my childish stories of *Seabright Island* - any desire to be, was first laid aside and at last almost forgotten. By the time I left St. Catherine's School, the reality of the island had receded so far it might never have existed.

My school life passed quickly and was unremarkable – the only distinction was earning the medal for Service and Sacrifice at our final prize-giving. Verena and Rose had become Head Girl and Deputy Head Girl, but I floated through the years, aimless as a leaf on a river, with no particular ambition, competent only at subjects natural to me, such as English, French and Art. I took ballet classes, but though they improved what Alice called "my deportment", I had neither my mother's passion nor her talent for dance.

At school, everything was prescribed and that suited me. In my teenage years, like several other girls, I considered becoming a nun, but was advised by Sister Miriam that seeking God must never be used as a means of escape. Later, I would realise, she had spoken wisely and truthfully. Thrust out into the world as a young adult, I understood that entering the convent would have been a way of covering up my failure to develop a strong sense of my own identity.

Going to university in London with Rose and Verena ensured we remained a tight-knit group into our early twenties. Verena's father permitted her to use his flat in Marylebone and it became the place where we socialised and studied. There I met an English student, Neil Sutherland, and fell for him hard. But when introduced to Rose, it was clear they were meant for each other - there was nothing for me to do but stand back and give in gracefully to the unpredictable ways of love.

Rose's marriage took place the summer after we graduated and she and Neil went to work for a publishing company, *Harp Press*. That same autumn, Verena moved to Oxford to train as a teacher, while I went to France for six months, to Nantes, to work in a bookshop owned by the Perrot family. Alice had arranged for me to stay with distant, elderly relatives, who were willing to provide bed and board provided I made no further demands of them.

Jean-Marc Perrot, the owners' son, was given the task of initiating me into the art of bookselling. We believed ourselves passionately in love and then as quickly our love had died. When my stay in Nantes was over, we parted with a certain *tristesse,* but without serious heart-break and I returned to England with no money, no job and no choice other than to resume my former life in Dulwich.

Alice was gradually losing her sight and had been forced to retire from St. Catherine's because she could no longer maintain discipline in class. Flora too, lived in a twilight world and her efforts to manage our domestic arrangements were inadequate, even in my eyes. I found myself caught between concerns for their welfare and the fear that my life would be circumscribed by caring for them, before it had really begun.

When we left school, Sister Miriam had given "her girls" a card with a scripture passage, mine had read, "Mary treasured all these words and pondered them in her heart." My life as an adult, she predicted, would not be one of high drama or heroism - but of endurance.

At Wren House, I discovered the sort of endurance needed to deal with laundry, cleaning and cooking on a day to day basis was something I hadn't yet acquired. I began to search for work - after a few months, making the transition from the *librairie* in Nantes to Morton's Bookshop, near Tottenham Court Road.

Mortons was an old, well established business but it lacked the vibrancy of the Perrot's shop, which had attracted writers, critics, students and teachers who gathered there to engage in heated discussions about the literary life and drink coffee among the ramshackle, overcrowded bookshelves.

Mortons, established by Russell Morton at the end of the nineteenth century, was a throwback to the Dickensian age. The façade was antiquated, with ornate gold lettering on the windows. The heavy door with its shiny brass fittings triggered a tinkling bell every time a customer entered or left the shop.

I wasn't sure how long I would stay. Though the job provided an income and opportunity to inhale, like any addict, the musty scent of books and paper – without the attraction of Jean-Marc, the intricacies of running a business induced a numbing sense of ennui.

My boss, the third Russell Morton was anxious to resist the influence of the American avant garde on our native literature and had formed a society called *The English Poetry Group*, through which the values and principles of more reactionary writers could be upheld and their work promoted.

He had arranged a series of evening readings to take place in a room above the shop and when I had been working there for about five months announced that the next speaker would be the poet, David Sayce, whose book *Midnight Shadows* had recently been published.

I had heard David reading his work on the radio – his Welsh background produced an attractive lilt in his voice and I liked his poetry. Impressed, I decided to break with my habit of going straight home to Dulwich after work and find a way of attending the reading. The subscription to *The English Poetry Group* was too expensive and I would have felt inadequate among the writers and intellectuals who formed the greater part of its membership, so I offered to help. I'd heard Russell complain more than once that the academics and poets didn't enjoy getting their hands dirty.

Though conservative in his politics and his habits, Russell was fundamentally kind and didn't raise objections to my transparent ploy to attend the meeting. As it turned out, my volunteering would be timely, Russell had a young family and one of his children was unwell – it would save him an enormous amount of bother if I could do everything from introducing the reader to saying a few words of thanks at the end.

Setting up the room took longer than expected and I was disconcerted when David arrived to find me still occupied arranging rows of chairs in a semi circle around the stage. Russell had scavenged a collection of props for these occasions - table lamps with orange shades, which bathed the audience in a warm, intimate glow – there were a few racks of books - a red leather armchair and a standard lamp, which created the illusion of the reader addressing a few friends from the comfort of his private library.

I'd barely finished putting the pieces in place when the first of the group members could be heard making their way up the narrow wooden staircase. David seemed an undemanding guest - he asked for a glass of water to be placed on the table on stage and then mingled - rather awkwardly - with his audience as they arrived.

Russell had scribbled a page of notes for me on the back of an order form, so I would know what to say to the erudite gathering of his Society. The reading was poorly attended; there were less than twenty people in the audience, though I'd been told me to expect forty or fifty. Most who came were women, who like me were mesmerised by David's performance and at the end they flocked round him asking questions about his poetry and proffering copies of *Midnight Shadows*, to be signed.

When I handed him my own copy, instead of an inscription David wrote a message on the fly leaf: Iris, *if you would smile, that single grace, that one true note, would be a refuge from my dark dreams, dreams cast by midnight shadows...*" it was a quote from the title poem. When he'd finished writing, he replaced the cap on his fountain pen, blew on the thick black ink strokes to dry them and handed the book to me.

I busied myself clearing away the discarded plastic coffee cups and the untouched plates of biscuits, which I had set out as instructed by Russell.

'Well?' David asked when everyone had gone.

I smiled at him.

'I suppose you have to put all those chairs away again,' he said with obvious amusement, 'I'm sorry I didn't manage a full house.'

'Perhaps more people will come next time.'

'You'd have me back?' he asked in mock amazement.

'If it was up to me, of course you'd come back,' I felt my face redden - he was making fun of me.

David pushed his papers into a battered leather briefcase. Everything about him was shabby, his corduroy jacket needed a button sewn on, his jeans had frayed and threatened to break into a hole over one knee - he seemed to have lost the battle to tame his tousled fair hair.

He began to help me pack the chairs against the wall at the rear of the shop.

'I shouldn't be letting you do this,' I objected, knowing Russell would have disapproved.

'I thought we might go for a drink - do you know a good place round here?'

I had occasionally gone to *The Green Man* during my student days, but it had been full of trainee doctors and nurses, was that likely to be a good place for a poet?

'Your stillness fascinates me...' he went on.

I smiled inwardly. David might think that was an original chat-up line, but I'd heard it before - several times - and on this occasion, it was wildly inaccurate, so far he had observed me flustered and moving furniture.

'I watched you during the reading, grave and peaceful, and then there was your hair, your conker coloured hair and your clear grey eyes, like pebbles under water.'

I laughed at him. 'Don't tease.'

'I'm deadly serious,' he said with a smile.

The truth was I had also watched him and absorbed the details. David was tall and well-built. His blue-green eyes, like the ever changing moods of the sea, had passed through every shade from aquamarine to jade as they registered his emotions throughout the reading - David was an enchanter - he had ignored the leather armchair Russell had provided and had stood, his body swaying with the music of his words.

While I continued to stack up chairs and sweep the floor, he leaned against the wall and chatted about writers he admired from Yeats to Larkin. Listening to him, I thought he was a person I would like, if I had the opportunity to know him better. He spoke with passion and knowledge - my ignorance humbled me - though his manner was friendly, never superior.

As I finished tidying the room, I considered my options. If I hesitated too long over his invitation, David might change his mind. At the same time, I was afraid to appear too eager - though if I turned him down, I couldn't see how our paths would ever cross again. Used to having to account for my movements, I was also worried about Alice. If I phoned to say I'd be home late, she would wait up to interrogate me - if I didn't phone she would be angry.

Depositing the contents of the dustpan into the wastepaper basket, I realised how much I wanted to have a drink with David Sayce, wanted it more than I'd wanted anything for a very long time – I just didn't know how to manage things and soon it would be time to leave.

I lifted my coat from the stand and slipped it on, then locked the door of the upper room and went downstairs to the shop.

'Where do you live, Iris?' he asked, shadowing me.

'Around Dulwich...' I was deliberately vague, unsure where the conversation was leading.

'...With your parents? Would that explain your look of consternation?'

I turned my face from him; I must seem such a child, so transparent, David must think me a complete idiot.

'I live with my aunt and grandmother,' I said - regretting the compulsion to be honest.

'How would it be if I see you to your train and instead of a drink at the dubious *Green Man* we go for a meal tomorrow night? My parents live in Surrey, I could visit them, collect you, say hello to the aunt and grandmother, convince them you're safe in my hands – how would that be?'

'Good,' I said, scarcely able to believe what I was hearing. 'But you don't need to collect me - you could meet me here after work.'

I had calculated that if our date was postponed for a day, I could warn Alice I would be out all evening. During my lunch hour, I could go to Oxford Street and buy something new to wear to the restaurant.

Meeting David seemed to offer the possibility that the world might open up, that I might have a future more exciting than my present existence of lonely lunchtimes wandering around Bloomsbury and lonelier evenings spent helping in the house and garden at Dulwich.

The next evening, we went to an Indian restaurant in Victoria. David was generous, charming and struck the perfect balance between being older and more sophisticated and showing an interest in my youthful exploits and nebulous ambitions.

We discussed poetry and the French writers we admired – he was impressed I had read Proust. He asked if I'd written anything and reluctantly I admitted I hadn't – not yet.

'If you want to write, you should,' was his only comment and the discomfiting moment passed quickly.

But later, David told me he'd been married and it came as a sharp blow. I stammered out that I "respected his honesty" and tried to hide the shock and disappointment as each detail struck me like another slap in the face. Hoping to appear a woman of the world, I listened attentively as he described his daughter, Zoë, who was four years old and lived with him. He said his wife, Lesley, from whom he was "almost divorced", was pregnant with their second child, but he expressed no remorse at having left her.

David portrayed Lesley as an ardent feminist, independent and strong, but the truth was he had abandoned her and his unborn child and I couldn't help seeing the situation from his wife's point of view. My dreams of a life with David hadn't encompassed the fact he would be older than me by almost twenty years. At the reading, he had been so energetic - so vital - I'd estimated he could only be, at most, in his early thirties, not someone old enough to be my father.

Less successful at dissembling than I'd hoped, I felt David withdraw as he gauged my reaction. 'Think about things,' he said and my heart raced - he must think me a terrible prig.

David was a lecturer in Victorian literature at a Polytechnic not too far from Tottenham Court Road and agreed he would call for me again at Morton's after work, the next week. I could tell him then if I'd like to join him for another meal or would prefer to go straight home.

I was grateful not to have to make a decision right away, I didn't want to discuss the question of David with Alice or Flora and wasn't ready to confide something so new and fragile to my friends. I needed time to think - to try to develop an ability to see clearly into the future. During the week that followed, I slept badly, lost my appetite and was in trouble at work for making mistakes when I cashed up at the end of the day.

But by the time David collected me on Saturday afternoon, I had decided to give him a chance. He interested me - his care for my well-being was reassuring and I enjoyed the sensation of being propelled from the edge of the literary world to the very centre.

We started to meet two or three times a week. His mother, Barbara, was prepared to look after Zoë, when David wanted to go out. Verena had returned from Oxford and when I needed to, I could stay with her overnight and go straight to work from Marylebone the following morning.

David's restless energy excited me, he gate-crashed parties where we met literary "names" whose work I admired and I was sure I could learn from the clever women and opinionated men to whom David was attracted. If he drank too much, so did everyone else and like everyone else he flirted - flattering and praising, using words in precisely the way he knew would please.

David was urbane, cultured and in the space of a year the pattern of my life had altered so radically, I could no longer expect to keep our relationship a secret. With Verena back in London, Rose and I met her each month at an Italian restaurant called Brizio's, situated off one of the narrow alleys behind Oxford Street. We gathered in the conservatory, shared our confidences or as Rose preferred to put it, made our confessions.

Rose was pregnant with her second child and worried Neil might tire of her when the ravages of child-bearing had taken their toll. Verena was in her probationary year at a school in the East End. She claimed she was too exhausted to think about men and working so hard she had no time for a social life, though in the next breath she had invited us to go with her to see a production of *The Merchant of Venice,* in which James Millford was to play the role of Shylock.

I made something of the fact I had known James on Littern Island, but when it was my turn to confess, I came close to relinquishing the chance to tell them about David. They could both be outspoken and I felt my new life was something completely different from their safe and conventional existence.

Hesitantly, I admitted David had been further from obtaining a divorce than he had led me to believe. Verena warned that in her experience, men like David never got divorced and ought to come labelled with a warning "beware, serial romantic at large". She'd had her own share of unsatisfactory love affairs.

Rose argued from a theological point of view, that unless David's marriage was annulled – and there was no chance of that – I would spend the rest of my life living in sin. Whether we married or not, it would make no difference – my choice was to be a fornicator or adulteress and in either case to be damned.

My defence was that David and I were in love – *could love be condemned?* Rose's narrow perspective represented the old world I had left behind to be absorbed into David's, in which he demanded more and more of my time. Resentful of her remarks, I might have echoed my father's words about the Pirans - Rose had been brainwashed by her Catholic education and was blind to the new freedoms the rest of us enjoyed.

David liked to take part in the various literary festivals around the country, which were becoming increasingly popular. He said it was important he attended to help provide a counterweight to the Beat poets and performance artists, whose presence would otherwise dominate. We drove about in his battered car, often making lengthy detours on the way home so he could show me his favourite places.

He said my company - refreshingly youthful and innocent - had given him the gift of a clean start. I was everything Lesley couldn't be and that he stressed was the greatest compliment he could pay anyone.

The more frequently I was away, the more difficult things became at home. It was important to me not to practice deceit - in relation to my past there were already too many secrets. If David wanted to stay away overnight, I would travel home by train from wherever we had ended up. If I was going to be very late, I stayed at Verena's flat, so I could tell Alice and Flora truthfully where I'd spent the night.

For my twenty-third birthday, David gave me a silver bracelet made of interlocking hearts and a matching ring which I wore on the fourth finger of my left hand. Though he had explained he had no desire to re-marry, I felt as bound to him as if we had made solemn vows in church. David had been as reticent about mentioning me to his family as I had been about introducing him to mine and the first time we made love was in the shabby bedroom of a Bed and Breakfast in Cardiff, where we could be certain of avoiding discovery.

David was hurried and clumsy and perhaps being drunk, forgetful of the fact I was a virgin. I found the experience painful and humiliating, a negation of the romantic vision I'd had of our physical union and noticed with sorrow that he made no declaration of love.

Though David's divorce had come through and he was free, it made little difference to the way we led our lives. I grew to know him better and dismissed many things - the hours he poured into his work, his obsessions and his black moods - his excessive drinking which was becoming habitual.

Despite what I observed, I believed in David – believed many things. If he seemed detached, less than attentive, I reasoned he was a mature man, a man who had been through a painful divorce, who had children and heavy responsibilities at work. He needed to channel any spare energy into his poetry. If he never mentioned love, he had, at least, begun to say it would be better if I lived with him. He argued that our extended courtship – over a year – needed to mature into something else or would become pointless. The next logical step was that I would "move in", so that maintaining our relationship wouldn't demand so much of him. He outlined the situation in such a way that I felt needed and was blind to the possibility that his underlying meaning might have been taken by someone else as an insult.

I'd survived the criticisms of my friends and at David's insistence prepared to inform Alice and Flora I would be leaving Wren House and living with him. The naive intention to be honest with them had long ago become flawed. I had withheld information about David so carefully it was inevitable they would be hurt and disappointed when presented with the truth.

His contribution to our discussions proved to be less useful than I had hoped. His assurances to Alice that I had the moral satisfaction of having nothing to do with his broken relationship, didn't impress her. What use was that if he had no intention of marrying me?

Alice, nicknamed "the demon dictator" at school, had, since she'd retired, become more dictatorial at home. David was hot-tempered and I could see his face growing red, the patches of scarlet on his neck and forehead, as he tried to contain himself and not shout or swear.

'Iris is an adult...' he said, 'she can make up her own mind...'

'Does she know her own mind?' Alice asked, a question really directed at me and one which I was unable to answer, torn between the love and security I'd received from her and Flora and my challenging relationship with David.

I hesitated, but David's sea-green eyes dared me to let him down. 'I want to live with David,' I said.

Alice, half blind, turned away from me.

Seeing my dilemma, Flora said, 'How lovely to have a poet in the family.'

Her generous spirit pierced mine with shame. We had cared for one another over the years with loving patience and loving exasperation, how would she manage if I wasn't there to keep the peace? Who would run the house now that they were both in poor health?

Conscience ridden, I delayed my leaving and spent several weeks searching the advertising columns of *The Lady* magazine to find a home-help acceptable to Alice. Just before David lost patience, I discovered Mrs. Stuart, a widow, who lived with her son in Dulwich and came from a genteel Scottish family, who had fallen on hard times. Alice made a commotion about interviewing her and checking references, she claimed having help was an unnecessary extravagance, but despite her objections, when the arrangement had been made, she was clearly relieved.

*

David rented a house in Pimlico for a pittance from his father. Ted had resisted supporting his son and so becoming an unofficial patron of the arts, but his mother, Barbara, was more indulgent and reminded him of David's hope that he might in the future to be able to work part-time at the Polytechnic and focus on his writing.

7A Hurst Row stood at the end of a terrace of Victorian houses. Tall compared to its width, it was a tiny sliver of a house, which had fallen into a state of dilapidation. The primrose yellow door was faded and lumpy with peeling paint, the window frames were held together with wood filler - but the house had its virtues. Off the main bedroom there was a balcony, from which the Thames was visible and through the row of trees that lined the Embankment – across the river - towered the tall, cream chimneys of Battersea Power Station – we had a view. At the back of the house, a small courtyard garden provided a place where we could sit outdoors in the summer and Zoë, who would be living with us, had room to play.

Things seemed to have fallen into place. I visited Alice and Flora regularly and could see Mrs. Stuart had quickly become an integral part of their household. I continued to work part time at Mortons while Zoë attended a kindergarten at the local school. The new baby, Eve, had remained with Lesley.

Each day, when I arrived home from work, I would find Zoë perched on a stool in the kitchen having her tea, her red-blonde hair in two stringy bunches and her blue-green eyes drilling into me. David promised her hostility would pass. When it didn't, he apologised and went on apologising - Zoë was insular because she'd been an only child, he had perhaps spoiled her since his marriage to Lesley had failed, he'd felt sorry for her as Lesley wasn't a natural mother.

Zoë made no effort to hide her feelings about my presence in her home, but I remembered how much I had disliked Geraldine and resented Shirley Fredericks, interlopers in my life as a child, and made allowances for her. After weeks of her campaign to frighten me away, I had simply laughed. Zoë's face had become so distorted with rage, her act so overblown - I'd held the kitchen mirror in front of her and waited until she began to giggle at her ridiculous appearance.

One Friday afternoon, I arrived home late from Morton's and finding the kitchen empty went to look for David and Zoë in the back garden. It was a hot, humid day during the long school holidays and David had told Zoë he would fill the paddling pool, so she could play in the water.

I opened the French doors from the dining room, wondering why David had closed up the house when it needed to be kept aired. As soon as I unlatched the doors, I heard Zoë crying. Her face was a ball of scarlet fury as she kicked through the water in her plastic pool splashing Eve, whose pushchair had been parked nearby.

David had set out two deckchairs under the cherry tree we'd planted at the centre of the garden, not long after I moved in, to provide a little shade. Lesley lay back in one chair, ignoring Zoë's screams. Her sandy hair was clipped back behind her ears, her pasty face shiny with suntan oil and her cotton skirt pushed high up onto her thighs. Beside her, David nursed a glass of iced coffee and was staring into its depths, anything rather than look up at me.

Around Eve's pushchair, where she sat blinking in the sun, the garden was strewn with baby paraphernalia - a dismantled cot, a folded high chair, a large suitcase and several carrier bags from which I could see nappies, toys and baby clothes escaping onto the ground.

As soon as she heard me open the doors, Lesley jolted upright; her hard eyes darted from me to the heap of stuff, 'As you wanted David so much, I thought you might like his brat.'

I felt a flash of anger, Lesley shouldn't speak about Eve like that and I didn't want Zoë picking up her ugly words.

'How long is Eve staying?' I asked, keeping my voice level.

'Eve's just staying,' David said.

From the unpleasant atmosphere in the garden, I could guess there'd been a row.

'Eve's coming to live here,' Zoë shouted. She stamped her foot and pulled a face, then pushed her fingers into her mouth and bit on them, hard.

Lesley's unwillingness to care for Eve was nothing new. Too often David or I had stepped in to take care of the baby – I'd learned quickly how to manage a young child and a well-thumbed copy of Dr. Spock's advice to parents sat on our kitchen bookshelf.

'Why didn't you discuss this first?' I asked. I assumed Lesley had turned up and made a pronouncement about Eve's future, that she had put David in a position where he could hardly refuse to give a home to his own child.

'Eve is David's too – what is there to discuss? Whatever you prefer to tell yourself, David left me and his baby for you.'

Lesley swung her legs round from the deckchair, grabbed the handle of her straw basket and stood up. With her, everything became a drama. I felt David's eyes searching my face as she shoved past me.

'You've no idea what you've got yourself into,' she hissed. 'Sometimes I think David's children are possessed.'

I glanced at David, expecting him to protest, but Lesley didn't stop, she'd gone before any of us could say a word, slamming the French doors as she made her exit through the dining room.

I lifted Eve from her pram. Her blond hair stuck up in short tufts - her blue eyes sparkled, as she settled into my arms with a deep sigh. Zoë's cries had subsided to a grizzle, leaving her red face streaked with tears, but I was shaken and angry, Lesley had done nothing to soften the blow of her leaving.

'What have I got myself into?' I demanded from David. 'Doesn't she care what she says or does? How can she be so heartless?'

David poured his drink onto the paving stones. 'Would you stop, Iris? There's been enough bloody trouble already. Do you think this is what I want?'

76

I was certain it wasn't - he hated to have the pattern of his life disturbed - it was one respect in which he could be accused of being ruthless. David had once said he should never have had children – now his lack of concern and Lesley's willingness to sacrifice Zoë and Eve disturbed me. The truth was neither of them wanted to take responsibility.

I carried Eve inside. Apart from David, no-one knew I was pregnant - our baby was due in February. Hot and tired, I felt overwhelmed by the mess of Eve's young life dumped all over the garden and the reality that by the New Year, I would be the mother of three small children.

When the children were in bed, I wrote my resignation to Morton's, convinced the chaos caused by Eve's arrival was only a foreshadowing of the inevitable disruption which would follow when our own baby was born, I could see no alternative. David wasn't pleased when I mentioned it to him but he didn't want to discuss the matter - so beyond a few protests, directed mainly at Lesley, I said nothing more.

Since the start of my pregnancy I'd felt unwell and David became cool towards me. Zoë could be spiteful - she got her temper from her father. She bit and pinched Eve when she couldn't get her own way and had one stock response to things she disliked, scarlet faced rage. My enduring image of her as a child would be the uneasy juxtaposition of her grubby red face, scored with tears, and her tangle of thick, marmalade orange hair.

David complained he found me distant and unresponsive and I'd begun to suspect he'd known what Lesley had planned for Eve and had lacked the courage to tell me. As had happened with his divorce, David's procrastination, coupled with his desire to avoid trouble, meant that too often important things remained unspoken or undone.

At the end of December, our baby, Tristan, was born prematurely and didn't survive. A tiny scrap of life, he was so fragile, his frail cry barely disturbed the air. For days in the hospital, I watched over him, with his pale, wrinkled face and halo of dark, downy hair. He lay isolated in the capsule of his incubator, lost among a web of tubes, while I desperately longed to hold him.

Allowed, at last, to cradle him in my arms, I both heard and felt his final breath - though his leave-taking was almost imperceptible. His soul slipped away and the world stood still, as if to make way for his departure.

Tristan was buried in the village churchyard at Leitchly, where David's parents lived. We had felt it better for him to rest among trees and wildflowers, animals and birds rather than in the noisy, dirty city.

As I mourned him, I remembered the baby my mother had lost and understood how the death of her child must have left her desolate. While

David was at work, either at the College or in his study, I brooded. *Why had God taken Tristan? What could be more innocent than a newborn child?*

Eve had a nap during the day and while she was sleeping, I would sit in Tristan's newly painted nursery, reliving the moment when my hopes for his survival had been crushed. Sometimes, I would go to the bathroom and fill the bath with warm water, sitting there weeping, too lethargic to get out until Eve's cries demanded my attention.

For David, life and work went on and my listlessness and grieving angered him. 'You're not the only woman to have lost a baby...' he said, as if Tristan had meant nothing to him.

Distraught, I demanded to know - what did he feel – did he feel anything? Couldn't he understand how in losing Tristan, I had been torn apart? I had loved my baby deeply - he had been – and still was - an essential part of me...

Driven beyond endurance by my obsessive mourning, David became enraged, 'I didn't want another bloody child, anyway...' he shouted.

The impact of his callousness, his brutality, released a flood of tears. My unrelenting sense of loss had lasted over a year and if I wasn't to go mad, I needed to find relief.

As if I could excise grief through walking, I roamed the streets taking Eve in her pushchair, having no destination in mind, only wanting to get away from the house in Hurst Row, where I felt the walls had begun to close in on me.

David's house remained as it had been in the 1960's when his parents had lived there. The kitchen was bold red and brilliant white, the sitting room bright orange and pink, the dining room stark in black and white with touches of Schiaparelli pink. Every surface was overrun with Barbara's china - sentimental pieces portraying shepherdesses or plump rosy children like cherubs.

The house was a setting in which I didn't feel at ease, but at first, venturing beyond the confines of home seemed just as disturbing. London was inhospitable; the grey, hard surfaces offered no comfort, Pimlico's residential blocks and rows of dark-bricked terraced houses seemed faceless and anonymous.

Each day, I walked further and further from Hurst Row – going beyond the greengrocer's stand with its colourful display of fruit, vegetables and flowers. Then past the stately Dolphin Square, until I discovered a playground where Eve could climb and run about with other children, while I chatted to their mothers, never admitting what had happened to Tristan, as if losing a child was as unmentionable as a contagious disease.

I longed for another baby and seeing how powerful and instinctual my need for a child, David relented. This time, I had trouble conceiving and when Eve was old enough to attend kindergarten, David thought my best plan was to return to Mortons. Though I was disappointed, his arguments were compelling. There was no point hanging about at home hoping to fall pregnant, he still planned to reduce his hours of lecturing, something he couldn't do so unless we had more money. Eager to encourage his work and to restore our relationship to the loving closeness of our early days, I agreed, though I wouldn't go back to the bookshop. I hadn't relinquished the hope of conceiving and believing that the strain of coping with Zoë and Eve had contributed to Tristan's death, I sought a compromise, something less arduous, which was unlikely to prevent another pregnancy or to cause a miscarriage.

Among the mothers I'd met in the park, one had mentioned her work as a publisher's reader. I approached Neil Sutherland. His marriage to Rose meant he had remained a part of my life, someone I could trust and turn to for help. As a mother of three, Rose supported my suggestion - working as a reader for *Harp Press* would provide income for the family but would allow me to stay at home and care for the children.

Once Neil had arranged things, I set myself up at the dining room table, where I could see the garden and watch the children when they played outside. Zoë had settled at school and Eve was contented, placid and unperturbed by the increasing muddle of our existence. Needing protection from the demands of family life, David shut himself up in his attic study, where he wrote to the miasma of background noise from his jazz records.

While the girls were small, I used to tell them the stories I'd written about *Seabright Island*, in which my main characters, Agnes and Jack, formed a close bond of friendship despite enmity between their parents. Living on an island, they had freedoms a London child could only imagine and embarked on their adventures with a recklessness which appealed to Zoë's impulsive nature and drew admiration from Eve, a more cautious and timid child.

David teased me; the stories were *Romeo and Juliet* without the sex. The children begged me to confess Agnes was me as a child. Not wanting to be questioned about the past, I told them that while my middle name was *Achness* – like a big sneeze - Agnes and Jack had been only a game. They were the imaginary friends of a lonely young girl exiled from her home and their adventures bore little resemblance to the truth about my life at Marisands.

The tales, which had begun as childhood fantasies, grew and were elaborated. I illustrated them with maps, sketches and little paintings of

Littern. When I babysat, I read them to Rose and Neil's children and was persuaded to lend copies of my notebooks to satisfy their demands to hear the stories again.

Neil was encouraging of novice writers and without telling me, showed my notes and pictures to the children's editor at *Harp Press*. I'd begun to consider a future career as a translator. It would be something more precise and measurable than my parents' or David's exploration of the dangerous underworld of the subconscious. While I'd been working for *Harp Press*, Neil had occasionally given me short translation pieces and the challenge of striving for accuracy while composing fluent, readable prose had been intensely satisfying and once Eve was at school, I was sure I would be able to summon up the necessary concentration.

When the *Seabright Island Adventures* were accepted for publication, I was astounded; without struggle, almost by accident, I had stumbled on something worthwhile I could do. With direction from the publishers, I continued to write under my childhood name, Iris Muys, and over the next few years, other books followed. *Copper Tops and Freckles* were about characters based on Zoë and Eve. I collaborated with David, illustrating two anthologies of poems, *The Breezy Book of Verse*, for children and *Sayce's Selection of Poetry* for adults and eventually there came a second and third series of *Seabright Island*.

Those years were to be the most settled period of my time with David – contentment had overtaken me by stealth. Though Tristan would never be forgotten, my life had changed for the better and I had shaken off the persistent mood of gloom which had infected everything I thought, felt or did. In the state of optimism which had replaced it, I believed I could look forward to an existence which would continue, indefinitely, to be happy, creative and fulfilling.

# Chapter 6

David's early poetry was arresting – he could capture a moment and hold it suspended in time – to read his poems was to experience a series of illuminations, through his intense sensuous images and lyric form. But poetry, like all the arts was undergoing a process of radical change and by the late 1980's David became aware that his work was beginning to fall out of favour.

Other poets found ways of bringing their writing in line with modernism, while remaining true to their vision, but rather than moving with the times, David became paralysed by his loyalty to respected poets of the past and by his resistance to the continued challenges of the British Poetry Revival, whose ideology called into question the traditional principles he valued. For a while he laboured with his familiar style and subject matter believing he could, by force of will, defend against being displaced, but as returns on his efforts diminished, he became dispirited and developed a severe case of writer's block.

Until then, being with David had offered a life which was indistinguishable from that of many people we knew. We worked hard all year and in the summer we took the children and spent a few weeks in a rented villa in Brittany. The scenery in Quimper and the sharp salt scent of the sea reminded me of the wilder parts of Littern. There was also a connection with Yvette, who had been born in a village nearby and over the years, I added several pieces to Alice and Flora's collection of faience pottery, which had been started by my great-grandmother.

Usually, we shared a villa with Rose, Neil and their children and I took on the role as an interpreter, as Rose's French hadn't improved since our schooldays and Neil was, in a very English way, self-conscious about speaking another language, though he was reasonably fluent.

For those weeks we lived simply, enjoying local seafood and cheap red wine. Rose and I would sit by the poolside airing thoughts about our children, mulling over our concerns that they should do well at school and keep out of trouble. Meanwhile, Neil and David discussed the changing publishing industry, while the children, indifferent to our worries, swam or played games, most of the time getting on well with one another.

Rose was an affectionate and patient mother. Her children were bright, the image of Neil with his fair hair and blue eyes, but though in him she had found a devoted husband and father, she could never quite shake off her insecurities. After a heavy lunch and plenty of wine, she had asked me if Neil and I had slept together at university. I assured her truthfully that we hadn't, but as I spoke, the unwelcome thought slipped into my mind that I envied her – envied her marriage to a reliable, straightforward man, a man who I had once loved and perhaps had let go too easily.

The escalation of David's problems as a writer coincided with our last trip to Brittany and the holiday was less than successful. David had suggested I went on my own; he would prefer to stay at home and work – believing his sustained lack of inspiration might be relieved in a house which was silent and empty.

His reluctance to take time off triggered complaints from Zoë - Rose and Neil's children were inclined to be bookish, by which she meant dull - and did we have to keep going back to the same place? Eve, she claimed, was always violently sick on the ferry and the thought of it made her want to puke. If David was staying in London, why couldn't she? She was old enough to be left at home, and besides, if her father was there, he could deal with any problems that arose.

In the end, they both made the trip unwillingly and we blamed any friction on the fact the children were growing up - we were caught in a process of change. Rose was studying for a second degree and had brought an enormous pile of psychology books with her, which she needed to read before she went home. David either took off in the car - which meant no-one else could go out - or shut himself in one of the bedrooms, refusing to enjoy the sun or the sea and sometimes not bothering to join us for meals.

It was the end of an era for our families. Rose and Neil's children were studious, whereas Zoë would be going to Drama School in the autumn - a natural performer, with the same tense energy as David. Creative rather than academic, she had refused to conform from a young age. I used to take her to Portobello Market, where we would rifle among the motley collections on the stalls to find garments for her to alter at home, and the market remained the source for most of her clothes. Causing heads to turn with her outrageous sense of dress was an activity Zoë enjoyed - especially if it embarrassed her family and friends and scandalised the conservative French, who regarded her style as outré.

More troubling was that Zoë and her sister had begun to grow apart. Eve was slight and fair, with a rash of freckles and a diffident, unassuming nature. She had been a delicate child, and in her early teens was still prone to long spells of bronchitis in winter. She coveted Zoë's street-wise manner and apparent confidence, her sister was well-liked at school, while she only just survived the waywardness of her peers through her innocent optimism combined with a tendency to be stubborn.

Eve kept away from Zoë, finding a quiet place to sit and draw or read. To her, Rose and Neil's children were intellectuals - they spoke about books she'd never read, films she'd never seen, they argued about current affairs, which didn't interest her – she told me they made her feel feeble and inferior.

That summer, I thought often of Tristan, wondering what sort of child he might have been. Would he have fitted in? Would we have been close? Would he have been a good brother and companion to Eve..?

Rose had announced she was expecting again, though it had hardly been necessary for her to mention it, she blossomed during pregnancy. Neil teased her that the baby was an "afterthought", but seeing her, the wish that I'd had another child struck me again and again with the force of an intermittent pain. Twelve years had passed since Tristan's death, I'd believed myself reconciled, but jealous of Rose's large happy family, I discovered that the loss of him had left a wound which had never quite healed - somewhere deep inside it festered, breaking through to the surface every now and then, just like the wound of losing my mother.

*

To compensate for his failure to produce new writing, that winter David threw a series of parties at home in Pimlico. There were fewer and fewer contemporary writers of whom he approved and his boyish ability to charm had perhaps worn thin. As his efforts to bring about a fresh interest in his poetry failed, he grew increasingly despondent.

Lesley still worked for Halkett & Haire, David's publisher, and it wasn't unusual for her to turn up to his gatherings, at which I spent much of my time in the kitchen on the pretext of refreshing people's drinks, finding more food or clearing away glasses and plates. If the party hadn't spilled outside and the pressure became too much, I took refuge in the garden, looking in at the sea of talking, laughing people who had overtaken our house and wondering what they had to do with me.

David was easily upset, but it was hard to adopt the right approach as he flattered the minor literati who had turned up for free food and drink, or flirted with young women whose talents weren't entirely in the field of letters. He complained about my lack of interest, but for days after his gatherings the house reeked of stale alcohol, cigarette smoke and pot. I'd find empty beer bottles stashed down the side of armchairs, cigarette butts dropped in the loo, food ground into the carpets and often wasted hours hunting down the owners of items of discarded clothing.

Hurst Row had changed, becoming gentrified and the new neighbours, most of whom I hardly knew, stopped me in the road to object to the penetrating noise of David's music and the increasingly decrepit state of the house. Rumours were circulating that David was having an affair with a third year student at the Polytechnic, but when the threat of dismissal put an end to the gossip I hoped that whatever might have been going on had finished.

If David and I were troubled, I continued to have faith in our way of rubbing along, tolerating one another and looking the other way. Already, we had made plans for David's retirement - an escape from London to live by the sea - and I thought those plans would carry us through for the rest of our lives.

My children's books felt as if they belonged to another age; the *Seabright Island Adventures* remained in print, but I had settled into the role of a freelance translator, backing that up with teaching French conversation at St. Catherine's, the school I'd attended and where Eve was now a pupil.

Often I felt lonely, but didn't like to bother Alice and Flora with my personal problems. They were now so dependent on Mrs. Stuart, that there was talk of asking her to move into Wren House to become a live-in housekeeper.

I missed being able to turn to my friends, our regular meetings at Brizio's had faltered, we could rarely find a date when we were all likely to be free. Verena was always busy, now deputy head of a tough school in a deprived area of London, her weekdays followed a nightmarish schedule and her weekends were something she preserved in order to recover. Rose had a baby of two years old and since our last holiday together had fallen pregnant again, despite which she had persisted with her studies.

With his failure to re-instate himself in the world of poetry, David's depression became so severe he was frequently off work and threatened never to go back. When Neil told me *Harp Press* was looking for a translator for Laurence Langlais the Art Historian and suggested he put my name forward, I agreed. Professor Langlais had two popular, long-running TV series, *The Everyday Connoisseur* and *Minor Lights in Art and Culture.* There were spin-off books planned to accompany those programmes, but the difficulty was that though Langlais was fluent in English, he insisted on writing in French.

I applied - lost my nerve - and decided even if the job was offered I would turn down the opportunity. Seeing me waver, Neil insisted I leave everything to him. He confided that my maturity was an essential consideration, as Langlais was regarded by everyone who worked with him as a pretentious pain in the backside.

The meeting with Neil, Laurence and other members of the team was held in the formidable building that housed the publishing company, with its marble pillars, high ceilings and a sweeping, elegant staircase which led to the offices upstairs. Neil had warned that Langlais would want to dominate the conversation, and I watched in admiration as in his calm, reasonable way he kept his difficult client firmly under control.

Laurence was smart in pressed denim jeans, white shirt and a tailored jacket. Though I'd seen him on television often, he was older than I expected, his tightly curled, receding grey hair, revealed a broad shiny forehead, which he said a phrenologist had told him was a guarantee of high intelligence. As we talked, he studied me with keenly observant eyes from behind his round, steel rimmed glasses. He knew of Bernard, Yvette and Flora's paintings and spoke about my background, which he imagined as quaintly bohemian.

Afterwards, Neil explained that was his way of making a pass at me - Langlais was the sort of man who felt obliged to flirt with any woman, but if I could tolerate that and agreed to the contract he had proposed, it could provide me with employment for a number of months, possibly years. "The resurrection of what could loosely be called your literary career," he had teased.

The job appeared more as a life-line than a way of resurrecting long suppressed ambitions. For David, inspiration didn't return and the threats to leave his lecturing job persisted, interspersed with threats from the Polytechnic and complaints from his students about his regular, lengthy absences. Watching him in decline was painful, he suffered with an intensity I'd never encountered in any other person and though I tried to understand and to help, mostly I felt guilty - I was failing miserably - failing to make David happy -

The strict moral code of St. Catherine's was known to make a deep and lasting impression on most of its girls. It had led me to believe if I worked hard and did the right thing, I would be safe, protected by God, and I was unprepared for the way in which both David and the life I had established began first to work loose and then fall apart.

David was convinced every new poet that emerged, every new book of poetry drove home the horrible truth that his work was outdated and he wasn't a man willing to reframe obscurity as an opportunity for personal growth or change.

When we'd first met, David had all the advantages of age and experience and I hadn't questioned his bleak humour or the threatening moods which hung in the atmosphere like storm clouds. I hadn't comprehended how ambition consumed him or how the darkness of envy and possessiveness could overshadow his better nature.

David drank - chain smoked - and lived on strong black coffee. Incarcerated in his study he mourned his inability to work with the same intensity I had mourned Tristan. Some days, he left the house without warning and didn't come home at night. He was suspicious, almost paranoid, but when I asked where he'd been, he answered by levelling accusations of infidelity at me – *did it matter where he'd been, wasn't I in love with Neil?*

Among our friends, the tale of my brief liaison with Neil at university had become nothing more than an amusing story and I reminded David of how our relationship had foundered the instant I had introduced him to Rose. David wasn't to be put off. If it wasn't Neil I was having an affair with, then it was Laurence Langlais, though despite his flirtatious manner, I was as Neil said "distinctly beneath Langlais's radar". In practice, it would have been difficult to tell which of us was most reclusive, the shy translator or the elusive author, and from the beginning, Neil had acted as an intermediary for our communications - like a medium he bridged our different worlds.

I continued to reassure David with facts, until I became sick of hearing my own denials and lashed out - *unlike him, I didn't need to sleep with my colleagues in order to work with them.* Laurence was an irritant. The desire to have a fling with a TV celebrity didn't exist. I loved David and despite our problems believed our relationship to be worth rescuing.

Without a focus, his jealousy became anger, and turning that anger inward David swung further down into despondency. Some days, I wept listening to his cries as he paced back and forth in the attic. If I went to comfort him, he wanted nothing from me - there was nothing I or anyone else could do for him. His crying alternated with bouts of rage. He directed his fury at me and the girls, especially Zoë, whose teenage angst had begun to manifest with particular ferocity.

David's outbursts were frightening - his face reddened, the cords stood out on his neck as a torrent of contempt poured over his victim. If Eve's strategy was avoidance, Zoë was willing to confront him, though his words of criticism were acid enough to expose her capacity to be broken.

When I found myself pregnant, I was faced with the reality of a baby being born into the mess of our relationship, I was afraid for David, but more afraid of what he might say or do in response to the news.

I counted Verena as my closest friend, but she had remained single and had little experience of the dynamics of family life, so I confided in Rose. Rose had continued her study of psychology – *with six children how could I not?* And when I described David's behaviour she assured me he could be helped, his was a classic case of depression.

Her analysis of our situation acted as a salve, David's behaviour towards me and the girls was a function of his illness, an aberration which might pass. Knowing Rose and Neil's last two children had been unplanned, I mentioned my thoughts of abortion to her in the knowledge that she would disapprove fervently on personal and religious grounds and might prevent me from doing something I would regret later on.

"This "unwanted" child could change your life - change it for the better,' she said.

It seemed unlikely, but I wanted to remain positive. My relationship with David might not at present be what I hoped for - but there was always the future to look forward to and I clung to that possibility.

Unwilling to risk an outburst from David, I concealed my pregnancy for almost five months. We slept together rarely and my discouragement of his advances was both expected and familiar. The baby could - for now – remain my secret and I enjoyed the feeling of its tiny body floating in the warm, fluid protection of my womb. When I caressed my belly in a gesture of tenderness, it brought me comfort too.

Then one evening, after supper, when Eve and Zoë had gone out, I made up my mind to confess and lingered by the dining room door, hoping to prevent David storming off, which had become his consistent habit when annoyed.

He was pouring scotch from the decanter, a cigarette hanging from his lips. His hands unsteady, he spilt whisky on the carpet – I would clean it up later, just as I would clean up the flecks of ash which flowed down his shirt front onto the floor.

'We need to talk,' I said, 'I'm pregnant.'

Swinging round to face me he asked, 'What the fucking hell did you want to do that for?' and banged his glass down on the table.

There were times when I wished David was dead - at other times I was haunted by the fear he might take his own life – and sometimes, as in that moment - the two ideas merged into one.

'Is it mine?'

'...Of course.'

'Why "of course"?' he demanded, glaring at me, 'how the hell would I know what you get up to?'

'You might trust me...'

'I don't want another bloody child,' he said, his jaw tightly clenched. He had said the same about Tristan.

He stepped forward. His once slender body was heavy and lumbering, the mass of him threatening as he pushed his face towards mine, towering over me.

I edged away, as he began to shout. 'You knew how I felt and you deliberately acted against my wishes...'

'It wasn't deliberate,' I said, my heart racing. I had interrupted him but blundered on, 'it's your fault as well.'

I was about to add that conceiving a baby took two, when David stepped forward again and yelled in my face, 'How is it *my* bloody fault? I thought you were taking the pill?'

'It didn't seem necessary.'

He grabbed my hair and thrust me back so violently, I lost my balance and fell, knocking my head against the sharply angled corner of the sideboard.

My knees folded and I slid to the floor with a thud.

David stepped over me and I was terrified he might kick out. But in a few seconds, I heard the metallic jangle as he lifted his keys from the hook in the hall and left the house, slamming the door behind him.

In the silence that followed, relieved he had gone, I lay on my side looking out of the window, where petunias with their bright jewel colours, shone among green foliage. My heart wouldn't stop pounding. Something warm was dripping down my left cheek and when I put my hand to my temple, my fingers came away sticky with blood. I knelt, getting slowly to my feet, legs trembling. I breathed deeply, but it didn't calm me. My limbs shook uncontrollably as bright red stains appeared on the front of my t-shirt and I prayed, *please God, he hasn't harmed the baby.*

Stumbling through to the kitchen, I pulled a clean tea cloth from the drawer pressing it hard against my head to stop the bleeding. Faint and dizzy, I examined the cut in the mirror – my face was blenched stark white, my eyes ringed with shadows. And in my reflection I saw my mother – her ghostly face as she received William's slap, delivered in the kitchen at Marisands, where they had been arguing about Shirley and Geraldine.

I sank down onto a kitchen chair, my hand stroking the place on my belly where I could feel my child moving, I murmured, *it's all right, it's all right*. When I was sure there was no bleeding from my womb, I went upstairs - step by step - on my knees. In the bathroom, sitting on the edge of the loo, I cleaned my face. My hair was clotted with blood - but it could wait – I'd wash it out in the morning.

Head throbbing, I changed into a nightdress and slid into the coolness of the spare bed in the room once to have been Tristan's nursery and soon to be occupied by the new baby.

David's words had been cruel, crueller than his violence - my feelings for him were confused, conflicted. I loved him, I hated him. I didn't know if any vestige of love for me survived in him – I couldn't tell if I wanted him to come home or to stay away - to stay away perhaps forever.

Thoughts amassed in my mind. I had tried to protect Zoë and Eve, to provide them with a safe, secure childhood. I had wanted my family to resemble the Pirans, as they had been before my mother's death, close and caring and somehow I needed to create that sense of security and wellbeing for our new child.

Full of questions - I had no answers. If I left David, where could I go? What would happen to Zoë and Eve? I could think of nowhere to seek even temporary refuge - Rose and Neil's house was overcrowded, Verena had her own busy life, Alice and Flora were now elderly and frail, they couldn't be expected to deal with my arrival on their doorstep with two teenagers and a tiny baby.

Alice had once said, the Armsted family were no good at love – her words had felt like a curse and she might as well have added that in that living with David I had made my own bed and had better lie on it.

I had endured years of disquiet and was weary of many things, from Lesley's presence in our lives to David's zealous interest in young female writers and the humiliating gossip about his relationships with his students. That evening David had put our baby's life at risk and yet my inclination remained what it had always been - to keep quiet, lie low and trust that in time our difficulties would be resolved.

\*

David didn't apologise and neither did I, instead we circled each other warily and he embarked on his own project, to create a new collection of poems, to raise his profile on the poetry scene.

I said nothing to discourage him, though he was no longer asked to do readings, nor to conduct workshops and his poems were being rejected by the usual small magazines he'd felt he could rely on. At the time when his reputation had started to wane, David had been subject to some of the bitchiness that can exist in the incestuous world of literature and had taken it to heart. He insisted now that he had put all that behind him and was ready to develop fresh ideas.

When approached, his publishers proved uninterested in the idea of his new book and David was outraged. He spoke to Neil, but Neil told me he had tried to prevent David from struggling with work he suspected might prove a waste of time. He had been tactful, but David needed to come up with poems that were less reactionary both in style and content.

David wasn't going to be advised by anyone. He had given the collection the title *Blue Rhythms,* and it would come into being whatever the pundits said. Neil was struck off his list of contacts as pseudo literate and *Harp Press* dismissed as publishing only third rate, trivial and inconsequential trash.

Meaning to help, I suggested we might collaborate as we had on the poetry books we'd produced in our early days together, but David was resistant. Didn't I think he was capable of working on his own or of doing anything without my bloody interference?

He shut himself up in the study for longer and longer each day, jazz blaring through the house as if to drown out the presence of his family. If he could be persuaded to talk about *Blue Rhythms* at all, it seemed the harder he worked the less he achieved. He was exhausted, bad tempered, morose and in the face of his obduracy, Zoë became increasingly unapproachable and Eve withdrawn.

David had always worked hard, now he worked compulsively, he became sensitive to any external, obtrusive sound, even the familiar hum of traffic, a constant background to our lives. I made efforts to persuade him to go to the doctor, but he refused. I went to the doctor on David's behalf, but he said there was little he could do if David was unwilling to co-operate. I spoke to Rose, but she said what I knew she must say, there was nothing anyone could do for David by proxy.

Needing sanctuary, the church became my refuge, not in the religious way of my childhood but in a sensual way. I rested in the quietness, the soft flickering candle light and the sweet, spicy smell of incense. What was taking place with David was the slow erosion of love and respect. He didn't sleep and was sluggish physically and mentally; his sense of humour had vanished as if a flame had been extinguished.

David was often out and I took to working upstairs in his study. I was watchful for signs of progress with *Blue Rhythms,* but all I found were lists of poems, poems altered beyond legibility, lists and lists, filling the waste bin, covering the floor in tightly screwed balls. The hours he spent isolated from his family had resulted in nothing but a morass of discarded paper.

As the year sank down towards winter, David's mood darkened. Zoë he claimed was impossible - she emanated bad vibes, which meant he couldn't work when she was in the house - Eve moped – and seeing my pregnant state got on his nerves. It was as if he was raking through our lives seeking anything we had ever done to annoy or upset him.

Minette was born in January, a strong, healthy baby, dark haired, grey eyed and pale - a little moon-face. Rose had come to the hospital and stayed during the birth and we had chosen her name together, it meant star of the sea or protector.

Then, David's absences from Pimlico increased, he couldn't cope with Minette's crying or the disturbed nights and disordered days. When he returned to Hurst Row he was irritable and distracted. He blamed me for the chaos but offered no help. I began to agree it was better for everyone when he stayed at Leitchly with his mother. He told me, he was getting on well there with *Blue Rhythms,* though months had elapsed without any sign of a finished manuscript.

The situation at home was becoming intolerable. Zoë was vociferous in her disapproval of my having a baby and though quieter and more earnest in her views, I suspected Eve felt the same. In getting pregnant, they believed I had been careless and my carelessness carried a heavy price - it had driven away their father.

*

David and I continued our uneasy state of separation without either of us initiating change, until one afternoon, when I went to visit Flora and Alice with Minette, who was by then almost four years old. Minette was a favourite with them - she had been an accommodating baby and had grown into an affectionate and lovable child - Flora doted on her and even Alice thought she was exceptionally well behaved. Minette was companionable and went everywhere with me, including to St. Catherine's where she played happily while I chatted in French to the small groups of girls I taught.

As soon as we arrived home that day, Eve informed me, 'Dad's disappeared.'

David had apparently taken off without a word, though more often lately he told us if he was having dinner in Leitchly or planning to stay with his mother.

Eve was standing by the stove, heating her usual snack of macaroni cheese, a pallid, glutinous concoction she bought in a tin and the sight of it - let alone the smell - made me feel nauseous.

'I suppose Dad's gone to Granny's again,' she said.

I thought she was probably right, though there were times when David's behaviour was alarming and I imagined him vanishing in a state of mental fugue or doing harm to himself.

Minette settled at the table and began to fiddle with the pieces of a wooden puzzle, while I cleared the kitchen of the stacks of crockery, discarded food and wrappers which had appeared on the worktops since lunchtime. Zoë had been home with her friends.

Eve helped wash the plates, dishes and pans, but she seemed distressed. Every so often, she swept her long fair hair back from her face with her hand as if she might speak - but when I glanced up expectantly, she deliberately avoided my gaze.

'What happened, while I was out?' I asked.

'Some publisher phoned. They told Dad his book was incoherent and disorganised - I can't remember the exact words he used.'

My stomach was rumbling and Minette was grizzling about being hungry and bored.

'Was Zoë all right?'

Eve pulled a face. '...Moaning as usual... Dad told her to shut up and she threw some ornament of Granny's at him, I think it was *The Bluebell Children*. After that she went out and so did Dad...' Eve looked at me, her clear, blue eyes full of concern, 'I've been making plans,' she said, 'but if you Dad aren't okay...'

'Dad's going through a bad patch, but it needn't affect what you want to do,' I said.

I'd trotted out the same lame excuse for David countless times, but I felt sorry for Eve. Her artistic ability had appeared like a rogue shoot on the Sayce stem - it was something David blamed on my influence and with which Eve found it difficult to make terms. She'd chosen to study art conservation rather than fine art, as the school had recommended, but I sensed an unspoken desire for something more, the suspicion that she might have betrayed her talent.

Eve moved gracefully as she wiped down the kitchen surfaces. 'Some people I know are going to Cornwall, to a sort of artist's commune...' her words were slow and considered.

'...And?'

'I thought I might join them, see how it goes.'

In my mind, I ran through a list of worries. If Eve left college and went to Cornwall now, she'd have no qualifications, she might get pregnant, drink too much, take drugs, and owe impossible amounts of money - but the truth was I would miss her.

'I'm meeting my friends in half an hour,' she went on, 'they want to know if I'm going to join them - I don't know what to say.'

'What would you like to say?' I asked. Eve was so tender-hearted, she found making decisions hard.

She shrugged in reply and sympathy welled in my chest, she was about to dissolve into tears. 'Do you have to give them an answer today?' Eve lacked David and Zoë's certainty about their ability and right to practise their art, but perhaps, in time, self-belief might come.

Minette abandoned the puzzle she'd been doing and tugged at my skirt, if I didn't give her something to eat at once, she was going to be sick.

Eve wasn't by nature evasive, but grasping her opportunity she slipped out into the hall, then I heard footsteps on the stairs and the click of her bedroom door as it closed.

I handed Minette Eve's macaroni on toast, which she ate with the relish of someone presented with a plateful of slugs. When she'd finished all she could stomach, I found chocolate biscuits in the cupboard and bribed her to have half an apple in exchange for a reward.

It was early, but Minette was tired and grumpy, so I ran her bath and put her to bed by half past six. She was a sensible child and after three stories lay down to sleep. Kissing her goodnight, I hoped she didn't sense my desolation or my coldness towards David; I didn't want the girls burdened with responsibility for what was happening to our family.

My appetite had gone, but I heated a can of stew and some rice and took a tray into the sitting room. A few fragments of *The Bluebell Children* figurine lay scattered across the hearth, where someone had done a hurried job of sweeping up.

I'd long ago given up admitting breakages to David's mother. Privately, I agreed with Zoë who said, "Living with her crap in the house offends my aesthetic". It was in the garden that I'd made my mark, dispensing with the pots David's mother had filled with annuals each year, replacing them with roses, iris, clematis and honeysuckle, plants I had known and loved from my childhood, both at Wren House and at Marisands.

I heard Eve leaving the house, escaping through the side door. Switching on the TV, I watched a programme in which Laurence

Langlais discussed the Impressionists. As a presenter, he was something of a poseur – playing up his French accent, gesticulating more than was necessary and managing to combine French-ness and eroticism with the image of a mad but learned professor.

The programme turned out to be one I'd watched before and I soon dozed off. I'd been working into the early hours of the morning for several weeks, only to sleep badly when eventually I made it to bed.

More than two hours later, the sound of a thumping bass line reverberating through the living room ceiling woke me - Zoë had returned and put on her favourite Jimi Hendrix track, recorded onto a cassette so she could wind it back and replay it - again and again and again.

The clock on the mantelpiece read quarter past nine; I'd intended to phone David after supper, but though it was late, I dialled his mother's number and Barbara came to the phone.

'I don't know why you're calling at this hour,' she complained - as I knew she would.

I apologised. Since David's father had died, life at Leitchly was run according to a strict timetable, but despite the lateness of my call, I asked if she thought David might be willing to speak to me. David's grumbling response was audible in the background.

'I expected you'd be here when I got home,' I said, not meaning to sound reproachful, 'the place was in a terrible mess.'

'Is that why you're so irritable? Mother says you're snapping.'

'Am I irritable?'

'*Bloody* irritable,' David said, his voice slurred as if he'd been drinking.

'We were worried about you – we wondered when you might be coming back?'

'Mother needs shopping in Croydon tomorrow - I thought I'd help her.'

I told him about Eve and the artists' commune in Cornwall, but he seemed unconcerned. 'She said one of the publishers you'd contacted rang...'

'I'm taking my work elsewhere...'

Our conversation felt like a duel - a constant exchange of retreat and attack. 'What I'm asking David is - are you all right?'

'Was I all right when you left home this morning? What's changed?' he asked sarcastically.

'Nothing *here* has changed.'

'So why did you phone? I'm staying in Leitchly, with my mother, as I've done innumerable times...'

'I thought you might be upset,' I said, faltering. 'I wasn't checking up on you.'

David's laugh was bitter, 'Are you sure? The problem isn't what I am doing, is it? It's what you think I might be doing. Your insecurity is like a bloody disease.'

'That isn't true.' I said - biting back words which would have reminded him of the unjust accusations he had levelled at me over the years and of *his* many flirtations, which I had largely ignored.

'God - what difference does it make?' he said. 'I've got to go. Mother's poured us another drink.'

I put the phone down. 'What an impossible man!' I said out loud,

Zoë was coming downstairs and heard me. 'Lost it Iris?'

'Somebody's lost it, but I think it's your father.'

Zoë crouched down and pulled on a pair of Afghan boots. Her grey coat was several sizes too big for her. She wore a scarlet woollen cap, which clashed violently with her ginger hair and a matching knitted scarf which was so long it trailed on the floor.

'I don't know why you take any notice of him,' she said.

'I suppose because I love him, I love all of you.'

Zoë mimed sticking her fingers down her throat and then smiled brazenly. 'All alone with nothing to do..?'

Her comment reminded me that I ought to be working. Laurence Langlais had recently begun writing a series of detective novels, *The Kenholme Mysteries*. He claimed the hero, Peter Kenholme, was his alter ego and that writing fiction provided light relief from the stress of being an art historian. My role in his work had developed into that of a translator-cum-ghost writer and as he was as fast, prolific and demanding an author of fiction as he was of non-fiction, I was left constantly up against the next deadline.

'Where are you off to?' I asked.

'Cameron's,' Zoë said. And in a flash of scarlet, ginger and grey disappeared out of the front door.

I'd only meant to express a friendly interest - with Zoë I no longer knew when I ought to be anxious. Cameron Monroe shared a basement flat in Stockwell with other music students from his college and she often stayed there. As far as I could tell, he seemed to be her boyfriend, but among her large group of friends, relationships, though passionate, were usually fleeting.

I made coffee and headed upstairs to the study, my mug in one hand and a cardigan in the other. I'd decided to read through text I'd written the previous day, it would be progress, even if I couldn't write anything new.

Hands full, I went into the room backwards, pushing the door open with my elbow. When I spun round, I faced devastation. Books had been thrown or dropped all over the floor, their pages splayed open. Some had pages torn out, crumpled and tossed down to join the scattered pieces of David's manuscript. David wrote with a fountain pen and there were gashes of black ink splattered onto the walls and across the carpet, ink had leaked onto the desk staining the wood.

I put down the coffee and slipped on my cardigan; suddenly I felt icy cold and needed to comprehend the scene in front of me, to try and interpret the meaning of it. On the chair, he'd left a pad of paper covered in scribbled reviews of other writers' poems. I picked it up and read what he'd written - David hadn't been asked to review anything and what he'd said was mean-minded and vitriolic, as if he could relieve his own sense of failure by the sly and provocative means of undermining other people's success and talent.

All thoughts of Laurence's script flew out of my head. Should I phone David again? Should I tidy the mess - or leave it to him?

I sat in front of the computer as if mesmerised by the blank screen. After a few minutes, I decided to begin by taping torn pages back in the books they'd come from – when I'd done that, I could put the desk and the rest of the room in order.

Sorting papers and scrubbing at ink stains, I wished I'd stayed at home that afternoon. If David had suspected that whatever brain storm he was experiencing might be interrupted, the knowledge might have prevented this pointless destruction.

Replacing books on the shelf, I stopped to read some of his poems – many were love poems - but where I was concerned, his words were spent; they had become empty vessels. A part of David beat hard against the bars of commitment and as I read on, doubts began to escalate. *Were his visits to Leitchly a cover up? Was he having an affair? Was it possible David and his mother could be acting together in a conspiracy?* As he was now, David cut a ridiculous figure as a womaniser; both his waistline and his reputation were sagging. *If he could barely manage ordinary family life - could he cope with the clandestine?*

Downstairs, I dialled his mother's number resolving to be constructive - to communicate my love for him - something I had failed to do when we had spoken earlier.

This time, David answered, and I mentioned it would soon be the anniversary of our first meeting at Morton's – couldn't we go out for a meal together?

'I'm not sure I feel like it...' he said - his voice expressionless - and briefly I thought his lack of irritation might signify he was mellower, more relaxed after a drink.

'Are you feeling depressed?' I asked, wanting to be understanding.

'...For God's bloody sake..! Shut up!' He shouted. His anger was like a wasp buzzing madly - banging its head repeatedly against a closed window.

Staying calm, I suggested, 'We could have lunch at the Indian restaurant where we had our first meal together.' He didn't reply, so I repeated myself, 'We could have lunch – talk - then you could come home.'

'I heard you the first time. But I'm not coming home - I'm staying here with Mother.'

I couldn't think straight – *What did he mean? ...Did he mean now, did he mean forever?* How had I failed to perceive the point when David had given up, when he no longer considered our relationship worthwhile?

'I'd like us to sort things out,' I said, 'why can't we do that?'

'Just leave it alone...'

'David...' I pleaded, feeling helpless.

'Damn you...' he roared.

'I'm sorry...'

I wasn't sure what I'd been going to say. But before I could find more words, he had dropped the receiver and the silence that followed had the quiet finality of a guillotine blade slicing down.

# Chapter 7

A letter from my father arrived early in May, forwarded from Wren House. William always wrote to me care of Alice and Flora, though I'd lived in Pimlico for many years. He suggested we meet when he visited London for the Royal Academy Summer Exhibition in June and promised to write again when he'd fixed on a suitable time and place for us to have lunch.

Work, family, and fears about my future occupied much of my mind. The weeks sped by, until at the beginning of June a second letter arrived, signed as the first had been - *William Muys* - with that formality of my father's, which suggested that in-between meetings, I might have forgotten his name. His message was brief and to the point. He would be coming to London and would like me to meet him at Pettit's Restaurant, near Paddington. He'd noticed an article in *The Guardian*, the newspaper had said the place was under new management and he'd thought it would be a good place to eat and to talk.

Usually, after a few civilities, our conversations were notable for the embarrassing silences which punctuated the polite questions we posed each other, having no real interest in the answers. Now he suggested I allow a couple of hours, making something of an occasion of it and would appreciate a reply to let him know if I'd be there. Feeling unsure, I pushed the letter back in its envelope - and went to sit in the garden.

As it matured, the garden had become a leafy bower – or what David regarded as an overgrown wilderness. Every space, vertical and horizontal, had been filled with plant life - roses, clematis and vines grew up the fences and the cherry tree now cast deep green shadows over the paving stones.

Placing a chair in the shade I closed my eyes and tried to dispel the distraction of William's letter. His impersonal words had summed up the emptiness which characterised my relationship with him - yet when we met - I found myself eager to elicit his affection, hoping things would be more open and that we might discover a common bond which we had so far overlooked.

Before very long, it was too hot to sit outside even in the shade and I retreated into the house feeling a headache coming on. Turning on the kitchen tap, I caught my reflection in the small mirror over the sink - red faced and frowning. I splashed my cheeks with cold water, fingering the white scar on my temple, left from when I'd fallen against the sideboard the evening I'd told David about Minette.

I filled a glass with water, went upstairs and located a packet of pain killers in the bathroom cabinet and took two. My head was pounding as I stretched out on top of the bed with an electric fan blowing cool air over me. I tried to nap, but my father's letter replayed in my mind. I couldn't stop gnawing at the scant details, trying to detect a hidden meaning or to define why it suggested something unusual and worrying.

Pettit's was a smart bistro, with white cloths, glass candlesticks, and a menu of classic country food. I arrived first and waited outside - my father had a habit of being late and sometimes forgot to turn up at all. But then watching him approach, I couldn't miss the change in William since I'd last seen him. He was of a slight, wiry build and had been quick in his movements, but now he walked haltingly for a man not yet in his seventies.

When he drew level with me, he said, 'Let's go inside.' There was no kiss, no hug- it was straight down to business.

He strung his canvas shoulder bag over the back of the chair and sat down, his linen jacket hung loosely on his shoulders, as if his body had shrunk and he had little flesh left on his bones.

Pettit's had only two other customers, we were early for lunch. William ordered a bottle of wine and I enquired after Geraldine. She'd remained my father's companion since Juliet had died and they'd continued to live at Marisands.

'I'd say Geraldine was less fat, more senile,' he told me without a smile, 'but I'm glad she's around. What are you up to these days?'

I explained nothing had changed - I was still Laurence Langlais's translator.

'Hasn't Langlais already said too much in any language?' he asked, 'All he's concerned about is fostering his public image...'

Though it was true Laurence was in many ways self-promoting, he'd set about demystifying art for the wider public and I respected him for that. 'I have to support myself and the family...' I told him, I didn't want to cause an argument.

'No-one's questioning *your* ability, Iris,' he said.

The waiter brought the menu, a basket of bread and plates of salad. I recounted news of the family, skirting round the troubling bits about David, but could tell William wasn't listening; he seemed more than usually preoccupied.

'I need you to forgive me,' he said. 'When you were a child, I was selfish and insensitive.'

Taken aback, I asked, 'Why do you say that now?' In our conversations, we were careful to avoid straying towards the personal, particularly matters involving the past.

'Sending you away after your mother died was necessary, but unkind,' he said. 'You have the same clear, grey eyes as Juliet, the same quality of stillness and at the time, I found that hard.'

'I've always hoped you might tell me what happened to my mother,' I said – wondering - was this the moment when the circle of silence around Juliet's death would be broken?

'Have you ever behaved badly?' he asked. '...Really badly..?' His breathing was shallow and uneven.

Disappointed, I realised my father was set on a course of his own. 'I don't know what you mean,' I replied, he was talking in riddles. My view of William had been strongly influenced by Alice and Flora and their disapproval had crystallised into my own harsh judgement of him.

At first, he didn't answer - he was coughing and couldn't catch his breath. While I waited for him to recover, I sipped my wine and picked at the bread on my plate.

'One day you'll probably inherit Marisands,' he said at last. 'I've told Geraldine, when I'm gone, she's to take nothing except what's hers.'

He dabbed his eyes with a napkin, his coughing fit had made them water. Though I had been thinking of my mother, I was beginning to comprehend – my father was telling me he was dying.

William lifted his glass - a few drops of wine spilled onto the perfect white tablecloth staining it purplish red. 'We don't always behave in the best possible way,' he said, his voice stronger.

'If I knew why you acted as you did, things might be easier...' I was afraid the chance for the truth to be spoken would be lost, yet I clung to my arrogance as I offered him the sort of forgiveness which involved only an effort of will not a sacrifice of the heart.

William reached across the table and took my hand. 'Things aren't always as they appear - Juliet made a choice, didn't she?'

'Did she choose to die?'

Having lived with David as he fought depression, I'd increasingly considered that whatever my role in her death, it was possible Juliet might have committed suicide.

William turned away as if thinking of how to reply as our main course was brought to the table. 'Some things are better not known,' he said, when the waiter had gone.

My hand was caught in his, but I drew it away. I'd been striking against this barrier of evasion since childhood and it was making me angry.

I asked after his work, that he was doing something was obvious from the tiny splatters of paint on his hands, the faint, encrusted rim of blue round his fingernails – but he refused to be drawn on the subject of his painting or on his opinion of that year's Summer Exhibition. As I questioned him, he coughed and framed curt answers. He was growing tired.

'Geraldine says I've gone soft in the head, but I've spoken to a priest,' William said.

I said nothing, if there was one thing about my father I would have held certain, it was his atheism. What had he glimpsed of the next world to arouse his desire to turn to religion?

'I suppose you might say I panicked' he said, apologetically. 'There've been too many points of departure, each more frightening than the last. I wanted to know what might happen next.'

Trying to read his expression, the gauntness and the greyness of his face told the whole story – I was looking at a man in the final stages of life – a man who was my father and yet a stranger.

We'd left most of the food on our plates and seeing we had laid down our knives and forks, the waiter cleared the table.

'We'd like pudding,' William said and ordered for us both as if he wanted to prolong our meeting.

During my childhood we had rarely touched, but now once again, I felt the warmth of his hand as it settled on my arm.

'I'm not asking to be let off the hook,' he said, 'that would repel me.'

A new group of people came into the restaurant and were shown to a table, close behind us.

'This is hardly the place...' I whispered, not wanting our conversation to be overheard.

'But you came here to see me?'

'You're my father - I can't help it.'

He looked uncomfortable - and I stared down at my hands, resting on the white table cloth - William hadn't let go of my arm. *Could love survive disappointment, indifference, rejection – could my feelings towards my father have ever been called love?*

I asked, keeping my voice low, 'What about my father loving me?'

When he gave no answer, I pulled my arm from his grasp, toppling my wine over. William's free hand pawed the air, but he was too slow and the glass smashed on the floor. Red-faced, I stood so the waiter could clear away broken glass and spilt wine, scraping my chair across the tiled floor and attracting more unwelcome attention.

When the fuss was over, William said, 'I was no use after your mother died - the women I liked weren't the motherly kind.'

'You sent me away...'

'...In your best interests.'

'All these years, I've needed to hear the truth from you, the truth about my mother and preferably without having to ask for it.'

'We're both haunted by Juliet.'

'And will be until you find the courage to speak,' I said. 'You've asked for forgiveness, but you refuse to tell me what I need to know. I grew up believing I was responsible for Juliet's drowning and you've done nothing to offer comfort or to relieve me of guilt or responsibility. I find myself asking is it possible she committed suicide – but I also have to ask, in what way might that be your fault?'

I spoke with deliberate cruelty. A deep crack split off the person I believed myself to be from this new and unpleasant person, who could be malicious and unkind to a sick old man. I'd come to meet William expecting a conversation, but when he needed me to, I'd been unable to hear his confession.

My eyes flicked up to meet his. In them I observed the sharp, metallic glint of his despair and it touched the flesh of my own hopelessness so that for a second a thread of understanding formed between us: we each wanted something from the other that they couldn't give.

Later, I would realise I should have said something - something kind - before the connection was broken. Instead, I refused his proffered hand and closed myself to him. After that, we hardly talked and as soon as we'd had coffee, William became restless and anxious to leave.

'Would you walk with me to the station?' he asked.

He held my arm as we set out along Augur Street towards Paddington. I carried his canvas bag, thinking it might be heavy.

As his weight bore down on me, I asked, 'How long have you been ill?' He was walking less well than when he'd approached Pettit's only two hours ago - small drops of perspiration formed on his temples and ran down his cheeks, his face was ashen.

'Shouldn't you see a doctor?' I asked, tentative because we had never been close in that way.

'I've seen plenty of doctors.'

We turned out of the sunlight into the dim, grey interior of the station - William was travelling home on the two-thirty train.

While we waited for his platform number to appear on the departures board, he said, 'The things you do or don't do – the things you regret - they're all part of the journey...'

His voice was scarcely audible in the hubbub of noise on the concourse, but I considered his words and thought how easy it would be to absorb the failures of a life into that glib, reassuring philosophy.

'I've never stopped loving Juliet,' he said, 'the others were insignificant, even Geraldine, though she's incurably loyal. If I'd behaved differently, your mother and I might have made something of ourselves...'

His train was announced and a crowd of people surged in the direction of the ticket barrier - I steadied him against the jostling – William asked the ticket collector if he would allow me through to say good bye. Afraid he might fall as we hurried along the platform, I supported him until we had reached the carriage, where he had booked a seat.

Seeing him so frail, aware our meeting had been painful and inconclusive I said, 'I'd like to forgive you, but I'm not sure what I'm forgiving you for...'

William rocked on his feet as if he scarcely had strength to stand. 'Go back to Marisands, you'll find the truth there...'

I had little interest in the house or the island - apart from the family paintings, what could I possibly want? I helped William climb the steps into the carriage. He stood in the open doorway gripping hard onto the handrail.

'Take this,' he said passing me a slip of paper with a phone number written on it. 'The priest I mentioned,' he added by way of explanation, 'when the time comes - call him.'

I pushed the note into the back of my handbag. The guard blew his whistle and began slamming the doors.

William said, 'I expect nothing from you – don't write or phone it would only make Geraldine agitated.'

His words felt like a rejection - I pretended I hadn't heard. But as his train pulled out and I waved to him, I found myself in tears.

# Chapter 8

I wrote to my father at Christmas and sent him a book on contemporary art from *Harp Press,* recommended by Neil, but received no reply.

Then in February, a printed card arrived from Geraldine giving the date and time of William's funeral, which would take place at Safford Bridge Crematorium.

Flora and Alice had also been informed of my father's death, but Alice seemed mainly anxious about the house, Marisands, and had contacted the family solicitor. For years, there had been arguments about the property, but as Alice evaded my questions, I didn't know why.

Now, she was angered by my indifference to her concerns and said, 'This situation involves you directly, Iris. Don't you think you should demonstrate a sense of responsibility?'

My aversion to going to Littern or to establishing the current state of Marisands was in her eyes a dereliction of duty. But in the event of William's death, I was unable to decipher what I felt about him - let alone the house and island. Worn down by my estrangement from David, I'd withdrawn into a hard, brittle shell – I didn't need my emotions to be bruised by anyone else or battered by the need to negotiate awkward situations on behalf of the family.

Geraldine's card reminded me of the slip of paper my father had handed me at Paddington. I'd placed it into a book by Laurence Langlais - using it to mark text about *Art Brut,* the style of painting my father had so admired.

William hadn't written a name with the phone number on the paper, and fleetingly, I considered calling Geraldine to find it out, though I had the impression he didn't want me to consult her on this particular matter. After several days, more from guilt than a desire to do as he'd asked - I plucked up the courage to dial the number. The man who answered introduced himself - Father Terry Hart - he'd been expecting me. My father, he explained, had wanted a simple funeral, but had asked if I could write a eulogy and read it during the service – would I be willing?

I hesitated, not sure what Geraldine would say as she had made all the arrangements - I didn't want to expose my reluctance to attend William's funeral or even greater reluctance to take part.

Terry Hart said. 'You could take a few days to consider - but I think you'd regret it if you didn't come...' My father's priest, it seemed, was a mind reader.

Tentatively, I made plans to be away for the funeral. Life remained difficult and demanding. David was unwell, his mother had managed to persuade him to see a doctor and the heart condition which had been diagnosed left him feeling exhausted so that he made little contribution to the family.

When I phoned and explained my need to be away for one night, he refused to stay at Hurst Row with the girls - he didn't think he couldn't cope. David's unwillingness to co-operate meant I would have to take Minette with me to Safford Bridge and my misgivings about going to the funeral deepened. As we argued, I asked, couldn't he at least call at the house while I was away and check Zoë wasn't holding a rave party or setting up an opium den in my absence?

'Explain to me why you're going to the funeral of a man you hate,' David said, 'and for God's sake don't tell me blood is thicker than water...'

He continued to wrangle over every detail. I would need to borrow the car, but David wanted to control my use of his clapped-out Peugeot, even though it would be for less than forty-eight hours.

'Couldn't you just say yes?' I begged in the end, I'd run out of inventive ways to coerce him and finally, he had agreed.

The night before I was due to leave for Safford Bridge I sat up composing William's eulogy. The wastepaper basket overflowed with discarded versions of what I'd thought I could truthfully say about him, but my words, when I read them, sounded false, meaningless and garbled.

I drank countless cups of coffee and shed a few tears before Laurence's books *Minor Lights in Art and Culture* swam into my vision and I realised the potential of translating someone else's words into my own.

In the pages, near where I'd put William's note, Laurence paid tribute to the work of several painters of my father's era. Flicking through, I believed I'd found a safe path – I could speak about my father's philosophy and work and avoid the subject of his private life and relationships.

By the time I'd finished, it was five in the morning and there was no point going to bed. The previous night, I'd hung a navy jacket and wool skirt ready in the bedroom and tiptoed along the landing trying not to disturb Zoë or Eve.

In the bathroom, I turned on the light and pulled the cord on the electric heater then stood beneath its scarlet glow for a few minutes allowing the warmth to seep into my skin. After a quick wash, I brushed my hair and braided it into the long plait that reached down to my waist – recently a strand of silver hair had appeared at the front, which depending on my mood I considered either distinguished or macabre, but could no longer hide.

Minette lay with her long hair spread out across the pillow, her doll tucked under her arm. Asleep, she looked tranquil, untroubled but when I lifted her from bed, she was so dazed and drowsy, I stayed to help her wash and dress.

After tea and toast, we left the house. I looked back at Hurst Row - there was a soft glow at Eve's window - she was a light sleeper and despite my efforts to be quiet she must have woken when I'd shut the front door.

We soon reached the scruffy back alley where the garage was situated. I wrenched open the stiff wooden doors, scraping out twin arcs on the frosted ground. Minette was shivering so hard her teeth were chattering. I strapped her into the back of the car and wrapped her in a thick blanket - as soon as she was warm, I was sure she would doze off and probably not wake until we arrived in Devon.

I didn't want to listen to the radio and sank into my thoughts. Terence Hart had been right about regrets. Despite William's reservations, I regretted not speaking to or seeing my father again before he died. When we had last met, I could have been more charitable, more willing to listen - and as futile as it was now, I regretted that too.

Behind me, Minette fidgeted and fidgeted, until she was uncomfortably bound up in the folds of the blanket, which she tore off and dropped angrily onto the floor.

'I'm bored,' she complained as we sped down the motorway. I'd forbidden her favourite occupation, reading, because it made her car-sick.

Hoping to settle her, I switched on the radio to a music station and reached over to open the glove box and retrieve the packet of chocolate ginger biscuits I'd stowed in there.

She took the whole packet, still moaning, 'I can't eat biscuits all the way to Devon.'

'Try to sleep,' I said, 'I know you're tired.'

'No you don't,' she argued, 'you *think* you know I'm tired.'

'Minette...' I cautioned, trying to keep my patience – remembering that she was the age I'd been when William had taken me from Littern.

'If you could drive, I'd be glad to sleep,' I said and smiled at her in the mirror.

'Don't be silly, I'm not old enough to drive,' she told me and scowling, slumped further down in her seat.

For the night of the funeral, I'd booked us into The Seamark, near the Quay in Safford Bridge, a distinctive building with toothpaste pink walls and turquoise blue shutters; it hadn't changed since I was a child.

As we passed through the town, the shops in the main square with their elegant Georgian frontages were bright with lights and trinkets. Many of the traditional food shops had been replaced by gift shops or expensive boutiques, but The Bridge House Bookshop remained exactly as I remembered it – the windows filled with piles of books, the glass reflecting the rippling surface of the river.

I pointed out the riverbanks to Minette, where I could see the striped leaves and tight buds of swathes of crocuses; they would soon be in flower. The crocuses had spread through the grass and encircled the grey stone hulk of St. Safan's Priory, where in the school grounds, adjacent to the church, a few children were visible through the railings strolling across the forecourt in their smart royal blue and maroon uniforms.

We parked outside The Seamark, where an icy wind was gusting inland off the sea. I hurried Minette inside out of the cold and found her a seat in the foyer, while I checked in and ordered a few sandwiches. I thought we could eat in the lounge, sitting by the open fire.

Minette was pale and silent, her grey eyes underscored by dark rings. I worried I'd been unfair, dragging her away from her normal routine to attend the funeral of a man she had never known. The girls showed no interest in my father's death and I couldn't blame them, he'd shown no interest in them while he was alive.

When it was time to leave the Inn and go to the Crematorium, I said to Minette, 'Cheer up, it'll soon be over.'

'Can't I stay here on my own?' she asked. 'I could sit and read by the fire, I wouldn't move, you could ask the lady on reception to keep an eye on me...'

Though I could see the logic of her argument, could sense that probably she would be all right at The Seamark, I intended to go to the island after the funeral, as Alice had asked, and had no idea when I might get back. I pointed out that the lady on reception was busy answering the phone or poring over papers – it seemed unlikely she would have time to babysit.

Minette stood up, her face a mask of patient martyrdom.

'I need moral support,' I told her.

'Then Dad should have come with you,' she said, 'he's a grown-up.'

The Crematorium was to the west of Safford Bridge off the coast road. It had all the lugubrious qualities of such places - manicured grass unbroken by trees or bushes, low, modern buildings – the falsely-religious atmosphere, cultivated to cover up the real business of the place - the mechanical efficiency with which they reduced the dead to a heap of ashes.

A brisk wind whipped across the car park as we walked towards the chapel. My raincoat billowed like a sail behind me and I held tightly onto Minette's hand as if she might be blown away.

When we reached the chapel porch, I didn't, at first, recognise Geraldine, a thin figure in a dark mauve coat and narrow brimmed hat, trimmed with purple feathers. I thought of my father's unflattering description "less fat, more senile" as we nodded to each other and then waited side by side, unspeaking.

The hearse advanced slowly down the Crematorium drive. On the coffin lay a large spray of bronze chrysanthemums with the wreath of white hellebores and glossy green foliage I'd chosen.

The priest, a tall scarecrow of a man, stepped forward – Father Terence Hart - he signalled we should follow the coffin.

Inside, the chapel was painted a pale turquoise that once must have been fresh and calming but had grown grubby with age. As the pall bearers brought the coffin to the bier they set it down awkwardly with a metallic clunk. There was no music - only the sounds of squeaking shoes, throat clearing and shuffling as the undertakers moved discreetly to one side.

Sitting in the front row of seats, I pulled Minette close to me, as without offering a welcome, Terence Hart stood at the lectern and began intoning the words of the service. I couldn't have imagined a ritual so devoid of feeling – William had wanted a simple funeral, but surely he hadn't meant such a raw occasion - pared down to nothing.

There was no-one else in the congregation except Geraldine, Minette and me, but after a few minutes, the chapel door opened and closed. Minette turned her head, but I didn't like to glance round, we were almost at the point in the service where Terence Hart would invite me to go to the front of the chapel and read the eulogy.

The moment came and I stepped up onto the chancel and faced the nave. When I raised my eyes from my notes, I saw who had come in late – Shirley Fredericks, my father's lover - instantly recognisable with her thick blonde hair, heavy make-up and colourful clothes – *were they a comment on my father's passing away?*

I smoothed my sheet of paper with its borrowed words, smiled at Minette and began to speak:

*Many creative people seek meaning through their art and this was the theme of my father's life and work.*

*He experienced a chaotic world. He needed, as a man and as an artist, to explore disparate elements and through his imagination find ways of expressing the possibility of a cohesive interpretation or understanding.*

*The need to make sense of life and shape it could perhaps be traced to the fact that when my father left The Netherlands, he felt he had become estranged from his country and his family – he had no background.*

*After his marriage to my mother, Juliet, he cultivated the seclusion offered by Littern Island, which allowed him to pursue his first love – painting – with the least possible restrictions on his freedom.*

*The conflict between order and disorder, I believe, was a difficulty my father grappled with throughout his life and was reflected in his love for the island, renowned both for its violent storms and its natural beauty.*

*Perhaps the measure of a life may be found in the extent to which we discover harmony within ourselves. William regarded that search as his final task - and though he will be missed by those who loved him, I trust he has finally found rest – a home in a place of perfect repose.*

Terence Hart cleared his throat - his thanks were peremptory. Geraldine hadn't raised her head once while I was speaking and from the corner of my eye, I registered a flash of bright colour as Shirley Fredericks disappeared through the back doors of the chapel.

Without ceremony, the flowers were removed and William's coffin slid on its conveyor belt towards the open curtains. Thinking she might be anxious, I had explained to Minette what would happen and held tightly onto her hand.

What moved me was the starkness of the funeral - there had been only conventional prayers and readings, no hymns, nothing personal apart from my few stilted, inadequate words. Now at the worst moment, there was no music to soften the poignancy of William's body being edged closer to the hatchway and the slowly closing curtains. I reached into my bag for a tissue and wiped my eyes.

After a few moments of respectful silence, I told Minette to stay seated while I went to Terence Hart and thanked him for conducting the service.

'This is what my father wanted?' I asked my voice unsteady.

109

'It seems bleak,' he said, 'but perhaps that was William's point. We can't ameliorate death with canned music and easy sentiment. Is that what you would have liked?'

'I don't know,' I said, flinching at his abruptness. 'But if it's what my father would have liked...'

Behind me, I heard sounds of the next funeral arriving - the low murmuring chatter, the lame attempts to be cheerful, to find some comfort in weak humour and platitudes. Through the open side door I could see the funeral directors laying William's flowers on a small paved area in the chapel garden.

'I think Geraldine was right to manage things as she did,' Terence Hart said, 'and thank you for speaking. I suppose you know that William would have preferred to feel he'd made peace with you - he was concerned you were unable to progress beyond remonstrations.'

Heat rose to my cheeks. 'We tried to talk last time we met,' I said, not wanting to lay out my own distress with our failure to find any resolution.

'You needed to talk further? You didn't resolve the issues between you?' he asked, echoing my thoughts.

'I don't think you know everything about my father...' I said.

'...And neither do you,' he replied, 'perhaps at some time in the future we should discuss that, try to form a complete picture.'

I gathered our belongings and led Minette out of the chapel. In London, it had been a clear, frosty day, but here, heavy clouds threatened rain. As the light began to fail and gloom descended on our surroundings, it rendered them lifeless and two-dimensional – an apt metaphor for William's funeral.

'Is that it?' Minette whispered.

'Almost,' I said, 'thank you for being good.'

She gave a deep sigh of impatience, exasperation at the annoying ways of adults, as I grabbed her hand and hurried to catch up with Geraldine.

'William didn't want a fuss,' Geraldine told me, as if defending herself against an accusation I hadn't made.

She emanated such hostility I couldn't think how to raise the question of going to Littern to discuss the future of Marisands.

'I wondered if any of the Pirans would come,' I said, hoping to circle our conversation gradually towards the subject of the island.

'You know perfectly well William didn't socialise with the Pirans,' she said, 'and neither do I.'

She spoke sharply and I apologised - the island community was so small, I hadn't imagined the two families could have remained enemies for all these years.

'You'll drive back to London now?' she asked.

'We're staying in Safford Bridge until tomorrow,' I said. 'I know how much you did for my father - I wanted to thank you...'

Geraldine's expression was one of contempt. 'Actually, you have no idea what I did for William, especially at the end. He couldn't crawl up the stairs to bed or use the lavatory - he didn't slip away quietly, he died wretched and in pain.'

Shaken by her words, I said, 'After we met in London, I didn't think he wanted to see me again...'

'I'm not surprised,' Geraldine told me, 'William said you had an unforgiving nature.'

I took Minette to the car. The wind cut its way across the Crematorium grounds more sharply than before. Even with my coat pulled tightly around me, I shivered and as Minette had forgotten her gloves, the tips of her fingers had taken on a bluish tinge.

Sitting in the car with the heater full on, I watched as a taxi collected Geraldine and drove away at speed.

'Can we go back to the hotel now?' Minette said, 'I don't like it here.'

'Soon,' I soothed, uncomfortable with my half truth. 'Alice wanted me to go to Littern.'

I started the car and headed out of town on the coast road which ran along a high ridge for nine miles, until it reached Narescombe.

'Would you like to see where I lived as a child?' I asked, 'Seabright Island?' She had read all the stories.

Minette shrugged and her miserable face was sufficient reply.

She fiddled with a loose thread on the hem of the blanket pulling it so hard it began to unravel. Feeling sorry for her, I thought I should have arranged for her to spend the night at St. Catherine's with her friend, Yuuka; it might have been fun, infinitely more fun than being taken to funeral which had no meaning for her.

The landscape of hedgerows and fields was drab in the lowering light. The road ran level until almost without warning it descended into Narescombe in a series of narrow "S" curves to where the small town was splayed across two hills, spreading down towards the natural horseshoe harbour.

On a winter's afternoon, Narescombe was deserted, buffeted by wind and waves, inhospitable and scruffy. Scraps of paper and empty plastic carrier bags ballooned and then blew along the promenade, where they gathered beside empty shelters. On the hills stood rows of half-built new houses, their abandoned state only partly obscured by trees.

The turning for Osford Lane was from the western edge of the town square, leading along Palk's Reach, to the island. As the lane reached the end of the promontory, the landscape grew more barren, though a belt of woodland on the seaward side survived the salt winds and battering storms and offered some protection.

Geraldine's cottage, Whitcroft, stood beside the causeway, it was isolated except for two ruined stone shelters - one each side of the water - remnants of the last war. I pulled up the car by the signpost to Yew Tree Farm, on the square of wasteland that edged the shoreline.

As the wind rose, the bare trees bent and shook their branches with an angry rustling sound. I hurried across to the notice-board, where a coloured chart flapped madly in the breeze. Holding it steady, I read information about the time of the tides, and the dangers of crossing to the island in inclement weather.

The tide was swirling in steadily from Whitcroft Cove - an eerie grey light caught the crests of the waves, as the moon appeared and disappeared between racing clouds. Since I'd left the island as a child, the causeway appeared to have sunk deeper into the gully and about half way across, a rough metal grid had been set into the road and filled with cement to repair the surface.

'Are we going to the island or not?' Minette shouted to me, leaning out of the window of the car, her dark hair fluttering in the wind.

I swung round and smiled at her, thinking her interest in the island had been aroused, but when I caught sight of her face, it wore a cross, worried frown.

'Can't we go back,' Minette asked, her voice a tired whine.

'Just wait, please,' I said, trying to decide what to do.

The channel that cut the island off from the mainland seemed two or three times wider than I had remembered and in the failing light, the road on the other side looked sinister as it vanished into the dark, dense belt of trees.

I could see lights at Whitcroft and smoke drifting into the sky from the chimney. Perhaps Geraldine hadn't gone to Marisands after all.

Lingering at the edge of the shore, I held onto the post of the notice-board to steady myself against the wind - the sea as it advanced towards the causeway looked as threatening as the stormy sky. I stared down at the waves as they rolled relentlessly towards the gully.

*Could I make a dash across?* With Minette in the car I didn't know if I ought to risk it and David would be furious if I ruined his beloved Peugeot.

I heard the car door slam shut and Minette ran towards me. She clasped my arm, holding herself tightly against my body for warmth.

'Can we go back now?' she pleaded.

'I can't make up my mind,' I said, knowing if I didn't decide soon, the choice would be made for me by the tide. 'I'm not sure if it's safe.'

Water flowed thinly across the road. I wrapped my arms round Minette to shield her from the cold. The chart on the notice-board indicated I'd need to allow at least three hours *after* high tide before attempting a return to the mainland. If there was no-one at Marisands, we'd be stuck on the island and it would be pointless driving round, we wouldn't see anything in the dark.

Minette started to cry, 'I'm freezing.'

In the boot of the car, I found an old cardigan of David's and handed it to her, 'Wrap up in that,' I said helping her put it on over her coat. I could hear her weeping softly under her breath, though she wasn't a child easily given to tears.

'I want to go to back,' Minette sobbed.

'Sshh...' I said.

'Please?' she asked.

I lingered for a few more moments at the rim of the gully until a wave swept right across the causeway swamping it. Cowardice, a sense of duty to Alice, curiosity, memories of Juliet's death had all been at war in me and cowardice had won.

'Stupid old island...' Minette said.

Her hair had worked loose about her face and her large grey eyes searched mine imploringly. She couldn't be expected to understand how discouraged I felt, how disappointed - she needed comfort - and I dismissed both the prospect of Alice's anger and the idea of calling at Geraldine's cottage. We'd both had enough.

'When we get to the hotel we'll warm ourselves by the fire - have an early dinner, would you like that?'

Minette nodded. 'I was scared.'

'I'm so sorry,' I said and dropped a kiss onto her head.

Back in the car, we waited and watched as two horse-riders came towards us from the island.

'Aren't they beautiful?' I said.

The horses – one chestnut and one pure white - trotted through the water, before passing so close to us I could hear their breath.

Minette eyed me uncertainly as if she thought I might change my mind and drive us over to Littern.

To reassure her, I said, 'Horses don't have engines, like cars - they're not ruined by salt water - it does them good to be in the sea. Would you like to learn to ride one day?'

Minette shook her head vigorously, 'Why would I? I live in London, don't I?'

The food at The Seamark was substantial homely fare, perfect for a cold February night. When we'd eaten, Minette struggled to keep awake in the warmth of the fire and as we had an early start the next morning, I suggested we went to our room so she could have a bath before bedtime.

The bedroom was well furnished and warm, a comfortable refuge after a difficult day. Once she was tucked up in bed, I read several chapters of a *Famous Five* adventure. Her face, once she'd relaxed, was beautiful – pale, soft and round, *a little moon face* - her body strong, sturdy and indomitable.

I rested on my bed, listening until she had fallen asleep and then wished her God's protection. When I was sure I wouldn't disturb her, I crept out of the room onto the landing to phone Hurst Row and make sure everything was all right.

My mobile phone received no signal inside, so I fetched my coat, locked the door and went out – Minette would be fine for the few minutes it would take me to establish Zoë and Eve were managing at home.

The wind had dropped and the temperature had plummeted - the pavement sparkled with frost and was slippery underfoot. I stepped cautiously along the path towards the waterfront.

Overlooking the quay, I leant, resting my arms on the wall, staring out at the rippling sea with its bright moon-path. With a sense of shame, I acknowledged that faced with the reality of Littern, feelings I had buried about Juliet's death had broken through my defences, until fear of those emotions had become as real as my fear of the incoming tide flooding the road.

Shame struck again and again, like the waves slapping against the seawall. I recalled my unresponsiveness, my lack of humanity to William. Geraldine had suggested my father had found me unforgiving, her accusation brought tears to my eyes, brimming over and trickling down my cheeks. The whispering of the waves sounded so sorrowful that soon I could no longer bear to look at the sea and the harsh white moon.

Standing with my back to the shore, I rang the Pimlico number three times until Zoë answered, but she was in a monosyllabic mood and I asked her to call Eve to the phone.

'Dad's been here,' Eve said. She sighed. 'Zoë's in a stress, Dad was with someone, he said he thought we'd have gone out for the evening and the house would be empty.'

'Who was with him..?' I asked.

Eve answered too quickly, 'I don't know. She looked young enough to be a student. You'd better ask him.' It was unlike her to be offhand, 'I didn't want to tell you,' she explained, 'but Zoë said I had to...'

I thought it was probably better if I didn't hear more, I'd only jump to conclusions and already, I'd left Minette for far too long.

Sleep was elusive that night; I lay in bed, hearing the rhythm of Minette's soft snores, thinking how fragile everything was – including life itself - unsure how much longer I could maintain the cool-headed image of myself I strived to preserve, the "unbreakable" me that I presented to the world.

As dawn broke, thin grey light appeared at the window and I asked God to help, not allow me to fall apart. But without thinking, I had spoken aloud and Minette stirred then slipped out of her bed and into mine.

I slept briefly then, as she lay beside me - until overhead, gulls wheeled and cried and brought in an icy, bright morning.

After breakfast, while I packed, Minette watched through the window where people were working on the quay, walking dogs, scurrying along in the cold – soon the town would be busy, it was market day.

The sky a delicate cerulean blue was flecked with white clouds; it reflected the pale waves of the sea as they curled onto the shore, clean, fresh and exhilarating.

I slipped my arms around Minette's shoulders, glad she was with me. I had forgotten the intense blueness of the water here and how the sky and the sea seemed to shine with silvery light, they were so clear.

As I stood for a few moments, resting my chin against Minette's soft hair, Flora's advice came back to me - *look for the light* – and I understood it was important to remember the light was always there – to *know* it was there – to believe in the light as Flora did, even when it seemed to have disappeared.

115

# Chapter 9

Back in London, trouble rumbled like distant thunder. I didn't confront David about his visit to Hurst Row with another woman, convinced any answers to my questions could only make me unhappy.

We were poised on the edge of emotional crisis and I could think of no other remedy than to persist with protestations of my and the girls love for David, hoping he might grasp how dividing his life between Pimlico and Surrey was threatening to destroy his family.

Talking to his brother, John, I'd discovered that while David was in Leitchly, Lesley had been helping him with *Blue Rhythms*. John thought she might now have persuaded Halkett & Haire to take an interest in his work and I envied her position of influence. The understanding that David didn't need me was becoming deeply woven into our relationship.

Meanwhile, Alice was annoyed with me regarding Marisands. She had placed responsibility on my shoulders and I had failed to deal with it in a satisfactory manner. At a safe distance from Littern, I appreciated how - to her - my fears must appear exaggerated and my hesitancy feeble, so as soon as could, I made my way to Wren House intending to apologise.

Without describing the awfulness of William's funeral I explained to Alice how inadequate I'd felt to the task of discussing Marisands with Geraldine, how I'd been overcome by emotion when I reached the island and had needed to take care of Minette, who was tired and overwrought.

'I can't see why you couldn't have called at Whitcroft,' Alice complained.

It was tempting to make excuses, but there seemed little point. Flora's sympathy had been quickened by my feelings and that mattered more than Alice's determination to remain ill-tempered-

'Since your mother became pregnant with you, we've had nothing but disquiet,' Alice said. 'Your grandmother had an arrangement with your father – he and Geraldine could stay in the house if they would maintain the property. Over the years, they've reported the house to be in good order, but I'm afraid they may have let her down badly, very badly indeed.'

I'd heard accounts of how Flora had given the house away to my mother on her marriage, and how afterwards, upbraided by Alice,

Bernard had taken complicated legal steps to ensure Marisands would always remain the property of the Armsted family.

'You'll have noticed we're moving?' Alice said.

I looked round the room as if it might hold a clue. As I'd arrived that morning, I hadn't noticed anything was different. Entering Wren House had produced the usual sensation of being wrapped in cotton wool, of entering an atmosphere of shelter, where lives were bookish and other-worldly - a place of muses, spirits and esoteric interests.

'Once we knew Mrs. Stuart would be retiring, it became imperative Wren House was sold,' Alice went on.

Mrs. Stuart had by then been taking care of Alice and Flora for almost twenty years and discussions about selling Wren House had been aired for almost as long.

Alice's plan that she and Flora should move to The Maples residential home had always been contentious - Alice's old friend, Edith Pearson, was already living there and she had been eager to join her for some time - while Flora, who had grown to love Wren House - especially her garden - found the prospect unbearable.

'Mrs. Stuart gets nothing done because of Flora's pestering and I'm no longer of use to anybody,' Alice told me.

I felt concerned for them both, but mainly for Flora, I wasn't sure she would fit in at The Maples or that once Alice had Edith for company, that she wouldn't exclude her sister.

'Consider things carefully,' I advised.

But Alice wasn't listening. 'There's a lovely garden at The Maples, Flora will be able to enjoy it without the hard work of its upkeep.'

She seemed to forget, Flora's garden was a labour of love. 'Couldn't Flora stay here?'

Alice dismissed the thought with a gesture of her hand, I had the feeling she found my sympathy for her sister deplorable. 'The Maples is rather exclusive, and therefore expensive. Unless we sell Wren House, we couldn't possible afford their fees. I've worked things out very carefully, very carefully indeed. At The Maples, we'll have everything we need and I believe we'll be cared for with kindness and respect. Miss Pearson is very happy...'

Flora had been silent throughout our conversation, sitting, head bowed over her lap – she might have been asleep.

I glanced at her, 'Won't it be difficult for Flora?' I asked, 'She tends to worry...'

Alice bristled. 'You need to realise, Iris, we all have to undertake tasks which are unpleasant or worrying. The next stage of my life will be the most dangerous of all – dying – and yet I feel quite at peace about it.'

'How is dear David?' Flora asked and I wondered if she had been listening to Alice's diatribe at all – she had a way of taking refuge in the labyrinth of her own mind.

'Nothing's changed,' I said, 'though I keep hoping.'

Alice pursed her lips, 'If you had asked me, I could have told you from the start that your happiness was likely to be short lived.'

She had hit her mark - and in her view, I was sure - felt my failure to go to Marisands had been suitably reprimanded.

Alice's harshness could be painful - I continued to feel guilty not only about Littern, but about David and our family. Neil, Rose and Verena formed a ring of security around us, but their love could only touch the surface of our loss and we seemed unable to touch David's suffering at all - he had become unreachable.

The situation wore on, leaving us down-cast by David's persistent absence. Minette was loyal to those she loved and as her father didn't relent, became increasingly attached to school and to practising Service and Sacrifice by caring for her friend, Yuuka. Eve, always intensely private, kept her thoughts and feelings to herself and focussed on her work, which left Zoë stranded in the middle of the situation, receiving little support from Lesley or her father and refusing it from me.

My weekly routine hardened into an unbreakable pattern which both chafed and comforted, but allowed no time to brood. Like Eve, I used work as a means of distraction and consolation, wanting to be bedrock for the children.

Communication with David - when it existed - was brief and dangerously mined and I was completely unprepared when John phoned to tell me his brother was in the coronary unit at the Royal Hospital, having collapsed at Leitchly Station.

David's doctor had diagnosed exhaustion caused by overwork and he'd been prescribed one set of drugs to manage his depression and anxiety, and another to treat his heart condition. I wanted to see him, but when I broached the subject, John assured me David would be all right, 'My feeling is in a few weeks this will all be forgotten - a one-off glitch in the system.'

Despite his assurances, I couldn't shake off the belief that I shouldn't have left David to work things out alone. His lifestyle had been sedentary for years and involved smoking, living on black coffee and drinking too much – it had plainly been unhealthy and yet those things had become so much part of David, part of how he was as a writer and as a man, that I'd become complacent in a way that now made me feel complicit in his illness.

The extent of the danger David had been in only emerged gradually - the Sayce's were determined to play his illness down. But then, after he'd been out of hospital for a few weeks, John asked if David could come to Pimlico to convalesce; the strain of caring for him was proving too much for his mother.

David loathed the sense we were all watching him - but I was vigilant – sometimes he forgot to take his pills and sometimes I was sure had had taken too many. I was also concerned about the effects of his illness on the girls, especially his continued emphasis on the understanding that his presence at home would never be more than a temporary measure.

He was restless and made fractious by boredom with life as an invalid. He resented the way I sheltered him from other problems, such as the fact it had become impossible to keep tabs on Zoë and that Minette was frightened by his fragile health and equally fragile temper. Only Eve, whose compassion was readily elicited by the suffering of others, seemed to have the right touch - reading to him, finding music he liked and discovering things of interest he could do without strain or anxiety.

His condition swung between seeming to be well and being obviously off balance. When he was depressed he desired death and yet the threat of his heart condition had induced in him such intense fear, he could barely conceal it. He told me he'd given up *Blue Rhythms* - it was his disappointment with words which had turned against him. But then I would find him sifting through notes John had sent from Leitchly - he scribbled on scraps of paper that came to hand, though nothing he wrote seemed cogent or purposeful.

When he began to agitate for a return to Surrey, I suggested that when he went back to his mother's house he should work there, but consider coming home in the evenings more often, so we could continue to live as a family.

Without meaning to, I had cornered David and by the end of the year he was once again spending most of his time away - consenting to stay in Pimlico only on the nights when he and John went to their favourite jazz club in Soho.

Eve's birthday was at the beginning of June and I persuaded David to join us when we went out for a celebratory meal. He stayed overnight, but the following morning was eager to return to his mother's. Rather than letting him leave alone, I suggested Minette and I should go with him - we hadn't seen Barbara for some time – and he and I could take flowers to Tristan's grave together.

There had been an epidemic of flu that summer, I'd picked up the bug and had been struggling for days to keep going. When I woke up feeling rough, David thought I should postpone the visit - London was stifling and the day so humid, I wouldn't stand the journey either by car or by train.

Determined not to be put off, I said I could manage. David argued that if I was trying to achieve family unity, we would be better to sit outside in the shade of the cherry tree and have coffee together - there wasn't a whisper of a breeze and whatever I felt, Minette would be made utterly miserable by a hot, dusty journey to Surrey.

Cross and ill, I refused to listen. We'd spoken to Barbara - she was expecting us and we'd never hear the end of it if we ruptured her plans. Starting to get ready, I changed into a cotton dress, assembled my hat, sunglasses and bag in the hall and then called out to David that I would go to the local florist to buy flowers for Tristan and for his mother.

Out on the street, the heat burned through the soles of my sandals. Perspiration dripped from my forehead and down my neck, though the walk was no more than a few hundred yards. At the florist, I bought two bunches of roses – yellow and white and cream and apricot, quite tightly in bud - thinking they might survive a trip in the soaring temperatures.

On the way back to Hurst Row, my legs threatened to buckle and I stopped to rest against the wall of the newsagent's, sheltering beneath the canopy, where there was a strip of shade. I waited, eyes closed, as the heat intensified and pain built in my head until I felt it might explode.

David was irritable when I got back to the house. Minette had been fidgeting and asking him where I was every few minutes.

'I didn't feel well, I had to stop,' I explained.

'Then why don't we phone Mother? You can visit as soon as we get a cooler day, for God's sake...'

I sank down onto the hall chair and sat with my head in my hands.

David stood over me. Roughly, he lifted my chin with his finger, 'You look terrible,' he said, 'stay here with Minette and go to bed...'

He checked his watch – wondering which train he might catch.

'Don't rush, David,' I said, 'this heat isn't good for you and please - come back tonight.'

He leaned down and kissed me on the cheek, the most affection he'd shown for months.

My head muzzy, I watched as he took his keys and wallet from the hall table and plonked an old straw hat on his head, before leaving the house, forgetting to take the flowers.

I poured a glass of iced water for myself and made squash for Minette. In the heat of the kitchen, the roses were drooping already; I put them in a vase and found a cool place for them on the hall table.

By then it was late morning and too hot to enjoy sitting in the garden, so I made Minette's lunch and when she'd eaten, sent her to her room to play, while I had a lie down.

Stripped to my underwear, I stretched out onto the cotton bedcover falling asleep almost at once in the sweltering heat. I didn't hear Zoë come home - I barely heard the phone ring - but was disturbed by footsteps as she thumped downstairs to answer the call.

Her yell woke me fully, 'Iris! Uncle John's on the phone. Hurry up! He wants to speak to you.'

I pulled on my wrap, tied it round me and stumbled down to the hall – *had David collapsed again?*

Minette appeared at the kitchen door, 'Zoë let me out,' she said, 'I'd been in my room forever.'

'Look at you with your bedroom hair.' Zoë mocked, grinning as she thrust the receiver at me.

I could have returned the compliment; Zoe's red-gold hair was tied up in a bunch on top of her head and fell like a fountain round her face. She was wearing a red bra over a white cotton top, black baggy shorts and desert boots.

'Is everything okay?' I asked John, 'I was expecting David home tonight, is he on his way?'

'...Not exactly.'

'Is David there? Is he coming home?' I asked. The more John was evasive, the more afraid I became.

'Look - David asked me to give you a message.'

'What's happened..?' My heart began to race.

In the kitchen, Zoë was fiddling with the grill; she lived on toasted cheese sandwiches, having them for breakfast, dinner and tea. Now the smell of scorching bread and cheese filled the hall and Minette peered round the door, wafting the smoke away from her face with her hands, her eyes watering.

Knowing she was listening, I spoke slowly and carefully, composing my voice, not wanting to alarm her.

'David's all right?' I asked - *why didn't John just say yes?*

'I think it might be better if I come over,' he told me.

121

While I waited for John to arrive, I had a shower, brushed my hair and put on a clean dress. After a long sleep, I was feeling better, but John's reserve on the phone had made me apprehensive.

A single man, John enjoyed being looked after so I made chicken sandwiches, cooled a bottle of wine, then found crisps and a jar of olives.

When Eve came home, I suggested she take Minette to the local park to play - it would make up for her being confined all afternoon and might prevent her asking unwelcome questions.

'What's this about?' Eve said.

'John didn't tell me - it could be anything...'

Zoë was at the kitchen table eating the olives I'd put ready in a bowl, I saw her pull a face at Eve, 'I think I'll disappear,' she said, she considered her Uncle John a gigantic bore and did her best to avoid him.

Once the girls had gone out, time dragged, but at last John arrived and I showed him into the sitting room. Like his father, he was a kind, affable man but looked so uncomfortable that evening, I felt sorry for him.

John's face was expressive when he was stirred up and as he spoke his skin flushed a violent red from his neck to the place where his ginger hair had receded to a point level with his ears.

'There's something you need to know,' he said and I recognised the apologetic tone of his voice.

I set my glass of water down on the table beside me.

'David's been seeing someone.'

Trying to retain a scrap of dignity, I said, 'I know, John, he brought her here when I went to Safford Bridge, Eve told me.'

'Her name's Helen Goode, she was a student at the Poly, a red-head, something of a Pre-Raphaelite beauty.' He coughed, realising he'd said the wrong thing and his expression became a picture of despondency.

Thinking of the rumours that had been circulating, years ago, at the time of David's series of literary parties, I said, 'I can't pretend I'm surprised.'

John appeared slightly relieved, 'You understand how David can be - I think he's always felt he had to prove something – my father didn't have much respect for poetry and David has flogged himself to demonstrate that his chosen career is of as much value as Dad's work in accountancy.'

'How long..?' I asked, bringing him back to the point.

John glanced up at the ceiling and then at me, 'David's been seeing people on and off since Tristan – he finds someone attractive - their paths keep crossing and I suppose, one thing leads to another.'

Slowly, the meaning of his words began to sink in – the reality that the whole of my life with David been based on a falsehood. 'I don't want to believe you,' I said, my breath coming in jagged gasps.

'You have to believe me because it's the truth...'

'All this time, whatever happened, whatever people said or implied, I've tried to keep an open mind, to have faith in our future.'

John's eyes slid away from me. 'David couldn't bring himself to tell you – he's weak like that.'

When I had been in labour with Tristan and Minette – in the space between pains - I'd thought *not again, please not again* - but the next pain had come anyway, and the next and the next. Now, I felt my own weaknesses pitted against years of broken trust and I had no strength or resistance to deal with it. My mind filed through the events of the day - David not wanting me to go to Leitchly - the kiss on the cheek - a Judas kiss -

'I understand...' I said, as if by clinging to civility I might find a way of surviving in a collapsing world. I had once been one of those young women who David found attractive and he had abandoned Lesley just as he was now abandoning me.

John cleared his throat, 'It must seem unforgiveable that we knew and said nothing.'

I let his remark pass. When David had walked into my life, I'd thought he was changing it for the better. My head throbbing, I went and stood by the window, resting my forehead against the cool glass, my eyes closed. In a few moments, I felt John beside me, but he didn't touch me, he wasn't an affectionate man.

He said, 'David and Helen seem to love one another - they intend to get married. Things became serious when you were carrying Minette - David didn't want another child...'

'I've made mistakes and I've been punished for it..?'

John sighed. 'I don't think that's how David sees it. In his own way, he probably still loves you...'

'Do you think so?' If David still loved me, it was in the same way my father had gone on loving my mother – to the point of destruction.

'Helen encourages David with his work - I suppose he's come to rely on her.'

'And I didn't encourage him?' Unable to hold back a burst of anger, I demanded, 'Does Helen Goode know anything about poetry?'

'Iris...' his voice carried a note of reproach at my bitterness.

I looked at him, ill at ease, out of his depth, 'I'm sorry you had to tell me. David should have done it himself. He's a coward - infidelity is the easy way out of a failed relationship – isn't that why so many do it?'

'For what it's worth – I think you deserve better, much better, but I couldn't betray my brother.'

'What will happen now?'

John paused before speaking, 'David wants to move here with Helen, Mother will explain to you.'

Low sunlight streamed through the window, deepening the bright colours of the sitting room and dyeing the monochrome street in a lurid pink and orange.

'You know how much I love David, don't you?' I said.

'You've been very loyal.'

'I'll need to know David's plans - may I speak to him?'

The red hue of John's face provided an answer. He promised he'd phone and I knew he would. The Sayce family prided themselves on their efficiency - they had been extremely efficient, allowing David to maintain his deceit for so many years.

My mind leapt from one unpleasant thought to another - while I had been upstairs, sleeping away the afternoon, had David and Helen been together? What could I say to the girls..?

'Unless there's anything else I can do...' John said stiffly – I'd fallen silent and he wanted to leave.

I watched him walk away down the path to his car and thought of my mother's death and how our first experience of loss becomes the measure of all subsequent loss, each adding its own intensity, until grief, fear and anger threaten to destroy us -

Alone, I gave way to tears. If my mother had taken her life to escape her unhappy marriage, she'd at least shown courage, would I have the courage to do the same? The feeling that I'd failed David and failed the children alternated with a different sort of self-reproach - why in God's name had I stuck with him all this time? Too afraid to leave him and start again...

When I could weep no more, I cleared away the uneaten food and untouched wine I'd set out for John.

The two girls had come home and were under the cherry tree, side by side on the sun lounger, sharing a bowl of strawberries and ice-cream. Minette was pink-cheeked from playing in the park - her legs projected over the end of the seat as Eve sprayed water from the hosepipe to cool them.

Eve called out, 'Should I put Minette to bed?'

Minette's expression beseeched me to say no.

I'd rinsed my swollen eyes with cold water, but when I appeared at the kitchen door, I saw Eve glance away; the atmosphere was heavy with doubt and fear.

'Dad isn't coming back tonight?' she asked.

I shook my head.

'Is that why you're sad, Mummy?' Minette asked.

Later, in the evening, Eve, Minette and I sat in the living room and watched a video - Rose had recently passed on a box of films her children had outgrown.

Eve had phoned Zoë and she came home before the film had finished, early and without Cameron. She hammered on the front door and when I let her in, began to confront me at once, 'This is about Dad isn't it..?'

'Stop shouting,' I said, not sure I could deal with Zoë in a state.

She pursued me into the sitting room, treading accidentally on my heels, 'What's going on, why isn't Min in bed?'

I reached out to touch her arm, but she shrugged off my hand and stood, shoulders hunched, glaring at us.

Ignoring Minette's cross face, I switched off the television. In my mind, I'd practiced several versions of what I needed to say, but none would help to soften the blow. 'Uncle John told me your Dad is planning to re-marry. Her name's Helen and they're coming to live here.'

Zoë kicked hard at the low cupboard we used as a magazine table. The drawer caved in, it was a cheap piece of furniture.

'It's the pouty red-head?' she demanded.

'What difference does that make?' Eve asked.

Minette sidled over and clung to my arm, I drew her close to me.

'Why didn't Dad tell you himself?' Zoë said.

'I suppose he didn't like to upset me...'

'So you're *not upset* then?' she sneered, 'The trouble with you is you never fight for anything. You'll never change - you'll just go on being sacrificed like some dumb animal...'

I expected her to run up to her room and slam the door, but she dropped down onto the footstool and started to sob. I knelt beside her and slipped my arm round her thin shoulders. Minette rested her head against mine. My throat felt thick and swollen, but for me, the time for tears had passed. We didn't speak, but stayed there unmoving, the remnant of a family, behaving not as if David had left, but as if he had died. After all the arguments, the shouting and bickering, it seemed strange that the end should come so quietly.

Eve sat cross-legged on the floor, her face the image of David's as a young man. In that moment, my daughters seemed perfect: Zoë with her wild orange hair and outlandish clothes, Eve with her sensitivity and apparent composure and little Minette, sad and confused.

'I suppose there's nothing we can do,' Eve said at last.

'Not unless you can perform bloody miracles,' Zoë snapped, her pain, as always, emerged as anger.

The jarring tone of her voice made Minette cry and Zoë scowled at me. Her hands were clenched into tight fists and defied me to reproach her, but my thoughts were elsewhere - turned constantly to David. *If he had seen our distress – would he have sacrificed us to his desire for Helen?*

# Chapter 10

John counselled it would be wise to leave David alone, he'd moved from Leitchly and was living with Helen at her flat in Gipsy Hill. As if I had an intractable blind spot, I couldn't think how to negotiate my need to speak to him, afraid if I handled the situation badly, I might alienate Zoë and Eve - perhaps even Minette.

One Saturday, John drove David's old car to Pimlico – he didn't need it any more, he could borrow Helen's convertible – I was grateful, but thinking of David and Helen together was like touching a raw nerve.

Two weeks later, a letter from Barbara's solicitor arrived. I was having a late breakfast and Zoë dumped the mail down in front of me. While I read, she sat tearing at a croissant, head down and intent on the thoughts which constantly preoccupied her, thoughts from which the rest of us were excluded.

'Barbara's written about the house,' I told her. The letter informed me I had a "generous" six months to find somewhere else to live.

'It's a poisoned chalice,' Zoë said, 'how typical of Dad's family. I *hate* them.' She had responded to David and Helen's relationship with unabated fury.

I absorbed the implications of the letter - it encapsulated my worst fears for our future. David's silence had been threatening, but I had pushed any practical matters to the back of my mind instead of insisting, as I should have done, that he let me know what was happening.

'What are you planning to do?' Zoë demanded, 'you'll never afford a house in London...'

'You're not helping,' I said, trying to keep my sense of humour.

'Do you need help?' she asked - her knife clattering onto her plate. 'Just find a flat, somewhere out of town...'

She asked for more coffee and I refilled our cups.

I asked, 'What about you, Minette and Eve? You'll need to be able to get to school or college.'

Zoë shrugged. 'You talk as if the world will end if you make the wrong decision. Once you start *thinking*, you'll go on thinking forever....'

I couldn't contradict her, she was right. Since David and I had first separated I'd been uncertain - unwilling to shoulder responsibilities I once would have carried lightly.

Zoë, a brooding presence, remained slouched over the kitchen table. Through the window, I watched Minette, who had gone out into the garden to water the cosmos, stocks and nicotiana she had grown from seed in the spring. Her small figure moved purposefully among the white, pink and purple flowers. Her hair fell to her shoulders in tangled waves. Still in her blue dressing gown - she was unselfconscious as she let the hose drench the soil, transforming it into a sea of muddy puddles.

'Barbara could have phoned - there was no need for such formality,' I said, certain David's father would have handled things more humanely - he'd been fond of the girls.

'Why don't you phone and give her a piece of your mind?' Zoë suggested.

'...Because I don't want to stir things up.'

Zoë had been to see David at Gipsy Hill and the enmity between her and Helen was as keen as her enmity with her mother, Lesley. In the worst of her teenage years, Zoë had called her mother, whose maiden name was Sleeman, "Sleesy", Sleesy she insisted was a "tart", but I knew Lesley had been deceived by David, just as I had been.

'You do realise, Dad and Gran have probably been plotting behind your back. Dad says Helen and Gran get on like a house on fire,' Zoë said.

I'd resisted the temptation to question Zoë about her visit to David. She was prone to exaggeration, though in her contentious way, she meant well.

Pink-cheeked, soft ginger hair askew from yesterday's hairstyle, wrapped in a baggy old jumper of David's, she appeared so brittle. I watched as she began to pick peel off an apple with her fingernail causing minute, crescent-shaped tears to collect in a heap on the table in front of her.

'I've written a letter,' she said without looking up, 'to the drama school - I'm not staying on.'

I drew in my breath sharply, 'I wish you'd spoken to me first, Zoë.'

'I knew you'd say *that*, and in that tone of voice, Iris,' she mimicked me.

Over the summer, Zoë had become increasingly adamant she wouldn't be returning to college to complete her degree. She'd made such a fuss, complaining incessantly her course was a waste of time that her grumbling had become no more than half-forgotten background noise.

'You could wait till the New Year to decide. You didn't have to write to the college *now*....'

My thoughts were full of the possible consequences of leaving Hurst Row, consequences which couldn't be anything but uncomfortable for us all and I wasn't really listening to her.

'If I'd waited, I'd probably have forgotten to write and just not turned up...' she said.

'You'd better get a proper job then.'

'You'd better get a proper job then,' Zoë echoed with the tone of sarcasm she'd perfected. '...How profoundly boring...'

The mood in the room darkened as she grew steadily more argumentative.

'Cameron got a van, yesterday. His parents sent him money in exchange for the promise he'd finish college - but he isn't going to college, not even when we come back.'

I didn't need to ask *come back from where?* Zoë and Cameron had been discussing doing the hippy trail, following the route of one of the commercial bus tours.

She went on, 'The money was a bribe - go back to college and you can have a car. Cameron said O.K. and they gave him cash. But instead of a car, he bought the van - the sort we can live in - he got it off a friend who went travelling last year.'

As she explained what they'd done, Zoë was smirking, pleased with their trick. I couldn't help thinking Cameron's parents had been ingenuous, trusting their son in his present incarnation.

'You needn't look so disapproving. The Monroes have loads of dosh. Anyway, we're going to live in Cameron's van, one of his mates...'

I interrupted, '...I've been hearing all this for months - it feels like years. I'm finding it *very* wearing...'

Zoë waggled her head from side to side like an Indian dancer and pulled an ugly face, 'Actually, I'm finding you bloody wearing, moping around looking fucking miserable all the time. Why don't you take an interest in what we want to do?'

'I promise you, I'm interested,' I said, 'more interested than you can possibly imagine.'

She stood up, jolting the table, almost knocking her chair to the floor.

'Don't speak to me like I'm bloody two years old - I can do as I please, and anyway, fuck you!'

She launched herself out of the room and after a few seconds, her bedroom door slammed shut. In the wake of her anger, I realised I shouldn't have patronised her - should have taken her seriously. She'd found a job as a waitress in a restaurant to raise money for their trip and Cameron had been saving his earnings from busking and street theatre.

Over the last few weeks, Cameron had by stealth become a resident at Hurst Row - he and Zoë spent most of their time holed up in her bedroom with the door firmly closed. Cameron played the guitar and harmonica relentlessly and I'd become accustomed to working to the accompaniment of his favourite group, *Juxon*. Zoë had painted several large canvases in black, across which she had written in gold, the words of one of their songs, *What can you see in the dark all alone?* The paintings were lined up along the landing, where they stood like a row of abandoned tombstones.

Re-reading the solicitor's letter, I wished I could share Zoë's pragmatic view of the situation. In six months we were going to be homeless and no amount of slogging at Laurence's art books or the *Kenholme Mysteries* was going to put me in a position to buy a house or flat in London - I would struggle to find sufficient for rent. Since David and I had separated, my savings had been dwindling and even though I received a discount on Minette's school fees for running the French conversation classes, I'd still needed to ask Flora for help.

Minette came in from the garden, her slippers covered in mud. 'Why do some flowers give off their scent at night?' she asked.

She had inherited my tendency to ask questions - she liked facts and dealt in precision, even in the unpredictable matter of flowers.

When I couldn't answer to her satisfaction, she said, 'Never mind, we need to go now...'

As had happened too often, lately, I'd forgotten what I was supposed to be doing and when I checked the calendar, discovered Minette and I were taking Yuuka for a birthday treat, collecting her from St. Catherine's and then going to Seaholme.

Yuuka was an orphan, her grandmother had wanted her educated in England and she spent the holidays living at school with other children from abroad. She was half Japanese and Minette was outraged on her behalf because she was teased unmercifully about her name, which however strange it sounded to English ears, meant gentleness.

I asked Minette to get ready quickly, in something suitable for the beach and preferably clean. We were having lunch at Nightingales, the tea-shop near the school, before going to the seaside for the afternoon.

While she dressed, I hurried to the local newsagent and bought a birthday card, reading book, and pencil case in pink, which seemed to be the only colour in the girls' palette. When I'd rushed back to Hurst Row, I wrote the card and quickly wrapped the presents.

Minette ate her breakfast nagging all the time. 'Mum, we need to go *now*. Yuuka will cry if we don't go, *now*, you'll ruin her birthday.'

'Just give me a few minutes,' I pleaded, 'I'll phone the school and ask them to tell her we're coming.'

I sipped at a hastily made drink and Minette hung about in the hall nibbling a slice of toast.

I could hear her, pacing up and down. 'I hate being late...' she chanted between bites of toast, 'I hate it, I hate it, I hate it...'

St. Catherine's School occupied a prominent position in a suburb called Stonall, south-east of Dulwich, in what had once been the manor house of the area. Yuuka was by the wrought iron gates, a bright figure in pink jeans and a blue school anorak - fidgeting and swinging her rucksack aimlessly round and round.

Behind her, the austere school building, set into a broad asphalt playground, made a formidable backdrop, with its rows of symmetrical windows and imposing pillars flanking the entrance.

I waved to her, she was a quiet, polite girl and a friendship had sprung up between us, like the relationship between mother and daughter.

'Minette..!' Yuuka called.

A young nun, demure in her blue and white habit, was holding Yuuka's hand, restraining her, trying to distract her from the fact she'd had to wait so long for us to arrive.

'Happy Birthday..!' I said.

Yuuka reminded me of an exotic flower - a lotus floating on tranquil water perhaps – but that day her usually passive face was full of consternation.

'Are you ready?' I asked.

'She's been ready for almost an hour,' the nun told me, with a reproachful smile.

Yuuka let go of her hand and slipped out through the metal gates. The girls ran ahead of me and when I shouted to them to slow down, linked arms and began walking five steps and then skipping five.

The way to the tea shop passed through a broad avenue of chestnut trees and grand houses, set well back from the road, but as we turned into the main street of Stonall, the architecture became more modest - brick terraces, a parade of small shops and Nightingales, set slightly apart.

'What presents did you get?' Minette asked.

When uncomfortable, Yuuka had developed a technique of avoidance. She focussed her eyes in the middle distance so she wasn't

131

ignoring the person speaking - which would have been impolite - but achieved her aim of not having to engage in conversation.

After several minutes stand-off, Minette fumbled in her back-pack for the presents we'd bought and Yuuka clutched them in her arms as the two girls zigzagged their way along the pavement.

The unchanging character of Nightingales was reassuring. Its deep bow windows filled with arrangements of dried flowers, its tables each with their tiny crystal vases of red roses hadn't altered since I'd started going there as a child. The aroma of tea and sugary cakes, its atmosphere of traditional elegance, had been maintained through years of feeding hungry schoolgirls and their families, with no concessions to the trend for fast food.

We sat at a table in the corner and Yuuka began at once to unwrap her presents. The pink felt pencil case had a concoction of embroidery and sequins, depicting flowers and butterflies. Yuuka took ballet classes and I'd bought her a copy of *Ballet Shoes* by Noel Streatfeild. She loved to read the books I'd enjoyed as a girl, and in the past, I had given her children's versions of the classics as well as a set of the *Seabright Island Adventures.*

When I'd booked our table, I'd asked Nightingales if they could make a birthday cake. Presented with the cake on a silver board - the candles lit - Yuuka shook her head in disbelief. The pink cake had been decorated with white roses – I passed her our plates and a knife, but she paused before touching them. A sensitive child, she could be a complex mixture of pride and humility.

When she didn't move, Minette explained if she blew out the candles and made a wish, then I would cut the cake for her.

Yuuka blew out the candles one at a time, 'I wish I could live with you and Minette - I'm a very useful person to have around,' she said.

Minette fixed her gaze on my face expectantly.

'Make another wish – it's meant to be a secret,' I told her, smiling.

Yuuka's eyes closed like the petals on a flower - the lotus I'd thought of earlier - her face had the blankness of suppressed, secret fears.

Minette reached out and held her hand. I put down my teacup. Without meaning to, I had dismissed Yuuka's wish – the hope she had expressed for a different and happier life – it was a request which must have cost her enormous courage to express.

'You must come and stay with Minette, if the school agrees, we'd love to have you,' I said hoping to cover my mistake.

Yuuka didn't speak, but her body and face made her disbelief clear and her doubts were justified - our lives were about to alter radically, so radically, that Minette and I might end up living anywhere, miles out of town, unable to see her at all.

Down on the beach, the two girls changed into flowery swimsuits and paddled in the shallows wearing sparkly jelly shoes bought from a beach stand. They were happy and excited, playing at the water's edge, while I watched and listened to the churning waves, the constant motion of ebb and flow - a rhythm which would persist throughout time, whatever else might change.

It was a warm, close day. The sea was calm and the shore crowded, colourful and alive with the sound of children's voices – but I felt a deep unease, my mind returned again and again to Barbara's letter and to Zoë's bad mood. Distracted, I lost sight of the girls and panicked, until I made out their dark heads, as they chased a dog that had strayed onto the beach.

When they'd tired of paddling and jumping waves, we headed for the arcade in town with its row of souvenir shops, where I traipsed behind them advising on shell-covered boxes, plastic dolphins and giant pencils with scenes of Seaholme printed on the side. Shopping done, they were hungry again and we looked for the nearest cafe, where they were soon occupied eating ice-creams.

I kept checking my mobile phone. As we'd left Pimlico, I'd shouted a goodbye to Zoë and had received no reply. Anxious to make things up, I typed a text to apologise for the row we'd had that morning – I didn't want her disappearing as she did sometimes for days, especially not while there was bad feeling between us.

The girls were content and there seemed no reason to hurry home. We rode on the open-topped bus three times and decided we would wait until the coloured lights were switched on at the sea front, in the meantime having a round of fish and chips for supper.

By the time we returned to school, it was almost dark. Without thinking, I had texted Zoë more than ten times, but she hadn't answered. Minette was quiet and Yuuka exhausted and grubby from the beach - the remnants of a second ice-cream had dripped down the front of her school jacket. The white box containing her birthday cake looked as if someone had sat on it, but she was insistent she would share it with the other girls in her room.

As we drove to Pimlico, Minette slouched across the back seat, her dark hair hanging limply round her face, pale with tiredness.

'Why can't I stay at school with Yuuka?' she asked, 'now Dad's gone, I'm practically an orphan.'

'But not quite.'

133

'If I can't stay at school, why couldn't Yuuka have Zoë's bedroom? She's going off with Cameron, she said so.' Minette must have overheard my conversation with Zoë that morning.

'You wouldn't like it if you went away for a while and I let someone else use your room.'

'Yuuka could fit into my bedroom - we could have bunk beds.'

'There's no space – the ceiling slopes,' I reminded her, 'and besides, we don't know what kind of bedrooms we'll have when we find our new home. I'll do what I can for Yuuka, but she can't possibly move in.'

Minette folded her arms across her chest, her lower lip formed into a deep curve of dissatisfaction and I suspected the two girls had been hatching a plot between them.

'Let me stay at school,' Minette urged - her voice defiant.

'...Stop it...' I said, 'this conversation is going round in circles.'

Minette slumped down further in the seat, her feet digging into my back. 'If we move out of Hurst Row and you make me leave St. Catherine's, I'll never speak to you again.'

Back at Hurst Row, Cameron's battered van was parked outside the house, mostly on the pavement, incongruous among the smart four wheel drives and shiny BMW's of our neighbours. The sound of Zoë's rock music – *Led Zeppelin* - blared from her open bedroom window. I'd checked my phone several times, but she hadn't replied to the texts I'd sent her.

I ushered Minette into the kitchen and made her a bedtime drink. In the background, Zoe's footsteps thudded down the stairs, each step followed by a loud thump. I went to the kitchen door to see what was happening, meaning to take the opportunity to apologise to her.

Zoë's ginger hair had flared out like an elongated halo around her face, a face scarlet with rage, an image familiar from her babyhood - she'd always been a fierce child.

I began to say I was sorry.

'Don't say anything!' Zoë interrupted, 'We're leaving *right now* and I'm not coming back.' She threw the words at me like small grenades and cool drops of spittle landed on my face.

'Where's Cameron?' I asked.

'Grabbing his stuff - God, you never listen.'

'I do listen, Zoë...'

'Well, listen to this then - we're spending a few days with Cam's brother before we leave the country for good, got that?'

Zoë had packed her things into an assortment of plastic carrier bags, which she had been throwing downstairs into the hall - they lay there now in a heap as depressing as a landfill site.

Minette scooted behind me as a Cameron hurled a sports holdall over the banister, narrowly missing knocking her off her feet.

'Be careful!' I warned him.

He disappeared into the bedroom without an apology and Zoë ignored me too, scurrying upstairs before returning almost immediately, empty handed.

She lunged at the handles of her bags, gathered them up and knocked the latch off the door with her elbow.

'We're going, there's too much madness round here, it might be catching.' Her sharp little comments always took on their keenest edge when she was in a temper.

I tried to grasp her arm but missed, 'I've said I'm sorry, I was upset about the house...' I called after her, as the door flung open.

'Gran's threatening to chuck us out is like some weird curse...' she yelled back.

'Zoë...' I objected.

'Zoë, Zoë, Zoë,' she echoed, 'with Cam and me gone you'll have two less people to worry about, won't you?'

She struggled, breathing heavily - hauling her bags along the path with a scraping sound, before lurching out onto the pavement, where the streetlamps cast an amber glow over the houses, cars and road.

'What does Zoë mean she's not coming back?' Minette was asking, tugging on my sleeve.

'Wait, Minette...'

Cameron appeared in the hall, dressed in the shapeless garments he wore day and night - grey, washed-out, baggy tracksuits. It was unfortunate Cameron himself had a pasty, baggy appearance.

'This is goodbye, then,' he told me, a vague, bemused expression on his face, as if he couldn't quite believe it himself.

He handed me two dirty mugs balanced on a pile of plates rimed with dried food, no doubt they'd been mouldering in Zoë's bedroom for weeks.

His guitar strapped over his back, he reached towards the enormous holdall he'd thrown downstairs, scraps of grey clothing peeking out where they'd caught in the zip.

'We're off round the world,' he said as if they were going on a two week package tour.

'Come on!' Zoe shouted to him. She was waiting by the van, bags in hand, her hair burnished by the orange lamplight.

The front door banged shut, 'Stay there...' I ordered Minette.

I deposited the pile of crockery Cameron had handed me onto the hall table, wrenched open the door and rushed out onto the street as I heard the van engine start. The van looked as if it was made of any constituent parts that could be fitted together. Cameron was in the driving seat with Zoë beside him and before I could reach them, they took off with a roar and a billowing cloud of black smoke; I wondered if they would make it out of Pimlico.

Stepping back onto the pavement, I felt defeated. Zoë in a rage was unlikely to have been swayed by appeals from me, but Cameron was more reasonable, he might have told me where his brother lived and how I could keep in touch with them while they were away.

'Can I move now?' Minette asked impatiently, she had remained exactly where I'd left her.

She had seen her sister in a temper often and the impact had probably worn off. Zoë and I'd had many rows and Zoë had stormed out before – though this time she had taken all her stuff and the only consolation was that she was with Cameron, who I hoped was as stolid as she was impulsive and headstrong.

The commotion had disturbed Eve, who peered down on us from the landing, 'What's going on?'

'Zoë's run away with Cam,' Minette said, 'I think it's because Granny's throwing us out of the house.'

'Does that make sense?' Eve asked, rubbing her eyes, heavy with sleep.

I no longer knew what made sense, but my heart had gone out to Zoë. She'd never found a comfortable place in the family or perhaps anywhere - set loose, God alone knew where she would go or how she would live – though God alone knew how any of us would live. With David's departure, our world had dislocated and no-one seemed to know how to fit it back together again.

*

Once Minette was settled in bed, I went to lie down - the throbbing pain in my head and the sensitivity of my eyes to light an inevitable consequence of my row with Zoe.

The darkness around me seemed vast, as if I was lost at sea with no landmarks of time or place. I dozed and dreamt I was in the music room at Marisands with its rippled glass mirrors. I was looking for Zoë, but no-one was there - nothing was there - only an impenetrable, swirling mist - and if I reached out to touch the mirrored glass, my hand grew invisible, then my body, until I had become so insubstantial, I was terrified I might disappear.

My waking with a loud cry brought Eve to my room. She'd been phoning Zoë's friends, in case she was staying somewhere in London.

'She's nowhere to be found,' Eve told me, and it was as if her voice had emerged straight out of my frightening dream.

Too restless to sleep again, I went to the study and found an old atlas, researching on the internet the route of the hippy trail via Istanbul, the Silk Road and Kathmandu.

'I think Zoë was just making a point,' Eve said.

But unable to stop speculating about Zoë's plans, I resolved to explore her room - there was a chance I might find a scrap of paper or a note which would provide a clue to her whereabouts.

Piece by piece I took Zoë's room apart, lifting the mattress and rugs, rummaging in the drawers and wardrobe, pulling the chest away from the wall. Most of the drawers and cupboards were empty, but there were cardboard boxes pushed under her bed. They contained unwanted clothes Zoë had at some time bundled away - an embroidered tunic in rich shades of red and orange, a pair of leather boots, a satchel bag and eleven pairs of evening gloves in an array of clashing, incongruous colours. When my rampage had yielded nothing useful, I wandered listlessly round the bedroom, carefully replacing her possessions exactly where I'd found them.

Zoë could be a perfectionist and had made the perfect exit - I didn't have the address of Cameron's parents or the registration number of his van - I'd never found out where his flat in Stockwell was and so couldn't enquire of his friends where they thought he might have gone. Torn between the hope Zoë might come home that night and fears about where she would stay while she and Cameron were on the road, I retreated to my bedroom to look for my headache pills only to discover a hundred pounds missing from the old purse I kept in my bedside table in case of emergencies.

Sipping the coffee Eve brought me, I asked her to search among Zoë's things again, 'Try to humour me,' I snapped when she suggested I was over-reacting.

Eve found nothing and came and sat cross-legged at the foot of my bed. We watched through the open curtains as moths flew in the night, their wings catching the orange light from the streetlamps like darting fireflies.

'Do you think you should see a doctor?' Eve asked, breaking the silence.

'Why?' I said - there was no need – the pills I'd taken would help me sleep.

'I've been wondering about when *I* might move out – then you'd only need to find somewhere big enough for you and Minette...'

Her words, echoing Zoë's sentiments, upset me. 'Do you all have to take off - abandoning the sinking ship?'

Though I was angry, where Eve was concerned my remark was unjustified. She hadn't mentioned leaving home for a while and her plans had seemed so unformed and desultory, I'd wrongly assumed the idea had gone underground.

'There's a village called Zethar Creek, in Cornwall, where my friends are living. It's isolated, literally up a creek, but there are workshops – well boatsheds - with rooms over...'

I tried to imagine it, but realised I had no idea who Eve's friends were - she rarely brought anyone home - I wasn't sure if she had a boyfriend.

'I wouldn't go right away, not till you're feeling better,' she assured me. 'It's just that I've decided I want to paint - see what happens. I'll get a job in a shop or bar - make some money to live on...'

'I'd miss you...'

'Would you? I've felt sort of invisible, since Dad left...' Her fair skin flushed easily and a tide of redness flowed up from her neck to her cheeks as she spoke. 'Uncle John says he thinks you're probably depressed.'

'You talked to John?' I asked - Eve and Zoë were always making fun of his old womanish ways.

Eve shrugged. 'We had to talk to someone, and he's better than Granny.'

'You don't need to worry, Eve...'

'Sorry - but one of us had to speak up and everyone thought it had better be me.'

She uncurled, stretching her long legs and stood up - I wasn't sure what I could say, *I'm grateful for your concern*..? It sounded ridiculous.

'The trouble is, you don't do anything to help yourself,' Eve said, 'the mail's been piling up in the hall for weeks - the house is a mess - I've had to put my life on hold to take care of you...'

She waited by the bed, her head hung and her hair falling over her face, just like Minette when she was distressed.

'I'm sorry,' I said – ashamed because whatever I had been doing in my efforts to survive had so obviously failed - it had been bad enough imagining Zoë and Cameron dossing down in a squat, now Eve wanted to take up residence in a fisherman's hovel, and even Minette, it seemed, would prefer to stay at school.

There were times when it seemed only hours since I'd learned that David intended marrying Helen - since understanding that through his betrayal he had been absent from our lives for years. But if the dark kiss of David's final departure had failed to awaken the need to establish life on more solid ground - however much I wanted to - I could no longer resist change.

'I'll do something...' I said, reaching out to touch Eve's hand, 'I promise...'

'Don't you always say promises mean nothing, unless you're willing to take action? You're always so uncertain...'

'I know what you're saying, Eve.'

What she meant was that I was frightening my children.

# Chapter 11

Zoë didn't come home or get in touch. I left a message with John, asking if he would explain to David what had happened. Zoë and I had been trapped in a cycle of combat, provocation and thoughtless reaction for months - possibly years - but now she was practising a new form of torment – prolonged silence.

Following my conversation with Eve, I'd been to the doctor - there was nothing wrong he concluded - nothing but stress. I spoke to Rose, who was now working as part of a team in a busy therapy practice. She suggested if I took lunch for us both, I could visit her new office and we could eat and chat at the same time.

Her consulting room was near Euston, in a Victorian Gothic house fronted by a small front lawn and a single silver birch tree surrounded by a neatly clipped lavender hedge. I arrived just after twelve o'clock, rang the doorbell and was sent upstairs by the receptionist to Rose's room - Rose was on the phone, but she motioned me to sit down in one of the armchairs.

Her room was painted in a fresh aquamarine and hung with a few tasteful prints of flowers. Since she'd returned to work, Rose's unruly dark hair had been cut close to her head and she had abandoned the uniform of tunic and jeans she'd adopted as practical clothing for child-rearing. The new Rose was neat and professional - a patterned silk scarf rested on the shoulders of her emerald green top and her grey slacks fitted perfectly.

When she'd finished her conversation, she spoke on the intercom and indicated she would only be taking urgent calls. Used to seeing her at home, surrounded by the muddle of her large family, I felt nervous meeting her in an unfamiliar role - it was as if she had become a stranger – a stranger in whom I intended to confide my deepest fears.

We spent a few moments catching up on family news and discussing the relative merits of salmon and dill or cream cheese and gherkin sandwiches.

Then I wasn't sure where to start. I didn't need to explain what had happened, only to describe how inadequate I felt to deal with situations from David's leaving to Zoë's departure. I told her how my headaches had become more frequent, how I suffered from insomnia and when I did sleep had terrible dreams. As my state of mind refused to improve,

I'd become afraid of the tide of darkness which seemed to be flowing through my life and gaining momentum.

'Those are the problems of people who hide their feelings,' she said. 'You can't live your life on its old terms – it's time to take stock.'

'I feel guilty, as if whatever happens, I'm to blame.'

'But none of this is your fault. David's had an affair - he's marrying someone else, that's his choice. Zoë and Eve are growing up and doing their own thing, and David's mother is exercising the right to lay claim to her property. It's possible, isn't it, that the girls are telling the truth – they've decided to move out in order to help you?'

It seemed I'd lost all sense of discernment.

'Did you ever talk about your childhood to David – do you talk to the girls, share your feelings with them?'

I shook my head.

'What's happened recently, I think, is playing into the cracks caused by the loss of your mother - you're suffering from an accretion of grief.' I glanced up and saw Rose's face was full of sympathy. 'Do you know, when we were at school I used to envy your colourful past – mine seemed so dull, so ordinary – coming from your funny little island with all your secrets gave you a certain mystique.'

I laughed, but her attempt to cheer me up had failed. 'I worry about the children, especially Minette, she needs a mother who's coping, she needs a father and she needs stability...'

'Your girls are strong and that's thanks to you.' Rose said, looking thoughtful, 'Perhaps the real question is - who do we believe we are when everything we've depended on has been stripped away?'

I took her question as a rhetorical one - I had no answer. 'I no longer believe anything - I've lost my faith.'

'It can't have been much of a faith then,' Rose said with a smile.

The core of a headache began to pulse behind my right eye, I had reached the point where I scarcely knew when one headache ended and the next began. My scalp and face tingled as if there might be a thunderstorm coming, and any attempt to form words was foiled by the refusal of my lips to move.

'They say there's a point in all relationships where we fall out of love and have to make the decision whether to go or to stay – sadly sometimes, like you and David, each half of the couple makes a different choice.' Rose leaned forward and took my hand. My heart beat so loudly, I was sure she must hear. 'There were complications with your mother's death, weren't there? The atmosphere of unhappiness surrounding your parents' lives, the possibility of suicide, the sense you'd failed to prevent - or had even caused - your mother's drowning.

I suspect all those issues and the feelings around them have remained buried until now and David's behaviour has brought them back to the surface.'

I wasn't sure how to respond to this incisive version of Rose and in many ways was more comfortable with the harassed mother and the chats we'd had at her kitchen table, when I'd commanded only a fraction of her attention.

She said, 'You're a writer - why not explore your questions on paper? Write a journal about your life as if it was a story. If we don't reflect, we're inclined to drift – we get involved with things we shouldn't and don't get involved in things we should...'

Under her cool appraisal, her words seemed to carry a veiled reproach. Though we were good friends, Rose had disapproved of my relationship with David - my ghost writing for Laurence Langlais, she regarded as reprehensible - a form of fraud.

'Perhaps you feel what has happened is abnormal, that your reactions are abnormal, but isn't this just life?' she asked.

'It's a very difficult phase of my life,' I said, forcing myself to speak. 'I think endlessly about my situation but I've no idea what to do. I used to have ideals of how I wanted to live, but I've moved so far from them, I'm alienated not just from David and the children but from myself – things feel worse than when Tristan died.'

'Change is painful,' she said. 'I've been through a rapid succession of changes recently and wondered how I'd emerge and whether Neil would keep up. Would he love the new version of me..?'

'You're not in trouble?' I asked. I couldn't bear the thought.

'We're fine,' Rose assured me. 'But for a long time, I thought I couldn't cope with all this...' she made a gesture to indicate her room, the stacks of books and the neat piles of papers on her desk. 'Perhaps you need to do as I've had to - stop seeing yourself as someone who can't manage. The real Iris, the one who is temporarily lost, could manage perfectly well – don't you think?'

Looking down at my hands, I said, 'I try not to think, I'd just like to feel better.'

'A good cry might help.' Rose reached for the box of tissues on the coffee table and pushed it towards me. We were near the end of her lunch break - her eyes had flicked up discreetly to the face of the clock on the wall behind me.

I'd come to see her believing there might be a better way of grieving, but she had reflected my image back to me in a broken mirror – all I could think was that when I left, she would be reabsorbed into her work while I continued to live an empty, meaningless existence, still swamped by my troubling feelings.

Rose's eyes searched mine. I put my hand to my head in a futile effort to stop the pain. 'I don't know how to go about finding my lost self, or even how to go about crying.'

'You do,' Rose insisted. 'We all know those things, but sometimes we feel it serves us better to forget, think about that...'

'Maybe I don't want to think about it.'

'Running away from life, from our past, is never the answer,' she said, growing impatient. 'If you can't face where you've come from, how will you face where you're going?'

My headache worsened. I felt dizzy and was afraid when I stood to leave I might collapse on the floor. I fixed my gaze on the velvety blue carpet, trying to count the flecks of gold and cream, but they persistently redistributed themselves, forming random, confusing patterns. I stared up at the window where the silver birch tree was framed - its yellow leaves, vivid against a dull sky, pulsed and vibrated unnervingly.

'I'm struggling to look after my family and myself, I'm struggling to work,' I said. I didn't tell her how at night, I felt the almost irresistible urge to go out and wander the streets, never to go home, as if by walking I might exhaust my mind until I no longer felt in a state of terror.

Rose studied me, her brown eyes soft now, 'You have support from friends and from your family, you're healthy, you have work that interests you, work you can do anywhere, you're young enough and attractive enough to meet another partner...'

'I hadn't thought of it...'

'...But you know I'm right. All these worries and doubts aren't inherent in your situation - they're in your mind. Take my advice, don't wait too long to start living again.'

I agreed with her out of courtesy rather than acknowledging the truth of her words, 'I don't think I'll ever forgive David or Helen,' I said. I was expecting her to remind me that forgiveness was a process, that in time I would find a way to accept that David had been unfaithful me for most of our life together.

'Perhaps Helen feels she can't forgive you for the years you and David enjoyed,' she remarked. 'Look the dragons of your childhood in the eye and you'll understand why you've reacted so negatively – if you can do that - I'd put money on it - your headaches will vanish and your confidence will come back.'

143

'Thanks,' I said, but my voice, sounded distant and strange, a voice someone might use to practice before going on stage, an exercise in inflection, quavering and uneven.

'Come on - we've had a good chat...' Rose said eager to encourage me. 'Being willing to recover is the least that's necessary, there's nothing anyone can do unless you're strongly motivated to get well.'

My headache made me clumsy and my handbag slipped off my lap onto the floor and spilled open. I crouched down, level with Rose's knees and scooped up my cheque book, lipstick, purse, and lastly, the black glass rosary, which had belonged to my mother.

'Do you still use that?' Rose asked, 'You could try *The Sorrowful Mysteries*,' she added and had the grace to smile.

Letting myself out of the room, I'd just reached the top of the stairs when she came onto the landing and called to me.

'It's an old fashioned idea,' she said, and even in the dim light of the landing I thought she looked embarrassed, 'a holiday can do a lot of good - fresh air, the sea, peace and tranquillity, why not go away for a week or two? Give it some thought.'

I promised I would.

'Send me a postcard,' Rose suggested, but her attempt at humour sounded flippant and when I'd made my way out of the building, I was more depressed than I'd been before.

*

Reluctant to go straight back to Hurst Row, I phoned Eve and asked if she could collect Minette after school. Meandering through the back streets towards Bloomsbury, I thought I would make a pilgrimage to Morton's Bookshop and buy a notebook in which – at some time in the future - I might do as Rose suggested and explore the nature of my existence on paper.

The ornate, old-fashioned façade of the bookshop was unchanged - the gold lettering on the window, the heavy door with its brass fittings - but the youngest Russell Morton had retired and the shop was now run by a manager.

The bell behind the door clanged and the tall, lanky young man at the counter looked up without speaking. The interior of the shop had been redecorated and the fittings rearranged. A shelf had been set into one of the back corners where customers could make tea or coffee and help themselves to biscuits. Nearby was a squashy lime green sofa where they could sit and read in comfort before taking their purchases to the cash desk – in a rather self-conscious way, it reminded me of the Perrot's book-shop in Nantes.

I poured a strong black coffee, added sugar, took a headache pill and then pulled a book entitled *British Marshlands* off a shelf in the Natural History section. The assistant seemed uninterested in my activities, so I piled five coconut biscuits onto my saucer and sat down on the sofa.

The text of the *Marshlands* book was illustrated with photographs and subtle watercolours and gave detailed accounts of plant and bird life over the cycle of the year. When I'd picked it off the shelf, it was with no special interest other than to pass the time, but as I flicked through the pages there was a reference to the marsh between Hagdon Hills on the north-west of Littern Island, a place where I had walked as a child. I scanned through the list of contributors and found Nicholas Piran's name among the photography acknowledgements.

Reading the descriptions of the island and studying the pictures for familiar landmarks, I came across a photograph of the round stone tower with a view of Clave Valley. Seeing that place, the drift of dusky blue irises, evoked bitter-sweet memories and feelings of sadness ran through me.

I wanted to buy the book, but it was expensive, so I put it aside on the sofa and turned my attention to the Psychology section – Rose seemed to have life wrapped up in neat manageable parcels – perhaps I would unearth a formula which would guide me.

Refilling my coffee cup - several times - I browsed and read, noticing how many of the self-help books offered rapid, if not instant, transformation brought about in ten simple steps or five or even three...

I thought if only there could be *a single* revelatory moment, one which identified the central theme of my life and made it clear what I needed to do next. My mother's death had set a different way of life in motion and David's departure would influence the person I would now become. It didn't take much – just a slight movement - the brush of an angel's wing - to change our familiar circumstances irretrievably and forever.

I stayed on, drinking coffee and brooding until I'd been in Morton's so long, I felt guilty about the amount of coffee and biscuits I'd consumed. I put a green leather-bound notebook into one of the net baskets the shop provided and then, on impulse, added the book on marshlands. I picked up a copy of the novel that was currently number one in the popularity ratings - though I'd never heard of the author - and then carried the heavy basket to the cash desk hoping I'd bought enough to justify my presence in the shop for almost three hours.

When I arrived home, the house was empty. By the phone in the hallway was a note from Eve to say she would be taking Minette to a burger bar in Victoria for her tea.

On the dining table, I laid open the *Marshlands* book at the page with the photograph of the wild irises – then unlatching the French doors - let in a draught of fresh air, standing on the step, watching as the sky turned a deep purplish grey, dreary and bruised.

In a sudden cloudburst, rain hissed against the paving stones and struck the windows. Spots of rain landed on my face and I breathed in the scent of wet earth as the storm cleared the air.

The garden was ready for winter; I had staked up the last of the autumn flowers - a few roses and Michaelmas daisies - and had dug over the tiny patch of garden I had given to Minette.

The refreshing rain brought a reminder of my love of the natural world just as the *Marshlands* book had re-awoken the sense that whatever had happened on Littern in the end - the years before my mother's death had shaped my ideas of how our existence should be - especially childhood. Minette needed freedom based on security, qualities which had been the hallmark of family life at Lyncross. From somewhere, I needed to draw strength to create a sense of well-being for my children, to find a house which could be gathering place, a place to which they could come knowing they would always be safe and welcome.

I closed the French doors and took from the sideboard the small figure of the White Virgin of Thrifswell, which had once belonged to my mother. Sitting with the *Marshlands* book in front of me, I lifted the figure, touched it to my lips, and asked the Virgin for help to achieve what I couldn't accomplish on my own – not just the locating of a house, but the creation of a home.

It wasn't much to go on, but at least I knew now that I couldn't bear the thought of raising Minette in a city flat with nowhere safe for her to play outside. She liked to grow things, to tend her plants and throughout the troubles of my relationship with David, the tiny garden at Hurst Row had sustained me. Now, distressed by David's leaving, we all needed to be earthed and in those quiet moments, it made sense to me to take that expression literally.

# Chapter 12

I no longer dreamt about Zoë, but instead began to have a recurring nightmare about pot-holing. Deep under the earth, rocks towered above me like a stone forest. On a ledge over a fast flowing river, I stood dressed in a black wet suit, wearing breathing equipment. My task was to swim under a shallow archway in the rocks, which was shaped like the eye of a needle.

As I contemplated the narrow space, I knew my oxygen tanks would jam and trap me in the hole. I had a terror of dark places and deep water and at the very moment when I was meant to plunge in, remembered I couldn't swim and panic pulsed through me like an electric shock.

That feeling of panic became real and familiar as I viewed over-priced garden flats, maisonettes and houses located all round London. They were mostly dismal and there were none I could afford or imagine us living in. With Minette to consider, I didn't feel comfortable renting a place in a run-down area or on a busy road and certainly didn't want to share a home, even if doing so meant we would have the garden, which now felt so important to me.

Every weekend, Minette and I made excursions further and further from the city until I thought I'd found a suitable house in Whitstable, though the town was far beyond the limit I had set for us, hoping to make it possible for Minette to remain at St. Catherine's School.

Minette was sulky and rebellious. She was bored by house-hunting, unsettled by the idea of moving and insistent she and Yuuka shouldn't be parted. We drove for what felt like hours to reach the house in Kent, but arrived at the property only to be told they'd had five other potential tenants to view that morning and one of them had taken it.

Frustrated, exasperated, I said sourly that even if the house had been available, I wouldn't have wanted it. Crammed into a small plot on a new estate, it was overlooked by neighbours from every direction. The garden was north facing and would be permanently in shadow and by the time I'd met our essential expenses we would have ended up living like paupers.

As I drove back towards London, tears seeped from my eyes and though I didn't want to distress Minette - I was helpless to prevent them. A reproachful voice in my mind asked persistently - *Didn't women in my position have to take what they could get and be grateful for it?*

Minette sat in the back of the car with her head hung - her dark hair hiding her face. I'd been bad tempered since we'd left Hurst Row that morning and needed to make it up to her.

'Shall we stop for a pizza?'

'No, Mummy, let's go home.'

I turned off at the next service station anyway and insisted she have lunch. While she ate, I considered what we could do. Having wasted the best part of the day, all I could think of was to go and see Barbara to ask for leniency over my eviction from Pimlico. David's mother wouldn't appreciate an unexpected visit, but perhaps with Minette's presence as an obvious reminder, she might be persuaded to consider the welfare of her grand-children.

Minette played listlessly on the playground equipment at the service station while I phoned Leitchly and explained to Barbara I'd like to call on her while visiting Tristan's grave. There was a long silence until she had made up her mind, but then she decided as John was out for the day and David and Helen wouldn't be visiting that weekend – she could think of no reason why not.

I explained to Minette we'd be taking a detour to her grandmother's and she was downcast. All she wanted was to get back to Pimlico, but calmer and more purposeful, having made a decision - I dragged her back to the shop and bought flowers for Tristan and Barbara. David's mother enjoyed reading, so I chose two novels and then selected a colouring pad and pencils for Minette, who would inevitably be bored by our conversation.

The last few miles of our journey were through pretty countryside. Autumn sunshine streamed through ragged breaks in the clouds. The trees had begun to change colour, their green canopies touched by red and gold - rainwater glinted on their leaves and berries, making dazzling sparks of light.

Among snug rural surroundings, at the end of a street of low thatched cottages Barbara's house stood foursquare in its swathe of lawns, like an intruder on the edge of the village.

I parked in the road, woke Minette and sent her ahead to ring the doorbell, while I gathered together the flowers and books I'd brought. The path to the house was edged with what must have been a vivid show of marigolds and nasturtiums, which had been bleached and faded by long spells of summer sun and then battered by heavy showers of autumn rain.

Minette reached the front door and Barbara was already in the hallway, her ginger-grey hair and the dull colours of her dress visible through the patterned glass.

'...At last..!' she said, stepping aside to let us in. 'What are these?' she asked pulling at the orange and cream chrysanthemums I'd chosen for her – the range of flowers at the service station had been limited. 'I'm not sure I like orange flowers,' she said.

I bit back a remark about the profusion of flowers in her front garden, which must have been every shade of orange from apricot to brown.

Barbara suffered from arthritis and walked with the aid of two sticks. Minette trailed behind me as I followed her along the hallway into the kitchen, a depressing room, which hadn't been altered or improved since the house was built - "retro is the latest thing" - David's father used to joke.

With painful slowness, Barbara fetched a bucket and filled it with water so the flowers would keep fresh. 'I hope there are no earwigs on those chrysanthemums, have a look, Minette,' she ordered.

Minette had a horror of creepy crawlies. So I went to the kitchen door and shook the flowers vigorously, upside down, so any earwigs would fall onto the crazy paving and could make a run for safety.

When the flowers had been sorted to her satisfaction, Barbara asked, 'Is that all?'

Sometimes when I visited, I had baked a cake or biscuits and apologised for having brought nothing to eat. To distract her, I mentioned the books, which I thought she might enjoy looking at later, but she said her eyesight was poor these days and she didn't much care to read.

'I suppose you're hungry?' she said to Minette.

Minette shook her head, refusing the offer of a green apple from the bowl on the kitchen table, 'It would give me a tummy ache,' she explained.

'Why don't you go upstairs and freshen up?' Barbara asked, 'you look flustered, Iris.'

I put the novels I'd chosen for her on the hall table and took Minette to the bathroom. More than once during a visit with David, I'd been tempted to lock myself into the toilet and hide as Zoë used to when she'd had enough of her grandparents.

'Do we have to stay long?' Minette whispered.

'Not long,' I promised. And related the story of how Zoë had once become trapped in the loo and had to be bribed with peppermints to climb out of the window and down a ladder to where her grandfather was waiting on the patio.

Coming to Leitchly was disturbing and I knew Minette must feel it too – the loss of David. Being in his mother's house brought home how

I still craved intimacy with him - how I'd wanted to cry on his shoulder when Zoë walked out, had longed to discuss Eve's planned move to Cornwall and the intensity of Minette's attachment to Yuuka. David's approach to life had once seemed worldly-wise, and I missed his perspective, which had been characterised by intelligence and a wry sense of humour.

Barbara was waiting for us at the foot of the stairs. The interior of her house was a grander version of Hurst Row - with over-elaborate furniture and a more extensive collection of china figures, which had spread through the rooms over the years, taking over every surface.

Minette sat at a half-moon table, facing the wall, doing her colouring surrounded by a collection of cherubs in various poses. The room was unheated and she'd pulled the cuffs of her jumper over her hands. Feeling cold too, I wrapped my cardigan closely round me before settling on the sofa as Barbara manoeuvred herself into a special raised chair.

'I don't suppose you have any news?' she asked.

I assumed she meant about my intention to move from Hurst Row.

'Not really,' I said.

'I heard about Zoë, and Eve wanting to leave home. They've been such difficult children. I think that bothered David, he needed a quiet, orderly life - no wonder he couldn't work...'

'In the end, David couldn't work anywhere – he wasn't well...'

'What a pity you had so many children, living in such a little house - David mentioned that to me, several times.'

I could have reminded her that two of the three children were David's, not mine, but that felt disloyal to the girls, so I answered carefully, keeping my voice neutral, 'If David wasn't happy with things, he would have been better to have discussed it with me.'

'Perhaps he felt he couldn't discuss it with you,' Barbara said, 'you were always preoccupied with Minette, or doing your work. David confided in me, you know, he said you'd never understood him. I used to think perhaps if you'd been different he might have made more of himself – been more successful as a poet.'

'How is David?' I dared to ask.

Barbara eyed me suspiciously, 'He's worried about Helen, she's having no end of trouble with her business partner - he's an antiques dealer and they're all rogues, aren't they?'

I didn't know much about antique dealers or about Helen, except Zoë had explained that she came from a privileged background and now ran Wilde & Goode, a vintage clothes shop, in Gipsy Hill.

'I'm sure David doesn't need to worry,' I said – feeling there was something bizarre about my discussion of the woman who'd seduced – stolen - my partner - as if she was any concern of mine.

'The trouble with you, Iris, is you don't worry enough.'

I didn't answer. David's lack of concern about his children had caused plenty of anxiety and was still doing so – our conversation was heading towards dangerous ground.

'The best thing you can do is put your relationship with David behind you,' she said.

'Maybe - but that isn't going to work for the girls. David will always be their father.'

Minette stopped colouring, her crayon poised over the paper. Outside, a heavy shower of rain, blown by the wind, drove large drops of water against the window pane so it was impossible to see out. I knew Barbara was upset and I reminded myself, whatever might take place during our encounter, she loved David too.

She said, 'When David was depressed, I used to tell him "come here and stay for a while, you'll soon feel better".'

'You wanted to help and he appreciated that...' I assured her. But if I sounded calm, I was losing control - we always ended up fighting an emotional battle for David. 'Now I need your help,' I said, 'whether Eve leaves home or not, there's Minette to consider. I think she'd benefit from staying at St. Catherine's until the summer, after the long holidays, she might feel more philosophical about a move.'

'I hardly see the girls from one year's end to the next,' Barbara complained.

I thought *I can't make them come to see you*, but to say it would have been unkind. 'Eve and Zoë are adults...' I began.

'If they're adults, then they can take care of themselves and as for Minette - if you're not careful she'll grow up into a spoilt little madam.'

Minette darted a look at me, her eyes questioning. I shook my head wanting to communicate that Barbara was wrong – she wasn't spoiled.

Barbara must have noticed the exchange. 'You'd like an ice cream now?' she asked Minette.

Minette nodded.

Barbara eased herself up from her armchair, groaning, moving awkwardly with one stick to support her as she progressed towards the kitchen with small, shuffling steps.

While she was out of the room, I went to Minette and hugged her, 'Don't take any notice,' I murmured.

In a few moments, Barbara returned with a sundae glass of ice cream and tinned fruit salad.

'I've made you a knickerbocker glory,' she announced.

Minette looked perplexed, but I smiled encouragement at her to at least try it.

Then I attempted to steer our talk onto something different - the current news, Barbara's annual coach trip to Llandudno, her Bridge friends, the garden -

'David thinks it would do Eve good to leave home, toughen her up a little,' she said, refusing to be sidetracked.

'Perhaps...' I agreed, though I found Eve's attraction lay in her mild nature.

As Minette had almost finished her ice-cream, I decided to make a final appeal, to speak to Barbara in a way which was simple and direct.

'It would really make a difference if we could stay at Hurst Row until next summer. You've been very generous, not expecting me to leave straight away, but please think of Minette, she's only seven. Hurst Row is her home...'

'...It may be your home, but it's *my house*, don't you forget that. It's my house to do with as I please. Your hanging on there is an embarrassment. Helen came to see me about it, you know. David will be much better off living in Pimlico than in her horrible little flat, all dank and poky...'

Pleading had been a tactical error - I'd placed myself at Barbara's mercy, handing her all the influence and power. 'I haven't found anywhere to go,' I said, though the expression on Barbara's face should have told me I was wasting my time hoping she might relent.

'Helen wants what's best for David and so do I.'

'But David's ignoring his responsibilities towards his children...'

'Ah,' she said in a way that meant she knew better. 'Helen tells me freedom from unnecessary responsibilities is proving good for David and his work. Helen's like Lesley – she has her head screwed on the right way.'

This was old territory. Barbara had admired Lesley, who was ambitious like David's father and John, and though their accomplishments were for her only second hand, she collected them like trophies.

'There were times when David regretted leaving Lesley,' Barbara told me.

'David never expressed regrets about his marriage to me.'

'He'd hardly express his regrets to you, would he?' Her voice had taken on the note of self-righteousness which was her habit. 'Your insecurity drove David to distraction, your nasty suspicious little mind...'

'David was unfaithful to me for years – though he knew how much I loved him and how much his daughters loved him...'

'Lesley still loves him,' Barbara objected, 'even now she's helping with his career.'

She was missing the point. 'This isn't about Lesley - it's about David being unfaithful to me with a woman half his age and you and your family condoning it.'

Barbara looked offended, 'You have no consideration for David's feelings, or for mine.'

'No..? Between you, you're destroying my life and that of our children...' I shouted.

'And you clung on to David when it was obvious he didn't want you anymore. Now David's "slumming it" in Gipsy Hill while you're living at my house in comfort – the situation is ridiculous.'

'I don't believe you care what happens to any of us,' I said.

'You wouldn't. You believe the worst of people – you believed the worst of David and it came true – a self-fulfilling prophecy. Did you ever stop to consider - you might have got what you deserved?'

I signalled to Minette to pack up her colouring things, it was time to go. I carried the sundae glass through to the kitchen while Barbara followed, her sticks tapping on the parquet floor.

'Wouldn't you like tea?' she asked, anxious to perform all the offices of etiquette, irrespective of how we were feeling - insensible to the consequences of our row.

I retrieved my bag and our coats from the hallway. Then taking the spray of flowers I'd brought for Tristan from the kitchen, I let us out of the front door, leaving it to fall closed behind us, cutting off Minette's polite goodbye.

Grabbing her hand, I turned down the main street of the village, past the cream painted cottages and the grey church, towards the churchyard.

The wrought iron gate creaked on its hinges as we pushed it open. A cold wind ruffled the box hedge and shook the cheerless Yew trees. As we walked, the long grass sent droplets of rain showering down, soaking our legs and feet.

Tristan's grave was beneath a group of sycamore trees. Just beyond the churchyard wall was a meadow, which in summer was full of daisies, buttercups and dandelions, though now the dandelions had gone to seed and their delicate, tiny parachutes were being snatched away and tossed by the wind.

Minette watched as I crouched down and arranged the flowers in the vase which was built into Tristan's headstone. There was a bench close to the grave which attracted the young people of the village, who hung round there in the evenings, when they had nothing better to do.

I tidied away the litter of drink cans, posting them into the waste bin, kicked a heap of cigarette butts out of sight and then swept drops of rain away from the seat with my coat sleeve, before sitting down.

Minette stood leaning against my knees, frowning. 'If Tristan hadn't died, would you and Dad have had me?'

'Of course,' I said and smiled up at her, 'think what we would have missed if we hadn't...'

'Is it my fault Granny won't let us stay at Hurst Row?'

I slipped my arm round her waist. 'No - of course not,' I said. I was struggling to exorcise the conversation with Barbara from my mind, to recover from the many accusations with which she had ambushed me. Eve had once suggested that her grandmother, in pain and housebound, was surely harmless, but while she was able to think and to speak, Barbara would never be harmless.

I'd intended to be a patient, loving partner to David, riding out a bad phase in our relationship, yet she implied I'd been nothing but a bloody nuisance, hanging around when everyone wanted me to leave.

David had told me I was the antidote to Lesley and everything he disliked about her - now he probably told Helen Goode she was the antidote to everything he hated about me.

Through the dripping trees, Barbara's house was visible, its tall chimneys jutting out above the church and the main street. I couldn't envisage on what terms we might stay in touch and yet didn't want to cut Barbara off, she was part of the girls' family and to never to come to Leitchly meant never to bring flowers for Tristan and that was unthinkable.

I dropped a kiss onto my fingers and pressed them into the mound of turf above Tristan's body, remembering the tiny white coffin in which he'd been carried away – so small, I could have held it under one arm.

The rain had stopped and planes flew overhead, leaving their white vapour trails like a signature across the cold blue sky. Wood pigeons hopped down onto the grass, flapping their clumsy wings and raising mud and debris from the ground as they searched for food.

Minette yawned as she waited patiently for me. Perhaps she believed everything might remain the same, though my world had shifted on its axis - in the course of the afternoon, David's new life with Helen and our exile from Hurst Row had ceased to be images in a bad dream and had become stark reality.

I apologised, 'I don't know why I'm crying again.'

154

Minette patted my shoulder. 'When we cry at school, the nuns say God always has an answer.'

'Let's hope they're right,' I said, blowing my nose.

'They're always right,' Minette insisted, 'Sister Gabriel says it's no good standing about moping, you need to take some initiative...'

Laughing, I asked, 'What does it mean "to take some initiative"?'

'In Minette language it means I'm hungry now, can 1 have that pizza? But in your language it means daring to do something on your own,'

I smiled at her then and she smiled back at me, her clear grey eyes soft with love and sympathy. I missed having all three girls at home, chattering and arguing like magpies in a tree. When Eve was at college and Minette at school, the silence and the loneliness could be overwhelming.

'Before he went away was Dad your best friend?' she asked.

'I used to think he was...'

'So why wasn't he really - and why couldn't you tell?

It was a question I'd considered, many times – searching my memory for signs that I'd missed - as on Littern Island, I'd failed to discern the subtle changes in the sea as the tide turned -

'It's a mystery - and you're a mystery,' I told her – though the mystery of Minette was one I hoped to unravel before she had ceased to be a child.

I slipped my arm round her shoulders as we walked back to the car – grateful to her for giving me something simple to do – something I could handle – taking her to the nearest pizza parlour.

# Chapter 13

Verena had been elusive, impossible to pin down, but finally we had agreed to meet for lunch at Brizio's.

Arriving at the restaurant, I found her sitting at a table on the patio - the old conservatory from our student days had long ago been taken down. Around her, strings of coloured lanterns hung in the bushes surrounding the area. Parasols and patio heaters made it comfortable to sit out, even in the chilly autumn weather.

Verena was reading notes from a folder and sipping wine. Her honey brown hair was caught back at the sides and her wine red sweater and woollen slacks were elegant and understated - the image which had become her trademark.

She was now headmistress of a girls' school in north London, a role with incessant demands – and as she noticed me weaving my way towards her through the tables, she tucked the folder back into her briefcase, as if to say, you've caught me out - working again.

We kissed - a touch on each cheek - an acknowledgement of our affection, which had survived so many years.

'I've ordered our usual, no point wasting time,' she said.

The menu hadn't altered since the 1970's and neither had Brizio's interior decor. The Chianti bottles in straw baskets remained, as did the red candles and artificial vines that draped the walls and wound up wooden pillars - familiar details which were part of the ritual and made meeting there easy and uncomplicated.

The wine glasses sparkled, catching light from the lanterns - the wine, a Barolo, glowed like liquid rubies.

'How are the girls?' Verena asked.

I sighed. 'Minette wants nothing to change, Eve's full of angst about joining a commune and Zoë, if I hear from her at all, is simply being Zoë - rebellious, abrasive and upsetting.'

'I would have liked to have children,' she mused.

'No you wouldn't.'

Our food was brought to the table – Spaghetti Carbonara and an Arrabiatta. As the waiter refilled our wine glasses - Verena's gaze flickered over him - a tall, slim, darkly handsome young man, with deep brown eyes.

Brizio's was full, and the buzz of chatter drifted through the open door to melt into a grey London day - so many conversations set loose to wander the streets and back alleys of the city.

'It's as good as ever,' Verena said, indicating the Carbonara with her fork, 'Yours?'

'Delicious...'

'We should drink a toast to Brizio's,' she said and we touched our glasses together.

I asked Verena if she would be going to see her father again soon. In old age, his physical health and mental acuity had begun to decline and for over a year she had been travelling to Geneva every school holiday.

She looked uncomfortable, 'I can't make up my mind when to go or whether to go. He doesn't mean to be, I suppose, but since he's been unwell, Father's become very difficult. I try to attend to his needs, but with the problems of distance and travel, I can't do as much as I'd like and still meet the demands of my job...'

It was unlike Verena either to be indecisive or critical of her father. I remembered him as charming. When we were at school, I had sometimes joined the Plaschy family for summer holidays in the Swiss mountains and when her father was in London he used to take us out for meals in restaurants far more expensive than Brizio's.

When we'd met lately, we'd often spoken of regrets. Verena had, in her own words, been seduced by the desire for a successful career. Her rise to the top of her profession had been sharp and unwavering, but she hadn't found love. For my part, life with David had been complex and unsatisfactory and life without him was turning out very much the same.

Verena's eyes followed the waiter as he moved among the tables with the slightly awkward, staccato movements of the young. She was beginning to stare and I nudged her foot with mine under the table and frowned a warning to her not to be embarrassing.

'You're looking tired,' she said.

'So are you...' I countered.

'Am I? When I left home this morning, I thought I was looking quite well.' She reached into her handbag and took out a tiny, gold-backed mirror and examined her face. 'I hadn't noticed before, but the lighting here isn't very flattering. We should find a restaurant that makes us look twenty years younger or where the waiters are twenty years older...'

I put my finger to my lips as the waiter appeared at the table to clear our plates and take our order for pudding. Verena snapped her little mirror shut and dropped it in her bag, then smiled broadly at him, saying she didn't require the menu - we'd have Pannacotta, as usual.

When he'd gone, she whispered, 'Despite my age, I've got good teeth.'

'You're perfectly all right,' I said, amused by her small vanities, the moments of self-doubt which betrayed her.

'I see you haven't tried my hairdresser, yet,' she remarked.

I put my hand to my hair, caught back loosely in a long plait - the streak of white at the front had worked loose and hung untidily round my face, while her "bob" was impeccably cut and coloured, without a touch of grey anywhere.

'I don't want a change of style,' I said, smoothing the stray lock of hair back into place.

'Now you're scowling - at our age it doesn't need the wind to change for our faces to get stuck. Let's drink to our collagen.' We raised our glasses and touched them together again with a soft clink, 'Love, happiness and elasticity,' she said.

The Pannacotta had been made in heart-shaped moulds and the puree of autumn fruits which had been spooned on top had spread violet-red juice across their creamy white surface, like blood filling veins. We ate pudding without speaking, savouring the delicious creaminess and the sharp contrast of the berries and currants. At a side table, the waiter prepared our coffees, his hands moving rapidly as he adjusted the barista machine causing a cloud of steam to rise in the cool air.

I slipped my coat over my shoulders and Verena put on her jacket and drew a wisp of cream chiffon from her pocket and tied it loosely at her throat.

'You asked me about going to Geneva,' she said her voice low, 'the thing is I've met someone...'

'Tell me,' I said. The course of Verena's love-life was usually anything but smooth and I felt we'd been skirting round our real concerns all evening.

She waited until our coffee cups had been deposited in front of us, the pudding plates whisked away. 'I never thought my relationships would be reduced to a sexual act – pleasurable if I'm lucky, appalling if not,' she began in a whisper, 'but this time it was pure lust...'

'*Was?* Is it finished..?' I asked.

'Mmmm - it's on and off - mainly off, but I'm trying not to resort to desperate measures to get him back.' She stirred sugar into her coffee and took a sip. 'You were outstandingly loyal to David, if only I could find that quality in a man...'

'I wasn't that good,' I said, dismissing her compliment. My sense of failure where relationships were concerned had deepened further since my conversation with Barbara.

'Rose told me I have an Electra complex and I'm in denial,' Verena said laughing. Earlier, I'd remarked on Rose's earnestness in her new role as a therapist.

'Perhaps you *have* got a complex...' I said teasing her, 'but sometimes life just fails to deliver what we'd hoped for...'

Verena frowned, 'I call that defeatism, I see it all the time in my staff and pupils and my job is to change their attitude...'

'Then give your mystery man another chance...'

'It's more a matter of him giving me another chance,' she said, then paused for a moment to gather her thoughts. 'When you first met David, did you think he was perfect?'

'It was love at first sight.'

'I think I'm like a machine with a component missing, the one that releases a flood of hormones to overwhelm your brain and convince you the man you've just met will be the perfect mate.'

'What a cynic,' I said. We knew each other well enough to trade insults without causing offense.

She shrugged, 'You say that, but how long have I been going through the motions? The cosy dinners for two, the theatre, concerts, bed - I'm bored with it all, from the chat–up to the moment of terror when I have to take my clothes off in front of yet another man, who may or may not find my body attractive.'

'I know,' I said sympathetically, 'or rather I can imagine...'

Verena looked away. 'Wouldn't it make you afraid? The thought of living the rest of your life alone, dying alone? You have a family - when my father's gone, I'll have no-one. I can't go on working for ever, filling my life with other people's children.'

Her eyes shone; her lashes rimmed with tears. I couldn't remember the last time I'd last seen her cry - and she was always so busy, I'd never thought of her as lonely.

'Don't give up on yourself or on other people...' I said, though it was a philosophy I struggled to maintain.

She shook her head, and took a handkerchief out of her handbag. 'I didn't want my life to be like this.' She dabbed at her eyes and said, 'Nothing lasts. Though you didn't let David go until he'd made you ill and miserable - you stuck your teeth into that relationship like a rabid dog...'

I couldn't help laughing and was relieved when Verena began to smile too.

'Love should be constant...' she said, 'if only I could live up to my own maxims...'

159

'Shall we order another coffee and ask the waiter for something strong to go with it?'

Verena caught the waiter's eye and signalled him to come to our table. He was beginning to look nervous - perhaps we appeared to him as gorgons, predatory older women. I asked if he could bring us some grappa.

'You spoke of being a machine with a component missing – my relationship with David was like that. There was a level of understanding we never reached, it didn't seem to come naturally.'

'I thought my father loved me with complete understanding....' she said, 'but there are things I'd like to know from him – did he resent me for robbing him of his wife when I was born – how did he feel having to bring up a girl child alone – why did he send me to London, when I could have gone to school anywhere in Geneva?'

Unanswered questions were something we had always had in common.

'Rose said I should face the dragons of my history - my father thought if I wanted the truth, I should go back to Littern...'

Verena smiled. 'The answers to our present dilemmas lie in the past? Rose recommended something similar to me.'

'Let's promise never to become bitter...' I said and we emptied our glasses of brandy.

'It's easy for you. You must have learned the capacity to love from your mother...'

'I wish I could remember,' I said, 'Juliet seems distant and unreal, though I think of her as warm and kind. Flora says she moved beautifully – she wanted to be a dancer - I've been told we're very alike...'

'I suppose you are quite graceful,' Verena said distractedly.

'...For a rabid dog?' I asked, referring to her earlier analogy.

A second glass of grappa had gone to our heads and we both erupted into helpless laughter.

'Sshh...' Verena said, 'you're becoming hysterical. I'll order more coffee.'

This time, I caught the hint of a grimace on the waiter's face as we summoned him yet again. We were the last customers sitting outside; the others had drifted away, getting up to pay their bills, calling out their goodbyes. Soon the waiter would signal that they wanted to close the restaurant for the afternoon.

After a few moments reflection, Verena said, 'I thought your mother was a sculptress?' The grappa had affected her badly - her eyes were glazed and unfocussed. 'Was she a dancer or a sculptress? I can't make the connection.'

My mind was also hazy - my thoughts disjointed and confused. Making a supreme effort I said, 'Perhaps the connection was a love of form...'

As I spoke an image of the spectral white statues my mother had made at Marisands, drifted into my mind, those eerie shapes that had flowed with the wind. Solid stone turned into something as fluid as the chiffon scarf Verena wore at her neck, shapes that suggested existence could only be ephemeral.

'What are you thinking?' Verena asked.

'Nothing, nothing that matters.'

'Those "nothings" are usually the most important...'

'Your childhood was safe and orderly...'

'Completely safe, orderly and terribly dull...'

I downed the last of my coffee. 'Mine wasn't any of those things - the atmosphere at Marisands seemed thick with sex and intrigue. But since I've seen Rose, I've been considering not only the bad parts, but the pleasures of growing up on the island. If my parents had got on better, if my mother hadn't drowned, I might have had the perfect childhood...'

Verena frowned. 'Those are very big "ifs". My father used to say you'd never find yourself until you became part of a happy family.'

'If I want a happy family, I'm going to have to make it...'

'Handle your problems alone?' she asked, 'that's usually how we end up making reckless and impractical plans.' Verena had a particular expression when she was weighing up something carefully, a look of patient neutrality, which she wore now.

'Let's talk about your work,' I said, changing the subject – my real problem was I had no plans, reckless and impractical or otherwise.

'I'm tired of parents, pupils and teachers - most of them want the school to improve, provided they don't have to do anything to improve it. I'm afraid I've reached the point where my lack of enthusiasm is beginning to show.'

'I'm sorry,' I said.

'I'm so restless - I've read all the books I could ever want to read, heard all the concerts that interest me and seen all the films and the plays - even my beloved Shakespeare. I've been threatening to go back to Geneva and live with my father.'

Shocked at the prospect of losing her, I spoke hastily, 'We can't become children again. Surely Rose didn't mean we should *literally* go back into the past – she only meant we should reflect on it...'

161

'Some of us need to do more – but I don't want to become a child again. I want to nurture someone I love, in this case, my father, who is slowly becoming childlike.'

'You said "difficult" earlier...'

Verena smiled, 'Aren't they sometimes the same thing?'

'When you're going through a crisis, things appear skewed...' I argued.

'It won't be for long – just a few months.'

'Well, if you've made up your mind...' I said, irritably, 'are you planning to stay in touch?'

'Of course, it'll be like a sabbatical. The only thing that's stopped me before now is the fear that if I nurse my father until he dies, I'll grow old myself - my life will be over...'

'In a few months..?'

'Caring for my father involves a deadly routine...'

'Don't give up on life, not yet...' I repeated, echoing Rose's injunction.

I didn't want to leave, but when I checked my watch, it was almost three o'clock and I needed to collect Minette from school. 'I'd better go...' I said wishing we had more time to discuss her plans.

'How's Laurence these days..?' she asked. 'Admit it – you're attracted to him - just a little bit?'

'I admire his intellect,' I said defensively.

Verena groaned. 'And I suppose at our age, that's the most we can hope for?'

I smiled at her and started to count out enough cash to cover my share of the bill.

Outside Brizio's, the narrow alley that led from the restaurant was so cold and draughty, we both quickened our step as we headed towards Draper Street, where Verena had parked in a narrow area of waste ground between two office blocks.

'Let me know when you're going away,' I said.

'We should agree to meet next summer...'

'Write *and* phone..?'

'You too...'

I stood and waved. As she drove away, in her little yellow runabout, a cloud of dust flew up into the dingy street. I hurried towards Oxford Circus, head down. As I walked, my shoulder swept against a buddleia bush, which had seeded in a scrap of dirt, its long, lanky branches overhanging the pavement. Its purple blooms were faded and rusty, but as I jostled into it, something small and white rose up into the air, almost into my face, disturbed by my clumsiness. I brushed it away, feeling a delicate wing, soft as feather against the edge of my hand.

The butterfly flew into the greyness of the city, moving ahead of me for a few yards before it disappeared, its wings fluttering like the petals of the white irises in the garden at Marisands.

I'd once watched a butterfly emerge from its cocoon. It had taken hours of hard work and the constant risk of death before its wings dried in the sun and it could fly and live out its brief, fragile existence.

It seemed a perfect image of the experience of beginning something frightening and new. Running down the steps into the underground, I missed Verena already. She would have said I was being fanciful, seeing an icon in the flight of a common white butterfly to which I couldn't even put a name – but its survival into the cold days of autumn was symbolic and in its frailty and endurance, I recognised both my own condition and my own need.

\*

One morning, a few days later, Minette was fussing about getting ready to leave the house. She was supposed to take something to school which had belonged to a parent or grandparent. I'd suggested she look for the flower press I'd used when I was growing up at Wren House, which had also belonged to Flora. When we couldn't find it, Minette refused to accept a reasonable alternative and just when I was about to lose patience, asked me to think of something for Yuuka, who couldn't possibly complete the project because she had little contact with her grandmother and even if she had, it would take too long to send something from Kagoshima.

For my birthday one year, Flora had given me her desk complete with its contents. Her hands were so shaky she was no longer able to write or to draw and she had felt the escritoire - once Yvette's - should be passed on to me.

I kept the small brass key to the desk in a ginger jar on the dining room mantelpiece. Minette knew where it was, had taken it without asking and unlocked the cupboard doors in the lower part of the desk, scrabbling among my things and leaving sheaves of papers spilled out across the carpet. The blue ribbon of my school medal for Service and Sacrifice was tangled round the leg of the chair.

Annoyed by the mess, I found a set of paintbrushes which had belonged to Flora and a Japanese paper fan for Yuuka and told Minette they would have to do or she would be late for school. We had an arrangement where she met with a group of older girls at Pimlico station - if we missed them, I had to travel with her all the way to Stonall.

When I returned to Hurst Row from the station, the postman had called – I picked up the mail and carried it to the kitchen. While I waited for the kettle to boil, I flicked through the pile, dreading finding another missive from Barbara or her solicitors. There was little of interest, except a cream envelope, addressed in the careful copperplate hand of an older person - writing which I was sure wasn't Alice or Flora's.

I took the letter through to the dining room, with my mug of coffee, and sat down at the table, elbowing the *Marshlands* book to one side.

The address, *Castle Rise, Esterlea* meant nothing to me, until I glanced at the signature, *Silvie Armsted.* As I turned to the second page, a faded photograph had dropped out from between the pages of the letter, substantiating the hazy image of my great-aunt, which hadn't quite faded from my mind. Dark haired, with a calm sensitive face and luminous grey eyes, she had long-fingered, hands, prematurely aged - her legs were wrapped in a tartan rug and her feet rested awkwardly on the foot-plate of her wheelchair.

With the photograph was a small watercolour painting of a dragonfly hovering above a pool, signed on the back by Silvie, I put it down on the table and began to read.

*My dear Iris,*

*You may not remember me, the eldest of the unholy trinity of Armsted sisters, which includes your great-aunt, Alice, and your grandmother, Flora. I'm usually referred to as 'the adopted one'. Your mother used to send me scent, Devon Violets, for my birthday and at Christmas – I have several of the painted glass bottles - the gifts were a kind thought - I was pleased she had taken the trouble to remember me. The drawing of Marisands you gave me as a child is still in my possession. Your grandmother didn't bring you here again, but I have heard news of you. Flora is too frail to travel to Esterlea these days, but we speak to each other on the telephone.*

*I have reached my eighty-eighth birthday and can scarcely realise I have lived so long, though it seems unlikely I will live for much longer. I wonder - what have you made of yourself? Is it possible you might be willing to visit an elderly woman, who has thought of you fondly and often?*

*Over the years, the family has treated me as a confidante - I have nowhere to go and few friends with whom to share their secrets. Your mother wrote to me regularly, until her tragic death, an occurrence, by the way, which I have never fully accepted or understood.*

*It is presumptuous of me, but I think we may have things in common – our roots in that strange place, Littern Island, our exile and the experience of losing our mothers. I have made a study of art, folklore and history - I retain a vestige of faith - and know we are both lovers of words. Like you, I am fluent in English and French and equally devoted to both languages.*

*Might we become friends, despite our difference in age? Such things happen and might have happened, had Alice not forbidden contact between us, threatening me through Mercer, the solicitor if I interfered.*

*Forgive me, if I sound bitter and disagreeable. The truth is I have struggled to establish my place in the family, to form a sense of identity beyond that of a lonely, single woman, an invalid. Isolation has been something of a vocation.*

*Please enjoy the small gift, a little painting of a dragonfly. A symbol of change and transformation, the dragonfly invites us to sift the meaning of our lives and if necessary to begin afresh.*

*I believe we may enrich or change the course of each other's existence, even now, as mine draws to its close. Flora has told me that you are in trouble – I may be able to help and have a proposal to put to you – we are sent to this earth to assist one another.*

*I have come to understand that the secrets of our being are like water – they emerge from a hidden source, become a spring and then flow outwards to become a stream - a river – an ocean –*

*If we can trust in that thought - who knows what might happen?*

*Please write soon - affectionately yours,*

*Silvie Armsted.*

The house was still and quiet, on a damp autumn day - the branches of the cherry tree in the garden were unmoving against a dull grey sky. The *Marshlands* book I had pushed aside remained open on the table at the photograph of Clave Valley.

I examined Silvie's tiny painting of the dragonfly - as delicate and as potent a symbol as the white butterfly I'd encountered on a dusty London street only a few days ago. That she wrote well and painted seemed natural – we came from a family of journal keepers, story tellers and artists.

I felt for Silvie and sensed she was imprisoned. Yet from the restrictions of her life had come her idea of the secrets of our being, a philosophy which moved me and gave me hope, though her letter had also pricked my conscience. Over the years, I'd made no effort to seek her out or to enquire after her welfare.

Now, I was unsure of the wisdom or kindness of visiting her – how would I find time to go to Esterlea once – let alone regularly? I was perhaps not the person she had constructed in her mind and might disappoint her - after all - I had ignored her existence for all these years. Receiving Silvie's letter reminded me of my childhood and had aroused my curiosity. But I couldn't think how she might be able to help me when she could do little for herself, without the support of others.

I'd long ago stopped practising my rites to remember Juliet. Alice had returned the carved box my father had sent me as a child, when I'd left Wren House to live with David. Though my mother's plait of hair had mysteriously disappeared, I'd put the box away connecting it with unhappy memories of the island. And when Flora had sent me her desk, I'd hidden the box in there with other things from Littern and Marisands.

Kneeling in front of the desk, I pulled out the wooden box and placed it on the floor beside me. Underneath was a manila folder containing old postcards, written in childish handwriting - spidery and leaning in every direction. Each one began, *Dear Granny, I hope you are well,* but the pictures were of scenes local to Littern - Narescombe Harbour, Sunset over the Marshes, The Priory, Safford Bridge. In simple words I'd attempted to describe what each place meant to me and I'd been touched to discover that those cards, along with letters, birthday and Christmas greetings I'd sent to Flora had all been kept, just as I had kept the many small things the girls had given me.

I sifted through the sheaves of papers Minette had left on the floor and rescued my school medal from under the chair. Among the papers were packets of seeds, hair ribbons, a pile of school reports and the flower press Minette had been searching for that morning. I gathered them together - Minette might like the seeds, she might like to use the flower press and ribbons – she had already told me she wanted to keep the medal, hung on her bedroom wall.

The top of the desk contained a row of cubby holes with an arrangement of stationery, pens and pencils. I sat at the desk and drew down the flap which formed the writing surface - the centre covered with a neat rectangle of green leather embossed with gold.

Lifting the box from the floor, I examined the lid with its strange carvings of interlaced trees and crossed keys, then turned it upside down, feeling along each of its sides until in one corner, my fingers found the tiny sliding hatch and the recessed lever which released the lock. With my fingernail, I flicked the lever outwards, the mechanism clicked and the lock sprung open.

I breathed in the soft powdery scent of tuberose; my mother's perfume, trapped inside the box, faint and slightly musty. The note my father had written remained there, neatly folded. With it were the yellowed newspaper cuttings recording details of my mother's drowning. *A Tragic Afternoon at Morrow Bay* the headline said and with the article were photographs of the Piran boys, Antony and Patrick, aged twenty one and fourteen, who with "heroic" effort had saved me and tried to save Juliet - both it proclaimed were "champions of the County Youth Swimming Team".

I studied the photographs – smudged, blurred images – their faces were clear and vivid only in my mind. Occasionally, I had heard of Antony, who had become conductor of an orchestra in the north of England. James Millford had also been successful, appearing in a number of Shakespeare plays – they had flourished and it should have been no surprise to find Nicholas Piran's name listed in the *Marshlands* book.

For most of my life, Littern Island had felt no more than a figment of God's or the devil's imagination. Keeping away from the island, refusing to think of it - refusing to cross the causeway after my father's funeral - had ensured that the past didn't intrude – but now when I least needed disturbance, memories of the island had begun to present themselves – as if to insist that whatever I felt, they didn't intend to be ignored.

I turned to the hand-written card my mother had made, the one she had pinned up in the outbuilding, where she worked on her sculptures, giving a brief account of the beliefs she shared with the artist, Arnaud Brisbois:

*Life is composed of fragments of experience shaped as much by imagination as by memory. When we examine those pieces we should try not to force them into any prejudged form, but allow them to arrange themselves into their own pattern.*

*If we are patient, the motif or theme of our life or work will suggest itself as quietly as a diffident guest and reveal the meaning of those fragments so that they catch the light like brightly coloured pieces in a stained glass window or the tesserae of a mosaic.*

With my finger, I traced her elegant writing and the narrow border of birds and flowers she'd drawn, as if by doing so I could touch her - as if the very ordinary things that have belonged to someone you love can become imbued with their spirit. As I did so, a sharp pain pierced through my left temple and eye, the prelude to a headache. I loosened my hair and let it fall free. Zoë would have said I'd been spooked, and though I'd read Juliet's quotation countless times, it was as if she had just spoken directly to me.

Littern and all that had happened there had been pushed to the margin of consciousness, but I could understand how the island had also remained at the heart of my existence. My childhood experiences were discarded fragments which I had forced into a pattern of loss and separation. Juliet had walked into the sea and the powerful waves had swept her away - as if she was as light and as insignificant as a piece of driftwood. Yet her death had been the source from which so much of my own life had sprung.

I closed the carved box, replaced it in the cupboard and shut down the desk top.

In the garden, the paths were speckled with orange and yellow leaves fallen from the cherry tree. I pictured my mother by the window of my bedroom at Marisands, contemplating the silver birches and white cherry trees in the oratory garden. I recalled the hours she had spent studying the differences of form and colour in plants all over the island and her excitement when James had taken her to Clave Valley when the wild irises were in flower.

Soon I would have to leave this house and find sanctuary in another place. My objections were no more than a faint cry of distress, a cry heard by no-one - a cry I would have to steel myself to disregard. But like the diffident guest of my mother's philosophy, a motif or theme had begun to suggest itself. If I went to see Silvie, open-minded, prepared to re-interpret the past, wasn't it possible I might see a new pattern?

# Chapter 14

I wrote a card to Silvie thanking her for her letter and promising to visit as soon as I could make arrangements with Eve to care for Minette.

Almost two weeks elapsed before I could get away from London. I'd told no-one where I was going and set out for Esterlea full of misgivings. I wondered if I had read too much into what Silvie had said. Her offer of help might prove no more than a way of persuading me to go to Sussex and relieve her loneliness and boredom. I wasn't sure if I could afford to complicate life with another frail, elderly lady when I was already concerned about Alice and Flora. Had my sympathy been aroused only because since David's departure, I too felt an outsider, someone isolated and abandoned?

I took the train to Esterlea and on the walk from the station to Castle Rise, stopped at a florist's shop and brought flowers – pink roses, gypsophila and purple beech leaves.

The nursing home was in a converted Victorian villa that fronted onto a leafy residential road. I rang the doorbell and stood on the step, waiting anxiously until a nurse in a maroon and white tunic answered the door and let me in.

'Miss Armsted is in her room,' she said and showed me the way to the back of the house along winding corridors. She promised to find a vase for the flowers and disappeared with them in her hand.

I tapped on Silvie's door and went in. She was dozing, resting on the bed - her legs stretched out straight and covered with a pale blue candlewick bedspread. Her folded wheelchair stood by the bookcase. Above the bed was a rosary of olive beads on a silver chain. The seascape which I had seen hung over the mantelpiece, thirty years ago, was still there, as was the painting of Clave Valley opposite her bed.

I admired Bernard's work, the river of dusky blue flowers flowing down to the valley floor.

'You must have that picture, when I'm gone,' Silvie said. 'Your great-grandfather was one of those early twentieth century painters, who undeservedly went out of fashion and faded into obscurity.'

I turned to find her smiling at me. Her hair was pure white, but the skin of her face was fresh and rosy, like the skin of a much younger woman. Strangely, though Silvie had been adopted, there was a resemblance to Flora and Alice and it struck me she had been the beauty among the Armsted sisters.

'I've never seen the wild irises...' I said raising my hand to touch the painting, 'though my mother knew where they grew...'

'My father took me there,' Silvie said, 'he could be enormously kind.' She reached out her hand and rang a bell, 'they'll bring us tea soon – perhaps you could carry the armchair closer – sit beside me.'

The garden was tinted deep gold in the low sunshine. Sparks of light flew from the shimmering fountain as it rose towards a clear sky of cerulean blue – I lifted the armchair across the room and set it down by her bedside.

'Would you pass my glasses?' she said.

I fetched them from her desk.

Under the coverlet she had concealed a small leather-bound photo album. When tea had been brought and the flowers placed on the desk, we looked through it together. Many of the photographs I had never seen before – there was one of Alexander in his soldier's uniform, 'Such a sweet, vulnerable man...' There were several pictures of my parents' wedding. Juliet had worn Flora's cream dress; she was so slender her pregnancy was no more than a suspicion hinted at by the fullness of the lace, where it gathered in folds at her waist. 'She was so like my mother...' Silvie said.

She told me how Alexander's family had fled religious persecution in Soviet Russia, how they had come to England, almost destitute and had made good, working their way out of a hard life in a slum area of London.

'I don't think your grandmother or Juliet ever recovered from Alexander's leaving – poor man – things might have been different if they had...'

We lapsed into an awkward silence as Silvie closed the album.

'I feel I should apologise,' I said, 'I should have taken the trouble to find you out – to make sure you were all right – my grandmother didn't mention...'

'...Anything about me?' Silvie laughed, 'She wouldn't and I blame Alice,' she said, 'but then I blame Alice for many things.' She glanced at my face to gauge my reaction, 'Tell me what's happened to you.'

I spoke briefly about David and the girls, and showed Silvie the photograph of the children I carried in my handbag. I told her about my work for Harp Press and at St. Catherine's School, 'I need to be independent, focus on my work, take care of Minette...'

'...And manage it all alone, because you trust nobody..?'

I felt my cheeks flush at her directness.

'You must wonder what happened to your mother before she died. She trusted no-one in the end. She was afraid, very afraid, though I

170

couldn't tell if she was more frightened of herself or of those around her. Whichever it was, perhaps she guessed the consequences which might ensue, if the truth was exposed. She must have preferred not to stir up a hornet's nest...'

'What do you mean?' I asked. As anger and grief for Juliet sprang from the dark place where I'd consigned them, I questioned Silvie's motives - *had she brought me here, not to help, but to undermine, to practice a form of retribution for the way she had been ignored?*

'You know, Iris, I believe in the right hands, the family's past could be healed. It carries wounds which require exposure to fresh air, cleansing and the application of love – if you were willing to do that, it might also heal you.'

'I'm not the right person...' I said.

Silvie smiled, 'Do you remember the story of St. Thrif? I think rather than being a simple servant girl, she was an intelligent young woman, strong, determined to overcome any obstacles in her path, to forge her own way in life – she was a survivor.' She stared out into the garden, 'I hardly care to admit it, but there are ways in which I could have escaped my circumstances. I've had my dreams, but found myself unable to create a different life, a life in another place. What a terrible failure of courage...'

'You would have liked to go back to the island?' I asked.

'Perhaps, though not now. I don't suppose I shall go there again.' She squeezed my hand, 'would you fetch something from the chest of drawers for me?'

Among Silvie's possessions was a silk envelope of starched linen handkerchiefs, which emitted the sweet, elusive scent of *Devon Violets*. In a covered shoebox, was her collection of tiny bottles of milk glass painted with violet flowers and of clear glass tied with a purple ribbon, some still with traces of the perfume inside, the liquid a startling chartreuse green.

'You might like to have these...' she suggested and the bottles awoke a lost memory - Juliet preparing prettily wrapped packages of the scent, never saying where they were going or who they were for.

'I expect Juliet told you the story of how Bernard discovered the island?' From her bedside cabinet, she took out the booklet, stolen by my great-grandfather, *The Legends and History of Littern Island*. 'I should like you to have this now – it might come in useful, everything you need to know about the island is there. She paused thoughtfully, 'You must be asking why I invited you here. When Flora told me you were to become homeless, it occurred to me, you might like to go to Marisands.'

I touched my hand to my forehead – it was inexplicable, but her suggestion had made me feel dizzy, disorientated. For years, Marisands had been a house I didn't wish to live in and Littern a place I hoped to avoid, but as my thoughts swung between the past and present, I felt both a great fear and the small germ of a desire to go there again.

'It wouldn't be possible,' I said, hoping to recover my equilibrium.

Silvie's eyes searched mine, 'I can see it would require a considerable upheaval and that your perspective on the island may not be a positive one, but I have a hunch if you can make sense of your mother's life, you'll make sense of your own.'

'What about all the arguments about Marisands?' I objected.

'There are arguments only because Alice resents the fact Bernard persuaded Juliet to leave the house to me - in trust. He was concerned I might, in the future, need more money for my care. On this matter, Flora for once has the final word, and Alice has no reason to complain, she's inherited her share of Wren House...'

Silvie was forthright, blunt, as I imagined her father to have been, and I tried to extricate myself from the embarrassing situation she had put me in.

'It's kind of you to think of me – but my ties are in London, Minette's at school is in Stonall...'

'But you have nowhere to live and I promised Juliet that whatever was left at the end of my life would be passed to you.'

'Your life isn't over yet,' I said. I had no knowledge of an agreement between Silvie and my mother.

'But it will be soon and the provision my father made has been perfectly adequate for my needs. I have no children - what could be more fitting than I should leave my possessions to my great-niece? I was quite fond of you, when you were a baby...' she added, her eyes sparkling.

Silvie could be provoking, but I had begun to like her. Despite her troubles, she had a lightness of spirit which made me uncomfortable with my own tendency to melancholy.

She touched my arm. 'Iris, look at my father's painting. Go back to the place where the wild irises grow, those flowers gave you your name, it's the place where you are - literally – rooted.'

'How can I..?'

'By trusting that my intentions are good – if you prefer, I'll find something you can do for me, in return.'

I focussed on the flowers I'd brought, which now seemed to remind me of Marisands' garden. Despite my doubts, the idea of returning to

Littern had begun to rise in my mind like a cork in water and however I pushed it down, it bobbed back to the surface and floated there.

Silvie said, 'There are certain things the family will never know, unless someone returns to the island and finds them out – I mean specifically about your mother. Neither Flora nor I will rest in peace until we know the truth of what happened to her. There'll be work to do in the house, but in-between, you could make enquiries. I thought you could write to me – once a month – keep me in touch with your progress.'

Confused, I asked, 'What does Flora think?'

'I imagine she'll think it's an excellent idea. I'm offering you an opportunity - too often we miss the signs that point to our destination. We ignore the trail of crushed leaves, snapped twigs and upturned stones that call to us to take a particular path. Do you believe our meeting has no significance?'

I cleared my throat - it was difficult to speak, 'With David gone, all I want is to continue as normal, to allow the girls to get on with their lives...'

'Can't you continue as normal on Littern? You might think you were never happy there, because losing your mother obscured everything – but it isn't true - before her death you were happy. Don't you see? This is the moment to be daring rather than merely stoical.'

'What's left of my family would fall apart...'

'Perhaps – but it would remake itself in a new and better form - that's an irrefutable principle in life.'

'If I had your faith, perhaps...'

Silvie tutted, signalling her impatience, 'Look at my father's painting again, Iris, I've learned so much from that picture.'

I did as she asked, but however hard I studied the painting, I seemed to learn nothing.

'Would you like me to pray for you?' she asked. 'It's no good dithering - the only way to find faith is to put it to the test...'

I said nothing, no longer sure what I wanted. Silvie was perfectly serious and I had the feeling that spoken to in her no-nonsense manner, God might feel obliged to act on her requests.

*

The tile-hung walls of Wren House glowed ember-red in the late autumn sunshine. The *For Sale* sign planted among the bare trees in the front garden read *Under Offer* and I had heard the details on the phone from Flora, their lives she claimed were in complete disarray.

I had a key to the house and let myself in. When I opened the door, Mrs. Stuart, was in the hall to greet me. She had put on a considerable amount of weight as she aged and it had slowed her down, but she was kindly and efficient and I had always liked her.

She informed me Flora was still getting dressed, but Alice was waiting in the drawing room. Alice made a striking figure, tall and upright in her chair, her white hair combed into a neat bun, her navy wool jumper showing off the well-defined angles of her face. I stroked the back of her hand, and she opened her eyes, eyes that were dove grey with just a touch of blue. I kissed her cheek and caught the familiar, sharp scent of lavender from her skin and clothes.

'Iris...' she said as if I was the person she most wanted to see.

'Are you well?' I asked.

'I'm very well,' Alice said, 'apart from a slight tiredness and I think that may be due to these cool autumn days.'

I had the advantage of being able to study her unobserved and thought the shadows beneath her eyes and the hollows in her cheeks had deepened – she was perhaps more concerned about their house move than she cared to admit.

'Sit down and tell me - how have you been?'

'I'm fine,' I told her, hoping the slight catch in my voice would go unnoticed.

Alice was astute. She had the habit of leaning towards me as if she wanted to catch every subtle inflection of my voice.

'Are you *fine*? I thought you might not be, with this wretched business about your home. Life rarely presents us with one difficulty at a time. We have to keep finding a fresh well of hope and courage...'

Her words flew straight to the heart of my distress. 'Everything seems to be changing,' I said.

'If change is happening, then it's time for change,' she was fond of aphorisms.

Mrs. Stuart arrived at the drawing room door bringing a tray of coffee and biscuits. While she presided over the coffee pot, she informed me how Alice and Flora were doing. Alice's face wore a longsuffering expression as Mrs. Stuart explained she was unsure of her claims about seeing coloured light and shapes and was convinced Alice was now completely blind. Flora's forgetfulness, she added, had progressed beyond the comic to the hazardous.

Usually I read the newspaper to Alice, but that day she declined my offer and soon Flora had joined us. In old age she'd shrunk until she was more like a little brown bird than ever before. I kissed her soft cheek and helped her into an armchair by the fire. Her hands shook so badly, I poured her a half cup of coffee and broke up a biscuit, placing the pieces in the saucer.

'Our life is in complete disarray...' Flora said to me – repeating what she had told me on the phone.

But any sense of disturbance was within Flora herself. The familiar things were in place, the shelves of books and Bernard's landscapes, flanking each side of the chimney breast. On the mantelpiece the heavy wooden clock with its measured tick, marked out time as if it had slowed it down.

Alice sat with her eyes closed and Flora stared into the fire, sipping her coffee, occasionally spilling it onto the front of her dress as her hands trembled violently.

'We shan't take much to The Maples,' Alice said at last, facing me in the unnerving way she had - 'but there are things you must have from here, things which belong in the family.'

'You must have all the paintings,' Flora said.

'Aren't those are the things you'll want around you...'

'It isn't what we *want*, it's what we feel is right,' Alice pointed out.

Flora's cup slipped out of her hands. I retrieved it and mopped at her stained cardigan and dress. Her strangeness and delicacy seemed to have hardened Alice's reason into something so solid it couldn't be questioned - as if her sister's belief in the correctness of her opinions had turned to stone.

Alice instructed me to fetch a pen and paper and write down everything she and Flora wanted kept in the family.

I chose a book to rest on and while I wrote Alice's list, said, 'I've been to see Silvie, she spoke to me about Marisands.'

When I glanced up, Alice's face was taut and Flora's perturbed, 'She can't sell Marisands,' Flora said, 'not without my permission.'

I tried to put her mind at rest - Silvie had no desire to sell the house.

Alice looked pityingly at her sister, 'I doubt Marisands is in a fit state to sell. We've had a letter - in fact several letters - about the decrepit condition of the place.' Alice fixed her blind eyes on me, 'Your father was a feckless man, not to be trusted with anything, especially not money or property.'

'He left the house in a terrible state...' Flora confided in a whisper.

'...There are holes in the roof of Thrift Cottage...' Alice said. 'However, I can't think what possessed Edgar Piran to write *to me* about it, that property is no business of mine.'

'Perhaps I could write a reply for you,' I offered.

Alice bridled, 'Edgar told us it would take months of skilled work to redeem Marisands, on top of which, your father owed money for the upkeep of the road on Littern, thousands of pounds - it's a disgrace – '

'The Pirans shouldn't have bothered you and my father's debts were his responsibility. I'll write and explain...'

'I'm sure Edgar didn't mean to upset us...' Flora said.

'Of course he meant to upset us,' Alice snapped at her, 'he wants *you* to take appropriate action.' To me she said, 'I've had no end of trouble preventing Flora being a fool over Edgar Piran. She's a terrible flirt, just like your mother.'

The image of Flora as a shameless coquette was ridiculous, but they were both clearly distressed.

'May I see the letters?'

'Alice threw them on the fire.'

Shading her eyes, as if she was exhausted by the memory of burning the letters, Alice said, '*I'll* deal with Edgar Piran, when I'm ready and not before...'

I didn't want to cause more anxiety, but I needed to raise the subject of Silvie's offer and there seemed little chance of speaking to Flora on her own.

'Silvie has suggested I go to Marisands,' I said.

'Poor Silvie,' Flora said, 'I really should visit her...'

'You can scarcely get out in the garden.' Alice reminded her.

I rested my hand on Flora's arm to comfort her, afraid she might weep. 'Silvie was curious about Juliet's death,' I said.

Alice glared at me. 'That's because she has nothing better to do than to rake about in other people's lives.'

Her voice tremulous, Flora murmured, 'I'd like to know what happened to Juliet.'

'You want the impossible,' Alice reproached her.

'And you forget the dead are never silent...' Flora replied, with unusual crispness.

'Did you mind very much when my father brought me here?' I asked hoping to distract them, if only briefly.

Alice said, 'Your being here helped your grandmother - she cared for you, nursed you when you were sick, you brought out her kindness and compassion. That's a gift, you know, bringing out the best in others.'

She had never been quick with praise, but even if I possessed such a gift, it hadn't influenced my father or made much impression on David.

'You were such an engaging child,' Flora said and smiled.

'Do you remember your blue coat?' Alice asked. 'The one you wore when William brought you here? It suited you very well.'

'I've no idea what became of it...' I said.

'You'll find it among my clothes,' Flora told me, 'please go and fetch it.'

In Flora's bedroom, I found the coat hanging in the wardrobe, swathed in polythene and still in perfect order. I touched the cool satin lining to my cheek and smoothed my hand over the soft texture of the black velvet collar as if comforting the grieving child, brought unwillingly to Wren House by my father.

Downstairs, I handed the coat to Flora who draped it across her lap, her wrinkled hands stroking the woolly texture.

Alice reached down the side of her chair, felt for her handbag and then took out her purse. She gathered a sheaf of banknotes and handed them to me.

'That little coat will do nicely for Minette - buy a blue coat that fits you. It can be your birthday present.'

Her generosity was unexpected, Alice had given me a hundred pounds, and I began to say that it was far too much...

'Put the money away,' Alice said crossly, 'It's from us both.'

Through the window, soft sunlight spread a veil of gold across Alice's pale face and Flora's rosier one – Mrs. Stuart topped up the coffee pot and for a while we sat companionably and at peace.

Taking a deep breath, I said, 'I came to ask Flora if I might go to Marisands and stay there for a while as Silvie suggested.'

I'd spoken quietly and wondered if they'd heard. For a second, the silence in the room was absolute, like the space between the steady beats of the ticking clock.

In the hot stuffy room, my head began to throb. I was under Alice's scrutiny and as soon as she'd gathered her wits she began to question me.

'Have you forgotten your work is in London? Minette has to go to school and Eve hasn't yet left home. How could you possibly stay in Devon? Besides, I thought you couldn't bear to go to the island...'

I felt the colour rise to my cheeks, 'Everything was so difficult with William's death - that awful funeral...'

'If you're thinking of living on Littern, you'll need a sign so clear that no amount of wavering on your part could cast doubt on its meaning.'

'I have to leave Hurst Row in January...' I reminded her.

'When she first came to Dulwich, Iris wanted nothing more than to go back to the island, she knew her mind, then,' Flora said.

'How could she have known her mind? She was only seven,' Alice retorted.

'Silvie can't go to the island - she needs someone to go for her, that's why she's asked me.'

Flora spoke gently, 'Iris no longer has David to protect her. This is something she could do for the family, and the family could do for her - if she takes on the responsibility willingly - why shouldn't she go?'

Alice's face hardened, but Flora must have known that once the suggestion had been reframed as a duty it might appeal to her sister, perhaps become an imperative.

'Minette needs stability,' Alice said, 'she needs deep roots and to feel secure at a fundamental level - as do all your girls – especially Zoë.'

Her insight surprised me. I'd believed Alice disliked David's children, finding them subversive and none more so than Zoë, with her overt acts of rebellion.

Flora said, 'I don't suppose Eve wants to live in a commune, and Zoë I'm sure, doesn't want to live in a van. They must feel those are things they *need* to do because Iris has no home...'

Alice interrupted, 'If you want to go, Iris, I don't suppose I can stop you. You're headstrong like your mother. But take heed, the first request from Silvie is always the thin end of the wedge - she's an extremely difficult and demanding person.'

Flora gripped hard onto my hand, 'Marisands can be lovely in spring.'

'But there are storms on Littern at any time of year, don't forget that...' Alice added.

'It would mean so much to us to know you were taking care of Marisands. We used to enjoy hearing about the house and garden, you wrote very well, even as a child...'

'Marisands is full of family treasures and they need to be preserved,' Alice said. 'They may be of considerable value, and I do have some say in what happens to the contents of the house...'

I felt like a ball, being batted back and forth and wondered what the conclusion would be when I landed on earth again.

Flora was growing drowsy in the warmth of the fire. 'You would have to discuss arrangements with Geraldine, of course. You could do that by letter or on the phone...'

'You'd have a duty to ensure anything that belongs to the Armsted family remains at Marisands and doesn't find its way into Geraldine's hands...' Alice warned.

'I wonder if the girls will be happy there...' Flora murmured sleepily.

'You do realise Silvie is no better than an interloper...'

I waited for Flora to speak again, though Alice enjoyed having the last word, Marisands wasn't hers.

'I see no reason why you shouldn't go, if you would like to, none at all,' Flora said and smiled at me, 'a house can be a comfort, a companion, as much as a person...'

I shivered and Flora cradled my hand in hers, rubbing my fingers as if I might be chilled. 'Don't be afraid,' she said. 'Do you remember what I used to tell you as a little girl? The things you believe will overwhelm you are nothing but tricks of the mind.'

*

Once I had given her news of my plans, Eve spent her time huddled at the kitchen table, reading books about Cornwall and studying photographs of Zethar Creek sent to her by the leader of the commune, Luke Porter. She was convinced her lack of confidence as an artist came from the strictures of living at home and of her studies as a conservator. She was sure that by going away she would discover a fresh source of inspiration and didn't seem worried about living alone in a remote place - the other members of the group would support her.

Zethar Creek lay in a deep gully approached across bleak moorland. Down by the creek, where Eve would be living, was a pub - The Angel Inn - its blank windows suggested it might be permanently closed.

My impression of the place was of brown muddy banks slashed by muddy water, except at high tide, when the margins of the creek disappeared under a thick, oily river. Enclosed by hills, largely featureless, Zethar Creek offered seclusion, consisting of not much more than the pub, a row of boatsheds and a few boats moored against a stone quay.

The main village was on a hill overlooking the water and according to Luke Porter could be reached only through a network of winding lanes so narrow, there was barely room for a single car to pass between the hedgerows. Luke's account of their friends' lives made them sound unstable; their plans marred by squabbles both within the commune and between the commune and the village.

Eve's place could only be approached along a boardwalk that skirted the gully and formed a narrow bridge across the river. Hers was the last of the row of boatsheds, distinguished by wooden cladding on the upper floor and what appeared to be its perilous proximity to the water. Jutting out over the river, a metal staircase ran up the outside of the building to the door of her flat, a primitive stone walled room, heated by an open fire.

'I can go to the pub to keep warm,' Eve said, when I expressed concern.

Peering at the photographs of the interior of the flat, I could make out an unsavoury brown sofa with a thick quilt folded at one end and an old army field cot - a heap of wooden struts, canvas and webbing - on which Eve was expected to sleep. The kitchenette had a collection of blackened saucepans, while the bathroom consisted of a toilet and basin fitted into a tiny cupboard.

Outside her studio door sprawled two cats, strangely marked - brindled - black on fox-brown. Eve explained they lived in the boatshed among the chaos of nets, floats, wooden boards and tools, which currently occupied her workspace. On the floor and the walls of the studio was inescapable evidence of damage done by the floods, which Zethar Creek suffered, every winter in heavy rain.

'Why not go in the summer? I suggested.

Eve's expression implored me not to interfere. 'Stop worrying...' she said, '...please?'

But I couldn't stop. Her flat had been intended as a store room, not as a dwelling. At the windows were the thinnest possible cotton curtains, there were no rugs on the floor. Eve's life in Zethar Creek would be penitential and living down in a swamp, I was certain the bronchitis she had suffered regularly as a child would inevitably return.

Eve couldn't be dissuaded from leaving. And less than two weeks later, we took a taxi to Paddington Station on a blustery November morning. She had sent her belongings to The Angel Inn, where they would be taken in by someone called Matt, who ran the pub and kept the keys to the flats. Luke Porter had sent instructions scrawled on a scrap of newsprint – he would meet her at Zethar Creek station in a van that had *Paradise Pottery* painted in flowery letters on the side – she couldn't mistake it as there would be no other vehicles parked within miles.

On her back, Eve carried a large rucksack. She wore a thin, faded blue anorak, a remnant of her school days, with a long scarf in rainbow colours wound round her neck. She was so anxious and excited we arrived far too early for her train and took refuge in the steamy warmth of one of the station's coffee shops, perched at the bar on stools. Eve's fair hair was gleaming in the low light, even against the drab background of the station she had the sort of good looks which would always shine, perhaps even in the muddy hole that was Zethar Creek.

Suddenly hungry, Eve said she would like a cooked breakfast. I had no appetite and ordered a black coffee. That morning, Minette had been upset about her sister's departure and had gone off to school in tears.

While she was eating, Eve took a phone call from Luke and in a subtle and chilling way her mood changed. When he'd rung off she was quiet and subdued, pushing her half-eaten meal about on the plate and not speaking.

'How are you feeling?' I asked when she said nothing.

'I'm all right.'

She looked not at me, but across from the cafe at the busy station, teeming with crowds of commuters.

'I hope nothing's changed.'

'Luke says it's deserted down by the creek,' Eve said. 'They've had more floods and a few people decamped to Truro - it's a kind of Marie Celeste situation, with me as the last ghost on board.'

'Is there anyone left?' I asked, trying to keep the panic out of my voice.

'One or two – Luke's stayed. People lost their work, or their materials and equipment were badly damaged, you can't blame them for pushing off.'

'But why didn't he tell you what was happening?'

'I knew things weren't going well,' Eve said, her pale cheeks colouring a bright red, 'but I didn't want you to worry.'

'You don't *have* to do this...' I said.

'I do – I need to live simply and do my work...' Eve met my gaze with her large blue green eyes. 'In Zethar Creek, I'll be free - able to explore my own ideas – if they're crap, then I'll see that they're crap - there'll be no running away.'

It seemed a painful process, but she was full of hopes and ideals and her clarity was so striking I felt it would be wrong to argue. Eve would reach a conclusion on life in Zethar Creek in her own time.

Morning light had begun to filter into the station and our waiting became uncomfortable, full of apprehension, there seemed nothing else we could say.

In the last minutes before she boarded the train, Eve dashed to a take-away to buy sandwiches, sausage rolls and a pie, enough to eat until the next day.

'Luke says the village shop is closed half the time, but I can scrounge off him or get a few basics from the pub – I might become a vegetarian.' Seeing the expression on my face, she said, 'Sorry, I'm really sorry.'

181

A mixture of laughter and sadness welled up in my throat, I thought *only you could live like this, Eve -*

She smiled at me, uncertainly. 'Luke's going to leave me a bucket of wood and coal - he's put milk, tea and bread in the flat with a few tins of macaroni cheese...'

Touching her face with the back of my hand, I repeated my instructions for lighting the open fire, something she had never done before. As we neared the platform, I slipped a hundred pounds into her bag – the amount Zoë had taken from my purse when she left home. With any luck, Eve might avoid starvation or freezing to death, at least, in the immediate future.

At the ticket barrier, I asked if I could see Eve onto the train. A cold wind funnelled down the platform. Eve clambered onboard with her heavy bag, shut the door, pulled down the window and leant out to talk to me.

During the week, I'd been to an art shop and handed her a paper bag containing the oil paints I'd bought in intense shades of blue, green and yellow. I'd thought they might counteract the brown muddy landscape of her surroundings. Eve pulled a face, her work tended to be done in watercolour using soft, neutral colours.

'Try them,' I said, reaching up to take her hand, 'try something different.'

Up and down the platform, train doors slammed shut.

Eve said, 'Luke's photographs show Zethar Creek at its worst - people do go there for holidays, you know...'

The train inched forward and I blew her a kiss. 'I shouldn't mention it, but you can come home – anytime - I'll drive down and fetch you...'

Eve's face threatened to crumple.

'Please - don't - you'll set me off,' I said.

'I won't...' She wiped her eyes with her sleeve. 'Give my love to Minette - and Zoë if you hear from her.'

I stood, waving until the train had disappeared. Eve was my friend, my companion and support – I was going to miss her terribly.

As I left the station, I prayed that the reality of Zethar Creek would match her dreams of artistic freedom and independence. Eve had demonstrated courage and a sense of vocation well beyond her years – she deserved not to be disappointed.

And with her leaving, my hopes of a future at Marisands took on a firmer resolution. If she could survive life in a desolate place, so could I - Littern Island couldn't possibly be worse than Zethar Creek - and Marisands was sure to be more comfortable than a fisherman's hovel.

# Chapter 15

December seemed to rush by and most of the items I was to have from Wren House were delivered to Pimlico, so I could take them with me to the island.

I had been open about my plans and Minette had only one thought in her mind that she must stay at school with Yuuka. She felt she needed to protect her from being bullied, but also from some other threat, which she refused to confide.

We had a row the day the van arrived from Dulwich, bringing furniture, books, a stack of paintings and two large leather suitcases of papers. I'd crammed them all into the already over-full dining room, making it impossible to walk from the hall to the French doors to get out into the garden.

Flora had sent Bernard's *St. Thrif's Holy Well,* a painting of mossy stones, trees, ferns and mystery, a green world with pure, clear water. I propped it up on a table in the hall so Minette could see.

But when I brought her home from the station that night, she was already in a bad mood and seeing the mess asked, 'What is all this stuff?'

I explained how the family's possessions had been passed down through the family and how one day they would be mine - then in time - hers.

'I don't want them,' she said and left the kitchen table where we were having supper together, leaving her food untouched.

I found her lying on the sofa in the sitting room, swaddled in a mohair blanket, curled into a soft woollen ball. The radio was playing in the background – she'd been asked to listen to the news for a week to complete a school project on world affairs, but I switched it off as the newsreader began to discuss how aid workers had been abducted, somewhere in Africa.

'That was my homework,' she moaned, 'I'll get into trouble now...'

Under the blanket she had two blue school exercise books, as I'd sat down by her feet - she'd hidden them in the side of the sofa. Recently, she had been given a detention for helping Yuuka with her homework and though I could guess one of the books was her friend's, it was an issue that could be dealt with another time.

'I know you're fed up, but we should try Marisands – just for a while.'

'I don't want to!'

'We don't have much choice,' I said, though I knew Minette wasn't being petulant, her feelings on the subject ran deep.

As happened often now, Minette's eyes were brimming with tears - her unhappy little face seared itself into my mind - she appeared so small and vulnerable, her thick hair falling about her shoulders.

'What's going to happen to me? What about Yuuka?' she demanded.

'You'll be with me on the island. There's a good school close by – very like St. Catherine's - would you like that?'

'More nuns?' she asked, shaking her head as if in disbelief.

'Minette...' I began, not really knowing what else I could say. And before I could think of something, she had launched into a list of complaints.

'I don't want to live on your stupid old island, I've seen it, and it's horrible. And I don't want to leave Yuuka, she'll be all alone, who's going to look after her?'

'If the school agrees, perhaps Yuuka will be able to visit us...'

'Why can't she *live* with us?'

'We've discussed this before – I can't kidnap Yuuka and take her to Littern...'

'I wish *I was* an orphan and then I could live at school. Couldn't I stay with Yuuka while you go away?'

I studied her face - leaving her behind was a possibility I'd never considered, 'You're only seven...'

'I'm nearly eight,' she reminded me, 'I could stay at school while you make up your mind what we're going to do.'

Her cheeks were damp with tears - I passed her a tissue. I'd been critical of parents who abandoned their children to boarding school at a tender age. Minette already took the concept of Service and Sacrifice far too seriously and I thought the school wrong to have allowed her to assume responsibility for Yuuka, especially as her friend, like all pupils, had an official auntie.

'Please ...' she begged. The tissue I'd given her was screwed up into a tight wodge in her fist.

I would hate it if she stayed in London - I couldn't really afford St. Catherine's anymore. Yet Minette formed profound attachments - she missed David and Eve – and parting her from Yuuka seemed brutal.

'Dad could look after me - or Granny,' she suggested.

'No...Minette, they can't.'

'It's what I want – I want to stay with Yuuka. You could ask Rose and Neil, I'll live with them.' Minette folded her arms across her tummy and her face took on its most stubborn expression.

184

'It's no good putting off facing up to something which makes you unhappy – we can't always do that, can we?'

'You'll break Yuuka's heart,' she said.

*And you're breaking mine*, I thought. Perhaps because Zoë and Eve were so much older, Minette had always longed to be an adult - often she was more grown up than the adults who surrounded her, including me.

'You'll have to come to the island,' I said, 'I can't see how this would work.'

'I don't want to go to the island.'

'We need a home, a place where we feel happy and safe.'

'I feel happy and safe with Yuuka,' she said and leant forward, hugging me round the waist, 'I promise I'll be all right at school.'

Scenting the possibility of capitulation, Minette began to make more promises: she would phone every week and write every day... 'I'd never forget you...' she said, 'Please..? I want to earn the Service and Sacrifice medal like you did - I've been trying really hard.'

Thoughts tumbled round my brain. *Could I ask David for help, might he be willing to make a financial contribution? Could I take out a bank loan?*

Minette, though she protected Yuuka, clung to their friendship as if it was the one sure thing in her life and I could see why. From her perspective, I must often appear unsteady, a woman whose capacity to trust had run out - as Silvie had suggested, relying on no-one, yet no longer sure I could rely on myself.

'Perhaps I'll talk to the school,' I said, 'it would only be for a few weeks.'

Minette broke into sobs, so intense it was as if she was weeping for all the years of her short life. Tears flowed out of her in an unstoppable stream. I held her close and let her cry her feelings out.

'I'll see what I can do,' I said, rocking her in my arms, 'I'll try...'

'Please try *very* hard,' she said, 'very, very hard. God won't let you be lonely without me...'

\*

As I prepared to leave Hurst Row, there were endless phone messages from Barbara and Helen and arguments were never more than a careless word away. Barbara reminded me repeatedly that no furniture or ornaments of hers were to be taken and seemed unable to comprehend how a human being can become so tired they're unable to make the simplest of choices.

185

I balked at being expected to deal with Helen – where was David? Helen was full of queries I couldn't answer and I became angrier the more I failed to hide how exasperated and futile she made me feel. When I couldn't face another conversation with her, I approached John, whose steady predictability made him the ideal intermediary, but wisely, he told me he didn't want to be involved.

The task of moving took over my life – the need to make one decision after another. I wasn't sure what to do with Zoë's possessions. When I'd e-mailed to ask, she hadn't replied and so I'd packed everything of hers, including the row of black paintings from the landing, symbols of unrelieved darkness, the aftermath of an eruption from the small volcano that was my eldest daughter.

The list of items I felt compelled to pack grew. Apart from my personal belongings, I wanted to take plants from the garden. Alice and Flora had sent more things from Wren House: William's drawing of St. James's Park, the rug from my childhood bedroom and the chair - then three large boxes of papers. Piles of things stood all over the house waiting to be transported to Littern.

During the week before Christmas, Minette and I were invited for supper at Rose and Neil's house in Bayswater. They had agreed that if Minette became a weekly boarder, she could stay with them at the weekends to keep their youngest son, Simon, company until she joined me on the island at the end of February.

At home, Minette had hung a few streamers and draped tinsel round the rooms, but Rose had decorated her house for Christmas in an unrestrained style, with vases of scarlet and cream flowers, bowls of holly and fir cones and an enormous Christmas tree which almost filled the hall. I'd brought a bottle of whisky for Neil and champagne truffles for Rose and left them with other gifts on the hall table.

'How's life?' Neil asked as we went through to the dining room.

'Completely chaotic...'

'You're probably exaggerating...' he said.

'I wish I was.'

I sensed Rose's reserve. She brought food to the table as soon as we sat down - beef and ale stew. She was a good cook and I was looking forward to a proper meal, we seemed to have been living on snacks for days.

Simon and Minette were handed plates of pizza, crisps and chocolate biscuits and sent down to the basement, where there was a den for the children with a TV and video player.

We chatted for a while. Rose was planning to set up her own therapy practice next year, to go it alone.

'I can't believe I'm re-launching myself at nearly forty, I feel like an eighteen year old again - naive and lacking in poise...'

'You'll be fine, stop feeling sorry for yourself,' Neil said and smiled at her.

He produced a large, neatly wrapped package from the sideboard, 'A late happy birthday and an early Happy Christmas and something of a going away gift,' he said to me.

I un-wrapped the parcel; it contained a book on survival and a pair of wellington boots.

Neil leaned forward and kissed my cheek, 'They seemed appropriate...'

'You shouldn't have...' I said.

'I bought the book from Morton's, in one of my increasingly rare lunch breaks. I don't know when I last paid for a book,' he teased. 'Let's play epitaphs,' he suggested, lightening the mood. It was a silly game we'd devised at university to mark major changes in our lives.

'You *can* teach old dogs new tricks,' Rose said.

After some thought, Neil said, 'His name was writ small in other people's books.'

'Once a ghost always a ghost,' I offered.

As we caught up with news, I studied their faces. Softened by candlelight, Neil's fair hair was a flattering ash blonde – he remained youthful because he was content. He'd had a good marriage, a brood of bright, happy children and a successful career and if Rose's face had become more severe with age – she remained what people referred to as handsome.

'You're quiet,' Neil said to me.

'All I seem able to think about is leaving people behind – leaving all this,' I said, indicating the candlelit room and sparkling glasses and the dishes of delicious food. I took a large sip of wine.

'Returning to Prospero's island? Will you be all right?' Neil asked.

'I will - but I'll need time...'

'Time for what..? Is there anything to do on Littern?' Rose asked.

Neil put a restraining hand on her arm. 'First of all, does the island really exist?'

I produced from my handbag the booklet, *The Legends and History of Littern,* which Silvie had given to me, I'd anticipated an interrogation.

Neil took it from me, 'The quality of the print and the paper are terrible,' he commented and peered at the fuzzy black and white photographs, which with the passage of time had become so faint they had almost no distinguishing features. 'Not much help, I'm afraid.'

Rose took the booklet from him and thumbed through it. 'This is what happens when you say, "I'm never going back to a place as long as I live", though I suppose David has put you on the spot.'

Neil seemed to understand I'd prefer to talk about something else, he was by nature a kind man. 'Ask me about work later, I've got good news,' he said.

He'd promised to put my name forward as the translator for Laurence's next *Minor Lights* series - I was in the final stages of completing the latest of the *Kenholme* books.

'Couldn't you tell me now?' I asked.

'As you well know, the first requirement of a ghost is complete discretion, but it's an ideal job for you, given your circumstances. Apart from receiving instructions from me occasionally, you can "bloweth where you listeth"...'

'...That's the Holy Ghost - Iris is hardly the same thing...' Rose objected.

But I didn't mind their bantering; Rose's sharp intelligence gave her character and Neil remained as amiable as when I'd known him in our student days.

'Rose tells me David's persisted with the idea of *Blue Rhythms*,' he said.

I'd passed on information Helen had given me.

'Maybe the moment for a comeback has already gone,' she suggested.

'Sometimes there can be a revival of interest or it becomes possible to generate one - I assume that would be Halkett & Haire's approach...' Neil said.

'Perhaps it doesn't matter - *Blue Rhythms* was something very private - personal to David,' I said feeling I no longer had the right to comment on his feelings or actions.

Rose passed *The History and Legends* back to me. 'Why don't you write something about Littern? You could weave the story of your family into the island's geography and history, throw in a few illustrations.'

'I'm not sure that would work,' I said, pushing the idea aside.

'Then what about, "An Artist's Journal: A Year on the Isle of Littern",' Rose persisted.

'That's not a bad concept - it's bound to be an unusual experience...' Neil said.

'But not necessarily the kind of experience I want to share.'

Amusement and concern flitted across Neil's face, 'I'm interested in your work, whatever form it takes, and there are plenty of people around who'd give both their eye teeth and their right arm to hear me say that.'

'Of course,' I replied. Neil was a gentle, lovely man - like a shadow the thought passed through my mind, if I only could find someone like him.

Our conversation rumbled on for another half an hour before Rose brought through pudding - lemon tart, with blueberries and cream.

While Neil cleared the table, she questioned me more about Littern and Marisands.

'I can't think of another thing to tell you,' I said lightly.

'Promise me, you won't do anything stupid. Do you seem depressed?'

'No more than usual.'

'Isn't there a history of depression in your family?'

'You mean David?' I asked.

'You can't inherit a psychological condition from your partner - I meant your mother.' Rose rarely saw the need to dress up her words.

'I have my daughters - I have a reason to live,' I said.

'Your mother also had a daughter – didn't she?'

Rose's words reminded me of the commitment I'd made when I was nine years old and had wanted *to be my mother* – could that bring happiness or would it lead to tragedy?

Neil poured me a glass of brandy.

'Perhaps you need a love affair,' Rose was saying, not realising how much her previous question had disturbed me.

'Why not..?' Neil asked.

'...Because having an affair wouldn't mend anything.'

'Not now it wouldn't, but there's no call to dismiss your entire future,' Rose argued.

'But I don't want a complicated life, my only idea is to go to Marisands and see how I get on. I want security for Minette, though I suppose Littern could hardly be described as safe...'

'Is there other sentient life on the island?' Neil asked.

'There are two or three houses, otherwise only a few abandoned cottages and farms,' I told him.

'If you go to an island, you never know who or what might wash up on the shore. You'll need to watch out, not lose your head, like St. Thrif,' Rose warned.

'I doubt there are any temptations on Littern.'

Rose laughed. 'As Sister Miriam used to say, "Girls - there are temptations, everywhere",' and she mimicked, her portentous tone, perfectly.

Neil offered to make coffee and Rose and I went down into the basement where we found Simon and Minette asleep in front of the TV. Simon, with his tumble of fair curls, lay sleeping on a cushion beside Minette who was curled up with her dark hair fanned out across the floor.

'I suppose going to the island is an improvement on spending the rest of your life in London wallowing in self pity.' Rose said. She was being deliberately provocative.

'You think I'm being selfish?'

'Minette's told me how unhappy she is about the prospect of leaving St. Catherine's. If you go to the island and can't bear it, her life and yours will have been messed around for nothing.'

Rose was my conscience - I wasn't sure how to defend myself as she detailed the many aspects of my decision which were unsatisfactory.

'I've reached the point where I feel there's little to gain by staying in London and little to lose by going,' I said. 'I've given myself a year.'

'I'll miss you...'

'Minette needs to be carefree – not shouldering responsibilities which are far too heavy for her.'

'And so do you. But don't let yourself go – most of us are reaching our peak, just at the age when women used to cease to function.'

'I'm keeping an open mind,' I said.

Rose pulled a face. 'You always say that when your mind is most closed.' But then she relented - it was like her to conduct a painful cross-examination and then to offer help, 'If Minette is coping, we could have her here until the end of the summer term - I'm not launching my new practice until next autumn...'

Neil had brought our mugs of coffee and stood at the foot of the stairs. 'It'll be fine,' he said, 'Iris is doing her best and Minette's a sensible girl. Now, Iris and I need to talk work for a few minutes.'

Rose's face tautened, but she left Neil and me to chat while Simon and Minette slept peacefully on the floor.

'Rose is on good form, tonight...' he said apologetically.

But I didn't want him to criticise her. 'Rose is just being Rose – honest, forthright and a good friend.'

'The new *Minor Lights* contract, it's looking positive, but I have to warn you, though you have considerable freedom, Langlais won't deal with elusive authors and neither will I. In the meantime, Laurence has a lot of papers that need sorting and translating, if you're willing, you could make a start on those and be paid for your trouble. Fortunately, he's come to see you as part of his coterie - he feels he needs you and that you understand his way of working. My advice is to agree to anything he suggests...'

'Within reason..?'

'Definitely within reason... But in your spare time, you could make a record of your life on the island and add some illustrations. People seem to lap up that type of thing – you can show me when you've finished.'

'Neil...' I began - I didn't think I would have any spare time on Littern, but I couldn't know that yet - I might be desperate for something to fill the empty hours alone at Marisands.

'Take care, Iris, promise me?' he said and kissed my cheek.

'I'm only going to Devon – and yet I scarcely feel like myself.'

'You may find you're very much yourself - this could be your moment of resurrection. Do you still believe in that?'

# Chapter 16

On Christmas Eve I'd arranged to take Alice and Flora to Midnight Mass, something I'd done each year, since I'd moved out of Wren House. Christmas at home was going to be quiet. Zoë had no plans to return from where I'd last tracked her down in France and though I'd sent money for her train fare from Cornwall, Eve had gone down with a chest infection and didn't feel well enough to travel.

Minette and I arrived at Wren House just after nine o'clock. Alice was a stickler for punctuality and was ready to go out dressed in her smart navy suit and the hat she reserved for winter best. When she went to church, she persisted in wearing her tortoiseshell glasses on a chain round her neck, though she was unable to read even with them on.

As we went inside the house, Flora was flustered, looking for gloves, scarf and hat. Alice had told her she must have things ready, not discover she couldn't find them at the last minute. While she searched, with Minette's help, I went to join Alice in the drawing room. Mrs. Stuart was spending the evening with her son and Alice was determined, in her absence, not only to look after her own needs, but Flora's as well.

'You're a little late,' Alice said, 'are you suffering from one of those terrible headaches?'

'It's nothing – I've just had a lot to do.'

'The Devon sea air may help.'

'I hope so...' I said, though I was growing apprehensive at the prospect of having to sort out Marisands. My memories of the contents of the house were sketchy and consisted only of those things that had been attractive to a child. How would I know what was of value, what should be kept and what shouldn't?

'Is there anything in particular at Marisands that you're concerned about?' I asked.

'Apart from household effects, I'm hoping the family's work is safe. There must be paintings or sculptures of Juliet's, perhaps some we've never seen. You'll have to obey your instincts.'

My instincts suggested she and Flora hadn't eaten properly that evening as there was no sign of their supper trays, so I excused myself and went to the kitchen to make something for them.

Cutting sandwiches, heating mince pies and peeling oranges, I found myself wishing we could have stayed at Wren House after all - things would have been companionable, so much easier, and I wouldn't have needed to leave Minette behind at school, something I was dreading.

While we had a light supper, Minette drank a mug of hot chocolate - she was overtired and couldn't eat. In the warmth of the drawing room, Alice dozed and while she slept, Flora helped me with the washing up and Minette put the plates and cutlery away.

'Really I don't want to go,' Flora murmured as she worked, 'but it would upset Alice if I didn't.'

Her silver hair had formed a halo round her head, in the soft yellow light of the kitchen she appeared like a rather elderly angel.

'We always go to Midnight Mass,' I reminded her gently.

'But I don't want to go to The Maples...' she explained and her eyes became hazy, 'So often I've dreamt of returning to the island, I didn't ever want to come here, it was Alice who made me...'

'You allowed my parents to move to Littern - that was a sacrifice, an act of love...'

'William was always my greatest spiritual challenge, though we must try to love everyone...'

'I think you do love everyone.' I said and smiled at her. Flora's faith and compassion were a mystery and came from a place beyond the world of reason or of the senses.

'Did I say that the dead are never silent?'

'You did...' I assured her – she'd made the same remark when I'd come to see her about Marisands.

'The dead continue to speak when their silence would break the spirit of the living...'

I slipped my arm round Minette's shoulders to reassure her, but like Eve, she was tolerant of Flora's conversations that drifted across time, history and place, as if they had no boundaries.

'I have something for you,' Flora said. Her hands shaking, she took down a large envelope from the dresser and handed it to me.

Inside was a small framed print of Aphrodite, mirror in hand - the goddess of love, rising from the darkness of the sea.

'First the darkness and then the light,' Flora said, 'it's like that for all of us being born and re-born.'

Minette nodded gravely as if she had understood. I kissed Flora on the cheek and asked Minette to put the picture carefully beside my handbag in the hall.

While she was gone, Flora told me to look into the envelope again. I pulled out a handful of legal documents. When I opened them and read a few lines, I realised I was holding the title deeds to Marisands - Flora had handed them to me as if they were a trinket.

'I've written to the solicitor, to make sure everything's settled.'

I wasn't sure I wanted to *own* Marisands, not even in the future. Silvie's Christmas card had contained a letter asking that I should promise, whatever happened, to remain at Marisands for a year – and that I felt was enough. It was perhaps superstitious, but I hadn't forgotten how Flora had once given the house to my mother, hoping to secure her future and yet things had turned out badly.

Alice had woken and made her way through to the kitchen. She stood tall and upright, framed in the doorway, looking severe. 'Something's going on,' she said.

Flora put her finger to her lips to silence me and I posted the deeds back into the envelope.

'Flora..?' Alice demanded, 'What are you doing?'

No-one spoke. Minette's eyes darted warily between Flora and Alice.

'It's all right,' I said, 'Flora was just showing me something.'

'Old papers,' Minette informed her, '*very old*, with curly-whirly handwriting and big letters...'

Alice's face cleared as she perceived what had happened. 'The right to own Marisands should be earned - and not simply given away.'

Minette guided Alice as she draped a knitted stole round her shoulders and eased on her leather gloves.

I took Flora's arm and led her into the hall, 'Thank you,' I whispered as she slipped her fur coat on, 'but I can't accept - I'd much prefer to wait – see how things work out.'

'The house will come to you one day, whether you want it or not,' she said. I rolled up the collar of her coat to keep her warm, securing it with a pale blue scarf. 'At Marisands you'll find a watercolour of the garden by Juliet, *The Oratory Garden*...do you remember?'

'I think so...' My mother had made a painting of the garden after we'd returned from our visit to Dulwich to see Bernard.

From her handbag, Flora took out a set of keys to Marisands and passed them to me. 'Alice has made a list of things she'd like you to do,' she murmured, handing me several sheets of folded notepaper, 'but I don't expect they're important,' she added, her eyes bright with subversion.

At the church, a Christmas tree stood by the main door, glowing with white fairy-lights draped among its dark green branches. We were in good time and I led Alice and Flora to a pew with Minette, before going into the Lady Chapel to light candles for my children and whatever our future might hold.

I had no words for prayers but sat watching the candle flames. It would take a miracle to restore my life to what it had been and miracles rarely happened to those who had ceased to believe in them. After David, loss of faith had been the last unbearable touch - prayer had become a final resort, something to turn to only when my own strength and ingenuity had once again failed.

The bell in the clock tower struck a single note and I rejoined the others as the organ began to play *It Came Upon a Midnight Clear*. Minette was huddled between Alice and Flora, wearing the blue coat I'd taken from Flora's wardrobe, her hair brushed into a broad fan, flowing over her shoulders.

Beside me, Alice was as strong and upright as the white alabaster angel that guarded the steps to the sanctuary. Flora's figure was a bundle of brown fur, like a small woodland creature exuding, not the scent of musk, but the astringent odour of mothballs.

At the altar, the priest's cope, white damask embroidered with gold, glistened in the candlelight. When he stood on the chancel step to deliver his sermon, he told the story of the nativity, from the annunciation - the moment when Mary was confronted by her destiny in the form of an angel - to the birth of her baby. He spoke of how the sacramental nature of everyday things too easily passes unnoticed.

Flora's gloved hand closed over mine with a touch, light as a bird landing on a twig. She had sensed my sadness that when Minette and I went home, David wouldn't be there − it had occurred to me also, that we might never, in future, be together again as we were that night.

I absorbed the loveliness of the church, the pale, ancient stones and the unadorned, whitewashed walls. They represented endurance and simplicity, qualities I would need to sustain me. There were no excesses, only the soft glimmer of polished wood and silver and the modest arrangements of leaves and flowers. I breathed in their beauty wanting to take away something of their grace and unaffectedness − I remembered Eve's words, *I want to live simply and do my work* − as good a rule of life as any creed might offer.

Towards the end of Mass, Minette's head had begun to droop as she drifted in and out of sleep, so we stopped only briefly at Wren House to say goodnight. Mrs. Stuart had returned to help Alice and Flora to bed.

Then having slept in the car on the way to Hurst Row, when we arrived in Pimlico, Minette was no longer tired. It was a sharp, clear night, so we sat in the garden on the bench, huddled together for warmth, studying the moon and stars. The scent of mahonia, drifted into the air as the yellow flowers were moved by gentle swirls of wind and brushed against the house wall by the French doors. In the moonlight I could see the cherry tree already had a few tender buds.

Flora communed with the spirits of the earth and plants and I'd felt their presence as I worked among the pots and flower beds of my small garden - leaving it would be painful, like relinquishing a friend. As we'd parted, Flora had reminded me again of the watercolour Juliet had painted at Marisands – a summer painting full of light and colour. I'd added a note to Alice's list of tasks to search for it when I was there.

We soon began to feel cold and I fetched a hot chocolate for Minette and poured a glass of wine for myself. When they came to Hurst Row, Helen and David might tear apart what I had created - but even so I wished David could share our moments among the sleeping plants and flowers - the peace and wonder of the night sky. While we sipped our drinks, a few flakes of snow fell, landing as fine as fairy dust on our coats and melting instantly. Minette smiled up at me and rested her cheek on my arm – I put out a hand to touch her soft hair.

'I don't want to leave Yuuka and I don't want to leave you,' she said.

I leant down and kissed her forehead. 'I know what you mean - if you change your mind – I'll come straightaway and fetch you.'

'I won't change my mind.'

I smoothed her hair back from her face. Minette was determined and impossibly stubborn. 'Shall we go indoors and open a present?' I whispered, 'wouldn't that be magical?'

We had a tiny Christmas tree - I turned on the fairy lights and lit candles on the mantelpiece, our presents were spread out on the sitting room carpet.

Minette chose her parcel first, a collection of Greek Myths from Flora. I sent her to fetch the little painting of Aphrodite from my bag and together we read the story of her birth. Then it was my turn, and I opened a little box containing earrings of lapis lazuli and silver from Verena. Inside was a note, "Wear these for good luck on the island..."

I sent Minette to bed, we were both exhausted. When I'd tucked her in, I read the story of Psyche, watching until her eyelids began to droop and her eyes fell closed.

'Are we going to be all right?' she asked sleepily.

'We're going to be all right, you and me - I promise.'

When I was certain she was asleep, I went into the study and stood knee deep among the piles of books and memorabilia. These were the fragments of my old life, the remnants, all I had to make a new existence on Littern Island.

*

By the New Year, most of my possessions were packed and the house looked not empty, but as if it had been put to rights. The only room that still spoke of my life with David was the study. With the windows shut, the room still smelt of cigarette smoke and coffee. While that familiar scent lingered, I could imagine him bent over the desk and when I knelt on the rug to gather my books, I felt the trail worn in the carpet as he had walked up and down reading his poems.

I was stranded at the centre of a canyon made of stacks of books - some like low rocky outcrops - others tall, narrow pillars. For years, I'd listened to the sounds of David's restlessness, had been driven mad by it. But then the absence of his tread on the floor, the quiet evenings, had brought about a different kind of emptiness.

As I placed books into cardboard cartons ready for their journey, I thought they might form a bridge between my old life and the new. I was taking anything I dared lay claim to: childhood classics, reference books, Messenger's *English Poetry* and David's slim volumes of poetry, including the signed copy of *Midnight Shadows* with its cryptic message and memories of when we had first met. From the shelf above David's desk, I took down a photograph of the three girls – their hair all the different shades of autumn leaves.

In the bottom drawer of his desk, I discovered a box containing a muddle of notes and papers relating to *Blue Rhythms* - David must have discarded them before he moved out. In a rush of sentiment, I found I could neither throw them away nor leave them behind - if they turned out to be important, I'd send them to him through the post.

Big Ben struck three and the resonance of each single note reached me, not much more than a vibration of the night air. I rolled up the rug on which I'd been kneeling and secured it with tape. I had finished. But the fear I'd overlooked something among the too-familiar clutter of Barbara's porcelain, glass and crystal kept me prowling the rooms for another hour.

Wrapped in an old overcoat of David's, I stepped out into the night garden where I could feel the touch of frost on stone, could sense the twining stems in the darkness, the sleeping remnants of the plants I'd placed there with love. One by one, I carried pots of plants through the house and stood them by the front door ready for the removal man to take in the morning – an assembly of dead looking sticks and twigs, the germ of life hidden beneath the dark earth to which their roots clung in hope.

Next morning, I woke after two or three hours sleep and when I had dressed and cleared the bedroom, watched sunrise tint the horizon with warm pastel colours. The cream chimneys of Battersea Power Station reached up into the apricot sky. That solid block of a building had accompanied my waking for half my life and visible through the trees, the Thames had lent its sombre presence – an unkempt, grey river - dividing the city, yet at the same time holding it together.

Pain hammered in my head as I gathered the last of my personal belongings. I had to stop every few minutes to allow the persistent nausea to settle. As if I was sea-sick, I clutched onto furniture so as not to fall down.

I opened the doors onto the balcony of the bedroom and let in a draught of cold air. There had been a rainstorm in the night and the fragile cherry blossom had been dashed to the ground. Too tender to survive, the blossoms lay bruised and transparent, forming pale drifts of white against the kerbs of the flowerbeds – while beyond the garden, traffic followed the curve of the Thames and streamed by unaware of this small devastation and the woman who stood at the window to witness it, silent and alone.

It was eight o'clock, when Helen arrived at Hurst Row; she let herself in and shouted upstairs to me from the hallway. I peered down on her over the banister. Petite, slender, with long, curly red hair, she wore a short skirt and fitted jacket, looking every bit the student, though I'd been told she was twenty five.

I carried my cases downstairs and she inspected the house from top to bottom until she was satisfied nothing had been taken which shouldn't have been and nothing forgotten.

'My God,' she said, seeing my stuff gathered in the sitting room and hallway, 'do you have room for all this at the other end?'

'I wish I knew.'

Helen perched on a stool in the kitchen watching me pack food for the journey. I felt her regarding me, as she had the house, with a critical eye. It was a fitting end to my life in Pimlico - my days there had begun with Zoë sitting in the same spot glaring at the strange young woman who her father had brought home.

'Will you have coffee?' I asked.

'Do you have fruit juice?' Helen said. She stretched her long, legs out in front of her and yawned.

There were two oranges left in the fruit bowl, so I squeezed them into a glass for her and made coffee for myself.

Helen slid down from the stool and joined me at the kitchen table. 'You're resigned to going to the island now?'

I thought she might make more effort to hide the truth that she could hardly wait for me to move out and we eyed each other like combatants. 'Do you ever feel you *have* to do something, even though you don't know why?' I asked.

'I never do things and don't know why,' she said.

I swallowed two headache pills with a glass of water and then loosened my hair so there was no pressure on my aching forehead.

'David told me you'd worn your hair in a plait since you were a child.'

'I find it convenient,' I replied, not meeting her eyes.

When she'd finished her orange juice, Helen poured coffee for herself. 'David said to tell you, if things get too much, call Eve.'

I hoped Eve would visit me and not only because I was falling apart.

'I suppose you blame me...' Helen said.

'I kept hoping things with David might get better,' I told her, managing to get the words out without bitterness.

'But you couldn't hang on forever,' she said. 'The trouble with living in someone else's house is that they decide when you have to leave...'

The removal man from Kilbarrons banged on the front door. Relieved to get away, I showed him all the places around the house where I had put my things and in a few minutes, my life began to stream before me in a succession of cases, plastic bags and cardboard cartons.

The city was in the grip of winter, cold, hard and grey – so different from my image of Littern with its dripping fecundity. Beyond Bristol, the richness of the countryside, the lush green hills became more pronounced and there was a deepening atmosphere of hiddeness and mystery.

The day had been one of heavy showers and as I left Safford Bridge, sheep huddled into the hedgerows, sheltering from the damp and cold. I followed the road along the ridge above the coastline, until it descended into Narescombe in a series of sharp switchback bends. Beneath me, I could see over the roofs of the houses and shops which clustered round the harbour - in the distance was the wide sweep of sandy bays, the scalloped edge of the coastline, scattered with clusters of dark rocks ringed by white foam -

Then as I cleared the last bend, the sun gave out a burst of burnt-orange, setting the hills and the trees on fire, fire which flowed over the grey stone buildings and the quay, to be doused almost immediately by another cloudburst.

Narescombe out of season was deserted, scruffy, a ghost town. I drove across the main square, skirting the town hall perched on its pyramid of steps and then turned into Osford Lane - the road to the island - which ran along Palk's Reach to the causeway.

The dense belt of trees hung over the road and beneath them, the lane was muddy, rutted and pitted with deep puddles. The woodland of sycamore, birch and oak stood behind a mossy stone wall, overarched with wands of brambles and edged with ragged grass and rusty ferns.

Once through the hamlet of Osford there were no other houses before the lane dipped down to the sea where Geraldine's cottage, Whitcroft, stood with the stone shelters on either side of the water, guarding the margins of land.

The causeway stretched in front of me, the surface of the road more worn and damaged than I remembered from the day of my father's funeral. I stopped the car and walked over to the board where notices flapped like sails in the wind. I found two posters which hadn't been there before - one gave details of a concert by the pianist, Sarah Almond, raising money to improve the island's road. The other – handwritten - advertised a stall selling fruit and vegetables at Lyncross.

Rain stung like needles of ice on my face. I'd brought my old school cloak with me, heavy wool with a warm lining; I fetched it from the back seat of the car and wrapped it over my raincoat, like a blue shroud. Pulling up the hood, I remembered how Zoë used to call it "the cloak of invisibility" and that was the effect I aimed for, standing by the waterside, staring out at the distant line of grey water as it licked the surface of the sand.

The marker posts, which had once showed the way across the gully, had rotted down to jagged stumps, but I'd timed my journey carefully, accessing tide tables on the internet so I could be certain it would be safe to cross. As I hesitated, a silver estate car passed me and eased onto the causeway before disappearing into the arching trees on the other side. The car seemed full, several children were visible through the back window, and from the rear three dogs stared out at me as the tail of the car disappeared.

When Bernard had first come to Littern, I imagined he'd had few expectations, wanting only to explore - and I'd resolved not to speculate about who might be living there or how things might be, but to wait until the life of the island revealed itself naturally. I'd come prepared to be independent, stocking up with food and kindling, matches, firelighters, candles, a torch, paraffin lamps. I'd remembered how when a storm blew in from the sea, the power went off to the houses and the telephone lines went down, sometimes for days.

Long fingers of water began to stretch across the sand reaching towards the causeway - if I was going to cross, I needed go now. I edged the car down onto the narrow concrete strip, my hands gripping the steering wheel hard and my heart beating fast. I revved the engine too hard when I reached the other side and as I took the steep slope up to the island, a plume of black smoke trailed behind me through the damp air.

It was less than two miles to Marisands, the first of the island houses. The car bumped and jolted along - the road was full of potholes and the hedges so overgrown, there was little room to manoeuvre out of the way.

An oak tree stood by the gate of Marisands and marked the place where I should turn from the lane. I had crept along the road, not wanting to miss it, but as each detail of Littern struck me, I'd realised it was familiar - the imprint of the island had remained, traced on my memory, through all those years.

*

The gate to the house had been left open, jammed back into the muddy earth, visible beneath the thin layer of gravel that covered the drive.

My recollection of Marisands hadn't been distorted by time - a white house, beneath a slate roof - the tiles as dark as black glass after the heavy showers of rain. The garden was enclosed within a blackthorn hedge and an inner circle of trees, which protected it from gales and provided privacy from the lane and the footpath which ran beside the garden, down to the shore.

Bare branches filtered the low afternoon sunlight and gave the house a veined appearance, as if it was built of white marble, like a tomb.

The trees had encroached on the land. The garden once neatly divided by curved pathways into lawn, flower-beds, fruit and vegetables had become so overgrown, any distinction between one area and another had disappeared. The uncut grass was brown and matted - the pergola that divided the garden choked by the thorny stems of a rambling rose.

There was no sign of Kilbarron's van or my possessions, except for the pots of plants from Hurst Row, lined up beneath the kitchen window. They seemed out of place in the wilderness of Marisands and I wondered if they would survive here, unused to salt laden air and lashing storms.

Leaves had formed into drifts and lay rotting all around the garden; they had blown inside the porch and carpeted the tiled floor with a sludgy brown mess that was slippery underfoot. I took the keys Flora had given me and after several attempts found one which turned easily in the lock of the front door, which was swollen and stiff to push open.

The deep porch made the hallway of the house gloomy, the small, square-paned window above the door too dirty to allow in sufficient light to relieve the darkness of walls painted a deep holly green. Flora had offered to ensure there was power to the house and that there would be sufficient oil for the central heating. I flicked a switch – relieved as the light bulb above my head began to glow.

The house no longer carried the familiar scent of beeswax and lavender polish. With the light on, I could see the oak furniture, which had once gleamed with a soft patina, was now thick with dust. The glass on the pictures seemed to have grown dull and milky and the odour of damp and mould irritated my nostrils and throat.

Put off by the smell, I retreated into the porch, full of broken flowerpots, dead houseplants and garden tools, scarred with rust. With my foot, I pushed the clutter under the bench, so that I could pass through easily with my luggage.

I walked round to the back of the house. The lock on the conservatory door was broken and some of my belongings, including Flora's desk and the suitcases of papers from Wren House, had been dumped in there among piles of newspapers, rubbish and broken cane furniture.

When I searched again, I found the rest of my possessions shoved into the garage, an open fronted wooden shed, where they had been arranged round an old brown car, which must have been my father's.

A mountainous black cloud loomed overhead and my raincoat, which had been adequate in London, couldn't stand up to the sudden deluge of rain that hammered down as I transferred things from the car to the house. I filled the hall with suitcases, boxes and holdalls and as I worked, icy drops of rain ran down my hair and trickled onto my cheeks and neck.

I slammed the doors of the car and locked it, but heavy rain was driving onto the things in the garage. I scavenged until I found a tarpaulin, then pushed the boxes back as far as I could out of the weather, draping them and weighing the tarpaulin down with bricks and discarded tins of paint I'd found on the shelves.

At last, cold, wet and hungry, I unpacked the bread, cheese and olives, I'd brought with me, eating them in the hall, straight from a plastic box. The kitchen was coated with a layer of grime - grease had become ingrained into the cream walls and terracotta tiles, there was a lingering smell of frying and onions mingled with an unpleasant note of decay.

The dilapidation of Marisands was deeply rooted and to venture further into the house would be to initiate the next part of my journey. So I took my time, standing in the shelter of the porch, where I could breathe fresh air and inhale the clean scent of rain soaked earth. Huddled in the shadows, I listened to water dripping off the bare branches of the trees and heard the whispering of the sea and creaking branches of the Virginia creeper as it fretted the walls of the house. A squirrel startled me with its rippling movements, running soundlessly across the roof of the wood store and disappearing into the garden with its tangle of brambles and weeds.

*How would I manage on my own?* The garden needed complete restoration. Watering and weeding a few pots and small flower beds at Hurst Row had been no preparation for the scale of work needed here.

Returning inside, I wandered through the house where nothing could have prepared me for the filth and disorder, the stench of mice or the heaps of dead flies and wasps lying on the floor beneath each window of the downstairs rooms. Though I'd hated leaving her, I kept thinking *thank God Minette stayed at school*. Marisands exuded neglect and decomposition and its condition hit me like the final assault after a succession of blows.

I longed for a hot drink, but the kitchen had been abandoned as if a sudden disaster had struck. On the deal table were plates with scraps of bread, encrusted with mould beside a plate of rancid butter dotted with dead flies. I found an empty carrier bag in a drawer and swept the revolting mess into it, tying the handles of the bag tightly to contain the odour of bad food.

Trying not to retch, I put the kettle on to boil. I needed hot water to clean the surfaces of the kitchen, so I would have a safe place to eat and prepare food. I scrubbed at the kitchen table with a washing up brush and then laid out a cup and jug of milk on a tray covering them with a clean tea-cloth I'd brought from London.

Before night closed in, I wanted to go down to the sea. The rain had slowed to a soft drizzle, so I made my way along the narrow, stony path that led to the beach, stamping down weeds – mainly brambles and thistles - that clawed at my trousers as I walked.

The tide was almost in, leaving only a thin spit of sand and I couldn't go far without the danger of being cut off by the incoming sea. Littern had a dark side to its nature. There were rip tides, coves where you could drown in minutes - the marshes could be treacherous, with deep swampy places that had the appearance of solid ground.

I scrambled across rocks slippery with seaweed, listening to the sighing of the waves and breathing in the sharp, salt air. Steadying myself against the cliff face, I clambered round to the foot of the steps that led up to the oratory - they looked crumbling and unsafe and the handrail hung loose in several places.

Resting for a few minutes on the bottom step, I looked west towards Morrow Bay. In the distance, I could make out a black dog running along the beach, splashing through the ragged edge of the water. But in those few moments, while the dog had caught my attention, the sea had flowed in so fast it was lapping at my feet.

Paddling my way back to the safety of the footpath, I watched as waves shattered against the rocks at the foot of the cliff, where I'd been standing - their deep aquamarine and indigo dispersed in a cloud of creamy foam tossed high up into the air.

The island and the sea had been the backdrop to my early life, but I'd forgotten the wildness of Littern. The translucence and the many colours of the water had faded from my memory - the way that the waves rolled onto the shore in lines of pure white curls - the sea's beauty marred only by its treachery.

As the sun dropped towards the horizon, the clouds parted and closed like heavy grey curtains and the darkness drew nearer warning me it was time to leave.

The first few yards of the footpath were steep and struggling to catch my breath, I climbed towards Marisands, its slate roof fading into the dark grey sky as if the house was vanishing into the night.

It was too late to explore the other buildings, but as I passed the wrought iron gate to Thrift Cottage, I glanced up and noticed a faint yellow glow from the windows of the studio. Curious, I pushed the gate hard and it scraped open, rasping against the worn stone step.

Beyond the studio, in the oratory garden, I could see the tops of the cherry trees showing a few lemon coloured leaves clinging to the tips of their branches. White hellebores were in flower among the long grass, giving off their strange luminescence in the failing light - *hellebores for the healing of mental pain* – the thought came to me in a whisper.

A path had been trodden down across the overgrown lawn of Thrift Cottage to the studio door - I swung the door open to find Geraldine Ottley, in front of an easel, paintbrush in hand. She looked towards me but didn't speak - I thought she must lead a solitary life without my father.

In the corner of the room was a makeshift bed - Geraldine must spend the night there sometimes, sleeping in a nest of old blankets like a wounded animal. She began to wipe her paint brushes with a stained rag. On the easel was the outline of a landscape of the island – the stone tower above the marshes - stark against a background of twilight sky.

'I don't know why you came here, nobody wants you,' she said.

Geraldine's presence had blighted my childhood; I'd found her cruel and frightening. After Juliet's death, she might have wanted William to herself. *Had she persuaded William to send me away?* Soon the sea would trap us on the island and I wanted her gone from Marisands – but couldn't find the right words to say.

'Why did you come here?' she asked again.

And though I said nothing, I could have fired the same question at her - W*hy did you come here? Why did you come to the island and wreck our lives?*

# THE SPRING

## Chapter 17

A dull, gold sun hung in the sky like a monstrance, and then as the light faded, I felt God had abandoned this rocky place to be battered and broken by the sea's pounding waves.

In the sheds, I found a stack of logs and trudged back and forth to the house carrying wood for the open fires. The trees grew invisible against a darkening sky, and as night slowly covered the island, dusk echoed my sense of being poised between two worlds.

Locking myself into the house, I spent half an hour deciphering the controls on the antiquated heating system, until I'd succeeded in setting the boiler to turn on in the morning. Then, I wandered slowly through Marisands, the walls of its rooms painted in shades of rose pink, cafe au lait, apple green, aqua, and lavender - the colours of the sea, sky, earth and flowers. The house was full of bibelots - the few treasures, as my mother had suggested were landmarks of our family history. My past was written into the paintings and ornaments, into the garden and out-buildings and into the surrounding woods and landscape of Littern.

The sitting room was scattered with art journals, books and old newspapers, but my father and Geraldine had changed nothing of the fabric of the place. The oak furniture chosen by Flora remained from when the house had been her family home, as did the curtains and cushions she'd embroidered with leaves and flowers. There were figures sculpted in wood by my mother, including one of me cross-legged on a cushion, they had been placed in corners or on side tables and had never been moved.

Facing north, the dining room was the coldest place in the house, damp and dank. The chairs, upholstered in turquoise, leaf green and coral, when touched sent a cloud of dust floating through the air, catching in my nostrils and throat. A sombre landscape of Bernard's, showing Hagdon Hills and the tower, hung above the sideboard, its ornate gilt frame veiled with cobwebs. Miniatures of Alice and Flora, painted by Yvette, lined each side of the fireplace.

At the back of the house was the music room, once Silvie's room, where *The Mirror Portrait,* a painting of my mother, by Flora, had been placed in an alcove. Luminous and full of tenderness, it showed Juliet sitting with her long braid of chestnut hair falling to her waist, her grey eyes softly lit as she gazed into a mirror, which she held balanced on her lap. The mirror reflected not only her image, but the image of Flora as she gazed into another mirror, in which was also reflected my great-grandmother, Yvette, thin, dark and delicate, misty-eyed as if she was focussed on a distant world. Held within that painting, were three generations of women who were part of me, just as I was part of them. Each life held within it the imprint of the life that had gone before - an imperfect replica - yet carrying its image across time.

Though its atmosphere had made me nervous as a child, the music room had natural warmth. The walls were a soft coral pink - each hung with a large mirror, the glass spotted, watery, and rippled with age. When I moved, reflected images streamed backwards and forwards as if into infinity.

Yvette's rosewood piano stood at the centre of the room, covered in a gold chenille cloth. I drew the cloth aside and lifted the lid of the piano, fingering the silky smooth surface of the keys. A pile of music had been left on the stool - *was it possible my mother had been the last person to play the piano, had it been silent all these years?* I replaced the lid afraid that any sound I made might disturb the house and the many ghosts which lived in it.

I brushed away cobwebs which caught in my hair as I climbed the stairs. The study was above the front porch, overlooking the drive, and clearing that room would be a way of establishing my territory. I planned to fill it with the books I'd brought from London, replacing the art volumes, which my father had once studied so intently, as he sought inspiration.

Peering into each of the bedrooms, I decided to sleep in my childhood room for now. Until my mother had died, that room with its creamy pink walls and soft sea-blue floor, had held me, made me feel safe and protected. I opened the windows and let in a wave of icy, astringent air. In daylight, I would be able to glimpse a narrow triangle of sea through the tops of the cherry trees in the oratory garden. To the west, Osford Lane would be visible as it wound in gentle curves up Holtleigh Hill towards Lyncross, before descending to Morrow Bay, where it met the path to the marshes and petered out into an earth track leading past the tower towards Clave Valley.

The isolation of the house unnerved me. Without moon or stars, the faint glow from my windows was the only light penetrating the darkness with insignificant, quivering patches of pale yellow falling on the roof of the porch. The loneliness of Marisands struck me again and again and I traipsed round the house checking all the windows, pushing

207

bolts across on the doors and piling discarded furniture hard up against the broken entrance to the conservatory.

As the wind gathered strength, the house creaked like an old sea vessel. My thoughts were disturbed by the repetitious, tremulous cry of an owl hooting in the interludes between showers.

The unfamiliar sounds of the night were alarming. Afraid to go to bed, I sat at the kitchen table warming my hands on a mug of coffee and praying that the creaks and groans of the old house would soon seem no more worrying than familiar notes from a well-loved piece of music.

*

Thin, grey light filtered through the bedroom curtains and woke me - finally, in the early hours of the morning, I'd become drowsy and had slept disturbed only by the mice I'd heard scampering behind the skirting boards.

I padded across the blue lino floor to the front window and peeked out through the gap in the curtains. The sky was overbearing, mottled with the grey-brown colour of cygnet's wings - the only sounds the dripping trees and a lazy sea, churning in the background. Through the orchard and pergola, I could see the roofs of the studio and Thrift Cottage and beyond them, the branches of cherry trees in the oratory garden, swept back and forth against a troubled sky.

The mess in the house looked no less daunting after a night's sleep and as I re-visited each room, it was as if Marisands had become dispirited - if a building could speak, the house seemed to beg me not to allow it to fall into further decay.

The rooms felt a few degrees warmer than the previous day and when I ran a tap in the bathroom, hot water gushed out. As there was no shower in the house, I scrubbed the bath and filled it, sinking deep into the steamy, scented water.

Then when I'd dressed, I took Alice's list of tasks downstairs. She believed I might find a collection of my mother's work at Marisands, though apart from the carved wooden figures, I'd seen no sign of it. I'd intended to search the studio straight away, but as I grabbed a coffee and a quick breakfast, rain blew in from the sea, heavy and persistent, and I couldn't face another drenching.

I cleaned the kitchen, washing and drying the china - remnants of dinner and tea services in the Armsted patterns designed by Bernard - the few richly coloured pieces which had survived my parents' arguments. Behind the crockery was an ancient cookery book, which had once belonged to Yvette and had then been passed to Flora, their names were inscribed on the fly leaf. I emptied ranks of storage jars - soft cream china with a rose pink band of colour near the lid and gold writing to indicate the contents. I'd once broken the jar marked *Raisins* - my mother's repair had been almost invisible - but now as I rinsed it, the two halves of the lid parted in my hands.

A trapdoor led from the floor of the larder into the cellar. I lifted the door cautiously, as if it might release a tide of vermin, as in the children's story *The Pied Piper*. I shone a torch into the gloomy space - the beam of light revealed stacks of trunks and boxes, thick with mouse droppings. I clambered down the wooden steps and opened one of the trunks, but when a fat brown spider ran out from among the papers, I leapt back, letting the lid drop with a loud bang and stumbled against a large wooden chest, pushed into a corner of the cellar.

Focussing the torch onto the trunk and sweeping the dust off with my sleeve, I recognised its patterned inlays and carvings, familiar from the small box my father had sent me when I was a child of nine. The catch which released the lock was hidden on the underside of the small box - but the chest was far too heavy for me to lift or turn over. Dragging it out of the corner, I tipped it slightly on its side, slipping my hand underneath to feel for the mechanism - frustrated as it became obvious I would need help if I was ever going to find a way of opening it.

Back in the kitchen, I continued washing pots and pans, until a ring on the doorbell disturbed me. Switching off the radio, I moved aside the piles of rubbish I'd assembled in the middle of the floor and brushing myself down, answered the front door.

On the doorstep stood a man in green overalls, his face concealed behind a large bouquet of flowers - he was juggling his umbrella with one hand as it caught the wind and clutching the flowers in the other.

'Iris Armsted? These are for you,' he said.

His portentous tone of voice reminded me of a television show, in which an unfortunate celebrity was confronted with their past and the people who had been a part of it.

Taking the bouquet from him, I undid the top of the cellophane wrapping, held the roses to my face and breathed in the faint scent.

'Hot-house flowers,' the man said, 'we'll all be that soon with global warming. Not that you'd notice round here, it's the coldest, wettest winter for decades.'

I thanked him for making the delivery in such terrible weather, but he hung about in the porch, as if he wanted something.

'You're moving in?' he asked. 'I heard the old man died and his woman haunts the place.'

'I hope I'll soon be the only ghost here,' I said.

'You've got a bit of a job on,' he commented, glancing round at the garden, 'it'll take a lifetime to make anything of this. I wouldn't live on Littern Island if you paid me. Give it a couple of years and the island will be deserted or swallowed up by the sea. You'll have noticed the new sea defences..?'

I hadn't and reluctant to listen to any more of his dismal predictions, didn't reply.

'I'll leave you to it then...'

I waited until the noise of his van had died out as he turned the corner of the lane towards Osford. Then I read the card attached to the bouquet, 'For your new home! With love from Silvie..!' Whoever had written the message hadn't appreciated that Silvie neither spoke nor wrote in exclamation marks.

There was a large, crystal vase at the back of the larder - filling it with water - I arranged the roses, placing them on the mantelpiece in the sitting room, in front of the mirror. I stood back to admire the arrangement, but the roses seemed to have melted into the shadows. Easing the vase forward, I adjusted the white buds so they would catch the pale glimmer of light from the windows each side of the fireplace, but still they looked grey and forlorn.

From my box of supplies, I retrieved two candles, pushed them into the silver candlesticks on the mantel shelf and lit them. All morning, the heavy showers of rain had been broken fleetingly by flashes of white-gold sunlight and for a few seconds, watery sunshine filled the room bringing the roses alive and then, as quickly, as if a shutter had dropped, the light was gone.

The moment of illumination had been transitory, but I needed to believe Marisands could still possess beauty, to be assured I had done the right thing in coming to the island. I went out to the back garden, weaving my way through thick tussocks of sodden grass to set the bird bath straight on its pedestal. Skeletal leaves shifted across the lawns and paths - I collected the best, those with a remnant of colour, and took them inside.

In one of the flowerbeds, there were snowdrops. I crouched down to tear at the weeds and dead stems. I scrabbled at the soil with my hands until my fingers were sore and bleeding, but the tiny white flowers had room to breathe. Filling my pockets with conkers and pebbles, I broke off stems of forsythia, which could be forced into flower in the warmth of indoors.

With purple hellebores, which grew in that part of the garden, I arranged the forsythia in a cream, enamel jug. The conkers and pebbles, the leaves with their delicate tracery, I placed on a glass plate in the sitting room, beside the photograph of the girls I'd brought from London. Finally, I fetched *The Mirror Portrait* and hung it behind the sofa to represent the connection between me and those who had lived at Marisands before.

I'd eaten nothing for hours and heated a tin of soup for lunch, carrying a tray to the conservatory. Though the sky was dense with clouds, the rain hadn't returned and snatches of birdsong broke the silence, if I listened carefully, I could catch the distant bleating of sheep, as they grazed on Littern's grassy hills.

The sound of a voice startled me. I slopped soup onto my shirt and the hunk of bread I'd balanced on my knee fell onto the dirty conservatory floor.

'The door wasn't locked, so I came in,' Geraldine said.

She was dressed in a man's overcoat, unbuttoned, and worn over a tweed pinafore dress, with black leggings and leather ankle boots. Her thick white hair, barely combed, crept out from beneath a brown felt hat. With a kit bag over her shoulder, carrying a flask and a package of food wrapped in grease-proof paper, she had the appearance of a woman of the road.

I mopped awkwardly at my spilled lunch, picked up the bread from the floor, broke it into fragments and threw it out through the conservatory door for the birds.

'Would you like coffee?' I asked - steering her towards the kitchen.

That Geraldine was more at home on Littern and at Marisands than me, made me uneasy − I knew it would be naive to underestimate her sharp mind, shrewdness and energy, all of which she would use to her advantage, especially while she regarded me as an adversary.

I put the kettle on the stove and sponged my stained shirt and trousers at the sink. When I turned round, Geraldine was no longer in the kitchen; I could hear her in the dining room, where she was leafing through a heap of papers I'd left on the table earlier that morning.

'Is the coffee ready?' she asked when I interrupted her.

'Coffee's in the kitchen,' I replied. I didn't want to encourage the idea that intimate chats might become a regular habit, yet I needed to be careful. Geraldine had been close to my father for most of his life - she must possess information about him and about Juliet and was perhaps the only person left who might tell William's story with any understanding or sympathy.

'What brought you here?' Geraldine asked.

'Someone had to sort out the house,' I told her. I hadn't quite recovered from her rudeness the previous evening.

Geraldine studied the kitchen where I'd been working - the room had begun to take on an aspect of wellbeing.

'With old places, it's best not to interfere too much,' she said.

Before she could give any further unsolicited advice, I asked, 'What are you doing now with William gone..?'

'What should I do? I might as well die here as anywhere else.' Geraldine regarded me with lowered eyes, 'My God - you remind me of your mother, that superior bloody silence...'

Her scrutiny made me uncomfortable.

'I'm assuming it's all right to continue to use the studio? I had an arrangement with your grandmother.'

The request sounded polite, but there was a hint of insolence in Geraldine's hazel eyes, we both knew she hadn't kept her side of the bargain with Flora and I didn't want her hanging about Marisands.

When I hesitated to reply, she stared at me, her eyebrows arched, 'Surely, you won't object if I finish the work that's on the easel? Trash for the tourists, it's the only income I have.'

'You've nowhere to work at home?' I asked.

'Of course,' Geraldine said, 'but the light in the studio is incomparable, and the sense of William's presence – I don't have that at home.'

She picked up her khaki kit bag, there was a hole in the side, through which I could see tubes of paints and brushes. 'I have something for you,' she said. She fumbled in the bag and brought out an envelope which she handed to me.

The envelope wasn't sealed and a newspaper clipping fell out onto the table. I picked it up and unfolded the paper to find Antony Piran's obituary - taken from *The Times* and dated November of the previous year.

I scanned the article which described how Antony had made a successful career as a conductor; he'd inherited his musical gift from his mother. There was speculation about what he might have achieved had he not broken his back in an accident in his early twenties – a young hero - who had fought hard to save the life of a drowning woman...

My eyes drifted to the closing paragraph, Antony was mourned by his wife, Eleanor, but it seemed there were no children and no mention was made of the grief of his family, still living on the island.

'Thank you,' I said, adding, 'I haven't decided about the use of the studio, would you like me to drive you to the causeway?'

Geraldine's face showed no expression.

As we made our way to the car, I said, 'I'd prefer it if you let me have any keys to the house and outbuildings.'

Geraldine groped in the pockets of her overcoat, produced a large bunch of keys and dropped them into my hand.

Driving down the lane, neither of us speaking, I began to feel guilty. 'This is difficult,' I said, 'I'm not sure how long I'll be staying at Marisands or what will happen when I go...'

'If you sell Marisands, the Pirans will buy it,' Geraldine said. She lit a cigarette. 'The Pirans don't want you here, they'd like to own everything on Littern – what would the Armsted family think of that?'

I slowed the car as we reached the causeway. The tide was out, the sea only visible where it had pooled in the rippled sand, reflecting the cloud-filled sky. When we stopped on the other side of the gully, Geraldine opened the car door and threw her cigarette on the ground.

'Did my father do paintings for the tourists – bread and butter work?' I asked. I'd noticed there were no paintings of William's in the house.

'He didn't need to, did he?' Geraldine said, without a trace of a smile. 'He had me to do it for him...'

I watched as she meandered towards her cottage. When she reached the gate, I turned the car and drove back over the broken road. Manoeuvring jerkily up the steep slope on the other side, the car engine laboured, sending out a cloud of black smoke to be dispersed on the wind. I wondered how long David's old Peugeot could survive the rigours of life on the island.

# Chapter 18

I collected everything in the house that was damaged or broken and stacked it in the carport besides my father's old brown Vauxhall. After a few days, the pyre of rubbish towered above my head. I wanted to strip back the contents of the house until it was free of the accretion of Geraldine and my father's living.

The suitcases of papers I'd brought from Wren House had been emptied onto the dining table with other papers I'd found at Marisands and the teetering heaps of letters, notebooks and diaries multiplied and occasionally toppled over and collapsed onto the floor.

At the back of a drawer, I'd discovered a few photographs of Juliet before her marriage to William, taken with the Pirans and James Millford. There were so many things I hoped to find out, but my early days at Marisands were centred on physical needs - keeping warm, making sure the house was clean, drying my washing despite the ceaseless rain, turning out bowls of soups and stews, chopping wood and hauling it into the house to lay the fire. At night, I was relieved to go to bed tired and put a few hours of sleep between myself and the day's quota of painful feelings -

The island might be full of mystery, but I needed to remain earthed and practical to maintain a grip on reality and not be subsumed by the otherworldliness of Littern. In my twenties, I had latched onto David and Hurst Row for security, but now I needed to be strong and rock-like, solid and immoveable, someone able to manage without assistance from anybody.

One morning, tired of being indoors, I rummaged in the boxes of garden tools in the porch and found a rusty pruning saw. Where the pergola had become overgrown, I hacked at branches of rose and bramble so I could ease my way through to Thrift Cottage and the studio.

Rain beat down on my head and back, splashing onto my face as I explored the lower garden. Though the vegetable patch appeared – inexplicably – orderly, in the oratory garden my mother's white statues stood like broken stalagmites rising out of a bed of rotting grass. Under the bare trees, the single grey tombstone reputed to have been St. Thrif's, leant to the ground where it had almost disappeared among the ranks of weeds.

Circling Thrift Cottage, I could see there were slates missing from the roof and the gutters were leaking so that water fell in a series of cataracts making muddy hollows in the earth below. The front door of the Cottage opened straight onto the living room, where a mess of canvases, boxes of paints, paper and brushes had been dumped and blocked my way.

In the studio, cigarette butts and matches littered the floor, dried out paints and brushes were scattered everywhere. Geraldine had claimed she felt my father's spirit in there as she worked, though his spirit, as I remembered it, had been one of cleanliness and order. On the easel, she had left the landscape I'd seen the first evening I'd arrived, the tower on Hagdon Hills. Other paintings of the tower – dozens of them - were stacked round the walls, the colours murky and suggestive of lurking gothic horrors - *trash for the tourists* - who perhaps had heard stories of the local wreckers.

For Geraldine, the tower was a recurring motif, but the paintings were trivial and badly rendered. Flora's portraits had been both delicate and radiant - the studio had been built for her as a place of light and inspiration. With Geraldine as its occupant, the atmosphere reeked of cynicism and when I'd made a half-hearted search for evidence of my mother's work, I gave up and returned to the house, sombre beneath a pall of smoke grey clouds.

Raindrops gathered in rows along the edge of the gutters and windowsills. The surrounding trees, unchecked for years, made everywhere dark. The sides of the house were hidden beneath a nest of Virginia creeper that obscured the windows making the rooms oppressive. Towards the end of her life, Yvette, had felt imprisoned on the island - yet she had grown so full of fears she couldn't leave. Silvie said Littern had sapped her mother's will to live, with its overbearing greenness in every shade from palest lime to pine. If Yvette had been melancholy, Juliet had perhaps inherited that sadness and might have passed a streak of pessimism onto me.

To escape the shadowy house, I tried walking from Whitcroft Cove to Morrow Bay at low tide. But where the two beaches were separated by a finger of rock, water cascaded down from the pool in the woods, pouring across the sand, making it impassable.

When I returned to Marisands, I set up the computer in the study and unpacked my dictionaries and reference books ready to begin work on Laurence's notes – Neil had warned me to expect a parcel from him soon. Some of the books I'd brought from London, including the *Marshlands* book, were piled onto a side table. On a shelf above the desk, I placed Silvie's copy of Messenger's *English Poetry* and the slim collections of David's work – *Midnight Shadows*, *Indigo*, *Not Black but Blue*, and *Drowning the Silence* – a reminder of the David who had functioned as a respected member of the literary community - the David I had loved.

The study had been decorated in warm autumn colours of moss and burnt orange and I took refuge there, unwilling to admit I was tired, upset and lonely. Apart from driving Geraldine home, I hadn't been off the island. Except for the man who had delivered Silvie's flowers and Geraldine, who turned up most days to ask for the studio key, I'd spoken to no-one. Beside me was a list of telephone calls I'd promised to make and hadn't - but I had sent an e-mail to Zoë and was glad to receive a reply, "How's life on the rugged rock?" she asked.

Zoë's messages were infrequent and cryptic, but she had included an image of herself, standing by Cameron's van, scowling at the camera. Scarlet faced, wearing a white headdress, her bright pink cheeks were surrounded by tendrils of ginger hair and the piercing gaze of her eyes, even in the picture, seemed difficult to meet.

I began a letter to Minette, copying sketches I'd made of the house and garden, showing the squirrel that startled me when I first arrived and the blackbirds I'd heard singing in the garden. I drew a cartoon of Geraldine stomping down Osford Lane, her felt hat whisked off by the wind and flying high into the trees.

I'd found several small, carved wooden figures of animals, made by my mother, with other objects she'd crafted – among them an apple core, a toadstool, a fir cone. I thought the girls might like them and wrote to Minette that I would put the little woodland creatures in her room, ready for when she came to the island in February.

Reading Antony's obituary had shocked me, as I was certain Geraldine had intended it should, but I'd decided to write my condolences to the Pirans at Lyncross, acknowledging the sense I had of indebtedness to them, of an obligation which had never been admitted or repaid – though Juliet had died - thanks to them, my life had been saved.

While I chewed on my pen and struggled to express my feelings in the right way, I noticed a pale, rectangular patch on the wall above the desk and wondered what might have hung there. Alice's advice that I should use instinct to discern where Geraldine might have helped herself to Armsted property had so far proved useless and my failure to visualise which picture had once occupied the empty space served as a reminder of both lack of success and effort.

I hadn't looked yet for Juliet's watercolour of the garden, the painting which Flora had been eager I should hunt down. So when I'd finished the Piran's letter, I spent two hours searching, until I discovered the painting at the bottom of a cardboard box in the conservatory.

The frame and glass were broken and the painting damaged, marked with rusty brown spots. The colours had faded so badly, it must have been hung in strong light and I could only just make out the path which wound through the orchard and pergola towards the oratory garden.

The studio and Thrift Cottage had been surrounded by deep beds of brightly coloured cottage flowers, contrasting with the white planting of the oratory garden. The painting had been made before my mother had set out her strange white statues on the lawn and as she portrayed the garden, the paths and flowerbeds all formed a trail which led towards the gate above the steps to the oratory.

I carried the painting through to the kitchen and carefully removed the shards of broken glass. *Could I resurrect Juliet's garden -- use her painting as a blueprint to carve out its original form from the mass of brambles and weeds?* The earth was buried beneath layers of rotting fruit and leaves that smothered everything, except the vigorous clumps of hellebores. There were tangles of bushes and vines, bramble wands several feet long, and thickets of couch grass. Bindweed had wound itself through the shrubs and taken a strangle-hold on what remained of the white statues.

Standing by the kitchen window, I stared out at the rain and the ruined garden and wept. Silvie believed what had been broken could be mended. *Did I believe in resurrection?* Neil had asked that, the last time we met.

An easterly wind shook the trees and rounded the corners of the house with a plangent wail - the house responded mournfully. The church clock in Narescombe tolled out its single notes to mark the dying of the day. The house and garden – the island - were all imbued with sadness – the threads of sorrow so deeply woven they felt entangled with the fibres of my own being.

\*

The next day, rifling through the desk looking for envelopes, I came across a small notebook, in which Juliet had kept a record of work she'd had in progress or had sold. Early in the year of her death, she mentioned a series of paintings which she'd intended to donate to All Soul's Church in Narescombe.

The paintings meant nothing to me, but I was curious to learn if her work had been hung in the church or if anyone might know of it. I'd been considering contacting people on the mainland who might remember me – my friend from St. Mary's School, Breda Reynolds, and Sister Odelia, Juliet's friend and my teacher.

There was no sign of Breda's family in the local telephone directory, but possibly she'd married and had a different name. So I rang St. Mary's School to enquire after Odelia and was directed to the Hintham Ridge Community in Safford Bridge, where she now a member - she had left the convent.

When I spoke to her, Odelia suggested we should meet soon and when I explained about my mother's paintings possibly being in Narescombe, she said, 'We'll meet at All Soul's, then.'

Since arriving at Marisands, I'd been living in scruffy clothes and without make-up, but in anticipation of seeing someone, put on a dash of lipstick and mascara and braided my hair, which in the damp weather frizzed out like spun sugar.

We'd had a week of torrential rain and as I pulled the car out onto Osford Lane, the road was running with water. Mud and stones had washed down from the banks – if the temperature dropped and the water froze the lane would be lethal.

A strong sea-breeze blew in brisk flurries, driving showers of heavy raindrops onto the windscreen of the car with a loud spitting sound. By the time I stopped at the causeway, the rain was so intense I could barely make out Osford on the other side of the gully. Rain hammered on the roof of the car, drowning out the noise of the sea as it crashed against the shore and I sat unsure what to do as I contemplated one of the bleakest spots on the island.

With the windscreen wipers going fast, I could just see beyond the bonnet of the car, but couldn't tell if there was water flowing across the causeway. Eventually, a vehicle, dark blue, loomed out of the greyness and flashed its lights as it drove past, indicating that crossing was possible. When the other car disappeared into the trees behind me, I started the engine and, crawled towards the gully, stalling as the car wheels slithered down the steep slope towards the cracked, water-logged surface of the road.

Narescombe was almost deserted. Sea spray flew over the harbour wall and rain bounced up from the streets and pavements. I parked outside All Soul's Church, but got soaked, making a dash to the post box with my letters.

A notice outside All Souls informed me the church had been decommissioned and had become a Community Arts Centre. I checked the list of events - there was a meditation session scheduled for that afternoon - but I had twenty minutes to look for my mother's paintings before meeting Odelia.

Until she had lost her baby, Juliet and I had attended a service at the church every week, I remembered stone plaques and heavily varnished paintings, the dimness of the interior relieved only by lavish displays of flowers.

The church was unrecognisable from the place I had known as a child. Where once there had been memorials and hangings, now there were ladders, workbenches and tools - the building was in the process of being restored and the Lady Chapel had already been transformed into a light, airy room.

On a wooden table, in what had once been the sanctuary, someone had placed a low copper vase of holly and ivy with white candles. The wall behind the table was shrouded in dust sheets – I thought perhaps to protect the carved wooden screen, which had been a notable feature of the church.

No-one was about, so I peeled back the sheets to discover underneath, three large paintings. Each painting was made up of fragmented images caught in a whirling flow of energy. One depicted the crucifixion of Christ on a cross engulfed by fire - flames licked at the broken body of the hanging figure without consuming it. Another was of Christ, stumbling as he carried his cross, surrounded by crowds, their figures fractured into segments of colour, like a stained glass window. The third painting drew on ancient myths of creation and resurrection, but there were shells and plants, animals, fish and birds native to Littern. Sketched into the background were places from the island - images of the sun and moon reflected on the sea. If these were Juliet's work - she had been telling her story in pictures as vivid as the words she had used to tell tales of the island to me.

Standing close to the paintings, each of the fragments appeared crammed with detail and yet as I moved to the back of the chapel, those details became no more than texture, a natural part of the whole. The symbols attempted to bridge the conscious and unconscious mind – yet - God was portrayed through an earthly Christ with clear, soulful eyes, fully alive in his relationship to the elements of water, air, earth and fire.

A plaque on a stand in the corner of the chapel described the paintings as part of an incomplete series, *The Stations of the Cross,* but the artist was un-named.

Questions rose off the canvases like so many spectres. If they were Juliet's, had she wanted to remain anonymous, if so - why..? What could the paintings tell me about my mother? Was there consolation to be gained from the images or were they irreligious and unsettling? Had they been created by someone unstable - someone who *couldn't* bring the fragments together because they themselves had been broken apart?

My mother could have been no more than twenty-four when she had planned to give her paintings to the church - at a time when she'd seemed on the verge of losing her faith. She would have been young to attempt such an ambitious project, requiring not only a profound understanding of suffering and pain, but the vision to imbue those emotions with hope rather than despair. I'd noticed, there were sections missing from all of the paintings – loose sketches were visible underneath. If she had been working on others in the series, *where were they?*

A few people began to drift into the church – the meditation group. I looked around, but there was no-one representing the Arts Centre, no-one I could speak to. A woman was scattering cushions in the space in front of the main chancel step, but when she had lit a row of candles along the altar rail, she spoke to the group and they began to chant - *Om* – a low, resonant sound.

I tip-toed past the circle of people towards a row of chairs set out inside the church door. The woman continued to chant and the group, who now sat cross-legged on the floor holding hands, gradually joined in, the sound rising in depth and volume until it filled my head.

The humming made a deep vibration which passed through my body, but then as it faded into silence, my thoughts strayed until I felt someone shaking my arm and found myself gazing up into a pair of earnest, light brown eyes.

'Hello,' the woman whispered.

'...Sister Odelia?'

'I prefer plain Delia, these days,' she said, 'I think you could do with a coffee.'

We made our way out through the glass doors into the foyer, where we sheltered for a while, staring out at the terrible weather. I noted her appearance - her brown hair was frosted with grey - a long tiered skirt and short knitted jacket, in shades of brown, had replaced the crisp blue and white habit of the Order of St. Stephen.

'I'd have known you anywhere, you're so like your mother,' she said. 'You've seen the paintings? Did you recognise them as Juliet's work?'

I couldn't claim truthfully that I'd have recognised the paintings as my mother's, except for clues such as the details of flora and fauna from Littern Island.

Delia said, 'I have no doubts, but Juliet died before she could finish the rest of the series. When All Souls closed, there was talk of moving the paintings to the Priory in Safford Bridge, but I don't think they met with approval...'

I smiled, 'Perhaps Juliet would have been pleased to think someone saw them as radical - I had the impression she'd put religion behind her.'

'Did you? As far as I know, Juliet never lost her faith - she was taking instruction to become a Catholic. Didn't it strike you - the paintings being called *The Stations of the Cross*? She was going to paint The Rosary – but given her unconventional style, I think that would definitely have been a step too far...'

Delia was bright, frank and open, qualities I had liked in her as a teacher.

'Were you worried about my mother in the period before she died? I mean about her state of mind.'

She looked thoughtful, 'I didn't see her much that last summer. Her life was complex. There were plenty of reasons why she might have felt depressed, but equally, many reasons for her to look forward. Are you asking me, if I think she committed suicide?'

I hadn't expected her to be quite so direct and backtracked a little. 'There's a lot about my mother I don't know, things I'd like to understand.'

Delia's eyes became shadowed with concern, 'What sort of things?'

'I've always felt Juliet's death was in some way my fault.' I explained what Beatrix had told her mother, saying I had caused Juliet to run into the sea in a place that was known to be unsafe.

'So with all the wisdom of a child – she understood precisely what had happened and condemned you?'

'I simply accepted what she said,' I admitted, colour rising to my cheeks.

'It doesn't do to be gullible,' she warned, 'you may need to practice discernment.'

Our conversation moved on to other topics. 'I usually take part in the meditation group,' Delia told me, 'how strange you mentioned coming here. Do you believe in coincidence?'

'All I know is that if I'd stayed on the island any longer, I would have gone mad...'

Delia laughed. 'The meditation group is for people with mental health problems, I lead it sometimes - perhaps you should join.'

I must have looked worried - it appeared it wasn't only my mother's state of mind that was in doubt but my own.

'I'm teasing,' she said, 'let's go and have a drink, and then we can talk properly. There's a cafe near Napier Street run by the community – as you can tell, we keep ourselves busy.'

We crossed town, the cold wind and icy rain whipping at our clothes, the streets colourful with dancing scraps of vegetables and litter left over from Narescombe market, which had taken place that morning.

Delia's thick hair was held back with a slide, but at the front, strands kept escaping and blowing onto her face, she swept them back impatiently.

'Do you know anyone else round here these days?' she asked.

'I've barely seen a soul on the island – I don't even know who else is living there. Do you remember Breda Reynolds? I looked in the phone book but I couldn't find her.'

'You wouldn't - Breda passed away five years ago. I used to visit her when she was ill. She had no family and that was her problem, her parents had died years earlier and she was their only child...'

Poor Breda, I thought, saddened by her story. Grateful Delia had been there to care about her illness and her passing – glad that she hadn't been left entirely alone in the world.

We turned into Napier Street, where there were a number of art shops and galleries tucked in-between rows of colourful painted cottages, with plants in tubs flanking their doorways.

Delia pointed out a gallery called Petra - its window full of bulbous grey sculptures, landscape paintings and gothic fantasy art recognisable as Geraldine's from the work she had in the studio at Marisands.

She said, 'You'll remember the sculptress, Shirley Fredericks? She lives in the flat over the shop - her studio is round the back somewhere.'

I'd never known whether Shirley had carried out her plans to move to Devon and open a gallery - had scarcely given it a thought - not even when she had turned up at my father's funeral.

'Shirley helps run the Arts Centre – you could ask her about Juliet's work,' Delia said.

We entered a narrow alley leading to a courtyard, where there was a café called Quay 11. Delia knew the staff behind the counter and chatted as we ordered drinks and then squeezed into a corner table. On a wet and windy afternoon, the place felt enclosed, airless, the windows running with condensation and the walls festooned in knitted objects the same colours as Delia's clothing. She told me they had been knitted from the wool of Jacob's sheep, by members of the Hintham Ridge Community to which she now belonged.

'Did you and William ever make up?' she asked.

I described how the last time we'd met, I'd wanted answers to questions about my childhood, but my father wouldn't or couldn't give them. In return, though I'd regretted it since, I'd been unable to grant the forgiveness he had asked for.

'Is forgiveness conditional on having answers?' she asked sounding surprised.

My cheeks burned. I hadn't expected her to challenge me and recalled Fr. Terence Hart with his reproaches, his invitation to talk, which I had, so far, completely ignored.

Delia asked, 'What did you think of the meditation? Did you like the chanting? I hope you'll come, the group needs people like you.'

'Like me?'

She laughed. 'I meant mainstream, "normal" people, meditation is something that benefits everyone - you don't have to be Buddhist, New Age or even mad.'

She talked about the Hintham Ridge Community, who had taken over a farm on the other side of Safford Bridge and carried out charitable work in the towns and villages of the area.

'This cafe gives work to people who couldn't find jobs anywhere else...' she said.

She delved into her shoulder bag and retrieved a leaflet about the community.

'Have you come to Devon to live or to visit?' she said.

'I don't really know – I came seeking a sense of direction...'

She nodded, 'When I retired, I felt at a loose end until I left the convent to become part of Hintham Ridge. The locals think we're a strange, esoteric cult, but we're only doing the ordinary things...' she listed the projects the community was involved in.

I was anxious to steer the conversation away from the community's many good works, knowing that nuns – and probably ex-nuns - could have a long reach when it came to enlisting volunteers.

'When I separated from my partner, I had to leave London,' I told her, 'but I'm finding the island in January a dismal place to recover.'

'How sad for you...' Delia's eyes shone with sympathy - her expression was warm and concerned.

I brushed her sympathy aside, 'I was young and inexperienced. I made a mistake, but plan to be more careful in the future.'

'Can you be careful in love?' she asked, frowning. She paused before speaking again, 'Why don't you come out to the farm one day? Don't be lonely - you can phone me any time, especially when Littern becomes too lugubrious. Your mother would be pleased that we've got in touch.'

She asked after Silvie, Flora and Alice. I told her Silvie had been in a nursing home in Sussex for over thirty years and that Flora and Alice had plans to move to The Maples, in Surrey.

'I hope Alice won't terrorise the other residents,' she said and laughed, 'we were afraid of her as children and even as colleagues. She was really something of a tartar – poor Flora.'

Delia needed to get back to Hintham Ridge, she was on kitchen duty, so when we'd finished our coffee, we walked together back into the centre of Narescombe, where she had left her moped, near where I'd parked outside All Soul's.

'Do you remember Kelda Sullivan, your "auntie" at school?' she asked. 'Look over there.' She nodded her head towards the doorway of a dry cleaning shop across the square, where a group of figures had huddled together, sheltering under a makeshift tent of blue plastic sheeting.

'Kelda's probably there with them. You'll see her around on the streets, here and in Safford Bridge.'

'What happened?' I asked. Kelda had been intelligent, gifted musically, held up as a source of hope and inspiration by the nuns.

'What usually happens?' She paused to put on her crash helmet, strapping it tightly under her chin. 'Kelda came from a respectable Catholic family but got in with a bad crowd. After some trouble with her parents, she took to the streets, the bottle and probably worse...'

I glanced across at the group jostling in the doorway to keep out of the rain. Last time I'd seen Kelda, she'd been with James Millford on the beach at Morrow Bay, had he been part of the "bad crowd"? If I approached her – would she speak or even acknowledge me?

'You'd be wasting your time,' Delia said, guessing my thoughts, 'I've tried to help and so have many others. Take my advice, steer clear, or you may find yourself up to your neck in her problems.'

She seemed to imply Kelda had deliberately chosen her path and there was no hope of change or redemption. Feeling uncomfortable, I changed the subject and spoke briefly about Antony Piran. Delia had read his obituary in the paper, but said she could offer little news of the rest of the family.

Black clouds had been gathering over the town while we were talking.

'You'd better get home,' she said.

I waited while she slipped her waterproof cape over her shoulders. Then she revved her moped's putt-putt engine and rode off out of sight, wisps of hair streaming behind her in the wind.

I was tempted to cross the square and see if Kelda was in the group of street people, I could give her the price of a meal and a bed for the night. I rested my umbrella on my shoulder and slipped off my gloves to open my handbag and find my purse. As I did so my bracelet with the tiny silver hearts caught on the clasp of my bag, broke and spilled into the gutter, teeming with fast flowing water.

The chain – David's gift to me - was swept away with clumps of dead leaves and litter. I ran along the kerbside, making awkward jabs at it - once I almost managed to catch it in my fingers - but then it disappeared down the drain, as shiny and slippery as a silver fish.

I stared at the metal grid in disbelief, but the bracelet had gone and when I turned round, the huddle of figures across the square had also disappeared.

Pushing my gloves into my pockets, I hurried towards the shops. In the supermarket, I filled my trolley with tins and packets - the kinds of things Eve and Zoë had survived on and which I would never have eaten while living in London.

As I packed my shopping into the boot of the car, my eyes were drawn to the gutter, where the bracelet had disappeared. I scanned the drain uselessly as if the silver hearts might be spat out, as Jonah had been ejected from the mouth of the whale. I felt I'd been self-indulgent - continuing to wear the bracelet, when David had made it clear he wanted to be free. I still wore his ring on the fourth finger of my left hand, hanging on to the groundless hope that even now, he might relent and come back to me.

Reluctant to return to the island, I wandered down to the harbour where boats bobbed in the rough water, their sails folded, their ropes beating and singing in the wind. The pub, *The North Star,* stood out, bright and welcoming – it was the place where my father had first met his student followers, "The Disciples", who had annoyed my mother, with their untidiness and unreasonable demands. I hurried inside, glad to get out of the cold and wet, and ordered a glass of wine and a meal from the bar. There was a table free near the window, so I sat intent on listening to the turbulent sea, scarcely visible in the descending twilight.

The interior of the inn had once been well-polished and ship-like, but the mahogany furniture and shiny brass fittings had been replaced by modern tables and chairs against a backdrop of wallpaper patterned with splashy flowers. The menu was no longer made up of homely fare - cottage pie, steak and kidney, chicken pie, apple crumble - instead, the main choice was pasta served on an enormous plate, like a flying saucer, with everything, including the rim of plate, sprinkled with flakes of freshly chopped parsley.

My meal took ages to come – the pub was busy. I ate quickly, growing anxious about the tide. Before I'd finished eating, my fears had escalated into panic – it was dark and I could see nothing outside except for the harbour lights. The pub was filling up with customers and when an elderly couple asked if they could sit at my table, I excused myself and abandoned my meal.

Scurrying along the quayside, my umbrella obscuring the view, I collided with a figure loitering by the public loos. At first, I couldn't tell if the person was a man or a woman. They wore a shapeless overcoat and a black hat and carried a bulky collection of bags. The odour they emitted, however, was pungent and unmistakeable – unwashed body and alcohol.

I turned to apologise, but as I started to speak, the figure rocked on its heels and slumped down in the entrance to the Ladies' toilets, dislodging the hat and revealing a tangle of hennaed hair. I crouched down, picked up the hat and touched the woman's shoulder.

'Are you all right?' I asked.

'Do I fucking look all right?' she asked, her breath rancid.

I straightened up - she didn't seem ill, just angry. Looking down at her, I said, 'Do you know Kelda Sullivan?'

The woman's mouth twisted into a strange smile, she burped and then said, 'Why the hell don't you just fuck off?'

# Chapter 19

A few days after meeting Delia, the package of notes arrived from Laurence. A cursory look at the contents revealed them to be unsorted and written on scraps of paper, which varied from table napkins to the inside of a toothpaste box – I needed to start work immediately.

The weather had changed and was bitingly cold. I fetched plenty of wood for the house fire from the shed but it took me half an hour to thaw out over a mug of coffee, huddled against the kitchen radiator, before I could bear the prospect of going upstairs to the freezing study.

My Pimlico hours of rising before dawn, were a thing of the past. I didn't want life to be as rigidly defined as it had been in London, though I wasn't settling at Marisands. Full of contradictions, I had no sense of belonging, yet didn't root myself by joining Delia's meditation group or seeking out my neighbours. Not wanting to be cut off, I still preferred to remain an outsider, focussed on the concerns I had brought with me to the island – how Minette was doing at school - whether Zoë had made contact - and whether Eve had recovered from her latest bout of flu.

One morning, the telephone rang; it seemed deafening in the usually silent house. Eve was calling from The Angel Inn, where she'd struck up an arrangement with Matt, the innkeeper, for free meals and the use of the pub phone in exchange for a few hours working as a barmaid.

'If I catch the next train to Safford Bridge will you come and collect me?' she asked, 'If I don't leave now, I might not make it – you've heard the weather forecast?'

I hadn't, but the sheer unexpectedness of her request made it a joy. Eve wasn't given to sudden impulses, I hadn't seen her for almost three months, and could think of few things I would like better than to have her company.

Switching on the radio, I listened for a weather report after the next bulletin of news. Snow was sweeping across the West Country, Cornwall had already been hard hit, and the wintry weather was likely to last for several days. Eve's call meant there was a need to consider what from my meagre selection of tins and packets of food we might eat, especially if we were likely to be snowed in.

Icy rain turned to sleet and it took me over an hour to drive to Safford Bridge. When I arrived at the station, Eve was sitting on a bench by the entrance, wearing torn jeans and her thin, blue anorak.

'I was beginning to think I'd been abandoned,' she said, 'I'm starving hungry.'

Her face looked cold and pinched and I was anxious to get her into the warm. As we walked to the car park she pulled her hood up over her woollen hat and shouldered her rucksack, too heavy for her fragile frame.

I suggested we went to The Pilgrim's Inn to have tea, though we wouldn't have much time, because of the tide. When I'd put more money in the parking meter and stowed her rucksack in the boot of the car, we set off towards town.

As we crossed the river, I pointed out where the swathes of crocuses on the bank had spread out as far as the eye could see – though their striped leaves were now gradually being blanketed by a thin layer of snow. In a few minutes, we were at the entrance of The Pilgrim's Inn, inviting, with its plush carpets in gold and soft red and the rooms lit by electric candle lamps, which gave off a deep yellow glow.

'I'm hardly dressed for this,' Eve whispered as we went in.

'It's not as grand as it looks,' I assured her.

I led the way into the dining room, where a scattering of guests sat enjoying plates of sandwiches and cakes. Soon, we were shown to a table overlooking the square.

Eve said, 'I can't imagine how you must have felt arriving here, all alone. It isn't good to be alone. Who said that?'

'I think it was God...'

'...The ultimate authority then,' she replied. 'Have you really met no-one on the island?'

I described how when I'd first arrived at Marisands, there was a car ahead of me with people in it. Occasionally, I'd caught sight of a tractor or some sheep in the fields - on the first evening, I'd even seen a dog running along the beach.

'Sorry I asked,' Eve said, laughing at the state of my social life since coming to Littern.

While I was reading the menu, she slipped off her jacket and removed her woolly hat and when I glanced up I saw that her long blonde hair had been cropped into an elfin cut and stood up in short ragged tufts all over her head.

'Eve!' I said. With her hair shorn, she was more like David than ever.

She pulled a face, 'Sorry, I should have warned you - I sold my hair - I was broke - more broke than usual...'

I ordered tea for us both and cheese scones with cheddar for Eve. She'd been telling me how she'd become a vegetarian like the commune leader, Luke Porter, and I wondered if they were living together.

'Are you well..?' I asked. I'd noticed Eve lacked her usual brightness, the healthy lustre that made her eyes and skin glow. With her hair cut close to her head, like a skull cap, her eyes appeared enormous and were ringed with smudges of black.

'Everyone's had colds,' she said and reached out and touched my hand, '*Please* don't fuss, I want to hear how things are with you.'

I didn't trouble her with an account of days spent scrubbing, polishing and moving furniture - instead I encouraged her to tell me about her painting, which had been her reason for going to Cornwall.

Eve said her work hadn't been going well, 'Perhaps Littern will inspire me.' Her smile lit her face with a gentle radiant energy.

Outside, snow whirled in the light from the street lamps and watching through the window, it felt as if we were sitting in a snow-globe. Across the square I saw a figure huddled under a tree. I'd been shaken by my encounter with the woman outside the pub in Narescombe, convinced she had been Kelda and ashamed because I hadn't done more to help her.

Eve shook my arm, 'A penny for them?' she said.

'How can people sleep rough in winter? I worry about Zoë. After your Dad left, I couldn't seem to find a way of talking to her...'

She shrugged, 'I picked up an e-mail from Zoë at The Angel, she thinks you've become a property tycoon, she spelt it "tie-koon" – she's in Morocco, where I expect she's quite warm.'

Eve was doing her best to raise my spirits, but as soon as she'd eaten it was time to leave. My eyes searched the streets as we left The Pilgrims' Inn, but the figure beneath the tree had vanished into a doorway or down one of the narrow back roads of the town.

Arm in arm, we hurried across to the covered market, where I stocked up with extra vegetables – enough for what Eve suggested could only be a global catastrophe, but snow on the island was rare and usually meant severe conditions on the mainland.

While I shopped, Eve tagged behind, chatting about people in her commune. Apart from Luke, two others had remained in Zethar Creek, someone called Finn and a girl called Gemma. Eve mentioned Luke often, giving the impression of a dominant personality, whose views on life and art were having a powerful influence on her.

We left Safford Bridge in the half-light and the landscape was transformed, the hills laced with blue-white, the snow drifting against hedges and trees, blurring their outlines like a winter scene in a children's book.

I took the car at a slow pace down the steep, winding hill into Narescombe, driving was difficult and we were both quiet until we reached the end of Palk's Reach and the causeway.

The car wheels jolted over the rough road and I winced at the sound of the labouring engine as we drove up the other side onto the island.

'It's perfect...' Eve said as enormous snowflakes fell steadily into the dark mass of trees, where they lodged on bare wood or the drooping branches of evergreens.

When we had reached the oak tree, she jumped out of the car to open the gate - Geraldine must have shut it when she left. Eve pulled back the ivy that shrouded the gatepost and underneath was a brass plate, giving the name of the house, *Marisands*. 'This needs a polish,' she called out, rubbing it with the sleeve of her coat.

'Everything here needs a polish,' I warned and wondered what she would make of the rest of the house.

I handed Eve the front door key and carried her rucksack into the hall, easing my way past the pile of wood in the porch.

Eve asked if she could look around while I laid the fire in the sitting room, ready for the evening.

'What a job - clearing this place up,' she said when she came downstairs again. 'Couldn't you pay someone to do it?'

'I need to see off the ghosts myself, it's what Silvie wanted,' I told her, though I hoped with Eve at Marisands I might not feel their constant presence, the noisy chorus of voices from the past, like in a Greek tragedy.

'At least it's warmer than Zethar Creek...' she said and sat down by the kitchen radiator, with her jacket on.

I put a tray of tea and cake on the kitchen table, Eve was hungry again.

'I saw you brought Zoë's paintings,' she said. I had set out Zoë's black paintings in one of the spare rooms. 'I should give you something of mine...'

'Bring something, next time,' I said - anxious not to inflame competition between her and her sister, though I had no intention of hanging Zoë's baffling work on the walls.

I'd given Eve the bedroom which had once been Flora's, decorated in violet, soft green and cream. I'd hung a portrait of Juliet in there – *In Marisands' Garden* - and two landscapes of Bernard's - *St. Thrif's Holy Well* and *Winter Marshes*.

When Eve had unpacked, she wanted to explore the garden and then to walk down to the sea - she thought it would be atmospheric - the snow, the ocean and the lowering sky.

I lent her a wool coat of mine and a pair of warm gloves and while I washed up our cups, watched her trudge round the garden making patterns with her footprints and shaking snow from the overhanging branches of the trees.

After a few minutes, she called, beckoning to me. I grabbed a jacket from the hall and followed her outside carrying the torch I kept near the door, in case the power went off.

'There's a dog here! Come and see. I heard him whimpering...'

Eve was by the garage. I switched on the torch and searched the darkness until I could just make out the shape of a dog where it lay shivering on the concrete floor, tied to the bumper of William's old car.

'Be careful!' I said, 'He might bite.'

The dog I had seen wandering on the beach had been black, like this one - but how could he have got here and who had tied him to the bumper?

'You wouldn't like a dog?' Eve asked. 'He'd be company for you.'

'No thanks,' I said. 'Has he got a collar with a name?' I was hanging back nervously as Eve crept towards the dog, offering the back of her hand for him to sniff - a gesture of friendship.

'I've found a rope and a collar with no name on it – there's a worn out lead on the ground. He's seems friendly...' she said.

I was puzzled - surely this wasn't some sick joke of Geraldine's? When I moved in closer, the dog stood up and was about hip height, with thick black fur, a bushy muzzle as if he had a moustache, and feathered ears. He was good-looking in a scruffy, vagabond way, but I knew nothing about dogs - we weren't a family of animal lovers.

'Please, give him a chance,' Eve begged. 'If you don't like him, I'll help you find him a new home. He can't stay tied up out here, not in this weather.'

I visualised the dog in the house and in my imagination he grew larger, hungrier and more unmanageable, until he was the size of a small horse.

'A cat would have had some purpose - catching mice - I've found plenty of those,' I told her.

I caught Eve smiling at me - she obviously thought negotiations were going well.

'I didn't come here to take in waifs and strays,' I objected.

'Of course you didn't - though you've taken me in. I was on my way back to the house when I heard him.' She imitated the dog's pathetic, squeaking cries, 'he needs to get warm.'

She untied the dog and led him towards the front porch. He showed no sign of anxiety at entering an unknown place with two strangers.

In the kitchen, Eve poured water into a plastic bowl and he seemed desperately thirsty - she refilled the bowl three times. Having finished drinking, the dog shook his head sending drops of water flying everywhere.

'You could keep him in Zethar Creek,' I suggested.

'No room,' Eve said. She ruffled the dog's fur, 'His coat's full of sand, I wonder if he's been living on the beach?'

It seemed probable, as half the beach was now on the kitchen floor.

Eve said, 'This is lovely – like receiving an unexpected gift.'

She could be ingenuous at times. I was concerned not only by the presence of the dog, but by the fact someone had been on the property while I was out collecting her from Safford Bridge.

'He could sleep in the conservatory,' Eve suggested. She was kneeling down, fondling the dog's ears and rubbing his chest. In the light, his black fur was tipped with reddish brown - his face rather foolish, as if he wore a silly smile. 'You've said it's no distance from the house to the beach, so there wouldn't be a problem exercising him...'

'A problem could be he belongs to someone else,' I pointed out. The Pirans had kept dogs - he could easily have escaped from Lyncross.

'They clearly don't care about him...'

I left her and went through to the sitting room and put a match to the fire. When the sun went down, the house soon grew cold and in winter all light had disappeared by early afternoon.

Eve was moving about the kitchen, probably finding something for the dog to eat. She was as bad as a little child trying to persuade her parents to buy her a pet.

'He's starving,' Eve said, coming to the sitting room door, 'I've given him bread and tuna.'

I felt a rush of impatience, 'I'm not going to keep him,' I insisted. 'Geraldine thinks she can barge in here when she wants, people think they can abandon stray dogs on my doorstep...'

'Don't shout, you'll scare him,' Eve scolded.

'I'm sorry, Eve, but I don't like dogs and I don't like that woman.'

'The dog is probably nothing to do with Geraldine. And anyway, you can't blame her for being difficult about things - Marisands was her home for years – think how you felt about leaving Pimlico. Maybe Geraldine was banking on no-one coming back here...'

'I'm sure you're right about that,' I said.

The dog was in the kitchen whining and when the sound rose to a heart rending wail, Eve let him out at the front door. Almost as soon as he'd gone into the garden, he bounced back into the house leaving a trail of icy water on the tiles of the hall floor.

'Stop him! He's undoing all my good work.' I snapped, raising my voice again.

'I'll take him out properly.' I saw a look of pity flit across Eve's face.

From the kitchen window I watched the two of them in the garden playing with a stick, treading down the snow. Eve was tall and lithe and the dog full of energy as he leapt and chased the stick she tossed in the air for him – he charged the atmosphere with life and it was impossible not to smile, seeing the two of them revelling in their game, like children.

When the dog had tired, Eve called to him and tried to lure him into the conservatory with a ginger biscuit, but he refused to go.

I'd begun preparing dinner. Chatting to Eve in the market at Safford Bridge, I'd discovered vegetarian cuisine entailed a considerable amount of ingredients and a lot of chopping.

Eve rested her arm round my shoulders.

'You're tired,' she said, 'this is how you were in London, when Dad was being awkward. My work is crap at the moment - maybe I need a break – maybe I could stay on a bit and help you see off those ghosts..?'

'You must do what's best for you,' I murmured, but she was right, I was tired and wound up.

Coming to Marisands, I hadn't calculated for endless lonely days, nights of troubled dreams or for the memories which crowded in, overwhelming my thoughts like an incipient madness that refused to go away. With Eve's company, I hoped I might find respite from the urge to go round the house checking I'd locked up – doors and windows – windows and doors - once, twice, three times - as I'd done every night since I'd arrived.

'I'm sorry,' I said, 'it's not your fault or the dog's.'

Eve patted my shoulder, 'That's right,' she said, 'let me take over...'

She removed the knife from my hand and began cutting a mountain of carrots, swede and parsnips to make a vegetable gratin.

I sat at the kitchen table. The dog lay beside me and absent mindedly I began to pat his head and caress the soft, wispy fur around his ears.

*

During the night, there was a snowstorm. Thunder rolled directly over Marisands and sheet lightning obscured the sky, but the next day brought a cold, sharp morning and a clear sunrise, suffusing the snow laden garden with a soft ethereal pink. Standing by the porch, waiting for the dog, who Eve had named Quirk, I became aware of the subtle colours of the garden - there were fading red berries - holly, rowan and firethorn - and the brown remnants of late roses, rimed with a layer of sparkling white snow.

On the cherries and silver birches of the oratory garden, snow had frozen into airy shapes, like sea-foam; it shrouded the shrubs and capped the white statues accentuating their strangely distorted shapes. The hellebores had raised their heads - a pure, clean white against the blue shadows, where snow had drifted against hedges and tree-trunks. There was a romance about Marisands in the winter weather which was seductive - the isolation of the place made bearable by the knowledge that Eve was sleeping soundly upstairs.

Later, Eve insisted on helping me to move in properly. We put the figure of the White Virgin on the table by the front door. Then she carried the remaining boxes of books from the hall to the study.

'This'll make you feel at home,' she said tearing the boxes open, bringing out children's classics, *Alice in Wonderland*, the *Just So Stories*, *Heidi*, the *Famous Five, Swallows and Amazons*. As Eve handed them to me, I arranged the books on the empty shelves, in the spaces where I'd removed large volumes on art to the music room.

While Eve made coffee, I cut stems of witch hazel and put them in a cream vase on my desk. I hung Silvie's dragonfly painting in the place on the wall, where a picture had been taken down and propped up the print of Aphrodite, Flora had give me, at the back of the desk.

When I joined her in the kitchen, Eve was crawling on the floor of the larder, trying to trace where the mice were coming in. Quirk watched her anxiously, his tail wagging in long slow arcs of consternation. I'd meant to buy mousetraps, but Eve thought they were barbaric. She'd found a gap around the pipe work, tiny, but sufficient for a small creature to squeeze through, and was busy making a temporary cover, using the bottom of a discarded washing-up liquid bottle, sticking it tightly into place with electrical tape.

'What's down there, Bluebeard's den?' she asked, pointing at the trapdoor.

'...Boxes and trunks of papers - an old wooden chest and some very large spiders...'

We sat to have our coffee with Quirk settled under the kitchen table, lying on our feet. I'd put out a plate of biscuits and caught Eve slipping him a gingersnap, placing it where he could reach it on her knee - supposedly unseen by me.

'Perhaps we should empty the cellar,' Eve said.

I hadn't ventured down there again on my own, but agreed we could retrieve the contents of the trunks, even if we left the trunks where they were. Eve had an inventive mind and I thought there was a possibility she might discover a way to open the lid of the wooden chest so we could look inside.

With Eve helping, the cellar seemed less threatening and we brought up bags full of papers and old diaries adding them to the piles already in the dining room. Among the trunks were cardboard boxes containing miniatures by Yvette, portraits of her French family, executed with a restrained sense of colour – translucent, intuitive and gentle. I found the silver holy water stoup which had belonged to my grandfather, Alexander, with prints of icons, which had also been his. There were paintings of *The Sacred Heart* in dismal colours and other religious artefacts, which had once belonged to Flora.

Between us, we managed to up-end the wooden chest, but there was no sign of a secret compartment on the base - nor could we find any other mechanism to release the lock. After twenty minutes, I was growing discouraged and Eve was so fed-up she suggested I research the problem on the internet.

Eve's attention was mercurial, she wanted to see what she referred to as "the rest of your estate", and so we dressed in warm clothes and made our way through the orchard and pergola, snow tumbling onto our heads as we stepped into the garden of Thrift Cottage.

Quirk followed us like a shadow, though our movements must have made little sense to him. As we went up to the studio door he barked and I half expected to find Geraldine there. She hadn't come to the house that morning for the key, but her absence felt predatory, as if she was a hawk sitting on a nearby branch, waiting for the right moment to attack.

Relieved to see the studio empty, I let us in. Eve glanced at me without speaking. She stood straight and tall, caught in the light that poured in through the windows making her fair hair and skin glisten.

'Geraldine's "incomparable light",' I said.

'My room in Zethar Creek is so gloomy - perhaps that's why my paintings emerge pale and wan,' she said. She fingered some of the work that had been left leaning against the racks that ran round the lower walls, 'These can't be Juliet's?'

'Geraldine's...' I explained.

I picked up one of the tower paintings. The background bore a resemblance to the landscape by Bernard, in the dining room, except that Geraldine's version lacked the skilled use of light and shade with which he had imbued the scene with atmosphere. Her work stressed the uncanny - I could imagine hobgoblins emerging from behind the reeds of the marshlands and Geraldine was not unlike a hobgoblin herself.

I described the paintings in All Soul's Church to Eve and Juliet's intention for further work in the series, *The Stations of the Cross*. She searched through a collection of folders she'd found in the shallow drawers, where William used to keep drawings. Most of the folders were empty containing neither his sketches nor anything of my mother's - in the case of my father it was beginning to appear that three decades of work had simply disappeared.

While Eve rifled through racks and cupboards, I began to sweep up cigarette butts, ash, discarded plastic wrappers and paper bags from the floor. The pile of old blankets Geraldine used as a bed lay in an untidy heap in the corner of the room. On a trestle table was a dirty primus stove - crockery had been abandoned in the sink and now displayed a colourful selection of green and orange mould.

'I've found three sketches - signed "J.A.",' Eve said.

I leant the broom against the wall and went to look, 'Juliet Armsted - my mother used the family name for her work...'

Eve laid the sketches on a table. The pen lines were faint, as if they had been made tentatively or else had been rubbed away by time – but there was no mistaking their purpose as preparatory drawings of paintings planned for *The Stations* series.

'The trouble is you can't speak to the dead and ask them what they meant...' I said. A part of me hoped I might uncover Juliet's story embedded in her art. 'I suppose, I'll have to ask Geraldine...'

In a corner of the studio, pushed behind a cupboard was a large metal frame on wheels, protected by a torn white sheet. Eve wheeled the frame out and turned back the sheet revealing a painting - a rough version of a work with a religious theme.

'It's like someone being blitzed by ideas so fast they have to hurl them down on the canvas,' Eve said.

And if there was any sense of unity, it had been achieved only through the colours – green and sapphire, emerald and amethyst – so dense they were almost black. The lack of light, the lack of sympathy was striking, as was the ultimate failure of the painting and its resemblance to the *Art Brut* style, favoured by my father.

'Let's cover it up,' I said. At Marisands, the membrane between past and present was delicate – it was too easy to be drawn into morbid speculation.

Eve studied the back of the canvas. Across the top of the wooden carrier it said, "The body of Jesus is taken down from the cross" in William's handwriting.

'It uses the colours of grief, is that what you were thinking?' she asked.

I shook my head. I'd been thinking less of grief and more of insanity. Then Eve showed me how at the bottom of the carrier Juliet had written, *The Resistance Movement* – but resistance to what – and could that depressing painting possibly be her work?

'Let's explore the cottage,' I suggested, the painting had unnerved me.

Quirk trailed us as we traipsed across the snowy grass to the front door of Thrift Cottage. As I opened the door, Eve coughed, choking on the smell of damp and clouds of dust, wrapping her scarf over her mouth to protect herself.

The main room had walls of rough, bare stone. We pushed aside the stacks of canvases, paints and jars of chemicals and manoeuvred ourselves inside. Clambering over boxes, we made our way to the foot of the staircase. There were water stains on the ceiling and on the walls, the rain was coming in through the roof and it appeared at some time a pipe may have burst. Upstairs, the bathroom was badly affected by mould, so I shut the door, opened a window to air the place and retreated downstairs.

The stench and small brown droppings everywhere suggested the cottage had become a lodging place for mice and rats and I was anxious to leave, but Eve had forced her way into the kitchen and discovered a broken window. To prevent more rain and snow blowing in, we covered it with a drawing board, wedged in place with a wooden frame. When we'd finished, I removed the corpses of two birds which had fallen down the chimney into the fireplace.

'An estate agent might say it has potential,' Eve commented.

*The potential to fall down*, I thought – I didn't have the resources to have the cottage repaired, redecorated and made habitable.

'This is too much,' I said, 'Silvie could have had no idea.'

Eve smiled. 'It might be nothing to an expert in DIY and if the fire was going - it could be snug as a beehive.'

I wished I could share her optimism, but the chimney was almost certainly blocked and her plan to make the cottage snug would probably set the whole place on fire.

We wandered through to the oratory garden, where the white sculptures were shrouded with a mantle of convolvulus and ivy. In the snow, one figure looked like a woman wearing a huge wig and a flowing cloak of white leaves. The statues had been severely damaged - fragments had been split off by wind and rain and had fallen into the grass. Some had been eroded until they were figures of lace, unrecognisable as the sculptures Juliet had first made, while others were translucent, like frozen light.

Eve ran her hands over the shapes of the figures. As she lifted the ivy away from the stone, part of one statue crumbled to the ground

'What *are* these?'

'...An obsession of my mother's,' I explained about the stillbirth of my sister.

'They're made of alabaster, they should never have been left outside – you could pretty well calculate the damage they would suffer over the years. Could they be self-portraits?' Eve asked. 'Did your mother feel she was losing her sense of herself, her sense of identity?

I didn't know, but agreed that she could have done, for that was how David had made me feel - invisible, insubstantial – preying on his relationships with other women - a presence he wanted to banish or better still annihilate. It was possible - even likely William had affected my mother in the same way, our partners had both been relentless in their infidelity.

As we passed through the small copse of silver birch trees, I scraped snow away from their roots and could see how the base of the each trunk was smothered in a tangle of ivy and weeds. When I tried to right St. Thrif's gravestone, it wouldn't shift.

'What's through there?' Eve asked.

She pointed to where Quirk stood whining, his nose poking through the wrought iron gate at the top of the oratory steps. I unfastened the padlock. Holding the dog's lead tightly, I warned Eve to be careful not to fall.

Stepping out onto the cliff, I'd forgotten how vertiginous the steps appeared from the top, how if you looked down, seagulls flew past you at eye level and how the oratory was perched on a ledge of rock so narrow, there was little room to stand to open the door.

St.Thrif's statue remained in its niche and I related the story of her persecution and decapitation. Her shorn head, we decided was an indication that she had despite the obstacles in her path, fulfilled her desire to become a nun.

Wanting to take Eve down to the oratory, I put my foot forward onto the first step and ran the sole of my boot across the surface to check how slippery it was. As I did so, Quirk tugged on his lead, eager to run down to the beach and my feet slid out from under me.

'Iris..!' Eve shouted.

I grabbed onto the gate to stop myself sliding further towards the edge of the cliff. I tried not to pull Eve with me as she clutched at my other arm and deliberately didn't look down at the dizzying sea breaking on the shore below. No animal or human could survive that fall - beneath me were jagged rocks, churning water and certain death.

Tumbling back onto the cold, wet ground, I'd winded myself. While I caught my breath, Eve took the dog and sent him back into the garden. My legs trembled as I stood - a bruised feeling in my ankle made it tender when I put my foot to the ground.

'Let me help you,' Eve kept saying. 'Go back to the house - I'll take Quirk down to the shore, we'll go by the footpath.'

But though my ankle hurt, I didn't want Eve to go to the beach alone. The tide was coming in and I wasn't convinced she took the matter of the dangerous currents seriously or understood that nature here had its own arcane wisdom, a wisdom that wasn't necessarily benign.

We slid and slithered our way down to the beach on the stony footpath; the blackthorn hedge was iced with snow. Quirk gambolled ahead as Eve and I held on to each other with our gloved hands, taking tiny steps so as not to fall.

The waves, a milky turquoise blue, rolled inland, their crests like flocks of white birds, flying low, driven by the wind. Quirk spun round in circles trying to catch his tail, then took off towards Morrow Bay with a sudden burst of energy. I shouted after him as he bounded into the distance but he didn't seem to hear and in a matter of minutes, had disappeared out of sight into the dunes.

We ambled along the sand and Eve linked arms with me, 'We'd better find him,' she said.

'Perhaps he's scented someone he knows, perhaps his owner...'

Eve smiled. 'Admit it - you'd miss him if he ran away.'

'I'm not sure...' I said, amused, aware that she was trying to take advantage.

Eve sounded exasperated, 'Dad always said you had the ability to make something straightforward into something complicated.'

'Did he?' I asked and felt the familiar pang in my chest that troubled me when I learned of yet another way in which I'd failed to satisfy David.

Eve squeezed my arm, 'Sorry,' she said, 'it just popped out. I thought the worst might be over...'

We'd reached the western edge of Whitcroft Cove, where the cliffs had been reinforced with metal baskets of rocks – the new sea defences mentioned by the man who had delivered Silvie's flowers.

Quirk had by now reappeared, but he was far ahead of us. Eve released my arm and ran on, whistling and calling as the dog scampered up and down the beach into the dunes, then back to the water's edge.

I didn't try to catch up with them; my ankle was sore and I didn't want to walk as far as Morrow Bay. Waiting for Eve to return, I tried to estimate the time of high tide, when the sea would rush in, making it dangerous to continue across the beach beneath Marisands.

Eve was skipping backwards towards me, encouraging Quirk to follow her. Unselfconscious as a child dancing on the sand, her cropped fair hair was ruffled by the wind like little feathers - the sleeves of her blue sweater dangled below the cuffs of her coat and fell over her hands.

When she turned to face me, I made frantic beckoning motions with my arms and called to her through my cupped hands to hurry up. Eve sauntered forwards, with Quirk slowing her progress as he crashed about at the edge of the woods.

I yelled, 'Quirk!' at the top of my voice, hoping to be heard above the waves, relieved when he hurled straight up to me, pressing a cold, wet, sandy nose into the palm of my hand.

Eve drew level with me, red-cheeked and breathless. 'I think Quirk's been living in a sort of cave along there, near where the stream comes down to the beach,' she said. 'There's food on the ground and an old blanket, someone must have taken pity on him. I found this...' she handed me a flattish stone with the word "Skipper" painted on it in red.

'Looks like a child's writing,' I said.

'He doesn't answer to Skipper.'

'Nor to Quirk,' I pointed out, as the dog had taken off again, despite my calling to him. 'Let's go back.' I didn't want to linger on the beach any longer, where we all might drown.

We turned back towards Marisands. Ahead of us waves were already breaking at the foot of the pyramid rock, splashing spray high into the air.

'We can't go that way, it's too late' I said.

'It's not far,' Eve told me, grasping my arm. 'Quirk's here now, we can wade through the water.'

Quirk was circling our legs, bowing his head and leaping about as if he wanted to play a game. Eve began to pull me towards the rock through the deepening water, 'Come on,' she said coaxing me.

'We need to get off the beach – *now*. We won't be able to reach the cove - we'll have to cut through the woods...' I said.

I could see Eve didn't believe me, but beyond the rock the entire beach would be under water, a reminder that here on Littern there was a need for sensitivity to the natural rhythms of each day, especially the tides. Quirk's disobedience would cost us a long walk - Osford Lane curved and looped round Holtleigh Hill almost doubling the distance back to the house.

I had never liked the woods on this part of the island, they were dense, dimly lit and to me felt sinister, but I hurried towards an opening in the trees and bushes, relieved Eve had stopped arguing.

'I don't know what I would have done if anything had happened to you, when I was a child,' she said.

She seemed to know intuitively that I had been thinking of Juliet. I'd been remembering how after she'd died, I'd thought either she didn't love me enough to stay alive or that I hadn't loved her enough to keep her alive.

I picked up a stout branch and used it to batter down the brambles that caught at our clothes as we pushed through the undergrowth. Snow tumbled down on us as we walked, but Quirk seemed resilient to any discomfort. Scratched by twigs and tripped by low branches, he flattened himself to the floor of the woods, moving forward with an ungainly crawling movement.

Eve and I trudged on in the semi-darkness without speaking, navigating by keeping the sea directly behind us, until we came to a clearing where someone had built a place for a fire with a ring of stones. A scrap of an orange tee-shirt, damp and mouldy, clung to a low branch on a sycamore tree - like a prayer flag torn from too much flapping in the wind. There were remnants of burnt logs and ashes in the centre of the stone circle and a few empty tins left in a heap under the bracken; someone was living in the woods and had probably set up camp for the winter.

Further on, deep among the trees and bushes, we came across a green van, camouflaged with branches of evergreen and vines of ivy. There was a dim light at the windows, and a spiral of smoke rose from the chimney. I urged Eve to move away in case it was gypsies, the gypsies who used to camp on the common in summer hadn't always been friendly.

The van had made wide tyre tracks on the muddy floor of the wood and I thought we could follow them towards Osford Lane. Before long we had reached a place where the wall that edged the road had tumbled down and the gap had been widened by pulling out stones to allow the van to pass through.

I called to Quirk softly. His appearance was more disreputable than ever, his fur full of scraps of leaves, tiny twigs and burrs.

'I'm glad to be out of there,' I said, stopping to catch my breath.

'They're only New Agers - that van's like Zoë and Cameron's - they all look like that, don't they?'

'If I was going to live in a van all winter, I wouldn't choose Littern.'

'Maybe it isn't as bad as you remember. When you're a child things seem more dramatic than they really are...'

On our way to Marisands, we passed Lyncross, the gatepost still showing the rough repair where Kathleen Piran had gouged a stone out on the day of Juliet's death. A corner of the house was visible through the naked trees, an imposing grey stone building with dark green shutters. In the flowerbeds that lined the curve of the drive were green spears of daffodils poking up above the snow.

'That was the house where your great-great grandfather lived,' I told Eve.

'And where you used to play as a child? I haven't forgotten *The Seabright Island Adventures* – you'll have to confess now - Agnes was really you...'

'You think so?' I asked, teasing her.

The garden of Lyncross was bordered by a laurel hedge. On the grass verge was a stall for selling produce, which I'd seen advertised on the notice-board by the causeway, a wooden construction with an ornately decorated, arched roof that reminded me of a roadside grotto.

Eve uncovered the boxes of vegetables, which were protected from frost by pieces of thick carpet. She sifted through the potatoes, carrots, swede, turnips and sprouts. There were baskets of apples and pears, boxes of eggs, jars of pickles and jams under the table.

'These look good,' she said, 'fresher than the stuff you bought from the market.'

I had no money, but Eve found a five pound note in her jeans pocket. I waited while she filled two bags from the collection of plastic carriers that had been pinned under a brass bell to prevent them blowing away. When she'd finished, she dropped her money into an old coffee tin, with a wide slit cut into the lid.

'You ought to call in – they are your nearest neighbours,' she said.

I shook my head, I'd hoped they might call on me, but I'd had no response to my letter of condolence for Antony's death. 'According to Geraldine, I'm not welcome on the island.'

'Why wouldn't you be?' Eve objected.

'William upset people and I'm his daughter – then there were the circumstances around my mother's death. That would be enough. Geraldine says the Pirans would like to have Marisands.'

'Do you believe everything she says?' Eve asked.

Embarrassed, I admitted that it hadn't occurred to me to doubt her.

# Chapter 20

Eve's cough became persistent, her cheeks flushed and her eyes feverish. The snow hadn't cleared and no one came to grit the roads on the island, but after a week, I was able to drive into Narescombe to West Hill Surgery, where she saw a Dr. Mike Acworth, who advised her to stay indoors, keep warm, rest and drink plenty of fluids.

There was little to distract Eve from following his advice. The temperature fell sharply and remnants of snow froze over until the roads and paths were unsafe. While she was ill, I set up a make-shift bed on the sofa in the sitting room, where she would be warm - for once, she didn't argue or say "don't fuss".

Eve sipped her way through mugs of lemon tea, looking dazed, as if she could hardly keep her eyes open and being unwell made her gloomy.

'I feel terrible,' she complained, tears seeping out from under her eyelids.

I was afraid she might be regretting her offer to stay on the island and was growing anxious to return to Zethar Creek, but her distress ran deeper. As I'd anticipated, the problems with her work hadn't disappeared because she had moved from Pimlico to another place.

'My ideas aren't any better than in London...' Eve said staring into the fire, 'I thought I was doing okay for a while, but then I realised I was just imitating the others and the worse thing is, they're all imitating Luke.'

Quirk jumped onto the sofa and lay against Eve's legs. I didn't stop him. Her quiet weeping and the raffish expression on his face were endearing.

'You would tell me if there was anything I could do..?'

'What could you possibly do?' she said avoiding my gaze, and I sensed that the subject was closed.

For days, Eve continued to sleep in the sitting room. She coughed through the night - I would hear her from my bedroom and go downstairs to stoke up the fire and make her a drink. After a disturbed sleep, we would both lie in late the next morning. When I opened the bedroom curtains the windows would be iced over with frost ferns covering the glass. We had another night of heavy snow and the garden disappeared under a thick white mantle, undisturbed except by bird's footprints and tracks of animal's paws leading in and out of the trees.

I let him out at the front door and Quirk moved noiselessly through the garden. The sound of the sea was muffled, the birds didn't sing. When snow blew down or fell from a tree or bush it landed with a barely discernible thud onto the soft white blanket below. Standing shivering in the porch, I watched a cobweb which had caught a scattering of snowflakes and trembled in the wind as if it too was cold. As Quirk was reluctant to come back, I went inside to make breakfast, leaving the front door ajar so he could push it open with his nose.

Eve convalesced over the next week and I began to sort out the papers that I'd piled up in the dining room. I separated personal letters from business, bills from receipts and organised scraps of paper and notebooks into date order, if it was possible to establish when they'd been written.

The dining room faced north and was one of the coldest rooms in the house. Until Eve had fully recovered, I kept the sitting room fire going day and night and didn't want to deplete my dwindling stock of logs by lighting a fire in another room. So I sat at the dining table, wrapped in my blue wool cloak with the hood pulled up to keep me warm.

I'd made a pile of Alice's diaries – she dissected the daily lives of the Armsted family with her sharp observations. I'd hoped to learn new things about my mother, the small details which would bring her alive, but Alice seemed full of grievances - her most powerful belief was that she had been hard done by - Bernard, she implied, had consistently favoured Silvie and Flora and ignored her most basic needs.

I fixed bundles of correspondence with rubber bands and resisted reading the letters - just scanning a few lines, enough to tell the subject matter and who was writing to whom. My father seemed to have kept all the mail that had ever come into the house. There were carbon copies of his and some of my mother's outgoing correspondence, whether handwritten or typed, and I discovered that the papers I'd brought from Wren House were often the counterpart to those I'd found at Marisands.

Some of the letters dealt only with orders for art supplies and other trivia and I added them to the mounting pile of rubbish I'd accumulated for burning. There was frequent correspondence between my father and Alice, mainly about money for my upkeep, while I was living at Wren House. I became preoccupied labelling the bundles of papers and laying them out chronologically. Alice would have called it busy work, appearing to do a task while actively avoiding it.

When I heard a sound in the hall, I thought Eve must have got up to make a drink and hoped she would bring me one.

I called out, but there was no response. I felt a moment of panic, *was she all right?* I went out into the hall to see what was happening.

'...My God!' I said.

Geraldine Ottley was standing by the kitchen door. She was dressed in an odd assortment of clothes, staring at me – probably looking equally bizarre, wrapped in my long blue cloak, the hood drooping over my face.

'How can I help you?' I asked, pushing the hood back. 'I don't want you or anyone else just walking into my house...'

Geraldine didn't apologise, 'You're not in London now,' she said, 'no one here bothers to lock their doors.'

Quirk sniffed at the hem of Geraldine's coat, where a thick layer of snow clung to it, like a band of white fur.

'I see you found that stray dog, I turned him out on the beach.'

'Wasn't that rather cruel?' I asked.

Geraldine's eyes were hard and seemed to say, she didn't care what I thought.

She didn't ask for the studio key, but showed no sign of leaving, so I made a pot of coffee and we sat together in the cold dining room.

Geraldine lit a cigarette. She barely looked up, let alone spoke to me and I was equally lost for conversation. I glanced towards the window and made a mental note that I must cut back the creeper - the room was doused in a green, subterranean light.

At last I said, 'We found sketches in the studio drawers and a painting on the metal frame, I wondered, were they my mother's?'

Her face showed no flicker of interest.

'My mother's notebook suggested there was to be a series of paintings – *The Stations of the Cross* - there are three in All Soul's Church, but I wondered if you knew where the rest were...'

Geraldine didn't answer. She sipped her cup of scalding coffee, stubbing out her cigarette in the saucer.

'I've found very little of Juliet's work and none of my father's. I've searched the studio and looked in Thrift Cottage...'

Her face wore an expression of profound indifference, 'I have no interest in your mother's work. If Juliet discussed it at all she would have talked to Shirley Fredericks.'

'I understand Shirley's living in Narescombe - I was in Napier Street the other day and saw her gallery. Was she the inspiration behind the sculptures in the oratory garden?'

Geraldine made a dismissive noise, 'The sculptures were entirely Juliet's idea - if you understood your mother you'd recognise that at once.' She lit another cigarette. 'William preferred his women to get along with each other, he asked Shirley to nurture your mother's work, but Juliet was determined to go her own way.'

In a haze of smoke, she drew deeply on her cigarette, she narrowed her eyes as if thinking, but said nothing more.

'I thought the paintings in All Soul's were passionate, spiritual works,' I said.

'Fear isn't passion. Juliet was afraid.'

'Why was she afraid?' Unknowingly, Geraldine had echoed Silvie's words about my mother.

'Use your imagination...' she said.

But sometimes I imagined too much – there were many things which must have oppressed my mother - her baby's death, William's affair with Geraldine and then also with Shirley.

'You may regret digging about in the past.' Geraldine moved her arm in a broad gesture to indicate the bundles of papers on the dining room table and swept several of my neat heaps onto the floor, leaving them strewn across the carpet.

'Surely it isn't unreasonable - wanting to know what happened to my mother...' I said, but I'd miscalculated. Geraldine wasn't going to be subjected to an inquisition and she had no concern for my feelings. 'You must miss my father.'

'I'd lost William long before he died - he changed beyond all recognition.'

She had described my father's suffering at his funeral and at Marisands there were times when I'd had felt his pain was almost tangible, as if it lingered in the rooms. Her regret seemed genuine and her words ignited a spark of sympathy - illness could change the person you loved into a stranger, I knew that from David.

'Don't go into the studio today,' I said, 'it's too cold, go home.'

'Are you planning to work there in the future?'

'I don't know...' I'd been thinking not of myself but of Eve and her struggles, wondering, would it help her to paint in that exceptional, clear light?

Geraldine nodded, as if she'd read my thoughts. As she rose from her chair, Quirk stretched and gazed up at me expectantly.

Outside, the surface of the snow had crisped over with a layer of frost so that with every step it crunched and creaked beneath our feet. Geraldine had leant her bicycle against one of the uprights of the garage. Despite my dislike for her, I was worried by the thought of her riding down the lane in the snow – I'd observed she was rather unsteady on her feet.

'You'll be all right?' I asked.

'Perfectly,' Geraldine replied.

I swung back the gate and she mounted her bike and wobbled down the lane towards the causeway, disappearing among the trees, her black blanket-coat covering her back like a beetle's carapace.

*

Eve was warm and comfortable on the sofa, so I left her resting while I took Quirk for a walk in the lane. If a dog's face could express disappointment, he appeared downcast when we turned west rather than heading down onto the beach as we usually did each morning.

With the new fall of snow, there was little hope of getting the car off the island so I'd thought I'd visit the stall outside Lyncross. Eve had been living on vegetable soups, stews and scrambled eggs and I was running out of fresh food. The pile of logs in the wood store was getting low and I had almost no kindling.

The archway of trees above the road glistened. Clods of snow, caught on the bushes, shimmered white-gold, but the pallid sun had no warmth and when the branches of the trees parted, they revealed a sky filled with heavy clouds.

Quirk soon settled down and was content sniffing round the snow-covered verges and banks. His gait was loose and easy and with his black hair flowing he achieved a kind of grace.

As we approached the gates of Lyncross, I could see a man there, bent over the vegetable stall, stuffing a tartan kit bag with produce, working at speed. He wore a thick, hooded parka in a fusty green colour and heavy black gloves. The hood of his parka had fallen across his face, but he must have heard my footsteps crunching in the snow. When he spotted me coming up the lane, he grabbed another bag, filled it as fast as he could and before I could speak, vaulted over the wall and vanished into the woods.

There was no sign of anyone at the house - no-one else had seen what had happened. Pinned to one of the wooden uprights of the stall was a note to say to ring the hand bell if help was needed. I considered whether help was needed, but decided not to tell tales on the young man who had run off without paying - we had something in common - I too would prefer to leave Lyncross, without encountering any of the occupants.

There wasn't much left on the stall – two dozen eggs, a few potatoes, leeks, onions, a cabbage and a bundle of carrots, showing signs of their age. Beneath the table were boxes of kindling, buckets of flowers – holly, ivy and Christmas roses - some with their petals fallen onto the snow.

I began to load the best of what was left into carrier bags. Then just as I was putting the eggs on top of one of the bags, a green Land Rover, with snow chains on its tyres, appeared along the lane from the direction of The Retreat. It swerved into the drive, taking the corner sharply and scraping the side of the gatepost.

Hearing the grating sound, Quirk twisted back in fright, knocking the table, so that boxes of eggs and a large jar of pickled onions fell hitting the stones which marked the edge of the verge. They smashed making a mess of the flower buckets, the kindling and splattering my legs and feet. Quirk cowered and tried to lick the mess away, but I jerked him back from the area where there was broken glass lying on the ground.

A woman emerged from the car, striding down the drive towards me. She wore navy wool slacks that were stretched at the knees and a black body warmer, underneath she had on a plain navy fisherman's sweater and her hair was cut in a short, masculine style.

She looked over the wrecked stall without expression, her dark eyes inscrutable, 'What happened? Has that delinquent been here stealing things?' It was obvious the stall had been ransacked - the money tin had fallen into the snow and lost its lid revealing its empty interior.

We spoke across each other. I said, 'I'll need to pay you for the eggs and pickled onions…'

'Did you see that young man?' The woman's question came out as a short angry bark and Quirk barked back.

I opened my purse and took out a twenty pound note and stuffed it into the tin, 'I hope that will cover everything, including what was taken by him.'

'You do realise who I am?' the woman said brusquely, 'Beatrix Piran.'

The woman in front of me bore little resemblance to the girl I'd last seen when I was seven years old – but she clearly had no doubts about my identity.

'Time has inevitably taken its toll,' she said sharply.

And after so many years it could hardly have done otherwise. Her hair once a rich peat brown was now completely grey - her oval face and lithe figure had blurred with middle age - she must have seen similar changes in me.

'We were very young when we last met...' I said, my words tailing off.

Bitterness had risen in my throat as I remembered her accusation, "Iris walked into the sea where she knew she shouldn't go..." and the unspoken corollary that I had caused Juliet's death and Antony's accident – the sting of her reproach had never faded, and never would.

I stared down at the broken eggs, the onions and vinegar staining the snow.

'I'll see to this,' she said. 'But don't encourage that hoodlum to steal my stuff,' her peremptory tone of voice was the same she had used as a child, when she'd ordered me or her brothers not to call her Trixie.

I gathered my bags and wrapped the loop of Quirk's lead round my wrist, then started to walk down the lane towards Marisands, heavily laden, tugging on Quirk's collar to make him hurry, trying not to slip over.

I'd only gone a few yards when I heard Beatrix shouting, 'I'll fetch the car and take you and the dog home. Wait there - I hit that bloody gatepost every time I take the bend.'

I waited on the grass verge while Beatrix reversed onto the road. She gave the impression she was acting less out of kindness than exasperation at my incompetence. She parked in front of me and then loaded the boot with my shopping, including a dozen more eggs from the stack of trays she had in the car. She threw an old rug on the back seat of the car and Quirk jumped in and lay down.

As we set off down the hill, she said, 'Perhaps I should consider a delivery service, passing trade isn't brisk, especially in winter, though a few people from Osford and Narescombe come here specially to buy from me.'

I was having difficulty encompassing the idea of Beatrix Piran as a market gardener - but could hardly say so. I was grateful for the lift, though her manner was cold like a cube of ice slithering down my spine - she had resorted to the form of courtesy I'd seen practiced by the Pirans before - the more they disliked you, the more they were meticulously polite.

'Your father must be getting on..?' I said in a desperate attempt to make conversation.

'He's ancient - I retired last year to take care of him.'

I began to gabble, 'My mother appreciated the support of your family – we both did - it provided us with stability...' I was hoping to make peace.

'My family is no more stable than anyone else's,' Beatrix replied irritably, 'and since Antony died we've been falling apart at the seams. I think you should know how much your letter upset my father.

'I'm sorry,' I said, 'I hoped I was doing the right thing...'

'Well, I can assure you, you weren't'.'

The journey from Lyncross to Marisands took less than five minutes. Beatrix turned into the drive by the oak tree and pulled up in front of the garage where William's car stood, with its covering of leaves, algae and bird droppings. I released Quirk from the back seat and he bounded up to the front door. Beatrix opened the boot, picked up the bags of eggs, vegetables and kindling and dumped them in the porch.

As Quirk wandered back and forth whining, she asked, 'Mongrel? He could have a touch of Schnauzer in him.'

I didn't know what breed he was - if any - and told her the story of finding him tied to my father's car.

'That's nothing to do with me,' she said.

There was an awkward silence and then she turned round to survey the garden. 'Do you know anything about gardening?' She eyed me up and down in an appraisal that obviously found me wanting.

'A little,' I said.

'Then you'll realise, sometimes you can't bring a garden back - things go too far...'

'Someone had kept up the vegetable patch...' I said.

Beatrix betrayed herself only with the slightest flicker of acknowledgement, 'The vegetable stall was the one thing in my life that caused no trouble, until the arrival of that young man, who's rapidly become a thorn in my flesh.'

'And is hungry and broke?' I suggested.

'I see you've absorbed your family's feeble-minded, liberal philosophy...' she said. Then slammed the car door and revved the engine hard as she took off through the gate.

Beatrix's company had been uneasy. Marisands could be oppressive. The clocks in the house ticked out time at a measured pace that reminded me of Wren House and by association with old age and death.

When I looked in on her, Eve was sleeping, so I called Quirk out into the garden, where he jumped through the deep snow in fluid arcs, like a porpoise moving through water. I stamped a pathway through the pergola to the oratory garden, where the pitted surface of the statues glistened through their covering of snow laden weeds and some of their heads and limbs shone like misshapen moons as pale rays of sunlight were reflected from exposed patches of white stone.

*Figures without identity* – Eve had said – there were many experiences which could leave you feeling hollowed out. I wondered if for Beatrix Piran taking care of her father gave meaning to her life. I wondered about Verena, who since she had gone to Geneva to nurse her father had been strangely silent.

There was a wooden bench beneath a honeysuckle bush which scrambled over the hedge behind it. I pushed the tangled vines out of the way and swept the snow off the bench with my sleeve before settling on the seat.

Closing my eyes I considered how, if I was to remain living on the island, I might weave the threads of a life that would make me happy, not bitter and disappointed, as Beatrix seemed to be. *Were my dreams impractical..? ...Or too prosaic to inspire faith and vision..?* I'd sought peace of mind after the hurt of losing David, to regain my daughters' trust, to find a place where I could feel safe and at home.

I leant down to fuss Quirk's head. As I touched him he swished his tail and made a wide arc in the snow. His brown eyes were as innocent and trusting as a child's as they gazed into mine.

Coming to the island, with its legends of healing and pilgrimage, I had perhaps expected too much - a magic cure instead of months of hard work, work which might in the end prove fruitless. Beatrix had expressed my own doubts about Marisands – *had it gone too far?*

It would be difficult to admit that to Silvie – who believed that not only the house and garden but our family life could be redeemed. But I wasn't sure if I could survive the climate of hostility between me and Geraldine, between me and the Pirans. Like the wind and waves wearing Littern's rocks into tiny grains of sand, might it not end in my own disintegration?

*

The snow thawed, slowly at first, but then as a mild wind blew in from the west, it disappeared in a few hours leaving puddles the size of small ponds on the lawns. Water ran off the hills in rivulets and filled the ditches to overflowing.

Rain whipped against the windows, wind whistled down the chimneys and through cracks, where the doors and windows didn't close properly. Every now and then, the lights in the house flashed on and off. As a storm gathered, the atmosphere became electric.

Eve had offered to help me sort papers in the dining room, but I was feeling restless.

'We could go to Narescombe. Would you like to come?'

'You want to go out in this?' she glanced up from the sheaf of letters she was sorting to the rain spattered window and the sodden grey world outside. Her fair hair and red sweater were the only points of colour in the watery light of the dining room.

'I'd like you to see Juliet's paintings...' I said - unsure how much longer Eve might stay at Marisands.

She pulled a face in reply, 'I've spent hours organising these.' She had been patiently matching letters and their responses, trying to build a story.

'But you don't have to...' I wished I had the courage to throw the papers away.

'Why not take Quirk out for a few minutes, before the weather becomes impossible?' Eve said. She spoke to me as if I was a child who'd grown fractious having stayed indoors too long.

Taking Quirk, I walked down to the shore. The wind hurled the waves at the beach as we made our way along a strip of sand only a few feet wide. In minutes, I was soaked both from the rain and the drenching I received each time a large wave crashed down on the edge of the beach.

I stood at the foot of the oratory steps, while Quirk scampered about where he could find solid ground. The steps looked lethal - running with water, which carried down mud, scraps of leaves, sticks and stones to be washed away by the sea.

'That's enough for today,' I called and Quirk pottered up to me as if he'd understood.

He hauled himself up a few steps towards the oratory, giving soft low barks. I called him back at once, but as he scampered towards me, saw out of the corner of my eye a flash of rich blue against the dark wood of the oratory door - surely no-one was up there on such a wild day?

I cupped my hands and shouted up the cliff side, 'Who's there?' But the wind carried my voice away with the cry of the gulls, far out to sea.

With a gale blowing, the steps were unsafe even for Quirk, so I clipped his lead to his collar and hurried back to the footpath with him bounding along beside me.

When we drew level with the gate of Thrift Cottage, I decided to call from the top of the oratory steps to see if anyone was there. I was concerned for their safety, but also worried in case someone was prowling about again, trespassing on the property.

Out on the cliff top above the oratory steps, I hung onto the gatepost to steady myself and shouted uselessly against the swirling wind. I couldn't hear or see any sign of a person. Quirk pulled at his lead wanting me to go back to the house – and as the oratory was intended for the use of islanders and pilgrims, I resolved if he wasn't worried, neither should I be. My intruder might be the person living in the woods, though I couldn't think why they'd prefer a rough stone hut to the warmth of their van. It might be a tramp taking refuge from the weather or perhaps nothing more than a figment of my imagination.

Eve and I sat in the dining room for an hour or two more reading the family's correspondence. In recording details of domestic repairs, my father had been precise down to the last screw and washer, though his bills were rarely, if ever, paid on time.

I spread the letters Eve had matched into pairs in front of me. Reading them, it became clear the Armsted family hadn't been entirely straightforward over the matter of William's marriage to my mother. The inducement of Marisands was to be no more than a chimera. At the time Juliet had taken me to Wren House to visit Bernard, he had insisted she make a new will, so that in the event of her death occurring before her husband's, the property would return to the Armsteds – in this instance, Silvie and Flora. The implication was that the change had been made without William knowing.

The allowance which had been given to William by Bernard had been stopped by Alice on Juliet's death and it must have been the threat of a dwindling income, rather than grief for my mother, which had made William consider seeking work at the college in Safford Bridge, at the time of her drowning.

Arguments passed to and fro as William made it clear he believed he had been duped into a loveless marriage. Eve spread out further bundles of letters – letters between Flora and William in which he begged to be allowed to stay at Marisands, to be free to continue his work. His words resonated with a cry from the heart - a cry of anger and pain, *Do I have to pay for my mistake forever..?*

Then the bargaining began. William could remain at Marisands as a tenant, but there were conditions. He was to maintain the place and would be required to give me up permanently into the care of Flora. Though the property wasn't hers, Alice acted as Flora's spokeswoman, and laid out her requirements in fine detail: I would see my father once a year in London, but I was to have no further contact, nor to keep in touch with anyone else on Littern. In a brief note, my father had replied agreeing to the proposals, without raising a single objection to the thought of relinquishing his daughter.

The truth of what had gone on shouldn't have surprised or appalled me. Alice was manipulative. When I thought of William, what came to mind was coldness, anger, selfishness - his callousness towards me as child confirmed that - but behind his indifference, there seemed to be something else. I had believed my family acted on principle but the letters showed them to be devious – relentless in the pursuit of their own aims. My father, who I had observed as shocked by Juliet's death, had written of a "loveless marriage". *Did he mean that Juliet had never loved him, or only that he had never loved her?* It seemed I might need to reinterpret what had happened - adopt a new perspective - in which William appeared as the victim of my family's scheming rather than the victimiser.

'Are you okay?' Eve asked, I'd been lost in thought and hadn't spoken for several minutes.

'I'm fine.' I retied the letters into bundles, hoping Eve hadn't grasped their significance.

While we worked, she had been listening to the radio. 'Did you hear?' she said, 'The weather forecast is terrible, more rain...'

I hadn't been paying attention and said, 'It doesn't matter - you can stay here as long as you want to...'

Then, preoccupied with my discoveries, I spoke without thinking, listing my concerns about her living in Zethar Creek - the mud, the damp, the loneliness, her weak chest, her lack of money - adding her recent illness as a reason why she might consider moving elsewhere – to Marisands, for instance - where she could make use of the studio...

'For God's sake...' Eve said stopping me. 'Zoë told me you'd try to gather us all back under your wing – but that's not going to happen. Perhaps *you're* the one who should think of moving elsewhere - you scurry round the island like a scared little mouse. What are you afraid of?'

Eve was the mildest of my children - an outburst from her was rare. A truthful answer to her question would have been that I was afraid of almost every aspect of my new and unfamiliar life. Especially now, as I was beginning to suspect that much I had believed about my past was going to be undermined by staying on Littern -

Since coming to the island, every person, everything that happened or was said, left a deep and often painful impression. Beatrix's coldness and Geraldine's intransigence about Juliet hurt me. Juliet's incomprehensible statues appeared as ephemeral and amorphous as the drifts of snow that had covered the garden and then disappeared. Some were as delicate as tissue dissolving in water - others solid enough to be stone babies, figures for a child's grave - and however hard I tried, I came no closer to comprehending what they might mean -

Before the white statues, before the paintings of *The Stations of the Cross*, my mother's work had been as tender and full of sympathy as Flora's or Yvette's. I couldn't yet tell what - but something had changed her - and unless I could summon the courage to find out the true circumstances of her death, the cause of that change might never be revealed.

*

The next day, Eve rang Matthew at The Angel in Zethar Creek to be told the river had flooded again. He'd tried to rescue her work, but her ground-floor workshop had been left in a filthy, stinking state and as everyone was busy clearing up their own place, he advised she would need to go back and clean it herself.

I wasn't convinced Eve had told me the whole story, but we agreed it was right she should leave and I gave her money for the train fare. I felt responsible, I'd encouraged her to stay on at Marisands and though she tried to hide it, I knew Eve blamed me too. Since our quarrel and her "little mouse" remark, we'd been reserved with each other and she could no longer contain her anxiety to return to Zethar Creek.

We set off for Safford Bridge the next afternoon, as soon as the tide was out. It would be dark when she reached Zethar Creek but Luke Porter had promised to meet her and drive her to the village.

As her train pulled away, Eve said, 'Take care...' but she sounded wearied by her situation and perhaps by a sense of duty towards me.

I stood on the platform and waved until I could no longer see her leaning out of the window, her fair hair shining in the low sunlight. I'd offered her the warm coat she'd borrowed during her stay at Marisands, but she'd insisted she would be all right, and had refused to accept money, above the cost of her fare. As Minette's stoicism had done when I'd left her in London, Eve's independence and bravado made me want to weep.

While in Safford Bridge, I thought I would walk to the Priory. I hadn't yet visited my mother's grave - it was one of many things over which I had been procrastinating. Outside The Pilgrim's Inn was a street vendor selling fresh flowers from a cart. I bought a bouquet of irises, early narcissi and evergreens and he gave me a few extra flowers because I'd caught him just before the close of day.

The Priory dominated the centre of town. Flanked by the girls' and boys' schools, it had a robust presence suggesting austerity, discipline and strength. I peered over the bridge to the riverbank. With the snow gone, the town's display of yellow and white crocuses was carpeting the banks down to the water, their colours reflected in a broken image, as a pair of swans glided by.

At the entrance to the church, beggars gathered, holding out their hands to passersby. I hurried past and as a policeman approached, the area cleared as swiftly as if a sudden gust of wind had swept them all away.

255

A cobbled lane led through an archway in the wall which surrounded the Priory. The graveyard was a maze of paths leading first to more imposing tombs, and then to humbler memorials tucked away behind the church building. I made my way to the north corner, where my mother had been buried - William had taken me there in the last weeks, before I had been exiled from Littern.

The stone marking my mother's grave was stark and simple, inscribed only with her name and the dates of her birth and death – *was it too late to have some loving words added?* At the foot of the grave, lay a small bunch of winter pansies, tied together with a long blade of grass. I picked them up but there was no message - the message must be in the posy itself though I couldn't interpret it.

I set down my flowers near the headstone. Darkness was encroaching, seeping across the sky. One day, when I returned in daylight, I would clean the stone and tidy the grass, meanwhile, the dismal state of the graveyard fitted my mood.

With the light almost gone, I slipped into the church for a few moments. Inside the door, a board informed me that Evensong was in progress and the choir were singing an anthem to a handful of people gathered in the chancel, their faces bathed in candlelight.

Not wanting to make a sound, I crept along the side aisle and chose one of the small chapels, where I knelt in a back pew with my head in my hands. Eve had gone - we had quarrelled - and I wasn't sure how I could outlast the loneliness and isolation of Marisands without her.

Anxious, like the little mouse she had described, I couldn't see how I might fit into life on Littern. My life in London now appeared, in contrast, to have been well-defined by work, family and friends, while at Marisands, my days were shapeless. I had failed to uncover the wealth of treasures Alice had anticipated or to do as Silvie had asked and restore the house. The weather had been so atrocious, work on the garden was impossible -

When the choir and congregation began to sing the final hymn I left. The grounds of the Priory were floodlit as night fell. In the shadows cast by the strong beam of light that illuminated the west face of the building, a cluster of street people loitered by the wall.

A man asked for money. He was dressed in a long belted raincoat, once smart, as if it had belonged to a business man, but now incongruous with his knitted balaclava and striped sports trousers. In London, I wouldn't have stopped or opened my bag for fear of being mugged, but I took out my purse and handed him a fistful of loose change.

Squatting on a black bin bag by the school railings was the emaciated figure of a woman, playing a flute. Her music case, lined in gold crushed velvet, lay open in front of her and a black hat was upturned on the pavement, ready to collect money.

The woman stood up. Thin and reed-like, she reminded me of the slender figurines of Krishna I'd seen for sale in New Age shops. I smelt the stench of stale alcohol and unwashed body. She was playing music that was vaguely familiar – Bach perhaps – the soaring notes drifted towards me along the path.

Drawing closer, I saw it was the woman I'd encountered in Narescombe by the pub. As I passed her, I felt her eyes on my back. Turning to take another look, I was certain I'd found Kelda Sullivan. Beneath her bird's nest of hennaed hair, Kelda's eyes were scrutinising me, eyes that were full of questions. *Would I stop or speak to her?*

In the harsh streetlight, her expression seemed one of devilish humour and I couldn't tell if it was born of the sense of fun she'd had as a girl or whether some other demon had since taken hold of her.

'Kelda..? ' I said, 'It's Iris Armsted – Iris Muys.'

Her lips formed a lopsided smile and my heart contracted. She stank of booze and sweat, but beneath her unkempt hair and raddled face was the girl I had known at school and while she played her flute with such competence and grace, the integrity of her mind and faculties was clearly intact.

'Think what would have become of you, if you'd stayed around me,' she said, her voice heavy with sarcasm.

She began undoing her flute and placing the separate parts in the case.

'Can I buy you a drink, something to eat?' I asked, though scanning the town square - the haunt of middle-class respectability – I knew Kelda wouldn't be welcome anywhere in that part of Safford Bridge.

'Do you know somewhere we could go?' I asked - a note of desperation creeping into my voice – I was floundering. I wanted to talk to her but couldn't think what to say.

She shrugged - a dismissive gesture. 'I watched you in Narescombe,' she said, 'I've watched you today, you were at the station, and then you came here. When you live on the streets you're invisible, but you can observe, make judgements...'

'You followed me..?' I asked, disconcerted.

She shrugged again. 'Forget it. I'll see you around.'

'Do you ever go to the island..?'

'No thanks - maybe in another lifetime.'

'I met Delia...' I told her.

'Fucking do-gooder,' Kelda said under her breath and spat on the ground.

She rocked slightly on her feet, scowling as I reached out to steady her.

Kelda wouldn't speak again or look at me and eventually she staggered off, clutching at the railings for support. She'd put the black hat on her head, the weight of her back-pack made her stoop. Her sleeping bag was rolled up in the bin liner she'd been sitting on, her flute case packed under her arm. I walked behind, keeping my distance, afraid of eliciting a torrent of abuse.

Kelda shouted, 'I was always trouble, wasn't I?'

In the half-light, the effect was of a disembodied voice and before I reached the car, she'd vanished into the hinterland of town.

Driving back to Littern, I couldn't get the image of Kelda out of my mind. Her complexion coarsened by living outside, by drinking, and whatever else she used to blunt the pain of life. Her expression had been at once waif-like and hard and our meeting felt as confusing and enigmatic as she was.

I thought if she had come to Littern as I had suggested - had a bath, a hot meal and a bed for the night - what then? *Who had I intended to help - Kelda or myself?*

# Chapter 21

I sheltered in the porch - moonlight cast eerie shadows in the garden - the trees shivered against the sky-line at the rim of the woods. The night sky was clear and I could count the stars, trace constellations - I could see the bushes swaying as some small animal or bird moved about in the woods nearby, an owl's hooting shuddered out from among the trees.

Quirk had heard me return and was whining, but I felt reluctant to go inside where my loneliness would only deepen as I shut the curtains and closed myself in for the evening. Flora had implied that the house might ease my isolation, but Marisands seemed to belong to another soul or mind, which imposed the existing pattern so strongly, I felt if I failed to comply, in some palpable way it might exact its revenge.

When I couldn't bear the sounds of Quirk's pleading anymore, I let him out of the conservatory. In the moonlight, his glossy black coat shone like silver, the waving tip of his tail sent sprays of raindrops up into the air as he sniffed his way across the damp grass.

He disappeared through the pergola - he had found something interesting, rootling about in the shrubs near Thrift Cottage. Fed up, I retreated indoors and put a pan of soup on the kitchen stove, too tired to prepare a proper meal. When I'd arrived at the house, I'd found a letter on the doormat, the envelope addressed in such tremulous handwriting, I thought it must be from Flora or Silvie, until I noticed it had been delivered by hand.

The letter was signed *Edgar Piran* and contained a response to my words of condolence - "don't concern yourself with what is no longer your business - your concern should be for the future of the island."

A whole paragraph was devoted to criticism of the neglected state of Marisands and Thrift Cottage. Then came what appeared to be the main purpose of the letter, to remind me of the considerable amount of money owed towards the upkeep of the island's road by William and the fact that Edgar was considering pursuing the matter of his debts through the courts.

This I imagined was the kind of missive Alice had consigned to the fire at Wren House. The Pirans were campaigning for repair of the causeway. In the longer term, they wanted a single-lane stone bridge, in keeping with the landscape of the island, allowing for an extended time period during which Littern could be accessed each day.

A closing directive informed me that in future, any correspondence should be addressed not to Lyncross, but to Nicholas Piran at The Retreat. And the harshness of Edgar's words struck a blow to the tender part of me, which hadn't let go of my childhood affection for his family. No wonder Alice and Flora had been upset - like them I felt under attack – I had no money to spare for repairs to the road. My savings and what I hoped to earn from Laurence's books would only cover our needs for the year, if I lived frugally.

I pushed the letter back in its envelope. Perhaps I wouldn't bother to reply, perhaps I'd throw the letter on the fire and try to forget about it or ask Alice to make contact with our family solicitor. Absorbed by my bad mood, I'd forgotten Quirk. I switched off the heat under the soup and stood in the porch calling him, waiting and listening. I kept shouting his name and rattling his food bowl - reluctant to venture into the garden – what if someone was lurking out there in the dark?

When he hadn't returned after my evening meal, I shut the front door, leaving the porch light on and went upstairs and flicked on the computer. I checked e-mails hoping for news from Zoë, glancing out of the study window every few minutes in case Quirk's black figure appeared on the drive.

Zoë had mailed to ask why I hadn't written for days. I tapped out a quick answer, describing Eve's visit. Then I started a letter to Silvie about Juliet and William's marriage, but grew more and more anxious about Quirk as I wrote, missing his presence, his disconsolate form pressed flat to the study floor, his eyes following my every move, his closeness allowing me to stretch out my hand to fondle his head and ears.

I couldn't concentrate and went downstairs, pulled on my coat, scarf and gloves, found the torch and went out into the night. I shouted Quirk's name again and again, explored every corner of the garden, called for him from the top of the oratory steps and from the footpath that led down to the beach. When he didn't come, I walked along Osford Lane as far as the causeway, but Quirk had vanished and my fear was that I might never see him again.

Unable to settle, I drove the length of the lane to the marshes. As I crept along slowly in the car, I stopped every now and then to yell Quirk's name into the woods. Sometimes there was a rustling in the undergrowth that seemed to be a response to my shouts, but in the end, he hadn't appeared.

Parking by The Retreat, I walked a short distance along the path that led towards the marshes. A signboard had been put up to say parts of the area had become a nature reserve and beyond the tower, dogs should be kept on the leash. I could make out the jagged outline of the tower, as it reared up into the sky. I went a few yards along the track at the foot of Hagdon Hills, yelled for Quirk and then looped back, clambering down over the dunes onto the beach.

As I wandered towards the water's edge, I could just see the shape of the black rocks against a dark sky. The Piran's boat, *The Silver Arrow,* was moored to the quay by a long rope and bobbed up and down on the choppy waves. As moonlight flashed through the clouds, I thought I saw a figure diving from the rocks, the cold light tracing the arc of their body. I heard the splash of water - voices shouting in the background – my heart began to race – it was as if the contents of my memory had spilled out to become reality. Upset, disconcerted, I hurried back towards the lane shouting impatiently for Quirk - if he didn't turn up I would ask round the island the next day.

All night, I lay awake worrying, wondering when I had grown to love Quirk so much - to rely on his unquestioning loyalty and affection. While I wasn't paying attention, he had wormed his way into my heart.

When I rose the next morning, I opened the curtains to sunshine filtering through mist, creating a nimbus of light so that the trees and hedges glowed with a gauzy, golden yellow – it was the first intimation of spring - but the fact that Quirk wasn't – as I'd hoped - waiting in the porch dampened my mood.

I searched the garden, opening the studio and Thrift Cottage in case he'd somehow managed to get trapped inside. When I didn't find him there, I unlocked the outhouses, including my mother's workshop. I looked in my father's car, before retracing my steps of the night before and calling for him from the oratory steps and the footpath to the beach. He was nowhere and there were no clues to indicate what might have distracted him or enticed him away.

Beginning to lose hope, I thought I should check as far as Osford – *was it possible Quirk could have swum the causeway?* At the gully, light poured through a gap in the clouds making a path of gold across the sea, fractured by waves into dazzling streaks, as if it had been painted by an unsteady hand. The breaking wavelets cast a shiny net of foam across the sand and the shadows of birds wading in the pools of water were clear and sharp edged – if Quirk had been there in the bright sunlight, I knew I would have seen him at once.

Still, I kept shouting. Quirk liked to play deaf, sticking his nose into a clump of seaweed or undergrowth so he could pretend he hadn't heard.

'Come on!' I called.

Disobedience was part of his nature, I had a bag in my pocket, full of cubes of cheese and as I walked back towards Marisands, I waved his favourite treat in the air, hoping his keen nose would catch the scent and it would bring him scampering out of the trees. I continued beyond the oak tree, walking a short way up Holtleigh Hill, before finally giving up and returning to the house.

The hedge around Marisands had become overgrown so that I struggled to open the gate to get the car out. When I took the footpath down to the beach, thorns caught in my hair and clothes. I reasoned if I worked outside, Quirk might hear me and make his way back. I fetched an empty sack from the wood store to hold hedge clippings and retrieved a pair of rusty secateurs from the porch. I freed the blades and began to chop at the overgrowth near the gateposts. The secateurs were blunt and the hedge tough - thorns tore at my hands, making them a mess of bleeding scratches, but the entrance to Marisands began to take on an air of respectability - in spring, the simple white flowers of the blackthorn against its dark stems would be poignant and lovely.

I tidied the tools away, polished the brass plate, then set out for Lyncross, though Edgar's letter, full of recriminations, left me in no doubt that my enquiries about Quirk wouldn't be welcomed.

Along the lane, holly bushes glistened in the sunshine. Hellebores, which had hung their heads in the rain, straightened up and held their white and purple chalices high, as if to catch every drop of light.

As Lyncross came into view, I thought of Bernard returning to the island and restoring the farmhouse, which stood like a stronghold on its land. Kathleen's garden, simple and elegant, had softened its fortress-like appearance and now the lawns were sprinkled with purple, white and yellow crocus and the spears of daffodils that lined the drive needed only a few more days' warmth to bring the buds into flower.

The front door of Lyncross was of studded oak - I lifted the black iron knocker and rapped three times. The dogs growled and rumbled in the hall and I stood well back in case they came dashing out. I was about to knock again when the door flew open and I was confronted by Beatrix. She was wiping her floury hands on her apron and from the expression on her face it was obvious I had disturbed her at the wrong moment.

I said, 'I've lost my dog - I wondered if you'd seen him, I've searched everywhere, all over the island.'

'There are only three dogs here and they're all ours.' she told me. 'Why don't you ask that delinquent in the woods – he's probably *stolen* your dog.'

'He lives in the van?'

Beatrix didn't hesitate to make a point, 'Where else would he live?'
I blushed at my own stupidity.

'You received Pa's letter?' she asked before I could leave.

'Yes...' I said and a further wave of heat flowed up my neck and face.

Beatrix had kept her keen edge and the tirade which followed was relentless, 'My father's fought a long, hard campaign against anything that threatens to disrupt our way of life - from the building of a modern road bridge, to the idea of setting up a tourist centre by the nature reserve.

'Despite his age, he hasn't lost his determination or his vigour, and even you must have noticed we can barely get on and off the island because of the tides. If things go on as they are, Littern will be uninhabitable and the properties on it worthless.

'What we want is a *suitable* bridge and to have the changes in the coastline looked at by an expert. We don't want every Tom, Dick and Harry discovering what we have here - but we do need to be able to live our lives...'

She paused, at last, 'I'll give it some thought,' I said. Before committing to one cause or another, I'd wanted to consider the facts, find out more information.

Beatrix rolled her eyes heavenward, 'Take my advice - don't spend too much time thinking. Thrift Cottage or the oratory might be the first to crash into the sea. What's needed now is action.'

I bought a bag of vegetables from the stall – thinking it would act as a sign of goodwill when I knocked on the door of the van in the woods. The day I'd caught him pilfering, I hadn't seen the face of Beatrix's delinquent, but her insistence he was disreputable did nothing to encourage me to believe he would be pleased to receive a casual visit from a stranger.

Entering through the place in the lane where the wall was broken, I followed the deep tyre tracks into the woods, until I reached the encampment. The van appeared shut up - there was no light at the windows or smoke from the chimney and no sounds of human habitation. Wandering round the clearing, I shouted Quirk's name, but there was no answer except for birds fluttering through the branches.

A wooden crate acted as a step to the van door. I banged with my knuckles against the blank window, covered inside by a piece of tie-dyed fabric. When no-one came, I knocked once or twice more. Then taking a scrap of paper from my pocket, I scribbled a note asking about Quirk. When I'd finished, I left the note inside the bag of vegetables, wedged between a bunch of earthy carrots and a cabbage, where I hoped it wouldn't be blown away by the breeze

*

An e-mail from Neil warned me to expect another package of papers from Laurence Langlais. He was ready to begin serious work on the *Minor Lights* series and had mentioned to Neil that, in his opinion, I'd been extremely slow translating his last collection of notes.

There were so many things that needed my attention. A few days of fine weather had inspired me to try weeding the garden, though the earth was cold, damp and heavy – too heavy for me to dig - and the weeds broke off at the neck, remaining free to continue their damage underground.

Quirk's absence lay heavily on my heart and I walked in our favourite places and called for him each day. One morning, after another fruitless search of Whitcroft Cove, I resolved to let him go, I needed to get on with my life. Sitting on the bench in the oratory garden, I began to sketch a plan of how I might restore it to conform to my mother's painting.

My mind acted like a faulty receiver, ideas of reshaping and replanting coming through in intermittent bursts. But the whisper of the pen moving across paper distracted me from the loneliness of being without Eve and missing Quirk and offered relief from the intensity of sorting and translating Laurence's endless and almost unintelligible notes.

A week or so later, there was a knock at the front door. *Please don't let it be Geraldine or Beatrix Piran,* I murmured as I went to see who was there. On the doorstep stood a young man with a wan face and long hair, dark as blackbird's wing. I recognised his dull green parka - this was the raider of the Piran's vegetable stall. Quirk rushed round excitedly on the drive, then launched at me, a missile of black fur, barking and beating against my legs with his tail. Crouching down, I circled his neck with my arms and gave him a hug.

'I received your note,' the man said, 'and the vegetables, which are more than I shall need – I give them to the soup kitchen in Safford Bridge.'

I stood up, had he been stealing vegetables from Beatrix, not for himself, but for the soup kitchen? Was he some sort of twentieth century Robin Hood?

He'd parked his bicycle near the house and behind it was attached a small trailer. 'My name is Kostyantyn Zelinski, people call me Kos,' he informed me and handed me two carrier bags. 'I have good things for you.'

Inside were eggs, leeks and squash, much more than I'd left on his doorstep. I lifted the bags onto the bench in the porch.

'You must let me know how much I owe you...' I said.

Kos shook his head. 'Those are a gift, all paid for, completely above the board.'

His voice was light, not unpleasing; a subtle Slavic accent underlay his words like a gentle drone, but Kos's English was competent – slightly cracked perhaps - but not broken.

'Where did you find Quirk? Thank you for bringing him back.'

'He found me in the woods and followed me to the van. I was the person who tied him to your car...'

It was a relief to have one mystery solved and I thought possibly it had been Kostyantyn Zelinski I'd seen near the oratory during Eve's stay.

'I'm looking for work,' he said.

Inside the trailer was a collection of garden tools.

'Is that why you came here?'

'The woman at Lyncross said I should do something useful - find someone who needs help. Everyone on the island knows you have this mess...' he indicated the garden with his hand, 'and I have everything, these tools belonged to my father.'

I didn't want to be press-ganged into offering work to a complete stranger. He had appeared like a genie from nowhere and genies could turn out to be less benign than they at first appeared.

'How long have you lived on the island?'

'Last summer I worked on Yew Tree Farm, they have fields on the far side of Littern. I did Christmas work in the town, also I help with building at The Retreat, but that is off and then on, not enough to make a living...'

There was something about his open manner that made me hope he was honest.

'Tell me what you charge,' I said, playing for time.

'Not money.'

I felt uneasy again, '*Not* money?'

'I would like to play your piano, please, and sometimes have something to eat.'

Kos smiled and there seemed little point in asking *how* he knew I had a piano, probably the whole island knew my most intimate business – we were a small community and information spread by osmosis.

265

Kos had deep brown eyes - he fixed them on me, 'Everyone knows this piano is excellent. I have to confess,' he said, the smile fading from his face, 'I broke in through your glass lean-to, I was curious, the house was empty...'

'Did you also break into the cottage?' I asked.

'Perhaps - I am sorry. Shall I begin work now?'

Though he was disarming and there was plenty of work he could do, I was unsure. Quirk seemed to like Kos, but I wasn't convinced he was the most reliable judge of character.

'Do you go into the oratory ever?'

Kos looked confused.

'The stone hut on the steep steps from the beach,' I explained.

Kos said, 'That isn't me.'

'You know how to grow vegetables and fruit?' I asked, remembering my original intentions to live frugally at Marisands.

'I know such things as are necessary,' he said, 'you'll see...'

I was still uncertain, but decided to give him a chance, find out if he could succeed with the weeding where I had failed.

'You can dig out the weeds in this flowerbed,' I indicated the bed under the kitchen window. 'If you make a good job, I'll give you a meal. The garden needs a tidy up,' I added, in a shameful understatement, 'but I might manage that myself.'

Amusement played across Kos's mouth, 'When I have dug, I can see the piano?' he asked.

'I'm not sure.'

I hated to be petty minded, but I was living on my own - apart from Quirk. Allowing Kos into the house was to imply friendship - however casual – and I was afraid it might open the way to some threat not yet apparent from his courteous manner.

Kos hacked at the dead grass with a billhook, until it was possible to make out that the flowerbed had once possessed shape and form. To keep an eye on him, I pottered about cutting branches of Daphne from the garden to put in the living room – by the evening, the downstairs of the house would be filled with scent.

Peering out through the kitchen window, while I made lunch, I saw Kos taking stock of the whole garden and realised that what was to me a problem must appear to him the perfect opportunity. But when I took him tea, it was obvious he knew what he was doing. The plants remained undamaged - he hadn't disturbed or lifted bulbs accidently.

'One day this garden will give very much pleasure,' he said. 'I will come in the morning, early, play the piano and then improve your land.'

'I'll see,' I said, though I admired his audacity.

'I do the job,' he said indicating the garden with a broad sweep of his scythe, 'I keep going until I have finished. With all this you *should* grow vegetables and fruit – no need to buy from the gorgon.'

I smiled and said nothing.

Kos downed his tea, handed me the mug and began tackling the weeds again with energy and enthusiasm. There was no point in distracting him, so I went indoors with Quirk to finish making the beef stew I'd begun earlier in the day.

I was deep in thought, questioning my trust of a stranger, when Kos tapped at the kitchen door. He stood in the hall looking hot and decidedly less respectable than when he'd first arrived.

'You would like to look at the progress?' he asked.

The flowerbed had been transformed from a tangled mass of rotting foliage and mud into a neat crescent of plants and cleanly turned earth.

'It's a miracle,' I said and laughed.

Kos smiled, 'I've never performed a miracle before. Some of the trees and shrubs in this garden are sick with diseases - they should be burned as soon as possible.'

The idea made me nervous, 'Perhaps another day,' I said and suggested he cleared up.

During the cold weather, I'd got into the habit of taking hot food down to Geraldine, in the studio at lunchtime. Returning to the house, I asked Kos, 'Would you like to eat now?'

'Of course,' he said, 'I am bloody ravenous.'

He took off his boots and came into the kitchen. When he'd washed his hands, I showed him the watercolour my mother had made of the garden and the sketch plan I had drawn, I explained that I wanted to restore the garden so it looked exactly as it had in her day.

'This will be very much work,' he said, 'Too much for one person.'

I cut hunks of bread to go with the stew. Kos said little while we ate and I guessed he would have preferred to have eaten alone - he spent most of the time hidden behind the curtains of his black hair.

'Where are you from?' I asked - I saw Kos as a pilgrim like myself, washed up on the shores of the island.

He eyed me suspiciously, there was a deep reserve in his nature and I decided it might be better not to probe whatever was bothering him.

'I just thought you must miss your home,' I said when he didn't reply.

'I think not of home but of your piano. You're not a pianist?'

'No - and I suppose it would be a shame for such a fine instrument to be left unused...'

'I have been thinking the same – but perhaps your piano needs a tuner..? I will discover one, who is sensitive to an instrument of such quality.' Kos glanced at me, for a moment and a troubled expression played across his face. 'One day very soon, you will hear your piano at its best, I promise you...'

I wanted to believe him – believe my instincts had been right – that Kos was an honourable man who wouldn't want to be in debt or to do harm.

We finished our meal and I led him along the hall and opened the door to the music room. Watching from the doorway, I noticed how gently he raised the lid of the piano, as reverently as if he was lifting a veil on a beautiful woman.

He stroked the keys without making a sound. I turned away and left him, shocked at having witnessed something so intimate - too intimate to be shared.

Waiting in the hall, I listened to the silence. His tenderness to ivory and wood confirmed his story as unquestionable fact - he had been in Marisands before and this was not the first time Kostyantyn Zelinski had touched the keys of Yvette's piano.

*

I had put Laurence's notes in order, but Quirk was bored by my endless reading and writing, day after day. He whined for me to take him out earlier each morning, until it was barely eleven o'clock before he was nudging my hand with his nose and whimpering to persuade me to move.

Life at Marisands had at last begun to adopt its own form. Kos came every few days to garden and play the piano, filling the house with music. I had reached a fragile truce with Geraldine, who worked in the studio when and if the mood took her. We exchanged a few words when she collected and returned the key. At lunchtime when I delivered her food, I noticed, she had continued to paint the tower above the marshes with little variation from the canvas I'd seen on the easel, the first day I'd arrived on Littern.

One evening after she'd left, I carried Bernard's rendering of the view out to the studio to make a comparison. In his work, the stones of the tower reflected the soft reddish light of a low sun, whereas Geraldine had painted it shrouded in brown shadows, enhancing the eerie effect she aimed to evoke, which obviously gave pleasure to the tourists.

Whatever her viewpoint, she made a background of the sea rather than the hill and the marshes, and the mass of rocks in Morrow Bay was always visible in the upper corner of her landscape. She added them for effect, exercising artistic license, perhaps to suggest more powerfully the evil deeds of the ship-wreckers.

Since his disappearance, I made sure when I was outside, Quirk followed on my heels; I didn't want to lose him again. If I went to the studio, I ordered him to lie on the step, from where he gazed up at me balefully. I'd been through Thrift Cottage again and had ransacked the studio, searching for paintings, finding nothing except for a few more of Juliet's sketches and the unfinished canvas - *The body of Jesus is taken down from the cross*, which Eve had discovered during her stay.

I removed the sketches to the house for safekeeping, they'd already been damaged by light and there were areas of spotting on the paper. I hoped Eve might be able to clean them so I could frame and display them. The lack of my parents' work perplexed me. Though in childhood, I'd had the impression my father wasn't prolific - I did recall his paintings, the explosion of images - ideas hurled onto the white space of the canvas – his need to explore the idea that from chaos might come a semblance of order. That creative energy must have drawn "The Disciples" to him and should have resulted in a profusion of work, but as I continued to search without success, I could only conclude I would be spared one of the many tasks I'd felt incompetent to handle - the need to act as an artistic executor.

Over several days, I had cleared the outhouses, including my mother's workshop, where I had cleaned her chisels and hammers. As a child, watching as she formed shapes from a lump of wood or stone had been like seeing a creature being born. It had seemed almost sacred and it pleased me now to leave her tools arranged on the work bench, as if she might come back, as if I might once again hear her rhythmic tap-tapping – the sound of metal striking stone.

The soft leather gloves she had worn, I'd smoothed and folded neatly besides the chisels. I retrieved Juliet's old red paisley mug, with the cracked handle, which had been repaired many times. There was a cake tin containing a series of photographs of the white statues, photographs which were dated neatly in my father's hand and catalogued their steady evolution, as the wind and rain eroded them.

Above the bench was one of the cards Juliet used to make. The black ink of her handwriting had bleached out to a pale brown, but I liked the quote, taken from Shakespeare's *Pericles*, suggesting that what was important about a life was woven into the lives of others. I unpinned the card carefully, I would keep it in my study, thinking the words might be suitable to have inscribed on Juliet's gravestone.

Since Kos had brought him back, Quirk barked whenever anyone came up the drive and seemed to relish his role as watchdog. Usually, it was the postman, or Geraldine lurking in the shadows of the porch wanting the key to the studio.

'Rootling around?' she'd asked when she'd learned I'd been searching again for my parents' work.

Her appearance was always bizarre, a sharp contrast to her refined accent - that day she wore a red and green turban, a brown tweed coat, patterned leggings and Doc Marten boots.

'Would you like coffee before you start work?' I'd resolved not to approach our every conversation as if we were engaged in mortal combat.

Geraldine followed me into the house where I ushered her into the dining room and handed her an old saucer she could use as an ashtray. I'd unearthed an electric fire in the conservatory which I used to heat the icy room. I switched it on and set it pointing towards her, though she never complained of the cold, not even in the studio.

The dining room table was laden with the piles of correspondence Eve and I had made. Geraldine picked out two or three letters, which she read before dropping them back in the wrong place. I moved the heaps carefully aside.

'Did you know Flora used to send William money after Juliet died..?' Geraldine asked.

I didn't know, but Flora lived in a world governed by her own rules, rules that were benign and so usually went unquestioned.

'...Meanwhile, Alice persecuted William for your school fees, fees for a type of school he abhorred - privileged and based on a religion he despised...'

I interrupted her, '...There was an arrangement - William was allowed to remain here despite what had happened to my mother. And didn't he hand over responsibility for me to Alice and Flora - all too willingly?'

Geraldine glared. 'Alice always thought she knew how other people should live their lives. Surely you realise William was placed in an impossible position? The whole issue of his marriage to Juliet was a sham...'

'My understanding was that William...'

'...Seduced your innocent mother? Your family rubbed his face in that fiction!' Geraldine lit a cigarette. 'William was besotted, for a while, but later, if Juliet hadn't been pregnant, he might have got rid of her. The problem was, it would have looked bad for him - worse than it did already - attitudes were restrictive in those days, despite what you read about sixties liberation.'

'Did my parents ever love one another?' I asked, thinking of my father's reference to their "loveless marriage".

Geraldine made a sound of dismissal, 'It was a bad habit of William's - being blinded by his desire for a beautiful woman.'

I sipped my coffee – weighing anger against the possibility Geraldine might reveal something I wanted to know. When I had written to Silvie about Alice and William's letters, she had replied that she had always been suspicious of arrangements made by the family to protect Juliet's reputation.

'I've been wondering why you keep painting the tower,' I said.

'Why?' she snapped. 'Because I can't be bothered to start anything new – it's too much effort and I'm too bloody old. The local Heritage Association in Narescombe takes the tower paintings and sells them through the Tourist Information Office.'

'...And Shirley Fredericks sells them at Petra Galleries...'

Geraldine shrugged.

Quirk lay on the floor between us, his soulful eyes fixed on my face. 'Was my father's work sold or hung anywhere? Apart from Petra, there must be reputable galleries in Safford Bridge...'

'William's early work didn't do him justice and he knew it.' Geraldine re-lit her cigarette.

'...And the later paintings..?' I asked, trying to keep calm. Under pressure from Silvie and Alice, the more Geraldine resisted, the more some demon took possession of me, urging me to extract information from her.

'The problem with your mother's paintings was that they lacked verve.' Geraldine said - she often used diversion as a form of counter attack.

'The white statues didn't lack verve - they were different from anything else my mother had done...' I argued.

Geraldine narrowed her eyes, 'Juliet was never the same after she'd lost her baby, her world was full of ghosts and shadows.'

'She never believed in herself again?' I was thinking of Eve's theory that Juliet had lost her sense of identity.

Geraldine drew hard on the stub of her cigarette and ground it out in the saucer.

I asked, 'What about my father, did he believe in himself after Juliet's death?'

'...For William it was one thing to lose Juliet, another to lose his vocation. The result was a series of meaningless paintings, badly executed.'

Her comment was cruel, but even though she was hardly dispassionate, I didn't doubt its truth. William had struggled as an artist and without belief in his talent his existence might well have lost its meaning.

'Did he never find a new source of energy?' I asked.

'Isn't sex the energy behind what most of us do, until we're too decrepit to be bothered? Some of the local culture vultures would have liked to adopt him, but William had no desire to become their pet. Worse still, he didn't want to be a marginal note to the Armsted family.'

'He was envious of my family?' It had never occurred to me my father might have felt threatened by the Armsteds, none of whom had made much impact on the art world, except possibly Bernard.

'William was a consummate draughtsman, but he made a fundamental mistake. He believed he could will himself to become an artist, whatever that means. The truth is the gift is given or it isn't and even the most cynical of us have to make terms with that. He didn't want to return to teaching art, so I covered for him. That's one way of loving isn't it?'

It was an honest answer and an honest question. Though I doubted the nature of my parents' relationship, Geraldine's love for William had begun to appear not only true but also heroic.

'What happened to my father's work?' I asked, 'When I met him in London – there was paint on his hands...'

'There's nothing,' Geraldine said, 'not of William's own.'

'The painting on the frame in the studio – is that one of his – one that was not quite his own?'

Geraldine didn't answer at once, 'William got some damn-fool idea in his head about completing *The Stations of the Cross,* a total bloody waste of time - he wasn't up to it - the concept was alien...'

'So he went to a priest for advice – Terry Hart?'

She looked away, 'Perhaps confronted with death, most of us will find ourselves in a state of shame and terror...'

Frustrated with her way of side-stepping questions, her show of indifference to the things that mattered, I could have snatched up the wooden tray I'd used to carry our coffee and smashed it against the edge of the table. 'You're telling me William and everyone around him suffered for a vocation that amounted to nothing?'

'You take an interest only now, when it's too late...' Geraldine said, standing up.

'I wasn't encouraged to take an interest. William wouldn't talk about his work. For most of his life, he behaved as if he had never fathered a daughter.'

She eyed me curiously. 'Things aren't always as they appear. I'd remember that, if you intend to carry on poking about in your family's affairs.'

I reached for the studio key on the sideboard, showed Geraldine out through the front door and shut it firmly behind her. Despite my best efforts, conversations with her were inevitably disturbing; I struggled to listen with an open mind, to hear the sub-text of her account of my parents' life and not to react with outrage.

When I returned to the dining room, I noticed a photograph on the table in the place where Geraldine had been sitting. The photograph was dated – *Marisands Summer 1964* - in William's handwriting. It was of my father in the oratory garden. He was sitting by a table laden with food, his Panama hat set at an angle - there could be no doubt that the occasion was the lunch party which had taken place, just hours before my mother had drowned.

Studying the image of William, it was evident from his eyes that he was deeply unhappy – his unhappiness at variance with the memory I had of him joking and flirting with Shirley. The photographer – I assumed Geraldine - had caught him in an unguarded moment – must have taken it without his knowledge.

Geraldine had intended to make a point - just as she had in handing me Antony's obituary. *Had William foreseen the misery that was coming? Had the misery had been of his own making?* Littern Island had been his hideaway, but nevertheless through his failed vocation, the loss of my mother and his final illness, trouble had come to this peaceful place and found him out.

# Chapter 22

After a succession of dry days, I thought I would risk taking the steps up from the beach, after Quirk's afternoon walk. Silvie had reminded me that while I was living at Marisands I was responsible for the oratory and for ensuring it was accessible to anyone who wanted to use it. She had asked for a report on the state of the steps and the building, especially the interior, which had enchanted her when Bernard had taken her there as a child.

At the foot of the steps, I unhooked Quirk's lead; I didn't want him pulling me over. Some of the steps were overhung with gorse and remained damp and slippery and I clutched at rocks and bushes on the side of the cliff to keep my balance, especially in the places where sections of the handrail were broken or missing.

Ahead of me, Quirk charged up to the plateau of rock on which the oratory stood. He explored behind the building before reappearing, staring down at me, his face quizzical because of my slow progress. I had no head for heights and had to stop several times to re-focus attention on the steps in front of me and filter out the booming sound of the sea breaking on the rocks below.

I'd almost reached the oratory, when I noticed, in the shadow of the building a hunched figure crouched down on a driftwood log, wearing a royal blue jacket in the same shade of blue which had caught my eye on the steps, one night during Eve's visit.

My mind raced through several possibilities - was it Geraldine or Kos, a tramp or gypsies? But as I drew closer, common sense informed me this diminutive figure didn't belong to an adult. The oratory might be little more than a stone hut, but inside it was lined with shells, hundreds of shells that glowed with their soft pinks, creams and purples, attractive to any child.

I arrived at the oratory door breathing heavily and reached out to take hold of the ring handle on the door to support myself.

'Don't go in!' The girl said, before I could ask her why she was hiding there.

'... Why not..?'

My query received a withering look, 'It isn't yours *and* you stole my dog.'

'You look cold and uncomfortable,' I said, 'you shouldn't be here, it's dangerous.'

The girl was clutching her knees so that she formed a small scrunched up bundle of blue anorak, the hood pulled as far forward over her face as it would go.

'Who are you?' she asked rather rudely.

'I'm staying at Marisands and while I'm here I need to look after the oratory,' I informed her.

'You can't *own* an oratory,' the girl said, 'it belongs to God. Do you own Thrift Cottage and the tree house?'

'I may do, one day. Are you alone here?'

The blue hood nodded. Quirk had run up to the girl greeting her as an old friend, so it seemed there might be some truth in her assertion I'd taken her dog. Watching them together, I felt a pang of disappointment - I couldn't bear the thought of giving up Quirk's company.

'Why don't you come to Marisands? I'll call your parents and ask them to fetch you. We can talk about the dog.'

'I'm not supposed to go with strangers,' she said, looking very solemn. But she stood up and stepped out into the light, I thought she was aged about eight or nine.

'I won't do you any harm.'

'That's what they all say,' the girl muttered and I found it difficult not to smile at her show of spirit. 'Why did you call out "Quirk"? That dog's called "Skipper".'

'I've got used to Quirk now ...'

I put out my hand again to open the oratory door. The girl sprang forward.

'I said don't!' Her blue hood fell back from her face revealing peat brown hair and dark blue eyes, features that were almost certainly of Piran blood.

'I don't mind if you've been using it as a den, it doesn't matter.'

'It isn't a den - I use the cottage and the tree house for that,' she blushed as she realised she had given away her secret.

I smiled. 'That's all right. The Robin's Nest was built for my mother, when she was a girl.' But I knew I wouldn't have wanted Minette roaming the island alone and would have been terrified to think of her playing on the oratory steps - I was already concerned for her safety when she came to Marisands at half term.

'I'm going back to the house for a hot drink,' I told her. The oratory would have to wait for another day when it wasn't being guarded by a ferocious young person. 'Perhaps I could bring you a drink out here - I'd be much happier if I knew who you were and where you've come from.'

The girl trailed after me. I asked her to go ahead up the steps, thinking I might be able to catch her should she fall - but she was sure footed and arrived at the summit and was standing by the garden gate, while I was still labouring to haul myself up to the cliff top.

'What will you do if I tell you who I am?' she asked.

'Phone your mother, or your father.'

'My mother isn't here.'

'Your father then... Would you like to hold Quirk?' I asked, thinking it might make her less likely to run off, 'You could come just inside the garden if you feel safe.'

'I'll wait inside the gate with *Skipper*,' she said.

Her large, dark blue eyes studied my every expression. Her blue anorak – several sizes too large - was part of St. Safan's uniform, the school badge, embroidered in red and gold was sewn onto the chest. She looked as if she had started the day tidy, with her hair pulled back into a ponytail, but now she was decidedly bedraggled, like an urchin.

'Shall I bring you tea or hot chocolate?' I asked.

'I'd like chocolate, please.'

'And shall I phone your father from the house or would you prefer to use my mobile?'

'My father isn't on the island,' she said and her eyes filled with tears.

'Don't cry...' I said uselessly. Something about her reminded me of a bird with a broken wing – there seemed no better analogy for her wounded innocence.

'Sometimes Dad forgets about me, he doesn't mean to, but since Mum went away he's been peculiar. He used to be "Aggravating but trustworthy", that's what Mum always said.'

'Tell me your name...'

'My name's Ursula.'

'I like the name Ursula - I'm Iris. I used to live here a long time ago and my father lived here until he died. Did you know him?''

'I didn't,' Ursula said and shook her head gravely. 'Did you know you look like a badger?'

'Do I?' I asked, taken aback.

'Your hair,' she said softly.

I put my hand up to the centre of my forehead and realised she meant the stripe of silver that ran across the top of my head and down into my plaited hair, 'You're right,' I said with a laugh, 'I don't know why I didn't think of it myself.'

I left Ursula holding Quirk, while I went inside and made two hot chocolates. I couldn't see her from the kitchen window and had to trust she would stay in the garden. When I carried our drinks out to the wooden bench by the honeysuckle, I was relieved to find she was still there.

'Let's sit down - we could let Quirk off the lead now.'

Ursula unclipped the lead and let Quirk go. 'I'm staying at The Retreat with my cousins,' she said, 'My Aunt Sarah's in London and I was at Lyncross having lessons with Aunt Beatrix. My uncle's called Nicholas Piran, he takes pictures of things like tiny bugs and flowers and twigs and leaves. He calls me Little Bear because of my name, it means that, he says.'

'He'll be worried about you.'

'He'll know I'm on the island somewhere,' she said nonchalantly.

'Someone should know *exactly* where you are.'

Ursula's legs swung back and forth under the bench, 'Uncle Nicholas might not be home - he had to take Rowena to the dentist.'

I checked my watch – it was almost three-thirty. No-one had come looking for Ursula and I sensed she was playing for time.

'Should I ring Lyncross?' I asked.

Ursula's eyes widened in alarm, 'Aunt Beatrix said if I didn't behave she'll tell my dad.'

'And that's exactly what you don't want?'

The fresh pink of her cheeks deepened to red. She stared down at her shoes - well polished black lace ups, probably new, but now scuffed at the toes and covered in sand and mud. As she sat there, leaning forward, occasionally sipping her drink, huge tears began to plop onto the shoes and roll off into the grass.

Wondering if they were real or crocodile tears, I asked, 'Do you come here often to play in The Robin's Nest?'

Ursula shook her head, 'I go to the oratory to ask God why my mother went away and to keep her safe.' She offered the information as if it explained everything and I suppose for her it did. 'Did you come to Marisands to be with your father?'

It was a strange question from a child but I tried to answer honestly, 'In a way I did – but I came here especially looking for my mother. I find my mother in her things - there are so many reminders of her on the island.'

'My mother's travelled all over the world, she collects shells.'

'Do you collect shells?' I asked.

Ursula shook her head more violently, 'Dad wouldn't like to have shells in the house, anymore.'

'I suppose because he finds your mother in them and it makes him sad...' I said, 'is it because of the shells you like the oratory?'

Ursula nodded in reply.

Quirk had sauntered off on some quest of his own, but I didn't want him to wander out into the lane and disappear, so I began to make moves to go back to the house.

'Please don't go,' Ursula said.

For someone so young, Ursula Piran was an alarming mixture of candour and calculation - but perhaps all children were - I had only to remember my own daughters.

'What shall we do then, Ursula? I could drive you to Lyncross or you could give me a phone number and sit in the kitchen with Quirk until someone comes to pick you up...'

Ursula walked with her head hung, but she followed me indoors. I fetched a selection from the children's books I'd brought from London and found paper and coloured pencils among the things on my desk in the study. After what seemed to have been a distressing day, I thought she might be hungry and put a plate of buttered toast on the table in front of her.

When she'd eaten, she searched her anorak pockets and produced a torn, grubby piece of paper with a phone number on it and a mobile number written beneath.

I dialled and waited, but there was no reply from The Retreat. Ursula was pretending not to notice me, her face pale and anxious. I dialled the mobile number.

'It's Iris Armsted,' I said when Nicholas Piran answered. 'I'm calling from Marisands. I met your niece, Ursula, while I was out for a walk. She's here with me, at the moment.'

There was a sound of impatience, a sort of 'tssh', 'I left her at Lyncross,' he said.

'She told me.'

'Would it be possible for you to take her there?' Nicholas asked.

'I don't know,' I said. I didn't want to go to Lyncross and face Beatrix again, and Ursula, I suspected felt the same, 'Perhaps later...'

'In that case, Ursula had better stay with you until I can get back to the island.' His tone was approaching rudeness, 'I'll be back, late afternoon.'

'You'll phone Beatrix to let her know where Ursula is...'

'Certainly,' he said and rang off.

Ursula was observant, but I tried not to show what I was thinking, which ran along the lines of wondering what had happened to the good humoured, friendly family I'd once liked and respected.

There was little opportunity to ponder the question, while I was on the phone, Geraldine had crept in through the open front door and now stood in the kitchen, nudging Quirk with her foot, where he had stretched half in and half out of the protection of the kitchen table.

'Babysitting?' she asked. 'She looks like one of the Piran brats - it's a local joke, the island's overrun with them and you can't tell one from another.'

'...Coffee..?' I asked, thinking *perhaps I should open a cafe*.

I fetched the key for the studio from the dining room and handed it to her. Geraldine had sat down and was rolling a cigarette on the kitchen table, while Ursula watched fascinated as the rectangle of thin paper was filled with a trail of tobacco, before being rolled up into a narrow tube.

'Please don't smoke in here,' I said.

Geraldine grimaced, but she put the roll-up back into her tobacco tin and snapped on the lid.

When the coffee was ready, I passed her a mug, 'You could take it to the studio,' I suggested.

Through the front door, I watched her beetling off down the garden. Ursula stood beside me with Quirk, who had settled into the warmth of a patch of winter sunshine on the flower bed Kos had recently dug over.

I'd washed some of Minette's clothes that morning, thinking they might have grown musty, shut up in suitcases for weeks. The clothes were fluttering in the wind – when I'd checked they were dry - I began un-pegging them from the line, giving them to Ursula to fold and lay carefully in the basket.

'Do you have a little girl, like me?' she asked, 'I'm nearly eleven.'

'Minette's eight - she's at school in London.'

'Doesn't it make you sad that she's so far away?'

'Very – but she'll be coming to the island at half term.'

'May I help you stack the logs?' Ursula asked, 'Uncle Nicholas won't be able to get his car in.'

I'd been so distracted, finding her on the oratory steps, that I'd almost forgotten the load of logs delivered to the house that morning. The delivery man had been in a hurry and refused to drop them in the garage, instead, tipping the wood out in an enormous pile that blocked the drive.

I looked at her in her untidy school uniform, 'If you spoil your clothes any further your uncle won't be pleased.'

'Couldn't you find you me clothes?' she begged, 'I can change back before my uncle comes...'

Ursula was so keen to help, I gave in. She was taller and thinner than Minette, but I searched through the clothes in the basket to find leggings and a jumper then sent her to the cloakroom to change. When she was ready, we began taking armfuls of logs into the shed and piling them up.

Ursula was wiry and economical in her movements, clearly a hard-worker when the task appealed to her.

'...When does your uncle normally get back to the island?' I asked.

Ursula shrugged. 'About five o'clock, if the twins haven't got into trouble during the day.'

'Does that happen often?'

'Most days,' Ursula said and smiled uncertainly. 'Granddad says twins are always naughty. Benedict and Dominic are just like my dad and Uncle Nicholas when they were boys.'

'Perhaps we'd better have tea, then,' I said, registering the fact that she was Patrick's daughter.

Quirk needed a final walk before the tide came in, so after soup, bread and cheese for tea, I left a note pinned to the front door to say we had gone down to the beach.

Meandering towards Morrow Bay, playing ducks and drakes, picking up shells, throwing sticks for Quirk, I'd almost forgotten the pleasure of a child's company. It seemed a life-time since I'd taken Minette and Yuuka to Seaholme – half a life-time since Minette and I had parted in the New Year.

Later, we finished our meal with biscuits and cake. Ursula had found her appetite, once there was no prospect of having to return to Lyncross and her lessons with Beatrix. I'd persuaded her to brush her hair and had attempted to tidy her clothes. Sitting at the kitchen table, quiet and demure, she now appeared a perfectly composed little schoolgirl - which was how Nicholas Piran found us, when he finally arrived at quarter to six.

I recognised his car as the silver estate I'd followed across the causeway the day I'd arrived on Littern – when it had been full of children and dogs. Now, he peered in through the kitchen window and seeing him, Ursula stuffed a final jammy dodger into her mouth before taking her coat from the back of the kitchen chair. She was crunching her biscuit, crumbs spilling onto her jacket, when I opened the front door.

I wouldn't have known Nicholas. The slight figure of the boy had become the very solid figure of a man, a tired, angry man. His hair and neatly trimmed beard were speckled with grey.

'Where did you find Ursula?' he demanded.

'She'd walked from Lyncross - she was by the oratory. I phoned as soon as I could,' I felt as if I was giving a statement to the police. 'She's been very polite and well-behaved...'

'Would you call running away from her aunt polite and well behaved..?'

'Children are impulsive…' I said, remembering how I used to make excuses for the girls to David.

'It isn't safe for her to wander the island,' he replied.

'What would you like me to do if it happens again?'

'Do as you have done today, I suppose,' and beneath his curt manner he sounded weary.

'She's a lovely child.'

'Really..? She refuses to settle down.'

*Perhaps no-one has helped her to settle down*, I thought, as we moved onto the drive.

I held Quirk's collar firmly with my hand, nothing had been said about him and I didn't want him escaping with the Pirans, if I could help it.

In the passenger seat of Nicholas's car was a girl of about thirteen - Rowena. Ursula had clambered into the back with the boys, who looked in their mid teens.

'Are you managing here?' Nicholas asked. A covert smile flickered round his mouth - he obviously thought I wasn't coping at all.

'You can see how I'm doing, progress is slow. It will need time and patience, lots of time and patience, just like settling a child…'

'I'll pass on your advice on to my brother,' he said and it was clear, whatever else had changed, Nicholas Piran hadn't lost his barbed tongue.

# Chapter 23

About ten days later, I returned from walking Quirk and found a message on the answer phone from Eve; I'd missed her call by half an hour. I pushed the button and played the message back - Eve's voice was so muffled I couldn't tell if she was crying, had a cold or if it was just a bad line.

'Could you come and collect me...' she was saying, but then her words were blurred and I couldn't make out any more.

I dialled the number of The Angel Inn and waited for the ever-obliging Matt to reply. He said Eve had just left, but he would send someone to fetch her so she could call me back. I waited by the phone watching through the kitchen window as sleety rain slashed down on the garden.

Eve's voice was tremulous, 'Everyone else has moved out because of the floods - I feel like shit - I can't work - my workshop's knee deep in water...' Her words were followed by the sound of her blowing her nose. 'I wondered if I could stay with you for a bit - I'd have to bring the cats...'

Before I could answer, she burst into tears and explained she'd been in hospital for a few days with pneumonia. Matt had told her if she paid a portion of her rent, he would let her keep her belongings in the flat while she decided what to do. She wouldn't have any money, but she would work for her keep - help me with the cooking and cleaning. 'I miss everyone,' she told me, sniffling, 'I even miss Zoë.'

'Then, of course you must come here...' I soothed, knowing that leaving Zethar Creek must feel like the end of her dream – the death of the artist's commune would surely mean her stay in Cornwall was over.

Since I'd been working on *Minor Lights*, the post had piled up in a big heap on the kitchen table. Not wanting to be scolded by Eve, I began to sort through the circulars and free newspapers that had accumulated.

Apart from junk mail there was a note from Mrs. Stuart, to say Flora had been unwell and she thought I ought to know. Feeling guilty that the letter had lain unopened for days, I phoned Wren House to discover Flora had been suffering from a feverish cold, which had left her confused and rambling about people and events from the past. Until she was better, the sale of Wren House had been put on hold.

A letter from Minette, in a bright pink envelope, had become lodged inside a flyer for ready-made curtains and blinds. I tore the letter open – annoyed with myself for missing it - I'd assumed she hadn't bothered to write because she would be coming to Littern soon.

Minette usually had plenty to say, but this time her writing was brief and subdued, *I WANT TO SEE YOU,* she'd printed, repeating the phrase ten times, underscoring each line in a blotched wave of blue-black ink. I composed a quick reply without any of the little drawings I normally enclosed and said Minette could tell me what was bothering her, the minute she arrived at Marisands.

Just before I was due to collect Eve from Safford Bridge, the door bell rang. Kos was there, his thick mop of black hair brushed and shining, falling in waves around his face and over his collar.

'I have to go out for a couple of hours,' I told him.

Kos's face fell - I hadn't seen him during the recent rainy days, normally when he couldn't work outside he didn't play the piano.

'Please - I will play and then lock up - leave everything perfect - I keep an eye on the dog and the house for you.'

I'd grown to like him and disregarding our first encounter at the vegetable stall, his behaviour had been impeccable.

'All right,' I agreed.

'You are very kind and very trusting.'

*Or an absolute fool,* I thought.

As I finished getting ready upstairs I could hear Kos in the music room, practicing scales, making a smooth transition into a Liszt *Sonata,* then into a snatch of Ravel, *Gaspard de la Nuit* – The Treasurer of the Night.

Often after he'd finished playing pieces by well-known composers, the music changed to something strange and unfamiliar - compositions of his own, I assumed, as he tried one phrase after another after another. He tended the garden in the same dogged way, bringing load after load of seaweed up from the beach and digging it into the heavy soil. His persistence had a dignity that had earned my respect, and though I was curious about both his life and his music, I didn't intrude. Kos disliked being disturbed in the music room, he dismissed any compliments with an angry shake of the head - so I let him alone, shut up in his private world, where he seemed completely at home.

I arrived at the station just in time to meet Eve's train. She was loaded with luggage. She'd brought most of her paintings with her and could hardly struggle down the platform carrying her backpack, two heavy portfolios and a cardboard box, with the cats mewing loudly and insistently from inside.

When I'd stowed her belongings in the boot of the car and put the cats on the back seat, Eve thought she'd like to have lunch at The Pilgrim's Inn, so we left the car and walked together across town.

As we waited for our food to be brought to the table, Eve said, 'I wanted to apologise to you for last time I was here – I was stressed out about the floods – I know I was really rude.'

'I wanted to apologise too. I kept you at Marisands when I should have let you go home.'

Eve smiled and said, 'I wasn't your prisoner. I make my own choices, don't you?'

'How far can any of us really do that?'

She looked uncomfortable but told me how life had altered for her in Zethar Creek – how her relationship with Luke had faltered and then collapsed - when she'd been ill in hospital he'd been no help to her at all.

I described Kos's arrival, my encounter with Ursula Piran and the things Geraldine had said to me about William and my mother. She agreed we should stop on our way back to the island in Narescombe and look at Juliet's paintings.

When we arrived at the Arts Centre, there was a craft sale in the lobby of All Soul's with tables of handmade jewellery, small panels of stained glass, pottery and paintings - we inched our way through the cluster of people who'd gathered round the stalls and made our way into the church.

The renovation of the building didn't seem to have advanced much since I was last there. I led Eve through to the side chapel and lifted the dust cloths that shrouded *The Stations of the Cross*. For a long time she stood on the chancel step, her head held to one side as if she was considering something she found baffling.

'The Christ figures are unusually feminine. And each fragment has a picture within a picture,' she said, pointing to some of the figures and faces in the background of the paintings. 'If you look closely, each image is reflected endlessly - like two mirrors opposing each other – like in the music room at Marisands.'

I had missed the way one face might appear as a reflection in the eyes, or in something metallic on the clothing of the figure next to it, and the way colours had been used to echo one another.

'Why would she paint something of such complexity?' I asked.

'You were looking for a message? Perhaps there is no message - Juliet was simply playing with pattern and form...'

'... or performing an illusionist's trick.'

Eve laughed. 'I'm not quite sure what you mean.'

I explained how Geraldine had warned that in regard to my parents, things weren't always what they seemed. Had Juliet intended to suggest our lives were made up of nothing but a series of illusions? Using such an intense layering of images, she might have hoped to create richness of texture - or equally to blot something out.

'The intricacy of the work and tiny details, are almost obsessive,' I said, although obsession was a quality I associated more with William than with my mother.

'Be careful *you* don't become obsessive,' Eve said with a smile, 'the paintings are probably meant to be a puzzle - like the white statues - maybe Juliet didn't mean you to solve it.'

We sat together on a front pew. I wished I could accept my mother's work at its face value, like Eve, but couldn't let go of the notion that if I studied the paintings long enough they would speak to me, deliver an understanding of Juliet, which she could no longer give in person.

Slipping my arm through Eve's, I asked her, 'Despite Geraldine's biased view isn't it possible Juliet's art might be one place where she told the truth?'

'Do people do that? Tell the truth in one place and not in another?'

'We aren't all of a single piece like you,' I teased, 'though it would be better if we were.'

'Tell that to Luke Porter,' she suggested, 'he thought I was difficult and complicated – he even used the word "impossible".'

*

While Minette was away at school, I'd spoken regularly both to the headmistress, Sister Gabriel, and also to Rose. The school had complained about David and Helen disrupting Minette's weekends when she had been happiest staying with Neil, Rose and Simon. Minette had also been in trouble again for "cheating" by helping Yuuka during an exam and Rose had taken time off work to go into the school for a discussion with Sister Gabriel.

Concerned, Rose had told me she thought Minette should move to Marisands after half term, but Sister Gabriel had observed that she would be better to leave the school on a positive note - there was little hope of her adapting to a new place and new people if she left St. Catherine's "under a cloud".

I didn't want to make up my mind until I had seen and spoken to Minette and more immediate was the need to make arrangements for her journey to Littern at the end of February. I'd phoned and asked if David could bring her half way from London, thinking we could meet near Bristol, but Helen had refused on his behalf claiming he wasn't well enough to undertake a long drive and implying I should have known better than to ask. I assumed would be the end of our discussions.

As the ostrich is fabled to do, I had preferred to bury my head in the sand where David's marriage was concerned – if I didn't think about it, it might not happen. Then I received a call to say that their wedding was planned for July and as Minette was to be a bridesmaid, Helen had checked on the internet and thought she might find a suitable dress for her in Safford Bridge. She was willing to drive Minette to Littern, take her out shopping and then return to London the same day.

Her offer threw me off balance and I said I'd prefer to make other arrangements for Minette - an older girl from school might be travelling to the West Country or I could arrange an escort through the train company.

Helen became insistent. David was going to stay at Leitchly for a couple of days and she would be glad to get out of London. The more willing she was to make the journey, the more uneasy and suspicious I felt - *was she curious to see how I was living so she could report back to David?* When I suggested as much to Eve, she pointed out that Helen was behaving in a mature, civilised manner, while I was being ungrateful, mean and narrow minded.

Minette was to have the small room that was a twin to my childhood bedroom. Painted green and white, it was fresh looking and there were pictures on the walls of pressed flowers and leaves made by Flora. I'd arranged the little wooden animals carved by my mother on the windowsill.

Worried in case fate decreed that Helen should become stranded on the island, I made up the master bedroom. Its deep honey-gold walls made it look warm, and it was cosier than any other room in the house as the airing cupboard, built into one corner, provided a constant, gentle heat.

Minette had asked me to stock up on her favourite foods. I'd planned for us to go to the swimming pool in Narescombe, perhaps to the cinema, and to have tea either at The Blue Mountain Cafe or The North Star – I'd also intended to phone Delia and see if we could go to Hintham Ridge and explore the farm. I couldn't wait to see Minette leap from Helen's car and run across the drive to greet me, her grey eyes alight, her dark hair streaming behind her. In her letter she'd said, *I WANT TO SEE YOU,* underlined ten times and I was equally desperate to see her.

Then, at the last minute, there was a phone call from Sister Gabriel to say Minette, Yuuka and several of the other girls had chicken pox, did I think she should travel to Devon? I spoke to Minette. She sounded drowsy, as if she could hardly bring herself to talk and didn't much care if she came to Littern or not, but hearing her voice I knew, however selfish, I couldn't bear it if she didn't come to the island.

A few days later, Helen swerved her lime green convertible into the drive and parked in front of the kitchen window. She jumped out of the car looking outré, wearing a purple velvet coat and mustard coloured tights. Her copper hair shone in the sunlight, she was as colourful as an exotic bird and as dissonant, among the soft browns and greens of Marisands' garden.

The air round Helen seemed to bristle and her greeting was perfunctory, 'God, it *is* cold down here...' she exclaimed.

I opened the back door of the car. Minette had been asleep, wrapped in a duvet, lying across the back seat. I helped her out and gave her a hug. Her face and hands were covered in spots which were just beginning to crust over, her dark hair was lank and unwashed and I could see a scattering of sore places on her scalp.

'This is the country mansion?' Helen was asking, 'And these are the grounds?'

'It's hardly a mansion...'

Helen ignored me, staring round at the overgrown garden, leaving me embarrassingly aware of the many areas Kos had yet to transform, where brambles grew in abundance, smothering everything around them. What would she make of the house where so little had been achieved?

Helen unloaded Minette's blue school holdall from the car and her own collection of bags, far more than seemed necessary for a few hours' visit. She dropped them onto the gravel as if a servant might appear from the "mansion" pick them up and carry them into the house for her.

'Eve's here,' I said, 'she's come to stay for a while.'

'Almost a family reunion then,' Helen remarked.

I sent Minette inside to get warm and piled their things in the hall. Minette asked to go straight upstairs to bed - she didn't want to sleep on the sofa in the sitting room as Eve had done when she was ill - she wasn't hungry - she wanted nothing except a glass of water and lots more sleep.

Eve took Minette to her room and I showed Helen into the kitchen. I'd begun to view the ritual kettle-boiling with amusement - perhaps my life at Marisands was to consist of the humble service of making hot drinks for people - though where Geraldine was concerned, the aroma of coffee usually spelt trouble.

Helen looked frozen, so I flicked the switch on the central heating. She sat in the chair closest to the radiator, huddled into her purple coat, rubbing her hands briskly together as if she might never get warm.

Quirk barked from the conservatory, but Helen had made her distaste for dogs apparent on the phone before she came. I was relieved we'd made a safe place for the cats, Boa and Brio, out in the woodshed and that before Helen came, I'd remembered to clear the porch of their early morning offerings of several decapitated mice and a half eaten rabbit.

Eve chatted to Helen for a few minutes - then signalled to me behind her back that she was taking Quirk down to the beach. I wished she wouldn't go - already I was in such an edgy mood, I responded to every word, expression and action of Helen's with suppressed annoyance. Rather than being stuck with her, I wanted to go upstairs and comfort Minette.

Helen made a study of appraising the kitchen; her sharp eyes took in all the details and I guessed she was calculating the cost of putting the place right.

Before she could say anything tactless, I asked, 'Is David well? He used to retreat to Leitchly when he was feeling down.'

'There's nothing wrong with him,' Helen said. 'John's taken him to stay with his mother - it was my suggestion - David thought it was a good idea.' She gave the impression that when she offered a proposal, David simply capitulated.

'What's happening with Eve?' she asked.

'She's living with me for a while, until she knows what she wants to do,' I had no intention of mentioning her break-up with Luke.

'Why here though? It's so inconvenient...'

'Zethar Creek wasn't any better,' I said, trying to remain composed. Helen had a way of appearing to be frank, while hiding what she really wanted to say behind a cloud of bluster.

'David thinks Eve's problem is she forgets she's a Sayce and thinks she's an Armsted.'

*Perhaps she wants to forget*, I thought.

I asked Helen if she would like to freshen-up and showed her upstairs to the room I'd prepared. I pointed out the sea view from the window, but she barely glanced at it, she was sizing up the furnishings and ornaments.

'This house is like a junk emporium,' she said laughing, 'if you kept only half the rubbish it would still be overstuffed. I've made lots of changes in Pimlico, got rid of Barbara's gee-gaws – I told David I couldn't possibly move in without clearing out and redecorating. My business partner has taken a load of stuff off our hands - he'd probably do the same for you...'

As I had no intention of allowing Helen or her business partner to loot Marisands, I left her and looked in on Minette who had fallen into a deep sleep. I sat on the edge of the bed watching her for as long as I dared, before kissing her forehead and leaving her to rest.

While Helen was out of the way, I brought in firewood ready for the evening. Leaning over the hearth, laying the fire, I didn't hear her come into the sitting room, but when I stood up found her watching me - now bundled into several thick cardigans.

'I feel like a vagrant,' she said, indicating her multi-layered clothes.

'You don't look like one,' I told her, the image and smell of Kelda rising in my mind.

'Do you go through this palaver every day?'

'Sometimes more than once,' I said, sweeping the ashes into a metal tray.

Helen had sunk into a corner of the sofa, surrounding herself with cushions - the house hadn't really warmed up since I'd switched the heating on, so I put a match to the fire.

'I suppose Eve's still playing the starving artist?'

'I don't think Eve will ever change,' I said, 'I hope she doesn't.'

Just as I spoke, Eve returned with Quirk and put him in the conservatory, but Boa and Brio had followed her indoors.

Helen cringed at the sight of the cats. 'Don't let them touch me,' she warned. 'Do you really want those little beasts in your life?'

'I really don't know,' I said feeling exasperated. 'Two cats here or there seem a minor part of my problems...' Dogs, cats, delinquents, other people's children, my own children, my ex-partner's lover all seemed to be fragments of my life on Littern, and I had no idea how in the end we might all shake down together.

Helen raised her hands as a sign of truce. 'I promise not to interfere - I'll be good...'

'If you did that we'd hardly recognise you,' Eve murmured but fortunately Helen didn't seem to hear.

The morning had brought in a bright, brisk day with the wind chasing white puffy clouds from across the sea. The trees in the garden were showing the first soft fuzziness of new leaves and seemed to stretch up as if to touch the clear, blue sky. I'd thought of suggesting we go for a walk, but wasn't convinced Helen would be interested in looking round the island. Not sure what to do with her, I made another pot of coffee.

As I set down her cup on a side table, Helen grabbed a throw from the back of the sofa and swung her long legs up onto the seat.

'Why don't you persuade your grandmother and aunt to sell this dump and find a bijou place somewhere? It'll take you forever to get Marisands to an acceptable standard - not to mention the cost.'

'Perhaps Narescombe standards aren't as exacting as London standards,' I said, in self-defence.

'If you sold, it would probably be some idiot from London, who bought it, looking for a country idyll,' Helen said and yawned.

'Well, I'm the idiot from London, who's living here at the moment,' I reminded her.

Helen smiled. 'You don't *have* to stay - it's just a house...'

'To you it's just a house and Hurst Row is just a house, but a home is something different and that's what I intend to make here.'

'Oh dear - David thought you'd be preaching about the country life,' Helen said looking bored.

She became more animated as we discussed their wedding. The reception was to be held in the garden of Barbara's house in Leitchly and they were having a blessing in the church there, where David had married Lesley in the 1960's.

When I'd heard enough, I excused myself, 'I'll be in the kitchen making lunch,' I said and found her a few magazines to read.

I'd done most of the preparation for the meal the previous day. As soon as I'd put the stew to heat on the hob, I slipped upstairs to see Minette again. She'd slept for over an hour, but didn't think she wanted to get up. She definitely didn't want to go into Safford Bridge to buy a bridesmaid's dress – Helen, she told me, had already dragged her up and down the length of Oxford Street, while she was feeling really unwell.

I helped her wash and change into fresh pyjamas and straightened her bed.

'Helen can't make me go shopping, I'm still poorly,' Minette moaned, 'that's no way to treat someone who's ill. It isn't right and Helen's marrying Dad isn't right. I don't understand why he isn't marrying you - I don't want to be *her* bridesmaid. I want *you* to tell Helen I'm not going to do it, not even for Dad.'

'Don't think about it now,' I said, 'I'll speak to Helen.'

Minette asked for a piece of paper and a pen to write a letter, she'd promised Yuuka she would send one every day. I fetched what she needed from the study and found a large book she could rest on then left her to set the table for lunch.

Helen was waiting by the kitchen door, 'It's so cold everywhere,' she complained, 'but you needn't turn up the heating, I suppose you can't afford it.'

She spoke disparagingly, but I could guess she was as uneasy as I was, we were both under stress and she was obviously out of place, like a tropical plant in a cottage garden.

She slid in behind the kitchen table, where the radiator was now lukewarm. 'David wondered what sort of man you'd have a relationship with now...' she offered conversationally.

'The sort of paragon who'll never exist...' I retorted, 'I still love David, despite what's happened.'

'Sorry, sorry - sacred ground - it's just he wondered if there was anyone in your life, most of us have a morbid curiosity about our ex-partners, don't we?'

I handed Helen a plate of stew and homemade bread. Eve wasn't joining us - she'd discovered Minette's supply of chocolate ginger biscuits in the cupboard and had disappeared upstairs to share them with her sister.

'I suppose you'll always have someone, Helen - you have that vital spark men like...' I told her.

'I blaze and you smoulder?' she suggested with a laugh.

This was the version of Helen I'd met on my last morning in Pimlico - ruthless and hurtful - I resented her comment – and was angry that I'd created the opportunity for her to make it.

But Helen's attention had flitted elsewhere, she said, 'I always thought David fed off you and in certain ways he enjoyed that.'

'I'd hoped we complemented each other.'

'It's as if you've been in bud all your life, but haven't yet flowered.'

It was a clumsy analogy. 'And now the bud is so wizened and brown it's hardly likely to bloom – more likely to drop to the ground?'

'I reckon you've got about ten years before that happens,' she replied. Her gaze was drawn to the kitchen window and the view of the garden beyond, 'What *are* you going to do with all this? It must be so dull here compared to London...'

'Does it matter? I may only stay a year...'

She didn't comment and once we'd eaten, grew restless. While I cleared the kitchen, I noticed her looking me up and down - under her scrutiny I became conscious of my clothes - torn jeans and a thick black sweater that had once belonged to David.

'Safford Bridge has the nearest decent shops?' Helen asked, 'You look like a woman who needs to shop.'

'Minette isn't well enough...'

'Couldn't we just take a look?' Helen asked, 'I've written down Minette's measurements, she doesn't need to come, and I've a few more things to get for the wedding. You can't refuse when I've driven all this way to help you.'

I suspected the worst thing that could happen to Helen was to be bored - I'd encountered children like her in the French conversation classes at St. Catherine's, you failed to occupy them at your peril, so I agreed we should go to town.

In the bathroom, I put up my hair, and changed into a wool print dress in shades of deep blue and turquoise. I'd probably freeze to death, but at least I wouldn't feel ashamed of my appearance. I heard the phone ring, but left it while I finished applying my make-up, if it happened to be David, I didn't want to speak to him.

When I went downstairs, Helen said, 'There's a message from the piano tuner.'

She had probably meant well, though I thought she had a nerve answering my phone. 'What did he say?' I asked.

She shrugged. 'Sorry, I wasn't really listening.'

I slipped on my coat and opened the door. I was growing tired of fighting my corner and hoped she also would soon have had enough and go back home.

Helen's work made her an avid bargain hunter; she liked to browse and to haggle, so we spent the afternoon shopping, apart from a brief break for tea at The Pilgrims' Inn. It was market day and Helen wanted to hunt for vintage clothes at a good price, or fabric she could use to repair things or make accessories to sell in her shop.

She elbowed her way through the crowds - raking the stalls for jewellery, beads and trimmings she could up-cycle and sell for a better price in London. She touched everything, passing the fabric through her fingers, smoothing it to feel the texture, weighing it in her hands. She held up a roll of navy velvet and offered to cut it for me into a jacket – but I couldn't think when or where I might wear blue velvet in my new life on Littern - besides which, I still had birthday money from Flora and Alice to spend on a new coat.

When we'd exhausted the market, Helen asked where we would find the smart shops in town - she was looking for something stylish to wear in her hair for the wedding.

In a boutique called *Stuff & Nonsense* she bought herself a fascinator, a cream silk jacket and an evening bag in a swirling pattern of burgundy red, complemented with a dash of chocolate brown and lime green. She found a flounced cream silk frock for Minette and said she would take it to show David - if he approved - Minette could try it on when her spots had healed.

Having found what she wanted Helen seemed in a better mood, but I felt like a traitor. I hadn't yet explained that Minette would prefer not to be her bridesmaid, in which case David's opinion of the dress scarcely mattered – she wouldn't be wearing it.

We left the shop and walked across the town square to where I'd parked behind the Priory. As we drew near to the car, I heard Kelda's flute, a faint trace of music in the air. I looked all around, until I made out her figure, crouched down by the wall of the Bridge House Bookshop, beneath the window, where an enormous poster advertised their sale. I dropped a ten pound note into her black hat as we passed. Kelda nodded and her eyes stayed on me, they seemed to follow my progress along the street as if she was watching over me, like a dark angel.

'You shouldn't encourage those people,' Helen said, making sure Kelda heard.

'...Why not?' I asked, 'If I was down and out, I'd like to think someone might do the same for me...' I didn't tell her that I also viewed almsgiving like a talisman, in the hope someone on the other side of the world would help Zoë if she was in need.

'You've wrecked David's Peugeot,' she said, bundling her packages onto the back seat, 'though I suppose a clapped out car goes well with muddy wellingtons and Jesus sandals. David wonders how long you'll stick the rural life style...'

Though it was a reasonable question, I couldn't give a straight answer. One day I thought I could stay at Marisands forever, the next I wished I'd never come.

As we left the car park and turned onto the Narescombe Road, Helen said, 'I'm not like you. I couldn't contemplate spending years putting up with someone I didn't like, but neither could I imagine spending the rest of my life alone.'

I felt she was criticising me – emphasising the fact that I'd hung on beyond the point where any reasonable person would have seen that my relationship with David was over.

'I acted as I did because I loved David. Perhaps one day you'll discover that you don't...'

Helen's face set into hard lines - I'd gone too far. 'David will never come back to you,' she said, 'if he thinks about you at all, it's only idle curiosity...'

'Doesn't it occur to you or to David that I might not want or be willing to have him back?'

'No, because that isn't true...'

'Isn't it? David can be very aggressive - you'll need to watch out if you make him angry...'

We arrived back at Marisands having passed the rest of the journey in silence. I didn't like to leave Eve at Helen's mercy, but Minette was miserable, her spots itched so much they made her cry and I'd spent almost no time with her.

I discovered a bottle of calamine lotion in the bathroom cabinet, the chalky pink sediment had separated from the clear liquid and sunk to the bottom, but I gave it a good shake and dabbed it gently on to her rash.

'Yuuka has more spots than me, we counted and I've been looking after her, until she gets better, I hope I'll win the Service and Sacrifice medal.'

'It's Yuuka that matters, not the medal,' I reminded her. 'Sister Gabriel and Rose say you've been in trouble again, helping Yuuka in exams, what will she do when you've gone away?'

'I'm not going away,' Minette said stubbornly.

And it wasn't the right moment to pursue the idea of her not returning to school. Instead, I promised to find an envelope for the encyclopaedic letter she had written her friend and to post it the following morning.

'I wish I could have brought Yuuka here with me,' she said, 'I didn't want to leave her behind on her own.'

'I'm not sure I could have coped with two spotty girls ...'

'You could – you're very good with children, Sister Gabriel said so.'

'It's lovely to have you to myself.'

I read to her and soon she grew sleepy.

While she dozed, I sat at her bedside, resting my head in my hands. *When were things going to come right?* Helen's visit had shown me Marisands through a stranger's eyes and my cleaning and tidying efforts seemed pitiful - the house was still a muddle. Though Kos worked diligently in the garden, most of it remained no better than a jungle.

Eve disturbed me, tapping softly on the door - she and Helen had finished their meal. She settled beside me for a moment, resting her arm on my shoulder, 'Please don't do this again – getting in a state...'

'I can't seem to help myself,' I said, close to tears, 'I feel so hurt. If only I could hate David, then it wouldn't matter...'

'You love Dad and you probably always will...'

'Then if I could hate Helen...'

'She *is* very annoying...' Eve said.

I didn't admit how nasty I'd been that afternoon.

By the time I felt calm enough to go downstairs, Helen had taken her place on the sofa in front of the fire and despite the tense atmosphere, she showed no sign of leaving.

Eve brought us coffee and cake and then made her excuses to leave.

'Do you really intend to stay here, letting life pass you by..?' Helen asked.

'I've taken sanctuary, but it doesn't have to be forever...'

'Lesley said to tell you she's fixing a venue for a reading of David's work. She's negotiating a date for the summer, *Blue Rhythms* is almost finished and it's a sort of pre-book publicity event. She claims she's staked her career on its success, but she has a new friend in Halkett & Haire and I understand he's pulled a few strings.'

Helen was only gossiping, but her remark touched a sensitive place. Lesley had once referred to David as "a tart" where the publication of his poetry was concerned, but now she'd shown no compunction in exercising her own influence through means of a relationship.

'Aren't you pleased?' Helen asked.

'I hope the book's a success - for David's sake - writing it almost destroyed his health.'

Helen scoffed, 'David's terrible, worrying about his health all the time – I tell him it's like marrying an old woman.'

'You're marrying a much older man, whose health is vulnerable,' I reminded her.

'He's fine if he doesn't get stressed.' She turned her gaze on me and said almost casually, 'Eve doesn't think Zoë will come back for the wedding and she isn't sure if she'll make it herself. So I thought *you* could bring Minette, David will be devastated if none of his children is there...'

I thought Helen must surely be the most inconsiderate person I had ever met - expecting me to endure the humiliation of attending their wedding on the pretext of ensuring my daughter attended, even though she didn't want to.

'Minette's confused and upset about what's happening – she might not want to go either.'

'You're turning David's children against him?'

'Zoë and Eve draw their own conclusions and so does she...'

'Minette isn't old enough to draw conclusions. Are you saying you *won't* bring her?' Helen demanded.

'If she wants to be there, I'll make arrangements,' I said, finally losing my patience. 'In the meantime I'm taking Quirk for a walk and I'd prefer it if you'd left Marisands by the time I get back.'

While I was still in control, I made my escape into the hall, roughly pulling on my coat and walking shoes. Shoulders hunched, my hands making tight fists in my coat pockets, I hurried down the beach path, getting scratched as I stumbled into the overhanging branches of the blackthorn hedge.

On the beach, the full moon made a straight path across a calm sea; I slowed my steps as I reached the water's edge. Quirk began to bark at the moon – a senseless noise ringing out into the night. Hurt and frustrated, I let out a roar of exasperation because my loving feelings for David refused to die or even to lie dormant – because Helen was immature, arrogant and presumptuous – and because David managed to provoke me even from a distance of over two hundred miles.

Breathing in deep draughts of cold fresh air, I heard Helen approaching. She'd borrowed a pair of Wellingtons from the hall and looked ridiculous as she staggered across the beach, her feet making squelching sounds as they sank into the soft wet sand. I moved away from her, walking along through breaking waves, towards Morrow Bay.

Helen called out, 'My feet are killing me - your boots are too small.'

I stopped and waited for her from a sense of duty, she reminded me of a naughty child. I could hear her teeth chattering, she hadn't put on a coat when she left the house -

She drew level with me and said, 'David unnerves me - I need a fall-back position - some kind of security, that's why I want us to get married.' She wrapped her arms round her body, rubbing them up and down, trying to get warm.

'John told me you made each other happy.'

'We do - it's just that sometimes I'm afraid.'

'David's an expert in ambivalence, he probably enjoys frightening you. If you don't understand him fully, *should* you get married?'

The moonlight glinted in Helen's eyes, 'You haven't lost your spirit...' she said.

'I need my spirit to survive living here.'

'I noticed your holy relics - do you still believe in all that?' she asked.

Despite my anger, I laughed - Helen had been observant - Juliet's rosary was hung on the landing and the figure of the White Virgin was near Alexander's holy water stoup, in the hall.

'I'm not sure what I believe.'

'Could we go back to the house now?' she asked.

We climbed the pathway back towards Marisands and I heard her struggling for breath on the steepest part of the track.

I couldn't make sense of her visit. Had she come to Littern to enjoy my disapproval – or in some bizarre way - was she hoping for my blessing on their marriage?

Then as we went indoors, the truth seemed to rise to the surface, she said, 'I've wanted David for years and now I've got him. I've always had to have my own way, whether it's in my best interests or not...'

'Is it in your best interests - *or his*?' I asked.

Helen shrugged. 'It's what I'm going to do...'

Minutes later, I heard her making a phone call upstairs, the rumble of conversation audible through the bedroom wall.

Soon, she reappeared smartly dressed in her London clothes, fully made-up, her hair - a rich, flowing red mane - caught up in a ponytail.

Though she owed me no explanation, she said, 'John's driving David back to Pimlico tonight, he'll be waiting when I get there.'

In other circumstances, her eagerness to see David might have been touching, instead I felt a sharp stab of jealousy. I saw her to her car - a flamboyant creature dressed in purple and mustard yellow - and doubted she would ever want to return to Littern, where life was rough edged, cold and uncomfortable.

# Chapter 24

I'd suggested Kos should make arrangements with the piano tuner and the next morning, Mr. Nesbit, arrived promptly at eight o'clock. He was blind and a taxi had brought him to the island from his home in Safford Bridge.

He tapped his way along the hall to the music room using his white stick to guide him. I hovered behind in case he bumped into anything, but he needed no help, as if piano tuners had an instinct for finding pianos, just as a dowser detects the presence of water.

While Mr. Nesbit was busy, I let Quirk have a run round the garden. I wrapped myself in my cloak and looked over the flower beds which Kos had tended. There were cowslips and violets, scented and sweet – pale primroses, braving the north wind. I was sipping a mug of coffee, warming my hands, when Kos swooped into the drive on his bicycle and jumped off with a flourish, propping his bike against the wooden pillars of the garage.

'Mr. Nesbit is here?' he asked.

'Yes – go in,' I said.

Kos listened from the hallway, fidgeting with his long hair, brushing it behind his ears as if to hear better, as discordant sounds leaked out into the hallway.

'Someone should be with the piano,' he said.

'You...' I told him, 'I'll bring coffee, soon.'

Carrying a tray, I eased my way into the music room, elbowing the door open. Mr. Nesbit had shed his jacket over the back of a chair and was peering into the entrails of the instrument as if hoping to divine its future. Kos, close by, was leaning forward, his dark hair flopping over his face, his hand resting on the piano as if comforting a beautiful but fragile woman.

I set the tray down on the cabinet where the sheet music was kept. I'd been planning a few changes to the house including the idea of making the music room into a small library-study. With the piano moved to the sitting room, I thought I might fit in Flora's writing desk, a small armchair, a lamp and table; it could become my personal refuge.

In the meantime, neither Kos nor Mr. Nesbit required my presence so I left them. Eve came downstairs, dressed in a woollen dressing gown she'd borrowed from my wardrobe, her face swollen and rimed with smudges and trails of mascara.

'That racket woke me up,' she whispered.

'I'll make more coffee,' I suggested, feeling I might accomplish nothing else that day other than supplying people with drinks.

'Bring it to me?' Eve asked smiling, 'Minette thinks she might get up later...'

Mr. Nesbit continued to work and the tension in the house seemed to mount, as if we were waiting for a life-changing event, such as a baby being born. Feeling at a loose end, I brought a notebook down from the study and sat at the kitchen table by the window drawing the spring flowers I'd noticed earlier. So far, I'd failed to make even a half-hearted attempt at illustrations for the artist's diary which had been suggested by Rose and Neil, and before I could complete the drawing, a squall blew in and lashed rain against the kitchen window obliterating any view of the garden.

When she'd dressed, Eve joined me at the table, eating her breakfast of yoghurt and fruit, gazing at the rain.

'If Kos can't garden today, why don't you ask him to bring stuff up from the cellar? While I'm here, we can both help - it makes sense, doesn't it?'

I seemed to ask Kos to do everything and didn't want to take further advantage of his willing nature, but the idea took root and began to grow in my mind - I was anxious to discover what might be in the wooden chest and there was a chance that between us we might work out how it could be opened.

Picking up my pen, I made a few notes to my rough sketches and pushed the notebook aside. Kos had begun to play scales, which gradually progressed into snatches of a Prokofiev. With a sense of relief, I paid Mr. Nesbit and made arrangements for him to be despatched back to Safford Bridge.

When Mr. Nesbit had gone, Kos came through to the kitchen.

'Iris wants to ask you something,' Eve said to him. She was standing by the sink washing up plates and cups.

'You're happy with the piano?' I said.

'If the piano is tuned once, maybe twice more it will be *almost perfect* ...'

Kos's brown eyes flickered nervously from my face to Eve at the sink. When Eve was around it was as if he'd been hypnotised - he couldn't keep his eyes off her.

'There was something else,' I said, and explained about the heavy cases in the cellar.

Eve showed Kos where the trapdoor was set into the larder floor. She pulled on the ring handle and the door fell back with a crash. I fetched the torch and clambered down the steps far enough to allow Kos to see what the task would involve.

Minette appeared, looking for breakfast, 'Is this a rural custom?' she asked, 'Sister Gabriel says some very funny things go on in the country, like Morris Dancing.'

'Stand back!' Kos shouted and brought two of the heavy leather suitcases to the head of the steps.

I hauled them out into the kitchen and checked they were completely empty before moving them into the hall. Kos brought one trunk, case or box after another up the steps and Eve and I carried them away until after half an hour, the only item left in the cellar was the wooden chest.

'Where did this chest come from?' Kos called to me, his voice echoing in the empty space.

'It belonged to my grandmother. That's all I know.' I'd thought perhaps Alexander had given it to her on their marriage and that possibly it had belonged to his mother.

Eve and I climbed down into the cellar - the chest was too heavy for Kos to lift alone.

'We have many such marriage chests in my country,' Kos said, running his fingers over the surface of the box, tracing the deep carvings in the wood. He tried the lid of the chest in case it would open – but there was no movement – so we pushed it to the foot of the steps, where Eve squeezed past us and prepared to help hoist it up through the trap door.

We could only manage one step at a time and then the chest had to be edged through the gap carefully, without scraping its sides or crushing our fingers. But at last, we had pulled it clear of the larder and Kos and Eve carried it through to the living room.

Minette watched expectantly as I knelt down and we tipped the box onto its side. The carvings were fine, done by someone skilled and the design matched perfectly the smaller carvings on the box I'd been given - the trees with their entwined branches, the symbol of two crossed keys. I felt round the base for the narrow indents that would mark the place where the opening mechanism should be hidden in its small compartment. We turned the base of the box towards the light and searched for tell-tale lines in the wood, but nothing was visible.

I stood back and let the others try to find how the lock worked. Eve probed with the tips of her fingers to see if any part of the ornate carvings moved or slid aside.

'These boxes have many tricks,' Kos said. But despite our efforts none of us could find the trick to this one.

'Let's leave it,' I suggested. 'I don't want to try anymore.'

'Force it – force the lock,' Minette urged, she was excited, expecting the box to contain treasure, but I didn't want to spoil the appearance of the chest or break the catch.

'I'll phone Flora, later,' I told her, 'let's hope she can remember how it opens.'

It was an anti-climax, but we moved the chest to the music room and dealt with the pile of cases and boxes in the hall, which needed to be taken out to the garage.

Kos had been quiet and before he returned to his camp, promised he'd figure out how the lock on the wedding chest worked and would come back to tell me.

When we were back in the house, Eve asked, 'Do you really know who or what Kos is?'

'I only know he seems to be a good person...'

'It's just that he doesn't seem like someone who'd be happy living in a van – or having to scrounge for work, just to play a piano.'

I'd observed that quality in Kos too - he seemed well-educated and well-mannered.

'I know what Kos likes...' Minette piped up, 'He likes Eve – he kept staring at her.'

Frowning a warning to her, I put my finger to my lips, there were times when Minette didn't know when to stop.

'He did keep looking at her,' she insisted, 'and Eve wouldn't look back, except out of the corner of her eyes, that means she finds him attractive.'

Eve left the room.

'Don't tease,' I whispered, 'you're upsetting your sister, go and say sorry,'

But before she could do so, the door of the conservatory had banged shut - Eve was taking Quirk out. She hadn't got over her break-up with Luke.

'Sorry...' Minette said to me. 'Please don't tell me off.' She made a sad little figure in her dressing-gown and slippers. She shook her head, as if in deep distress, 'I think I want to go back to bed.'

'Why not keep me company?' I said to encourage her, 'Eve will be fine when she comes back.'

Late in the afternoon, Kos reappeared. He tapped on the kitchen window and out of his pocket produced a vicious looking implement, a hook made of heavy wire which he waved at me.

'Stay here,' I said.

Eve and Minette, amused by Kos's performance had both began to giggle, but if Kos thought they were laughing at him, I'd probably never see him again.

When I let him in, Kos announced, 'I can open the lock of the wedding chest, without doing harm.' He sounded like a magician about to perform a difficult trick.

In the music room, he crouched down by the chest, his head hung - his hair masking his expression. With deep concentration, he wriggled the wire hook in the lock – and though it didn't give way at once - after several minutes I heard a satisfying click as the latch was released.

Kos lifted the lid and the front of the box folded down, revealing several smaller boxes inside, like a series of drawers. On the top row was a cavity where the box my father had sent me when I was a child would fit perfectly -

I pulled out one of the drawers, I'd been afraid each might be locked in a secret way and Kos would have to solve the puzzle of opening them one by one. The drawer I'd chosen was empty, faintly musty – but the scent of Tuberose drifted into the air – my mother's perfume - haunting and familiar.

'Thank you, Kos,' I said closing the drawer quickly, anxious in case the trace of perfume should dissipate – disappear forever.

I wanted to be left alone to explore the contents of the chest and was relieved when Kos understood without being told. He produced a sliver of wood from his pocket and showed me how I could wedge the lid of the chest open, almost invisibly. The wooden piece had a hole cut from the centre; I could fit it between the two halves of the lock so that it didn't catch and open the lid whenever I needed to.

Kos nodded, in the quaint way he had - almost a bow. 'I'll leave you, now,' he said, with the faint smile which meant he was satisfied he had done a good job.

I knelt with my hands resting on the chest. Within its compartments I might find answers to my questions - or I might find nothing. I raised the lid, slipped out the filet of wood and opened the drawers. There were diaries of my mother's – blue covered notebooks. Other books were bound in brown leather, soft and powdery with age - those were filled with little drawings of plants and flowers, labelled in Juliet's handwriting. In an old chocolate box were letters and photographs, letters from Juliet to my father, written when she'd been his student and had admired him and his work.

The largest of the drawers ran right across the bottom of the chest. Inside was a polythene bag of my mother's clothes, her bright pink sundress, neatly folded - the dress she had worn the day she had drowned. I pressed my face into its folds and could just make out the lingering scent. Beneath the dress was a small parcel wrapped in green tissue. I lifted it out and separated the leaves of paper until a dark object fell onto my lap. This time, I knew what it would be - Alice must have returned it to my father. But still I cried out in shock - as disturbed as I had been in the kitchen of Wren House as a nine year old child - on the floor by my knees, lay my mother's severed plait, the braid of chestnut hair which had been cut off when she went to the tower.

The hair was secured at both ends with a rubber band - it felt dry and coarse, had lost its sheen and the rich red highlights which had made my mother so beautiful. I turned the braid in my hands, it had been roughly hacked off and the image of my mother as she had pushed towards me in the sea flashed into my mind – her silhouette against the bright summer sky - her head, not smooth and sleek as it should have been, but surrounded with a halo of spikes of hair.

My head began to ache; a sharp pain stabbed behind my right eye and temple. *What could have induced her to cut off her hair - and so brutally? Would anyone else have dared to do it - would my father?*

It troubled me that there must have been some warning of my mother's state of mind, a warning perhaps comprehensible even to a child. Wilfully or not, had everyone around her missed or ignored the signs of her despair?

Tenderly, I wrapped the hair in its green tissue paper and replaced it in the drawer – it seemed to represent both Juliet's shame and mine.

Silvie's words came back to me, that the wounds of the past could be healed by exposure to fresh air, cleansing and the application of love.

Lowering the lid of the wedding chest, I replaced the slither of wood carefully, making sure that the lock didn't quite click back into place.

\*

That night, in bed, I began to read Juliet's diaries. I learned how on first leaving Littern she had felt torn between the promise of the future and memories of the past - how returning to Marisands had been an agony of fear and anticipation.

After Geraldine's arrival, she described the atmosphere at Marisands as *rife with sex and unhappiness*. William expounded the concept of "Frith" - a state of well-being brought about by right living and right action - and yet he did everything in his power to negate the principle. Meanwhile, my mother had tried to live out her philosophy that the direction she should take would emerge on its own, only to discover that leaving her future to some external force, whether God or fate, had led her not towards joy but towards disappointment and pain.

She wrote of the time we had visited Bernard in London, just before his death. *Is it a blessing or a curse that I fall pregnant so easily? God forgive me - I don't want William's child - it would be like having something alien growing within me.* Two years later, she wrote of her stillborn baby - *I've been shipwrecked on a vast sea - this is God's retribution for what I have done.* An almost illegible note followed - *An innocent wrenched from the eternal waters of the womb into the sea of time.* What did she mean? The words could have been an epitaph for her lost child.

I read and re-read the page many times trying to make sense of it. Had Juliet's operation been an abortion? Was it possible she had acted against the mores of the time, against her own personal beliefs and conscience to rid her body of that *something alien growing within me...?* Would she have confided in anyone – Flora, Silvie, Delia, one of the Pirans? Surely not Kathleen - so devoutly Catholic - unless she had hoped Kathleen would dissuade her from an action which she sensed might cause her unbearable grief in the future.

The diaries related how, for years, Kathleen's illness had forced constraints on the household at Lyncross, how she and Antony and Tom had become less close and she had *talked instead to James Millford - who is attentive and listens to me.* They had become friends, soul mates. He had encouraged her to create the nature notebooks, sharing his knowledge and taking her to places on the island where the flora and fauna were especially significant - he had shown her the way to Clave Valley. It was unmistakeable - the drawings in those notebooks formed the source for the flowers, animals and shells in *The Stations of the Cross* paintings.

Later, when she'd returned to Littern with William, she discovered James hadn't dropped his plans to move to London and attend RADA. She had written - *my heart went cold* - as if James was abandoning her in a personal way, leaving her to manage her loveless marriage. Inside the diaries, I found letters from James to my mother. Other letters from Antony offered her consolation in a way that was part mentor, part friend and occasionally suggested the intimacy of a lover. But though Antony had intended to enter Holy Orders, it was James who taught Juliet his faith, the Catholicism to which Delia had told me my mother had aspired towards the end of her life. His company and his words had seemed to help her to forget about William, who was *constantly in a rage* and *by his own condemnation working with all the conviction of a performing monkey.*

By the spring of Juliet's final year, her writing amounted to no more than scribbled notes, without sketches and lacking her characteristic humour. *William maintains my frigidity* - she wrote, and perhaps with deliberate ambiguity - *he dislikes it now I have proven him wrong.*

*I used to have faith that sadness would be superseded by joy, but not anymore. When I acknowledge happiness for what it is – it evaporates, until I'm afraid of hoping or searching for joy, until I feel the absence of sadness would be enough for me to survive. Without pain and disappointment, might I feel strong enough to carry on..?*

Her words were followed by an arrow and the symbol of a 10 enclosed in a circle. I noticed then that on the spine of each of the diaries was written a number – I had all of them up to the ninth, but the last was missing. Had it been lost, destroyed - given to someone for safe keeping - or never started?

In the end, my mother hadn't concerned herself with facts – the dates were no longer exact - but the diaries revealed her emotional life to be more complex than I had imagined.

Though to onlookers, it must have appeared that my mother had followed me into a rip tide and been swept away - I was increasingly developing the conviction that Juliet had walked into the sea to drown and had dragged me with her - convinced the answer to her troubles was not only to bring about her own death, but also mine.

*

Finally, it had been agreed that Minette should remain at St. Catherine's until the summer and for the moment she was content. Eve had taken her back to school, planning to visit friends in London; she would stay with Alice and Flora for a few days.

Each morning, Quirk waited inside the door of the conservatory for me to let him out, licking my hand with his warm pink tongue as I reached down to scratch the tuft of black curls on top of his head.

While I watched him in the garden, he scented his way round the bushes and trees, startling fat woodpigeons which perched in the holly tree, though the bush had long been stripped of its red berries by faster, less clumsy birds.

Amused, I had drawn them balanced on twigs which could barely hold their weight and added the picture to the collection I was making for Minette's next letter. Quirk watched me too and tried to delay the moment when I began work, recognising the rituals which were a prelude to my going to the study - making coffee and putting on David's thick black cardigan.

I kept Juliet's sketches for *The Stations* on the side of my desk. I'd been poring over them, feeling there was something not quite right about the paintings, as if someone – perhaps William - had tampered with her original work, but had lacked her delicacy of touch.

Before losing myself in Laurence's papers, I checked through e-mails in case Zoë had written. There had been no news for ages, and I was schooling myself not to assume her silences were sinister, for when she did communicate, she usually had something to say which was witty, caustic or prophetic. Hoping to inspire a response, I tapped out a few lines, telling her about Minette's holiday, Helen's visit and the forthcoming wedding.

When, I could create no more distractions, I settled down to a session of deciphering Laurence's scrawled handwriting and opaque French prose. I sipped coffee from the faded, red paisley mug I'd found in Juliet's workshop. Only half aware of what I was doing, I allowed the mug to collide with my pile of reference books and the impact was enough to dislodge the body of the mug from the handle, sending a wash of coffee dregs across Juliet's sketches, where they lay on the desk beside the keyboard.

I ran to the bathroom, grabbed a towel and hurried back to mop up the mess, praying that the coffee wouldn't have dissolved the ink into a meaningless blur.

'Get away,' I scolded Quirk, clicking my fingers and signalling with a sweep of my arm he should move. He had the habit of hogging the fire, of lying so close that after a short while I could smell his fur singeing. He shuffled away lazily and flopped down in a corner.

Nudging him with my foot, I blotted at the papers so as not to smudge the ink and then switched on the desk lamp to see the damage. Thank God - Juliet had used waterproof ink - but the strong coffee had left brown stains where pools of liquid had formed. The drawings, already faint, were soiled and gritty with dregs and there were brown outlines where coffee had sunk into the imprint of pen strokes, I hadn't noticed before.

'What's going on?' Eve asked.

I spun round. She was standing in the doorway, wrapped in one of the blankets from her bed, her short fair hair standing up in peaks.

'What does it look like?' I snapped, 'I've spilt coffee on Juliet's work and everything's ruined.'

'Let me see...'

'Get away from the desk!' I shouted, still upset.

'Perhaps I can fix it – I know what to do...' Eve said.

I heard the hurt in Eve's voice. Since her return to Marisands she had been unnaturally sensitive - the trip to London had if anything left her more disconsolate than before.

Tears were seeping from her eyes, 'I feel so useless,' she said, sobbing into her hands, 'no-one thinks I can do anything...'

I pulled a tissue out of the box on my desk and handed it to her. 'Sorry – it was stupid of me – it means so much to have you here...'

Putting my arms around her, I felt the hopelessness of my words. David had told me that when he was depressed nothing could impinge on his despair – was that what Eve felt? Upsets with her used to pass like spring showers - light and brief - but this time, her tears wouldn't stop.

Quirk licked Eve's bare feet, full of sympathy, but she pushed him away with her knee.

'Why not get dressed, and then take a look at the sketches,' I said.

She didn't argue and wandered off to the bathroom, blowing her nose and taking in gulps of air. I put Laurence's notes back in their folder and gave up the idea of working for the day. What had happened at Zethar Creek had gone deep with Eve and some aftershock must have occurred in London. Concerned for her, I recalled the many things I'd promised and had failed to do – to have William's car repaired so that she could use it and to evict Geraldine, so she could work in studio.

Eve was soon back. She leant over the desk, turning the lamp towards her, 'There are other drawings underneath the ones you've seen – the coffee has sunk into pencil lines that have been rubbed out...'

'Can you make anything of them?' I asked.

'Not easily – but it's as if the first idea hasn't been erased exactly, but turned into something new – a woman's figure has become the basis of the Christ figure in All Soul's – other faces in the crowd have been altered...'

'Why would Juliet do that?' I asked, 'Why hide her original idea?'

'Leave them to me?' Eve suggested.

'In the meantime, I could make fresh coffee...'

Downstairs, Eve slipped into her place at the kitchen table, her back to the window. Quirk sat beside her and she fondled his soft ears, head bowed as if she didn't want to be spoken to or to speak.

'I haven't been able to make things better, have I?' I said, 'I hoped being at Marisands might help...'

'It isn't you,' Eve said.

Who then...or what..? I wondered.

Eve shook her head as if in response to my unspoken words.

'Do you know what would make a difference?' I asked. David would have said, *Fuck off and leave me alone.*

'Just don't take too much notice of me,' Eve suggested - it was the same message, more politely expressed. 'I'll look at the sketches another day. I thought I'd explore the island, take my camera and a sketchbook...'

'You'd like to go alone? You could take my car – I won't need it.'

'I'd prefer to walk.'

She started to get ready to leave and I hoped she would heed the warnings I'd given about the treachery of the island, the marshes and the beaches, the places where you had to watch in case the tide rushed in. Despite the bone-chilling weather, she set off wearing her light blue anorak over a thin jumper, which offered little protection from the penetrating cold.

As I closed the gate behind Eve, Geraldine's dark figure appeared in the lane. By the time she had reached the house, I had the key to the studio ready so I could give it to her without inviting her indoors. I had caught Eve's low spirits, dogged by a sense of dread, as if anything I'd achieved so far at Marisands might be swept away in an instant by an act of divine indifference.

Recently, Kos hadn't come to the house as often, despite the improvements to the piano and I suspected Eve's presence inhibited him – he was painfully shy. And though I tried to make terms with Zoë's silences, the truth was they wore me down, like Geraldine's persistence in turning up to use the studio, when I had dropped unmistakeable hints that I would prefer it if she worked at home.

It was drizzling as Eve left Marisands, but soon the hard edges of the garden were softened by a light fall of snow. I chopped vegetables and made soup - Eve would be hungry when she came back. While I was cooking, Quirk played in the garden, his black woolly figure padding across the snowy grass, his head turned up, mouth snapping at snowflakes, his eyebrows peaked with amazement as the world was silently transformed before his eyes. He dashed to and fro leaving a trail of paw prints in the freshly fallen snow.

When the soup was ready, I filled a thermos, cut bread and set it on a plate. Putting on my thick coat and boots, I set off down the garden to the studio, ordering Quirk to lie down on the step outside and wait.

'I thought you'd need something warm to eat,' I said to Geraldine.

'You needn't have bothered...'

The studio was full of an uncomfortable reflected light that hurt my eyes – but Geraldine seemed untroubled working in the harsh white glare. She stood on a piece of sacking she'd spread out on the floor by the easel. A spare figure, in her duffle coat - her wind-torn grey hair drifted out from beneath her tea-cosy hat, she wore fingerless gloves and her chest was covered in drifts of ash from the cigarette which dangled from her lips.

'This is nothing,' she said and made a broad gesture with her paintbrush to indicate the falling snow outside, 'by the time winter's over, most of us have been driven one step closer to madness by the cold and wind.'

She was painting the tower again and each picture she produced appeared to get darker, though they were all dim, brown and shadowy. She varied them only by changing the perspective from which the tower was viewed, though it always emerged with the same backdrop – the sea and the rocks at Morrow Bay.

'The day my mother died, you went for a walk to the tower with Shirley and my father,' I said as if discussing her paintings, not wanting to sound accusatory.

'...And?' Geraldine asked, lighting another cigarette.

'I've found my mother's plait. Someone had hidden it in a chest in the cellar.'

Geraldine paused in her work and stared past me into the garden towards the snow covered white statues, 'Some things are better not known,' she said; it was the same phrase my father had used, when we had met in London. 'That summer, your mother was unwell - she was depressed after losing her baby – she couldn't think straight, she jumped to conclusions...'

'You and my father formed a circle of silence around my mother's death and I don't understand why you won't break that silence, even now...'

Geraldine laid down her paintbrush and unscrewed the top of the thermos flask. As she poured soup into the cup, the steam of the hot liquid rose to meet the steam of her breath - she took the bread and broke it into pieces on the surface of the soup.

'You persist in believing there's something *I* ought to tell you – but you'll find the circle of silence is wider than you think – have you considered the role of Pirans or James Millford, your new friend Delia Colebrook or Kelda Sullivan?'

'When Kelda left the beach did she go to the tower? '

'She wanted to speak to William...'

'And what she said upset my mother?'

'What she said upset everyone.'

'What did she say?' I urged her.

Geraldine returned to her painting, screwing up her eyes as she worked. 'That was a private conversation. The tragedy was William spent the rest of his life subject to blame and blaming himself because of his reaction to what Kelda said.'

'Who cut off Juliet's hair?' I asked.

'Who do you think? She cut it off herself.'

'Do you know why?'

A look of impatience deepened Geraldine's frown, 'Juliet was fond of rituals – she believed in ritual expiation – I suppose it had some meaning for her, though to the rest of us she appeared merely hysterical.'

Geraldine had never suffered fools gladly and as she considered most people to be fools, few escaped the sharp edge of her tongue - I felt her dismissal of my mother keenly.

'There seems to be no way of establishing an objective truth about my mother's life or death or her work…' I was tired of us both repeating our entrenched points of view.

Geraldine asked, 'What does *objective* mean? I doubt it exists outside the minds of intellectuals.'

'I mean standing back, keeping an open mind…'

'…Really?' Geraldine countered, 'Haven't you been gathering up the crumbs of Juliet's life hoping to turn them into something unpalatable? William did his penance before he died – he wanted to finish Juliet's *Stations* - to carry on where she'd left off - and do it in her style.'

'Would he have been working on *The Stations* when we met in London?'

'You've seen the canvas,' she said, nodding towards the shrouded metal frame, 'William was beyond working by then, he had no chance of completing them, but he couldn't stop…'

'Because he loved my mother..?'

'Because he loved himself and didn't wish to go to hell.' Geraldine inhaled deeply from her cigarette.

Returning to her painting of the tower, she began to scrape and flick paint onto the canvas to represent sheaves of dried grass. I could see we might spend the rest of eternity conversing in questions that never got answered - perhaps that was my own definition of hell.

'Why won't you tell me what I need to know - the truth?'

Geraldine smiled - an expression full of wickedness. 'You deal in abstract concepts. You want to believe in absolutes, "objectivity" and "truth". If you want those you'll have to look elsewhere.'

'Shirley Fredericks? Do you think I'll find the truth there? She was in the tower on the day Juliet died.'

'You'll get nothing from Shirley.'

I gazed out at the oratory garden – at Juliet's white statues. *What were they – had they any meaning?*

'Your dog will be getting cold,' Geraldine said - bringing me down to earth.

I'd forgotten Quirk lying on the step and I'd forgotten Eve, out somewhere on the island in the worsening weather. When I opened the studio door, Quirk was crouched, patiently waiting for me, a layer of snow and ice across his back.

'Why don't you finish now?' I said to Geraldine, 'I'm going to lock up.'

Very slowly she wiped her brushes and scraped remnants of paint from her palette - the latest painting of the tower looked almost complete.

Knowing her loyalty to my father, it was hard to condemn her – she wanted to protect him. How many women could have tolerated William? How many years had she spent hoping to be at the centre of his world, while he forced her again and again to the perimeter?

She packed up at a sloth's pace, but when at last she was ready - I picked up the flask and plate, turned off lights and fastened the door.

Quirk shook himself and skittered through the snow, leaping every now and then to catch falling flakes as we trudged in procession across the garden.

'When that painting is finished, I'd like my daughter to use the studio,' I said.

'Has she asked to use the studio?'

Heat rose to my cheeks, I hadn't asked Eve - I'd assumed.

Seeing my discomfort, Geraldine said, 'Ask her, then let me know, I'm sure we can come to an arrangement...'

When we reached the house, I told her, 'You don't have the right to be here - you're only here because I allow you to be.'

She turned away with a smile of contempt. In an awkward movement, she mounted her bicycle and rode off down the lane. I watched her unsteady progress on the slippery surface of the road, but she didn't speak again or look back at me.

There was no sign of Eve, so I went down to the cove with Quirk, in case she had decided to walk back along the beach. The sky was the soft grey of pigeon feathers, the low light made my eyes ache as it glanced off white mounds and lacy hillocks of snow that had settled on the slope of the cliffs. It was growing bitterly cold.

I walked briskly towards Morrow Bay to keep warm, but when there was no sign of Eve on the shore, I didn't linger. In the distance, I could make out a small group of riders exercising their horses - water splashing up as they cantered at the edge of the sea - their dim figures shimmered in the failing light, spectral and unreal.

Before he could run too far, I whistled to Quirk and we struggled up the footpath, our steps a gory mush of earth-stained snow. When we reached the lane, I gathered a few pieces of dead and fallen branches to add to the wood in the store, while Quirk sniffed round happily, his muzzle thick with clumps of mud and ice.

As we turned through the gate, Quirk barked and rushed up the drive towards the house. Eve was there, stacking logs into the basket, the two brindled cats playing around her feet. And seeing her safe, the depth of my relief was a measure of the fear I had felt when she had set off alone across the island. In too many ways, her life had collapsed just as David's had done when he was suffering from writers' block. Luke Porter had hurt her – men were so easily attracted to her, but she needed someone who could love her deeply.

I threw the bundle of wood I'd collected onto the back of the pile in the shed. The wind danced through the branches of the trees; the rim of the sky had taken on a coppery hue – we were in for a storm.

Indoors, I shooed Quirk into the conservatory, muddy water dripped from his thick coat and formed into large dirty puddles. On the kitchen table was a box of apples, pears and root vegetables, under a bunch of spring flowers - lemon and white narcissi and purple irises.

''I've bought a few more things from Lyncross,' Eve said. 'The flowers are for you, to say I'm sorry.'

'You don't need to say sorry...' I told her, Eve's quiet suffering was hard to bear.

'You've been talking to Geraldine? You have that look of brooding intensity on your face.'

I smiled - I'd also been trying to gauge her mood. 'I told Geraldine I'd like you to use the studio...' I said.

Eve's face took on the stricken expression I'd noticed that morning. 'Sometime - not now...' she said, her voice faltering.

She sounded almost afraid and I reached out to touch her. 'You and Geraldine make peace about it - when you're ready – I shouldn't have interfered.'

Lighting the fire, I wished I could gather my careless words and burn them. Eve's gentleness, her receptivity, her awareness and compassion made her vulnerable – perhaps the island would prove too melancholy for her as it had for Yvette, as it might yet do for me.

While the last streaks of light lingered on the horizon, I went into the back garden, snow whirling against a dark sky. In the blowy evening, my face and hands were stung by sharp little arrows of ice as I cut a few beech leaves and hellebores – *hellebores for the healing of mental pain.*

When I'd arranged them in a jug and carried them to the dresser in Eve's room. I tidied her rumpled bed – small acts of kindness and love – acts which I hoped might ease her heart-ache as she had eased mine.

# Chapter 25

The snowy weather lasted for several days. While it was difficult to get off the island, Eve began to clear and clean Thrift Cottage. As soon as I'd finished my morning's writing, I would go and help her. The stone of the walls and the floors needed scrubbing and to make room to work, I moved the boxes of art materials and equipment, which had been stored there into the studio where they belonged.

I was piling the last of the boxes on the studio racks and was about to leave, when Quirk sprung up from the doorstep and began to whine. He stared past me and I swung round to catch sight of a flash of blue - some kind of apparition. Underneath the racks was a row of shallow cupboards. One of the cupboards had opened as Ursula Piran crawled out, covered in dust and cobwebs, dragging a schoolbag behind her.

'You frightened me..!' I said, but seeing her so bedraggled, I felt a range of emotions - amusement, irritation, concern.

'Uncle Nicholas left me with Aunt Beatrix,' Ursula explained, brushing her clothes down with her hand.

'And now she'll be worried and cross - shouldn't you talk to your dad about what's bothering you. Surely he'd want to help?'

'No one can help.'

I took in the details of her appearance, her pale face, her hair all askew - she'd grazed her knee so that blood had dripped down onto her clean white sock. 'You'd better come to the house.'

'Can I stay like I did before?' she asked. 'Aunt Beatrix makes me do lessons, but she thinks I'm rubbish. She says I'm way behind with everything. That's what Dad thinks and Uncle Nicholas. The twins and Rowena are too clever.'

'Where has your uncle gone today?'

'He's taking photos about how animals survive in the winter.'

As we walked up to the house, Quirk crawled in and out of the bushes, his black fur tousled and full of dead leaves, he looked rather as Ursula had done when she crawled out of the cupboard. They followed me across the rough grass, like two familiars.

Ursula seemed unaware of time, content to kneel on the tile floor of the kitchen, fussing Quirk. When I'd made her a sandwich, I phoned Lyncross, anticipating another awkward conversation with Beatrix.

'I was about to call you,' Beatrix said, 'could you possibly bring Ursula here? I can't leave my father, he's unwell.'

I checked the kitchen clock - I'd arranged to meet Delia at Hintham Ridge that afternoon - Ursula studied my face with an imploring expression.

'If it's any use, Ursula could come with me to Safford Bridge. I'll bring her to Lyncross, later.'

There was a long pause. 'I don't suppose her father would approve, but I can't see why not,' Beatrix said and despite her abrupt manner, I sensed she felt a reprieve - Ursula wouldn't be under her feet for a couple of hours.

'Thank you,' Ursula said as I put down the phone. She smiled - the first time she'd really smiled - I could see her likeness to Patrick, her father.

While I prepared to go out, I sent Ursula to the study where she could find children's books and drawing things - she would need something to occupy her at Hintham Ridge, where my conversation with Delia was unlikely to be of interest to a child. By the time I was ready, I found her sitting happily at the desk reading one of the *Seabright Island* books, sipping a mug of hot chocolate and crunching her way through a plateful of biscuits.

The drive to Narescombe took only ten minutes, but then we crawled through the centre of town, where the main square was clogged with road works and traffic lights, most of which seemed to have been set at red.

'Your little girl didn't come for the holidays,' Ursula said.

'She had chicken pox and had to stay in bed - but she was here. One day, I hope all my family will be at Marisands, but Zoë's travelling abroad, she's in Turkey, Istanbul...'

'I've travelled to Kenya, we stayed in Nairobi.'

Though I was curious, to question her about her family would have been to take advantage, so I asked, 'Are you glad to be back in England?'

She pulled a face. 'My cousins are much older than me - they're nearly grown up. I miss my mum.'

'You'll soon make friends at school...'

Ursula scowled and slumped down in the seat — I could imagine Minette giving a similar response to my well-intentioned platitude. 'There's no-one I want to know at St. Safan's...' she said, 'no-one at all.'

The Hintham Ridge Community was based in a converted farmhouse at the foot of a deep valley, just beyond Safford Bridge. The views, as we descended the narrow curving road down the side of the hill, took in a broad sweep of cultivated land - a patchwork of pale green and dark earth - with areas of snow lying under the hedges and in the hollows.

The track to the farm was thick with mud and muck, there were large frozen puddles and the car slid in an ungainly sideways movement for the last few yards as we ended the steep descent to the five-barred gate at the community entrance.

Straight in front of us, the community house stood in a paved yard, a long low building of plain grey stone. Ursula chattered away at my elbow as we walked towards the house, before darting ahead to ring the doorbell.

Delia answered, she'd been waiting in foyer and ushered us inside. Unlike the day when we'd met in Narescombe, she wore a navy tabard over a green sweater – some kind of uniform.

'You wouldn't get here easily in bad weather,' I said.

'Last winter, when someone needed an ambulance, they were airlifted – it was rather frightening - having a helicopter land on the farm.'

Ursula stared at Delia, wide-eyed imagining the scene. I introduced her, explaining she was spending the afternoon with me.

'You needed an ally for this strange experience?' Delia asked, 'Is Ursula the canary in the mine? Let's hope she survives.'

The interior of the community building was soulless and institutional, decorated in dull, serviceable colours - anaemic greens, blues and greys.

'What do you do here?' Ursula asked.

'That's a good question,' Delia said. 'I'm assistant chaplain to Father Terry Hart. Like some of our members, I work with people who have mental health problems. There's a centre run by the community in Safford Bridge. Others do practical work, we try to be self sufficient in fruit and vegetables, and we have pigs, cows, sheep, hens and goats to look after. There's no room for people who don't enjoy hard work.'

Delia showed us to her bed-sitting room, plainer, I imagined, than her cell would have been at the convent - with no decoration on the walls - and the curtains, like much in the house, a soft grey-green.

I'd taken a homemade cake and a bag of Cox's apples from Lyncross's fruit and vegetable stall. Ursula settled on the bed with a book, a drink and a slice of sponge. I hoped I wasn't going to be held responsible for ruining her teeth or making her sick - apart from the sandwich - she'd been stuffing herself with sweet, unhealthy foods all afternoon.

Over tea, we discussed Delia's work as a chaplain, and she spoke about Terry Hart, who seemed well-respected by the community. Her own role was a mixture of support worker and general dogsbody, but she too was full of praise for Father Hart, who she claimed was a good priest, adept at bringing wanderers back into the fold.

'Wanderers like my father?' I asked.

Delia laughed. 'I expect William encountered Terry in Safford Bridge Hospital – he would have been a sitting target...'

She gave no account of her reasons for leaving the convent, but Delia was eager to outline why she was happy at Hintham Ridge – she admired the way they were so active among the needy in the locality.

'I've been to see Kelda, recently,' she said. 'I went on a mercy run with food and warm bedding - I thought she might need help in this terrible weather but she wasn't at all grateful.' Delia glanced at Ursula before she went on, 'Kelda has talked to me in the past – I mean really talked. She was a bit of a rebel at school, though not too much trouble. Then she found herself pregnant and her parents sent her away. A few months later, she came back without her baby and after that I only ever saw her on the streets,'

'Sometimes I'm rather afraid of her,' I confessed, remembering Kelda's devious eyes and the expression which had been too knowing, 'I'm afraid *for* her too.

'I should have been more of a mother to Kelda, but some people just don't want to help themselves,' Delia said. 'Would you like to look round the farm now?' she asked Ursula. She explained that a sheep had gone missing and she'd been asked to track it down – everyone was busy because of the lambing season.

Ursula had been very quiet, probably receiving an education about aspects of life of which her family wouldn't approve. Now she leapt up enthusiastically as Delia led the way downstairs.

We left the building through a boot room, where Delia donned a pair of muddy green wellingtons, offering us rubber galoshes to put over our shoes.

The back of the community building had two long extensions and several barns, creating a farmyard that was more or less enclosed on all sides. There was a strong smell of manure and a few red hens pecked about in a pile of straw -

Delia showed us out through one of the gates, other members of the community were working on the land - all wearing blue tabards and green sweater tops. If we passed anyone, Delia greeted them with a signal of her hand but then moved on without saying a word. There was little conversation, even where people were together in groups. Ursula

316

stopped to admire lambs and piglets and I thought, even the animals seemed subdued.

From the farm, we took a cinder pathway across a grassy field with a cluster of beehives in a sheltered corner. We climbed over a wire fence and entered a broad meadow, which sloped down towards an area of woodland where a collection of ruined caravans stood in an untidy huddle.

Beyond, there were far-reaching views of rocky hills with snow lying on their upper slopes. This wasn't a landscape for the self-indulgent or faint-hearted or a landscape that could be ignored - it was wild and bleak, a natural reflection of the spiritual asceticism that seemed to be practised by the community.

Delia led us towards the enclosure of trees. The old caravans, once white, were now green with algae - one had a black chimney that protruded from the roof - most were like rusty tin cans.

'Not grand, I'm afraid,' Delia said, 'but we're thinking of doing them up, they would provide a home for people like Kelda if they wanted to move off the street. In fact, Kelda has stayed here sometimes. The assumption that all human beings want to live comfortable lives is flawed, there are people who believe they can only redeem themselves by leading a punishing existence - and perhaps for them it's right...'

While Delia was talking, I opened the door of the nearest van. The caravan was damp, the temperature inside colder than outdoors. When a gust of wind swept up the valley, it rocked the van as if something heavy had struck it on the side. A stove, crumbling with rust was meant to heat the sitting area, which housed a rotting sofa. A sink, a double hotplate and a tiny fridge comprised the kitchen - the bedroom was just large enough to house the narrow, built-in bed, which was stained from the runnels of condensation that dripped down the walls.

Ursula peered round the door and pinched her nose with her fingers against the odour of mould and mice.

'Hintham Ridge can be a good place to re-think and review your life,' Delia said.

I didn't know how to reply. Life in the community was austere and the caravans would never be much more comfortable than living rough, except they might keep out the very worst of the wind and rain.

We left the valley, circling the hill through a narrow ribbon of woodland. A squirrel bounded down from a tree and Ursula skipped ahead, chasing it.

While she wasn't listening, I asked Delia if she thought Juliet might have had an abortion – did she know if that had been the reason for our trip to London, supposedly to visit Bernard?

Delia sighed. 'I think Juliet could see no other way out of her situation. She didn't believe in divorce, she felt cornered by her desires and imprisoned by her sins. She desperately wanted to join the Catholic Church, but to do so would have wrecked all hope of following her heart or finding happiness...'

'Whatever she did, she'd felt condemned..?'

'After the termination, she was ill and depressed - she felt she'd been physically and emotionally violated. She'd suffered from bad headaches for a long while, but afterwards they became intolerable. She'd had enormous difficulty obtaining the money needed - she couldn't find a doctor who was willing to say the right things – essential if a backstreet operation was to be avoided.

'In the end, Shirley Fredericks advised her, I don't think without her, Juliet would have gone through with it, but the strain affected her mind...'

As Ursula ran back to meet us, Delia fell silent.

'I've found the sheep, it's dead - its eyes are all funny. I think it fell in the ditch and broke its leg, the baby's with it, do you want to see?' Ursula asked.

'Better to keep away,' I suggested, thinking she might be upset.

She hung her head, 'I thought it was very interesting...' she said, dismayed by my reaction. 'I've seen lots of dead things before – even people.'

The mixture of artlessness and earthiness were strong within Ursula and somehow shocking in a child. Delia promised to report the death of the sheep to one of the farm workers, but we went with Ursula to examine the body only to find that the lamb had also died.

I was relieved when Delia checked her watch, 'I'm afraid I have to go. I'm on duty in the house this evening.'

'Why not come to Marisands, one day?' I suggested, despite the strangeness of our visit, she'd been very kind.

'It must be years since I was on the island,' Delia said, but I sensed, for whatever reason, she wasn't keen to come to Littern again.

On the way back to the farmyard we chatted about a new project being launched by the community, who wanted to establish two clinics, specifically for street people, they were looking for doctors willing to act as volunteers.

'I might be a doctor one day, like my dad and Uncle Tom...' Ursula told her.

'Then I'll expect you to be at the front of the queue of people wanting to help,' Delia said with a smile, 'In the meantime, perhaps you could tell them about it.'

We'd reached the yard in front of the community building.

Delia said, 'Bring Ursula back on a fine day – perhaps with Minette – you could have a proper look round. There'll be calves and more piglets and who knows, I may have become a goatherd, though I'd much rather stay in the warm and bake bread...'

She waved goodbye as the car chugged up the hill in bottom gear. The road twisted and turned until we were looking down over the roof of the community house in its green swathe of land.

The light was already failing by the time we reached Safford Bridge, but I parked behind the Priory wanting to revisit the boutique, *Stuff & Nonsense*, where I had been with Helen. They were selling floor cushions at a reduced price and I'd decided to buy three to make the sitting room more comfortable, Eve enjoyed sitting cross-legged on the floor by the fire, especially when she wanted to read. I bought cream candles, for the mantelpiece in the music room. Placed in front of the mirrors, I thought they might create an atmosphere of gothic charm.

The flower vendor still had his cart out on the street so I bought bunches of anemones in deep jewel colours and we went into the moonlit churchyard to place them on Juliet's grave.

Ursula was thoughtful, 'My grandmother's buried in here and Uncle Antony. I visit them with my dad - he goes very serious and stares into space – just like you did.'

'My great-grandmother's buried here too, but I'm not sure where...' I said absent- mindedly.

'Shall we look for her?' Ursula asked, full of enthusiasm.

But in the twilight it would have been useless to search for Yvette's grave, it was late and we needed to return to Littern. Crossing the square, I scanned the side streets, but there was no sign of Kelda and no sound of her music. I hadn't liked to ask Delia, but couldn't help wondering who had been the father of Kelda's child.

Back in the car, Ursula began asking her own questions.

'What did Delia mean "a canary in a mine"? I can sing like a canary...' and she demonstrated with a trill of notes.

I explained the historic practice of taking canaries into mines to test the purity of the air.

'I am still alive,' she said, fidgeting in the passenger seat of the car as if to prove her point, 'but wasn't it a funny thing to say and a very funny place?'

'Did you like it?'

Ursula shrugged. 'There was too much silence - it didn't feel safe.'

With a child's perception, she had pinpointed my disquiet, I'd felt exactly the same.

We passed the Priory School and Ursula complained, 'I wish there was a school on the island. Why isn't there?'

'You don't like St. Safan's?'

She shook her head vigorously, 'Granddad says the Pirans always go to St. Safan's and once my work's up to scratch I'll like it, but I won't. My cousins stay in Safford Bridge with Uncle Tom all the time because of the tides - I want to stay with my dad.'

Hoping for a few minutes respite, I switched on the car radio and found some classical music.

'You might hear Aunt Sarah on the radio, she's quite famous,' Ursula remarked, and I realised it was going to take more than Radio Three to quieten her, now she was in a chatterbox mood. 'She's a pianist...' Ursula illustrated this by wiggling her fingers as if striking the keys, 'she's always in London, never at home and Uncle Nicholas has to do everything.'

'Like look after you?' I asked.

'Only for now - until my dad finds a job...'

At Marisands, Ursula wanted to take Quirk for a run on the beach, a delaying tactic to put off going to Lyncross. When I said no, she asked if we could walk home, but I insisted we take the car. She played with Quirk for a few moments, throwing a stick, encouraging him to race about in the garden. But then we drove up the lane through the beech trees, sturdy and ancient, their pale bark giving off a soft eerie glow in the headlights, their branches rustling in the breeze.

'Is your little girl, coming at Easter?' Ursula asked, 'do you think I could play with her?'

'That would be up to your family.'

'Will she go to St. Safan's?'

'She'll probably go to St. Mary's – though she'd prefer to be in London.'

'Why?' Ursula demanded, 'Is it near her dad?'

'Minette's dad left us last year,' I explained, concerned at the impact this information might have on Ursula, who seemed insecure.

'When we get to Lyncross, my dad should be there.' She said - her left hand held to her mouth as she gnawed the thumb nail. 'I *hope* Dad is there; if he isn't, will you stay until he comes?'

'I can't invite myself into the house.'

'I'll invite you,' Ursula said, sounding less than confident.

'Your dad might not like it.'

'Yes, he will.'

I could hardly explain the flaws in her argument and continued in silence until I turned into the drive, anxious not to clip the gatepost, as Beatrix had done.

As we approached the house, Ursula took my hand. 'Dad's car isn't here.'

Her anxiety made me anxious too. The dogs could be heard scuffling in the hallway. Ursula was eager to go round to the kitchen at the back of the house, but I felt I couldn't presume on a friendship which no longer existed - my plan was to deliver her to the front door and return to Marisands.

Ursula fidgeted from foot to foot and pulled on my hand. When I knocked, one of the dogs gave a low, deep growl - then Ursula rang the bell and rang again -

'That's enough,' I said. 'You'll annoy everyone...'

'I always do,' she said humbly.

The oak door creaked open and Ursula darted behind me, perhaps anticipating a telling off from her aunt.

'Why didn't you go round to the kitchen, Ursula?' Beatrix scolded. 'Will you come in - we're having tea?' she said to me.

I stepped back, sure that Beatrix would prefer me to leave, but Ursula tugged hard at my arm, forcing me to step inside or appear rude.

'I've phoned Patrick and told him how badly Ursula has behaved,' Beatrix looked tired and sounded strained.

'When *is* Daddy coming?' Ursula pleaded.

'Soon,' Beatrix said irritably, 'Sometimes I think there's only one word in Ursula's vocabulary and it's "Daddy".'

In the drawing room, Edgar was by the fire, blankets over his knees, reading *The Times*. His shock of white hair made a point of light catching the yellow glow from a table lamp next to him - despite his great age and frailty, he remained distinguished.

'Is that you Beatrix?' he called out, 'I can't see a thing.'

Beatrix switched on the overhead light, revealing the room with its solid, dark furniture, worn over the years to shabbiness - the red velvet curtains so faded they'd almost turned grey. The portrait of Kathleen, once in the study, had been hung over the fireplace. Behind Edgar, the bookcases were overcrowded, as I'd remembered, with the classics of literature stuffed in among music scores and tomes on anatomy and medicine. On top of the bookcases, the displays of butterflies hadn't been removed, nor had the stuffed birds and animals that had once belonged to James.

'Pa doesn't see or hear very well these days,' Beatrix said.

'...Nonsense!' Edgar objected.

Beatrix indicated a chair beside her father; I took it hesitantly, feeling unwelcome, though I supposed if I didn't sit near him conversation would be impossible.

He leaned back and closed his eyes, 'Do you have that naughty little girl with you?' he asked in mock annoyance.

Ursula giggled and squatted down on a stool by his feet. Edgar had always loved children and his kindness had meant a lot to me in my childhood.

'I didn't mean to intrude...'

'Are you intruding?' His retort, like light reflecting off the tip of a rapier, implied I'd been ill-mannered to suggest it.

'Shall we have tea?' Beatrix asked. 'We could have it in here, today.'

'Of course...' Edgar said, sharp with her too - the dynamic between them seemed edgy and unpredictable.

'Beatrix works hard,' I remarked, when she'd left the room.

'And I'm an ungrateful old codger? I know it's true, and if I should forget, I now have Patrick on hand to remind me.'

On a long table next to the fireplace was a group of family photographs, I glanced up at them.

'The ever burgeoning Barbarians,' Edgar said, following my gaze. 'Kathleen and I didn't think what having five children and James in the family might mean in terms of grandchildren and soon, perhaps, great-grandchildren.'

With a rattling sound, Beatrix pushed a tea trolley into the room and Ursula helped her lift it over a trail of rugs covering the well-worn carpet. Ursula handed out tea cups and plates, with roughly cut sandwiches. The sandwiches were followed by remnants of Christmas cake. The silver teapot, familiar from childhood, was tarnished and dented in several places - the china tea service reduced by thirty years of wear and tear to an assortment of cracked, unmatched pieces.

A tall, dark haired boy, one of Nicholas's sons, appeared in the doorway. When he saw there was a visitor, he stepped back as if he wished he could disappear.

'You must have smelt food,' Beatrix said to him, 'help yourself.'

After loading a plate, the boy vanished - he'd taken a double portion, half he claimed was for his brother, Dominic.

'Someone should do something about that boy's confidence,' Edgar said.

'And about his manners,' Beatrix commented.

'Benedict's always hiding in a corner somewhere,' Edgar grumbled to Nicholas as he entered the room.

'At his age most of us are hiding in corners.' Nicholas told his father, 'and some people start even earlier,' he added, looking at Ursula.

Conversations at Lyncross had used to be verbal battles, when despite an atmosphere of good will, words had flown round the room and lodged in the flesh like shrapnel - Edgar, not by nature a cruel man, could be tactless in the extreme.

Ursula was dispatched to fetch more cake. She came back with a Victoria sponge, which had barely risen and sat miserable and deflated on its paper doyley. Though Edgar thanked Beatrix for it with considerable charm, Beatrix - and perhaps nobody - could match her mother's elegance and grace. My impression was that the Pirans were hanging on to their customs, though they and the world had changed beyond recognition.

'Are you all right, son?' Edgar asked Nicholas.

'Fine... It was Tom's birthday - we took him out for lunch,' he was crisply courteous, adding the snippet of information as a meagre offering to me.

'If only Kathleen were here,' Edgar said wistfully, 'and of course Antony, Sarah and Honor...'

'It doesn't help to think in that way,' Nicholas said, and the atmosphere in the room grew a few degrees colder.

I finished my tea and said I should be leaving, but there was a fresh fracas in the hall as the twins scrapped noisily at the doorway and Rowena shoved past them and stumbled into the room.

Rowena and Ursula could have been sisters - they each had the heart-shaped face, dark brown hair and navy blue eyes, characteristic of the Pirans. Rowena had been crying - her cheeks streaked with mascara filled tears. She sidled across the room towards Nicholas and flopped down on the sofa. Copying her cousin, Ursula climbed up on the seat and though he was unsmiling, Nicholas put a reassuring arm about her as she nestled by his side.

I carried a few of the tea things out to the kitchen.

'I know what'll happen,' Beatrix muttered, 'we start out with four people for afternoon tea and it will be eight for dinner, and everything left to me.'

Her outburst had been intended to be unheard and my look of concern seemed to offend her.

'Why don't you go back to the others? In fact why don't you go home? Having you here brings back bad memories and whatever anyone says about Antony's accident and his death - I blame your mother and I blame you.'

I'd left my coat draped over a chair in the drawing room and went to retrieve it. Beatrix clearly hadn't changed her opinion about what had happened on the day of Juliet's death and had wanted me to know it.

In the warmth of the fire-lit room, Edgar had fallen asleep and was snoring softly. Ursula rested against Nicholas's shoulder, while Rowena lounged in a corner of the sofa, listening to music through earphones.

'Will you stay for dinner?' Nicholas asked, but the question was a matter of form, that cold politeness at which the Pirans excelled.

'I have to get back, my daughter's expecting me.'

'Thanks for seeing to Ursula.'

'She's always welcome at Marisands.'

Out in the hall, the three dogs crept up on me from a back room - they were enormous, Quirk would barely have reached their shoulders. Nervously, I stretched out my hand towards the front door, but before I could turn the latch, the door was pushed open from the other side.

I edged out of the way as Patrick came into the hall. My lips formed into a smile, but then I caught his expression - one of displeasure, almost distaste. As the door had swung back, the hall had filled with cold, unforgiving moonlight.

We stood there awkwardly. The wiry boy of fourteen now a tall, slight man, his fine, brown hair edged with grey, his skin sallow and his eyes surrounded by a hatching of fine lines.

Ursula rushed out of the drawing room and hurled herself at his legs, clasping onto him as if her life depended on it. He prised off her hands gently and smoothed her hair.

'Would you excuse me,' he said to me and with barely a flicker of recognition, hurried upstairs.

'I was just leaving,' I murmured.

I could think of no other response to this stranger, this unfathomable man, who had once been my friend – who had once risked his life to save mine.

At Lyncross, the props were the same, yet the overall feeling was of disintegration. The demise of the Piran family appeared every bit as real as the demise of Armsteds.

When I'd returned to Littern, I'd believed I could achieve a cessation of hostilities, the renewal of friendship on equal terms, but after thirty years, nothing had changed.

My encounter with Patrick upset me deeply. I'd thought he might be the one who would provide a bridge, a way of making peace – but he was no better than the rest of them and I resolved in future I should concentrate on my own life and leave the Pirans to get on with theirs.

# Chapter 26

As I began writing up the new *Minor Lights* book and worked on Laurence's latest *Kenholme Mystery,* I was incarcerated in the study for longer periods each day and had little time to give attention to the house or garden.

Kos was tough and never complained of hard physical labour, he'd begun digging over the flower beds near Thrift Cottage and had continued to bring seaweed from the cove to fertilise the soil. Using Juliet's watercolour for guidance he'd cleared the oratory garden, freeing spears of young plants and cleaning out the fusty overgrown pond. He called it a moon garden – a garden whose beauty was perceptible at night.

At ease now with Eve's presence, he was repairing and renovating Thrift Cottage. Already, he had fixed the roof and broken window, so the place was water-tight. Often he stayed at Marisands all day, but refused to accept more money - we had become friends, he said. At meal times he settled at the kitchen table, as part of the family, his boots discarded in the porch, his dark hair damp from exertion and clinging to his long pale face.

I encouraged him to tell us more about his family history, but he repeated the same story, with little elaboration. His grandfather and his father had been farmers.

When his grandfather had become a soldier in the Second World War, he had lost himself, like many good people, he'd been forced to act as a man of violence and he had deep regrets – a prisoner of his guilt.

Kos said, 'Until I came here, perhaps I was to follow in his footsteps...'

Kos had arrived in the country two years earlier and had travelled around until he visited Devon, where the cows were fat and the grass lush and green. He'd been seeking a place to call home and had taken a liking to Littern.

The story left considerable gaps in his account of his life before he had left Ukraine, but I didn't like to press him further. Eve had joined him working at the soup kitchen in Safford Bridge - another venture run by the Hintham Ridge Community - and he was well liked both by the other volunteers and the clientele. To discourage him from pilfering produce from Beatrix, we had agreed he could take some of the vegetables he grew at Marisands.

I'd asked if he had come across Kelda - describing her black hat and the flute she always carried with her. Kos told me she turned up for a meal occasionally and they'd talked because of their shared love of music. 'For some people more is needed than food,' he said mysteriously, 'they suffer not from sickness of the body but of the soul.'

*

Since my conversation with Delia, I'd been meaning to visit Shirley Fredericks. As I started the car, ready to leave Marisands, Kos gave a long low whistle and Quirk, who was whining at the gate, ran to him at once. In the rear-view mirror I saw him usher the dog back into the porch before they both disappeared inside the house to see if Eve would provide them with lunch.

It was market day and Narescombe was in chaos - people crowded the narrow pavements and cars crawled through the square looking for somewhere to park. The market stalls had spilled over the kerb making the streets so congested that vehicles could barely pass through the mass of shoppers.

When at last I was clear of the town square, I drove to Napier Street and parked outside Petra Galleries, admiring its neighbours, the smart little cottages that were the sort of place I wouldn't mind living in myself.

I tucked-in a few loose strands of hair and smoothed a slick of Vaseline across my lips, then craned my neck to see where the entrance to Shirley's flat was - the only way in was through a wide, black-painted wooden gate, secured by a Yale lock. As there seemed little chance of making a personal call - I would have to make enquiries in the shop.

By the door to Petra a notice requested that you ring the bell before entering. The gallery was served by a woman in her sixties, her grey hair swept into a neat chignon, her clothes all in black.

'May I help you?' she asked.

'I was wondering if it would be possible to speak to Shirley.'

'Miss Fredericks doesn't work *in here*,' the woman said, 'she'll either be in her workshop or she may be out - and you are?'

'Iris Armsted, 'I said, 'Juliet and William Muys's daughter.'

'How do you spell Armsted?'

326

I spelt the letters out slowly - there was no way of discerning from the woman's face if my parents' names meant anything to her.

'Would you like me to give Miss Fredericks a message?'

I considered leaving my phone number - but though I was certain any message I left would be passed on - the woman seemed a dragon of efficiency - I was less optimistic about expecting a phone call from Shirley.

'I'm gathering information about my parents,' I said, phrasing my intentions carefully, 'Shirley knew them quite well.'

The woman made a note on a pad of paper. 'I'll see if she's interested.'

Her remark was meant to put me off, but I stopped to look round the gallery. The work displayed in the window was unchanged since I'd walked along Napier Street with Delia and was part of a varied collection. Some galleries are imposing and Petra had a forbidding atmosphere. After studying a display of seascapes in unnaturally bright hues, I went to the desk and bought two postcards, one of the marshes and the other of the harbour at Narescombe - I would use them when I next wrote to Silvie.

As I paid for the cards, I said, 'I'll look forward to Shirley's response.'

'Response to what..?'

I turned to find Shirley standing behind me, statuesque, distinctive with her brassy hair, florid complexion and colourful clothes – she'd always had a penchant for drama.

'Iris Armsted?' The assistant said to her.

'Of course...' If nothing else, Shirley would have recognised me from William's funeral.

'I have a few questions - I hoped you might be willing to help...'

Shirley eyes flickered towards the woman at the desk. 'We can't talk here.'

I followed her into the street, her robes flowing about her as she walked. She approached the black gate beside the gallery and took out a key. The gateway led into a long narrow courtyard paved with brick and edged with tubs holding small bushes surrounded by daffodils. At the far end was her workshop. She let us in and flicked on a fluorescent light, showing a large room crammed with grey stone statues like those in the gallery window, there were several unfinished on the bench and something about the atmosphere of the place reminded me of a stage set.

'I'd heard you were around from Geraldine and wondered if you'd call.'

'Geraldine's still using the studio at Marisands. We've talked - but some things remain unclear.'

Shirley eyed me, a thoughtful expression on her face.

'I've been wondering why there are no paintings of William's at Marisands and very little of Juliet's work - Geraldine doesn't have much of an explanation.'

'One reason might be that William was easily influenced and by the wrong people - it was a weakness which affected his work badly.'

'I always saw my father as the strong, dominant one.'

'That's what he'd have wanted you to think,' she said unsmiling.

She'd made no reference to my mother's work – I'd been wondering was there any connection between her own style and Juliet's white statues.

Shirley turned on a powerful overhead lamp and began to dust the surface of one of her grey figures, as sinuous as a flexed muscle.

'I've been mystified by the white statues in the oratory garden. I understand you and my mother discussed her work. Juliet's despair – could that be their meaning..?'

Shirley's face wore an expression of amused irony, 'Juliet wanted to depict the sea, rocks and trees of the island stripped down to their essence. Think Hepworth.'

I considered her answer but could find no resemblance to Hepworth's work. It was more likely that Juliet, rather than imitating someone else, like Flora had believed in the nature spirits.

'The statues are badly damaged...'

'Juliet had them put outside – the garden seemed the most appropriate backdrop. After she died, they should have been moved indoors...'

'William's responsibility..?'

Shirley looked indifferent. 'Does it matter - why did you really come here, today..?'

'Geraldine suggested William was seeking expiation for my mother's death that seems to imply he was guilty in some way.'

'Do you think so?' she asked and I recognised the false manner, the blank-eyed stare which she used to mask her feelings.

'I need to know about Juliet – her life as well as her death. Did you help my mother in personal ways - did you help her procure an abortion?'

Shirley reached for her safety glasses from the bench beside her and applied a small sanding tool to the stone figure – as the disc whirred round, it made a high-pitched moan and I thought our conversation might be over.

328

I waited and in a few minutes, she switched the tool off and spoke again.

'William had clear ideas of how his life should be. He had believed the admiration of a group of students confirmed his artistic vision – and nothing, not even his obvious mediocrity, could persuade him he wasn't a painter. When the students drifted away, William was confronted with his self-delusion. Instead of accepting the truth, he renewed his efforts to create the right ambience to express his talent – that in his view precluded having more children...'

'So William asked my mother to have an abortion..?' I persisted.

Her version didn't agree with Juliet's diaries where I'd read of my mother's unwillingness to accept William's child, *the alien presence.*

Shirley avoided the question, 'I happened to know from friends about a particular clinic in London. Your mother thought it was the only way to save their marriage.'

I said, 'It was a pity William didn't care as much about their marriage, he did everything to destroy it – his relationship with Geraldine and with you. When my mother returned from the visit to Dulwich, there was no way she could have mistaken what had been going on – while she was putting herself through an emotional hell, you were all...'

Shirley interrupted my tirade, 'William needed love in his life. Juliet wasn't ever quite herself again after they moved to the island. Later when she suffered a stillbirth, she thought God was punishing her - she blamed William and me for what she'd done, but he blamed the influence of the Pirans and James Millford - their obsession with religion...'

'My family expected there to be a collection of Juliet's work at Marisands...'

Shirley looked away, 'Geraldine hasn't told you? A week before I came to the island for the last time, your mother had a bonfire and destroyed her paintings. William managed to rescue a few pieces...'

'The panels from *The Stations*..? Couldn't he have stopped her?' I asked angrily.

'He didn't find compassion easy where Juliet was concerned. But then, when he was already seriously ill, he wanted to finish the panels himself. You could say that was his way of seeking "expiation" for your mother's death - if you wanted to stretch a point.'

'I've seen the three paintings in All Souls...'

'Have you?' Shirley smiled in a way that felt patronising, 'When the church was decommissioned, William and I had the idea of founding an Arts Centre – he could make his mark and it was something the town needed. Our proposal was accepted, and funds were raised for the renovations that are going on now. William felt that as one of the key people involved, there should be some of his work on show – but really he had nothing...'

'But the idea for *The Stations* wasn't his – I have sketches made by my mother.'

Shirley appeared indifferent, 'William made little progress, so after his death we hung what Juliet had done and left them as an anonymous donation - it would have been difficult to establish their provenance – they hadn't been signed.'

I found her blasé attitude infuriating, but though I hadn't found an ally in Shirley, she was less aggressive than Geraldine and I wanted to leave the way open to talk to her again.

'Have I answered your questions?' she asked, her impatience becoming obvious.

I dared to slip in one more. 'Kelda Sullivan followed you, William and Geraldine to the tower on the day Juliet died - do you know what she wanted?'

'Shouldn't you ask her?'

'Kelda isn't always coherent...'

Shirley laughed. 'On that particular occasion she was completely coherent. She had things to say which she thought William ought to hear. There was a plenty of gossip and even more jealousy – more than one woman wanting the same man...'

'Who did Kelda want?'

'James Millford,' Shirley said sharply.

And I remembered how Juliet had said *Kelda hangs round James like a bad smell.*

'If you're coming again, give me a call, would you..?' Shirley handed me her business card, making it obvious she wanted to get on. As she showed me out of the workshop, she added, 'I heard you were evicting Geraldine from the studio. Didn't you realise she's almost blind? We take her stuff at the gallery, so she doesn't feel compromised.'

I felt embarrassed. I'd been uncharitable about Geraldine's need for the "incomparable light", which must be essential if she was to work at all. I'd been scathing about her endless dreary paintings of the tower.

Desperate for a cup of coffee, I called in at Quay 11. They sold stationery with other goods handmade by the community, so I bought a pack of paper and envelopes and while I drank my cappuccino, wrote to Silvie, enclosing the postcard of the marshes. I imagined Juliet feeling pulled apart in so many different directions and as the picture of my parents' lives began to fit loosely together, it didn't seem to offer the healing Silvie had promised. I saw my mother as lost and felt lost with her. I couldn't help wondering – who had known what – who might still be keeping secrets. Had Silvie been aware of the truth about Juliet's "operation" – had Alice or Flora?

Throughout my life, I'd accepted the myth of my father's talent, but if Shirley and Geraldine were right - his work belonged to the deadwood category of the talented amateur. Yet, my mother, who was gifted, had destroyed her work - had she been driven by depression? Were her actions a prelude to her suicide or a rebellion against William's artistic posturing, part of *The Resistance Movement,* the term scrawled on the carrier of the last of the *Stations* paintings? The questions seemed endless. Juliet had acted against her nature and beliefs by destroying their child - might she have expressed outrage and regret by burning her paintings?

I didn't know and was beginning to feel I couldn't know. The stories I'd heard jangled in my head, and as soon as I'd finished writing, I didn't linger at the cafe, but drove back through Narescombe, stopping only at the post box to send Silvie's letter.

By the railings of the recreation ground, I noticed a cluster of figures and was certain one of them was Kelda. I hesitated only for a moment, and then headed straight past them, out onto Palk's Reach along the deserted road towards the causeway. The effort of listening to Shirley had left me exhausted.

Eve was in the kitchen, poring over the old cookery book I'd found, that had once belonged to Yvette and Flora.

She looked up as I went in, 'You're white as a sheet, are you all right?'

I said I'd been to Petra Galleries and flopped down at the table, my hand to my head where pain pulsed behind my right eye.

Eve put a bowl of soup and a plate of bread in front of me.

'You need to think about something else or this whole thing will drive you mad. Whenever you've spoken to someone about your mother, you seem way too close to the edge...'

I gulped at my soup, though it burned my throat. There were too many pieces missing from the story, 'I need to find the truth,' I said, 'I've promised Silvie - and Flora – I've promised myself.'

'Let's hope it's worth it...'

'Shirley told me Juliet destroyed her work – she made a bonfire in the garden a few days before she died.'

'So? Have you thought - when it comes to it, you're exploring what a bunch of middle aged Bo-ho's did behind closed doors, *thirty years ago...*'

'But two of them were my parents. Was Juliet into the lifestyle of the others or was she pushed out, excluded? Was she uninterested, contemptuous, disgusted? Did her interests lie elsewhere?'

Eve sighed. 'Maybe the stories about what went on are salacious gossip. Maybe Geraldine peddles the idea of William being tortured and depraved the same way she peddles her paintings. People enjoy imagining artists are somehow different, liberated, especially when it comes to sex.'

'I thought Geraldine was more intelligent - I hoped I was...' I said.

Eve dumped a mug of tea down on the table in front of me - I could hardly blame her if she was growing tired of my constant soul-searching – a process that seemed to lead nowhere...

'You trusted your mother when you were a child – if Juliet had been like the others, would you have thought she was trustworthy?'

'Perhaps like everyone else, I only saw what I wanted to see.'

I left my soup half-eaten and after a few sips of tea, gathered my dishes and dropped them into the bowl of soapy water in the sink. I told Eve about Geraldine and how she was losing her sight, but she didn't seem surprised.

'...I need to go for a walk, clear my head – I'm sorry...'

I fetched Quirk and took the footpath to the beach, moving at speed, determined to make it to Morrow Bay and back before the tide came in.

A stiff breeze blew in from the sea, I gathered my hair in my hand, twisted it in a knot and folded it into the hood of my coat – it was so fine it soon clumped into sticky tangles in the salty sea air.

I kept calling Quirk's name, afraid of losing him. He ran to my side, shook his coat then chased the waves as if they were wild animals he was frightening away from the shore. We waded across the stream that flowed down from Thrifswell Woods and scrambled over the finger of rocks at the edge of Whitcroft Cove, Quirk scrabbling at the seaweed with his claws, trying to keep a foothold.

When we reached Morrow Bay, I hurried across the arc of white sand. Waves were already lapping at the foot of the old quay where the Piran's wooden boat, *The Silver Arrow,* was upturned on the pier.

The tide had begun to sweep in, I signalled to Quirk to run towards the dunes, then we walked the length of the pier, so I could judge our chances of making it back to Marisands walking along the beach. My plan had been to go as far as the marshes and climb the stone tower, hoping to see Clave Valley – in a week or two the wild irises would be in flower.

Looking back along the coast, it was obvious there was little hope of returning that way and yet something compelled me to try. I climbed down the ladder onto the sand and shouted for Quirk to jump from the pier. When I'd clipped on his lead, I jogged along the water's edge with him splashing beside me. We clambered over the spur of rocks at the fringe of the bay and headed towards the stream, but the beach was no more than a thin strip of sand, too narrow for us to walk side by side.

Catching my breath, I half-walked, half-ran through the cold water until a wave broke over my legs, soaking me up to my thighs. It caught Quirk unawares and I grabbed his collar as it threatened to drag him out into the sea.

Rubbing away a stitch in my side, I took refuge among the trees. We were stranded on the wrong side of the stream but with the tide rolling in - it wasn't safe to wade through the deepening water.

Even in winter, when the trees were bare of leaves, the woods were so dense I could barely see where I was going. Quirk crashed about happily, pleased to be exploring different terrain, forging his way through the undergrowth – he didn't share my fear of being in the woods alone.

In about twenty minutes, we had reached a place where the stream cut a deep course through the woodland floor. The water was edged with rocks, and as we followed upstream it narrowed, until we could jump across easily.

I was sure we were close to St. Thrif's Well, though there was yet no sign of the marker stone, only heavy gloom, whispering trees and rustling as we stumbled on through the dusk. I elbowed my way past brambles and bushes until, at last, I could hear the spring bubbling into the basin and caught the clean scent of water as it poured and splashed down into the pool below.

The spring rose in what had been a large open glade which had become little more than a thinning out of the trees. There was a scattering of white hellebores still in flower and underfoot, fleshy green leaves - in a few weeks, bluebells would carpet the woodland floor.

Thick mud made it awkward to clamber close to the pool, though Quirk had slithered his way down and was drinking noisily. Hot and dry mouthed from exertion – I hung onto branches and vines – making my way down to join him. Then as I let go of a branch, it sprang back, striking me on the back of the knees so I slipped, bumping into Quirk, who managed to stand his ground and break my fall before I slid into the still water.

Startled, two white pigeons fluttered out of an oak tree, their wings beating the air - there used to be a dovecot in the garden of The Retreat, they would probably fly home. Quirk licked my face as I lay in the mud, clinging to an ash sapling, which had seeded on the bank. I grasped at its soft, pliant branches and hauled myself up to where I could hold onto a rock and clamber to my feet. With Quirk's lead bound tightly round my wrist, I jerked and dragged him up the slope, back onto the path which led to the well.

The walls around the basin of the well were thick with moss, crumbling – a few stones had tumbled down and lay buried under rotting leaves. Kicking back a tangle of brambles, I knelt and put my cupped hands into the font. Though the basin was filled with twigs and earth, the ice-cold water was clear and clean. I rinsed my hands and splashed water onto my face, before drinking deeply and saying a prayer for calmness of mind.

I searched for the way out of the glade – above the well, from a birch tree, hung a string of African bone beads and a scrap of Kanga cloth in a black and white wave pattern. I fingered the smooth shiny beads as I passed – and wondered if Ursula had hung them there, strange and incongruous among the bare trees.

A narrow track meandered its way out of the woods emerging just west of Lyncross. I scaled the wall and jumped onto the lane, my hair full of twigs and my trousers flapping damply against my legs with every step. I meant one day to fill a bottle with spring water and use it for the holy water stoup in the hall at Marisands, so I picked up a sharp stone and carved a deep + onto the bark of a beech tree - next time, I would find my way easily.

When, at last, we arrived back at Marisands, Eve had been worried, 'What have you been doing?'

'Battling with nature,' I told her, towelling down Quirk's damp fur, 'sorry about earlier...'

'While you were out, I started to clean the coffee stains from Juliet's sketches. It's been quite interesting – the mirrored images suggest the panels were intended to make a continuous work – not a series. The way they've been hung at All Souls is wrong...'

'Geraldine and Shirley both said my father tried to do something with the paintings – to finish them...'

'...Maybe that explains why the canvas in the studio has only a vague connection to the original drawings, but I'm not sure yet whether he touched the others...'

I thought it would be disappointing if what was left of Juliet's work wasn't entirely hers. If William had interfered with them, the paintings would have lost any intrinsic value or integrity.

'So we're left with another conundrum – is it Juliet's work or William's?'

'If you're okay with it - I might remove some paint from the panel in the studio, see what I find underneath. When I've finished, I might have a better idea of who painted what...'

She couldn't do much harm and it would be better to try to prove what was really Juliet's, it would mean as an artist, at least, her life had some point – hadn't like the rest of her existence ended in nothing but unsolved mysteries.

'Don't let Geraldine and Shirley get to you,' Eve said. 'They're sabre rattlers - don't let them convince you they're more knowledgeable or more dangerous than they are. I think Juliet's paintings were meant to be about heroism, but for some reason they've been turned into a display of technique...'

I nodded. Though her ideas were no more than a theory, perhaps in time they would make sense.

'Shall we eat now?' Eve said – I have a surprise for you.'

The surprise turned out not to be the vegetable risotto she'd prepared from her expanding repertoire. Over supper, she explained that Kos had knocked out the built-in cupboards from the sitting room of Thrift Cottage, creating a space large enough for a couple of armchairs to be placed by the fire, with a small dining table behind the kitchen door.

When we'd had our meal, she was eager to show me and opened the cottage door with a dramatic flourish. Quirk, exhausted from our long walk, lay on his back on the hearthrug, the soft feathery fur of his belly exposed, giving out those odd little noises that sleeping dogs make, when they're dreaming. In a corner of the room, beside the fireplace, Boa and Brio lay curled in a basket.

'What do you think?' she asked.

I smiled at her transparency. 'You'd like to move in here..?'

Eve grinned.

'Promise me, you won't fall in love with the place - if I decide not to stay at the end of the year...'

Eve kissed my cheek. 'After all the sorrowful things don't you long for peace and happiness?'

'Peace and happiness seem rather elusive...' I confessed - thinking of my prayer at the holy well that afternoon.

'Perhaps you're so busy asking questions, you wouldn't know peace and happiness if they walked up and tapped you on the shoulder.'

I laughed, knowing she was right.

'I'm going to enjoy being here for as long as it lasts – not even ask what might happen next...'

The ability to face the future with such confidence, I thought, was a gift reserved for the young.

# Chapter 27

I was late for my appointment with the bank in Safford Bridge, where I needed to discuss a loan to cover Minette's school fees until the end of the summer term. While I was in town, I thought I would go to the weekly flea-market and call in at The Bridge House Bookshop. The sale at the shop was now their "final closing down sale" and Flora's birthday was in a few days time. Though I had nothing specific in mind, a book was always a reliable gift for her, she'd never been converted to watching television and reading was one of her few enduring pleasures.

I couldn't find a place to park behind the Priory, so I drove round the side streets until I found a space on Pierce Street – a steep hill flanked on both sides by terraces of elegant Georgian houses, with neat front yards and black wrought iron railings.

In a rush to leave the house, I'd skipped breakfast but there was no time to stop as I hurried into town, anxious not to make a bad impression with the bank manager. Discussions of my finances were likely to be thoroughgoing and painful, more of an inquisition than a debate, as I sought permission to borrow up to and beyond my limit.

The bank manager was young enough to be spotty and seemed unable to understand the human story behind the facts and figures as I tried to convince him that my work, though freelance, had provided a steady source of income for years. And taking on the latest *Kenholme Mystery* in addition to *Minor Lights* had significantly increased, if quite not doubled my salary.

My stomach rumbled in an embarrassing way throughout the interview. When I stood up to leave, I felt unsteady on my legs - glad to get out into the fresh air and find a seat on a bench in the town square for a few moments – the bank manager had said no.

I needed to find something to eat, but while I was recovering heard the sound of a flute nearby and knew it must be Kelda. My eyes searched the streets – the brightly lit windows of the smart boutiques and gift shops - then I spotted her, crouched down by the bridge, sitting on a blanket, with her upturned black hat set out by her feet.

Retracing my steps across town, I stood close to her, looking down at the river, where the grassy banks were now studded with the golden yellow of daffodils. Kelda played a piece by Debussy, one I hadn't heard her play before. Her black hat contained only a few coins, change she had probably put there herself, to encourage the punters.

She finished playing and laid the flute down beside her on the blanket, staring up at me, eyes dark and glittering. Her greatcoat was unfastened and the stench of alcohol and stale sweat rose towards me in waves each time she moved - her hands and fingernails were smeared and encrusted with dirt.

'I know somewhere we could go and eat,' I said.

Near the market, was a small cafe called Turn Tables, it had a few seats inside the premises but more out on the pavement. Through the crowds hustling round the market stalls, I could see the tables outside were unoccupied - there was no-one who might object to Kelda's presence.

Kelda didn't move, so I said, 'I haven't got long.' I had several errands to do before hurrying back to the island in time for the tide.

She fitted her flute into its battered case and pocketed the money from the hat, before putting the hat on her head and gathering up the blanket and bags of her belongings. Since I'd last seen her, she'd added a large black umbrella to her possessions - it was strapped to the outside of her back pack.

'If I wasn't so fucking hungry, I wouldn't come,' she grumbled - a warning not to be optimistic about our meeting.

As we walked towards the cafe, a wedding party emerged from the Priory, the groom in naval uniform and the bride in a froth of white, disappeared into a cloud of pink, blue and yellow confetti.

The market stallholders were noisy – shouting against each other to promote their wares. The passageway that led to Turn Tables was messy with discarded crisp packets and empty cans which clattered across the pavement as the breeze blew them into the gutter.

Kelda wouldn't meet my eyes - she behaved as if my being there was an unfortunate coincidence, so I went inside, ordered two mugs of tea, the large "all day breakfast" with extra bread for her, and a bacon sandwich for myself. Being with her reminded me of being with Zoë, in the worst phase of her teenage years.

I carried our drinks outside and Kelda emptied three packets of sugar into her mug and sipped steadily at the sweet tea. When our food came, though I was hungry, I struggled to eat, the aroma of salty bacon, burnt grease and tomato ketchup mingling with the less savoury odour of Kelda made me feel sick. I pushed my plate aside after two or three mouthfuls and waited while she took the edge off her hunger before expecting her to speak.

'What happened to you, Kelda?' I asked at last, I was hoping she might provide more than the rough outline of her life given by Delia.

'Mind your own fucking business, nosey cow,' she muttered. She chewed her food with her head down, shovelling it into her mouth, wiping her mouth with the back of her hand. 'You dragged me away from my pitch. Some fucking bastard's probably taken my place and I'm losing money. You could at least have taken me to The Pilgrim's Inn,' she added grinning.

The brief glimpse of the mischievous girl I'd known at school made my heart contract. It was the sense I had that the real Kelda was still there, imprisoned behind an ugly mask, as if some entity had taken her over, as if some devil had captured her voice and forced her to express herself in a string of expletives, which made me determined not to walk away or abandon her.

She finished her mug of tea and wiped her mouth on her sleeve.

'Where will you go tonight?' I said, thinking I could give her money for a hostel. Though there were signs of spring in the countryside, the nights were still bitterly cold. 'Could you go to Hintham Ridge..?'

Kelda eyed me suspiciously, 'I used to camp there before that fucking community moved in, now it's crap.'

She began to collect her things together and made a move to shuffle away from me. It seemed we were going to part already, after another depressing, frustrating and seemingly pointless encounter.

Reaching into my bag for my purse, I called after her, 'Wait..!' But when I held up a ten pound note she shook her head.

I'd paid for our meal when I ordered, so followed her along the street. People moved aside to avoid meeting her gaze or worse still - in the hustle of the crowd – having to touch her.

'What do you fucking well want?' she asked, veering round to face me, her eyes glinting.

'I want to understand what changed for you – what changed you so much...'

I waited for a rude rejoinder, but she shrugged and said, 'What has changed? We're the same, aren't we? Consumed by guilt over the death of your mother...'

The truth and lucidity of her statement caught me off guard – however confused I was by her, she clearly understood me.

I'd thought she would return to her pitch to see if it was free, but instead she wandered off towards the public park on the north side of town, away from where I needed to be.

When I fell back, giving up my pursuit of her, she called out, 'See you around,' and lurched into the road, to a squeal of brakes and a sharp blast on a car horn.

338

She looked over her shoulder when she reached the pavement on the other side and waved - she was mocking me – but perhaps Kelda's stance on life was to make a mockery of everybody.

The Bridge House Bookshop had been an institution in the town for years, a significant part of my childhood. Stepping inside, I relished the musty scent of books - books which could drift me into other worlds, where I could forget my troubles. But the shop had a dejected air about it – many of the shelves were empty, the remaining books leaning to one side, where stock had been sold and not replaced.

Passing the Poetry section, I caught sight of a slim volume, *Indigo*, an early book of David's. It had must have sat on the shelf for some time - the spine was bleached by the sun - but I felt the usual stab of pride, pleasure and pain seeing his work on display and thought later, I might buy it.

Heading for the *Biographies* section, I searched for something which would interest Flora, working my way methodically through the few volumes that were left. The doorbell tinged as someone came into the shop, but I barely glanced up except to notice they'd disappeared into the *Local History* section. I'd reached the shelves marked T-Z without finding anything suitable. Reluctant to give up, I removed a copy of a book on Tintoretto from the shelf, but flicking through the pages, thought the writer seemed to be saying nothing new – Laurence Langlais could be controversial, but his work was well-researched, original and his writing had become my benchmark.

At the back of the shop was the second-hand section, nearly as large as the area selling new books. Everything there was marked down to half price. Picking my way through the narrow aisles and teetering stacks of books piled on the floor, I came across a heap of monographs on art in a broken cardboard box in a corner of the room.

I blew the dust off each book as I lifted it out and examined it. Near the bottom of the box, was a monograph about the portraitist, Paul Carrell-Abbott, written by his sister Jean – both had been friends of Bernard and Flora. I wiped the book carefully with my hand, it wasn't in bad condition – some of the pages were brown at the edge, but not bent or ragged and the book was unmarked inside. There was no price written on the cover, but as the artist had been relatively obscure, I thought the book shouldn't cost more than a few pounds.

As I'd stood up, my legs almost gave way beneath me, I was still hungry and emerged through the archway into the main bookshop, fumbling for my purse, anxious to get outside and go to the nearby newsagent, where I could buy crisps or a chocolate bar, enough to prevent me passing out.

Moving towards the counter, I stumbled into someone – and when I looked up to apologise, found myself face to face with Patrick Piran. He was dressed in a smart navy overcoat, his face less strained than the day we had seen each other at Lyncross. Our eyes met and I thought he was about to smile, but then he and the shelves of books appeared to spin round me, to disappear into a sea of black. I steadied myself against the counter.

When I was a schoolgirl, Sister Miriam had counselled that the correct way to deal with an embarrassing situation was to leave with quiet dignity. Patrick stepped aside and I turned away, just as he had turned away from me at Lyncross - I moved swiftly towards the door of the shop.

My hand reached out for the brass handle of the door, then through the thrumming in my ears I heard the bell ting as I pushed the door open.

The shop assistant cried out, "Can I help you?" her voice full of outrage.

The monograph was still tucked under my arm and though I began to offer an explanation, the woman's angry face suggested she wouldn't be taken in by the shameless gabbling of a shoplifter. The monograph was clutched close to my body but I was tempted to drop it on the floor and run. Apart from Patrick Piran, two other customers in the shop were staring and the assistant had advanced from behind the counter, as if to apprehend me.

'I'm sorry,' I said to the accusatory faces, my cheeks burning, as laying the book on the top of the children's bookcase, I made my exit.

As I closed the door behind me, I heard the assistant say, "we get all sorts in here."

After calling at the newsagents, I hurried across town to the chemist shop, where I bought Flora a gift box of lily of the valley soap, perfume and talc. To have reached the end of the morning empty-handed, would only have served to make my despondent mood worse. In the stationer's, I bought a card, sellotape, wrapping paper and a Jiffy bag. I found a table in the Post Office where I could wrap the gifts and scribble an apologetic note to Flora. As I handed the package to the clerk, I felt a wave of relief – what should have been a simple job was finally completed.

I'd given up any thoughts of shopping in the market, but considered waiting until The Bridge House Bookshop was clear of anyone, other than the assistant, who'd witnessed my ridiculous performance. I wanted to go back and buy the monograph, but was too much of a coward, preferring to vanish among the busy people who crowded the pavements.

I blundered past shops selling haberdashery, knitting wools and magic tricks, and bumped into someone again, this time a well-dressed elderly woman, in a tweed suit and felt hat.

'Sorry, how stupid of me,' I said.

340

'If that's the most stupid thing you ever do, you're very fortunate,' she remarked.

'Sorry,' I said, I seemed to have been apologising all day.

In the delicatessen, I bought a ham sandwich to eat in the car on the way back to Littern. Taking a few surreptitious bites as I walked towards Pierce Street, I scurried up the hill. The last thing I needed to round off the day was to be cut off by the tide.

There was no sign of Eve at Marisands. She now spent much of her time in Thrift Cottage either alone or with Kos, joining me only for meals, but I was late and she'd eaten and left lunch on the stove. After a bowl of soup and an apple, I fetched Quirk and crossed the garden to the oratory.

Once through the gate, I tied him to the gatepost. I wouldn't allow him onto the steps, but felt more confident knowing he was nearby, as I descended the steep cliff. Clinging to the handrail, I eased my way down, fixing my gaze on the statue of a headless St. Thrif, in its niche above the oratory door.

I leaned against the rough stone wall, waiting for my heart to stop pounding. Quirk barked as I pushed open the door. I stepped into the interior with its lining of warm pink of shells in intricate curving patterns. A single shaft of light, struck the altar. Someone had placed two jam jars of sea glass there with a green glass fisherman's float - Ursula perhaps - or a beachcomber? Beside them were arranged candles, shells, feathers and driftwood and a jar of wild flowers with a few narcissi and primroses.

Where the oratory extended back into the cave, a clean blanket lay neatly folded on the sandy floor. I spread it out where the sun created a rectangle of lemon light in front of the altar and when I'd lit one of the candles, sat with my back resting against the low wooden bench, the oratory's only furniture.

There was quietness, though not silence. As the sea broke against the pyramid of rock on the beach below, the rhythm of the waves throbbed like a steady heartbeat.

The oratory had known centuries of prayer, of faith that beyond the outward starkness of life could be found a God of compassion and unremitting love. The shells and driftwood on the altar suggested the worship of a pagan god, but their simplicity touched me. Ursula with her fey wisdom had said an oratory belonged to God, not to any person, and she was right – the oratory was for any pilgrim who needed a place to pray or take refuge.

I closed my eyes. I'd come to Marisands with a heart in turmoil and the irony was, that after three months, it needed almost nothing to return me to the same turbulent state – Kelda's defensiveness, her boundaries so fragile that attempting to breach them felt like a terrible infringement - the annoyance of Patrick Piran, encountered in the wrong place at the wrong time –

Clasping my knees to my chest, I felt the vibration of the sea beating against the rocks. *Was it arrogant to have expected answers to have come easily or so soon?* If I carried out the tasks I'd come here to perform, could I leave the results to a God who seemed to speak no more intelligibly than the wind and waves? My father had been troubled by what he saw as the anarchic nature of the world, and I might discover that my future lay in chaos, not in the natural pattern, which according to my mother's philosophy formed the foundation of our lives.

I stayed in the oratory for a long time, waiting until I felt calm. When I was ready to go back to the house, I didn't extinguish the candle, but left it to pray on my behalf, to intercede until it had burnt out. As I began to climb the steps, I turned to see its flickering light at the oratory window.

Quirk barked encouragement as I scaled the steps. When I released him into the garden he shot off, a black streak of fur racing towards the house, while I paused to strip one of Juliet's statues of its coat of moss, sending slivers of soft white stone cascading into the grass. There was smoke from the chimney of Thrift Cottage, but I left Eve alone, I was going to the study to write a letter.

I hadn't replied to Edgar's request for money to repair the island's road, but now the bank had refused me a loan, I felt justified in making sure any outstanding business with the Pirans was concluded and would direct my response to Nicholas Piran at The Retreat, as I'd been instructed.

Fidgeting and chewing my pen, I grappled with the few words needed, wanting to write simply and directly. On a scrap of rough paper, I drafted a note to say that though I would have liked to fulfil my duty where the road fund was concerned, I wasn't in a financial position to make good my father's debts or to give the sum of money Edgar had demanded. When I was satisfied, I copied the notes out and put in a cheque for five hundred pounds; it was far more than I could afford but only a fraction of what had been asked for.

I signed the letter, addressed the envelope, then shut Quirk in the conservatory and drove out to The Retreat. The house, long and low, cream with turquoise blue window frames came into view where the lane curved towards the sea. The broad gently sloping garden, reached all the way to the margin of the beach and behind the house, the grassy slopes of the Hagdon Hills formed a quiet backdrop, with the tower the only outstanding landmark.

The gardens of neat lawns and mature trees ended at a row of pines and a steep ridge of rocks, intended to keep the sea at bay. The Retreat was beautiful, isolated, enchanting - I'd forgotten how lovely - and for a few moments it slipped my mind how unwelcome my visit would be.

Intending to post the letter through the door and leave, I didn't notice the three dogs lying in wait on the veranda. I was greeted by a chorus of low, deep growls and when they approached me, the dogs stood level with my waist.

The front door had been left ajar. Nicholas's family life was exposed in a display of colourful and disparate objects. Skateboards, cricket bats, racquets and games had been pushed to the edges of the hall, leaving a pathway through to a wooden archway, which led into the heart of the house. I pushed the door open a little further and laid the letter on the mat – only realising someone was there, framed by the arch, as I straightened up.

'What the hell are you doing?' Nicholas said.

'I've left a letter about the road...' I indicated the envelope on the doormat. 'I've explained - I didn't expect to find so many changes on Littern...'

'You need to adjust – and quickly,' he said, Beatrix had indicated the same. 'On other parts of the coastline they're building strong sea defences, but not here on the island. Give it fifty years or so and sea levels could have risen by a couple of feet making those gabions they've installed along the cliffs useless – not to mention the causeway.'

I bent down to retrieve my letter and handed it to him. 'This explains my position, I'm sorry to have bothered you.'

'You're like your father then..?' Nicholas asked - scorn in his voice. 'You're indifferent to the problems of the rest of us? The worst thing that could happen to Littern is to become the victim of apathy.'

'If there's anything I can do that doesn't involve large sums of money...'

Nicholas laughed and I felt the bitterness in him. 'Everything worth doing involves large sums of money, and everyone who lives here is equally responsible.'

'I've offered what I can,' I said.

'Really..? We're all waiting to see how soon you'll leave Marisands.'

I was tired, feeling low and he was taunting me.

My temper flared, 'If I decide to go - I'll go when I'm ready. I won't be hounded off the island by anyone - not even you – in fact, especially not you nor your family.'

There was a moment of silence, then he closed the door and I wasn't sure which of us had been most startled by my outburst.

# Chapter 28

Kos had serviced and cleaned William's old car and one morning, Eve decided to drive into Narescombe with him to buy plants and seeds for the garden and materials needed for decorating Thrift Cottage.

I stayed behind to work, but took a break when I heard the post arrive. Waiting for the kettle to boil, I looked through the mail and found a note from Verena and a letter from Silvie in response to the latest news I had sent her. Verena would be returning to England in June and I thought I'd invite her to visit the island. Silvie suggested it would be better to discuss my discoveries about Juliet, when we could meet, face to face. Since I'd come to Marisands, I'd noticed her letters had been brief and to the point, nothing like the detailed missive she had first sent me in London.

Quirk was restless, it was a cold, rainy morning and he'd only had a run in the garden. Ignoring his attempts to pester me to take him out again – I returned to the study and began to examine Laurence's text, ordering Quirk to stop nudging my hand with his head and lie still on the rug.

At about eleven o'clock the doorbell rang. I grabbed my coffee mug – I'd make a re-fill while I was downstairs – I'd been engrossed and hadn't heard anyone coming up the drive. As I opened the front door, I uttered my usual prayer that it wouldn't be Beatrix or Geraldine.

Quirk gave an exuberant welcome as he did to all visitors. But had I been a dog, I would have felt my hackles rise.

'What can I do for you?' I said wondering how Patrick Piran had the nerve to turn up on my doorstep. My heart beat faster, afraid of what he might say, considering the possibility that his appearance at Marisands was a result of the letter I'd written to Nicholas about the money for the road.

'Could I come in? The rain's blowing into the porch and I'm already soaked.'

It was raining heavily and the shoulders of his jacket showed broad patches of damp - his hair was speckled with rain drops. I wished I could think of a pithy comment that would diminish him as I felt he had diminished me at Lyncross, but as nothing came to mind, I led the way through the hall and into the kitchen and put the kettle on – it was becoming a reflex action.

'Have a seat,' I said.

Patrick unbuttoned his jacket, and slipped out a brown paper bag from an inside pocket.

'You left this in the bookshop the other day. I thought I'd bring it for you.'

He took the monograph on Paul Carrell Abbott out of the bag and laid it on the table.

'You didn't need to do that...' I said and reached for my bag, which was hung over the back of one of the chairs.

'... And you don't need to do that. The book is by way of an apology for my appalling rudeness at Lyncross - I think I might have upset you.'

'The book was a birthday present for my grandmother,' I explained, flustered by his unexpected kindness.

'Is it too late now? You could give it to her next year, perhaps,' he said and I recalled his tendency to tease.

I set a tray with the coffee pot and mugs and carried it to the table. In the bookshop, I'd gained only a fleeting impression of him - now I noticed once again, the slight drooping of his shoulders, the tightness of his voice, and the tiredness in his eyes.

'You'll have found much changed here...' he said.

'I tried not to have too many expectations.'

I put coffee in front of him and my hand trembled. I wanted to look at him, but had the feeling I was equally under scrutiny and that he wouldn't miss anything.

Eve had been baking - I fetched a tin of oat biscuits from the larder and put a few out on a plate.

'Was it your father's death that brought you back to the island?'

I sat down in the chair by the window. 'Partly – but I suppose I was taking refuge in one way and fighting dragons in another.'

'And I suppose I could say the same. When I came back I needed time to consider what to do next.'

Patrick had taken off his jacket and hung it on the back of the chair, revealing a jumper that was frayed at the neck and cuffs and worn into holes on the elbows. 'I wondered what happened to you - after you left the island...' he said.

'I lived with my grandmother and aunt in Dulwich,' I kept my reply brief, still feeling resentful.

'...And now?'

When I hesitated, he smiled in encouragement.

'I separated from my partner and couldn't stay living in his house in London. We have three daughters and I needed a home - an ordinary woman trying to come to terms with an ordinary sorrow.'

Patrick sipped his coffee and took a biscuit. 'It was good of you to write about Antony. I try to take comfort from the fact he had made the most of his life. He was happily married and fulfilled in his work - not many of us can claim that.'

'No...' I said.

'I expect Ursula has already told you most of my secrets,' he said and laughed, 'I was working on an aid project in Kenya with my partner, Honor. I met her out there, she was a friend of Nick's, a photographer - it seemed natural we should get together, but in the end there were problems.'

I tried to absorb this unfamiliar version of Patrick Piran. If I'd thought about it, I would have imagined him settled with a comfortable wife and lots of children, a family man, not someone unsettled and unsettling - someone whose intensity was redolent of pain, pain that was still raw - not unlike my own.

'Thanks for taking Ursula in,' he said. 'She misses her mother and wants to be with me all the time - her point of security, I suppose.'

'She reminds me of myself as a child, I sympathise with her.'

'Somebody needs to - the family are growing tired of her frequent disappearing act.'

'One of my daughters is a bit of a runner,' I admitted, thinking of Zoë whose extended silences seemed to grow longer.

'I wanted to apologise not only for myself but for my family's behaviour. Antony's death has brought things to the surface, especially for Beatrix, she and Antony were close.'

'It's losing people - after David left, I went a bit mad.'

'...How mad?' he asked with twinkle in his eye.

'Mad enough to come back here...' I said and smiled.

'I was sorry we lost touch after your mother died – it must have seemed cruel - losing your mother and your friends all at the same time...'

I thought of his last words to me *I can't be with you, Iris. I have to be with my family*. Had he forgotten?

I said, 'I also lost my father. What happened to Juliet and to Antony is woven through all our lives, perhaps one of the strongest threads - but as Beatrix blames me, perhaps the rest of your family do too,'

He looked thoughtful. 'I'm afraid, Juliet's death played into a series of unhappy events - my mother was seriously ill - Antony's accident was too much for her and for Pa - he couldn't deal with things rationally – none of us could. But life on the island isn't easy these days – it really is better if people can be on good terms...'

346

'I want to be,' I said. 'Since leaving the island, I've had the sense that at any moment, the structure of my existence could fall away, and when something bad happens, I feel that is has...' I hesitated, 'I've wanted to thank you for pulling me out of the sea, saving my life.'

'You don't need to...' He downed the last of his coffee and I wondered if he would leave. Instead he said, 'You must have felt lonely since you came here..?' He had no inhibitions about probing painful places, though we were virtually strangers.

'My daughter Eve is living in the cottage, Minette, will be coming at Easter - I have Quirk, two cats and a large collection of books to keep me company...'

'Ursula told me about the books - the *Seabright Island Adventures*.'

'I wrote those a very long time ago,' I said, embarrassed. 'I work for Laurence Langlais now, he's become something of a god in the world of art history – I've been lucky.' If my intention had been to keep my reserve, Patrick, like Ursula, had disarmed me with his openness.

'I heard about your visit to The Retreat, don't mind Nick, his life is rather complicated - and don't mind my father, he isn't well.'

I stared out of the window at the rain falling on the lush green of the garden. So many feelings had been suppressed since I'd returned to Littern and now I couldn't trust myself to hold them down.

'Are you all right?' he asked.

'I thought I would find peace here, but my presence seems to be disturbing the peace of others...'

'Perhaps they need disturbing...'

And despite our awkwardness, the Patrick who was sitting in my kitchen had begun to bear some resemblance to the Patrick I'd known as a child. I felt the spirit of kindness in him, sensed that the essence of him was unchanged.

I asked if he would like more coffee.

'As there haven't been any distress flares from Lyncross, I think I will,' he said. 'You've been extremely forbearing with Ursula...'

'I like her,' I said simply.

Patrick told me about his work as a doctor in Africa and how his belief that his family should come home and stay permanently had caused a rift with Honor. He described how Beatrix had left her beloved world of Oxford to care for their father and how Nicholas since returning to the island had become something of an eco-warrior, running a volunteer conservation group based in Narescombe.

It was late morning and as Eve and Kos hadn't come back, I said, 'Perhaps you'd join me for lunch? It would be some recompense for the book.'

Eve had made vegetable stew and a rhubarb pie, I switched on the cooker and fetched plates from the larder and set them to warm.

'Do you think you'll settle on the island?' I asked.

'I'm not sure. The others manage their lives round the tides, but because of the nature of my work, I have to be available, especially when I'm on call. We're a bit of a nuisance at Lyncross and probably at The Retreat, and Ursula needs to be settled. I'm open to all possibilities – you could say I'm seeking a new vocation.'

'I'm hope you'll find what you're looking for,' I said. But he had begun to edge his way back into my life and I knew if the new and tenuous thread between us should be broken too soon – that would be painful.

I found a bottle of wine and poured us each a glass. As I lifted the casserole dish from the hotplate, the rich smell of tomato, herbs and vegetables filled the kitchen.

Patrick sat, long legs stretched out under the table - Quirk down by his feet. We talked about philosophy and faith and I remembered how he, like Antony, had always seemed pulled towards God as naturally as the sea is pulled by the moon. I related some of the disconcerting truths that had emerged about my family and the difficulties I'd had persuading people to talk and hoped I didn't sound rancorous.

'Perhaps people want to protect you,' he said. 'But maybe we should keep that discussion for another time, do you agree?' Patrick's gaze was as penetrating as his questions.

'Eve says I've so become obsessed with other people's lives, I forget how my own life was a mess – the result of many things I'd brought on myself - things I'd done or not done...'

'Those are the worst sort of things...'

There was still no sign of Eve and Kos, I imagined they must have gone into Safford Bridge - perhaps William's old car had broken down.

We'd finished our meal and Patrick said, 'I've always been intrigued by this house, your father wouldn't allow us to cross the threshold.' I glanced up at his face where a barely suppressed smile played round his lips.

'My father didn't welcome any guests except his own friends.'

'And I expect Pa destroyed any possibility of us being welcome here. After you left the island there was yet more enmity over the road and the bridge. My father's written a few lambasting letters.'

'I've received one...' I said.

Patrick laughed. 'I've told Beatrix, more than once - she should censor Pa's correspondence...'

He helped pile the plates on the draining board.

'Would you like to see round Marisands?' I asked.

I took him through the downstairs of the house, into the dining room with its teetering stacks of papers and letters, the sitting room, and the music room, where the piano had been left open by Kos.

'May I?' he asked.

Patrick reached down, touched the keys and played a fragment of melody as if it were as much a natural part of our conversation as words – I remembered his mother playing with the same ease.

'The young man who lives in the woods – Kos - he uses the piano in exchange for gardening,' I explained.

'I wonder which skills I could barter?' he asked, putting the piano lid down. 'Pa gave my mother's piano to Sarah, Nick's wife, I miss it at Lyncross.'

It was time to take Quirk to the beach before the tide came in. The rain had slowed to a soft drizzle. Patrick lifted his jacket from the kitchen chair and we set off together, stopping to admire the newly cleared flowerbeds, the orchard and the vegetable patch before going through the pergola towards Thrift Cottage.

'All this is Kos's work,' I told him, 'he's been a God-send.'

'Beatrix said he was a lazy good-for-nothing. Perhaps she doesn't bring out the best in him.'

We crossed the lawn, leaving our footprints in the rain-spangled grass, Patrick found a clump of cowslips that had seeded themselves in the cottage garden; he crouched down to breathe in the fragrance.

'Isn't nature where reverence begins?' he asked, 'imagine if the scent of cowslips was the only air you had to breathe?'

'Someone told me your family would like own Marisands.'

He seemed surprised. 'It's true Tom's looking for somewhere to retire and my sister went through a phase of getting ideas about the garden here, turning it all over to vegetables. She's determined to grow sufficient food as a means of survival should the island become completely cut off from the mainland...'

'Having a bridge built – wouldn't it destroy the mystery of the place?' I ventured, I'd been thinking about the Piran's plans for a proper road from Palk's Reach.

'But we have to remain connected to the real world - that's important, isn't it?'

As we passed through the gate by Thrift Cottage onto the footpath, I said, 'Ursula goes to the oratory sometimes – it isn't safe – the steps are damaged, the handrail has rotted away in places...'

'I'll speak to her.'

'I've asked Kos to repair the steps - but he always seems to have something better to do...'

'He has no head for heights, perhaps...' Patrick suggested with a smile.

We followed the track down to the beach - the breaking sea resounding with a boom as wind-tossed waves crashed onto the shore. After a few moments, he stopped suddenly, 'Listen, in a few seconds you'll hear the tide turn.'

I stood, listened and heard nothing, only felt a change in the wind, which now seemed to brush my cheeks and ruffle my hair rather than drawing me out towards the water. 'You're teasing, but you can't fool me anymore...'

'I'm deadly serious,' he said.

He threw a driftwood stick for Quirk, who raced off towards Morrow Bay.

'So many things come back to me in this place...' I said.

'You must find it difficult...'

'Things didn't make much sense in London, either, I'd forgotten who I was, how to be...'

'Since Honor left, I've been asking how I should view myself. More than anything, I wanted us to stay together, but there was nothing I could do or say – she wouldn't be swayed by my pleas or even by Ursula's.'

'Thank you for coming to see me...' I said.

'...But I've left Beatrix at Ursula's mercy for too long - I'd better get back...'

We had almost reached the edge of Whitcroft Cove, so I called Quirk and we made our way slowly to the house by the oratory steps, so Patrick could see the extent of the damage.

Passing my mother's white statues in the oratory garden he asked, 'What are these?'

'The spirits of nature, the trees, wind, rocks and sea - apparently...'

'Really..?

We stood by his car on the driveway, the dark blue car I'd seen the day I had met Delia in Narescombe. He talked about his family, his nieces and nephews. 'There are far too many of us - in some people's opinion.'

'Yours always seemed such a happy house,' I said half to myself.

'All the ingredients for a *Famous Five* adventure - except there were six of us, if you include James.'

'Thanks for bringing the book - I was sorry I'd left it.'

'My pleasure,' he said with that smile of his, which lit his eyes and reminded me of the play of sunlight on water. 'And thanks for lunch – it takes an iron constitution to survive Beatrix's cooking.'

As he drove away, I felt shaken. When he'd come to the door of Marisands that morning, I had wanted to dislike him - but there was an innate quality of goodness in Patrick - he seemed to have lived a life of self-sacrifice and honour, qualities I found bitter-sweet and endearing.

We might never be friends, as we had been as children, but I understood that to have turned him away would have been like taking a carefully wrapped gift and rattling it violently in a mistaken attempt to discover if it contained something I wanted to receive.

# Chapter 29

Easter was at the end of March that year and Minette was travelling to Safford Bridge for the school holidays with an escort. I was to collect her from the station at lunchtime after stopping to do a few errands in Narescombe. Eve had recently had her hair styled at a salon called *Mopheads* and I'd decided to try them out by having a trim. At the Post Office, I sent off the Carrell-Abbott book to Flora. When I'd slipped it into a Jiffy Bag, the cheque I'd given Nicholas Piran for the road fund dropped out and I'd been unsure whether Patrick had left it there inadvertently, or if he had meant to hand it back to me. The most likely answer was that Nicholas had decided it was insufficient to be worth bothering about, so I'd tucked it into a cubby hole in my desk and decided to wait and see if the Pirans mentioned it.

As the train pulled into the station, Minette was leaning out of the window, her face full of anxiety. Her expression cleared momentarily as she noticed me on the platform, but when she jumped out and I offered a hug, she accepted it with obvious reluctance.

'Trains are boring,' she said.

'Was there nothing you enjoyed?'

She gave the merest hint of a shrug in reply.

In our letters, Minette and I had been engaged in a discussion about her bringing Yuuka to Marisands. I'd explained I would be happy for her friend to visit in the future - but not at this time - not until she had accepted and got the measure of the island herself.

Before we had left the station she'd asked gravely, 'When do I go back to school?'

'In just over a week, long enough for you to get used to Marisands and Littern, you hardly saw them last time.'

Minette closed in on herself and walked towards The Pilgrims' Inn, head down, studying the pavement. She was uninterested in lunch and complained when told we needed to shop for jeans and a waterproof jacket from the country store.

Leaving Safford Bridge, the countryside was fresh and lovely, as spring sunshine filtered through the shiny new-leafed branches of the trees, making them glow like little lanterns - beyond them the rolling hills, richly green, formed tantalising curves and folds.

We passed through Narescombe and when we turned from the square onto Palk's Reach, Minette asked, 'What happens if we're cut off by the tide *before* we get to the island?'

'The tide won't be in until late tonight,' I told her, 'but we'll walk down tomorrow and watch as it cuts off the island, if you like.'

'No thank you.'

I slowed the car and drove down onto the causeway. The sea distant and un-menacing lapped at the far shore. I pointed out to Minette the wooden markers showing the depth of the sea at high tide, but she hardly bothered to look.

The road rose onto the island through overhanging trees and Minette shivered so hard, I wondered if she was going to cry. Her bad mood left me shut out – she was hurt, disappointed and entirely vulnerable and the weight of that responsibility bore down heavily on me.

At the oak tree, we turned into the gateway of Marisands. Minette said nothing, her face sullen. Sweeping into the drive, I prayed Eve was around – perhaps she could cheer up her sister.

Minette was nervous of Quirk, so I shut him into the conservatory. He'd been over-excited by our arrival and had run up the stairs after us, making Minette shrink against the wall to avoid colliding with him.

'You'll soon get used to him - he's very friendly, isn't he?'

'Too friendly,' Minette said glumly.

I lifted her navy blue holdall onto the bed. 'Why not get changed now?' I put the bags of new clothes we'd bought on her bed by the pillow.

'Yuuka cried when I left, she wanted to come to the island.'

'I don't want to make anyone cry,' I said, 'but I can't take charge of Yuuka...'

'Who can take charge of her then?' Minette demanded, 'Nobody cares about her - how would you like that? I have to look after her all on my own.'

It would have been pointless to advise Minette that St. Catherine's was responsible for her friend, she was too miserable to listen. I had noticed the ribbon of my Service and Sacrifice medal hanging out of the corner of her bag.

'We can ask about Yuuka staying in the summer...'

'It'll be too late by then.' Minette tugged back the zip on her bag, 'I've tried on *that* bridesmaid's dress, Helen bought' she said, 'and I'm not going to wear it.'

Before coming to Littern, Minette had been to see David and Helen, to have the dress properly fitted.

'Did Dad and Helen talk to you about the wedding?' I asked.

'Helen doesn't talk about anything else.'

'Your dad wants you to be there, you can understand why...'

'But not in that stupid dress - you promised you'd speak to Helen. You're a liar...'

I could understand that while for me the problems which had been inherent in my life in London had begun to recede, for Minette they were close, threatening and very much alive. 'I'm not a liar, Minette,' I said as patiently as I could. 'I did speak to Helen and I'll speak to her again...'

Eve had been baking and plates of cakes and biscuits covered the kitchen table; after a glass of milk and a slice of cherry cake, Minette put on her new jacket and jeans and we went out into the garden to look for her sister. The studio was empty and there was no answer from Thrift Cottage. So I took advantage of the opportunity - there was something Minette and I needed to do before she was on the island for very much longer.

Through the gate from the oratory garden, I led Minette down the steep steps, until we were safely on the plateau where the stone hut stood, then ushered her inside. She wandered about, fingering the shells on the walls, tracing the patterns. On the altar were fresh wild flowers in a jam jar.

'Who put those there?' she asked.

'I don't know,' I said. Then grasped her shoulders and made her face me. 'You must *never* come down here alone, *never* - only with me or another grown up like Eve.'

She shrugged off my hands and nodded - her eyes bright with fear.

'Now let's go down on the beach.'

We approached the beach by the footpath to drive home my point that the oratory steps were dangerous. As we passed my mother's statues, Minette suggested they looked like snowmen, melting.

When we reached the shore and turned towards Morrow Bay, three figures were visible in the distance. Eve's fair hair shone, catching the sunlight - she was walking between two taller people – one I was certain was Kos.

'Can I run to her?' Minette asked.

The tide was out, but I didn't want her thinking she could go anywhere on the island unaccompanied, so offered the excuse that Eve was further away than she appeared. 'Let's wait back at the house,' I suggested.

Despite the sunshine, it was a bitingly cold March day and Minette's face turned scarlet in the icy wind as we retraced our steps up the path to Marisands.

In the dimly lit porch, I reached for my keys, but before I could unlock the door, Ursula leapt out from under the wooden bench that flanked the side of the entrance.

'Made you jump!'

'What are you doing?' I asked startled, 'I suppose everybody's out looking for you?'

She had scared me so much my heart was racing and Minette had retreated as if she'd been frightened by a wild animal.

'Don't be cross,' Ursula said. She was in her school uniform, the skirt creased and covered in dust, her blazer torn on the sleeve.

'How long have you been under there?'

'...Ages. I'm supposed to go into school during the holidays and work with one of the teachers.'

'Who are you?' Minette asked rudely.

'I'm Ursula,' she said, 'Who are you?'

Minette had rooted herself to the spot, but Ursula was already trying to drag her away from the front door, pulling at her arm. 'Can I show Minette how to climb into The Robin's Nest?'

'No,' I said, imagining them both disappearing across Littern on one of Ursula's walkabouts.

I hustled them inside and applied a clothes brush to Ursula's uniform.

'I'm really hungry,' Ursula said seeing the plates of food on the table.

'Being hungry is the least of what will happen, if you're not where you're supposed to be at the right time,' I said.

Ursula eyed me from beneath her thick, dark fringe, 'You're not usually exasperated - that's why I like you.' She made me laugh with her quaint, adult way of speaking.

I kept my mother's sewing basket in the larder and sat at the kitchen table trying to make a discreet repair of Ursula's blazer sleeve.

'That's my new uniform,' Ursula told Minette, 'Dad bought it for me.'

Minette looked bored.

'I'd better let him know you're safe – there seems to be a search party out on the beach,' I said, hanging her blazer over the back of a chair.

'Dad isn't on the island - I'm staying with Uncle Nicholas again.' She pulled a face to indicate that this wasn't an entirely happy arrangement. 'Your mother says you're going to St. Mary's,' she said to Minette.

I'd wanted to avoid the subject of school - Minette was hardly in a receptive state of mind. She'd been studying Ursula curiously as if considering a hundred possibilities to explain the presence of another child at Marisands.

'St. Mary's isn't *very* strict, not like St. Safan's,' Ursula went on.

'And in any case, when you're with friends the strictness doesn't matter, you stand up for each other,' I said.

'That's what Rowena told me,' Ursula said, wiping her mouth free of biscuit crumbs with the back of her hand, reminding me of Kelda. They'd been helping themselves from the plates Eve had left out.

'Can't we go and meet the others now?' Minette asked, 'I want to see Eve.'

Ursula looked worried, 'Couldn't we do something else instead of meeting the others?'

Through the kitchen window, I could see Eve, Kos and Nicholas had arrived on the drive. Ursula stood, her face pale and prim, avoiding looking at anybody.

'It might help if you apologised,' I suggested.

'Dad says it's no use saying sorry if you don't mean it.'

'He's right,' I agreed.

'Granddad says I'm incorrigible.'

I might have agreed with that too, but the front door opened and Eve and Nicholas came in.

'Where was Ursula this time?' Nicholas asked.

'Close to the house...'

His expression was a mixture of relief and anger and I felt some sympathy for his ambivalence towards Ursula, who was now hanging her head and clutching tightly onto my hand.

'You've got to stop this,' he said to her, 'one day either you or somebody else is going to come to serious harm.'

Ursula nodded.

He looked impatient, 'I have to get home, I left the twins and Rowena and they're inclined to fight.'

'I don't want to go,' Ursula said, her voice quivering.

'Ursula could stay with Minette for a while,' I said. I wasn't sure Minette had taken to her, but given time, perhaps they might find things in common.

'Ursula has to have lessons with Beatrix - she didn't make it to school.'

My heart went out to her, seeing her wan little face as they left.

As soon as she'd gone, Minette said, 'What a funny little girl.'

Eve seemed agitated. 'Does Ursula talk to you? Because if you know anything, you should tell her family...'

'I don't *know* anything,' I said, 'except that she misses her mother and her father when he's away. She doesn't want to go to St. Safan's, but it's hardly my place to interfere.'

'Sometimes we have to interfere,' Eve said.

'But sometimes things go better if we don't interfere and I think this is one of those times...'

'...Because you don't like the Pirans? I don't find Nicholas as bad as you say...' Eve argued, but I shot her a warning glance – I'd had enough.

The day seemed fractured - Kos didn't want to stay on at Marisands and rode away on his bicycle, towing his trailer of tools. When I asked what she would like to do, Minette made it clear she preferred being with Eve, so I released Quirk, went to the study and before starting work, scanned e-mails for something from Zoë.

I clicked through my inbox, in case I'd missed Zoë's name, but the last mail from her had arrived more than five weeks ago, when I'd written about David and Helen's wedding. Since then, I'd received nothing, not even one of her caustic one-liners.

Zoë's refusal to answer was wilful and deliberate. Despite her long silences, I'd sent news of what was happening at Marisands – brief notes - because her interest in others was limited. Though I couldn't think how - I'd considered trying to trace Cameron's parents, in case they received regular mail from their son. It was a risky strategy, Zoë, I knew, would have been furious with me for "stalking" her.

An hour passed, while I sipped cold coffee and stared at the computer screen. I tapped out a few lines to Zoë about Minette's arrival, and then on an impulse - though I'd sworn I wouldn't, except in an emergency - I e-mailed Cameron using the address Eve had managed to extract from her.

I asked if everything was all right and said how grateful I would be if he could find the time to write to me - Cameron, I suspected, unlike my daughter, was more of a people pleaser.

*

Minette seemed tired so I gave her tea on her own and put her to bed early. As she bathed and changed into her pyjamas I noticed the pale pink marks on her back, remnants of the chicken pox and was thankful there was no scarring on her face.

'I'm sorry Yuuka couldn't come this time,' I said – wanting to make peace.

I understood that Yuuka was damaged, at the heart of her was the longing for a mother, for a family, a longing which I knew painfully and intimately, but in Yuuka's case, couldn't meet.

'Is it because of that other little girl?' Minette asked.

'Ursula? Ursula pops up every now and then, she's staying on the island for a while, until her dad finds a new job.'

'You can't replace Yuuka with another girl - I don't need a friend on the island because I won't be living here...'

Without giving the uncomfortable details of my interview at the bank, it was time to be straight with her. 'I'm not trying to replace anyone - but I'm afraid you can't stay at St. Catherine's, indefinitely. Rose and Neil have been kind, but they can't be expected to look after you forever and I miss you, I want you at Marisands with Eve and me.'

Minette wriggled under the bedclothes, hugging her pillow tightly. 'Why can't Yuuka live here?' she said, 'you've loads of bedrooms not like in Pimlico...'

When I didn't answer at once, she closed her eyes tightly, signalling she had no intention of speaking either. My heart was heavy; I didn't know how to help her. She was by nature curious and friendly, yet she'd barely responded to the island or the house or even to meeting Ursula, except in terms of suspicion and jealousy.

I kissed her forehead, smoothing back her dark hair, and said goodnight, 'I'm going to talk to Helen, as I promised,' I told her.

Downstairs, Eve was busy in the kitchen making dinner. I was reluctant to phone Pimlico, but it was no use procrastinating, so I dialled the number for Hurst Row.

Helen began explaining that their wedding reception would be in the garden of Barbara's house at Leitchly, something she'd told me before - when I stopped her - she added that John was going to be David's best man. I didn't need nor want to hear any more details.

'Minette isn't happy about being a bridesmaid,' I said.

'But her dress is beautiful,' Helen objected, 'didn't she tell you I'd added a royal blue sash?'

'She didn't mention that...'

I was surprised Helen couldn't see that a cream silk dress, with a Peter Pan collar and flounced skirt - with or without a royal blue sash - didn't suit Minette or her personality. Neither was Minette simply being obstructive - she was hurt - her values upset by the whole business of their wedding.

'It isn't the dress – it's more how Minette feels,' I explained. *Hadn't I made the same point when Helen had come to Marisands?*

'What about my feelings or David's?' she asked.

'Has David talked to Minette?'

'He says if you'll bring her to Leitchly, he'll make things convenient for you.'

I bit back my response - David marrying his lover could hardly be described as "convenient" for me or for his daughters.

'Minette's only eight - she can't be expected to understand the complexities of adult relationships.'

'But have you tried to explain to her?' Helen asked - her voice accusatory.

'David needs to communicate his side of things,' I said.

She didn't answer.

'I'll take your silence to mean David *isn't* willing to explain himself to his daughter?'

'David doesn't want to end up in hospital again. People should get on and do the right thing - I'm trying to keep everything under control, but I'm finding it very difficult. When we went to buy rings the other day, there was a lot of standing and David nearly passed out on the floor, it was so embarrassing.'

'David loves you – couldn't that have been enough – did you need a ceremony to prove it?'

'I've told you...' she began.

I assumed she was going to remind me either of her need for a fall-back position or her life-long urge to have her own way. 'I'm not going to force Minette to do something she doesn't want to do. I won't have anyone pressurizing her and you shouldn't pressurize David.'

I felt Eve's restraining hand on my arm, my voice had risen to a shout and she had overheard me in the kitchen.

Helen said, 'Minette told me she doesn't want to stay with you for the whole holiday, I thought she could come back here for a few days.'

'Well, she isn't going to.'

I was tempted to slam down the phone, but Helen and David were talking in the background - the word *paranoid* was used and I could guess it was directed at me.

'You can't blame Minette for not wanting to stay at Marisands - she'll die of boredom,' Helen said.

'I'll find plenty to amuse her.'

'What though?'

'I've made plans...' I said defensively, 'what they are has nothing to do with you.'

'David says you're full of dark secrets.'

'How astute, too astute...'

'Can one be *too* astute?' Helen countered.

'We were talking about Minette,' I said. When any of the girls was unhappy, I found it difficult to stand back and take an objective view.

'David's just reminded me, Lesley wants to speak to you. The date, time and venue for his reading have been fixed. She wanted to know if you're willing to take part – as you'll be in London for the wedding, anyhow...'

'I'll call her,' I said, wanting the conversation to end before I exposed the heat of my resentment against all of them - her, David and Lesley.

When I'd put down the phone, I appealed to Eve, 'What can I do?'

I'd been trying to let go and yet some unwelcome and inexorable force seemed determined to keep me attached to David, to draw me back into his life.

She shrugged, 'Dad was furious when I said I might not go to the wedding – but I could take Minette, spare you. They say it's better to make a clean break...'

'There's nothing clean about it,' I said fighting back tears.

Eve rested her hands on my shoulders, 'I've wondered if Lesley ever cared for Zoë or for me – I've never had to ask that question about you – and that really matters - even Zoë admits it, when she's being sensible. As for Helen – we don't expect anything from her...'

I hugged her. '...But don't hurt yourself or your dad out of loyalty to me – not ever. Helen doesn't matter – given time - this might even seem funny...'

'Do you think so?' Eve asked, her face dejected - I thought, like me, she was treading a fine line between melancholy and irrational optimism.

Quirk instead of settling under the table had lain down in a corner of the kitchen, his chin resting on the rug. I crouched down to give him some fuss, needing the comforting touch of an animal. The island felt unsettled and I did too – edgy as on those days when the wind blew across Littern in nervous gusts – one moment calm, the next restless and disturbed.

When I let him out in the garden a few minutes later, Quirk raced round burning off excess energy, chasing up and down the lawn in huge zig-zag movements and I envied his ability to discharge his emotions so easily.

# Chapter 30

Before going to bed, I looked in on Minette, who was sleeping restlessly. When I put my hand to her head, despite the coolness of the night, she was hot and I wondered if she was still unwell and if that was contributing to her grumpy mood.

I was wakeful for most of the night. Sunrise was ushered in by a single bird breaking the silence, before the dawn chorus rose in a wave of sound.

When I checked e-mails, I'd received a message from Cameron. He told me he and Zoë had split up several weeks ago and gone their separate ways. *I had to get my head straight,* he wrote, *I left her by the Ghats of Benares...*

Images of death filled my mind. I was furious. Cameron had turned out to be irresponsible, like Zoë - he should have stayed with her. Now she was alone in India, refusing to get in touch and according to him had no intention of coming back – clearly, the fire in her - which had made her leave Hurst Row, had yet to be extinguished.

Engulfed by a sense of helplessness - I considered contacting Interpol only to realize I was being ridiculous - as an adult, Zoë could do as she pleased. I wrote an angry mail to Cameron and deleted it before I clicked *Send* and eventually replied calmly, asking him to let me have news of Zoë, if he should hear any.

Not wanting to disturb the rest of the household, I crept downstairs to put on the kettle for tea, but after a few minutes Eve joined me, wrapped in an old blanket to keep warm. Despite lack of sleep, she was bright eyed - a young woman it seemed who could only be lovely, while I felt worn out and hag-ridden.

'... Bad dreams..?' she asked.

'Thoughts whirling through my mind...'

'Perhaps life on Littern Island too exciting for you,' she said with a smile.

'There are too many "what ifs"...'

'I have a lot of those too, it's scary.'

I handed her a mug of tea and relayed Cameron's message.

'Wouldn't Zoë be moaning or asking for money if she wasn't okay..?'

That I thought depended on how *not okay* she was... 'I tried really hard to ensure you girls had stability...' I complained.

'Saints and martyrs..?' Eve replied. It was her expression for someone carried away with self-righteousness or self-pity. 'Zoë probably left Cam, not the other way round, going off in a huff was always her way of sorting her head out...'

'I wonder what my way is,' I answered.

'Why don't you go back to bed and sleep..?'

'Kos will be here soon wanting to play the piano,' I said and yawned, I couldn't seem to stop yawning.

While Eve dressed, I finished my tea, slung on yesterday's clothes and took Quirk down to the beach. I blamed myself for the argument with Helen the previous evening - though it didn't take much insight to realise I wouldn't want to be present at David's wedding or be involved in his poetry reading. Yet, a part of me would have loved to hear David read again. I could imagine him - see his expression as he glanced up to be sure he had the audience spellbound. I could feel each nuance of emotion expressed in his soft lilting accent, as he recited his work with insight and passion.

The sun floated high above the horizon, a diffused orange light gilding the cliffs and the smoky blue water. Quirk nosed through a ridge of seaweed and shells, the detritus of the beach that marked the last high tide, for him life was immediate and simple.

I'd washed up on Littern Island needing to come to terms with my future, my actions underpinned by nothing but the most fragile hopes. I'd believed I could learn how to live again, if I asked the right questions and received the right answers. But underlying each question was another question and too often the answers were only questions in disguise.

Summoning Quirk, I made my way back to Marisands. I'd promised to lend Eve the *Marshlands* book I'd bought in Mortons, and when I'd been up to the study to fetch it, called in at Thrift Cottage. Eve had set up a work bench in the box room and when I tapped on the door, Minette called down from the window for me to go up and see what they were doing.

Eve had been restoring Juliet's drawings and my mother's pen lines now stood out on the cleaned pages with new clarity. The coffee I had spilled on them had revealed the sheets to be a palimpsest and Eve had made separate drawings of the hidden outlines she had found – many relating to the legend of St. Thrif and the White Virgin. She'd read the story in *The Legends and History of Littern Island*. As she worked, she'd gathered evidence and had decided that the painting for *The Stations* in the studio was exclusively William's work – he'd over-painted a canvas of Juliet's that seemed unrelated to the panels hung in All Soul's Church.

On an old deal table, Eve had laid out her own paintings, taken from photographs and sketches of her walks round the island. She had borrowed some Armsted china from the kitchen, drawing my attention to the subtle and glorious colours, a richness which I'd ceased to notice, blinded by familiarity.

She had made a large painting of the sea intended as a housewarming gift for Marisands. Minette unveiled it, tugging aside the scrap of an old sheet with a grand gesture and a deep bow. I traced the swirls of iridescent colour with my fingers, they glistened like oil on water, but the painting was spectral, so quiet its voice was barely a whisper.

'It's beautiful, Eve...' I said.

'But..?'

'No buts...' I said, Eve was a perfectionist - chaste in her work - unforgiving when she failed to attain the standard she had set herself.

We carried the canvas to Marisands, removed Bernard's landscape of the tower from the dining room and hung Eve's work in its place. Pale light, filtered through the creepers that hung over the window, glanced off the mirror above the fireplace catching the surface of the paint so it glimmered and seemed to shift as if the water was moving.

'Look at that...' I said as the painting was transformed.

Eve blushed with pleasure, 'I thought I'd call it *An Eternity of Waves*,' she said, 'but I've no idea what to do next...'

'I was saying the same on the beach five minutes ago,' I admitted.

Minette folded her arms and her expression dared us to contradict her, 'You should both pray to the White Virgin of Thrifswell,' she said. 'If we *have* to live here on this horrible island, we might as well...'

*

Mid- morning the doorbell rang, Beatrix Piran was standing in the shadowy porch - her expression one of annoyance.

'I've lost Ursula, is she here?' she asked.

'I'll call you straightaway if I find her...'

Without preamble, she launched into a diatribe, 'It's time Patrick did something effective. I see no reason why a ten year old girl should hold every adult in the vicinity to ransom...'

Ursula's behaviour was becoming tiresome, but when I expressed my sympathy - once again, rather than placating her, it seemed to touch a sore place.

'I ferry Pa to the doctor's,' she continued, 'I do the housework and the gardening and though Mother's been dead for almost thirty years, nothing must be changed. In Pa's view, everything she did was entirely lovely and now I have Ursula and her ridiculous antics to contend with...'

I invited her in for coffee, but Beatrix had to get back to Lyncross, Edgar was demanding and couldn't be left unattended for more than a few minutes.

As soon as she'd gone, I scouted round indoors in case Ursula had slipped into the house and was hiding. I searched the studio, went back to Thrift Cottage and then checked the overgrown places in the garden, The Robin's Nest and the oratory. Ursula had seemed to feel Marisands was a refuge, but she wasn't stupid, and must have realised if her family had begun to assume she would be here, there was a need to find a less obvious hide-out.

Eve offered to look for her on the beach and in the woods and Minette said she would go with her. Meanwhile, I drove the length of Osford Lane up to The Retreat, then back to the causeway, making a tour of Osford village in case Ursula had crossed the gully while it was low tide.

Osford Chapel wasn't far from the causeway; it had been left marooned on the island side, at the top of a steep incline. As I drove past the foot of the hill, a sliver of bright blue among the trees made me stop and reverse the car to where a narrow lane led up to the chapel gate. Ursula was like a wraith. I hadn't so much spotted her, as seen a flash of colour, just as when I had caught her by the oratory. I pulled the car onto the grass verge and called to her impatiently. Ten minutes passed before she gave in and emerged from the bushes - covered in leaves and twigs - and meandered slowly down the path towards me.

'People are beginning to get cross,' I said.

'Don't make me cry,' she said, lips trembling.

'What about you making other people cry?'

'My dad only cries when big things happen, like my mum leaving.'

'Don't you think losing you would be a big thing?'

'If I never came back, I suppose it would be,' she said coolly.

I let her into the car and tried to think how I should handle the situation, I felt ill-equipped - after all - I hadn't dealt well with Zoë. I wondered what images and memories played through Ursula's mind – when I had taken her to Hintham Ridge, she had spoken of witnessing death – the death of humans -

'Is it just that you don't like school?' I asked.

Ursula shook her head. Her face had taken on a mulish expression that I recognised from Zoë - perhaps it was the mask worn by all runaways.

'I'd give anything for Zoë to come back and every time you run away, your family must feel the same.' I started the engine. When I turned to Ursula, she'd stuck her fingers in her ears and as irritated as I felt, I couldn't conceal a smile. 'Everyone's kind to you at home, aren't they?' I asked.

Ursula nodded, though her ears were plugged with her fingers, she'd obviously heard, 'They're very, very kind,' she said gravely.

At Marisands, Quirk came bounding down the hall to greet us, wagging his tail.

Eve and Minette were in the kitchen. Minette had stopped complaining about the dog, but she looked flushed and unwell and wasn't really eating. She picked at a slice of cake, took a slurp of tea and then put her head down on her folded arms, resting on the table.

I phoned Lyncross, while Ursula stood leaning against the back of a chair taking sideways glances at Minette.

'Ursula was up by Osford Chapel,' I said to Beatrix, 'she was hiding in the trees.'

'Iris knows where to find me,' Ursula said to Minette.

Minette lifted her head and sent me a puzzled look, she seemed hot and uncomfortable.

'It was purely chance, I saw you,' I told Ursula. 'You'd better tidy yourself – Beatrix told me your uncle would be here soon.'

Ursula dragged herself across the kitchen to the sink. I coaxed her to hurry washing her hands and brushing her hair. She'd barely finished when there was the sound of a car arriving on the drive.

As Eve answered the door, Ursula whispered to me, 'Can't I stay here?'

Minette was observing every detail of Ursula's behaviour and mine - as if we were engaged in some kind of conspiracy.

'Where's Ursula now?' I heard Nicholas ask from outside, he sounded as crabby as I felt and hearing him, Ursula had shot upstairs.

Then there was the sound of Kos's bike scraping against the wall as he rummaged in his trailer – I let him in and he nodded to Nicholas, before making his way to the music room. His desperation to play the piano had lately overcome his shyness – he'd obviously concluded that if he refused to play when people were in the house, he would never play at all.

*So much for my tranquil retreat* - I thought as people appeared and disappeared through different doors, like in a farce. But as the sound of

Balakirev began to fill the house, I remembered how I'd felt so alone when I'd first arrived on Littern, how empty Marisands had seemed.

While I was speaking to Nicholas, Ursula came scurrying down the stairs.

'If Ursula would like to stay with Minette, I'll look after them both,' Eve said.

Ursula stood absolutely still on the bottom step, clutching an armful of books she'd found in the study - Minette's face was expressionless.

Nicholas was taking the twins and Rowena out to lunch and had thought Ursula might like to join them, but Ursula shook her head, 'I want to stay with Eve and Minette,' she said and before I could make any comment, it all seemed to be agreed.

Quirk followed me to the study, where I switched on the electric fire and curled into the armchair wrapped in a blanket, looking out through the window at the cherry-tree tops, misty with white buds. Laurence had sent a new file of amendments – I was in the early stages of decoding them and had intended to read them through - but in the warmth of the room, I dozed off until I was woken by a soft knocking at the study door.

The door opened a crack to reveal Eve with Ursula.

'Ursula was worried she'd upset you,' Eve said.

I propped myself up in the chair, Eve had brought me a mug of coffee.

'I was tired and bad-tempered,' I said, 'I needed a nap.'

Ursula fiddled with Quirk's fur, folding it round her fingers. 'Aunt Beatrix says I make people sick with worry,' and I detected the shadow of mimicry in her voice.

'When we love people we don't want them to come to harm, a little girl who's surrounded by love can create a lot of worry.'

Ursula nodded but she was uneasy, fidgeting, perhaps not liking me to speak of love. 'I'm staying for lunch,' she said, 'Minette and I helped Eve get it ready.'

Eve and the girls had set cottage pie, fruit, cheese and biscuits on the table. Minette sat in the corner with a glass of milk, dressed in an old apron Eve had retrieved from the kitchen drawer. Ursula showed me how she had been wrapped in a torn blue sheet to keep her clothes clean. Her hair was in two long plaits with a blue velvet head band and as she busied herself, helping, she looked as innocent as an angel and I wondered if Eve had reconciled the two girls to one another.

The biscuits they'd made were in the shape of animals; Ursula showed me hers - a bear and a badger. 'Eve made a deer,' she said, 'like the ones that live in the woods behind Hagdon Hills.'

'What sort of animal did you make?' I asked Minette.

'A roaring lion,' she said and I understood that any reconciliation I'd hoped for could have been no more than a fleeting illusion.

When Ursula had gone home, Minette admitted she wasn't feeling well. I put her to bed for a rest and decided while she was sleeping, I would make an appointment for her at the doctor's surgery in Narescombe.

As I tucked her into bed, she showed me a letter Yuuka had written. The pink notepaper had been taken from Minette's writing set - it was covered with the stickers of hearts, rainbows and flowers, which I had given her when she had started boarding at school in the New Year. Yuuka had written to say how she'd liked hearing about Littern - she'd been re-reading the *Seabright Island Adventures* and wanted to come to Marisands and see the place for herself. The message was the same as on the day we had taken her to Seaholme on her birthday, it echoed her heartfelt words – *I'd like to live with you.*

'Something's going on, Min,' I said.

'Yuuka's being sent away, she doesn't want to leave.' She burst into tears and I held her close. Was this what Minette had been trying to tell me, since before half-term?

'I want you to do something...' she wept.

'Is it the nuns who say she has to go away?'

'The school says she isn't clever enough, but she is – she's leaving in the summer – but I want you to tell Sister Gabriel she mustn't go.'

I couldn't imagine anything I said would make a difference as far as Yuuka's fate was concerned, especially as Minette would be leaving in the summer too - but it was unlike her to give way to a hysterical outburst.

'Is this a result of the exams?' I asked. There had been no further complaints about Minette's cheating and perhaps it had become clear that Yuuka's schoolwork didn't stand up alone.

'I promised her you'd help,' Minette sobbed, 'so you'll have to phone the school.'

Minette's dogged loyalty was heart-wrenching, she believed herself to be strong and it blinded her to her own vulnerability.

I approached phoning St. Catherine's with the same level of enthusiasm, I'd felt phoning Helen, but after some persistence, eventually managed to contact Sister Gabriel. I couldn't think what to say, except to express my concern at the news about Yuuka's future.

There was a long silence at the other end of the line. The nuns disliked having their decisions or actions questioned, as I'd learned on more than one occasion, when I'd been teaching French conversation at the school.

Sister Gabriel explained with exaggerated patience that when Yuuka had been sent to England, the school had effectively become her guardian.

'Yuuka will be happier somewhere less demanding,' she said - she was a smooth operator. 'What is paramount is the welfare of the child, but we can't always arrange things from the child's perspective. We have a sister school in Nottingham, which we feel will suit her perfectly. Minette needs to be with you and she and Yuuka must be weaned from each other, as soon as possible. People and friendships come and go – it's important to learn that lesson early in life - wouldn't you agree?'

My own view was that it would be better to postpone coming to terms with life's transience for as long as possible, but I didn't say so.

'Have you contacted St. Mary's about Minette?'

I confessed I hadn't.

'I'll tell them to expect your call,' Sister Gabriel said - and knowing how efficiently the nuns' grape-vine operated - crossing continents and oceans without difficulty - I should have been ready for that manoeuvre.

I'd made an appointment at West Hill Surgery as Minette became gloomier and more enervated after my failure to prevent Yuuka's removal from St. Catherine's School. Eve volunteered to take her sister to see Dr. Acworth and I thought there was more than a hint of mischief in her smile as she made her offer.

It was a clear spring day with a lively sea-breeze and I'd decided to climb the tower on Hagdon Hill. I thought I might see Clave Valley from the roof, and the tower itself had become the centre around which many questions about my mother revolved.

While I laced my walking shoes, Quirk twisted round and round in the hall with excitement. One of his endearing qualities was that he would have followed those he loved anywhere - ears flapping joyously - emitting muted barks of pleasure - he would have walked through the gates of hell.

I settled him in the back of the car and drove out into Osford Lane. When I drew level with Lyncross, Beatrix was sorting the table where the produce was kept. I'd intended to stop on my way back and pick up a few vegetables, but tempting as it was to drive past with no more than a wave, I agreed with Patrick's sentiment that it would be better to live in peace while we were neighbours on the island and pulled the car over onto the grass verge.

'Did you want something?' Beatrix asked. She was filling a basket with turnips from a sack.

As I helped myself to onions, carrots and cabbage, I explained I was going for a walk – Quirk was barking furiously from the back of the car, as if he wanted me to hurry up.

'Our dogs are lodging at The Retreat,' Beatrix told me, 'I couldn't stand having them fussing about under my feet.'

While we were speaking, Patrick came down the drive carrying two buckets of potatoes - he pushed them under the table.

'Iris is going to the marshes,' Beatrix said.

Patrick smiled at me. 'If you'd like company, I could collect Pa's dogs and take them out.'

'All right,' I agreed, though my visit to the tower had been planned as something of a personal expedition.

Beatrix disappeared into the house and Patrick indicated he wouldn't be long - in a few minutes he returned and climbed into the car.

'I have a feeling I've sabotaged your plans, but Pa's passed responsibility for his dogs to Nick and he could do with a hand exercising them.'

'It's all right,' I said, 'I spend far too much time alone summoning up ghosts of a not very friendly kind.'

'How *is* the ghost laying coming along?'

'As quickly as I send one spirit back to where it came from, another appears in its place, more ghoulish than the last.'

'Like *Macbeth* or Dickens's *Christmas Carol*,' he said.

I started the car and we headed down Holtleigh Hill towards Morrow Bay, its crescent of white sand clearly outlined against the choppy, blue sea.

'I wish I could view the island in a simple way – just see it as a place shaped by wind, sun, rain and salt air - not a place where every memory jolts as if a nerve has been touched.'

'I don't think we can subtract the past from the present as if it was a mathematical problem...' he sounded amused.

'So how do we deal with the contamination of the past?'

'That's a good image - infected memories,' he said, 'but I don't know the answer to your question.'

'What's Ursula up to today?'

'She's at Tom's house. I'm trying to persuade her she'll be all right sleeping there during term time, fitting in with the others.'

'She doesn't like to leave the island.'

Patrick seemed troubled, the tips of his long fingers combing the dark waves of his hair, 'Ursula's afraid of her own shadow - she's grieving for her mother and the trouble with grief is it's like constantly bumping a sore place. I try to remind myself that my time with Honor had value because, if nothing else, we learned something from one another, but I can't expect Ursula to take such an objective view.'

We reached The Retreat and I waited while Patrick fetched Edgar's dogs. Quirk seemed to know he was in for excitement in canine terms and fidgeted about in the rear of the car, whining until Patrick appeared and released him. The four dogs shot off towards the hills, barking furiously, Quirk joining in their endless circling, weaving and ducking, playfully chasing his own tail.

'I never thought I'd become a dog-person,' I said as we set off to follow them.

'Permanently covered in mud, moulted hair and slobber?' he said. 'What did you think you would become, living here?'

'I saw myself writing quiet reflective pieces about the island, painting wildflowers in watercolour - maybe I couldn't envisage much beyond that stereotype – the lady artist and writer.'

Patrick whistled for the dogs and shooed them onto the path to the marshes. The birds and insects, the rustle of grasses blowing in the wind filled the air with peaceful sounds and in about five minutes we had reached the grassy track that led up towards the tower.

'Do you think it's safe?' I asked. The tower had been in a bad state when I was last there and had met James on the roof. 'I was going to climb up today and look for Clave Valley.'

'I wouldn't risk it. And James says the way to Clave Valley is completely blocked, there's an almost vertical wall of scrubby, impenetrable trees...'

I still wanted to see the view of the island from the tower roof, the whole of Morrow Bay from the dunes down to the beach and out to sea was visible. I'd wanted to understand the perspective of Geraldine's paintings, in which the outcrop of black rocks always featured in the background.

Leaving the path, I crossed the rough grass that surrounded the tower. Through a hole in the wall, where a window had once been, I could see birds nesting in crannies within the old stonework. The floor was scattered with packets and cans, cigarette butts and condoms – there were a couple of spent syringes lying by the wall.

'Watch out for the wreckers,' Patrick teased.

'Island lore says the tower is haunted - and so did Nicholas – I think he mentioned human sacrifice...'

Patrick laughed. 'My brother has an overactive imagination. I don't believe anywhere is haunted – it's us, we're haunted...'

I peered up inside the building trying to tell if the structure was sound. I wondered where my mother had found William, Geraldine and Shirley. Had they been sun bathing on the open roof - or hiding down in the shadowy base of the tower? And where had Kelda approached my father – what had she wanted to say?

Patrick touched my shoulder, 'I'd better call the dogs in case they wander into the nature reserve.'

I watched him clamber down the hill onto the track and stepped a little way back from the tower, unsure what to do. I stood with my arms wrapped round my waist as if encompassing the pain Juliet must have felt that day – trying to bear it without flinching - as I failed to hold back images of the ménage a trois that had excluded her – thoughts of my mother mourning the loss of her baby. I felt her guilt and remorse at the truth that her marriage was over.

The four dogs jostling round his legs, Patrick called up to me, 'I'm going to the beach - join us when you're ready.'

I looped round the tower and approached the entrance. The metal door had rusted on its hinges. Inside there was long grass growing up through the floor, where among the other litter, I could make out shards of broken glass glinting in the sunshine. I was wearing thick soled shoes and thought I could reach the foot of the staircase safely, but if I took the risk, what did I expect to find? After thirty years, there could be no clue to the actions of people who had climbed to the top of the tower perhaps meaning only to admire the panoramic views, on a summer's afternoon. There could be no hint of what might have happened there when Kelda arrived. I didn't even understand why James had been there alone, on the day of my mother's funeral -

I squeezed in through the rusty door, pushing it hard to force it open a few more inches. Stepping carefully, I picked my way to the foot of the winding staircase. As I began my ascent, a gull rose up, its wings shuddering against the air – as it flew away it dislodged a rough piece of masonry, which crashed down, grazing my forehead and landed just beyond my feet. I put my hand to my head but there was only a smear of blood. I used a tissue from my coat pocket to clean the graze with spittle - *was it some kind of warning?*

Swallows swooped overhead, as I slid down the slope onto the path leading back to the lane. From the hillside, I'd seen that Patrick hadn't gone to Morrow Bay, but to the next inlet along the coast, Coyle Sands, where he was sitting watching the sea.

I cut through the dunes and as I drew close, he spread his jacket on the sands and reached out his hand to help me down beside him. At the edge of the water, the dogs were playing a friendly game of chase and though he was only half the size of Hext, Luna or Mars, Quirk seemed to be holding his own.

'How are the demons now?' Patrick asked, 'I can see you ignored my advice, you've banged your head.'

'The ghost of the tower, disguised as seagull, tossed a stone at me...' I smiled at him. 'Forgive me, but I can't help wondering if there are things you or your family might know about Juliet's death - things I haven't been told.'

'I only know what I saw and experienced on the beach that day,' he said.

And I wondered - had the circle of silence closed again as Geraldine had predicted? 'I can't seem to find my mother as a person – was she who I thought she was - or someone quite different..?'

'When someone dies, we're caught between the world of what might have been and the world of what is – what would Juliet's life have been like if she hadn't drowned – how would things have been for Antony if he hadn't had his accident?'

'No-one knows...'

The sea was running in fast – driven by a north wind, it formed shallow, white crested waves that broke on the beach with a constant sound like a loud whisper.

'Your family must be pleased to have you back,' I said.

'I was glad to be home and it would have been wrong not to be part of the family's mourning.' He leaned forward, propping his folded arms on his knees, 'Things happened, all about the same time. Africa was no longer right for me or for Ursula. Hardship should be a personal choice, not something you impose on someone else, especially not on a child.'

He threw a stick for the dogs and we watched while they vied for ownership, chasing each other through the shallows.

He said, 'As a family, we've all suffered a sense of guilt that we couldn't save Juliet.'

'None of you could have done more,' I said. 'Perhaps we all feel as if we were to blame?'

'But you were only a small child - what took place that day with fatal consequences was caused by the dynamic between adults...'

'...My family with its illicit passions and irregularities? Yours seemed so much more satisfactory - you stuck together, protected one another.'

'I don't suppose you think that now?' Patrick said, his eyes shining with humour.

'I'm not sure what to think about anybody...'

'You've said you've struggled to find your mother. There was a time when Juliet seemed the only one who could communicate with James – they were soul-mates. Perhaps the question of who she was has to do with the quality of that relationship...'

I nodded – not sure where a consideration of Juliet's relationship to James might lead me – perhaps onto treacherous ground.

Patrick held out his hand, 'Let's walk...'

We strolled along the upper part of the beach away from The Retreat, the tower behind us as a landmark.

'Did you feel David was your soul mate?' he asked.

Gulls wheeled and cried overhead and the sea toiled in its endless motion - *would telling the truth mean committing the greatest act of disloyalty in my life?*

I chose my words carefully, 'I wanted to believe David was my soul mate. At first, I loved so much about him - I thought we had a relationship that couldn't be bettered...'

'But..?'

'...It – or I - lacked the vital ingredient which might have kept David content, never wanting anything else...'

'He was unfaithful to you?'

'Many times and in many ways...'

'When I met Honor, I hoped we'd found a love which would keep us never wanting anything else – until then - I'd given up any thought of marriage and children and my life felt empty. I wasn't interested in working purely for status or money. After I'd been abroad on a couple of projects, I discovered I had a taste for that kind of life and then I met Honor in Nairobi - we seemed happy, at first, both pursuing our own interests - until she became pregnant with Ursula.'

'Honor didn't want children?'

'Not really and I made matters worse by always insisting we remained as a family – going to Africa, leaving Africa – I wanted us to do those things together. She must have thought I was an arrogant fool who couldn't hear what she was saying about her need to keep her career intact. Honor thrived on working in the most challenging and dangerous places and I waited over ten years for her to change...'

'And then, when she didn't, the life you had hoped for was over...'

'I couldn't bear what was happening to Ursula. She'd had meningitis when she was a baby - she's never been easy - Honor couldn't cope with her strange little ways.'

I'd almost forgotten the relief of sharing experiences, especially the painful ones, with someone who is able to understand what you mean without explanation. Since my conversation with Rose, I'd barely spoken of my feelings about David.

'When David left, my belief in God, in life, changed irrevocably. I craved peace of mind, safety, security, but faced with life at Marisands – hardly their embodiment - I've sometimes felt more threatened than in London.'

'You have no clear vision for the future?'

'No vision and no conviction, that's what makes it hard to convince myself that we should settle here.'

The wind shook the coarse grass on the sand dunes. As we talked, I had sensed Patrick's light hold on life. A tall, slender column of a man he evinced strength, but a strength that was brittle and might, if God remained silent on his future, reach the point of breaking.

Where the dunes rose into small hillocks we stopped again, resting our backs against sand warmed by the sun, occasionally slipping as the sand shifted - laughing at each other like children. Patrick gathered a few tiny pink flowers and arranged them in the cleft of a stone.

He handed it to me, 'You should take that home – the hole goes right through – isn't that meant to bring good luck?'

The flowers flew away on the wind, but I slipped the stone into my pocket, 'I thought you weren't superstitious,' I said, 'you don't believe in ghosts.'

'But I know you do,' he teased, 'and to some extent, I'm my father's son, both scientist and dreamer.'

'Do you go to the oratory to pray?' I asked - thinking of the votive objects I had found on the altar there.

'Sometimes - when I came back to Littern, the oratory had been neglected for years. Sweeping out the mess of dust and sand, cleaning and clearing, taking in flowers seemed simple and good - it helped me.'

'The first time I went to the oratory Ursula was on guard...'

Patrick smiled. 'She can be very fierce...'

The dogs had run far ahead, perplexed by our lack of progress - nothing was visible of them except the waving black plume of Quirk's tail. Patrick gave a loud whistle and Hext brought the other dogs back at full gallop, to where we were standing by the dunes.

Patrick spoke then about his work – he would be at Safford Bridge Hospital for the next six months. During that time, he was hoping to find a house to rent in town and that Ursula would settle more easily at St. Safan's when they were living nearby. Once it was established if she was likely to be content, he'd decide whether to make the arrangement permanent or whether to move on.

'Did you know, before I met Honor, I was a Franciscan? Hence my late start in life - the delay in making a career, falling in love and having a family.'

'You're teasing,' I said.

'I wish I was - I was absolutely useless as a religious - it was an act of mercy when they chucked me out of the friary.'

He had captivating warmth – either speaking or listening attentively - his humour was gentle and often directed towards himself.

374

'What made you choose that way of life?' I asked, laughing.

'Antony. After his accident, I wanted to make up things to my mother - she'd lost the hope of having a son who became a religious or a priest. When I left the religious life, meeting Honor was heady. I needed to catch up on what I felt I'd missed, I was in a hurry, unfairly so, I wanted the kind of family life I'd grown up with, but Honor didn't...'

I tried to imagine what kind of person Honor could be – had she recognised the man I was beginning to know - a man who was intelligent, perceptive, kind and respectful – had she let him go easily?

'When I pulled you out of the sea, I hoped yours would be a life worth living,' he said. 'Has it been?'

'Can we answer that for ourselves?' I asked, unsure if he meant had I made a valuable contribution to life or had I been happy -

'I think it's important to know – we all need to know...' but his smile took the edge off what might have been a reproach. 'When my mother died, Pa felt he was nothing without his beloved wife. If we're going to withstand what life throws at us, we need to be sure we're something, even when we're on our own.'

'I came here to try to be something in the sense you mean, but it's proving more difficult than expected...'

'Give it time,' he counselled, 'as far as my family are concerned, they're trying to undo thirty years of prejudice against you.'

Patrick waved the dogs on along the beach, the way we had come and they raced ahead not seeming to care that we'd turned back.

When we reached the gateway of The Retreat, Patrick said, 'If you'd like to, we could go for a meal one evening, there's a place on the other side of Safford Bridge where the food's good - you're not too sophisticated for pub grub?'

'I'm not sophisticated at all...'

'Excellent...' he said, 'you know, I always enjoyed talking to you even when you were a child.'

'I'm glad you haven't changed.'

'And neither have you, not in the ways that matter. I'll have to find someone willing to take Ursula on for an evening, I'll phone or drop in to arrange a date and check you haven't changed your mind.'

I was certain I wouldn't - but I'd forgotten how tentative Patrick could be and how sensitive – how he had once been a person I had trusted completely and in a child's instinctive way had loved.

# Chapter 31

As the deadline for Laurence's book became more pressing I returned to my habit of going into the study early in the morning, before anyone else was up.

On those spring mornings, the sun rose above the horizon, glowing with a soft apricot pink. The pillowy clouds moved constantly and reshaped themselves, creating vistas of a tender blue sky beyond, streaked with wisp-like fronds of white.

Dredging through Laurence's corrections, my mind kept drifting – how might my life might have been different, if William hadn't sent me away from Littern? If I'd grown up on the island, would the seed of relationship have been planted between Patrick and me? *Had the seed been planted now..?*

I dragged my attention back to *Minor Lights,* and stuck with the text for two more hours before checking e-mails.

My heart missed a beat when Zoë's name popped up, but all she'd written was, "you won't get to me through Cam" - and my only consolation was the thought that at least I knew she was alive.

Eve was making breakfast and the scent of warm bread rolls filled the hallway. I had been working since five and it was barely nine o'clock when Geraldine arrived, knocking at the front door.

I directed her into the dining room, out of Eve's way. She seemed more dishevelled than usual. Her hat was askew and she didn't appear to have combed her hair, she'd buttoned her coat wrongly, like a small child, so the collar on one side sat awkwardly, tucked in beneath the lapel.

'Would you like breakfast?' I asked.

'I don't eat breakfast.'

I fetched two mugs of coffee and a few rolls from the kitchen for myself. Geraldine liked her coffee strong, with a tiny splash of hot milk and a spoonful of brown sugar.

I buttered one of the rolls and broke it into small pieces with my fingers. Geraldine lit a cigarette, flicking her lighter three or four times before the flame was steady. I pushed the ashtray towards her.

'I heard you went to see Shirley,' Geraldine said, blowing smoke into the air as she spoke.

'She explained your situation – I've been meaning to come to Whitcroft to say it's all right - at the moment - to use the studio for as long as you need to.'

'What else did she blab about?'

'She said Juliet destroyed most of her work before she died – she had a bonfire here at Marisands – I wondered why you didn't tell me.'

Geraldine glared at me. 'Perhaps it's because I resent your intrusion – I'd expected to live out the rest of my days without interference from you or anyone else.'

She was blunt, but it was an honest answer and I could appreciate her desire to be left in peace.

'When Juliet burned her paintings – didn't my father think it was odd, worrying?'

Geraldine's eyes fixed on Eve's painting of the sea, *An Eternity of Waves*, hung above the sideboard, but she made no comment and her face gave nothing away.

'William destroyed so much of his own work over the years he thought it was a fit of artistic pique - not unlike his own - for William, his life with Juliet was like a recurring dream in a long night, a dream that turned to a nightmare.'

'...Was it loss or guilt which made him feel that?'

'Isn't it enough that he blamed himself and that you blame him? You forget that many other people are responsible where your mother's death is concerned.'

'You imply that - but no-one will tell me who...' I said.

Geraldine finished her coffee and stood up to leave.

Tired of being tantalised, I said, 'Before I go from here, *I will* find out what happened to my mother.'

'You may wish you hadn't,' Geraldine said. 'If you continue your pursuit of rough justice, you may find it poisons everything...'

'I'm not putting anyone on trial...'

But for Geraldine, my efforts to elicit the truth were a contest of nerves, wit and endurance, and the endurance she'd needed to tolerate years with my father had given her the edge.

I handed her the studio key.

'You seem to have ruled out the possibility that William wasn't necessarily the father of all Juliet's children...' she said, catching me unawares.

Before the implications of her statement could sink in, I snapped back, 'I've ruled out listening to gossip, especially when it's perpetrated by well-known trouble makers.'

'William thought the gossip was well worth listening to...' Geraldine said coldly, 'And Kelda Sullivan had plenty to say on the subject of your mother and her many pregnancies.'

My head had begun to ache, I slipped the band off my hair and shook out my plait – no longer sure if Geraldine or I had steered our conversation into such a contentious area.

'Why can't we move beyond innuendo?' I asked, almost pleading, 'Couldn't you just tell me what you know?'

'I don't owe you anything,' she said.

'But I feel a responsibility towards you because you helped my father.'

'There's no need...And you needn't think permitting me to use the studio will make any difference,' she sniped, 'I won't be manipulated by you or by Shirley Fredericks.'

The inconclusive nature of our conversations reminded me of the battles I'd had with Barbara over possession of David, battles in which there could be no victor. I put up my hand in a gesture of truce. If Geraldine was right about anything, she'd spoken wisely suggesting that my search for the truth could poison my life – there were times when I couldn't see anything or anyone with eyes unclouded by the quest to know the facts about my mother. And maybe Geraldine had also suffered enough – she was going blind, an artist's worst fear - and all the while, I kept striking at her Achilles heel – her love for my father.

I showed her out of the house, watching as she ambled unsteadily across the garden, not sure if I was doing the right thing by having her at Marisands or landing myself in deeper trouble.

In the kitchen, Eve was sitting in the sunlight drinking coffee. Minette was cross-legged on the floor, in her pyjamas, Quirk resting his head on her knee. It was comfortable scene, completely at odds with my mood - Geraldine had left me thoroughly ruffled.

I glanced at the kitchen clock. 'You'd better get dressed, Min,' I said, 'We're going to Fernley this morning.'

'Why?' Minette asked fiercely.

'You know perfectly well why...'

Minette's face was mutinous as she grabbed a bread roll from the table and ran upstairs.

'That's going okay then,' Eve said with a smile.

'Don't...' I said, topping up my coffee, 'I was hoping you'd back me up.'

'I do back you up - both with Minette and with Geraldine – it's you – you're always  determined to swim hard against the flow of the current.'

'I feel I'm being swept away by a raging torrent,' I said irritably, 'trying to stay afloat and at the same time calm the wind and waves.'

Minette took so long getting dressed I knew she was dawdling and went to her room to help her brush her hair and find her shoes, which she'd hidden under the bed, behind her holdall.

All the way to the school she sat with her arms folded, staring straight ahead of her, refusing to answer my questions - even questions about what she might like to do after our interview with the headmistress, Miss Grieves.

St. Mary's was at the heart of the small village, Fernley, where primroses flowered by the roadside with periwinkle and violets. It was a perfect day, warm and bright, but as I pulled the car to a halt in front of the ivy clad walls of the school, my heart was heavy.

The wisteria covering the porch, the chestnut tree on the front lawn and the colourful display of children's work in the front hall of St. Mary's were familiar from childhood, almost as if I had never been away. Miss Grieves's office was at the front of the school and she'd been looking out for us – had possibly heard our progress as we approached - Minette was scuffing the toes of her shoes on the hall floor.

Miss Grieves's blue suit and plain white blouse seemed to imitate the nuns' blue habits - a tall, willowy woman, her fair hair pinned up, she had a gentle, decorous manner and I wondered how someone so refined survived the rigours that Verena assured me were an inevitable aspect of running a girls' school.

'How good to see you,' she said as we went in. 'I've heard from St. Catherine's what a lovely, helpful girl your daughter can be.'

Though I couldn't see Minette's face - she'd retreated behind me - I could visualise her scowl. In the corner of the office was a set of three armchairs arranged round a low table. I took the chair opposite Miss Grieves, but Minette refused to sit down and stood sulkily by my right arm, staring at the floor.

'I've spoken to Sister Julian and she's certain she could fit one more little girl into her class, in September,' Miss Grieves said and smiled optimistically. 'St. Catherine's tells me you've made a very close friend there, Minette. We know it can be very difficult saying goodbye, but there are some lovely girls in your class and I'm sure you'll soon make new friends.'

As she spoke, I recalled my own hollow assurances to Ursula Piran and was afraid that though well-intentioned, Miss Grieves had chosen the approach most likely to inflame Minette's loyalty to Yuuka.

'What I propose is that you meet Sister Julian and spend a few minutes with her, while I talk to your mother, is that a good idea?'

'No,' Minette growled, 'because I don't want to come here.'

Miss Grieves stood up, 'It's early days,' she said, with a knowing smile directed at me, and led Minette away to her form room.

When she returned, she continued, 'I understand from Sister Gabriel the other girl isn't particularly happy at St. Catherine's and it's undermining Minette's progress?'

This I thought was typical "nun-speak" for covering their failure with Yuuka.

I started to explain that since I'd separated from her father, Minette found security through looking after Yuuka, but my explanation was interrupted by a knock at the door of the office and the appearance of Sister Julian, plump and red-faced, with Minette beside her, tears dripping down her cheeks.

Minette slouched across the room towards me and I passed her a handkerchief to dry her face.

'I think we should try another day,' Sister Julian said.

A look passed between the nun and Miss Grieves that I couldn't interpret, or preferred not to.

'Perhaps it would help if I came to the classroom?' I offered.

Sister Julian shook her head as if I had suggested something indecent.

'Thank you, Sister,' Miss Grieves said, dismissing her.

Minette sat on my lap, her head resting on my shoulder and I felt sorry for her, she was caught in a series of events she hadn't wanted or asked for - as a child, she had less control over her life than the rest of us.

'I'll discuss things with Minette and I'm sure she'll see things differently after the summer holidays,' I said.

Miss Grieves's smile was obviously forced as she replied, 'Let's try another visit during the next half term, shall we? Perhaps Minette will be feeling better by then.'

As soon as we were off the school premises, Minette stopped sniffling.

'Was it that bad?'

'I'll do whatever you say when Yuuka's gone, I shan't care about anything then.'

'Oh, Min,' I said and took her hand.

'Why can't Yuuka come and live with us? Other girls from overseas stay with host families and they get paid loads of money. Yuuka wouldn't

mind St. Mary's, if I was there with her and I wouldn't mind it either...'
Minette's words tumbled out - but what she said was true - in recent years, St. Catherine's had encouraged overseas pupils – reinventing itself as an International School.

'Sister Gabriel was very definite about Yuuka going to Nottingham...' I said.

But Minette wasn't to be put off so easily, 'They're going to send her somewhere horrible like a prison just because she isn't clever...'

'The Sisters of the Order of St. Stephen's don't run prisons - but if you promise not to say another word about it, I'll speak to Sister Gabriel again and try to make a definite arrangement for Yuuka to stay with us over the summer.'

Minette's eyes were bright with satisfaction.

'Don't convince yourself you've won me over,' I warned, 'let alone St. Catherine's...'

We went to the Blue Mountain Cafe for a hot chocolate and while Minette was occupied, I phoned Delia and asked if we could drop in at Hintham Ridge. Despite reservations about the community, Ursula had enjoyed going to the farm, and I thought seeing the animals might distract Minette from our unsatisfactory morning.

I had expected Delia to tell me she was busy, but she said we could go whenever we liked, provided we didn't expect to be fed – the community ate their meals together. So before we left the cafe, we ordered a pizza and I was relieved to see Minette had regained her appetite.

On the way out of town, I bought Delia a bunch of spring flowers - pink and cream tulips. When we arrived at Hintham Ridge, Minette rang the bell of the community house enthusiastically, but I waited uneasily until Delia appeared, intimidated by the strange atmosphere of the place.

Minette handed Delia the bouquet, she was on her best behaviour. Upstairs in her room, Delia left us for a few minutes to fetch a vase, and then Minette helped her arrange the flowers and put them on the window sill behind her desk.

Delia said, 'We have a new young couple in the community with children about Minette's age, if you and she are happy, they'll show Minette round, they thought perhaps she could help to bottle feed a lamb...'

Minette tried to hide it but her face turned pink with anticipation, 'Please...' she said.

'As long as you're sensible and do as you're told,' a warning which until that morning I wouldn't have felt necessary for Minette.

When Delia returned, she made us coffee. 'Do you ever ask yourself - how and why did I get *here*, to this precise place at this precise time?'

'I ask every day and often throughout the night...'

'How are things on your melancholy island?'

'Much better with my daughters there...'

She smiled, 'When I saw you last, you were trying to make sense of the gaps in your past – I suppose we all have a tendency to crave consistency...'

'I'm struggling to find anyone who'll talk to me about Juliet and if they do, I struggle to find the meaning in it. After Juliet's death, so many lives were changed- but I'd like to know what started the chain of events and why was the chain broken on that particular day, in the way it was - with her drowning.'

'Your own story could have ended there and then,' Delia pointed out, 'but someone fished you out of the water and saved your life. That gives a message about the power of the sea, but isn't it also a parable of resurrection? God chose that you should live and surely for a reason.'

'I'm not sure I know the reason,' I said feeling despondent. Though by leaving the convent Delia's way of life had changed radically, she seemed untroubled by the doubts and uncertainties that undermined my own perspective on life. 'Before she died, Juliet burned her work – no-one seemed to consider the significance of that and though I don't remember her doing it - I feel I *should* have noticed, *should* have been aware. I was almost seven, isn't that the age of moral comprehension?'

'...Of an embryonic sort. But don't forget, I was her closest friend and with justification reproach myself for failing to notice the extent of her depression.'

Glancing away from her steady gaze, I felt the heat of tears, spilling onto my cheeks.

'You're exhausted Iris,' she said gently, 'and you don't even know it.'

'And I'm not sure what I'm upset about,' I said, crying and laughing at the same time, 'nearly drowning or not drowning, losing my mother, being despatched off the island - the way things were turning out..?'

But in a sense it was all those things – to which I could now add Geraldine's comments about Juliet and who might have been the father of her children. With that one question she had undermined the foundations of my past, made me question my love and respect for my mother - begin to regret the way in which I had grounded my identity in hers.

Delia put down her mug and rested her hand on my arm to comfort me, but now I'd started, I couldn't stop crying. Tears rolled down my face in a steady stream soaking my handkerchief. I wept because David and Helen were getting married - for my children, including Tristan – for my parents' loveless marriage and because of the loss and unwelcome changes the Pirans had suffered because Juliet had drowned.

'I just hope if Juliet took her own life she saw death as stepping not into darkness but into light – I can hardly bear to think of it otherwise – Flora always said in any situation – look for the light – wouldn't she have taught my mother to do the same?'

'If Juliet lost sight of the light, it was because she had many things troubling her conscience. The Catholicism of the time, which she learned from James Millford, had a profound influence on her and by the time she painted *The Stations*, she was well grounded in the symbolic language of damnation and the heavy cost of redemption, in relation to her art and to herself.'

'I keep hoping if I study the paintings closely, I'll find her.'

'I'm sure you will...' Delia said.

'But I can't make the James Millford I knew fit with a person who could inspire my mother to change her religion...'

Delia squeezed my hand, 'James was a bit of a wild card – but he admired the Pirans, they'd given him a home, their love wasn't lost on him and for the most part they were good Catholics whose beliefs must have had an influence – I understand he's quite devout, even these days.'

I took a deep breath before speaking, 'If as Geraldine Ottley says, William wasn't the father of all Juliet's children, would Juliet have known for sure who was..? Who else could possibly know, James Millford? Patrick Piran says they were soul mates.'

'Kelda told me James was the father of her illegitimate child.'

'My God,' I whispered, 'I found letters from James in an old chest at Marisands – I thought he was in love with my mother...'

'Your mother loved James that much I know to be true.'

'So many secrets...' I said.

'...And secrets can act like a slow poison, both to the person keeping them and to those they keep them from. Juliet was passionate, hot-headed and stubborn - those were the emotions which underlay everything she did. But we're responsible for ourselves - whatever went on in your parents' lives doesn't taint you.'

'Sometimes, I think, when she died, I should have written Juliet's name in the sand and let the tide wash it away - I should have just said goodbye.'

'For now, why not just wash your face? A splash with cold water can do miracles for swollen eyes.'

She showed me to the bathroom - but I didn't splash my face. I ran the tap fully and took my sodden handkerchief and rinsed out Minette's tears and my own. Things were complicated - the threads of my history so twisted and tangled I was afraid of separating them - what if in teasing them apart, I discovered something unbearably shocking?

I heard Delia calling, 'Are you all right?'

I patted my face with a towel and returned to her room. 'I haven't seen Kelda, either in Safford Bridge or Narescombe,' I said.

'She spent a few days here. We didn't think she should stay in the caravan in the bad weather, but Kelda has an innate resistance to the idea of a bath and a clean bed. The result was an argument - she attacked one of the community members and we had to ask her to leave.'

'I can't help thinking she could tell me everything I need to know.'

'I believe in the end Kelda will tell her story,' Delia said, 'She doesn't like pretence, if you speak to her honestly, as you've spoken to me, the truth will emerge and probably at the precise moment when you're ready...'

# Chapter 32

Minette returned to school in London and after my visit to Delia, I needed a break from the task Silvie had set me. I wrote to her describing everything I had found out so far about my mother and asking if she had any suggestions of what more I might do, or who I might speak to? I asked if she had seen Juliet's last diary, the one marked with a 10, or knew who might have it - the diary didn't seem to be at Marisands and when questioned, Flora knew nothing of its whereabouts.

Over two weeks passed and Silvie didn't reply to my letter. Upset, I felt she should comprehend how disheartening it was to feel she had withdrawn her support and interest. I was so angry, I was tempted to phone Castle Rise and speak to her, but before I could do so, they had called me. Silvie had been suffering from a chest complaint and wasn't strong enough to write or come to the phone – she'd instructed them to find out whether I thought I might visit her in Esterlea, if possible, sometime soon.

There had been many times when I had longed to leave the island, but that same week I'd received a note from Verena accepting my invitation to Marisands. Her father had died - she was worn out by caring for him - and now her services were no longer required in Geneva, she said she would be glad of a holiday. Unable to see when I might get away from Littern, I wrote to Silvie again and said it was unlikely I could visit Esterlea before I collected Minette from St. Catherine's School at the end of the summer term.

Patrick dropped in at Marisands one afternoon on his way home from the hospital, and apologised for having taken a while to get in touch. He'd been working long, hard days. Some of his colleagues resented the fact he worked part-time and a number of old-school autocratic types had congregated at Safford Bridge General Hospital – he felt with the express purpose of bothering him.

We decided to have dinner at The Crown and Anchor, a pub in the main street of Little Reeding, a small estuary village near Safford Bridge. James had recommended it as a good place, with excellent food and lots of atmosphere.

Before our meal, we were to have drinks with two of Patrick's closest friends, Richard Howe and Margaret Selwyn, who had worked with him in Africa. Richard and Margaret had been on holiday in

Cornwall together - Margaret was now retired and was looking for a cottage to buy at St. Just - she wanted to live near the sea. They were passing through Safford Bridge on their way back to London after another house hunting trip.

The Crown and Anchor was on a narrow road that dipped down steeply to a tiny quay on the river. The shops and houses of the village were decorated with tubs of flowers and hanging baskets that rocked gently in the breeze. The outlines of the trees and bushes were soft and ill-defined - the hazy orange light of the evening sun had tinted everything a deep red-gold.

When we arrived, Richard and Margaret were sitting at a table outside watching the sunset over the river. I'd imagined they might be a couple, but Richard, an Anglican priest, was in his early forties and Margaret, now in her sixties, had always been single - they enjoyed each other's company - and as Richard said, 'Rode out, the mistaken belief that we're mother and son.'

When drinks had been ordered, Margaret said to me, 'Those two will inevitably talk shop, but we don't have to...'

She described one of the cottages they had found in Cornwall which had seemed suitable - she was considering putting in an offer.

'The trouble is, now we're heading for home, I'm rather getting cold feet, I shan't know anyone in Cornwall...'

'You could consider Devon,' I suggested, 'then you'd know Patrick...'

'Is Devon wild enough for my inner wild spirit?' she said. When she smiled, Margaret had rosy apple cheeks - she had pale grey eyes and pure white hair, which she wore wound round her head in a neat braid.

'Have you been to Littern?' I asked.

'Not yet – but I have a feeling I might.'

I'd overheard Richard, trying to convince Patrick to do another stint abroad, 'There's always a shortage of anaesthetists,' he explained to me, 'couldn't you do something to persuade him?'

Patrick looked at me, waiting for me to respond and I felt awkward.

'Patrick's done more than enough - that part of his life is over,' Margaret said.

But I felt Richard had seen my reaction and taken note – at first, I had found him attractive – brown-haired with a clear complexion - he had an affable temperament – but now I thought he must dislike me.

'Richard should leave Patrick alone,' Margaret said quietly, 'I've never known him not to come back to the UK exhausted and ill. The refugee camps are dangerous, in a constant state of ferment and the body can stand to be overworked only so many times. If you persuade Patrick to do anything – persuade him to stay at home...'

'Patrick wouldn't be influenced by me,' I said, 'we've only just met again - after thirty years.' It was easy to talk to Margaret - I liked her kind and straightforward manner.

'After Honor, Patrick went into something of a melt-down – that shouldn't happen again – ask me if you need a few hints on how to manage him,' she added with a smile.

The two men became engrossed in discussing the minefield of hospital administration but our conversation didn't shift from the subject of Honor.

'I've known Patrick a very long time,' Margaret said, 'everyone except him could see she was a mistake. She needs to be heroic - he needs support and understanding - he's been marvellous with Ursula. When he left the Franciscans, he idealized her - she's a strong woman.' And though she was discreet, Margaret had managed to intimate that she believed Honor's separation from Patrick would in the long-term be a godsend.

The conversation passed onto more general matters, but then before long, Margaret thought she and Richard should continue their journey if they were to reach London before bedtime.

When we parted, Richard kissed my cheek and in a stage whisper said, 'Patrick can't remain on your magical island forever. He's lotus eating – he's needed in Kenya - all I'm suggesting is one final trip to Nairobi - what do you think?

I shook my head not sure how to reply.

But Patrick had overheard and said, 'A lot would depend on Ursula - it would mean being away for a couple of months...'

'You'd prefer to stay here and join the local golf club?' Richard asked.

Patrick laughed. 'So far, I've declined all offers to be recommended to the local golf club.'

'I quite like the thought of golf,' Margaret said, 'I might take it up myself...'

When she and Richard had left, we ordered food and more drinks - then moved inside to a table by the window.

Two swans glided beneath the weeping willow trees on the far bank, 'Isn't that beautiful?' Patrick asked.

I nodded. 'I wonder if I've been lotus-eating on the magical island of Littern.'

'I'm afraid Richard takes his role as ambassador for a worthy cause rather too seriously.'

'He means well?' I'd thought Richard unsettling.

'I wouldn't count on that,' Patrick said with a smile, 'but he's right about one thing – I do need to move off the island. Ursula and I spend a lot of time at Tom's, and Nina finds Ursula trying. I leave for work early in the morning and she's had to take Ursula to school – I think she agrees with Pa who's been lecturing me on the need to regain order in my life. He thinks I should be back to normal by now, forgetting he hasn't returned to normal since my mother died, over twenty-five years ago.'

I explained then about losing Tristan, something I rarely spoke about to anybody, 'I didn't realise that the distance between life and death is only the distance between breath and no breath...'

'The death of a child is very cruel...' he said and stroked my hand for moment, 'words are always inadequate...'

'The pain of being a mother without a child was indescribable...'

'...And the aftermath of loss is always intense loneliness.'

He spoke about how friendless life had felt when he first left the Franciscan community. 'It took me months to adjust - I was impossible to live with and that spilled over into my early days with Honor - I'd lost my way then, as I feel I have now.' We touched glasses and he took a sip of wine, 'As a religious, I missed easy contact with people and I missed my family - detachment didn't bring me any closer to God and it took me far too long to become human again.'

I felt the pieces of the puzzle that were Patrick were beginning to fall into place as I gained an understanding of how he had - as Delia put it - arrived in this precise place at this precise time.

'Ursula tells me you took her out to Hintham Ridge Community,' he said. 'I'd heard they want to set up a couple of health projects, that's something I'm considering - possibly combining it with working at the hospital. Delia taught Beatrix at the Priory School, when she was in training. Beatrix, I imagine, probably gave her hell.'

'I always thought Beatrix's behaviour would be exemplary.'

'Not entirely - she was a tree-climber and a giant spider on the nun's chair sort of person. Were you?'

'Grave and given to asking far too many questions, at least that's how I was described on my school reports. I couldn't tell if those qualities were virtue or a vice. Generally, I kept my head down.'

'But not anymore..?'

'When I came to the island, I meant to - but from the start Geraldine Ottley has been deeply upsetting and other people have made comments which undermine my sense of the past and then refused to justify them...'

388

I told him about Silvie and how she had helped me out when I had nowhere to live – and how the information she had asked for had been more difficult to come by than I could have imagined.

'I've been trying to remember how things were between Juliet and my family,' he said. 'I had the impression there were problems towards the end – James and Antony were both in love with her. I remember Antony crying because he felt James had stolen Juliet from him, possibly that was part of his motivation for taking up the religious life, he didn't feel he could compete with someone he saw as more glamorous and certainly, at that stage, more pushy.'

'My mother caused a lot of unhappiness,' I said. 'I'd hoped to talk to your family, but as things are...'

Patrick's hand rested lightly on my arm, 'I think it would help for you to speak to my father - but someone would need to raise the subject and to choose their time carefully...'

'Would you be willing to do that?' I asked.

'I'll give it some thought, though I expect for you, the questions will carry on round and round in your head - those pestilent ghosts and demons?'

He was right, but there was no choice but to accept what he offered – to give the matter consideration. I sipped my wine, while the waiter arranged the table and set down our food.

'Tell me what you loved about David...' Patrick asked.

'David's ghost wasn't one I intended to bring to the table.'

'Answer the question...' he said firmly.

'...David seemed exciting, he was dedicated to his work and I respected him for that. But by the time we separated, any love I felt was for a version of David who hadn't existed for a long time - possibly never existed – it's been hard on the children.'

'And on you,' Patrick said. 'When I met Honor, I overlooked her ambition, the fact she was both politically minded and fearless – she needed unshakeable nerves to work in the places and conditions she did and it took unshakeable nerves to live with her. She didn't want her life to be changed by love or by motherhood. She was willing to persist with her work, even if the end result was her death, while I felt I didn't want Ursula growing up in either over-privileged or horrifying circumstances, witnessing things which shocked and terrified her. I'd seen the effects of that on James...'

'How do you decide if death is your calling?' I asked. 'If God isn't indifferent to the feelings of those we love or who love us, surely we shouldn't be either?'

389

'Honor would argue God isn't indifferent to our personal visions and dreams and we should leave the outcome to Him...'

He described his own feelings of exile, the way he sometimes felt an outsider on the island and to some extent even within his own family. Ursula was different from the other children – less academic, less self-possessed – the soft underbelly of the Piran family, was how he termed her. I sympathised with his efforts to persuade her to fit in, I'd had my own obsessions, eager to cure Zoë's hot temper, Eve's shyness and Minette's self-sacrificing zeal.

The sun had long ago sunk down below the horizon. We talked and gazed out at the moon and stars shining over the water. Though we'd been speaking of difficult things, I felt at peace. Patrick had many different and subtle moods, but when he spoke, he spoke with absolute honesty and I wanted to respond with equal honesty when I described my own life, even my life with David.

'I wonder if the grieving will ever be over for Ursula - she's a very emotional child - whatever you do don't make her cry,' he warned.

I smiled at him. 'When I took Minette to St. Mary's School the other day, her behaviour was so reprehensible, I think the headmistress was overwhelmed and her form teacher permanently traumatised.'

Patrick laughed. 'I don't need to say anything about Ursula's behaviour – you've seen for yourself. It can't have been easy for you, bringing up the children virtually single-handed...'

'Eve helps and Minette has the kind of determination which must make saints impossible to live with - it's Zoë who worries me, always Zoë.'

'Ursula's sensitivity makes life hard for her. She reminds me of you as a child - somehow hiding - very quiet...'

But it seemed clear to me Ursula had inherited her sensitivity and her strength, from Patrick and I was grateful to her, who with her funny ways had begun the process of breaking down barriers between me and the Pirans.

'Quietness was one of the things I enjoyed in the religious life,' he said, 'and the practical aspects – tending the garden, keeping bees, bookbinding. There was something humbling about realising not everything important can be learned intellectually. Working with my hands added a new perspective – it made me want to practice not only the science of medicine, but the art, though I would probably have trouble articulating how I try to do that.'

'When we were children, we lived on the island like wild things and that experience of the physical world must have shaped our minds,' I said.

'I still find long walks on Littern the most relaxing thing...'

'...Coyle Sands?'

'Yes – I enjoyed our time there together.'

An understanding was growing between us and I dared to hope that the intuitive knowledge we'd shared as children might now branch out and grow into a deeper affection.

I had begun to enjoy every detail of the man who was Patrick – his smile, his habit of running his hands through his hair when worried – the blue shirt he wore that night, clean, ironed, not fraying at the cuffs – which brought out the colour of his eyes – eyes the colour of the night sky. Later, when we parted, I wanted to recall the shape of his strong, elegant hands, the contours of his face – to capture the timbre of his voice...

Patrick asked, 'Shall I take you home or would you like a walk?'

'A walk,' I said, 'unless you're ready to leave...'

'I'm not at all ready to leave, let's go outside and look at the stars.'

He lent me a warm jumper from the back of his car and I slipped it on over my cardigan and dress - a scattering of holes laced the sleeves.

'Still embracing Lady Poverty?' I asked.

'While I was away, the moths had a feast on my clothes. I've been clearing the house in Manchester – the sale should go through in a few weeks.'

'You didn't want to stay there?'

He shrugged, 'The connections I'd made with friends and colleagues didn't feel strong enough and I thought Ursula needed a better sense of her family. I'm giving Honor half of the value of the house, so she can set up a base for herself in the UK...'

We strolled down the village street to the quay, our shoulders jostling, touching now and then – Patrick moved in an easy loose limbed way. As we stood together, watching the moon reflected on the water, his arm rested lightly across my shoulders.

'We've led such different lives,' I said, 'I was poised between life and death - you chose that I should have a future, but the future seems to have no shape or pattern.'

'Then you can let events unfold - isn't that a privilege?'

'Does it feel like one to you?'

Patrick smiled. 'I'll tell you in a few months time...'

'... Since you asked, I've been considering the nature of my love for David - I admired his creativity, his passion - at first, even his melancholy - I wanted to be the best partner I could...'

'And I'm sure you were - I thought the same with Honor, but by the time we parted, I didn't much like the image she'd made of me -

391

narrow-minded and cowardly, always wanting, more than anything, for Ursula to be kept safe and happy...'

'She feels safe and happy on the island and with you.'

'And she feels safe at Marisands with you.' He hesitated before speaking again, as if suddenly reticent, 'Richard found you very attractive – but I suggested it was a case of hands off - did I say the right thing?'

I laughed, 'Do you need to ask..?'

And his response, reflected in the brightness of his eyes told the truth that whatever reason might say, it was already too late, Patrick and I had fallen in love.

*

Patrick called at Marisands whenever he was free. Sometimes he ate with us and then played Yvette's piano – or we walked the island together, throughout the fresh, lovely spring. We admired bluebells near St. Thrif's Well, the common land, where buttercups, dandelions and yellow daisies had turned the scrubby ground into a field of gold - and Beckhead Cliffs, from where in the clear light, we could see the small islet with its colonies of seabirds and enjoy grey seals playing offshore.

Towards the end of May, Patrick returned to Manchester to complete the business on the sale of his house. Early in the mornings, when the sand was touched with sunlight and the water reflected the soft eggshell blue of the sky, I would take Quirk down to Whitcroft Cove and think of him and the time we had spent together.

For weeks, there had been no storms on the island to wash things away and each rock and piece of driftwood in the cove had become a familiar landmark. Quirk was content running to and fro, following his nose - so before going back to the house, I would sit on the oratory steps and watch the gulls diving into the windswept surface of the sea.

One morning, I returned to the footpath to find Ursula there, hopping from foot to foot and staring at me.

'Are you alone?' I asked.

She nodded and jammed her fingers in her mouth as if to indicate she didn't intend to answer any more questions.

'Come to the house,' I said, 'you can brush the sand out of Quirk's fur, if you like.'

Back in the kitchen I gave her Quirk's towel and brush and left her to groom him. Eve still came to Marisands for her meals, she was having breakfast and sat at the table, sipping coffee and poring over her sketchbook, while Ursula knelt and rubbed Quirk vigorously with the towel, creating small sand dunes on the tiled floor.

Most days, I spent grappling with *Minor Lights* and Laurence's attempts to unravel the intricacies of yet another group of artists' lives. His ability to winkle out unsavoury facts was legendary and I wished I could use his talents or those of his detective, Peter Kenholme, to investigate my parents' history. For weeks, I'd continued to leave the search alone – feeling that unless Kelda or Edgar Piran would agree to talk about Juliet, I'd probably reached a dead end. I could hardly approach James Millford with a list of accusations made on the basis of hearsay, and I saw less of Geraldine, who now came to the studio only infrequently.

Needing to get back to work, I phoned The Retreat to let Nicholas know I'd found Ursula, but as usual, he asked if we could look after her until he had time to collect her from Marisands. Eve offered to occupy her in the studio - Ursula had decided she would like to write her own story about "Seabright Island".

At the study desk, I sharpened a selection of coloured pencils for Ursula as she stood at my elbow, and then found her a notebook she could use.

'Why *does* Minette like her school in London so much?' she asked.

'Because she has a close friend there who feels lonely without her.'

'But I'm lonely without her,' Ursula said, 'Rowena always wants to go riding and I don't want to - I liked it when Minette was here.'

'She'll be back before long - and your dad will be home soon,' I said, not wanting her to make a fuss.

Ursula looked tearful; in my anxiety to get down to work, I'd perhaps been dismissive of her feelings. 'Would you like a hug?' I asked, remembering Patrick's warning not to make her cry.

Ursula slipped into my arms and kissed my cheek, a tiny, insubstantial kiss. I rocked her gently, her frame bony and angular, awkward, 'When your dad comes back, he'll be staying, won't he?'

Ursula nodded, but as she wriggled out of my grasp, I had a feeling that nothing I said would console her.

Later in the morning, Nicholas phoned and asked if – after all - I would drive Ursula to The Retreat. Edgar was unwell – he'd taken him home for a couple of hours to give Beatrix a break, 'He's tired and querulous, like a horrible child,' he told me.

I agreed to take Ursula after lunch, but before abandoning Laurence's book, checked e-mails to find that, as usual, there was nothing from Zoë - her prolonged silence was beginning to cast a shadow over each day that passed without hearing from her.

I carried a tray of sandwiches out to Eve and Ursula, they stood in the brilliant light of the studio at the easel, drawing little cartoon figures to illustrate Ursula's stories. Set out on the racks was a new series of Eve's ocean paintings with their vibrant silver, blues and greens and also paintings of the marshes in which she had highlighted details with gold leaf to enhance the colours of the grasses and reeds.

'I'm going to try copper and bronze, a more burnished look,' she said when I complimented her.

'Do you miss having your friends to spark off?' She rarely mentioned her time in Zethar Creek.

'I love it here on the island - I don't want to be anywhere else.'

'Nor me... 'Ursula agreed.


At The Retreat, the dogs ran out to see who was at the gate but when they discovered it was Ursula didn't bark or bound up to us. Benedict was in the den working on his computer, but when he saw me, went to fetch his father.

On the wall of the den was a black and white photograph of a woman, her hand held up to her face, her fingers coiling a lock of her thick dark hair against her cheek - a portrait of Nicholas's wife, Sarah, a strikingly beautiful woman, with fine drawn skin and lustrous eyes.

Ursula lurked by the door and when Nicholas came, he greeted her with the mixture of impatience and affection I'd noticed in him before.

'How is Edgar?' I asked.

'Rather confused, but it makes a change, from spiky and difficult to live with...'

'I've wanted to thank you for giving back the cheque for the road repairs,' I said.

'Don't thank me - it was Patrick. He thought I was being unfair, but then he tends to err on the side of compassion.'

'It's a good fault to have,' I said.

'Patrick's a good man.'

'He always had the makings of a good man...'

'Then be sure you don't hurt him.'

Nicholas hadn't spoken in an unfriendly way, but his manner was disconcerting and I wondered – *had he always been so protective of his brother?*

Mars, Hext and Luna began to weave round my legs and in the small room, it felt menacing. 'Would you call off your dogs?' I asked - I didn't want to have to push through them when I left.

Nicholas clicked his fingers and the dogs went obediently and lay by his feet.

I tried to think how to reach out to him, a complex and difficult man.

'That's a stunning portrait of your wife, is it one of yours? She's beautiful,' I said.

'My wife's left me, but I expect you knew that...'

A flood of heat rushed to my face and I stumbled over my words. 'I didn't know - Patrick's discreet – it was a genuine mistake.' All Patrick had said was that a marriage between two creative people was inevitably volatile.

For once, Nicholas seemed to believe me, 'I'm afraid I've become insular and suspicious, perhaps it's a symptom of island living, though your house seems to have turned into something of a sanctuary...'

'More of a soup kitchen - but living on the island, it's easy to feel both people and the forces of nature are against you...'

'Aren't they?' he asked, 'aren't they against us?'

'Surely not all the time,' I suggested, 'Patrick would like us to live in peace...'

'Patrick has the imagination of a saint,' he said with a rare smile – 'the rest of us make do with reality.'

When I left, I drove straight from The Retreat to the log man's yard in Narescombe. When he'd delivered the last load, he'd done his usual trick of dumping wood all over the drive and sticking his bill in a grubby plastic bag weighed down with a stone, on top of the mound he'd created. I had no other business in town, so when I'd paid and arranged for the next delivery, I returned to the centre through the web of narrow, picturesque streets, which led down to the seafront.

I parked near All Souls and walked along the quay as far as The North Star, thinking I might go in for tea. The sea was vivid turquoise in the afternoon sunlight - the waves idle - as if they could scarcely be bothered to lap at the shore.

On the way to the pub, I passed the block of public conveniences, where I'd previously encountered Kelda. The block had a long wooden bench running along one wall, under the protection of a canopy. At one end lay what appeared to be a pile of rags until I drew closer and smelt the stale odour, saw the black hat, the music case and the overloaded back pack -

A grimy face appeared from the heap of clothes, 'Can't a person get some fucking sleep around here?' Kelda hauled herself into a sitting position, blinking away the light, and grumbling under her breath. 'Shall we have a drink together or a meal?' she mimicked, 'Which establishment shall we patronise this time?' she added, her glinting eyes exposing her sharp sense of humour.

What was certain was that we couldn't go inside anywhere. Kelda was in the worst state I'd seen her in, but there was a Fish and Chip shop by the harbour entrance and we could sit on the wall nearby, so I suggested we go there. She sank down onto the wall with all her gear and I hoped she'd stay put while I ordered food. It was almost time for the cafe to close, but the assistants were friendly and made up a box of assorted left overs – Kelda was likely to be hungry enough not to be bothered about eating sausage and beef-burger as an accompaniment to her fried fish.

'I heard you'd been to Hintham Ridge?' I said, careful in case I was in danger of using what Zoë used to call my interrogator's voice – a voice that was *too enquiring.*

Kelda was immediately on her guard, 'Bloody Delia,' she said, posting chips into her mouth.

'People look up to Delia – I think she's a kind of mother figure for the community...'

Kelda spat on the ground...

'It's somewhere to go if you need help...'

'...For someone who can't afford to be choosy?' she said and choked slightly as she laughed.

Kelda reacted to everything I said like a cat that had fallen in water and couldn't get out.

'Hintham Ridge was all right until that bloody community took over...' she mumbled, I'd heard her say the same before.

'I was worried - you haven't been around for a while.'

'Nobody fucking worries about me,' she said as if she was making a threat, 'What business is it of yours?'

I couldn't think of anything to say that wouldn't attract her ridicule - perhaps deservedly - but Kelda was in a state, cut loose from society, she had no anchor, no family or backdrop, nothing to protect her, apart from the aggression she used to protect herself -

'You'd have to live my life to know where I'm coming from...' she said – and I sensed anger wasn't far away.

'I can't do that - but I'd still like to know what happened to you...'

'Why should I fucking care what you want to know..?'

'...Because your friends and your family seem to have abandoned you...'

Kelda didn't reply – she'd finished her meal and drunk her tea. Cautiously, I put out a hand to prevent her leaving.

'You were friends with James Millford...'

Kelda spat on the ground again, this time more venomously. 'James Millford is a fucking hypocrite, he couldn't tell God from his own arse,' she said, 'flood-clear, bastard.'

'Why do you say that?'

Kelda gathered her bags together, muttering to herself about James.

'What would have happened if my mother had lived?' I asked.

'James fucking Millford would have done nothing for her – just like he did nothing for me...'

She wandered away rocking dangerously on her feet.

'I meant it when I said you can come to the island if you need help.'

'...Seems to me you're the one who needs help. If you want to know what happened to your mother, talk to old man Piran before he drops dead or loses his mind. Some people will do anything to protect the family honour and James Millford being an adopted member...'

Kelda shuffled off towards the town square and it crossed my mind that despite his age, Edgar Piran might well outlive her. I followed for a while in case she fell, but she wouldn't look at me and found a place in a doorway near the Blue Mountain Cafe, where she slumped down on her blanket.

She didn't unpack her flute, but set out her hat and began to sing in a haunting, throaty voice, a song with a strange wandering melody – redolent of the music Kos sometimes played on the piano.

Trying to provoke a reaction, I said, 'If I see him, what should I ask Edgar Piran?'

Kelda's glittering eyes fixed on a point just above my head. The painful notes of her song rang out. I repeated my question, but her eyelids were half-closed - a stream of hypnotic sound flowed round me, out through the cloudless afternoon.

I opened my purse and dropped a five pound note into her hat. She nodded – or I thought she did – but if her words or music bore any kind of a message, as with Juliet's paintings, it wasn't decipherable by me.

# Chapter 33

The day of Verena's arrival was stormy - the wind rattled the trees, making their pale leaves quiver ceaselessly against the threatening sky. The tourist season was in full flood and Safford Bridge station was crowded with visitors milling about, not knowing where they were going. I waited by the barrier as a swarm of passengers alighted from the London train.

At last, I spotted Verena as she emerged onto the platform from the overcrowded train, smart in cream slacks and a brown jacket and carrying an enormous leather holdall. She had been through an ordeal in Geneva and her face was drawn, her eyes dull and tired; she had taken her father's death hard.

We each grabbed one handle of her heavy bag – the town was so busy I'd had to park off Pierce Street, in a cul-de-sac – it would be a long, uphill walk from the station.

'I haven't eaten for hours,' Verena complained, 'the train food looked grim.'

The Pilgrims' Inn offered Devon cream teas, so we pushed through crowds, walking across the square in the blustery wind. Kelda was playing her flute, standing by the railings of an Insurance Agents' office. Her black hat was weighed down with a stone and her black tee-shirt and waistcoat flapped in the wind as it swirled clouds of dust around her feet.

I dropped a few coins into the hat but Kelda didn't respond. With her arms bare, I could see she had a butterfly tattoo above her right wrist and however incongruous, I thought of the story of Psyche – the story of a soul's journey. She wouldn't look at me, pausing only to take a swig from a bottle before returning to her skilful rendering of the passage of Bach she seemed often to play. We continued towards Pilgrim's, but I could feel Kelda's eyes fixed on my back and turned just in time to catch a nod of recognition, unseen by Verena.

The front of the Inn was bright with rows of hanging baskets, full of fuchsias, lobelia and Busy Lizzies, swinging like pendulums back and forth in the wind. The hotel had a courtyard garden for use in summer, but the weather was too rough to sit outside and as the place I liked in the restaurant, overlooking the square, was free we said we would wait while the detritus of someone else's meal was removed and a clean white cloth spread on the table.

'An oasis of civilisation in the wilderness,' Verena remarked as she took her seat, 'just what I need, I feel so very weary.'

I'd noticed her honey coloured hair showed roots of grey at the parting and temples and the fine lines on her face, usually well-hidden, were clearly evident. She seemed restless too, her eyes darting anxiously about the dining room as if taking in all the details – I hoped she approved.

At last she said, 'You're looking well, I hope being at Marisands will do wonders for me. Are you managing?'

'You'll see,' I said, 'Tell me about Geneva - I was sorry to hear about your father.'

Verena frowned. 'I miss him – though his demands for rigid order were stifling, not to mention the prohibition against expressing any emotions, especially the indecorous ones, such as enthusiasm.'

She had made similar comments before - her father's orderly way of living, as he aged, had progressed from well-regulated to fossilised.

'When I didn't hear for a while, I was concerned,' I said.

Verena sighed, 'I couldn't write, even to you, there was too much to do – too many arrangements to make. I found my father considerably more demanding dead than he'd been as an invalid.'

The waitress appeared bringing platters of scones, plates of cakes and a large pot of tea.

'Excuse me if I tuck in...' Verena said, piling jam and cream onto a scone. 'In the end, the problem wasn't only with my father making demands...'

'Don't tell me there was a man in the case..?' I said, laughing.

Verena ignored my question.

'Was there someone?' I persisted.

She smiled uncertainly and paused while the waitress brought a jug of hot water. As she poured the tea, Verena said in a low voice, 'He was the son of a friend of the family. He helped me when Father was really ill.'

I could sense a "but..." coming. 'He was married..?' I asked.

'Divorced, an engineer, rather serious... I think he viewed me as a project, he seemed very fond of projects.'

'He sounds an insensitive dolt,' I said teasing her.

She looked wistful. 'You know when you're young - you meet someone and on the first night you pour out your entire life story and he pours out his? Well, it was nothing like that - I suspect he had no interest in me – and the truth is he wasn't very interesting...'

'But he's hurt you?'

'To be hurt you have to be in love and I've come to the conclusion that I don't believe in love, let alone practice it.'

Something had altered in Verena and her words saddened me. I watched through the window as a crocodile of children from St. Safan's, smart in their blue and maroon uniforms, was led down towards the quay, I wondered if Ursula was among them.

Verena followed my gaze, 'I don't want the responsibility of a school headship again, if I go back to work at all, I'd rather work with the pupils than manage the staff.'

'Less impersonal..?' I asked.

'Less lonely,'

As she spoke, I felt that perhaps, for Verena, the successful career woman and the person with a woman's natural longings had never been reconciled. Those two aspects of her nature lived together uneasily – and at the moment they had declared war and were fighting it out, robbing her of peace of mind and judging from the shadows under her eyes, also of sleep.

After tea, we spent an hour looking round Safford Bridge. Verena was impressed by the shops as Helen had been and in *Stuff & Nonsense,* bought a cotton jacket in burnt orange and a matching print skirt in orange with chocolate brown roses on it. I browsed the rails of clothing and as she tried on her outfit pulled out a blue jersey dress with silver stitching round the neckline, I'd noticed it when I'd taken Helen there.

'That would be stunning on you,' Verena said, emerging from the changing room, 'it would go with the earrings I gave you for Christmas that you've probably never worn.'

'It would blow my entire budget for a fortnight,' I whispered, showing her the price tag.

'Try it – let me see when you've put it on...' she said, 'I'll make sure we don't starve...'

And so coaxed by Verena and the compliments of the shop assistant, I bought an expensive dress I would probably never wear while living on Littern and spent the journey back to the island wondering if I could sell it online to re-coup my losses or dream up a plausible pretext which would allow me to return it unworn to the shop.

The weather was worsening and the town grew sombre under mounting black clouds. I thought Verena might be ready to go back to Marisands, but she was eager to see the Priory. So heads down, huddled together as we carried her bag, we scurried across the road, the wind whipping at our hair and clothes and snatching at the branches of the trees, tearing off leaves and swirling them along the ground.

400

I hadn't visited Juliet's grave for weeks and now it was surrounded by pink and white Campion, red valerian and periwinkle growing wild among the grass. I picked a posy from the earthy bank by the graveyard wall and laid it close to the headstone.

'I hated leaving Tristan's grave behind in Leitchly.' I told her.

'All my father will have is a plaque set into a wall – I wonder if I'll ever see it.'

'You don't want to go back?'

'Apart from the boring engineer, I know no-one there...'

In the stormy weather, the interior of the Priory was gloomy and foreboding.

We wandered round for a while, Verena taking an interest in the history of the place as related by an over-keen guide.

Earlier, I'd noticed a poster in The Bridge House Bookshop advertising "the very last week" of their closing down sale. There was just time to call in before we needed to leave for Littern to catch the tide. When we entered the bookshop, I glanced cautiously at the woman assistant behind the counter. Thankfully, she didn't seem to remember me, so I browsed the art book shelves while Verena chose two novels and a guide to north Devon - she wanted to be well informed about the area in which she was staying.

As we left Safford Bridge by the Narescombe Road, she said, 'I can't understand why you were so against coming here, I've rarely seen such an attractive place.'

'You do know why - and it was nothing to do with the landscape.'

'I suppose so,' Verena agreed, but she was staring out of the window and wasn't really listening.

The wind chased threatening clouds across a dull sky and it began to rain heavily. The trees tossed their heads - the long grass rippled across the fields, like waves on a choppy sea. As Verena didn't want to talk, I switched on the radio for the latest weather forecast – the storm had reached Bude and was heading our way. At the causeway, the sea beat up against the edge of the road, water slapping loudly against the broken concrete.

'What does gale force mean in practice?' Verena asked.

'It means no-one can leave the island until the storm's blown over - the electricity supply and phone lines will probably go down - we'll have to huddle indoors and wait until it dies out.'

'How dramatic... Coming here is like passing through a series of portals – like dying and being reborn into another world.'

We crossed the causeway at a funeral pace, the car moving in the shallow water with a hissing sound. I didn't like driving through the woods when it was blustery and was relieved when the oak tree by Marisands' gate came into view and we could turn into the drive.

All around us, the trees shook and shivered with a wailing sound, the summer flowers Kos had grown were flattened and broken by snapping gusts of wind.

'Your poor garden,' Verena said, climbing out of the car. 'You must love all this surely? I shall get the truth out of you, Iris, before I go home.'

'You sound like Sister Miriam.'

'And I can be as thorough in cross-examination. You could let Marisands out as a holiday home, people would love it wouldn't they?'

'No and maybe,' I said smiling at her.

I showed Verena to the double bedroom which my parents had used. I'd left Eve to make the finishing touches while we were out and she'd had found a lace bedspread and had tied back the curtains so Verena could enjoy views over the tree-tops from the comfort of her bed. There was a vase of white and blue campanula by the mirror on her dresser.

Before the storm really took hold, Verena wanted to explore outside, so I led the way to the beach across the garden, taking Quirk, who loathing storms, had been making his presence felt by low moaning, interspersed with a high pitched squeaking designed to shatter our nerves.

We stopped in the oratory garden by my mother's statues and then looked down at the oratory perched on its ledge, hanging onto each other's arms to keep our balance in the strong wind. The last remnants of cherry blossom had been torn off and had fallen onto the lawn in drifts like snow. Verena described my mother's white statues as "extraordinary" and the oratory as "picturesque", Thrift Cottage, she thought was perfect for Eve.

Once through the gate, I released Quirk and he skittered off down the path to the shore like an over-excited child.

Verena grasped my arm, 'What have you got to tell me?'

'Where should I begin?' I asked and tried to describe the confusing mixture of good and bad incidents which had characterised my time at Marisands.

Conversation was difficult as the wind funnelled its way up the footpath and tore at our hair and clothes. Verena pulled up the hood of the waterproof jacket I'd lent her but had to hang onto it tightly with both hands.

'If Eve left the island would that influence your decision to stay?' she asked.

'Who knows? There are so many loose threads – and I'm more concerned she'll be disappointed should I decide not to stay.'

Down on the beach, black clouds mounted in threatening ranks on the horizon; the wind made a shrill whistling sound as it came inland and battered the cliffs. The dark sea crashed and fractured into fine spray against the rocks as the tide rolled in, pounding the foot of the oratory steps.

I turned up my collar and Verena wrapped a silk scarf around her neck – already the wind had brought a faint pink glow to her pale cheeks. We clambered across the rocks below the cliff face, never going far from the path, while Quirk dashed along the narrowing strip of sand following an invisible trail of his own.

Verena spoke, shouting against the sea and the wind, 'my father didn't need me in the way I thought he would – he was much better off in the nursing home – it was rather depressing.'

'You did what was right,' I said, our heads almost touching as I struggled to make myself heard. I slipped my arm through hers and led her back to the path, cupping my hands to yell at Quirk that he must come at once.

In the shelter of the garden, we stopped to catch our breath and it was easier to continue our conversation.

Verena said, 'I hadn't been long in Geneva before I realised my Father could have paid for the help he needed and as I'm no good as a nurse, my fussing got on his nerves.'

'But at least, you were there, he didn't die alone, without any family.'

'True - but I'm relieved to be back in London, though I can't seem to step into my old life - I'm not sure I want to return to teaching. And what London has to offer no longer interests me - culturally, things proliferate, but the new isn't always as innovative as it believes itself to be and at our age there are few surprises - don't you begin to feel you've seen it all before?'

I squeezed her arm, 'Since I've been on Littern, I seem to be constantly surprised.'

'Good surprises or bad?' she asked but didn't wait for an answer. 'I think I need a nest, a comfortable nest. Without Father, I have no kith and kin and nowhere to call home - except for a flat which has never really been mine.'

Rain began to fall steadily and the woodland surrounding the house appeared to be hidden behind a curtain of damp grey gauze.

Before we went indoors, Verena said, 'Do you remember our childhood promise, always to stick together?'

'Of course...' We had vowed to be friends and support each other into our old age.

'...And it appals you now?'

'You're my closest friend,' I told her.

'But...?'

'You're in mourning and I'm confused...'

She was despondent and I hadn't expressed myself well, but my new life on Littern was so fragile, I was afraid even Verena's welcome presence might tip the balance in some unexpected way – she represented life in London, a life I didn't want to intrude on the island.

'Let's go in,' I said. 'My first night at Marisands was so rough, the house felt like a ship tossed on a stormy sea...'

'...Iris's ark?' Verena asked with a touch of asperity and I knew then my reluctance to meld my future with hers had upset her.

The west wind blew itself out overnight, but the next day rain fell in torrents. The electricity came and went - lights in the house flickered, failed and then sprung on again.

I was anxious to keep Verena occupied, but after breakfast she said she'd be happy to sit and read. I suggested she might like to look at the *Marshlands* book, *The Legends and History of Littern Island* and also take the opportunity to study the guide to the area she had bought in Safford Bridge to see if there was anywhere she would like to visit. I left her in the music room with an oil lamp beside her on the table, in case the power went off completely. Eve promised to make sure she was all right, while I went outside to check if any of the buildings had been damaged.

There were slates lying broken in front of the house, but as far as I could tell they had come from the outbuildings and not from the main roof. A pool of water had gathered in my mother's workshop, in the dip in the floor where she used to stand. I swept the water out onto the drive with a broom then fetched a bucket and left it there to catch any drips from the leaky roof, covering her tools and leather gloves on the workbench with the tarpaulin I'd found on my first evening on the island.

I'd deliberately left looking at the garden until last – I'd already seen how the beds that edged the path to the orchard were a mess of ravaged flowers, broken stems and sodden leaves. In the orchard, two of the new apple trees Kos had planted had their tops snapped off and on the grass among the fallen leaves lay tiny green globes of set fruit, which would never mature. The pergola had been broken and hung to its posts by a few nails twisting this way and that like a snake crossing the lawn. Until

Kos could repair it, I posted spiny branches of the rambling rose through the diamond shaped spaces of the trelliswork, in the hope they would hold it together.

'Iris..?'

I turned at the sound of Kos's voice. He stood by one of the wrecked fruit trees, trying to raise it upright; the top of its slim trunk hung like a broken limb. The hood of his parka jacket was up against the driving rain, but water ran in rivulets down his face and dripped onto the ground.

'You are all right...' he asked.

'Except for this,' I said, indicating the garden with my hand. 'You were safe?'

Kos nodded, but I could imagine the terror of spending a night in the woods with the trees creaking and cracking all around you.

'I'm sorry - all your hard work,' I said.

Trays of plants Kos was growing from seed had blown over and scattered and spilt on the ground. In the oratory garden, two of my mother's statues had large chunks split off and another stood headless, the wounded neck raw and exposed to the wind and rain.

Kos followed me as I unlocked the gate to the oratory, but there was no protection and the wind buffeted my body, pushing me sideways. Kos sprang forward and grasped my arm, 'Not near the steps,' he shouted.

A stream was running down the cliff carrying rocks and earth, stones bounced off the cliff-face before tumbling into the sea. I steadied myself against the gatepost, leaning forward as far as I dared to look down at the oratory. The building seemed undamaged, but below the plateau on which the oratory stood, part of the cliff had fallen onto the rocks below and smashed into a mound of pieces rapidly being swept away by the waves.

Kos hung back nervously. I would check the safety of the lower steps next time I was in the cove, without the stability of the cliff, they were dangerously exposed and the damage was beyond anything Kos could be expected to mend.

Without speaking, we walked to the studio and found all the large panes of glass intact. At Thrift Cottage, the roof and gutters reinforced by Kos's repairs seemed to have stood up to the gale.

While we stared at the devastated garden, Kos's hood blew back and his hair streamed away from his face - a ghostly white – his lips pale and thin.

'I don't think there is anymore I can do here...' he said.

I reached out to touch his arm, '...Come back another day and we'll talk about how to put things right...'

'Sometimes there is no right,' Kos said, 'so perhaps I will go away.'

'Please don't say that,' I pleaded - he was so much part of our lives. Eve would miss him and I couldn't contemplate managing the garden on my own. 'We'll help...' I promised. But he'd pulled up the hood of his parka against the rain and I couldn't read his expression.

The lane was a mess of stones and broken branches, so Kos hadn't come to Marisands on his bicycle. I opened the gate for him and we walked a little way up Holtleigh Hill – 'If I don't see you, I'll call at the van in a few days,' I said and explained that Verena was visiting.

'Always there is someone here, I will see what happens,' and with the Slavic drone of his voice, he had managed to make the simple phrase sound sinister. 'Perhaps I have something important to do...'

'More important than Eve..?'

'*For* Eve...' he said and sounded sulky.

'Whoever comes to the house, no-one minds you playing the piano,' I said, in an effort to soothe his feelings.

Kos merely shrugged. And I watched until he had disappeared over the brow of the hill towards Lyncross - I had expected him to be frustrated, disappointed by the damage to the garden but not inconsolable.

I splashed my way down the lane as floods of water ran in rivulets from the woods and banks onto the road. Before I'd reached Marisands' gate, I heard a car coming from behind and stood aside with my back pressed tightly against the wall.

Patrick pulled to a halt and opened the passenger door; 'Jump in,' he said, 'I saw Kos – I was just coming to make sure you'd survived the storm, but he seems to have got here before me.'

I climbed into the passenger seat, glad to be in the warm car. Patrick leaned across and kissed my cheek.

'Kos seemed so upset, I wasn't sure if it was just the garden - or something else,' I said.

'Beatrix thinks where Kos is concerned you're too kind for your own good.'

'That's because she doesn't know him,' I said in his defence. 'How are things at Lyncross?'

'The garden's a wreck, but it's much worse at The Retreat – Nick thinks several trees near the house will have to be cut down. They're saying there are floods in Narescombe and parts of Osford are impassable.'

When we got out of the car, he pointed to the flower bed beneath the shelter of the kitchen window sill, which Kos had dug out the first day he appeared on my doorstep. 'Look – clumps of lilies, quite unharmed...' The green spears of the lilies had pushed through the soil and showed heavy buds - faintly pink - their stems bent with the wind, without breaking. 'Regeneration,' he said, 'isn't that the whole point of making a garden?'

'I wish I'd thought of saying that to Kos,' I told him.

Verena was in the kitchen, chatting to Eve. 'I really enjoyed Safford Bridge...' she was saying.

'Verena's wondering if she's tired of London,' Eve said.

I introduced Verena to Patrick and wondered how it would go - this meeting between two of my closest friends.

'I was just speculating about the future,' Verena replied, looking at me.

She had the *Marshlands* book open in front of her - she must have brought it through from the music room. 'Iris always has lovely books - she used to work in a bookshop, that's where she met her partner.'

'She told me - but we had an interesting encounter in a bookshop too,' Patrick said and I caught his look of amusement. 'What makes you disillusioned with London?'

Verena explained how she had left London to nurse her father. While they were talking, I fetched a bottle of white wine from the larder and glasses from the dining room.

'I hope you'll have the opportunity to explore the island,' Patrick said, 'the weather might improve in a day or two.' He opened the *Marshlands* book and flicked through the pages, studying the photographs and delicate watercolours. 'The marshes here are well worth exploring,' he told her, 'if you enjoy walking.'

Verena described her childhood holidays in the mountains outside Geneva, when her days had been spent hiking in the hills and by the lakes. 'Do you live on Littern Island?' she asked.

Patrick explained he was staying on the island with his father and sister. 'My brother lives here – he's passionate about Littern – he was an engineer, but became a naturalist and photographer by profession, there's some of his work in this book. Having a house next to a nature reserve was for him the realisation of a dream, though perhaps it doesn't seem so after last night's storm.'

'Being an engineer and a photographer seems an unlikely combination,' Verena remarked, she was still sore about her encounter with the boring engineer in Geneva, 'and either way, your brother's choice of occupation is very different from yours...'

Patrick met her gaze, humour lighting his eyes, 'Not so very different perhaps, Nicholas prefers tinkering with machines, I prefer something living – the human body.'

Eve announced lunch was ready and Patrick agreed to stay. Eve had been unnaturally quiet and Verena in an unreadable state of mind, the storm seem to have affected everyone's mood.

'What about your dreams, Verena..?' Patrick asked.

'When I was young, I wanted either to have a large family, or to be a nun.'

'A woman of extremes...' Patrick smiled at her.

'Perhaps that's my trouble, anything less than either of those extremes has seemed unsatisfactory. I am tired of London with its the filthy air, the fact that on a beautiful day there are so few places to go, the sense you have to keep up with events just to have social currency...' she was sounding rather crabby.

'Perhaps living in a city makes you tense – combatative - even if you don't want to be...' Patrick suggested.

Verena seemed to realise she had met her match and as Eve handed out steaming plates of risotto, the conversation began to flow more easily. Verena interrogated Patrick about his work in Kenya, and he deflected her questions explaining that dealing with the suffering of the poor and dispossessed was innately practical rather than heroic and our talk drifted onto the problems of the island.

When we'd finished coffee, Patrick had to leave.

He said, 'my daughter's with her cousins - they've probably had enough of each other by now...'

I excused myself to see him out and closed the kitchen door behind me.

'Thanks for staying,' I whispered.

'Anything to help – but Verena's not that bad - if you like headmistresses...' he stroked my damp hair back from my face. 'May I?' he asked and we parted with a long, slow delicious kiss.

*

There was a little improvement in the weather the next day so I suggested to Verena we visit Narescombe. I'd thought we could go to the Arts Centre and Petra Galleries and perhaps have tea at The North Star, but Verena was eager to return to Safford Bridge and spend the afternoon there.

That morning, a package arrived from Lesley containing an advance copy of *Blue Rhythms*, and a letter requesting that I reconsider my decision not to take part in David's reading. I flicked rapidly through the pages of poems and the brief sections of biography - seeing David's work affected me badly - but Verena had no such qualms and while I worked for a couple of hours, she said she would study the book and give her opinion later.

Verena could be ruthless and when I asked what she'd made of the poetry she said, 'It reads like an extended suicide note and I don't believe I'm the only one who would think so - but however melancholy – it's driven by anger.'

'Maybe David shouldn't have allowed Lesley to take over...' I said remembering some tasteless remark she had once made about suicide being good for publicity, 'unless we're viewing the poems out of context...'

'I defy you to read them without feeling depressed, whatever the context. Surely David knows if you want the truth, you have to tell the story yourself..? Or put it in the hands of someone who's worthy of trust, which probably isn't Lesley - or maybe anyone who's your ex-wife or partner.'

'I should say no to the reading then?'

'Definitely... I see you returning to your children's books, not agonising over Laurence's sleuth or *Minor Lights* and certainly not *Blue Rhythms...*'

'I didn't come here to enjoy myself.' I said without thinking.

Verena burst out laughing, 'Then perhaps it's time to begin...*I* came here to enjoy myself, so are we going to get some pleasure from the rest of the day or just sit here arguing? You implied coming to Littern was about your soul – but as it's turned out it isn't about your soul, is it? It's about a beautiful place, encountering some unusual people - and an interesting man - after lunch yesterday you can't expect me to swallow all that dreary, dutiful, soul making stuff...'

'If you mean Patrick, he's very kind - a decent person...' I said.

Verena tutted dismissively, '...That makes him sound comfortable, like an old shoe, but I don't imagine he's *harmless* – at least, I hope not - imagination means so much at our stage of life, doesn't it?'

When we arrived in Safford Bridge, Verena headed across the town with unshakeable determination, refusing to stop and admire the swans and their cygnets on the river as her feet led her straight to The Pilgrims' Inn and to the table by the window.

The table was decorated with a tiny vase of sweet peas in pink and mauve and gypsophila, 'How lovely,' Verena said. 'Couldn't you see me here? Living in one of those elegant Georgian town houses on the other side of the square?'

'I could,' I agreed, 'until you grew so bored with provincial life you were climbing the walls...'

Verena ordered a full cream tea for us both - she said she wanted to sample the local delicacy again. 'Since I was a child and first came to this country, I've always imagined myself living in a town house - candlelit dinner parties, tea on the lawn, so quintessentially English...'

I poured the tea and passed her the plate of scones.

'You think I'm clutching at straws? My father made me feel as if I had no place in what had been my home and when I came back to London, my future appeared bleak.'

'Your father used to like to give gifts and treats – that's some people's way of showing affection...'

'...But he wanted the recipient of his gifts to conform to his ideas and not to cause any trouble – I feel the need to be utterly selfish for a while, perhaps even for the rest of my life – it might be some compensation for being unable to find love...'

Her bitter words crystallised my concerns for her into a definable form – since going to Geneva, Verena had become desperate.

'I couldn't sleep last night for thinking about all you have here,' she said. 'Before you left London, you kept saying you had nothing and now you have this – the house, natural beauty surrounding you - your very good friend, Patrick Piran...'

'Things are never as simple as they look,' I said.

'You still feel only resignation? That isn't the same as being glad to be here, putting down roots in the place...'

'What are you saying?'

'...Only that you'd be a fool to throw all this away - don't end up drifting back to London, you'll only discover that everything which depressed you before depresses you now - I know you,' Verena insisted, 'you're not settled.'

'Perhaps until Zoë comes back, I'll never be settled...'

'Or perhaps it's the opposite - Zoë won't come back safely *until* you are settled. And if Zoë decided never to come home, would you would condemn yourself to a miserable existence for the rest of your life?'

I looked out at the rain dripping through the trees as the breeze stirred the branches, this way and that. 'Whatever I do, someone is going to be put out or hurt. Eve wants to live on Littern, but Minette doesn't and I have no idea what I'll want to do when the year is up...'

'See what happens...' Verena said. She hesitated, 'While I was in Geneva I found something out. I discovered my father had a lover – for years - long before my mother died.'

'Do you know who she was?'

'I tracked her down - she had a child – think of that – I have a half-brother.'

I was shocked - her father had been so establishment, so eminently respectable, 'I can't imagine how that would feel,' I said.

'It should have made me feel less alone in the world, but when I made enquiries Christian said he would have preferred not to know I existed.'

'Why?'

'Because like me he hadn't realised his beloved parent was leading a double life.'

After tea, Verena persuaded me to take her to the Library to research local societies and events. She stopped at the window of every estate agent to assess the housing market and once or twice went in to obtain details, when a particular property interested her. The rain had settled into a fine drizzle and I trailed behind her, following the circle of her red umbrella through the streets of the town.

'Would you want to live here if I moved elsewhere?' I asked. Though Verena was heart-sore from all that had happened in Geneva, I was unconvinced by her single minded pursuit of *reasons to move to Devon.*

'You could visit me,' she said.

'Come back in the winter,' I suggested, 'make your mind up then, yesterday's storm was nothing...'

'Shall I come for Christmas?' Verena asked brightly.

'If I'm still here...'

I tried to distract her by insisting we browse round the market. It was hardly Verena's milieu, but she was interested in the food stalls displaying continental breads and charcuterie – later, she bought several jars of olives and peppers – some to take back to London and some for us to have at Marisands.

I picked out a few summer clothes for Minette, inexpensive shorts and tee-shirts for playing on the beach and two swimsuits, she would need them when she returned at half-term.

'Will we make it for the tide?' Verena asked as we wound our way back towards the car. 'Do I sound like a local?'

'Definitely - worrying about the tide is a permanent affliction.'

'I couldn't live on the island,' Verena said, thoughtfully, 'not unless they build a bridge or improve the causeway. I'm used to doing what I

411

want, when I want - I suppose that's why I found it so difficult to get on with my father – with men in general.'

On the way back to Littern, we talked about Minette and how she'd been moping over Yuuka and how Yuuka was under threat of being moved to another school. I mentioned Silvie, Alice and Flora, and said that I felt I should take time from my commitments to spend a few days with them in the summer.

'Your commitments..? One of whom had lunch with us yesterday?' Verena asked sharply.

I didn't want to be drawn on the subject of Patrick again, 'We're good friends,' I said, 'it's a cliché, but true in this case.'

'...Do you think so? How very convenient – it gives you the perfect excuse to slink away without taking him seriously.'

I didn't say so, but though I had grown to love Patrick, a part of me was afraid to embark on a new relationship – he had hurt me when we parted as children. Would it be different now? *What would happen when my year on Littern was over?*

I said, 'Silvie's extracted a promise from me – so I can't slink away until I've discovered the truth about Juliet's death. And it is possible the Pirans are keeping the truth from me...'

'Do I detect shades of Peter Kenholme?' Verena said, referring to Laurence's novels. 'But you're a daughter wanting to know about the mother she lost at an early age, not a sleuth - nor a prosecutor.'

'I often wish I could pick Juliet's story apart, as Laurence seems to do with his subjects.'

Verena laughed. 'Well, for God's sake, don't allow *your* picking about ruin everything. Patrick Piran is extremely well put together, not to mention the fact that he's in very love with you.'

'Perhaps a little in love...' I said.

'Don't be ridiculous,' she scolded, resolved as ever to have the last word.

# Chapter 34

Verena returned to London, but had offered to bring Minette to Littern for the summer half term in return for an opportunity to stay on the island again.

'On Iris's ark..?' I asked.

'My remark was probably uncalled for...' she said and smiled apologetically.

During her time in London, she made herself busy on my behalf. She visited Flora, who was still adamantly refusing to be packed off to The Maples, though Alice was already resident there with her friend, Edith, and according to Verena, in better spirits than she had ever seen her.

She went to St. Catherine's to see Sister Miriam and had taken Minette and Yuuka to tea at Nightingales. The precarious state of Yuuka's position at the school had touched her and she had spoken to Rose, who had agreed that they should tackle Sister Gabriel together.

While Verena was away, I'd heard from Silvie, who was disappointed that I had delayed my visit to Esterlea, "when I see you, I want to tell you more of how life was for me on Littern," she wrote. I felt guilty that I was unable to provide her with any further news.

For days, the weather was unseasonably muggy and confined in the study, I felt suffocated, frequently tempted to go outside to help Kos, who had been labouring to restore the garden since the ravages of the summer storm.

I had almost finished checking the penultimate chapter of *Minor Lights* when there was a knock at the front door. Kos was waiting in the porch, instead of his gardening clothes he was smartly dressed in a clean black shirt and black cord jeans.

When I invited him in, he told me he didn't want to play the piano - he wanted to talk to me. When I suggested I make a drink, he refused - he said he would prefer to remain outside, though since he'd been working at Marisands, he'd developed a very English taste for tea.

We stood on the drive, Kos pulling dead-heads off the pink roses that flanked the path to the orchard.

'I have told Eve,' Kos said at last, 'in the summer I go away for some weeks travelling.'

Since he'd said no more about leaving the island, I'd pushed the thought to the back of my mind.

'I am to go on the road...' he said and I could detect a note of stubbornness in his voice.

'Not following the hippy trail?' I asked.

Kos smiled as if I had caused him pain, 'No...Not like your daughter, though I will ask around in case anyone has heard of her.'

'You've worked hard to put the garden right...' I said, 'do you have to leave?'

Kos shrugged, 'You will manage very well. Eve will help you.'

'But you will come back, Kos?'

'Perhaps I shall return to the island in winter – I enjoyed freezing in this place beneath the bare trees, the sky full of snow...'

'I don't want Eve hurt,' I said, I had sensed coolness between them.

'We have made our goodbyes. Eve has a friend elsewhere,' Kos's face darkened, 'This man is very conventional and boring...'

'Which man?' I asked, forgetting myself.

Kos looked away - his hair fell forward over his face. 'He is the doctor in Narescombe – who apparently knows everything – Dr. Mike Acworth.'

He looked forlorn and my thoughts rattled through recent events; Eve had mentioned in passing, a few weeks ago, that she had changed to a woman doctor, but I had assumed that was no more than a personal preference -

'You know this man?' Kos asked.

'Vaguely...' I'd been to see Dr. Acworth and hadn't much liked him - he *did* seem to think he knew everything. 'Kos...' I began, 'Eve's very young and life for her remains open - fluid...'

'...She prefers someone dull who thinks she should be a nursery school teacher -to me she is an ice maiden.'

I smiled - Kos had a penchant for melodrama. I wished I could offer him hope but couldn't risk being disloyal to Eve.

Misreading my thoughts, Kos said, 'You mustn't blame Eve, it is possible I would have gone anyway...'

'...I'll miss you and your wonderful music and all you've done for me...'

'I haven't repaired the steps to the oratory - you must be careful, very careful.'

'Won't you change your mind?' I asked.

'I must go now,' Kos said and though I'd thought he might be persuaded to play the piano, one last time, he was clearly anxious to leave.

I picked a few sprigs of forget-me-not which had seeded in a pot sheltered against the wall of the house. 'You know what these mean..? Don't forget me or anyone here and we won't forget you...'

Kos made a small bow and without speaking walked away, head down, through the pergola and past Thrift Cottage.

I imagined him striding across the beach, back to the shadows of the woods, where he had lived for so many months among the trees. I thought he might turn and wave, but he opened the gate onto the footpath and didn't look back. He was a man in a hurry, a man escaping something. I wanted to call out after him, *don't get into trouble* - I hated to think of him shiftless, adrift - I hated to think how easily the garden could revert to the wilderness it had been when I had first arrived on Littern.

When I'd made coffee, I sat in the oratory garden, by the honeysuckle and read the day's mail. With Mrs. Stuart's weekly report from Wren House came the usual complaint that though Alice had gone to The Maples, Flora fell 'ill' each time there was a buyer interested in the property and didn't recover until she was certain the sale had fallen through. Mrs. Stuart was becoming discontented and I was concerned for her, she could manage at present, but had been warned by her doctor that to continue working beyond the end of the year would be to put her health at risk. At some point, it seemed, however reluctantly, I would have to intervene, begin to make definite plans for an extended trip to London.

I knew I ought to return to work, but with Flora's situation and Kos's departure on my mind, my concentration had gone. I wasn't much of a swimmer, but thought I would visit the pool at St. Thrif's Well - the sticky heat of the day was unpleasant and exhausting, a dip in the cool water might revive me - I could spend time in the study later in the evening.

Driving along the lane, I passed the place in the woods which had been the entrance to Kos's encampment, but the gap in the wall had been filled in, the stones replaced, he had left the island already. Eve's love-life had always been something of a mystery to me, all I knew was that she had gone to Zethar Creek and been badly hurt and whatever had happened there probably held the key to her actions now.

I parked on the grass verge near the beech tree I'd marked with a + last time I had been to the well. I couldn't wait to change into my swimming things and slip into the water beneath the shade of the trees. The woodland floor was thick with broad, green hellebore leaves. I shouldered my way along the overgrown footpath, now nearly impenetrable, pushing aside overhanging branches and wands of brambles that caught in my hair and clothes. Every now and then I bent down to pick dock leaves to rub against my bare legs, soothing them where I'd brushed against clumps of stinging nettles.

The well seemed farther into the woods than I had remembered, so deep that even on a summer's day, the sun only penetrated the thick canopy in flickering points of light as the sea-breeze moved the branches of the trees.

When I reached the marker stone, I knelt down and dipped my cupped hands into the moss covered font and drank from where the spring bubbled up and pooled in the shallow basin. Below me, the water in the pool was still, and as clear as a mirror, reflecting fragments of blue among the outlines of fluttering leaves.

I splashed my face, stripped down to my swimsuit and found the place where once before, I had slid down the bank to the edge of the pool. Now the earth was dry and it was easy to part the reeds and slip into the water to float on my back looking up at the sky.

I had overcome my fear of water here, as a child. Now perhaps, I might overcome a fear of the path my life was taking. If I had known how difficult surviving life on Littern would be - would I have come? *Would I have known not to fall in love with Patrick?* I wondered - could I be healed of love? Did I want to be?

The thought came to me that Patrick might be the thread of gold to be woven into my life - a thread which I mustn't let go. Falling in love with him had been easy - as natural as breathing – as if love for him had been running though my life, always, an underground stream, even when my faith in David had seemed absolute.

I swam to the centre of the pool and in the quietness and solitude prayed to the White Virgin for wisdom, strength and clarity – for patience and forbearance.

In the treetops, fat wood-pigeons flew about clumsily disturbing a pair of blackbirds; on the ground, a thrush hammered a snail against a stone. Eyes closed, I listened to the music of the woods – the rippling stream, the creaks from the surrounding trees and the busy rustling sounds.

In a while, I heard a louder and more consistent rustling - someone was coming towards me through the undergrowth, from the direction of Osford Lane. I rolled over in the water, my heart beating fast, my gaze fixed on the point between two ash trees, where we had once hung our offerings for the Clootie Well ceremony, where the narrow track emerged into the glade.

The bracken swayed rhythmically from side to side, I caught sight of flashes of white through the bushes and stayed far out in the centre of the pool treading water. Seconds dragged by until between two hummocks of bramble a tall, figure appeared - blue jeans, white shirt and dark hair – and my heartbeat settled as I swam towards the bank, where I had left my clothes.

'I was on my way to The Retreat with the children and saw your car,' Patrick said, 'I assume you were the vandal who put the mark on the tree?'

I admitted I was.

Patrick had found a fallen log near the mossy stone basin of the well, and sat with his long legs swinging over the edge of the pool. I stepped out of the water onto the bank and rubbed myself down with my clothes before slipping into my skirt and top, putting them on over my damp costume.

'You frightened me - advancing through the undergrowth.'

'Aren't you pleased to see me?' he said - his eyes lit with pleasure.

'When I saw your white shirt, I thought I might be having a vision...'

'I'm afraid not, every bit blood, flesh and bone.'

I pulled on my shoes and picked my way through the bracken and nettles to settle beside him on the log. My hair dripping, I pulled it back with my hands and wound it into a braid.

'What happened here?' he asked, putting his finger to the scar on my temple, the scar left from where I'd hit the sideboard - arguing with David about my pregnancy with Minette.

'I fell,' I said.

'As in *I fell down the stairs*?' he asked, quoting the usual excuse people made when they'd been subject to violence. 'David hurt you physically?'

'Only once... David could be difficult - we'd lost Tristan, and I wanted another child - he didn't agree.'

'Love comes in strange disguises...' he said.

And I felt ashamed, 'I wanted to stop loving him, but I couldn't...'

'...Because you're a loving person...'

'I'm not,' I said, 'I've failed at love.'

'And I've failed too,' he said, 'we're human.'

We moved onto the flat boulder, where Bernard must have rested when he first came to the island and there we lay side by side on the warm surface.

'I wish we could stay here forever,' I said.

He leaned over and kissed me. 'You'd like to grasp time and hold it still?'

I nodded.

'I miss you so much when we can't meet – sometimes it seems impossible to get free – and to see you on your own, that's a miracle...'

'We're in the right place for miracles,' I said drowsily.

'I've already witnessed one,' he teased, 'you've learned to swim.'

I felt his warm breath on my cheek, Patrick kissed me, his hand caressed my neck and I felt the fluttering wings of desire, open and close at his touch.

'I have an idea,' Patrick said, 'why don't we go into Safford Bridge - I have something to show you.'

He refused to say more but suggested I park on Pierce Street. We walked into town, called in at the delicatessen and bought pastries. Patrick bought flowers from the street vendor and a bottle of chilled white wine from the general store. Then we walked back up the steep hill, and turned into the cul de sac, Aspen Terrace, with its row of Georgian townhouses.

He opened the front door of No.5. Inside, light poured through tall sash windows into well-proportioned rooms painted in pale primrose yellow and soft white. The house was simply furnished – but with the sort of simplicity that speaks of expense, luxury and good-taste. Nothing was there that shouldn't have been and nothing was lacking.

'This is James's place,' Patrick said. 'When he was home recently he suggested Ursula and I make use of the house as he's rarely here.'

I could almost envy him – certainly Verena would have done - everything about Aspen Terrace was elegant and peaceful.

'It's lovely,' I said.

There were drawings and watercolours in all the rooms, some by well-known contemporary artists. On the living room mantelpiece were photographs of James's family, his wife and their two children. From the upstairs windows, views reached far across the roofs of Safford Bridge, out beyond farmland to the green, open hills.

I stood in one of the bedrooms, resting my elbows on the window sill, enjoying the view beyond the quiet street below.

'As you can imagine, I'm finding it hard to adjust,' Patrick said. 'It's not quite the environment I'm used to, though James is thinking of selling the house and in many ways it would suit me. I can drive from here to the hospital in a few minutes and easily drop Ursula off at Tom's. When she's older, Ursula could walk to school...'

'But..?'

'I'm not sure I can afford it – or if it would be good for me to become accustomed to such luxury. James is a good man - he hasn't allowed his wealth to go to his head.'

'It would suit you perfectly,' I said and smiled at him, 'Does Ursula like it?'

'She prefers the island and in many ways so do I – I rather resent the need to be practical about my living arrangements.'

'I'm afraid practicality may drive me off the island too.' I was already worrying about how to manage Minette and school when the tides didn't fit in with St. Mary's timetable.

'When I first encountered you at Lyncross you were afraid of everything,' he said and put his arm round my shoulders, 'In so many ways you're still the little shadow, still full of questions.'

We went downstairs and sat at the table in the tiny dining room overlooking the courtyard at the back of the house. We propped the French doors open and chatted over a glass of wine and ate the pastries we had bought from the deli.

'Delia told me Kelda had James's baby – it seemed to be the start of her trouble...'

He looked uncomfortable, 'Whatever happened, James has tried to help Kelda, but there's nothing he or anyone else can do unless she wants to change.'

'Delia said the same,' I admitted, though Kelda's situation bothered me.

'I have something to tell you,' he said. 'I've arranged a trip to Africa, later in the summer. I'll be in Nairobi for about two months – two weeks of which will be holiday. Ursula can stay in the city with Honor and then I'm taking her to the Lakes on my own. I'm hoping if she and Honor can be reconciled, she might come to terms with things here.'

What he proposed was perfectly reasonable, but his words crept under my shell and irritated the tender feelings I'd allowed to grow – they seemed to have grown even in the brief time since we'd met at the pool, earlier that afternoon.

When I didn't speak he said, 'I don't want Ursula to feel all the links with her past have been broken, that's important isn't it? Isn't that why you came back to the island? I have to make things right for her, she's desperately unhappy and I understand she can't simply cast off our previous life as if it has no relevance to now – somehow she has to integrate the two. By going to the Lakes, I want to draw her attention to the positive things, teach her to use the experience as a resource against her sadness.'

I thought *we can all use our children to justify the things we want to do*, and then despised myself for the meanness of the idea. It was obvious Ursula needed help – the many refugees Patrick worked with needed help – but it was going to take strength and grace to accept his absence and not to doubt his motives for leaving.

Patrick said, 'Ursula has so many problems – I don't want what happened between Honor and me to blight the rest of her life. Nick and James's children are close, but Ursula is much younger both in age and behaviour – she's the outsider, regarded as a little strange and tolerated rather than accepted by the family.'

'I'd do the same for any of my children...' I admitted knowing it was the truth. 'It's just that the last time we parted, I didn't see you again for thirty years.'

I felt the warmth of his hand stroking my arm. Patrick's sensuality was easy and natural like that of the living world – as natural as the warmth of sunshine, the roughness of rocks, the softness of moss and lichen and the rich colours of the sea and sand.

'The time will soon pass. When I've finished my stint at the hospital, I'll need a break and I thought if I took her to a wild-life reserve Ursula would relax, enjoy the scenery and the animals.' He held out his arms to me and I felt his comforting strength, his head resting against mine. 'My going away isn't forever, is it?' he asked.

'You may be ill again or find you're seduced into an enticing project...'

'I won't let that happen...'

'Kos left and though he says he will - I'm not convinced he'll ever come back.'

'You don't believe anyone will ever come back, even though they say they will. But after I definitely do get back, in September, the family will be celebrating Pa's ninetieth birthday, there's a party at Tom's house - would you like to come?'

'I couldn't...,' I objected.

'...Why ever not...?'

'Your family wouldn't want me there...'

'My family will have to get over themselves – isn't that what people say?'

'I don't want to spoil your father's birthday.'

Patrick laughed out loud, 'Now who needs to get over themselves? My family is perfectly capable of ruining Pa's birthday without any help from you. Tom thinks Pa should move off the island for the sake of his health and will be promoting that view, which is inflammatory as far as my father is concerned. Then there'll be arguments about what Beatrix should do and who should move into Lyncross when Pa's gone - of course, I think it should be me - but unfortunately, Tom thinks it should be him and so does Nick...'

'Perhaps you'll be living here, by then.'

'The island is my home, I've always planned to retire there, I can't imagine, ever detaching myself from Littern, but neither can I live forever on the charity of my family.' He told me then he'd applied for another part-time contract at the hospital, starting in the autumn and would be involved, with Tom, in setting up the clinics being run by the Hintham Ridge Community.

He was trying to reassure me and I wanted to feel reassured, though it seemed as though the people I loved were abandoning the island.

'Iris - shall we take advantage of two or three hours alone? Does it occur to you we've had to find seclusion away from one of the most secluded places in the British Isles..?'

'Our families would be scandalised...' I said.

'I see it more as putting them out of their misery, all that watching and wondering. Do you ever consider how the vast universe continues to move and work without any interference from us? And how God, the sun, moon and the stars must look down and think "if they're happy, let them be"?'

'Our life together feels so fragile,' I whispered.

'Separately we're fragile – but together? Isn't that the point of love?'

'One of the points,' I said.

Patrick kissed me and guided me upstairs, 'Please spare me the rest of the points - at least for now.'

When I woke, Patrick slept beside me, his breaths soft and even, his presence as calming as the warmth that passed between our bodies in the airy room. He had placed the vase of pink roses he'd bought in town on the bedside table. I turned on my side, towards the window and through the open curtains watched as grey clouds drifted across a lavender sky.

Desire and joy were gifts I had believed would never again be mine - after David I had expected nothing. Now my body was heavy with pleasure and my eyes threatened to drift closed again in contentment. In the depths of physical love, nothing had mattered - the safety of Patrick's arms had been the whole truth, dispelling past loves with all their illusions.

I breathed in the scent of his skin - fresh and woody - I reached out to stroke his fine, dark hair where it rested against his cheek.

As he stirred he said, '...Too many thoughts to sleep..?'

'...Far too many...'

He touched my lips with his fingertip. His hands long-fingered, elegant... 'Where had you gone in your thoughts?' he asked

'...to Marisands, Kos filling the house with music...'

But then intensity of feeling and sensation made everything else recede and I understood how love with him would be - few declarations, just a steady series of proofs. As I learned to know him, I wanted to understand without words when he was upset, when he was exhausted - I wanted to sense not only his frailties, but also his joys – to delight in his smile.

I knew that while Patrick was away, the sea would churn endlessly, pulled by the moon and driven by the wind - the rocks and cliffs of the island would stand braced against the pounding water – nothing would be altered by his absence - I hoped not even my brittle belief that he loved me, as I knew for certain - now - that I loved him.

Before we left, I had a shower. The bathroom was upstairs on the top floor. As I came out, I noticed a small room where the door hadn't quite been closed. Curious, I looked in, it was a box room, there were suitcases packed neatly into one corner – but on the walls were three framed drawings of a baby, less than a year old.

As the art works in the rest of house were of good quality, I studied the drawings, wondering whose they were - they appeared to be unsigned. The tentative style struck me as familiar from the examples of Juliet's sketches which Eve and I had found at Marisands. I lifted one of the frames away from the wall and examined the back, but it gave no clue to the identity of the artist.

'Do you know about these?' I asked Patrick.

'I hadn't noticed them, but James might be at Pa's party, if you're interested, you could ask him...'

I hung the picture back on its hook and set it straight. When I stood back to check it was level, a pile of books in a cardboard box caught my eye – one of them a notebook marked with a number 10 in a circle.

'You do realise we missed the tide, almost two hours ago?' Patrick asked, distracting me.

I didn't answer. I was considering why Juliet's diary might be in James's house and how I might find the opportunity to make sure it was hers.

There was no chance that evening. Patrick suggested we had dinner in Safford Bridge and when we'd phoned home, we walked to The Seamark and stayed there until we could get back onto the island.

Patrick had given me the flowers he'd bought from the stall in town and we parted with a sense of poignancy. It wouldn't be long until he went away – and it seemed to me he would be away for very a long time.

Determined not to spend the summer moping on the island, I resolved the best way to make time pass would be to fulfil my plans to go to London.

# Chapter 35

A few days later, I discovered Ursula up in The Robin's Nest when I let Quirk out into the garden for his morning run. The fine weather had held and it was a warm day, though as always at Marisands, there was an insistent breeze blowing in from the sea.

I called to her that I would soon be fetching Minette from the station. She slid down the tree at once, grazing her knee as she landed on the lawn.

'Could I come with you?' she asked and I hadn't the heart to dampen her enthusiasm.

'If your dad says yes - does he know where you are?'

Ursula nodded her head solemnly, she seemed to believe a lie wasn't a lie if it wasn't spoken but only implied. When I reached Patrick on his mobile phone, he was at Tom's house, they were tinkering with his car, trying to repair it and he seemed satisfied with our plans - he'd collect Ursula from Marisands later.

'I'm just like a parcel,' Ursula said cheerfully, 'Dad talks about me as if I were a parcel.'

Ursula was smart in a navy blue t-shirt with white daisies embroidered on the chest and a pink skirt. Before leaving for town, I changed into a sundress with mauve and pink, splashy flowers on a navy background.

'Now we match,' Ursula said happily.

Eve hadn't appeared at the house for breakfast that morning, so I tooted the car horn as we drove away from Marisands, to let her know we were leaving. I'd allowed plenty of time for our journey because of heavy summer traffic, caused by the influx of tourists, but we arrived early at the station and Ursula danced up and down impatiently as we waited for the train.

'Can Minette and I play tomorrow?'

'I have to take Minette to see her school again,' I said.

'Couldn't I come with you?' she suggested.

'I'll see...' She didn't mean to be intrusive, but I couldn't run the risk of Minette having another fit of the sulks, Miss Grieves, I suspected, wasn't as patient as she pretended to be.

The station was bustling with visitors, so I took Ursula's hand and insisted she stay close by me at the ticket barrier, looking after her was like being responsible for a much younger child. When the London train pulled in, we could just make out Verena looking out of the window with Minette's small figure beside her. As I waved, Ursula slipped her hand out of mine, ducked under the barrier, and hared up the platform to their carriage. I followed her, pushing against the stream of passengers to where she was jumping about, excitedly, by the train door.

I helped Minette down onto the platform, she was tousle headed and pretty in her blue school dress.

'Are you really here?' Ursula asked her.

'She is – you're not dreaming,' Verena said.

Behind the mass of other passengers, Ursula twirled along the platform like a miniature dervish, and then slowly Minette began to twirl too - their dark hair flew round their faces, their skirts flared out in wide circles around their legs.

'You've survived the journey?' I asked Verena, laughing at the girls.

'Minette kept me amused.'

'She seems in a good mood...'

'I told her there might be news where Yuuka is concerned, though perhaps I shouldn't have - she's going to be unbearably let down, if the school won't agree to our ideas.'

It was almost lunchtime and the traffic in Safford Bridge had log-jammed round the town centre, so I phoned Eve to ask if she could put some food together, I had decided it would be better to go straight back to Littern, despite objections from both Verena and the girls about being deprived of a meal at The Pilgrim's Inn.

We bundled into the car, Ursula whispering to Minette while I chatted to Verena and we crawled in a line of cars around the town square. Ahead was a hold-up at the main junction that fed traffic out of the town towards the coast - it seemed congested in both directions.

As I pulled out onto the roundabout, from the corner of my eye, I noticed a dark figure sprawled across the pavement their belongings scattered into the road and instinctively knew it was Kelda. I couldn't help looking – nobody stopped to help - they just avoided her, giving her a very wide berth. Then a man crouched down to speak as she tried to lift her black hat onto her head – he seemed an unlikely good Samaritan - the contrast between his smart linen suit and Kelda's baggy, mouldering layers of black clothes was stark - startling.

'Watch out!' Ursula screamed.

I slammed on the brakes, to avoid a motor cyclist who had veered in front of us. Horns blared behind me and the motorcyclist sped off, holding up his finger.

'Iris, you need to move,' Verena urged and I came to my senses.

We hadn't collided with anyone, nothing had run into us, Verena was unharmed and the girls quite safe, huddled together on the back seat.

Apologising, I drove off, creeping forward - several cars had formed a queue behind me and continued to blast on their horns.

'You didn't swear like Dad does, or Aunt Beatrix, you were very ladylike,' Ursula said.

'Thank you,' I said, relieved - finally - to have filtered out onto the road for Narescombe. 'I'd never forgive myself if any of you came to harm...'

'My dad would never forgive you if I came to harm,' Ursula said airily.

'No...' I agreed, 'he wouldn't.'

Patrick was already at Marisands, waiting for us to arrive, Eve had made him a coffee and he was enjoying drinking it outside in the sunshine.

Ursula jumped from the car - I thought with unnecessary haste - and ran up to him shouting, 'Iris nearly killed a man on a motorbike. She was driving without due care and attention.'

Patrick smiled but his eyes searched mine, waiting for an explanation.

'It was busy - we were talking - it's easy to let your attention wander,' Verena said in my defence, 'No-one was hurt...'

'I hope it wasn't you chattering, Ursula,' Patrick said, but not unkindly.

I said, 'It was my fault - I wasn't looking and a motorbike cut me up,' I would explain about Kelda later.

'...I think we're lucky to be alive,' Ursula insisted dolefully, making everyone laugh.

But I was chastened - life on the island would be untenable without a car, I couldn't afford a new one and without Kos to maintain it, the days of William's old banger were probably numbered.

Patrick carried Verena's and Minette's cases inside while I released Quirk from the conservatory. I handed Minette a ball to throw for him, glad she seemed reconciled to his presence and that she and Ursula seemed to have made friends.

Eve had prepared lunch for us and had set out a picnic rug on the back lawn where it was shady. Minette and Ursula ate their food sitting together on the grass resting their backs against a lilac tree.

'This is like a magic world from a book,' Ursula said, 'with teeny tiny things in it like Eve's little cottage. One day, I'll show you the whole island...' she promised Minette, while I glanced at Patrick making a mental note, not to take my eyes off them.

Ursula asked for the notebook in which she had painstakingly written her story about *Seabright Island,* in spidery handwriting. Eve fetched the book from Thrift Cottage and Ursula read the story to Minette, in which two girls lived with each other on an island and formed a friendship, closer even than sisters.

*

Eve seemed to have formed a friendship with Nicholas based on their mutual love of photography and of the island. He had invited her and anyone else interested to walk out to Beckhead Cliffs with him one day during the holiday. The weather forecast was good for the whole week and there would be fantastic views of the island from the cliff-top.

I decided not to go - the oppressive heat had given me a headache, but Verena had offered to take Minette and Quirk, so I lent her clothing suitable for walking on the rough terrain at the western tip of the island. As they prepared to leave, she was *almost* scruffy, wearing an old polo top and a pair of socks, folded over the tops of her canvas shoes.

I closed the gate behind them and went up to the study, where I e-mailed Zoë and wrote a reply to Mrs. Stuart's latest letter. Usually, her account of life at Wren House was neat and painstakingly written, but her latest missive had arrived dog-eared and torn reminding me of my own efforts to keep up with correspondence when the children were small. Without Alice's presence, it was possible the discipline of the house had gone into decline - perhaps their circumstances were less under control than Verena had thought - and I added a postscript that I would probably be in London sometime during June and July. I scribbled a postcard to Silvie and suggested we could also meet during that time.

Beckhead Cliffs was a walk of five miles; when the hikers returned late in the afternoon, everyone was hot and tired. While I prepared supper, Verena sat resting her foot on a kitchen chair – she'd twisted her ankle on the way back and had slowed everyone down.

'I do hate appearing ridiculous,' she complained.

I'd already listened to three different versions of their day, but wasn't sure if Verena had enjoyed herself or not.

'But it was all right?' I asked, when she'd described - once again - sighting grey seals from the cliff tops and seeing onto the rocky islet so clearly, she was sure, even without a pair of field glasses, she'd spotted puffins on the rocks.

'It's been lovely to find someone who talks well about significant things.'

I assumed this was Nicholas. They had stopped at The Retreat on their way to Marisands so Verena could bind her ankle and she had returned with a collection of rare classical music C.D.'s and a newfound interest in coastal erosion.

After supper, Minette helped Eve with the washing up, but she was very quiet. It was already late, but when I suggested she went to bed, she said, 'I don't want to go...' and I thought she was close to tears.

I excused myself from the others and went upstairs with her, she was white with tiredness and I wondered if the long walk had been too much for her.

'We were gone for ages,' she said, 'I wanted you...'

'You didn't need to worry – I was here all the time...'

She changed into her nightdress, dropping her jeans and sweatshirt in a heap on the floor. I drew the curtains across her bedroom window, closing out the moon and stars – the night was so clear I could see the lights of Narescombe, glowing on the horizon.

While Minette cleaned her teeth, I turned down the bed for her. She was a child who had always wanted to be an adult and it was easy to forget how young and how vulnerable she was, 'I'm sorry, Min,' I said as she climbed into bed, 'perhaps we should have had a day together.'

'Why is Patrick going away?' she asked, 'Nicholas and Verena kept talking about it.'

I explained in a simple way what had happened to Honor and Patrick – they had separated - and Ursula needed to go back to Nairobi to see her mother.

'Everybody goes away,' she said and began to weep.

I curled up on the bed beside her and tried to take her in my arms, but she pulled away and buried her face in the pillow.

'Things seem worse when we're exhausted – you've had a long tiring day,' I said, stroking her temples to soothe her as I had when she was a baby.

'I want people to stay where they're meant to be...' she said, 'then I can think of them in their right place and I don't feel scared...'

'You wanted me to be at Marisands – and I was,' I said.

Minette nodded.

But then there was Yuuka - Yuuka who we were both trying not to mention – though my Service and Sacrifice medal was draped in clear sight across the chest of drawers.

'If Yuuka stayed at St. Catherine's, I could imagine her in the classroom and in the playground and I think I could bear leaving her,' Minette said.

'Verena says there's hope, no-one's promising, but there is at least hope.'

I pulled the sheets closely round her small body. 'Try to sleep now.'

Then I stayed on the bed beside her, curved loosely round her back until I heard her breath deepen into soft snores. When I was certain she was asleep, I crept out of the room, careful in the half-light not to stumble and wake her.

Eve soon made excuses to go back to the cottage for the night. She wanted to work, excited by the places she'd seen - Nicholas had taken them to caves and gullies, ancient patches of woodland, which I'd never heard of – he intended to write about hidden places on the island for the magazine of the local naturalists' society.

The humidity of the day had scarcely died down and I suggested to Verena we go to the sitting room, where it was cool. She'd been asking about the portraits of my family, including Yvette's miniatures of Alice and Flora; I explained to her about the mirror portrait.

'What Yvette, Flora and Juliet achieved with their art you could achieve with words – you have the same lightness of touch,' she said.

'I've thought of asking Eve to paint a new mirror portrait.'

'You should - four generations of women who have something in common as artists and as people.'

'...Eccentricity and fragile nerves..?' I suggested, smiling at her.

'I should apologise for my fragile nerves,' she said. 'I'm ashamed to admit to a touch of jealousy – Eve is young and full of energy, Nicholas has an arresting vitality and I felt exhausted and foolish, limping along with my sprained ankle.'

'No-one minded...'

'Except me,' she said ruefully. 'I can't help feeling cheated. My father is a fallen hero - and believing no man could match him, I've loved nobody. When the truth came out about his affair – I felt he'd showered us with gifts only to hide his indifference to me and my mother – while his true interests lay elsewhere...'

'I'm sure he loved you...' I said, but though I wanted to console her – how could I be certain? My own father had been worse than indifferent and there had been no gifts to compensate, only the carved wooden box - and who could comprehend what had driven him to send that to a young child?

'...When I look ahead, nothing but emptiness yawns in front of me,' she said. 'I've been forced to live as a stranger to my feelings - I've wanted to love - I've wanted to have children...'

'But you're mourning your father – with many conflicting emotions.'

'I'm growing to like Nicholas Piran - beneath all that bitterness is a deeply hurt man.'

'Nicholas is still married to Sarah,' I said, wanting to protect her.

'What happened?' Verena asked.

'There was a misunderstanding. Sarah has a flat in London, she works away from home, someone gossiped about a man, she says was a colleague and now there's an impasse - she's furious with Nicholas for not trusting her and he refuses to believe her side of the story...'

'His doubts could be perfectly reasonable – "there's no smoke without fire" don't people say that?'

'They do - but my point is Nicholas isn't available - the family believes things will blow over.' I paused before I spoke again, 'I can see that to you he's attractive and intelligent but don't set yourself up for more trouble...'

Verena responded irritably, 'I merely remarked on his state of mind and since when did you become the arbiter of other people's lives? You have Patrick to watch over you like a guardian angel - or a faithful dog.'

If one of my daughters had made that remark, I would have been tempted to slap her, but when Verena had come back that day, I'd recognised the symptoms of attraction I'd encountered in her before, and had added them to my list of concerns.

'All I'm saying is don't place your hopes in a hopeless situation, but perhaps I should have been more tactful.'

'When have we ever been tactful?' She leaned forward and rubbed her sore ankle, 'Was Minette all right?'

'...Fussing about Yuuka, if things don't work out it will send her into the depths.'

'And she isn't the only one to have the bottom knocked out of her world? I heard about Patrick going away.'

I rested back in my chair. When I thought about him leaving, life felt as aimless as it had once done when I'd been a teenager, I seemed to have lost the self-determination which had brought me to Littern.

Not wanting to dwell on our disagreement, I showed Verena my mother's sketches for *The Stations of the Cross*, her diaries and some of the letters I'd found.

'Geraldine's account of my parents' existence is quite sensational and in a way so is my mother's.'

429

'Hardly surprising,' she said, 'I read an interesting article in *The Times* about the damage caused to children of the sixties by irregular family set-ups and lack of order and discipline...'

'Obviously my problem...' I said and yawned.

'But hardly mine. Perhaps you haven't been asking the right questions...'

'I've been taking a break from asking questions – I can't think of any new ones.'

'But your enquiries must have been painful for everybody - Geraldine's talking about a man who spent fifty years misusing her - until he required her services as an unpaid nurse. You've come to this situation full of prejudice – but however much *you* might want to condemn William – Geraldine obviously doesn't...'

'I don't know if that is what I want - not any more...' I said, unwilling to acknowledge the truth of what she was suggesting.

'What do you feel your parents contributed to the art of the period?' Verena asked.

'Nothing, it seems they contributed absolutely nothing. Most of their work has been lost or destroyed and with it goes my image as the daughter of the poor man's answer to the Bloomsbury set...'

Verena glanced at me and laughed, 'Did you really think that?'

'Alice and Flora encouraged it, in as far as I could read between the lines of their silence. But the situation seems less about art and more about personal entanglements – and a part of me would prefer not to know the answers to questions that at first seemed vitally important.'

Verena stood up from her chair, stretched and hobbled over to the window, 'Just look at the stars - I don't think I've seen a sky full of stars like that since I was a child.'

'I noticed them from Minette's room when I put her to bed.'

'We went to The Retreat today – it's a lovely house...'

'...set in a beautiful garden...'

'Nicholas talked so regretfully about the island – as if its beauty invites desecration – some millionaire wanted to build an enormous club house on the site of The Retreat, there have been schemes to open a nudist beach...'

'But Littern hasn't much to fear with the Pirans fighting its corner...'

Verena laughed. 'Nicholas told me he can't seem to raise your enthusiasm for the new bridge...'

'I like the island as it is.'

She limped back to her chair and rearranged the cushions before sitting down - flexing her ankle - she winced as she wiggled her toes and then rested her leg on a stool.

'I hope I'll be all right to go back to London,' she said glancing at me sideways.

Her ploy was transparent. 'Of course you'll be all right, you have to be – Minette and I are relying on you.'

She pulled a face, 'Really? I would much have preferred to stay on Littern for a few extra days.'

*

Just before the end of the holiday, it was Patrick and Nicholas's birthday. Patrick had suggested we go to Morrow Bay for the afternoon and Nicholas said we could use The Retreat as a base, while we were on the beach.

The children went to change into their swimming things and we carried a tray of iced drinks to the summerhouse from where we could enjoy the vista across smooth, sweeping lawns, through the trees to the beach and blue sea at the end of the garden.

'This is idyllic,' Verena said, 'it would be immoral to be unhappy here.'

But we weren't allowed to relax for long before Minette and Ursula insisted we went to the bay so they could swim.

On the shore, a brisk breeze drove shallow waves inland, topped with spumes of white froth as they broke onto the sand. Benedict and Dominic hauled the *Silver Arrow* down to the water's edge and Minette and Ursula begged to join them in the boat to be rowed along the shoreline as far as the quay.

Verena's ankle had begun to improve but she had been advised to rest, so she built an enclosure with brightly striped windbreakers and stretched out on a rush mat to sunbathe with Rowena beside her.

'Are you going to swim?' Patrick asked me.

'I ought to watch Minette.'

'The others will watch her.'

I looked round to see everyone occupied - content. There was an occasional splash followed by a shout of protest as one of the twins leant over the side of the boat to run their hand through the water scooping it into the air and soaking Minette and Ursula.

'Everyone's safe,' he said and took my hand. 'Come on - put your feet in the water.'

We paddled along in the shallows towards the quay. Minette and Ursula had grown bored and had been landed on the beach, where they were now building a complex construction in sand. The twins had moored the boat against the pier and were heading towards Coyle Sands with their surf boards. Nick was lying apart from the others, reading, with the three dogs by his side. Occasionally he reached out lazily for his camera took a picture of the children playing in the sea and laid it down again.

'Minette and Ursula seem to be enjoying each other's company,' Patrick said. 'Minette asked this morning if I sit and read the newspaper all day, when I've finished putting people to sleep - Ursula will have put her up to that one. I said when she can pronounce and spell anaesthetist correctly without help I'll tell her. I'm hoping to have a long wait – I'd prefer not to think about work, at least until later.'

Patrick had "noticed a few things" at Safford Bridge General, and his compulsion to mention them meant he was being to some extent ostracised, in the expectation he would either choose to leave or become so uncomfortable he would make a mistake that would cost him his position – the friction was getting him down.

Despite the fine day, clouds were banking on the horizon slowly advancing towards us, gradually blotting out the pale blue sky.

Patrick put his arm round me and pulled me close, 'You'll hear the tide turn in a few minutes,' he said, 'then Nick and I are going to swim to the rocks, it's traditional, on our birthday...'

'Is that a good idea? I asked, remembering what Margaret had implied about his health, the evening when we'd met at the pub.

'I'd like to undo the bad memories of this place – I don't feel either of us will truly be free until that happens.'

As the time of his departure for Africa grew closer, I felt increasingly insecure - agitated. I said, 'What lengths do we have to go to - to break free? Swimming to the rocks might be too much - and though going to Kenya is important for you and for Ursula, for entirely selfish reasons, I don't want you to do that either...'

His eyes searched my face, 'That's very honest.'

'I want us to be honest...'

'Then I can only say that I have to go to Kenya – I'm certain it's for the best.'

'And you'll swim to the rocks, whatever I say?'

I was beginning to realise how uncompromising Patrick could be - his decisions were supported by his belief that the good intent of his actions was sufficient to justify any distress they caused to other people. To him, going to Kenya offered a suspension of problems. He was uneasy at work, guilty about living at James's house in unaccustomed luxury and increasingly concerned about Ursula's future at St. Safan's, where her struggle to keep up with her work left him nonplussed and her humiliated.

432

'If you didn't come back from Kenya – I'm not sure I'd come back from London.'

'You have my commitment to come back, don't you trust me?'

'Perhaps I don't yet trust myself.'

'While you're hurt, confused and looking over your shoulder, we aren't free to love,' he said.

'Am I the only one doing that?' I asked - his words had stung me. 'You rarely speak of love...'

'...Because I'm not interested in meaningless declarations or in trading endearments, love has to be demonstrated, it has to be strong and steady - touch on rock...'

But I felt my own foundations shifting and suspected his might be less firmly grounded than he imagined.

'Do I have a commitment from you to come back?' he persisted.

'I have to come back, I've promised Silvie...'

'And that's what matters?'

I heard the edge in his voice, but hadn't intended him to take it that way – had only thought to lighten our conversation. 'I meant I don't have control over every aspect of my future...'

'And I have? Isn't commitment about knowing that even if circumstances are against us we'll find a way through it together?'

Nicholas called to Patrick that he was ready to swim. I pulled on a cardigan over my dress - turning up the collar and tucking my hair in at the nape of my neck. The cool wind had begun to whip round the end of the pier and I couldn't stop shivering. Mars, Hext and Luna barked excitedly, watchful of our faces, as if by instinct they understood something of importance was about to happen.

I couldn't share their enthusiasm and wondered if Nicholas felt concerned, as I did, that Patrick wasn't strong enough to do the long, difficult swim.

'Couldn't you go in the boat?' I suggested.

Patrick laughed. 'That would defeat the whole object...'

'Wait in the house if you can't bear to watch,' Nicholas said and I felt the sting of his sarcasm.

But I couldn't bear the thought of *not* watching and followed them down to the water's edge. The sea was choppy and as the waves raced in towards the shore, it was difficult to distinguish where the dangerous currents clashed in the broad stretch of sea between the bay and the rocks.

Nicholas ordered the dogs to lie down. I waited on the sand beside them, holding towels and clothes. Patrick stepped into the water, taller and wirier than Nicholas, his fine brown hair blown back from his face, his dark blue eyes kind as he turned and smiled.

A strange white light had broken through the clouds and I had to screw up my eyes to see their progress. Nicholas shadowed Patrick as they struck out towards the quay. Luna, Mars and Hext stayed motionless, like a row of statues, their long sharp noses pointing out towards the rocks.

Verena stood close by me.

'Who could love such a man?' I asked her.

She slipped her arm through mine. I thought of Patrick's involvement with his family, his intensity about his work that made him distant at times, his fluctuating moods – mostly warm - but every now and then troubled by problems of which he refused to speak. I bit my lip anxiously as his figure receded – he and Nick were now no more than two bobbing dark heads, far, far out to sea.

A flash of pale sunshine passed in a moment and a heavy grey light tinted the white sand and sea a dull monochrome. My eyes watered in the chilly wind. Verena squeezed my arm as I fixed my gaze expectantly on the rocks – Patrick and Nicholas had disappeared from view and my heart had begun to beat wildly. To climb the rocks they needed to go behind them, to a place where they were certain to find a few footholds.

I looked impatiently, waiting for them to appear silhouetted against the sky. Luna had broken ranks from the other dogs and I was afraid she had sensed something wrong as the minutes ticked by and there was no sign of anyone standing on the hulk of rock.

I moved closer to the edge of the sea, as if going forward two or three paces would allow me to make out the figures I desperately wanted to see. Memories of Juliet clamoured for my attention, I fought back images of Antony's struggle in the water, the sea dashing him against the base of the rocks as he tried to reach my mother.

It seemed like hours, before Nicholas and Patrick crawled onto the top of the rocks and stood tall against the mottled sky. I waved, signalling they should return to the beach, the weather was now changing rapidly - surely this must be the final gesture towards that terrible day – the day of my mother's drowning?

At last, the twin arcs of Patrick and Nicholas's bodies made a synchronised dive into the water, as perfectly curved as a double rainbow. Intent on watching them, a wave caught me and soaked my dress up to the knees as the sky grew black and the rocks took on a foreboding darkness in the turbulent sea.

Shading my eyes with my hand, I saw Nicholas take the lead, but the swim to shore was no safer than the journey out and when they were half way across the expanse of water, Patrick seemed to tire.

Behind me, the girls were packing their things – scurrying round to gather their possessions, rolling up windbreaks, rescuing towels and buckets and spades. Rowena called out that she'd take Minette and Ursula to the Retreat. I asked Verena to go with them.

I kept checking my watch, focussing on Patrick's body, buffeted by the waves. Nicholas had stopped moving and Patrick appeared to be struggling, making an enormous effort, only to come no closer to shore as he floundered in the water. I urged him on silently as Nicholas swam beside him, guiding him to avoid the dangerous rip tides, going far over towards the quay - almost into Coyle Sands - where the twins were running up the beach towards home, their surfboards on their backs protecting them from the rain.

Nicholas didn't leave Patrick's side and as they came closer, I saw that every ten strokes they stopped to tread water. When at last they drew parallel to the pier, they turned towards the bay and swam steadily at a steep angle to the shore.

Patrick stumbled out of the water. Luna barked and leapt in excitement, like an overactive child running back and forth not knowing whether to go towards him or Nicholas. As he reached the shallows, Nicholas stood up, the water lapping his waist and the dog twisted and turned in ecstasy.

Patrick was winded, unable to stand except by leaning his arm on Nicholas's shoulder. He was rocking on his feet and when I wrapped the towel round him, I could feel the icy coolness of his skin - cold saltwater dripped from his rumpled hair onto his shoulders.

'Give me a few moments,' he said panting as he tried to catch his breath.

'I hope to God you never plan to do that again.'

'Ssh,' he said, taking my hand, pressing my fingers to his blue lips, 'I shan't do it again.'

Gradually, he began to breathe more easily, his face regaining its colour as a faint tinge of pink returned to his lips. He bent over and rubbed his hair and body dry, then slipped on his trousers and sweater. When he'd lost the white, pinched look he'd had when he emerged from the water, Nicholas left us, heading up the beach with the dogs hard on his heels.

'What did you hope to achieve..?' I asked crossly.

'What I *hoped* to achieve was to prove I was well again – but what I *did* achieve was the need to accept certain things in my life are over.'

He seemed amused by my concern, 'Couldn't this be part of an adventure? A tale of Seabright Island and Jack and Agnes..?'

'Even Jack wouldn't have been foolish enough to do what you did today.'

'But if he had been, Agnes would have cheered him on and then been charming to him when he valiantly made his way back onto the shore.'

'When we first came here today, I hoped I'd made peace with the bay.'

'And I've disturbed your peace..?'

'I've been trying to understand what shape our lives will take, but when you do stupid things, I can't get that clear.'

A rumble of thunder filled the air as lightning cracked to the west of the bay.

We took shelter beneath the wall of the quay and despite my anger all I wanted was to hold him – to explain that while I supported both his desire to regain his health and engage in his humanitarian activities, I'd prefer him to find something to do that didn't involve killing himself.

'I think I understand how Honor made you feel...' I said, 'when you couldn't persuade her not to take risks.'

'Do you?' he asked. He looked up at the black sky as another fork of lightning stabbed down at the bay, 'I think we'd better get back.'

He grabbed my hand, rain clinging to his skin and hair and making damp splotches on his jumper. He said something, but I didn't catch it, his words blown away on the squally wind. In a sudden cloudburst, rainwater thrashed onto the pier, coursed down our hair and cheeks, while behind us the sea churned, wild and unreliable.

At The Retreat, Luna, Mars and Hext were on the veranda, lying in a row like three sphinxes, unbothered by the rough weather.

The usual clutter in the hallway had disappeared beneath piles of wet sandy towels, surf boards and wind breakers - a series of obstacles to be negotiated between the front door and the living room.

'Thanks for letting us use your house,' I said to Nicholas when he appeared in the hall.

'Any port in a storm?' he asked, meaning it as a joke, but he didn't have Patrick's easy manner and I was wondered if the truth was that our presence was an intrusion.

Rowena had found a children's film suitable for Ursula and Minette, and they had settled down in front of the TV. Reassured they were happy, I went to the cloakroom to let my hair loose and brush it out. The thunder had closed in and was almost above the house and the pain in my head begun to build as the storm gathered force.

I helped myself to a glass of water from the kitchen - Nicholas had said we should make ourselves at home. Bored by the film, Rowena lounged in a corner of the sofa beside the two younger girls, painting her fingernails black, and conspicuously ignoring them. She blew so noisily onto her nails to dry them, Minette complained she couldn't hear the TV – then having upset Ursula by fidgeting - Rowena sprang out of the chair and left the room without a word.

'That's a terrible age to live through,' Verena said watching her vanishing figure.

'She won't be able to ride today,' Nicholas explained, 'if you're Rowena that's the equivalent of the end of the world – she prefers horses to people.'

I had given Patrick a blue wool sweater for his birthday, dyed and knitted by members of the Hintham Ridge Community, but had brought wine for Nicholas as a gift. He fetched glasses, poured us each a drink and everyone seemed to relax, the conversation moving round the room in an easy, companionable way. Nicholas spoke about his work as a photographer and film-maker. He explained to Verena the problems caused on the island by the changing coastline, how shifting sands in one area could cause freak tides and flooding in another. Playing devil's advocate to his brother's arguments, I felt how Patrick was deeply woven into his family and into life on Littern – the place where he was most truly himself, the place he had loved since childhood.

Patrick had been asked to be on standby for the hospital that night and had to get to Safford Bridge before eight o'clock. He'd been rather cagey about it, but had described the situation as not exactly being on call, but engaging in an act of vigilance – with a hint of the vigilante. I followed him into the kitchen, when he went to make coffee, knowing he would soon be leaving.

'You're quiet, are you okay?' he asked.

'It was good of Nicholas to invite us here,' I said, avoiding answering the question.

Patrick glanced up at me. 'The children have got on with their lives since Sarah left and Nick needs to do the same...'

'Someone else's problems help to put your own into perspective..?' I asked.

'That can work either way - make you feel much better or much worse,' he said.

'Will you be safe in Kenya?'

'Ursula will be fine, but I suppose I can't be sure. The camps are chaotic places – fights break out, people have accidents, people helping the sick become sick themselves and it's always exhausting – long hours, too few resources...'

'And you love it..?'

Patrick laughed. 'It doesn't make much sense, does it?'

What he'd said was no worse than Margaret had already told me and I'd noticed he had an infuriating compulsion to tidy up the loose ends in his life – he had unfinished business in Nairobi.

I thought how each person's life is a mystery - their identity always contains something hidden - something which can't be unearthed by assembling facts and applying reason. I couldn't lay out the parts of my own life - or Juliet and William's - or Patrick's – couldn't hope to assemble the whole through simply re-ordering the component parts.

The bright light in the kitchen made my eyes ache and as Patrick fed handfuls of coffee beans into the coffee mill, the low grinding noise seemed to reverberate painfully through my head. I pulled my cardigan tightly around me, pulled my hands back into the sleeves and turned up the collar.

'You look nice...' he said.

'So do you...' he'd put on the new blue sweater and I was pleased to see how well it suited him.

'You also look very pensive.'

'I'll be okay when this storm clears...'

Overhead, thunder growled, every now and then giving way to a downpour which left the garden sodden – the lawns spotted with puddles.

Patrick loaded a tray with mugs of coffee and disappeared into the living room. The dogs seemed calm, so I stepped out onto the veranda and stood breathing in draughts of cool fresh air, hoping to clear the dull ache from my head.

In a while, the thunder moved eastward towards Narescombe and a strong wind blew the clouds away. Through the trees, I watched the hazy sun go down – the burnt- orange glow reflected in drops of rain that clung to the leaves of the trees, bushes and blades of grass - at the foot of the garden the shallow waves on the surface of the sea flashed red-gold, like facets of glass producing flame coloured shards of light.

I was about to re-join the others when I heard a mobile phone ringing in the kitchen. When I glanced round, I saw through the window that Patrick had come to answer it and stayed outside, not wanting to intrude.

The kitchen window was slightly open, I heard him ask, 'What can I do?'

I moved away, trying not to listen, but his voice was raised and I realised he was speaking to Honor, discussing arrangements for his trip to Africa.

Nausea clutched at my stomach, the call felt like a violation of our life together – of life on the island. Patrick had spoken of the dangers of looking back over our shoulders – he'd said how focussing on the past implied we weren't ready to love again. *Had he not just been reproaching me - but issuing a warning - telling me that he too wasn't ready?*

As I stepped nearer to the dogs, they became restive; Luna gave a soft, low bark. Verena had said it would be immoral to be miserable on the island – but that was before Honor had called and the peace of our paradise had been disrupted.

I cleared my throat, feeling sick, and then Luna barked and wouldn't stop.

Patrick came out to silence her.

'What are you doing?' he asked sharply.

'I needed some air. Could you take me to Marisands? Eve can bring the others later in my car.'

When I went to say goodbye, Ursula and Minette were settled, Verena relaxed and content and as I handed Eve my car keys and thanked Nicholas for his hospitality – I could see my departure would barely cause a ripple on the surface of their enjoyment.

'How often do you have these headaches?' Patrick asked. He sounded tense, his question more a medical enquiry than an expression of personal concern.

'Not often since I came to the island, they started a few years ago, when there was a lot going on...'

He made no comment and started the car.

The woods were eerie in the twilight. We passed the beech tree I'd marked to show the way to the well and I stared at the narrow path, as if I might see a vision, a flash of white light, a ghostly figure - the White Virgin of Thrifswell.

Patrick drove carefully, but every curve of the road, every movement of the car, increased the nausea I felt and I only just made it to the house, where I bolted into the cloakroom. When I could stop being sick, I cleaned my teeth, fetched my pills and took two with a glass of water. I lifted my mother's black glass rosary from the wall and bunched it in my fist, hidden in my cardigan pocket.

Patrick had made tea for us and carried it into the living room.

'Has something upset you?' I asked, thinking he might tell me about the phone call, explain what had happened.

He ran his hands though his hair as he did when he was worried. 'No doubt you heard what I said...'

'I did my best not to...'

'Look - I'm sorry – but I'm going to Kenya sooner than I thought - it's what I feel I have to do. Something's come up – it affects Honor and several people I know out there.'

'And that takes precedence over everything?'

Patrick sat leaning forwards, his hands dangling loosely between his knees - the colour had drained from his face as if he'd been punched in the stomach.

'I know I'm hurting you, Iris, and I'm sorry. Circumstances change...'

Disjointed thoughts swum into my brain, Nicholas's words *don't hurt my brother* flowed through my mind – now he was hurting me.

'When people are in trouble, how can you not have compassion?' he said.

'You can't - but I've been waiting for something which would bind me here on the island, make me feel I couldn't possibly exist anywhere else...'

'Surely a sense of belonging comes from inside?'

'Not from friendship or love?' I asked. He'd said he wanted no meaningless declarations, no trading of endearments – *if I said I loved him, would he believe me, would it change anything?*

'I could have gone to see Honor without telling you...' he said.

'Perhaps that would have been better.'

'It wouldn't,' he said glancing up, 'you said you wanted us to be honest.'

'At least we've had the opportunity to say goodbye.'

He looked hard at me then, his hair ruffled by his hands. 'Iris – let's not do this, let's not part like this when we don't have to. Could you make it to James's place? We can talk tomorrow.'

'If it's what you want...' I said petulantly.

'It hardly matters what I want,' he snapped, 'I'm needed in Safford Bridge in an hour and a half and I have to get off the island while the tide's out...'

I threw a few clothes and my toothbrush into a holdall and left a note in the kitchen for Eve and Minette - I didn't want Minette upset when she came back and found I wasn't there.

Our drive to Aspen Terrace was overshadowed by my mood of hopelessness, as if our efforts to mend the differences between us were doomed to failure. The confidence I had felt in Patrick seemed to have drained away - I was full of doubts - as if a little demon was perched on my shoulder whispering mistrust into my ear.

I had depended on his transparency. I'd suffered since returning to the island, among people who communicated from behind a veil of nuance or through hints fuelled by anger or words honed to a sharp edge with double meaning. I needed my life with him to be different from life with David, not tainted by subterfuge and suspicion.

When we arrived at James's house, there seemed little to say and Patrick was business like, 'you're exhausted – so am I – let's go to bed and hope nobody calls me.'

We made love and slept for a while – later - I felt him, restless beside me.

Then a call came through at about five o'clock and disturbed us both. Though he slipped out of the room quietly, I heard him shut the front door. When I was sure he had gone, I got out of bed.

Wrapped in my cardigan, I went up to the box room and sat on the floor studying the drawings I'd found hanging there – the drawings of a child which I'd thought could have been made by my mother. I examined them more closely and this time found her signature, tiny and tucked down deep into a corner, almost hidden by the frame, 'J.A.', Juliet Armsted.

I pulled the notebook marked with a 10 from the pile where I'd noticed it before. Inside, I found page after page of drawings of the wild irises in Clave Valley. *Our trysting place...* my mother had written. She had copied out poems besides the drawings and inscribed the initials – J & J - Juliet and James –

Before long, I heard Patrick return, he'd been at the hospital for less than an hour. My heart pounded as I pushed the diary back in its place and went down to see him.

My mind was in turmoil – *what did Patrick know? What hadn't he told me?* James had lived in his family, they'd been like brothers. Was it possible he hadn't noticed what was going on – Patrick, whose observation was deadly accurate and all encompassing? His reserve on the matter of Juliet could only be a deliberate withholding of information – perhaps family loyalty demanded his silence, even on a subject that mattered so much to me...

There was no way I could ask him directly – I'd been snooping about in James's house in an underhand way, as no honourable person should have done.

I reached the foot of the stairs where Patrick was waiting in the hall and he leant forward and kissed my cheek.

'Feeling better? I needn't have woken you,' he said, 'I could have told them all they needed to know on the phone.'

He made toast and tea and we sat in the kitchen together – his eyes shadowed - he seemed deeply preoccupied.

'You have to trust me...' he said at last, 'I hoped our love-making was evidence that you did...'

'I do trust you, in that way...'

'In what ways don't you trust me?'

'I'm not sure you're as free of Honor as you like to think.'

'I have to see Honor is all right - if nothing else - for Ursula's sake. And for Ursula's sake, someone has to talk sense into her mother.'

'But why does it have to be you..?' I asked.

'Because I know her better than anyone - surely you can understand that?' He was becoming angry, his voice strained as he struggled to control himself.

But then, without warning, all the tension and distress I'd ever felt about coming to Devon, about David's leaving, Juliet's death and the things I'd found out about her, flooded out of me like water that had been dammed up and I questioned him without respect or restraint.

'I've asked you about Juliet and you tell me nothing. Why? Why are my mother's things in James's house?'

'I can only tell you what I know - I'll ask James if you like...'

'Just as you asked your father if he would be willing to speak to me?' I shouted.

'The time hasn't been right – Iris – if I broach the subject too soon – it might never happen. What's made you like this? Is it David? The effect of that relationship seems to have been extremely corrosive...'

Before I could say anything in reply, the phone rang.

'Hell and damnation,' he said and went to answer.

While he spoke to the hospital, I buried my face in my hands knowing our conversation was out of control. Though I wanted to, I couldn't stop myself provoking him. I could no longer hold back my fears, my anger with the secrecy and silence, the many things hidden in darkness, the lies and entrenched beliefs based on untruths, which had gathered together and become my enemy.

'I came home to see if you were okay,' he said, 'but I really do have to go this time, it's unavoidable, and I don't know when I'll be back...'

He was rattled, upset – neither of us was thinking straight.

'I'll be staying in London for several weeks,' I said, 'I need to get some distance from this.'

'Then have your distance,' he said curtly. 'Perhaps I'll see you if you decide to return to Littern...'

He left and though he had hurt me - I knew I didn't ever want to see that look of pain on Patrick's face again. My mother's rosary was coiled round my fingers - I lifted the smooth glass beads, touching them to my lips in a form of prayer - and wept for the frailty of human love – for the truth that I'd sacrificed the person who mattered most to me on the altar of suspicion and mistrust.

After a long while, I showered, dressed and phoned Marisands – Patrick hadn't come back and I had no way of getting to Littern unless I asked Eve to fetch me.

'What's wrong?' she kept saying, when she picked me up.

But all I could tell her was that I had made a terrible mistake - certain that the grief of parting from Patrick would endure forever – the painful legacy of two people who should have loved, who should have found their meaning in one another and had failed.

# THE FLOW

## Chapter 36

I heard no more from Patrick and didn't expect to. I had wanted our relationship to be distinct from the disappointments I'd suffered with David and he with Honor – marked by the quiet, patient love of which I believed we were both capable. I regretted not having found the courage to tell him what was in my heart.

Restless, distressed, I was unsure how to continue when each day seemed a void. I was grateful to Verena for staying at Marisands and being willing to make the journey to London with us. I'd kept Minette home from school for a week, but as soon as I had completed Laurence's work we made preparations to leave the island.

I'd been receiving letters and phone calls from Lesley Sleeman asking and then begging me to take part in David's reading. "There's a gaping hole in my programme where your name should be," she said, and feeling I had nothing to lose, I'd agreed to meet David to discuss it.

Wondering which poems I might choose and what I might say, I sat for hours brooding over *Blue Rhythms* and reaching no conclusions, until in the end, I packed all David's volumes of poetry into the car, with the box of notes I brought from Hurst Row and had never read.

The day of our departure brought a soft, bright summer's morning - dawn spread its flush of pink across the sky, making the landscape warm and hazy. In the garden, the late cherries shook the last of their white blossom in the breeze, as sunshine filtered through their leaves. In the distance, the sea broke on the shore with a rhythm as gentle as breathing.

Minette was up early and came to my room, dressed in a pale pink sweater-top and jeans - her hair brushed and tied back in a pony tail.

'Why are you frowning?' she asked, furrowing her brows in imitation of mine. 'Can I go straight to school and not to Wren House...*please*?'

'Flora's looking forward to seeing you...'

'But Yuuka's looking forward to seeing me too...' Minette protested, 'she's had to wait ages.'

I held out my arms to her, often she liked a cuddle in the morning, but she was annoyed with me and turned on her heel, leaving the room, slamming the door. I heard her ask Eve if she could go with her when

444

she took Quirk down to the cove, but Eve must have said no, as when I went downstairs, Minette was playing outside, her ball thump-thumping as she bounced it against the house wall.

Eve had opted to stay at Marisands until David's wedding. I wrote a long list of things for her to do including arranging care for Quirk and the cats and asking Geraldine not to make use of the studio while we were away. We had both e-mailed Zoë and eventually she had replied in a brief staccato message, "Sorry - don't believe in love or marriage – not coming."

All other concerns had been laid aside – I hadn't found out what had happened to Kelda on the day I'd seen her collapse in Safford Bridge – I'd given no further thought to questions about Juliet - those worries, like most other things, could wait for my return.

At Wren House, the drive was resplendent with yellow daisies and Madonna lilies, as it had been each summer for as long as I could remember. Minette ran to the door and rang the bell, eager for the visit to be over as soon as possible.

Flora was in the dining room by the open French windows, dozing peacefully. On the table beside her she had a little brass bell to summon Mrs. Stuart. When she woke, she talked to Minette about St. Catherine's and how Alice had once been a teacher there and Minette listened respectfully to her reminiscences, though she had heard them many times before.

Eventually, she started to fidget and I sent her into the garden to cut a posy of sweet peas for Sister Gabriel. I chatted to Flora about the garden, but she seemed vague and asked instead how things were going at Marisands, listening attentively as I described the changes I had made in the house and the places on the island I had visited.

'I should very much like to go there again,' she said wistfully.

'Perhaps you will...' I told her, though I didn't think now, when my year on Littern was over, I would stay. Instead, I might rent a cottage in Narescombe or Fernley - it would make life less complicated when Minette started at St. Mary's school not to be constantly worried about the tides.

Minette picked not a posy but an enormous bunch of sweet peas and Mrs. Stuart took the flowers to the kitchen and wrapped them in damp newspaper.

Hearing Flora's comment about Marisands, Minette said, 'I'm going to the island again and my friend, Yuuka, is coming to stay for the whole summer...'

I shot her a warning look - I'd been preparing her for the possibility that her ideas of how things *should* work might not be matched by reality. Minette scowled and took her book out under the willow tree, where she lay on her tummy on the grass reading, to pass the time until I was ready to leave.

Flora agreed we could sit in the garden for lunch. I noticed as we talked, I needed to speak to her two or three times before she responded.

When I carried our plates to the kitchen, Mrs. Stuart told me, 'Flora doesn't say much - some days I can barely get a squeak out of her.' She must have been observing my efforts to engage Flora in conversation.

She stood over the kitchen sink washing up our lunch things, her plump arms immersed up to the elbows in bubbles. Her powdery face, harshly framed by her black hair, appeared unnaturally white – she was keen that we discuss Flora's future. Her determination not to be moved to The Maples had resulted in the collapse of another house sale.

'Flora isn't quite as she should be,' I said. I was wondering how we could break the impasse on the problem of Wren House.

Mrs. Stuart nodded, her cheeks wobbling. 'When the latest people offered to purchase, she became *very* strange – naughty like a little child - making herself sick - the doctor wanted to send her for tests.'

Flora, I knew, would be upset by the fuss of having tests and a stranger was unlikely to be able to disentangle her normal state of mind, with its wanderings and sudden leaps of understanding, from what might be signs of an illness.

'She rallied when she knew you were coming, she enjoys your letters and calls,' Mrs. Stuart said. I could sense the approach of a sentence beginning with "but"...

'*But* at my age, I can't nurse someone who can do nothing for themselves. Flora's gone downhill so fast I had no choice other than to mention it. During the winter, I thought once or twice pneumonia might carry her off – and it would have been a blessed release...'

I disagreed - but could see how Flora's demise might provide a "blessed release" for Mrs. Stuart.

'Alice is very happy at The Maples...' she went on, 'she's very well cared for – I told Flora she won't find anything better – it will be just like staying here with me.'

'It was the right thing to say,' I assured her.

Mrs. Stuart's face now had two circles of pink on her powdery cheeks, she was becoming emotional. 'Don't take it to heart - it comes to us all in the end, doesn't it?'

I thought of Edgar Piran, almost ninety, with a mind still razor sharp and wanted to say - it doesn't come to us all - old age brings its afflictions without discrimination.

Outside, I explained to Flora that Minette and I would be leaving for St. Catherine's soon.

'People come and go,' she remarked her eyes misty.

'But I'll be back in time for dinner...'

'I expect I'll forget,' she said and looked up at me with a wavering smile. 'It's painful to lose your memory - you reach for a picture or thought but it slips away...' Her clear grey eyes moved swiftly from side to side, as if she was searching for something that she couldn't find.

In the half hour before we left, with some coaxing, Flora took my arm and we wandered slowly about the garden admiring the beds of summer flowers in pink and lilac and the fruit swelling on the trees. Every few steps, we stopped so she could rest and drink in the sweet scent of the roses, feel the cool, soft petals against her skin.

I described the work that had been done by Kos in the garden at Marisands, how it had begun to resemble the watercolour Juliet had painted, the one which Flora had told me about, before I went to Littern.

'We could sit in the oratory garden together...' she said and I thought, fleetingly, she seemed more lucid. Then whatever was clouding her thoughts descended again, 'I must visit Juliet,' she told me, 'Have you seen her? She seems to have disappeared.'

'Juliet went away,' I said.

Flora became agitated. 'Where did she go?' She tugged her shawl tightly about her chest, 'William won't look after her, you know...' Her voice rose and Minette looked up from her book, watching us anxiously.

Trying to soothe Flora, I said, 'Don't worry - there's nothing to worry about...'

Mrs. Stuart bustled out from the kitchen, 'Flora should rest, she gets worked up and we don't want that, do we?'

She led her back to her chair in the dining room, Flora still talking about Juliet, 'She was never strong - nor was my mother - you may have noticed, I am fragile in my mind...'

Lessons were over for the day when we arrived at St. Catherine's and made our way to Sister Gabriel's office. Refusing help, Minette dragged her blue kit bag across the empty forecourt and clutched her wilting sweet peas in her other hand.

'...Back from the wilds?' Sister Gabriel said. She sat behind her desk - hands folded neatly, her spotless white headdress falling in perfect folds onto the shoulders of her blue habit.

On the wall behind her were the faded prints of paintings by Constable, which had been there since my schooldays and on the warm afternoon, the familiar scent of lavender furniture polish seemed stifling. As we entered the office, I found as usual, I was almost overwhelmed by the obligation to curtsey as I'd had to as a pupil - though St. Catherine's no longer required that particular gesture of respect to the nuns.

'You look very well,' Sister Gabriel said as Minette handed her the flowers, 'you were a pinched-face little girl when you went away.'

She sent Minette to arrange the sweet peas in a glass vase – she hoped a drink of water might revive them. When Minette returned, Sister Gabriel placed the vase beside a pile of school reports, stacked on the desk, menacing in their shiny black folders.

Minette was growing impatient and after a quick hug and a kiss, she went off find Yuuka. She'd brought shells from Littern and souvenirs from Narescombe and was excited about showing them to her friend.

'A successful half-term..?' Sister Gabriel asked.

'It worked quite well...'

'For Minette..? But you feel upset and unsettled?'

The nuns were expert at detecting the merest scintilla of weakness, anxiety or guilt. 'I suppose I am unsettled,' I said, meeting her penetrating gaze.

'Now more than ever, I believe Minette's moving to St. Mary's School will be good for you both,' she said.

'Minette would like Yuuka to spend part of the summer holidays with us? It might help Yuuka to have a place to regard as home, somewhere she can always go to...'

Sister Gabriel's lips tautened into a straight line, her voice became severe,' The school is Yuuka's home, until she leaves – if you would like to take an interest in her future *then,* you'll be free to contact her grandmother. Incidentally, you had no right to ask Verena Plaschy or Rose Sutherland to interfere in school affairs.'

'I didn't ask them...' I said, but she didn't seem to hear.

'Young girls have to learn that they can't do just as they like, we have to be guided by common sense.'

'Not by God or love?' I asked, 'as a member of a community you have the loving support of your Sisters, Yuuka has no family in this country...'

Sister Gabriel stood up, she was tall, an overbearing presence, 'I understand that you want to protect Minette from being hurt, but we can't shelter either our children or ourselves from every vicissitude.'

Knowing Minette would be desolate, outraged, if I told her there was no hope of Yuuka coming to Marisands, I made one last attempt, 'All we're doing is offering to provide a sense of belonging for Yuuka – how can that be harmful?'

'Nothing in life is improved by resorting to sentiment, Iris, the subject is closed.'

*

During the long evenings at Wren House, I read David's poems and filed through the box of notes, hoping for inspiration. Nothing could have brought such a painful reminder of how David had struggled with the arrangement of his work - the many hours he had spent inserting poems first in one section of the book, then in another, moving them back and forth, taking them out of the manuscript and putting them back. Some, like strays, he had corralled into a category on their own only to discover they were strays which needed a proper home.

Among the handwritten scraps, I found roughs of many poems that had been chosen for *Blue Rhythms*. There was a printed page, which had been torn out of a copy of Shakespeare's *The Tempest* and clipped to a sheaf of papers.

David's handwriting was cramped, heavy and black, awkward from the thick nib of his fountain pen. He had made a few scribbled notes, just phrases – *sea change, transformation, death that isn't death, redemption,* and *consolation.* I'd studied *The Tempest* at school and remembered the storm in the opening scene, the shipwreck and drowning, which had turned out not to be real. In Shakespeare, as in life, things weren't always what they seemed.

A poem I hadn't seen before had become lodged among the layers of David's papers. Entitled *Laocoon* – its theme was the tragedy of an unjustified death following an act of heroism. Laocoon, a priest of Neptune, had tried to expose the trick of the "Trojan horse" - attacking it with his spear - but as a punishment had been killed by sea serpents sent by the gods.

I followed David's thoughts, tracing patterns, hearing the song-like qualities of the poem, with its refrain and incantatory rhythm. There were several versions of *Laocoon*; in one, I particularly liked the closing lines:

*As the sea remains faithful to the earth,*

449

*I have remained faithful to death,*
*Bone-white, destined to sleep,*
*Wreathed in a blue-green shroud...*

It seemed the poem was one David had intended to languish unseen – its theme would remain in the background. His notes were cryptic and my understanding tentative, but I began to consider using *Laocoon* for the reading, with its themes of mistrusted visions and fatal illusions - it would have a universal appeal for any audience.

With the poems, tattered and covered in coffee stains was an illustration of the famous statue of Laocoon and his sons. David had written on the back:

*I may not have long to live – how should I respond? Bear it alone or begin to say my farewells? I sense that already I wear a death mask and people fear me and the questions I pose by remaining alive-*

*How do I relinquish all I have to do? Can I relinquish love for my family – can I open my hand and let them fall from my grasp?*

*I take refuge in a new love, I suffer guilt. Yet, guilt carries its burdens of remorse more lightly than love bears its regrets – I find the regrets of love too heavy to bear...*

I brushed tears from my eyes as I read his words. They must have been written at the time when he had first become ill. He'd described the uncomfortable place he had reached, poised between his love for his family and for Helen – and more profoundly between life and death. His fear was raw and honest. It had sprung from his heart, a reminder of how the many strands of love can never be disentangled, of how the belief that love can be severed with one final blow was a falsehood - the truth was more subtle and more poignant.

\*

*The Fox and Hounds,* a country hotel, was where David and I had arranged to meet. Close to Leitchly, it stood in a long, leafy lane by a shallow brook. Crowds of people sat outside under a vine covered pergola, enjoying the warm, bright day. Among them stood John, as we met, he gave me a peremptory peck on the cheek.

'Mother's waiting inside with David,' he said.

'I thought it was nice enough to sit out.' I didn't mean to be contentious, but I was feeling nervous, more so because I hadn't expected David to bring his entire family.

'Mother never feels warm these days,' John said.

I followed him into the dim interior of the Hotel, where Barbara sat waiting in the foyer with David – there was no sign of Helen. Barbara

450

said nothing to me, as we made our way towards the dining room, but clutched onto John's arm as she limped along in the same bronze patent "going out" shoes she'd worn for years. Walking slowly in front of them, David stared into the distance, avoiding the need to meet my gaze.

As we were shown to our table, John said quietly, 'David has to be careful these days - he doesn't need stress or excitement.'

It was perhaps an explanation of his presence and Barbara's. And I felt David had changed, his blonde hair had turned the unhealthy grey of damp straw, his shoulders were stooped like an old man's and he seemed short of breath after a few steps.

'David had been doing very well...' Barbara said.

I tried and failed to catch David's eye, but he seemed not to care if people discussed his health in front of him, as if he wasn't there.

'I was pleased to hear *Blue Rhythms* is being published,' I said, hoping he would speak to me on the subject of his work – wasn't that why we were here?

David looked as if my effort to smooth things over had made matters worse and didn't comment.

'It was no surprise to me, it was published,' Barbara said filling the silence, 'I always told David he would finish it. I'm sure the book will be very successful, David's writing has gone from strength to strength since he's been with Helen.'

Barbara held up her family's successes as if they were personal triumphs – but her speech seemed to wake David up and as if he had suddenly remembered his daughters, he asked after Eve, Minette and Zoë.

I described Minette's new school. In my handbag, I had photographs Eve had taken of her latest work – her paintings of the sea.

Barbara opened the envelope painfully slowly, 'How pretty,' she said after a cursory look, 'so much better than those dull things she used to paint.'

'I'll tell her how much you liked them,' I said and passed the prints to John and then David, who flicked through the images rapidly before handing them back to me.

'Eve feels she's been inspired by the island,' I said.

'But I don't suppose you'll stay in Devon much longer - you must have taken enough time, by now, to find yourself?' Barbara sneered. She paused while the waiter brought our first course to the table. 'Shouldn't you be in London if you're going to find steady work? Surely, when you've finished sorting out that house you're not going to be idle?'

I wondered how she thought I would survive, if I chose to be idle – David gave no financial support, but Barbara's belief that she was the ultimate authority on any subject was so strong that few – including me - dared to contradict her.

'Minette told David you'd met someone,' she said - her eyes dark with disapproval.

I wished Minette had kept quiet, but she was only a child. 'If she meant the Pirans, they're family friends from the island,' I said.

'I thought your family didn't have any friends on the island.' John said and laughed at his own joke.

'I knew Patrick when I was a child.'

Barbara wasn't listening, 'We'd all like companionship, though I *never* thought of another man after Ted died,' she said.

I took a sip of wine, tempted to gulp down as much as I could swallow even at the risk of making a spectacle of myself. Barbara seemed – conveniently - to have forgotten that David had left me for Helen, that unlike her and her faithful husband, Ted, I had endured years of inconstancy.

'I'm pleased if Iris has found someone to make her happy,' John said.

'You're nothing of the sort,' Barbara objected. She laid down her soup spoon as if to swallow another mouthful would choke her. 'I suppose I'll never see my granddaughters now.'

'Minette got carried away, she doesn't understand, she made something out of nothing,' I told her.

Barbara left the rest of her soup and nibbled at scraps of bread, she reminded me of a goat the way her jaw moved from side to side.

When the waiter cleared away our bowls, she said, 'I don't seem to be hungry,' but when our next course arrived, she picked up her knife and fork and made a valiant effort.

Unwilling to let go of the subject, she asked, 'What does he do, this man?'

'He's a doctor – he's been working on various aid projects overseas,' I explained, assuming Barbara would lose interest immediately, rather than refuelling for another attack.

'Everyone seems obsessed with AIDS these days,' she said, 'Does he have children?'

'A daughter... And he does sometimes work with people with AIDS,' I added, to cover her mistake.

'He has no inconvenient wife to stand in your way?'

452

It was such an odd phrase, that in my overwrought state I was hard pressed not to laugh. 'He didn't marry, so no wife, inconvenient or otherwise.'

'I suppose that makes it all right then,' Barbara said and began to tuck into her Dover Sole.

The smell of Barbara's fish and the way she ate it blunted my appetite - I'd been more worried about this meeting than I'd realised and peacemaking with David seemed just as far away as when we had lived together.

Eager to avoid any more uncomfortable silences, I said, 'Perhaps you remember the concert pianist, Kathleen Forbes – now Piran - Patrick is one of her sons.'

'Then probably Antony Piran, the conductor is also a relation?' John said, trying to help me out, 'and isn't Nicholas Piran a wildlife photographer?'

'Quite a distinguished family,' Barbara remarked. 'I heard Kathleen Piran play once - I couldn't believe a slip of a girl could make such music...'

Perhaps slightly drunk both from the wine and my apparent success at making the conversation flow, I mentioned James Millford. Barbara had seen him on the television in various Shakespearian roles and offered her appraisal of his performance, which was as acerbic as the most vitriolic of theatre critics.

'Eve's agreed to come to the wedding,' John said, changing the subject, though to something scarcely less charged.

'That's right, she'll look after Minette.'

'The problem – as usual – is Zoë,' Barbara remarked. 'You've been far too lax with that girl - your tolerance of her bad behaviour has ruined her.'

'Young people can't help their age or their temperament,' I said, but then my reserve began to slip. 'Lesley has been worse than useless as a mother and David hasn't been much better as a father. If Eve wasn't such a caring person, she'd want nothing to do with the wedding...'

The easiest thing would have been to walk out of the hotel then and go back to Wren House. My outburst made the atmosphere edgy and the remainder of the meal was interminable - coffee dragged on forever. I willed John to take his mother back to Leitchly - though I pitied him - his life must be circumscribed since David and Helen had been living together.

Unable to read his mood, I was no longer sure if David wanted to see me alone or whether this would be it – a pointless confrontation that had got us nowhere.

453

But then, at last, Barbara expressed the wish to go home. She walked away, leaning heavily on John's arm and left us at the table. John tooted his car horn as he passed the window of the hotel. I waved at him and turned to David.

'Sorry about that,' he said, 'my mother's weekly dinner out with her sons – it was a mistake, trying to slay two birds with one stone.'

It was an unfortunate image. 'How are you..?' I asked.

'My health hasn't improved...' David paused while he signalled to the waiter to bring more wine. '...but I've been slowly killing myself for years - why stop now?'

The obvious answer was because of Helen and I refused another drink - I'd had far too much already.

'The irony is I used to *want* to die – I only discovered too late, if I had the choice, I'd much prefer to live...'

'Are you very afraid?'

'Almost as afraid as when I needed to tell you about Helen and knew you wouldn't want hear what I had to say...'

'So you sent John as your messenger?'

He raised his hands, 'One of the admirable things about you, Iris, is your sense of honour, but it can make things uncomfortable for the rest of us.'

'You have a new life and I'm trying to be glad for you...'

David laughed dismissively. '...And what a life - Helen's made more improvements to Hurst Row in six months than I made in twenty years.' He smiled at me.

'I wondered why you chose the story of Laocoon as an underlying theme for your writing...'

'*Blue Rhythms* will probably be the last of the poetry,' he said, 'Laocoon's story is the ultimate tragedy - he exposed a falsehood but no-one would believe the truth, he suffered for nothing and had a meaningless death...'

I hoped the David speaking was the man who could write about his torments without dissembling – the David who struggled not to take his despair too seriously.

'My heart's packing up,' he went on, 'to use a cliché - I've become a "ticking time bomb" - despite which Helen wants to be married - it matters to her.'

I had anticipated our meeting being brief, angry, but as David became more amiable with drink, I grasped the opportunity to say sorry for my part in our break-up.

'About Minette,' I began, 'I wanted to explain - though I loved Zoë and Eve, we'd lost Tristan and I longed for a baby of my own – I had hoped now that you could understand...'

As I spoke, my hands were trembling, I didn't want to feel I'd been guilty of the kind of trickery the Armsteds had practiced on William - but David made no reply and his silence was wounding.

'What about your new relationship?' he said at last, 'how's that going?'

'It isn't - I was telling the truth – I suppose it fell through because of my insecurity - "like a bloody disease", wasn't that how you described it?'

David re-filled his glass, he was uneasy, 'If it's really upset you, I'm sorry. But I suppose we're here to discuss my reading – Lesley thought without your input it would be incomplete – it's meant to be a full retrospective of my writing life...'

'You expect so much...' *and give so little in return,* I thought. I was on the verge of changing my mind.

He described the controversies that surrounded *Blue Rhythms.* There had been nasty rumours in the literary world that the work wasn't his and had been subject to "heavy editing", without which it wouldn't have been good enough for publication. Lesley had, he admitted, done a thorough job of assembling the poems and had helped revive his flagging creativity – but he argued - that didn't mean he was incapable of functioning – he'd simply become stuck.

'Verena said it read like an extended suicide note.'

David laughed half-heartedly, 'Lesley put a spin on it,' he said. 'But apparently it's only in the professional sense that I've killed myself. I need someone to speak in my defence...'

'And you're asking me?'

'Because of our long association, your reputation as a translator, Lesley thought coming from you, it might be convincing.'

'What about someone from Halkett & Haire – or a critic – I have no authority.'

'But you have integrity...'

'...Which you'd like me to compromise? To what extent is *Blue Rhythms* yours?' I asked.

'Impossible to say, but when I retire – or die – whichever comes first, I don't want to be remembered both as a bastard and a failure...'

David was such a heart-breaker – such an enchanter, with his mellifluous voice and those blue-green eyes which changed through all the colours of the sea – he was also drunk from the second bottle of wine – now empty in front of him.

'I wondered about reading *Laocoon*,' I said, not mentioning my idea of using his thoughts on death – they were so intensely personal, I was sure he would say no.

'*Laocoon* didn't make it into the collection,' he said.

'But it is genuine – your own work, isn't it?'

He glanced away, his pride hurt.

'Is there some sense in which you identify with Laocoon?'

He looked impatient then, 'I suppose when I was younger I had grandiose ideas. To me the new poetry was as false an invention as that of the Trojan horse and I wanted to expose it for what it was – is that the sort of thing you want me to say?'

'Only if it's the truth...'

'God, Iris, I don't know if it's true. But if you're saying yes to reading – you can do as you please.'

'I will,' I said, 'but this is the very last thing I shall ever do for you.'

# Chapter 37

The Maples was a drive of about forty-five minutes from Dulwich; it had once been a grand house, with its pillared portico and rows of symmetrical sash windows.

From the car park at the end of the long drive I could see the faces of some of the residents peering out of the windows, hoping for a visitor, their eyes fixed on me as I rang the doorbell and waited to be allowed inside.

The interior was decorated like a country house, with chintz curtains and linen covered chairs in dull gold. In the large, airy conservatory I found Alice sitting by the open door, where the scent of roses wafted in on a light breeze. As I leant forward to kiss her cheek, she remarked on the birdsong - she thought there must be as many birds in the garden at The Maples as there were at Wren House – I must be sure to tell Flora.

There was no sign of Alice's friend, Edith Pearson, but four other residents were sitting with her, though apart from one elderly gentleman reading a newspaper, they were asleep, heads back, mouths open. Alice made a striking contrast, upright in the chair, her white hair beautifully combed and neat, her face showing just a touch of powder and a thin veil of pink lipstick – the white collar of her navy dress was crisp and impeccable.

When I asked after her health, she said, 'I'm very well, and so is Edith, we're quite content and I think that may be due to sound sleep and good food. How are you and how are things at Wren House? Mrs. Stuart tells me Flora persists in playing the role of an imaginary invalid. I regret my sister's weaknesses.'

We discussed Flora's reluctance to join her at The Maples, and I suggested she might be happier somewhere near Marisands – I thought there might be a suitable nursing home in Fernley.

'You'll be staying in Devon?' she asked, as if surprised, 'even so, your plan sounds unreasonably complicated. I don't know why Flora has to make such a commotion, even at her advanced age, she never wants to conform.'

One of the helpers appeared, distinguished by her cropped hennaed hair, broad pink face and plump body, curved and indented like a pile of cushions. She began to tell me how Alice was doing and Alice's face wore a long-suffering expression as the woman recounted in minute detail everything she had eaten over the past week.

'What was I saying?' Alice asked loudly.

'We were talking about Flora,' I said, though I knew she hadn't needed reminding. 'Do you miss her?'

'Did you imagine I wouldn't?' Alice's voice was full of reproach. 'I do hope you've managed things properly at Marisands, Iris. I can't think what's happened to Juliet's paintings – Flora has found it all quite distressing.'

My observation was that it was Alice who had been upset by material concerns, if Flora was distressed it was at my failure to discover the truth of what had happened to her daughter.

'I've asked everyone who might know about Juliet's work,' I told her, 'people are tired of my questions. I've tried to persuade them to talk about what happened to her, but the truth remains elusive – always beyond my grasp.'

'But you're convinced now that your mother's death was no accident?'

'If it wasn't an accident, it was suicide and no-one wants to discuss that either.'

'Of course they don't.' Alice said - her words a murmur deep in her throat. She turned her face from me, as if studying the rose beds outside. 'Your father would never have found the courage to tell you what you needed to know....'

I glanced round the conservatory, thinking perhaps we should have gone to Alice's room for privacy, but the gentleman with the newspaper had fallen asleep. A string of dribble hung from the corner of his chin, he emitted a medley of grunting sounds and deep sighs.

'I found letters between you and William - as if some kind of bargain was struck for possession of me as a child – you were determined to persuade my father to give me up, but after all he didn't seem to mind...'

Alice made a tutting noise as if she disapproved of my version of events, 'I did it for your mother, it's what she would have wanted - and for Flora. Flora was out of her mind with grief. She'd lost her daughter, and through you she could in some way have her back. Juliet wanted you brought up as a Roman Catholic, but I explained to Flora it was quite unnecessary - she was already sufficiently enamoured of the Pope, miracles and saints to satisfy anybody...'

'My mother and James Millford were in love.' I said.

Alice's mouth tightened. 'All this talk of love – it's usually no more than an excuse for prurient behaviour. I frequently observed that with Juliet there was a lack of restraint in her manner and in her relationships with men.'

She had taken refuge in moralising. With Alice a question directed *to her* was regarded as a breach of good manners, though she was expert in interrogating others.

'When I was four – Juliet had an operation - an abortion.' I watched her face for signs of surprise or resignation - had she or Flora known what was going on? Juliet would have struggled to raise the money for a private consultation – one of them might have paid for it.

'Your mother's emotions overcame her conscience...' Alice said.

'Who was the father of that child?'

'Really, Iris...'

I explained that I'd opened the wedding chest at Marisands and found Juliet's severed plait and asked, 'Why would Juliet have cut off her own hair?'

Alice didn't hesitate. '...Because she had Flora's tendency to hysteria, just like our mother.'

An image of the mirror portrait depicting a line of frail Armsted women floated into my mind, if Eve painted a new portrait, could she paint in the qualities of faith, strength and courage?

Alice was saying, 'I've never been able to comprehend what goes on in Flora's mind. She says she wants her ashes scattered in Morrow Bay - she wants to be with Juliet. I'm perfectly happy to have my ashes scattered in the garden here – Edith and I have agreed it's quite the most suitable place.'

'I'll try my best to please everyone...' I said.

Alice clasped her hands together tightly, 'I find that a most irritating phrase, it implies a refusal to take responsibility,' her voice rung out so loudly, I turned round to see if she had woken anyone.

The carer appeared at the doorway of the conservatory and sent a warning look in my direction – her sturdy body now appeared less comfortable and more threatening – I imagined her grabbing me by the collar and throwing me out.

'I'm willing to take responsibility for Flora,' I said, 'I'd like to see her happy.'

'What suits everyone else never suits my sister. If you didn't stay at Marisands what would happen then? Flora would be stranded with no-one to visit her. You need to regain a sense of proportion - living on Littern Island can have a debilitating affect on the mind.'

I didn't want an argument - I didn't know what to do about so many things now - if I'd ever had discernment or a sense of proportion - it seemed to have deserted me. We talked about the activities offered by The Maples for its residents, Alice and Edith enjoyed music and talks on local history. Though Edith's arthritis was increasingly crippling, she could see clearly and read to Alice – Verena's assessment had been accurate – Alice was thriving.

The afternoon wore on and in the warmth I struggled to stay awake. Every now and then, Alice's head nodded. I took a cushion from the chair next to her and placed it behind her shoulders, so she wouldn't wake with a stiff neck.

The books in The Maples' small library were mainly by authors I'd never heard of, so I took a copy of *The Times* from the rack.

Alice's life, like Flora's and Silvie's was stretching thin. Soon time would run out for them all and I dreaded the diminished circle of my life, facing the world alone. Reading the paper, I began to regret the way I had breached Alice's private world that afternoon - her soft breathing told me she was fast asleep, but when she woke, I would need to apologise.

I turned to the *Overseas News* section where a short article gave an account of aid workers in Africa being attacked or taken hostage on the Kenyan border. I felt my pulse quicken and as if she had picked up my distress, Alice's eyes shot open and I folded the paper hurriedly with a loud rustling sound.

'Edith usually reads me the news,' Alice said.

I recounted the main headlines, then told her what I'd found – 'someone I know may be out there in Africa,' I said. A lump had formed in my throat and I tried to clear it with a discreet cough.

Alice shrank from me, 'I hope you haven't come here with a cold - you could decimate the population of The Maples with a single sneeze. I once had a friend who was a missionary, she and two of her colleagues were killed by the natives - they showed no gratitude for the selflessness with which they'd been treated...'

It was kinder to assume Alice was unaware of the likely irony of her statement, so I smoothed the newspaper, returning it to its place.

'It's time I went,' I told her.

'Come again if you can,' Alice said, 'perhaps you'll be able to see Edith.'

I kissed her, sorry for my interrogation, for appearing irresponsible, for being a disappointment. But I was sorry too because Alice claimed she had never understood love and that was perhaps the greatest tragedy of all.

*

Flora's routine with its simplicity and orderliness was comforting and I was grateful to Mrs. Stuart for taking care of us in her placid, even-tempered way. She had a key to Wren House and in the morning, before making breakfast for Flora, brought me tea in bed, drawing back the curtains of my room, allowing light to flood in.

'Looks like another lovely day. Not too hot. Flora isn't awake yet...'

Mrs. Stuart enjoyed delivering these state of the nation bulletins and I was always relieved to learn everything was well. But a few days after my visit to Alice, she told me she'd called the doctor. Flora had become muddled, her face was ashen and there was a tinge of blue at her lips.

'Perhaps she's ready to move on...' Mrs. Stuart said.

She believed she might possess the sixth sense, inherited from her Scottish forebears – but her belief seemed to encompass a very earthy kind of mysticism, in which her prophecies suited her own convenience.

I slipped on my dressing gown, thinking I should get up straightaway.

'Take your time,' she said. It was her way of letting me know she preferred not to have me under her feet.

By the time I'd showered, dressed and had my breakfast, Mrs. Stuart had delivered Flora's tray of tea and toast. Flora had taken one bite and asked for a few sips of tea to wash down her pills. While I made my bed, I heard Mrs. Stuart encouraging her to "try to eat some more" or "take another sip" but in a few moments she asked me to remove the tray.

Flora's room was a pale turquoise, the delicate colour of the sea at sunrise. As I went in, she smiled at me, an unsteady smile as touching and as innocent as that of a very young child. When I said good morning, she raised her hand a fraction above the bedcover, as if to wave, and then let it flop down again as if the effort had exhausted her.

Mrs. Stuart arranged Flora's hair, brushing the halo of wispy white curls away from her face in case they bothered her. I opened the window a tiny crack, Flora couldn't bear any draught. I thought, seeing her frailty that morning, it seemed impossible that only a few days ago she'd felt well enough to sit in the garden, wrapped in her shawl. I'd placed her chair near the orange-blossom, where she could enjoy the scent and she'd dozed off, reminding me of a little brown dormouse, sleeping in the sun.

I fetched a bowl of lukewarm water, a flannel and a tablet of lily of the valley soap, Flora's scent. I washed her face and hands very gently and dried them on a soft white towel, her skin was so dry and fragile it seemed it might tear. While I went to empty the bowl in the bathroom, Mrs. Stuart opened the chest of drawers and took out a fresh cotton nightdress for Flora, perfectly ironed and aired.

461

Waiting, perched on the top stair for Flora to change, heaviness fell over me. I pressed my fingers to my temples – the dull ache on the right side of my head had begun to throb. Reluctantly, I took a dose of pills and then, as Mrs. Stuart hadn't called me, went into the garden to pick flowers - the creamy *Peace* roses were covered in blooms.

Enjoying the warmth of a sunny day, I cut roses, with alchemilla and ivy and then sat on the wall by the pond, where there was shade from the willow tree. Bees hummed, burying their heads in the foxgloves that had seeded themselves in the herb bed, butterflies, mainly cabbage whites, had settled on a purple buddleia, their wings flashing in the clear, gold light.

No one would suspect Flora of genius or vision - but the garden remained a work of art - the lawn carved out like an island, in a sea of pinks, lavenders and white phlox, which brought the atmosphere and colours of Marisands to Dulwich. When she left Wren House, the garden would be as much Flora's bequest to the world as the portraits she had painted as a young woman. A tabby cat from one of the neighbouring houses ran across the lawn, a blackbird sang out a warning from the apple tree - Flora thought birds brought messages from the other side and I wondered what it wanted to say to me.

Upstairs, I put the flowers on the dressing table.

Flora said, 'How lovely to have my room filled with perfume.'

Mrs. Stuart watched my every move as I placed the roses in front of the mirror, she had more than once expressed her reservations about flowers in the sickroom.

I held Flora's hand. Her skin was as transparent and as sweet-smelling as a baby's. Her breathing wasn't easy - she struggled to draw in the next lungful of air and then her body juddered with the effort of breathing out.

'Is there anything you need?' I asked, but with Mrs. Stuart standing protectively over her, Flora's whispered answer that she needed nothing was expected.

I pulled her bed jacket more closely round her narrow shoulders, she was shivering.

'Shall I read to you?'

The love of words and of books had been nurtured in me by my mother and by Flora and now she asked me to read from *Morning Prayer*. She seemed clear-headed and murmured the responses without prompting – it seemed one of the ways in which I might accompany her on what Mrs. Stuart referred to as "her journey" - but before I'd finished, she reached out her hand and gently closed the covers of the book.

There was a photograph of my grandfather, Alexander, on the bedside cabinet.

Following my gaze Flora said, 'Alexander broke your mother's heart when he disappeared – and mine.'

'Did you ever know what happened to him?'

'Not for sure, but I loved him anyway.'

'When I went to see Alice, I think I asked too many questions.'

'Alice takes the family history so very personally,' she said and smiled. 'I always think if she and Edith had been born in a different age, they might have been lovers - certainly they were in love, though Alice didn't know it...' She closed her eyes. 'The day your father brought you here, you were so afraid and yet so full of wonder and curiosity - so like your mother.'

Her mind roamed through her life with no apparent logic or chronology. Every word she spoke seemed to exhaust her. I cradled her hands in mine; they felt cool, light and dry and fluttered against my palm like a little bird.

'After your father left you here, you wouldn't take off your coat and you wouldn't speak...'

'...We sat by the fire all day and you read Rudyard Kipling - *The Crab who played with the Sea.*'

'You were my very dear companion.'

'And you were mine.'

'...When Alice came home from work there was no dinner on the table.' Flora's mouth unfolded into a tremulous smile, 'Alice minded those things too much.'

She rested her head against the pillow and her eyelids drooped low over her grey eyes, leaving just a glint of the iris visible. *Was she sleeping?* I saw her chest rise and fall and my own breathing settled back into its natural rhythm.

'Alice doesn't need me at The Maples, she has Edith,' Flora said.

'She misses you.'

She shook her head. 'Are you in love, Iris? You have that feeling about you – as if the whole of you isn't here...'

'It's nothing...'

Flora sighed. '...Love is never "nothing". Would it be one of the Piran boys?'

'You're far too clever for me...'

'Love carves its way through our lives like the sea – it follows no rules and obeys neither justice nor reason...' her words emerged as simple and flowing as a poem.

'Were you really in love with Edgar?' I asked.

463

Flora smiled regretfully, 'So Alice tells me...'

I tucked her hands under the bedclothes; her fingers were white at the tips and cold. Her attention had wandered, so I rested in the blue wicker chair watching as Flora strayed from this world to the next and back again.

I pulled the bedcovers over her, when they slipped, touching her cheek with the back of my hand as I had touched the children's faces when they were unwell. I crept to the window, opened the curtains to let in the sun's warmth and breathed in a draught of fresh air, the room was growing heavy and stale.

'There's an angel in my room,' Flora said, 'a being of light.'

I laughed, 'I'm afraid it's only me, by the window.'

'May I have water?'

I poured a little from the jug on the bedside table and held the glass to Flora's lips, supporting her head with my hand. When she'd had taken enough, I patted her mouth dry with a handkerchief.

From downstairs came the sound of the doorbell's double chime.

'I expect that's the doctor,' I told her.

Mrs. Stuart was on the stairs, talking to Dr. Kelly and Flora shrank back into her pillows.

'May I join the party?' Dr. Kelly asked - his voice was deep and booming. He was a big-built man - white-haired, with a smooth ruddy face - and appeared to be the sort of doctor who was eager to convince his patients that, despite all evidence to the contrary, they would soon be up and well. 'How are you feeling today?'

'I'm not quite at my best,' Flora replied.

He looked from me to Mrs. Stuart, who had taken up her post by the other side of the bed.

'It's difficult,' Flora said, drawing in a quavering breath and releasing it with a sigh.

Dr. Kelly took her pulse and temperature. He put his case on the end of the bed, took out his stethoscope and listened to her chest, then took her blood pressure before asking how she was eating and drinking. When Mrs. Stuart answered, he nodded, taking in the information, an expression of amusement passing fleetingly across his face.

'Thank you so much.' He made it sound as if Flora had performed a great service by permitting him to examine her.

'I'll see you out,' I said, 'thank you for coming.'

When we reached the foot of the stairs he spoke in a low voice. 'Some old ladies can be really rather naughty. Considering her age, I would have to say there's nothing much wrong with your grandmother.'

'Flora isn't dying?'

He laughed out loud and I heard Mrs. Stuart close Flora's bedroom door. 'Has someone been to view the house recently? Isn't this is about not wanting to go to live with her sister? A spell in some nursing homes I could name or the local hospital would almost certainly cure her antipathy – but I can't write that sort of prescription.'

I felt a fool. Only days ago, one of the neighbours had suggested their son look at Wren House to see if it was suitable for his family - he had called round while I was out with David.

Dr. Kelly squeezed my arm as if to soften the impact of his news. 'The best thing for your grandmother would be to stop the mollycoddling,' he said, 'I thought Mrs. Stuart knew better, but Flora has *you* completely hoodwinked.'

I closed the front door behind him. When I returned to Flora's room, she was talking happily to Mrs. Stuart. 'Juliet should never have left the island. If she hadn't met that dreadful man, William Muys...' she was saying.

'There, there now,' Mrs. Stuart soothed her, 'never mind - shall Iris read to you again?'

# Chapter 38

In the days leading up to David's wedding, my headache became so severe I could only crawl from bed to bathroom on my hands and knees. I prayed, bargained with God, feeling I would give anything for the pain to stop, for a miracle to clear my vision, which had fractured the world into mosaic pieces. Mrs. Stuart was a good nurse, considerate and sympathetic, but I felt guilty adding to her work, despite the suspicion she preferred her charges flat on their backs in bed, where they were less trouble.

As soon as Eve arrived from Littern she took over, helping Mrs. Stuart and dealing with the solicitor – Wren House had a buyer and Alice had been advised to encourage things to proceed - though nothing was to be said to Flora about the likely necessity of her going to The Maples, until it became absolutely necessary.

Minette had asked if Yuuka could go to the wedding with her and remarkably both the school and David had agreed - Eve arrived back from St. Catherine's with the two girls, heads together, chatting earnestly. David had sent a message to say if I wanted to attend the reception, I could take anyone I liked. So I'd phoned Verena and she'd offered to drive me to Leitchly and transport everyone home to Wren House in the evening.

Yuuka was smart in her summer school uniform, and Minette wanted to wear the same, not the fussy cream concoction Helen had chosen for her, which had arrived at Wren House by courier. The dress didn't suit her – she carried a little puppy fat round her middle and the full skirted style with a wide blue sash did, as she claimed, make her look like a pudding,

'It's only for a couple of hours,' I coaxed and promised she could take clothes to change into after the wedding ceremony.

Minette ran through her repertoire of sulks – she pulled faces and scowled, she pouted and burst into tears, while Yuuka watched astonished by her behaviour. When my patience ran out, Eve took Minette to her bedroom, dabbed perfume on her wrists, brushed on a little make up and put up her hair in an adult style, with the result Minette agreed to wear the dress until precisely three o'clock – at which point she threatened to strip naked if she hadn't been permitted to change into her ordinary clothes.

When the taxi arrived to take them to the registrar's office in Guildford, I waved them off from the road. Eve was wearing a simple dress in sea-green. I'd lent her a cream straw hat that had belonged to Flora and a silver brooch – she looked lovely. As soon as they'd gone, I changed into a navy slip dress and cardigan. The expensive blue dress I'd bought in Safford Bridge, I would keep for David's reading; my aim at his wedding reception was to melt into the background.

Dosed with as many pills as I dared take, I sat in my favourite place by the willow tree and waited for Verena, trailing my hand in the pond, while around me the scent of roses and sweet peas filled the air. I could hear the hum of the vacuum from inside the house – Mrs. Stuart kept the house spotless, but was spring cleaning now, as it would soon have a new owner.

I'd invited Verena to lunch at Wren House; I was anxious not to arrive at Leitchly too soon. 'You look as if you need to lie down,' was Verena's greeting, 'perhaps when this is over you should go away for a few days.'

'I'm not in a holiday mood,' I said.

'Post-relationship blues or a bad case of PMT..?'

'I've missed my period...'

'Which coupled with bad headaches and irritability can be a symptom of the menopause – or even pregnancy,' she added.

I stared across the garden, not wanting her to see she had upset me.

'Just a thought... Why don't we take Minette and Yuuka out for a treat soon – to Seaholme, perhaps..?'

'I'm going to Esterlea to see Silvie – come with the girls, if you'd like...'

'I might,' Verena said lazily.

I asked, 'Sister Gabriel allowed Yuuka out - have you and Rose been working magic?'

'We've found a way of applying some gentle pressure – a scandal the school wanted to suppress – I can't say more...'

I recounted Dr. Kelly's embarrassing visit to Flora. Since then, I had spoken to Mrs. Stuart and insisted Flora get up in the mornings. Mostly she sat in the garden and dreamed – she had always favoured the summer flowers, the ethereal pinks, blues and whites, the colours of childhood, of the seaside, which captured the place she loved most, Littern Island.

'I can see why Flora doesn't want change,' Verena said, 'I've always loved this house.'

'But if change has to come, she might prefer to return to Devon rather than face the prospect of The Maples...' There were so many conflicting interests – I needed more wisdom than I possessed to sort them out.

The sounds of David's party could be heard on the village street. John led the way through Barbara's house into the back garden, where Helen was standing on the patio, tall and elegant in a pale gold suit and the fascinator she had bought in Safford Bridge, with its short dark veil. She was talking to her business partner, and a gathering of David's relatives. David was nowhere to be seen and something about Helen suggested that she would always remain essentially alone. She was someone who appeared to have few doubts, who rarely entertained uncertainty - and yet her susceptibility touched me in a way that was unwelcome – spoilt pretentious Helen, who would allow all this ceremony on her behalf simply to wash over her, as if it was no more than she deserved.

John poured us each a glass of champagne then said, 'I'd better get back to Mother.'

We joined Eve, Minette and Yuuka, away from the rest of the crowd, in a corner of the garden where the girls could play. Minette was still in her bridesmaid's dress, though any perfection was now marred by dirt and grass stains. She and Yuuka were chasing round a circular bed of a flowering annuals, as multi-coloured and as gaudy as a circus ring.

John had encouraged us to help ourselves from the buffet, which was set out on tables in the dining room. The room had been decorated with yellow-green lilies and the scent was overpowering in the oppressive heat.

'How was the wedding..?' Verena asked Eve.

'Tense...' Eve said. 'John was best man, but he obviously doesn't like Helen, Barbara on the other hand, seems to think Helen is God's answer to her prayers. Meanwhile, Dad's been flirting all afternoon with Helen's friends and I'm trying to keep away from Lesley – she's drunk too much already.'

While Verena was shepherding Minette and Yuuka away from the garden pond, I took Eve's arm.

'Lesley seems to have forgotten Zoë ever existed and she's ignoring me - Dad's so unreliable...' she said.

'Perhaps I should have come sooner...'

'You're here now, that's more than most people would have done.'

A gust of wind swirled round, fluttering our clothes and Eve put up her hand to save her hat from blowing away. Barbara and John were by the house, handling people with their usual efficiency - all around us was the buzz of chattering and above the background noise, the sound of Verena as she shouted to Minette, 'Please get down from there!'

Minette had climbed onto the stone slabs at the edge of the pond. She and Yuuka had been kneeling so they could part the pondweed with their hands, trying to find fish in the depths of the murky green water, while humming a tune they'd made up to lure them up to the surface.

Yuuka's smooth rosy skin had caught the sun and her dark brown eyes looked at me appealingly- she didn't like to be ticked off.

'Just do as Verena says,' I told them wearily.

I'd spotted David and watched him talking too loudly with a group of women. I was trying not to think *he's just the same, he hasn't changed.* When we'd met for lunch, I'd felt something might have altered – that he'd become aware of the flaws in his usual approach to life. But seeing him working his guests, as he'd done at countless parties at Hurst Row, I pitied Helen and regretted my agreement to defend his cause at the reading. My confidence waned as I considered that my faith in his integrity might be based on nothing more than the unsure foundation of what I preferred to believe and possibly a heap of lies -

'What on earth is Minette doing now?' Verena's voice rose as she shouted, 'She's fallen in, Iris - she's fallen in the pond!'

There was no sign of Minette on the surface of the water, Yuuka wide-eyed, stared at the blank expanse where she had overbalanced and toppled in. I dropped my glass and my handbag on the grass and leapt into the pond, my heart racing until I could feel Minette's body and clutching at the shoulders of her dress - haul her roughly up out of the water and set her on her feet.

Verena gave me her hand as I climbed out, stepping over the edging stones of the pond onto the lawn. Minette was crying and looked a pitiful sight - pondweed was stuck to her hair and face and draped round her ears like long, dangly earrings. As she stood there shamefaced, the cream dress dripped green murky drops of water onto her satin shoes. I saw Barbara bearing down on us - walking rapidly across the lawn, barely needing the two sticks she claimed were indispensible -

I grasped Yuuka's hand and hugged Minette to my side.

'I hope you've learned your lesson,' Barbara said sharply to Minette, 'look at the trouble you've caused with your ridiculous game.' Her glasses glinted in the sunlight.

'Children do these things...' I said, wanting to avoid a scene - Verena could be outspoken and Barbara would make an aggressive opponent.

Barbara was scolding Minette, but glaring at me. I must have made a ridiculous spectacle, standing there soaked up to my thighs, pondweed stuck to my legs - but soon everyone's attention focussed on the trivial details – Barbara wondering if Minette's dress could go to the dry cleaners - Minette concerned she might have crushed a goldfish as she slipped on the floor of the pond.

Eve and Yuuka followed Barbara into the house, Eve pulling Minette behind her as they went to retrieve her dry clothes. I brushed my legs down, but couldn't seem to get rid of the sensation of slimy green water.

'I should have been watching - thank God you were there,' I said to Verena.

Heavy spots of rain began to fall through the sultry air and the party started to break up. People gravitated towards the house and the tingle of electricity heightened the atmosphere as in the distance, lightning flashed out of a slate grey sky.

Lesley must have noticed I was on my own as Verena made her way indoors. She advanced towards me carrying a glass of wine in each hand and there was no way of escaping her. The pallor of her long face was dramatic against the brightness of a salmon coloured linen suit.

'...Need a drink?' she asked.

'No – thanks...'

'All the more for me, then...'

I'd moved away from the pond and was standing by a clump of bright orange crocosmia, a shade not dissimilar to the colour of Lesley's hair, which she now dyed.

'Rather low key wasn't it?' she asked.

'Perhaps appropriate..?'

Lesley took a sip of wine, 'I suppose David's reading will make up for any deficiencies here – and for God's sake - don't look so woebegone, David always was an old tart...'

'Perhaps like all those who prostitute themselves – he would claim it means nothing to him...'

Lesley laughed dismissively. 'Did you know David now *has* to work here at his mother's place? Helen won't tolerate his mess or his moods. She's insisted on this marriage to protect herself, she even asked Barbara if she would give them Hurst Row as a wedding present – she obviously hasn't figured out the extent of the Sayce's avarice.'

'I had the impression David wasn't writing at all now, with all the rumours about *Blue Rhythms*...'

Lesley scoffed, 'who could write anything with Barbara or Helen breathing down their neck? You were good for David's work...'

'But only at first...'

'That's just David - it's what he tells himself. Helen has no appreciation of poetry whereas you had a genuine understanding...'

'Which didn't help me much in the end..?'

She shrugged, 'relationships come and go - we have to find civilised ways of dealing with it. Anyway, the good news is that people are talking about David and the latest controversy adds to that – they've been digging around in the period when he was silent and coming up with some interesting gossip...'

'Do you think *Blue Rhythms* is an extended suicide note?' I asked, quoting Verena.

Lesley smiled. 'The angst ridden poet is still at the forefront of the public mind. David might not be sunk in melancholy or suffering from consumption but there are other ways in which he fits the profile.'

She'd begun to get on my nerves, Eve had been right - she'd had far too much to drink. She planted one of her glasses, now empty, in the nearest flowerbed among a clump of marigolds.

'I approached Eve about the reading...' Lesley said - she must have known the suggestion would annoy me.

'She's not interested...'

'Or as Zoë would have put it, if she bothered to reply, *fuck off?*' Lesley continued talking at me undaunted by my anger. 'David's told me how much he appreciates your agreeing to read.'

'I'm no longer sure when David's telling the truth. Perhaps his life will always be a conundrum – for example, precisely how ill is he..?'

'Not as ill as he likes to make out. But your being there is the only way anyone will ever know what you did for him – what he owes you – what the world of poetry owes you, perhaps.'

I couldn't help laughing - she was exceeding her usual capacity for empty words.

'We need to ensure that when David finally goes out, he goes with a bang not a pathetic little whimper.'

'Does it matter..?'

'I think it will – if not to you, to David's daughters. You can't airbrush twenty years of your life as if it never happened, can you?'

I'd always seen Lesley as an enemy, however civilised our behaviour towards each other – *was she offering me good advice?*

'I don't know if I fell in love with the poetry or the man...' I said.

'Certainly, the poetry was easier to live with...'

It began to rain persistently, so I left her drinking and went looking for Verena, who was in the sitting room conversing with an ancient aunt of David's.

'I'm going to find Eve and the girls - I'd like to go home,' I said.

Verena deposited her coffee cup on the table and made her excuses to the aunt, who was very deaf and couldn't hear what she was saying.

'Are you all right?' she whispered to me.

'I've been talking to Lesley.'

'I couldn't help wondering why Lesley had dyed her hair the same colour as those awful orange flowers.'

I smiled, amused that the same thought had crossed both our minds.

'Minette's had a bath,' Verena told me, and as I led the way upstairs and I could hear a hairdryer being used in Barbara's room.

I fetched a glass of water, swallowed two headache pills and went into David's room to sit on the bed, neatly made and folded down. If David's chaos had once frightened me, the sterility of his room was alarming. There were no books, his pens on the desk in a perfectly straight line, like an exhibit for a museum. On impulse, I began to move things, scattering the pens, opening David's notebook, leaving a few paper clips strewn across the desk, even screwing up blank sheets of paper to throw in the empty bin.

'Don't do that...' Verena objected.

I hadn't heard him come upstairs, but John appeared at the bedroom door.

'What's going on?' he asked and his tone of voice suggested my behaviour was an affront to his sense of propriety. 'I don't think David or Mother would like you being in here.'

'Your mother has done this?' I asked indicating the immaculate room, as if the concept in relation to David was entirely ridiculous.

'She meant to help...' John's face flushed a deep red.

'What do you think, John?' I asked.

John raised his hands in a gesture of defeat, 'Mother feels upset when David's upset – she does her best. I think you should come downstairs.'

'I'm not well - I need a few minutes quiet.'

John left us - his face troubled - no doubt dreading having to account for the situation to his mother.

I lifted a cluster of papers covered in David's writing and fanned them out. Reading a few words, I could see they had none of the energy I had found in *Laocoon* nor in the notes he had written, where his fear had leapt off the page as he explored the idea of his own mortality. There his emotions had been fully expressed – awkwardly - but hauntingly – and at the reading, I wanted to speak those words with trust, to convey the hope that the core of David wasn't irretrievably lost.

I sat on his bed, stroking the smooth cover. *Who was David now? Who was I?* A spectre that walked in her mother's footsteps - a writer reduced to writing other people's words - the woman whom David had abandoned – a woman who no longer knew how to love? If I returned to Littern, would London and David become dreamlike again and life on the island real and vibrant..? I had no faith in it.

I heard Verena speaking to me, 'Iris? We ought to go – Eve's taken Minette and Yuuka downstairs.'

I gazed out of the window as David must do when he was working. The rainstorm had come to nothing and mist had settled over the garden. The lawn was bleached out, the roses burdened with dying blooms – behind the cold grey mist, the trees and bushes appeared as if they had all life sucked out of them.

Only a scattering of people remained – Helen was with Lesley – *what is it with my father and redheads?* Zoë had once said.

'... Summer's gone..?' I asked - my voice breaking.

'Shush...' Verena said as I wept, 'shush, shush...' her words soothing and rhythmical like the waves of the sea breaking gently on the shore.

I walked to the churchyard with Verena. At the time of Tristan's death, I'd been so distraught - so weak - I'd relinquished control to David and his family. Left to them, we had gathered, a small collection of family and friends, in a cold church decorated with winter evergreens and few flowers – it had felt so ponderous, so wrong for a tiny baby. Tristan's grave had been dug in an area newly cleared of trees and shrubs. In the middle of winter, the ground had been raw, and after days of rain, had become a sodden mess, like an infected wound.

Now, we found the churchyard grass un-cut, the afternoon's rain had hardly touched it and the long stems scratched at our bare calves as we made our way through buttercups and dandelions - children's flowers – cool and sappy against sandalled feet.

At the grave, I untied the flowers I'd bought from Flora's garden: gypsophila, pink roses and love-in-a-mist. No-one could have visited since I was last there - the vase was covered with dried black slime.

'Who'll keep Tristan's grave tidy if I can't come?'

'Speak to John, ask him to help,' Verena said.

'If I could take Tristan with me to Littern, I would,' I told her.

I'd brought a jar of water and using a tissue swabbed the stained vase and arranged the fresh flowers in it. Then we sat on the bench beneath the trees.

I said, 'When David and I first met, we could never have imagined the pain we would cause each other, I used to wish someone had given me an instruction book for dealing with depressed poets. We orbited each other, never quite touching the heart of our relationship or its meaning. I feel the same with my life on Littern and with Patrick - whatever my intentions nothing comes to fruition.'

'Did you know fear can cause a drowning person to kill their rescuer?' Verena asked archly.

I understood what she was implying. 'So far, I've only been accused of killing my mother,' I said and shivered as sadness passed over me like a shadow. 'When Eve went to Zethar Creek, she wanted to live simply and do her work, that's my only plan. Maybe what I chose to call love only arose because Patrick had dragged me out of the sea - but rescue isn't a reason for loving, perhaps not always for gratitude - Patrick needs to explore every possibility of doing good, of settling Ursula, that's his nature and nothing will get in the way of his ideals – not his family and certainly not me...'

'Patrick's in his own crucible,' Verena said. 'If I move to Littern Island, will I catch the propensity for melodrama?'

'Almost certainly, it's endemic on the island. But if Patrick had feelings for me, he would tell me so and mean it...'

'Which is precisely why you shouldn't give up - Patrick and David are at opposite ends of the spectrum and I know who I like better...'

I thought the girls might be growing restless, wanting to go home and there was little reason to linger. I crouched down, dropped a kiss onto my fingertips and pressed them deep into the earth, whispering goodbye to Tristan.

William had once spoken of life's many departures. I considered how I had left Patrick without a word and had said nothing to prevent his leaving – yet my farewell to David, which would take place very soon and very publicly, would inevitably be made with far too many words.

*

Minette had broken up from St. Catherine's. At the school prize–giving, Yuuka had been awarded the Service and Sacrifice Medal – as Sister Gabriel had put it – S-S might, in her case, be taken to stand for sugar and spice, the nice things which summed up Yuuka's gentle, caring personality. That evening, I made a permanent gift of my own medal to Minette as she tried valiantly to be pleased for her friend - it was an acknowledgement of her loyalty and compassion towards Yuuka, something she richly deserved.

I'd arranged to take Verena and the girls to Esterlea and we collected Yuuka from school early in the morning. Stripped of notices and posters for the holidays, the school entrance was depressing, furnished with items that had been broken or rejected from the classrooms having outlived their usefulness. The walls were pitted with drawing pin holes and spattered with Blu-tack, like splodges of chewing gum.

The traffic on the road to Esterlea was heavy and the journey slow, it was a sweltering day and the car was stuffy even with the windows open. The girls seemed cheerful - singing songs they made up as we went along, perhaps trying to forget that the pain of separation was hanging over us all. If Yuuka stayed at St. Catherine's, there would be little opportunity for the girls to see each other soon - if she went to Nottingham, perhaps ever.

Esterlea was a smarter, more comfortable version of Narescombe, with the streets of shops giving way to a small harbour full of brightly coloured pleasure boats. Behind the town, the South Downs made a gently undulating backdrop and the sky spread a mantle of pale blue, which with the gold of the upland grasses, reminded me of the plumage of a blue-tit's feathers.

When we reached the shore, the girls ran free - paddling, jumping the waves, holding hands, screaming when a wave soaked their clothes. Yuuka stood transfixed by the sensation of her feet being sucked down into the sand. 'I'm sinking into another world...' she kept saying, 'the world under the sea!'

Verena and I sat on the sea wall eating ice cream. She explained how the school had felt under an obligation with Yuuka, who was supported by an obscure Trust, which placed a high priority on the child's achievements. If she failed academically or didn't show sufficient signs of promise, funding could be withdrawn. Verena had offered to give Yuuka extra coaching if she stayed at St. Catherine's and Sister Gabriel was in the process of discussing the matter with the Trust. I hoped they would draw the right conclusions - all I could see was a child who needed someone to love and care for her – something better than a committee of strangers supervising her welfare.

After lunch, I left Verena and the girls to explore the shops and walked to the edge of town, where Castle Rise was situated in a small suburb of Victorian red-brick houses. We had cut flowers from Flora's garden for Silvie, but Flora had been so generous, I had to cradle the bunch of roses, cosmos and white daisies in my arms like a rather large baby.

At the nursing home, a few of the residents were outside in the sun – some at small tables on the lawn, with trays of tea - others reading or dozing in the warmth. There was no sign of Silvie, so I rang the bell and waited on the doorstep as I had done before.

When the flowers had been whisked away by the nurse, I made my way to Silvie's room at the back of the house and knocked at her door. Silvie was in her wheelchair beside the bookcase, the curtains at the open window billowing in the breeze.

'It's Iris...'

Silvie swivelled her chair to greet me. Her face was gaunt, the sharp bones of her cheeks clearly visible beneath her parchment skin, accentuating the brown-black shadows that ringed her eyes. As she turned, it was evident the fresh, youthful look I'd noticed on my last visit had been wiped out by illness.

'I wondered when you'd come...' She gestured with her hand that I should sit at the desk, where my letters to her lay open, beside a small pile of brown envelopes.

'Wouldn't you like to go outside? It's a beautiful day,' I suggested.

'We'll talk first,' she said.

In the last months, we had been writing to each other less and less and I was afraid there might be bad feeling between us.

'You were very unwell in the spring...' I said.

'Nothing to bother about, sickness passes...' she replied and suggested I should ring the bell for tea.

When I'd first entered the room, I'd noticed that though Bernard's painting of *The Wild Irises* was in its place, Silvie had hung a another watercolour of her own, a portrayal of Thrift Cottage and the oratory garden in spring – the garden without my mother's white statues.

'I really couldn't manage in Thrift Cottage,' she said, 'I had a chair bed and a commode downstairs – Juliet brought me meals, when she remembered – but she was always busy, wandering the island - she spent a lot of time away from home.'

'Was it my father's idea that you should live in the Cottage? That's how I remember things.'

'William was always hostile - he referred to me as "a freak of nature". Juliet did her best, but she was, as Alice pointed out, rather spoiled and caring for an invalid went against her inclination towards pleasure.'

I felt I'd heard enough denigration of my mother, since I'd been on Littern and said, 'I had the impression when she went to Lyncross, Juliet needed a refuge.'

Silvie's expression was one of exasperation. 'I couldn't blame her for keeping away from her husband – but her preference for Lyncross only inflamed the situation. Your parents were alike in their brittleness and their rigidity - but as they couldn't recognise the resemblance themselves - their lives were full of conflict.'

The nurse brought the flowers, arranged in two green metal vases and then returned with tea, sandwiches and a plate of little sponge cakes. I felt ill at ease. Silvie's mood was difficult; the atmosphere of kindness and expansiveness with which she had greeted me previously had been replaced by a caustic resignation, which sapped my energy.

'Flora sends her love and Alice asked to be remembered to you,' I said.

'Alice wrote to me, she hoped if you found Juliet's work, it could be sold as a single collection – she's anxious about paying for The Maples.'

I described how Flora had been stalling the sale of the house with her imaginary illnesses - and the verdict of her doctor.

'How fortunate, only to be indisposed in one's mind,' Silvie said. 'But it might break Alice to be separated from Edith – she's been waiting to be with her lover for over sixty years. She caused quite a scandal at St. Mary's School, you know. Edith was the school secretary and it became clear they had to be separated – my father intervened and she's never quite forgiven him. I think she imagined herself living at Lyncross with Edith, when they retired...'

Silvie fingered my letters on the table in front of her. She had a pair of reading glasses on a cord round her neck - she slipped them onto her nose and read a few lines to herself.

'The flow of information about Juliet dried up...' I said, anticipating her criticism.

'When you fell in love? With whom, Iris..?'

Heat rushed to my cheeks.

'You entered the room today on a wave of sadness – assuming I wouldn't notice - intending to say nothing.'

'There is nothing to say, except that for a while I became friendly with Patrick Piran...'

'And how are the Pirans?' Silvie asked. 'Edgar and Kathleen were exceptionally kind to me. Without their intervention I might never have come to Castle Rise – they were disgusted by William's behaviour.'

'Edgar has his ninetieth birthday, this year...' I said for the sake of conversation, 'Beatrix looks after him – he has Nicholas and his family on the island and Tom living nearby...'

Silvie poured tea into delicate china cups, white, gold and blue, decorated with cherubs. My hands rested on the table, and I studied them intently, just as I had done as a child, when Silvie had embarrassed me with her questions.

'I thought Patrick Piran was a boy with a deep well of understanding – always calm and reasonable. Juliet told me you were close as children.'

'Patrick is calm and reasonable,' I said wearily, 'but I don't seem to be – not in the aftermath of David. I thought Patrick might be hiding things from me...'

Silvie looked thoughtful. 'However it appears now – I believe good is bound to come from all this - in the end...'

I couldn't think of a suitable reply so we talked about Minette changing schools, about Marisands and my efforts to restore order in the house, while Kos reclaimed the garden.

Silvie said, 'Although I grew up at Lyncross, it was always Marisands I loved – the oratory garden with its mystery and romance - and I was an avid admirer of St. Thrif. One day, my father carried me down those perilous steps, so I could see inside the oratory – the patterns made of shells. Can you imagine? He could easily have dropped me...'

Last time I'd visited, Silvie had told me she didn't want to go back to Littern - I wondered now whether she might have changed her mind. Did she miss the island or did it hold too many bad memories?

'Aren't you resentful of how you were treated by Alice and my father..?' I asked.

'And not only by them - but I don't feel resentful...'

'To know all is to forgive all?'

'It's possible to know too much and that also makes forgiveness difficult, sometimes inconceivable. In many ways, I adored my father - he understood that however feeble my body, my mind was untouched. He made sure I had excellent tutors and wonderful books – but there were prejudices which even he couldn't overcome - Alice would never accept my presence in the family - she disliked being expected to care for me.'

'Poor Alice...'

'Don't pity her,' Silvie said. 'She's got what she wanted with Edith – some of us are still waiting. Alice thinks she knows everything, but one day, I may surprise her.'

She seemed to imply there were more secrets, but I preferred not to ask what they might be.

'I've found drawings of Juliet's and the diary I mentioned, the one marked with a 10, they were at James Millford's house.'

'Did you take them?' Silvie asked.

My cheeks coloured at her suggestion, though the thought had crossed my mind at the time, 'I looked at the diary, there were pages of little drawings and paintings of the wild irises - nothing much else – but in a strange way, it confirmed more than anything the truth that Juliet and James were in love.'

Silvie appeared unsurprised. 'Kathleen was afraid that their love was the spur for Antony's decision to go into the church - he'd lost the woman he wanted to a man he considered unworthy and his jealousy almost destroyed him.'

'Juliet came to London to have an abortion – but I'm confused – one version is that William didn't want more children and my mother did it to save her marriage, yet Juliet wrote in her diary that she didn't want his child - she described the baby as an "alien presence". Either way, she despised herself and felt she was being punished later, when her baby was stillborn...'

Silvie's face had become tense, closed. She made no comment and I wondered how much she disapproved of my mother's actions.

'Geraldine Ottley suggested William wasn't the father of all Juliet's children, is it possible she didn't know who the father was? Or that James wanted her to get rid of William's baby or even his own..?'

'Only James would know the answer to that...' she said, 'why don't you ask him?'

She was being impossible. Already, I felt uncomfortable with the appalling intrusions I'd made into people's lives - interrogating strangers about their personal history.

'How could my mother have raised money for an abortion?' I asked. 'No-one had money at Marisands – James was a student. Might Flora have paid?'

'...She might, had she believed in the efficacy of money to solve problems.'

'It could have been Bernard - or Alice. She used Marisands to bribe my father into sending me to Wren House after Juliet died...'

'...Though neither you nor the house was hers to bargain with...'

Silvie poured fresh cups of tea and pushed the untouched plates of sandwiches and cakes towards me.

'I gave the money to your mother,' she said. 'She came to see me, she needed assistance, as we all do sometimes - she appealed to me, woman to woman, so I didn't ask questions, I simply provided a solution...'

As her words sunk in, I felt angry. '...Didn't you realise how destructive that might be – how it might unbalance her? You knew Juliet's temperament - impulsive but given to regrets – deep regrets.'

'It was a mistake, I see that clearly now, but once she'd confided in me she no longer carried her trouble alone. Juliet was under pressure from William and James on the island – from Alice, who insisted Bernard encourage her to deceive her husband by changing the details of her will. She was close to breaking point and came to me for advice. I acted on the wisdom I possessed at the time.'

We fell silent. Sunlight glanced across the table in an arrow shape, the narrow gold rim of the plates and cups glinted. Silvie's photo album had been placed on the bookcase, but there were no framed photographs in the room, not even of Bernard, the father she had loved. Was that significant? Were there too many things Silvie would prefer *not* to remember? Her life had been lived largely within the confines of this one room, the common rooms of Castle Rise and the places in the garden where her wheelchair could go. What wisdom could she have offered my mother about the ways of the world?

'I see you're angry with me - but please - don't renege on your promise to stay at Marisands until the end of the year...'

'If I must stay in Devon, living in Narescombe would make life much easier,' I replied.

Silvie eyed me closely. 'Shall we go outside as you suggested? I think we need a breath of fresh air.'

I found a shawl for her; her thin body scarcely made a mound beneath the blanket that covered her hips and legs. Wheeling her out of the house, I found a place near the fountain, where there was no-one else around and we sat watching water spouting up into the sky from the fish's mouth, fracturing into a thousand crystal pieces. The neat flowerbeds with their box edging were filled with pink Iceland poppies, ghostly with their frosted green leaves.

'I promised your mother I would give you Marisands and Flora agrees. It's a way of making reparation to Juliet and to you. What you choose to do with the house, after I'm gone, is no concern of mine. But I can give you freedom and independence through something that was Juliet's, something she wanted you to have...'

'I'm no longer sure what to think of my mother...' I confided.

'Don't fall into the trap of moralising – don't become like Alice. You need to remember that compassion is far more important than justice. We both love Juliet, isn't that one of the things that binds us together? You may not think it, but I longed for a child, if William hadn't stood in my way, I would have doted on you...'

Her words hardly sank in. I was considering the possibility that Silvie already knew the truths she claimed she wanted me to discover. Perhaps she had good reasons for hiding what she knew- hadn't she implicated herself where Juliet was concerned?

'Iris - who else could I ask to help but you..? I'm hoping one day you'll give an unexpurgated account of deeds of the Armsted family, weave all our stories together.'

I put my hand to my head. I was tired of feeling unwell, tired of the persistent, nauseating headaches and recalled what Alice had once said about the many ways in which Silvie could be demanding.

She leaned forward in her chair, and laid her hand on my arm, 'I'm sorry about your broken love affair, but you have to go back to Marisands for my sake and Flora's – even for your own sake and your children. You said Minette had made a friend and that Eve was happy there?'

I agreed, though Minette would no doubt be cut off from Ursula because Patrick and I had quarrelled.

'Whatever happened, it would be better for you to go back and face it - you gave your word, I believed you to be a person of honour...'

My eyes focussed in the distance, tracing the curving line of the South Downs, their fragile colours of gold and pale blue – the openness they represented was so different from the restrictions of Silvie's life.

'What's wrong, my dear?' she asked and took my hand.

I shook my head unwilling to share my fear, the fear that I was pregnant - my feelings were too confused. I reminded myself that my body might simply be protesting, as it had after David and I had separated – but if that was true, then I experienced deep sorrow - to bear Patrick's child should have been a joyful, beautiful gift, a symbol of our love.

'Something is bothering you,' she said, softly.

I looked straight at her, 'Is it possible William wasn't my father?'

'That's one of many things I'm waiting for you to tell me...' she said sharply.

With a hasty movement, she manoeuvred her wheelchair towards the house, pushing the wheels rapidly with her knotted hands. 'I'm chilled - I have no warmth in my blood these days.' When we reached her room, she said, 'Flora created beauty wherever she went – her paintings, her magnificent gardens – but though she loved Juliet, she was an incompetent mother, especially after Alexander had disappeared. Juliet needed a firm hand – someone to guide her – left to herself, she struggled with problems beyond her maturity and ability to cope...'

'But the truth of what happened to her still lies behind a veil of mistrust and suspicion. Hard as I try - I can't get hold of it and tear it away.'

Silvie sighed. 'You know, Iris, I've always felt I betrayed Juliet by leaving the island. If I'd had the strength and resolve to stay in Thrift

Cottage, things might have been different. And I don't have the comfort of being able to claim ignorance – I understood how things lay...'

I felt some sympathy for her, I said, 'You couldn't have stayed in Thrift Cottage - no-one could expect it of you, the Pirans were right to help you leave.'

'Dear Iris. You know - the breach between the Armsteds and the Pirans should never have happened, I thought you might be the one to mend it...'

'I'm sorry.'

Silvie moved her wheelchair to the desk and I sat with her – just as we'd done earlier in the afternoon. She opened one of the brown envelopes and took out a letter from the family solicitor, and placed it in front of me.

'Flora tried to give you my house,' she said with a smile. 'The deeds are now safe but nothing has changed – on my death, the house will be yours – or even before, if I should so choose.'

I wanted to protest – she didn't need to bribe me with Marisands as the Armsteds had once bribed William. I began to recount the difficulties of living on Littern, but she stopped me.

'Don't say any more, not now. Go back to the island - you must give it another chance...'

'You think I've let you and everyone down,' I said, holding back tears – Silvie seemed to believe she had some greater purpose both in sending me to Littern and keeping me there – to her my personal hurts and disappointments were an irrelevance.

She leaned forward to comfort me, to kiss my cheek, 'Look at me...'

I raised my eyes to see her face, perfectly at peace, beautiful – *was that how she would look in death?* I held my breath at the thought.

'You'll give it another try?' she asked.

Time seemed to stop and the world, which could be disappointing and full of pain, momentarily ceased its endless turning.

I wondered how I might use my anger when I returned to Littern – could I rouse a new determination to uncover the underlying cause of my mother's death? I longed for the peaceful spirit I had seen in Silvie's eyes - without that inner peace - regardless of circumstances - the future would almost certainly be marred by bitterness and regret.

\*

I'd spent far longer than I'd intended with Silvie and when I left Castle Rise hurried back into the centre of Esterlea, where Verena and the girls were waiting in the ice-cream parlour, overlooking the sea

482

front. I apologised, but the delay had only added to the girls' anxiety, Verena was annoyed and there was an unpleasant atmosphere as we faced the end of a demanding day.

On the way back to Dulwich, everyone was subdued. The prospect of separation had become an unwanted guest in the car and Minette and Yuuka sat unspeaking in the back, while Verena and I struggled to make conversation. My thoughts were full of my discussions with Silvie - which I couldn't share - and with the thought of another unwanted parting.

When we arrived at St. Catherine's, Minette carried Yuuka's backpack across the yard for her. I went with them to let the school know Yuuka was safely back.

Then, we stood in the bleak hallway, Yuuka's whole person an image of misery - her shoulders slouched, her eyes brimming.

I hugged her, rocking her and murmuring assurances. 'We'll write and phone – you and Minette will keep in touch - Rose and Verena will visit you here - I hope *very soon* you'll be able visit us on Littern.'

'I shan't ever be happy again,' Yuuka said and Minette dissolved into tears.

'We'll do all we can to make sure you're happy...' I promised and handed out tissues from my bag.

'Say goodbye to Minette, now,' I told her.

But Minette asked if she could take her friend to the dormitory.

Sister Gabriel, I was sure wouldn't approve - but watching them disappearing upstairs - two small girls trying so hard to be brave – I discovered I didn't much care.

# Chapter 39

David's reading was to be hosted by *The English Poetry Group* who had continued, over the years, to meet in the upstairs of Morton's Bookshop. Lesley had entitled the reading *A Retrospective for David Sayce* and it took place at The Frontline Repertory Theatre, in north London, at the beginning of August.

Lesley's voice rang out across the auditorium, 'To complete our programme, we have a reading from David's partner of many years, Iris Armsted...'

I walked from my seat in the front row up the steps and crossed the stage, noticing the low orange lighting, the plain box-like interior of the theatre and the familiar faces, including David's. I felt the flowing movements of my dress against my legs - the dress I'd bought in Safford Bridge, encouraged by Verena - midnight blue with a fine line of silver embroidery circling the deep curve of the neckline - mirroring the swathe of silver hair that grew from the peak of my forehead and wove its way deeply into the long thick braid that fell to my waist, where I'd bound it with a bow of black ribbon.

Stepping into the spotlight, I placed my notes on the lectern and allowed my arms to hang relaxed by my side, my hands lightly touching the curve of my hips. I raised my head and faced the audience.

'There has been much speculation and some misrepresentation of the circumstances of David's life and his writing. David's critics have suggested certain poems, including those in *Blue Rhythms,* might not represent his own work.

'I prefer facts – facts can be reassuring. As is well documented, David has suffered periods of severe depression and as a consequence writer's block - but *Blue Rhythms* is the culmination of many years of work arising from his desire to recreate and enhance his reputation as a writer, not to destroy it. His recent marriage to Helen should dispel any remaining questions regarding the possibility that he might wish to be the cause of his own death.

'Drawing on David's commentary I believe his poems to be about the fear of death, not about death itself. The poem *Laocoon*, which I shall read shortly, exists only in David's original draft, crafted in his own distinctive handwriting and is evidence of his continued creativity.

'Laying doubts aside, frees us to focus on David's heartfelt wish that the community of poets of which he is a longstanding member should reach an unbiased estimate not of him as a man, but of his poetry.

'I was twenty two when I first heard David read his poems and he mesmerised me, as he has mesmerised many of you this evening. He read from *Midnight Shadows,* and tonight, I would like to read a poem from that collection, a poem from *Blue Rhythms* and excerpts from the unfinished work *Laocoon.* The words of that poem demonstrate David's greatest gifts and this reading is my farewell gift to him.'

Pausing to allow people to fidget, cough and rustle their programmes, I waited before beginning the first line. I'd been practising in front of the bedroom mirror at Wren House, speaking slowly and clearly, taking care not to falter, being careful to pick up David's rhythm and reminding myself I was going through this ordeal because however David had hurt me, however he had changed, however diminished his reputation as a writer, he had once been a man who could be inspired.

Clearing my throat, I allowed the words to flow, reading until I came to *Laocoon* which I had learned by heart.

*'The lens through which I see my life*
*Creates a film of blue*
*Concealing love or sensation...*
*Far beneath the surface*
*Where turbulence cannot reach,*
*I am muted, there is silence...'*

As my lips released the words, long rehearsed, my mind drifted in the wake of their images. I inhabited each syllable, each line, and each mark of punctuation, using phrases as stepping stones.

I glanced up from the lectern and imagined how David would deliver the lines, an incantation of hope and despair:

*'As the sea' remains faithful to the earth,*
*I have remained faithful unto death,*
*Bone-white, destined to sleep*
*Wreathed in a blue-green shroud...'*

As I finished, I raised my eyes and the theatre had become a chasm of soundlessness into which I might tumble. I swayed on my feet, like a tree battered in a storm. My hands moved clumsily as I folded my papers. I clutched the pages tightly in my hand, as if they could bear me up - I faced two hundred people and felt the most intense loneliness.

Slowly, applause began, like the spatter of rain on hard ground and rose to a roar. I nodded a wordless acknowledgement and left the stage on feet that felt as heavy as stones. My ears filled with a noise like

485

rushing water. I eased my way down the steps, afraid the sensation would knock me off balance. I saw David watching me. I saw Eve, stand up to allow me back to my seat, caught her startled look, as instead of returning to my place I continued up the aisle, my gaze fixed on the exit, not wanting to see the rows of heads turning towards me in an unspoken question.

Lesley began her closing speech, "I'm sure we would all like to thank Iris for her perceptive and sensitive rendering of David's work, especially the poignant poem, *Laocoon*."

Out in the foyer, I grabbed at the brass handles of the main doors to the theatre, and forced them open, desperate for air. Lesley had arranged an informal get-together in a pub round the corner from the theatre. Drunken literati, the incestuous world of poets and the bitchiness which had broken David – I wanted none of it - I would prefer to go back to Wren House and forget everything.

The coolness of the late evening washed against my face and I realised my handbag and jacket were still tucked under my seat in the auditorium. I had no money for the tube and couldn't walk far in sandals which consisted of a few silver laces strung onto thin leather soles.

I stared at the row of blackened terraced houses across the street as if they might hold an answer, but this was London, no-one would take pity on a woman knocking on their door, begging for money. Clouds billowed in the overcast sky. A damp, chilly wind whipped litter along the pavements and raised goose-bumps on my skin. I returned to the theatre, unsteady on my feet, brushing against tattered posters of past events, rubbing my hands against my arms to warm them, alone in the empty foyer.

Lesley had said if the evening was going well she might "try to get interactive" with the audience, by inviting David back onto the stage. She had meant a session of questions and answers, a discussion of his work. To Lesley, colourful, energetic and charismatic, organising David's reading had been nothing – just part of her job to promote his work. While I gasped for air, she was in her element.

I loitered by the foot of the stairs on which lay a pile of abandoned programmes and wondered how David would survive the interactive session. Before the reading, I'd e-mailed Zoë and asked if she wanted to attend – but she'd replied that she had no wish to be present at what she referred to as "Sleesy's remake of *The Dead Poets Society*," one of her favourite films.

The foyer was drab, old-fashioned, with worn figured wallpaper, red plush, gold trim and dark wood. Behind me were displayed photographs of the cast of the last performance of the summer season at The Frontline Theatre, Shakespeare's *Pericles*. I struggled to remember the lines I'd encountered on the card written and illustrated by my mother – but all I could recall was the implication it was how we lived our lives in relation to others that was important – a stark reminder that in speaking as I had on David's behalf that evening, I might have acted well or equally, have sold my soul to the devil.

I considered how, until I met David, I had allowed my life to be borne with the current, like a leaf floating on a river - a leaf that had lodged in the deep shadows of a bridge and seemed to go nowhere. Our love had been tumultuous - and as I recited his poems, I had wondered - could his life - my life - be led towards a safe conclusion?

The door from the auditorium opened and shut. Eve appeared - her blue-green eyes, dark with concern. She had my bag and jacket slung over her arm and stood looking down on me, striking, with her fawn-like elegance - her short fair hair caught up in an intricate silver band.

'What are you doing?' she asked and settled beside me on the bench.

'I'm cold.'

Eve passed my jacket to me.

'Lesley's working the audience, several people are up on the stage, they were knocked out by your performance – no-one could follow that.'

'I'd like to go back to Dulwich.'

'What about the pub party?'

'You go – go with the others,' I said.

I took my bag, a ridiculously small concoction of navy blue silk, from Eve. As I stood up, the red and gold of the foyer swam into a blur.

Eve steadied me, 'Wait here – I'll ask Verena to take you home...'

I shook my head, 'She'll want to go to the pub...' Verena would want to meet and question everybody - I couldn't drag her away.

'But if I tell her you're unwell...'

'There's really no need - please just look after Minette.' I handed her the car keys, I could go home on the underground.

Eve made her way back into the auditorium. For a few moments, I continued to sit where I was - shivering - my jacket was unlined and had no warmth in it. I took out a small oval mirror from my bag and peering into it was confronted with a chalk white face, eyes ringed with black shadows.

Snapping the mirror closed, I fastened the bag and escaped through the front doors of the theatre. Once down the steps, I hurried along the street, the leather soles of my sandals pattering on the pavement. North of Camden I felt as if I'd entered unmarked territory, but as I'd driven to the theatre, we'd passed a station. If I followed my instincts I was sure I would find it.

For twenty minutes, I wandered the streets before looping back and discovering the station, much closer to the theatre than I had imagined. Inside my bag was a tiny coin purse embroidered with butterflies, borrowed from Minette. I'd pushed fifty pounds into it before leaving home. I bought a ticket and checked the map of the underground - things were beginning to make sense and relief flooded through me as I crossed the booking hall and made for the escalators.

Standing close to the edge of the platform, I stared down at the rails. In the dimly lit station they appeared like two streaks of silvery water in a dirty ditch. For a split second, I experienced both the pull of death and the fear of death – the compulsion to step off the precipice -

There was a rumbling noise in the tunnel and a change in air pressure that signalled the train was coming. As I stepped forward I heard the rapid click clack of high-heeled shoes behind me on the platform and then a hand clasped my arm.

'Iris..! You don't want to do that!'

I swung round to see Verena, angry and troubled, as she hung on to me. People pushed past us, the train doors slid shut and she pulled me away from the draught of the train as it left the station.

'You're frightening everyone – your children, your friends – even David asked what had happened to you.' She clutched my jacket sleeve, 'Couldn't you have stayed for one drink, just for the sake of form?' When I didn't speak she said, 'I suppose not.'

Keeping hold of my wrist, she led me back towards the escalators. She must have run from the theatre searching for me. Her hair had been blown out of place. Her once meticulous suit had become creased; it was as close as Verena came to being dishevelled.

'You were very courageous, speaking out for David,' she said.

'I want to forget everything...'

'Eve said you were feeling faint, did you eat before you came out?'

'Too petrified... I thought I'd catch up at the pub, drink and nibble my way through the evening.'

'I don't suppose Lesley considered how difficult this would be for you,' she said and in her loyalty, Verena made it sound as if my irrational behaviour was entirely Lesley's fault. 'I've parked round the corner – let's go back to the flat.'

'If you promise there'll be no interrogation.'

The escalators cranked their way up to the booking hall and Verena chatted on, making conversation. 'It was a respectable turnout wasn't it?' she said.

I agreed. I couldn't fault Lesley on her research - she had dragged out anyone with the slightest connection to David.

When we were out onto the street I said, 'That stupefied silence after I read - it was unbearable - they must have thought I was lying to save David's reputation.'

She looked at me in disbelief, 'Isn't silence the greatest homage of all..?'

Not long after we'd reached Verena's flat in Marylebone, Rose arrived.

'I'll find some brandy,' Verena suggested.

I was glad to be told I need do nothing, glad to watch Rose pottering about the kitchen making coffee, finding mugs, teaspoons, sugar while Verena climbed onto a kitchen chair, found the brandy and fetched glasses from the sideboard.

We went through to the living room and Rose sat beside me on the sofa, 'Where David's concerned this is closure, isn't it? You've changed and your life will change after tonight. You've paid your respects to what was the best of David, the things you valued in his poetry – even though David found them difficult to live out. Now you have freedom – David's gone from your life – isn't that what you wanted?'

I put my hand to my head – the familiar pain had started in my right temple.

'...Another headache..?' Verena asked, 'Don't you ever think those headaches maybe *your* responsibility?'

'I'm just tired.'

Rose shook my arm as if to wake me up, 'Iris - how can you contemplate living like this? Swallowing pills, always in pain..? Neil's been worried about you – your work's been late and inconsistent – you've upset him, he's always been able to rely on you.'

'Sorry...'

'Is that all you can say?' Rose demanded, obviously exasperated.

'What happened at the station?' Verena asked and this was the interrogation I had dreaded.

'I don't really know – I was light headed - a moment of fugue – suddenly I thought I understood how David must have felt when he was depressed – as if he'd lost his bearings and found himself poised on the edge of an abyss.'

Significant looks passed between Rose and Verena - but there was no point speculating on what they might mean, no point being paranoid.

Rose said, 'You informed two hundred people this evening that you were saying farewell to David – what did you intend, surely not *the end of everything*?'

'Perhaps I intended the *start* of everything – the need to find a new way of living.'

'As long as that *is* what you meant,' Rose said, speaking to me firmly as if I was one of her children. 'I think we should put you to bed, you can go to Wren House in the morning,' she added, confirming the impression.

\*

Eve returned to Littern and I missed her. Rose and Neil offered us a holiday with them in Brittany, Minette would be a companion for Simon. I thought it a good idea, something to take Minette's mind off the situation with Yuuka - but I didn't want to go. Quimper held too many memories of holidays with David and I'd promised to help Mrs. Stuart through the sale of Wren House and to support her with managing Flora.

I delivered Minette to Rose and Neil's house one day after dinner - they would leave for France early the next morning. As I returned to Dulwich, the clock on the tower of the local church struck eleven o'clock. In Rowell Lane, the houses all had their curtains closed and a bright half-moon transformed Wren House into a silhouette, its chimneys outlined sharply against a deep blue sky.

The porch lamp was on and there was a faint glimmer of light at the window of the upstairs landing. I pushed past the clump of shrubs that shielded the front door, catching the sleeve of my cardigan on the holly bush that Flora refused to have cut down. The night air was cool and fresh, so I stood on the doorstep and took a few deep breaths. The family buying the house was anxious to move in August, so they could settle their children at the local school and having now been told her removal to The Maples was imminent, Flora had become unwell again.

Inside, Mrs. Stuart's jacket hung over the banister, her floral shopping bag was on the bottom stair where she always left it. I slipped my feet out of my sandals and padded upstairs past the ranks of bookshelves on the landing and went to the door of Flora's bedroom.

In the soft yellow glow of her nightlight, I could see Flora asleep, lying on her back, her head turned slightly towards the pillows. Beside her, Mrs. Stuart sat on the blue Lloyd Loom chair - she had dozed off and keeled forward so her forehead almost touched her knees.

Flora's breathing was shallow, but I could make out the rise and fall of the honeycomb blanket, which lay loosely draped over her chest. Mrs. Stuart snored, not loudly, more like the rhythmical purring of a cat. If I left her to sleep she would feel dreadful in the morning, if I woke her, she would feel dreadful now. I touched her shoulder lightly.

'Mrs. Stuart?'

She straightened her back slowly and covered her eyes with her hands as if to protect them from the light.

'I nodded off for a moment,' she said, 'I didn't hear you.'

'Is everything all right?' I whispered.

'Flora's been troubled, she kept asking for you.'

'Thanks for staying, we'll be fine now.'

Mrs. Stuart's solid figure swayed down the stairs, comforting and motherly. In the artificial light of the hall, her face appeared pasty, except for two spots of orange rouge on her cheekbones. Zoë, with all the cruelty of youth, had once said she looked like a clown — but then Zoë was blind to her own propensity to dress and make up in ways that others found ridiculous — she had yet to understand the sovereign value of simple kindness.

In the muggy warmth of the kitchen, I drank a glass of water. I couldn't stop yawning, couldn't wait to get into bed and after a cursory wash and a final peek at Flora went to my room, hung up my clothes on the wardrobe door and slid in between the bedcovers in my slip, too tired to change into a nightdress.

I lay with my eyes closed but my thoughts persisted in wandering into the most sensitive places — jangling my nerves and keeping me awake.

Though the house was full of books, I couldn't think of anything I wanted to read. I took one of the pillows and lay it beside me, curling round it, so the bed didn't feel so empty. As a child I had used to pretend my mother had miraculously returned and come to hold me — now I was muddled - was it David's embrace I missed or Patrick's that I longed for?

Next morning, I was woken by Mrs. Stuart's tapping on my door, 'Flora is anxious to speak to you. I've put your tea in her room.'

I borrowed a dressing gown from the wardrobe. Flora put her hand to her forehead as I went to her, as if she was struggling to think of something she couldn't quite remember, 'Perhaps you would leave us,' she said, to Mrs. Stuart.

'You'll go back to Marisands soon...' she murmured her voice so low it was difficult to hear what she was saying. 'Marisands is in a very bad state - a little bird told me...' her mind was jumping from one association to another like a stone skimming the waves. She mustered the energy to speak again and mumbled words that sounded like – "Someone needs to redeem it," but then I thought she had said, 'I'm looking forward to seeing it.'

'I can't hear you,' I said, stroking her face, following the deep lines in her cheek, my hand brushing against the fronds of her hair.

'Please don't go without me,' she said. Her eyes opened wide as she breathed heavily, forcing words up to the surface so I could hear them more clearly, 'I didn't ever want to come here, I was happy on the island. They should have left me alone – I was sure Alexander would come back for me one day.'

Flora fell silent - she'd exhausted herself. Resting my hand on her arm it felt all bone, as if the flesh had melted away.

Minutes passed and then she said, 'I was sorry about you and David, it was so lovely, having a poet in the family...'

I smiled - she'd said the same thing when David and I had moved in together.

Her lips trembled, 'It's never too late - it only takes only a moment to fall in love - did you know that?'

I said then what I'd wanted to say for days, years perhaps, 'I love you - I've loved you since my father brought me here. Thank you so much for everything...'

I kissed her hand, then leant forward and kissed her cheek. Flora was humane, compassionate and capable of a depth of love that was rare – no wonder she could fall in love in a moment.

'Did you buy a new coat for your birthday..?' she asked.

'It doesn't matter how I look on Littern...'

Flora shook her head, 'You promised...'

'Then I'll promise again – perhaps I'll find something in Safford Bridge...'

'Before you leave, would you to sort through my things? It will be far too much for Mrs. Stuart when I go to The Maples,' she said and for a moment she sounded as if she had accepted our plans for her future. Then she sank back into her pillows. 'You will come for me – take me to the island, when you can?'

Careful not to raise her hopes, I said, 'I'll try to find a suitable place, perhaps in Narescombe, and then you could visit the island and we'd see each other often.'

Flora closed her eyes. 'Couldn't I stay at Marisands? Isn't there room there for one very old lady?'

Over the next days I sorted through her possessions. Flora told me I could keep or dispose of anything I chose. As I emptied her wardrobe, the smell of mothballs stole into the room from the terrible old furs, outdated dresses, skirts and blouses which she must have bought in the 1930's and had continued to use. Always small, she had shrunk as she'd aged, until her clothes had swamped her, but she'd remained attached to the faded prints, which had brought out the clear grey of her eyes, to the old woollen skirts and jackets, which she had mended and darned.

I folded Flora's shabbiest clothes into heaps - those unsuitable even for a charity shop would have to go in the bin. The cream straw hat which Eve had borrowed for David's wedding, I tried on, checking my reflection in the mirror and deciding to keep it. I took down cardboard frock boxes from the top of the wardrobe. In one, was the cream lace wedding dress in which Flora had been married and a photograph of her on her wedding day - my grandfather, Alexander, was a soft-faced, gentle looking young man with kind eyes.

In the bottom drawer of the chest were neat piles of hand-knitted sweaters in the soft, sweet-pea colours that Flora favoured. When I lifted them out, protected beneath the pile, I found one of Juliet's notebooks. The aged kid leather suggested it was a partner to the nature notebooks I'd found in the wedding chest.

I examined the first few pages studying the small drawings and watercolours of animals, birds and plants, touched by the tenderness and quietness of the work and the infinite trouble taken by my mother to record accurately what she had seen, both in images and in words.

'I found more like this at Marisands...' I said to Flora.

'Juliet was afraid the book might fall into the wrong hands - she sent it to me for safe keeping.'

'Drawings..? Who could object to that?'

'William – he was jealous in the way that only an unfaithful man can be...'

I hated to bother Flora – the delicacy of her mind meant a mere suggestion could unbalance her – but the urge to know what everyone refused to tell me had grown stronger since I had visited Silvie.

'My mother and James Millford,' I began...

'When your mother died, she was carrying his child...' Flora smiled at me, 'it was so sad - she'd lost one baby and had to get rid of another dear little soul - women did even then - there were ways - when they had no other recourse.'

Flora's words were unambiguous – I touched my hand to my belly. Juliet had been faced with a new life – was it a life she had feared because it would be a sign of her love for the wrong man? Had she

493

stood up to my father on the matter of James? If he'd had lovers - wouldn't she have demanded to know - *why couldn't she?*

I asked if I might keep the book; it was among the most intimate of Juliet's belongings, suggesting that within the timbre of her character there was an ingenuousness which would have been devastated by the impossible choices which had confronted her – choices which could have caused a serious rift in her character and had perhaps led to her death at Morrow Bay.

Flora, resting on her pillows had fallen into a light sleep. I went downstairs, not wanting to disturb her. I picked up the post, made coffee, and went outside, so I could read the mail under the willow tree, by the pond.

We'd had a few wet, blowy days, the leaves on the trees and shrubs were turning yellow and shaken by the breeze had scattered across the lawn. Among the letters, was one from David – his handwriting, clumsy and thickly black – I slit open the envelope – he thanked me for my contribution to the reading and asked if I would be willing to write a review or an article endorsing his work, as I had already publicly defended it.

I walked to the edge of the garden, through the nettle patch to where trees overhung the fence leaving an area of bare earth beneath them, where nothing would grow.

When I left London, I wouldn't see Wren House again. I'd drunk in the details, anxious to imprint them on my memory – the poppies that had seeded by the fence, the golden fronds of the willow tree dipping the tips of its branches into the pond.

Tearing David's letter into pieces, I held up the fragments, releasing them into the wind, watching as they flew away like paper birds.

Raindrops shone and reflected a pale sun – the soil was cold and damp as I crouched down and dug a hollow in the earth with my hands. Into the tiny grave, I put the ring David had given me – the narrow silver ring with its interlocking hearts that had stood for me as a wedding band.

The patch of scuffed ground would soon heal over – cover my memories of the impressionable young girl, who had grown up here and then seemed to have no purpose other than to collide with the life of a poet on the rebound – a man capable of creating the illusion of love - but not of loving me.

# Chapter 40

I returned to Littern on a still, grey day, when the island was quiescent, poised between seasons. The experiences of the summer had left me cut adrift from my old life and uncertain about the new – standing on a threshold, not sure which way to go.

Driving through Narescombe, I caught my first glimpse of the sea and wound down the car window to breathe in the sharp salt air. Turning onto Palk's Reach, the scent of damp earth beneath the trees was clean and fresh, and the tight band of tension, which had gripped my head, since I'd left London, began to ease.

By the edge of the causeway, I pulled the car to a halt. At Whitcroft, there were signs of Geraldine being at home, a light at the downstairs window and a thin trail of smoke rising from the chimney. While I'd been away, the state of the road had worsened and the channel through which the sea flowed at high tide seemed wider, making the island more remote, less a natural extension of the mainland.

I eased the car down into the dip and crossed at a stately pace – revving the engine hard to climb the steep slope on the other side. The lane was dank and dismal beneath the archway of trees. I didn't look forward to the closing-in that would come with the autumn and winter, but had resolved that neither Minette's coming to Littern nor my commitment to Flora to find a suitable nursing home need alter my intention to reconsider my future at the end of the year. Renting a cottage in one of the local villages, would offer a reprieve - there we could get on with our lives, untroubled by the undercurrents which had made an existence on the island challenging and unsatisfactory.

Eve had been sleeping in Marisands while I was away, so the house felt lived-in, welcoming. Quirk gave a rapturous reception – he'd spent a couple of weeks in kennels in Narescombe and hadn't enjoyed the curtailment of his freedom. He was skittish, dancing round as I unpacked my things from the car.

In the absence of Kos, the garden had an unkempt, overblown appearance - Boa and Brio played chase round a cluster of pink hydrangeas and as they tumbled and rolled, the long stems of grass swung wildly scattering seeds onto the ground.

'It's good to have you back...' Eve said.

'How have things been..?' I asked hugging her. 'You didn't mind being here alone?'

'It's been quiet, but I prefer Littern when it's just island people.' She helped carry my bags and suitcase into the house. 'I had a phone call from Zoë, she said something like, "I'm not far away" or "I'm nearer than you think". She asked if you were okay and she hasn't done that since she first left home.'

'Perhaps she's back in the country...'

Eve shrugged, 'She didn't say that – she mentioned she'd been unwell, but when I asked her about it, she hung up.'

Since she'd returned from London, Eve had met no-one and apart from Zoë received calls from no-one except Delia, asking if she had seen Kelda in town or at the soup kitchen – she seemed to have disappeared.

'Sorry about the garden,' Eve said, 'the stall at Lyncross has been empty, so I tried to keep up with Kos's vegetable patch - it took all my spare time with Quirk's demands for endless walks in the cove.'

'Bring back Kos?' I suggested.

Eve pulled a face, 'When Kos left, he was very mad at me.'

'When he spoke to me he mentioned Mike Acworth.'

Eve's face was lit with humour. 'Kos talked a lot of nonsense - my romance with Mike Acworth was all in his head. Mike had ideas – he thought I should live with him in Safford Bridge, but I want to enjoy the island and Thrift Cottage – maybe not forever - but for now. I liked things how they were, casual and friendly but Mike wanted more...'

'Not less than everything?'

'Pretty much, he was a distraction - lust is such an irritant,' she said and laughed.

'And Kos..? You know he's in love with you?'

Eve cheeks turned pink, 'You'd prefer me to be a gypsy like Kos rather than hitched up with someone respectable like Mike?'

'I probably would.'

I sorted quickly through the pile of mail, stacked on the kitchen table – there was a postcard from Minette, enjoying herself in Brittany, but nothing from Patrick or Ursula –

'You and Patrick quarrelled – but you never said why.'

'Patrick had to leave in a hurry and he didn't really say why...'

'The sympathetic sort is the worst,' she said, 'you fall in love with them before you realise they're not just sympathetic to you, but to everyone in the world and expect to be shared...'

'Sounds like bitter experience...'

'More observation,' Eve said, 'but with Dad married to Helen, at least you have room in your life now, maybe Patrick wasn't sure what you wanted.'

'Maybe we met too soon,' I said. 'Maybe after months of Zoë and her interminable silences, I'm weary of negotiating with people who refuse to communicate. Patrick hasn't been in touch and I don't feel it's my place to take the initiative...'

'I like Patrick, I think he's good for you,' Eve objected.

I hadn't meant to snap at her, but I wanted to close the door on something I believed was over - to fight down my absurd, childish wish that Patrick would suddenly appear at the door – to suppress my desire to phone Lyncross and see if he was there.

Eve left me alone at the kitchen table, as if I had disappointed her. Through the window, I watched her make her way through the long grass, Boa and Brio following on her heels as she disappeared through the pergola towards the studio.

Feeling restless, I went upstairs and unpacked my belongings. I had a large box of papers to go in the study. When I had taken Minette to Rose's house, Neil had given me directions for working on another volume of *Minor Lights* – or as Laurence had put it, "a further collection of disarming, hidden treasures". When he'd told me Laurence was also writing another *Kenholme Mystery* I'd offered to undertake both books - apologising for my lateness with the last one – promising to do better. Once Minette was settled at school, I was certain I'd have time to work without interruption.

Flora had given me Juliet's notebook from Wren House and I left it by my chair in the music room, thinking I could turn to it whenever I needed to feel close to my mother. Then I wandered through the garden with Quirk. In the vegetable plot, I could see Eve had been weeding and hoeing – I would need to help her - life would be easier if we were self-sufficient. While she'd had the house to herself, she'd made jams and chutneys from recipes she'd found in the old cookbook she'd been using since she came to Marisands.

I envied her ability to make herself content – I envied the simplicity and optimism that shone through her clear eyes. I thought of her remark, when she had first come to Littern, *Dad always said you had the ability to take something simple and make it complicated* – and knew she was right. Above anything now, I needed the capability to be single-minded in every aspect of my life.

The oratory garden looked tired, the white planting dusty - the petals of the phlox, roses and Shasta daisies were browned at the edges and had lost their freshness. I wandered round, picking off a few dead heads, Quirk ran to the gate by Thrift Cottage, wagging his tail furiously at the prospect of going down to the beach.

I followed him onto the path - concerned he shouldn't run too far ahead as the tide was coming in. When I reached the shore he had found a dead fish. Excited, he shook it and threw it about until the stench of rotting flesh seemed to fill the air. When I could persuade him to let go, I took it from him and buried it deep in the sand and placed a rock over it. Washing my hands in the sea, I shouted to encourage him to roll over in the shallow water and clean the smell from his coat.

Ungainly, he paddled away from the shore, his black fur floating round him like fronds of seaweed. In the distance, beyond the place where the stream flowed out of the woods, a single rider on a white horse trotted along the edge of the water - as elegant as Quirk was clumsy. I knew it was likely to be Nicholas's daughter and felt the pain of severance from her family, even from Nicholas who was edgy and difficult, and who would be furious with me because I had done the unthinkable and hurt his brother.

We retraced our steps and Quirk gave a few soft low barks, but there was no sign of anyone on the footpath or by the oratory. I missed the feeling that Ursula might leap out and startle me or Kos appear to do gardening or to play the piano. Patrick's silence, his absence, had created an emptiness which I feared might distil itself into the aching loneliness I'd felt when I first came to the island. If my only company on Littern was to be my children, the animals – the songbirds, crows and gulls – could I bear it..?

I called Quirk to climb the oratory steps with me - I didn't want bad feeling between myself and Eve to simmer overnight and tapped on the studio door. Quirk lay down on the steps to wait. Eve had made the studio clean, neat and tidy - she'd told me Geraldine hadn't visited Marisands at all in the last weeks and I wondered if she'd been unwell over the summer.

As I opened the door, we both said sorry simultaneously.

'I shouldn't have criticised you,' Eve said, 'but I'd been wondering how long you could manage *not* to mention Patrick.'

'I didn't want him to go away,' I said, 'I'd like him to come back. But Patrick's purposeful - if he wanted to see me or speak to me he'd do so.'

'Change of subject needed..?' Eve said, 'I've been working hard on my paintings. There's a new one of the marshes...'

'Things going better..?' I asked.

'I'm afraid it's not exactly inspired - I might have let the *Marshlands* book influence me too much.'

She set up the painting on the easel and I stood for a long time, studying her work.

'Tell me what you think,' she said.

'The subtleties of light are wonderful.' Eve seemed uninterested in the darker side of beauty, which might have made her work more challenging.

'But..?' she asked, standing behind my shoulder.

'Things grow in darkness - plants under the soil - a child in the womb – creatures in the fecundity of the depths of the sea...'

'It's lifeless and dull?'

'Never that,' I said, her work was competent, pleasing...

'Look at this then...'

Eve had a large canvas propped up on top of the row of cupboards. She pulled away the old sheet she had used to cover it and revealed a long panel mapped from the drawings hidden beneath Juliet's sketches for *The Stations of the Cross*. What was emerging would comprise a section of twelve scenes from the legend of The White Virgin of Thrifswell. I could see now how the figure of the Virgin underlay the peculiarly feminine image of Christ, which Eve had noticed in All Souls.

'I did some research into Silvie's notes and re-read that old pamphlet you keep, *The Legends and History of Littern Island*. A continuous mural, a meditation on the story of St. Thrif and the White Virgin – I'm convinced that's what Juliet originally intended.'

Eve had discovered more detail about St. Thrif, detail beyond the familiar legend. The persistent attempts of her employer's son at seduction had resulted finally in rape and had almost cost her sanity. She had cut off her hair to make herself unattractive to her unwelcome suitor. It was a symbol of her desire to remain pure, her willingness to sacrifice herself to achieve what she believed in – that she was called to life in a convent – life as a solitary. She had fled across the causeway to Littern, pursued by men who had been instructed to kill her, to prevent her disgracing the son of the house with stories of his depraved behaviour. But after her vision of the White Virgin and her healing, she had been installed as an anchoress in the oratory, where she had lived in safety and seclusion and had created a white garden – a Mary Garden - a sign of chastity - planting white hellebores for the relief of mental pain.

'This is glorious – Eve,' I said – admiring the richness of her work. The painting was bursting with life and activity - like a Renaissance fresco, it was full of vitality and eagerness to tell a story. She had given prominence to the little creatures and flowers that formed the background – images Juliet had drawn in the nature notebooks.

'No buts this time?' she asked smiling. 'I'm going to paint the whole series, all twelve of them – I seem to be better at someone else's work than my own.'

'This is yours...' I assured her. 'Juliet only provided the concept - almost accidentally.'

Eve covered the panel. 'While you were away, Delia invited me to Hintham Ridge, there's an arts project they're trying to get underway – when I've finished the panels, I thought I might get involved – it would be a sort of cross between teaching people practical skills and using them as therapy.'

'Would you be interested in that if you were satisfied with your own paintings?' I asked, uneasy at the prospect of Eve becoming bound up with Delia's community.

'I've always wanted to try my hand at pottery – I've been studying the Armsted china you keep in the larder – those vibrant colours. The community has the equipment I need and I can use it for free.'

I smiled at her simplicity and optimism – her hallmark qualities. 'Wait...' I said, 'wait and see.'

'It'll take me months to finish the panels anyway,' she said cheerfully, 'until then I'll only be going to Hintham Ridge every now and then.'

'Did Delia show you the caravans?' I asked.

Eve laughed. 'She told me you hadn't been impressed – anyway, at the moment, I'm perfectly content in Thrift Cottage.'

*

I'd begun sorting Laurence's notes as a prelude to translating his books. One morning, needing a break from disentangling what was important from the excesses of his overblown style - I went to the music room and began looking at Juliet's notebook which I had brought from London.

After a few minutes, I realised what I'd failed to notice before, that the entries about flora and fauna ended after about thirty pages. The book had been turned upside down and written from the end towards the beginning – a series of entries, some dated, some not.

This diary was different from the others in mood. Juliet seemed less concerned about the hurts she had received and more preoccupied with her own inner suffering. The sparks of humour – of spirit – were missing as she considered her life and reflected on her actions, from leaving the island at eighteen years old to the difficult weeks before her death.

She had left Littern and moved to Wren House in the spring of 1958 in the expectation that James would join her in London in the autumn to attend drama school. Almost immediately, he had written to say that he wasn't sure he was ready to leave family life with the Pirans, which had offered him security after the traumatic experiences he had undergone in Kenya.

My mother blamed Antony for James's change of mind, she wrote, *Antony's influence pervades the whole family, he's in love with me and I've always been afraid he would do or say something, which would destroy my relationship with James.*

She made no mention of why she had abandoned her ambition to be a dancer so easily and so suddenly, but described meeting William at the art school. He made a strong and immediate impression, and she implied she had been more open to that impression as she struggled with the reality that James was likely to fail in his promises to her.

Antony had also written - he advised her to give James room to grow - he was too unstable for love or marriage. Juliet reacted heatedly, Antony with his passion for God was unable to understand romantic love – she reminded him how she could have taken advantage – tested him to see if he would relinquish God for her - but she hadn't because she wanted not him, but James.

*There's something about James, who lives by his animal instincts that excites and frightens me. How can my love for James, which feels so right when we're together, tend towards everything that's wrong? He witnessed not only his parents' death, but that of his younger brother and sister and it's left him aggressive, vengeful but also vulnerable – he needs physical comfort – he needs to reproduce himself, as if by doing so he can restore what he has lost in other relationships...*

I wondered if James used Kelda for that purpose. Had he used my mother? Their feelings for each other were powerfully physical – their relationship passed through phases when they tried to contain those feelings – only to find when they met, their desire was instantly reignited.

The diary described Juliet's return to the island after her marriage. James had remained on Littern for the summer and it was obvious her love for him was unaltered so that Lyncross became a place of temptation, excitement and despair as she struggled to be faithful to William. *Where James is weak - I can be strong* - she claimed, but what wasn't clear was James's response - about that she wasn't explicit.

The diary gave more of a series of recollections than a chronological record and contained frustrating gaps. Juliet described how her values had been inverted - *to part from James seems immoral - to be with*

*William seems deceitful. William is self-conscious and mannered about his freedoms, whereas James pursues whatever ends his natural instincts drive him to...*

Finally, despite his reservations about going to London, expressed earlier in the year, when autumn came, James had left the island to attend RADA, abandoning my mother. She had longed for the holidays - which though they brought guilt, also relieved the frustrations of her life with William – as she wrote, it was *a life to which I had knowingly sacrificed myself...*

The final entry referred to the last summer she was alive. Juliet seemed almost maternal - *Despite his betrayals, I will always protect James, he can be so indiscreet, a lovely boastful fool. Like a child he is unable to help himself... Kelda throws herself at him like a young animal in heat - dangerous because she knows too much – knows how to flatter James into confiding, though he's aware of her reputation as a gossip and the possibility that she might do us harm...*

My mother's desire to protect the man she loved offered a small spark of light, as I weighed the uneasy truce between the Juliet I had loved as a child and the negative image of her so often portrayed by others.

Was she really a person who would have been willing to sacrifice not only her own life, but the life of her unborn child - and my life? What kind of love was that? Would such a sacrifice have been possible without the kind of mental breakdown Geraldine and Shirley had hinted at? Though they were hardly impartial observers, their stories in that respect agreed – and self-protection didn't preclude the possibility that their accounts were accurate. St. Thrif had cut off her hair as a symbol of steadfastness and purity – was it possible Juliet had become unhinged and in some way identified with her?

Reading the diary served to remind me that I'd returned from London with the intention of pursuing the truth about my parentage and about Juliet's death with energy and determination. In practice, I'd found the idea of waiting to see what information would come to me preferable to taking action. I wasn't certain I had the courage to speak to Shirley and Geraldine again – to approach Kelda, once more. I was uncomfortable with my failures so far, painfully aware of the truth that I might be holding back because a part of me was afraid to hear what they had to say.

The time I had spent away from the island had accentuated the need to find resolution, but something new had crept in – a craving to be released from my childhood vow to encapsulate my mother's life. The more I learned of Juliet, the more I feared that whatever Flora believed, whatever Silvie said about resisting the temptation to pass judgement, my mother hadn't been innocent - but in some way had made both herself and others a victim of uncontrolled passions.

*

I called Quirk for a run to Lyncross. I thought Beatrix might have set up the vegetable stall and wanted to buy provisions without the effort of going into Narescombe. The weather forecasters had predicted an Indian summer, but walking up Holtleigh Hill, signs of autumn were everywhere, in the tiers of dew laden cobwebs hanging from the bushes and in the layers of mist which wound and curled their way through the sombre trees.

Before I had reached the gate of Lyncross, it was clear that the stall was empty of produce - there was nothing except for the brass bell, weighing down a pile of plastic carrier bags that rustled in the breeze, and the gates to the house were closed.

Quirk tugged on his lead, trying to communicate that he wanted a proper walk, preferably down to the beach at Morrow Bay. But as Beatrix had implied that running the stall was central to her life – I couldn't help wondering if something was wrong.

I unlatched the gate, dragged Quirk up to the front of the house and knocked on the door.

Beatrix answered almost immediately, 'It's you,' she said, without enthusiasm.

'I was hoping to pick up a few things,' I indicated my empty shopping bags, 'Is everything all right?'

'Pa's become quite frail over the summer – with no-one here to help me, all my attention has been directed towards taking care of him.'

'I'm sorry,' I said.

'Are you? You needn't think you can come here and interrogate my father in the way you have Geraldine Ottley.'

'I had no intention of *interrogating*...' I said trying to remain patient.

'That's not what Patrick told me...' she said interrupting, it was as if she had been waiting impatiently for an opportunity to confront me.

'I asked Patrick to approach your father, to see if he was willing...'

'Then take it from me, Pa isn't willing,' she said curtly, 'we hoped when you went to London you wouldn't come back.'

Her rudeness was making me angry, 'Who hoped?' I asked, 'Your father..? Your whole family..? Or was it just you? I hoped when I returned to the island you might realise that we don't need to be enemies...'

In the background, I could hear Edgar calling, '...Beatrix..? You haven't brought my coffee...' he sounded querulous.

'Iris is here,' Beatrix told him, 'she wants vegetables.'

'Then let her in, you're making the house cold,' he grumbled.

I expected Beatrix to see me off, but she suggested I let Quirk loose in the garden and follow her inside.

The atmosphere at Lyncross was so different from when Kathleen had been alive - I couldn't get used to the half-drawn curtains and the slowly ticking clocks – the air of faded gentility. In the drawing room, James's stuffed birds and animals stared out from their cases - it was like entering a long forgotten corner of the Natural History Museum, heavy with morbidity.

Edgar sat in his usual place by the fire, huddled under a tartan blanket, despite the stifling heat of the room. As I went in, he leant his head against the back of the chair, pulling the blanket firmly round him.

There were sounds from the kitchen of Beatrix filling the kettle. Edgar seemed close to nodding off. I waited, standing before Kathleen's portrait. Over the years, the whiteness of her dress had been yellowed by the fire, but still she stood out in sharp contrast to the un-lit background, just as she had been a prominent figure on the island. I sensed she was and always had been the dominant presence in this home and that if the picture could speak - she would have informed me that I wasn't welcome. My mother had written of Antony's influence over the whole family, but that was perhaps only because he had been Kathleen's favourite.

'Some days, I can hardly wait to be reunited with my wife,' Edgar said, 'we were made for one another.'

'Anyone could see it was the perfect marriage...'

'Kathleen spoke and I did her bidding,' he said with a smile.

'She seemed to turn against my mother – and me,' I said.

'The family was her raison d'être. She was a lioness defending her cubs, in the case of your mother, with some justification.'

Beatrix bustled into the drawing room and put an instant coffee on the table beside her father, but offered me nothing and didn't invite me to sit down.

'I'll be in the garden,' Beatrix told him.

Edgar looked for a moment as if he might object to her lapse in good manners.

'It's all right - don't go to any trouble...' I said, expecting a venomous remark in return.

'Tell me what you need...' Beatrix barked.

I mentioned a few things Kos hadn't planted at Marisands, courgettes and squash - we'd used all our own tomatoes – we needed more eggs.

Through the French doors, I watched Beatrix leaning over the hen house collecting eggs, stopping every now and then to straighten up and rub her back. She moved across to the vegetable patch, stooped down and began to fill my bags.

Edgar's eyes were on me, 'Kathleen always grew flowers,' he said, as if to do otherwise was a heresy. 'I hear the garden at Marisands is becoming a jungle again. Sleeping Beauty's garden of briars?'

There was a mischievous glint in his eyes. His mood had improved with the arrival of coffee and two ginger biscuits, which he nibbled, crumbs littering his chest, though he was unconscious of them like a small child.

'Ursula and Patrick - is there news?' I asked.

'They're in London. Patrick hasn't returned from his latest errand of mercy...'

'He's not still in Kenya?' I asked, thinking of the reports I'd read in the paper.

'Actually, I'm not sure I should be discussing my son's whereabouts with you,' he said, removing all hope of finding out which particular errand of mercy Patrick was currently on and why he hadn't come home.

'I'm sorry,' I said, 'I shouldn't have asked.'

'You and Patrick have quarrelled - he won't bother you. He'd never make a nuisance of himself to anyone - especially not to a woman. It's old men who experience the continual urge to interfere...'

'You do nothing but interfere...' Beatrix told him as she came in from the garden.

She stood on the hearthrug - with her mother's portrait as a backdrop - wearing her gumboots, her hands rimed with earth. She had always been in Kathleen's shadow, gauche and perhaps never believing in herself as a woman.

'I need to get on,' she said eyeing me in an unfriendly manner, 'With Patrick away, I have to do everything.'

My shopping bags had been deposited in the hall, by the front door. Taking my purse from my jacket pocket, I paid her.

Then not sure I would be welcome at Lyncross again, I asked, 'When Juliet drowned, what made you tell your mother it was because of me?'

Beatrix's face tautened, but she was ready with a reply, 'I was a plain, awkward child, painfully aware of my shortcomings - my father and my brothers both favoured Juliet - and you – I wanted to make trouble.'

'But Nina knew what you said was untrue?'

'Nina was a little nincompoop...'

'Your words blighted my life...' I said.

And her failure to respond or refute my suggestion - let alone to apologise - was more shocking than her original lie.

# Chapter 41

Eve and I continued to call at Whitcroft to check Geraldine was all right and to leave a meal of soup or stew which she could heat up. Eve had heard Geraldine had been in hospital during the summer and there were rumours that the cottage was going to be knocked down. It had been badly damaged in the last storm - the sea had flooded the property - said now to have been condemned.

The windows at the side of Whitcroft had been boarded up, but a bright light shone from the sitting room into the dull, grey afternoon - Geraldine must be home and working - I knocked and let myself in.

Geraldine's thinness was accentuated by the drab dress she wore; like a long, narrow sack, it fitted her nowhere. The house smelt rank, perhaps not properly cleared and cleaned of flood water. Piles of books, journals and canvases covered the furniture in the hallway and the lower stairs. In the room where she was painting, an unfinished canvas was on the easel, a landscape of the tower, but with the perspective skewed and exaggerated, so it appeared to loom over the viewer in a way that was menacing.

'Eve sent more soup for you ...' I said.

'You can put it in the kitchen.'

The back of the house was unlit – in the gloom I saw the state of her kitchen was much as I had found Marisands the day I'd arrived - food mouldering in discarded dishes gave off a musty smell – cups of coffee, half-drunk, had been abandoned on the mantelpiece, hearth and on the window sill. I left the flask on the table and closed the door behind me.

I wondered how much longer she could manage to live there alone. I remembered the slow diminishment of Alice's sight, how she had coped at first in bright light until the darkness had snuffed out even the vaguely formed shapes she had claimed she could see...

Geraldine said, 'Light or dark, it makes little difference to me now.'

'I heard about the cottage, will you leave?'

'I have no plans to leave.'

'But is it safe..?'

Geraldine ignored me. I watched her painting - the movements of the paintbrush were deft and confident, though often missing the mark. The old canvas bag she had used to carry her things to Marisands had spilled open on the sofa, some of its contents had tumbled onto the floor – I picked up a wooden paint box and a bottle of oil, afraid she might step back and fall.

She lit a cigarette and continued to work, flakes of ash drifting onto her dress, some adhering to the wet paint on the canvas. When her cigarette dropped from her lips, she stamped it out with her boot, not bothering to look down at the burned out hole in the pile of the carpet.

'You're still here - did you want something? Her eyes darted from her painting to my face. 'Have you come to suggest I use the studio again or to waste my time with your endless, ridiculous questions?'

She lit up, flicking her lighter three or four times, struggling to hold the flame steady at the tip of her cigarette.

'I came to see how things are...'

'You can tell how things are – perhaps that gives you some kind of satisfaction?'

I considered going home, but as far as I knew, Geraldine had no family or friends who could help her. I knew of no paintings of hers, before she had begun to work as a hack to support my father – she probably had no resources to fall back on. Though she had done irreparable harm to others, she had sacrificed her life to love, had meant to do good to William - she was suffering and was someone of whom it might be said, she hadn't led much of an existence.

She carried on smoking and painting – occasionally talking - producing a litany of complaints against my mother. Geraldine had been dissatisfied for most of her life. The one thing she had wanted - my father's love - had always eluded her and both in life and death she saw Juliet as standing in her way.

'Why didn't you and my father just go off together?' I asked. As things stood, it might have been better.

'William was damned if James Millford was going to have his wife - God knows why, they were never going to be happy.'

'But after I was born, Juliet had three more pregnancies – would it be reasonable to assume James Millford was the father of her children..?'

'Hardly an assumption...' She said and turned to face me, lighting another cigarette. 'Has it occurred to you that William might not be your father?'

'It's crossed my mind, but the evidence is flimsy...'

'Not if you saw, as I did, Juliet making a target of William in London, at the art school - he was always a fool for a young and beautiful woman...'

'But you don't know for sure,' I insisted, 'they might have fallen in love...'

'Think that if you like. Nothing is sure, except that your mother's innocence has been greatly exaggerated.'

Her words, William's intimations of a loveless marriage, his resentment of Juliet and of the Armsted family all suggested something other than innocence. Yet I couldn't relinquish my longing for something substantial to sweep away the picture I was building of trickery, of adultery with its many lies and clandestine meetings. When James broke faith with her, had Juliet chosen to be disloyal to him with William? If so, her act of self-protection would also have been a terrible self-betrayal.

From William's correspondence with Alice, I'd understood that he'd been deceived by promises of money and property, but if Geraldine's accusations were accurate and my mother had used him to cover her pregnancy by another man, his outrage would be entirely justified and Juliet's actions unquestionably immoral.

'What else would you like to tell me?' I asked challenging her.

I didn't doubt her readiness to strike out, to respond vindictively, she had shown no compunction in tearing down the foundations of my identity, but I couldn't think where else my search might now lead. The Pirans were unwilling to talk, so was Kelda, and in any case, according to Delia, Kelda hadn't been seen for weeks.

Geraldine scowled as she worked, her eyes screwed up in an attempt to see the canvas only inches in front of her nose.

'I can tell you that before the end of the year I shall be totally blind - the fools at the hospital can't say precisely how long – only that there's nothing more they can do. But God knows I prefer isolation to being put out to grass. They can carry me out of here in a box.'

'The house can't be salvaged?' I asked.

'With what..? I have no money. Look at it for God's sake – look at me,' she demanded, 'I devoted myself to William and this is what I got.'

*

There seemed little more I could do for Geraldine except to make sure she was fed and for Eve and I to call in regularly to check she was still alive - but from that afternoon, when we went to leave food, the used containers were put out on the step, but Geraldine refused to answer the door.

I began to make enquiries about finding a place for Flora in a local residential home. I visited a few in Narescombe, all of which I rejected on the basis of the lack of a garden or of residents who were well enough to provide her with suitable company or conversation.

Hartbury Court, in Fernley I had left until last, hoping it might match the high standard set by The Maples. Run by the Sisters of St. Stephen, the plain walls, the colour of sugared almonds, reminded me of St. Catherine's - that and the acres of lavender polished parquet floors. The staff moved about quietly and treated the residents with respect and the rooms were warm, cheerful and comfortable. There was a small chapel on the ground floor and a large, well-tended garden with plenty of benches, where Flora could sit and enjoy the flowers, birds and butterflies, which gave her so much pleasure.

One of the Sisters showed me round - at eighty-six she was too sprightly to be a resident of Hartbury herself – but she answered my questions in a patient, kindly way and I felt confident that if Flora could manage the journey to Devon, this was a place she might call home.

When I left, Flora's name had been added to the extensive waiting list, which was operated not on a first come first served basis, but according to need, as discerned by the nuns.

'Leave it in the hands of God,' I was advised, and could only emphasise Flora's distress at leaving Wren House and my wish that she should be able to end her days with the support of family nearby, in the place which had always meant so much to her.

*

I had yet to find a way of reframing life on the island without Patrick – nothing felt quite right. Eve was spending most of her time in the studio working on the *St. Thrif* paintings and I tried not to disturb her except for taking coffee and food, as I had once done for Geraldine.

Marisands had been meant to be my sanctuary, a cocoon in which I could find protection from the world. Since Patrick and I had parted, I had felt that need more powerfully as I tired of grappling with one emotional crisis only to have another rise in its place - I had wept as I bathed, one morning, and noticed the tell tale cloud of red in the water – proof at last, that I wasn't having Patrick's child.

After two weeks of murky weather, the long promised Indian summer arrived and the gloom and mists that had shrouded the island melted away. On the first fine morning, I packed a picnic of bread and cheese and a flask of tea and set out with Quirk in the car, parking as usual, close to The Retreat. As I passed, I had noticed the vegetable stall at Lyncross was still empty and the wall by Kos's encampment hadn't been taken down, meaning he hadn't returned from his summer travels.

As I took my walking shoes out of the car, two hares bolted across the road towards Hagdon Hills, while Quirk tied to the bumper barked in frustration at being unable to chase such exciting quarry. Before going to the marshes, I wanted to collect spring water for the holy water stoup at Marisands. When I released him, Quirk nosed ahead as we pushed our way along the overgrown path to the clearing surrounding the well.

Thick reeds had grown up round the stone font and had almost overtaken the pool. I called Quirk away from the edge, where he wanted to swim - afraid he might get caught up where I wouldn't be able to reach him. For once he obeyed and leapt up beside me onto the flat boulder overlooking the water. I sat for a few minutes, listening to the birdsong ringing through the trees, while he lay - pink tongue hanging out - moving his head lazily every now and then to chase a fly, wasp or butterfly.

I rested my hand on his back. A heron stood poised on the bank – its feathers so pale it was almost white – in a flash it dived into the pool, before rising into the air, shaking beads of water from its wings as it flew off through the leafy tree tops. I thought of St. Thrif, in terror and panic, had her vision of the White Virgin been nothing more than an illusion - had she placed her trust in nothing more supernatural than a startled bird?

Leaving Quirk to rootle among the undergrowth, I made my way to the basin of the well, filled the bottle I'd brought and then washed my face. Despite my doubts - from habit - I said a brief prayer for the family and asked for clarity of vision.

Retracing my steps along the lane, I turned towards the footpath beneath the tower. In Morrow Bay, the sun made pinpoints of light on the glistening sea – inland, a soft wind rippled the grass and fluttered my hair round my face.

The marshes had a bleached-out loveliness, the azure sky a perfect foil for the pale corn yellow of the grasses and reeds. Above me, oyster catchers swooped and cried - a single swan glided on a long, deep pool of water. The air was humming with insects and overhead flocks of gulls turned through a helix of thermal currents - I envied their gift of flight, their aerial view of the world.

Heading towards the nature reserve, I climbed the sheep-track up to the tower. As I rounded the curve of the hill, I felt the deep isolation of the place. Using a rusty iron post secured in the ground, I tied Quirk's lead and left him - sheltered in the shade of a gorse bush. The tower had been damaged by the summer storm - the ground was strewn with fallen masonry, larger and heavier than the stone which had rolled down and struck me, when I had last been there.

I eased past the door - hoping my thick-soled shoes were sufficient to protect my feet from whatever might lie buried beneath the rubble, as I trod my way towards the foot of the staircase. Using rocks as stepping stones – I managed to jump across onto the lowest stair. Then leant against the wall of the tower to steady myself, as I inched towards the top, making sure no gulls were perched on the ledge of the roof, likely to hurl a missile at me.

The muscles in my legs trembled as I climbed towards the upper floor. Breathless, I clambered out onto the roof and then stood to gaze over the broken parapet, across the marshes and to the dunes towards Morrow Bay. From the tower, the whole of the bay was visible - the black rocks far out in the sea, the edge of the woods where James had once loitered by the line of trees, smoking and talking to Kelda, until she had left him to make her journey to the tower.

A jumble of images was summoned up - William with Kelda deep in conversation - Geraldine and Shirley watching them - and Juliet perhaps distressed, not only by what she had seen inside the tower, but by what was being said – the true meaning of that exchange known only to the people who had gathered here.

The trouble was those images never gave up anything new. Each character persistently undertook the same role they had always played - up until the moment I had been dragged down into the sunless undersea world. I'd taken a risk coming up here – the tower was unsafe - and yet however hard I tried to hear its message, nothing at the tower had spoken to me.

Heart pounding, I edged round the perimeter of the roof always looking out across the island, never down to the earth immediately below. The north side of the tower faced directly over the sea, Morrow Bay and Coyle Sands; the east faced Holtleigh Hill and the south revealed the topography of the marshes sunk in a wide gap, below the Hagdon Hills. I turned west to where Bernard had first spotted the dusky blue irises flowing down the hillsides – but could see nothing except a wall of scrubby trees and undergrowth that looked, as Patrick had told me, impenetrable - a threshold that couldn't be crossed.

There was no shelter on the roof of the tower and exposed to the full heat of the sun my face was burning and my head had begun to ache. I thought momentarily, I heard angry voices, people shouting, but it was only a skein of geese, taking off in the distance.

Afraid of slipping or losing my balance, I bumped my way down the steps on my bottom, relieved when I had reached the floor and could cross the rubble strewn ground out of the tower.

I untied Quirk, but the idea of a walk had palled. I hadn't slept well for days and my brain had gone into rebellion, I saw flickering lights from the corner of my eye, one of my eyelids had set up a persistent tic - my headache was making me feel sick and I needed to go back to Marisands and take my pills.

Quirk dragged behind me, his tail drooping with disappointment as he realised his run on the marshes had been postponed. We reached Osford Lane, where I gave him a drink of water and opened the bag of dog treats I kept as bribes, offering him a few on the palm of my hand. I could see into the garden of The Retreat. Several trees had been felled, leaving the area round the gateway of the house raw and scarred. Then, through the gate beyond the line of sawn-off trunks, I realised the dark blue of Patrick's car was visible at the end of the drive.

I let Quirk into the back of the Peugeot, climbed into the driver's seat, and sat trying to decide whether to drive off or knock at Nicholas Piran's door. Appearing on the doorstep of The Retreat, I could imagine would invite the unsympathetic scrutiny of Nicholas and Patrick, united against me.

The car windows steamed up with dog-breath, my head was still throbbing. Life might seem empty without Patrick, but I had only to think of my mother to suspect I might be better without the many uncertainties of love. Left to myself, I was free to live quietly as I had intended when I came to the island - yet however compelling my thoughts, I couldn't bring myself to move.

There was a low roar and then a whining sound as someone started up a chain- saw. Reflected in the driving mirror, I could see Mars, Hext and Luna playing, circling one of the pillars of the veranda. Quirk pushed his head out of the car window and barked - unlike me he regarded the Piran's dogs as favoured old friends.

Nicholas was working just inside the gate – sharp-eyed - he must have seen me before I could persuade Quirk to shut up. My heart sank as he walked across the area of rough grass at the end of the lane and came towards me.

He leaned his elbow on the open window of the car, explaining he was cutting logs and trimming some of the other trees, before the storms began in earnest in the autumn. I tried not to, but as we spoke, my eyes flicked up to the driving mirror where I could see the reflection of Patrick's car.

'Patrick's in the summerhouse, why don't you leave Quirk with the other dogs and go and see?'

'Because I'm not sure Patrick would want to see me.'

He shrugged. 'Whatever the rest of us think, particularly my sister, I happen to know that Patrick doesn't share our sentiments.'

'He knows where I am,' I said sourly and tried to quieten Quirk, shushing him. I reached for the key in the ignition.

'Don't do that,' Nicholas said.

'Patrick's made no effort to write or speak to me...'

'Then go and ask why.'

Nicholas opened the back door of the car and Quirk jumped out. He whistled to the dogs and all four trooped after him and lay on the path, while he returned to working on the felled trees.

We didn't speak as I made my way across the grass to the summerhouse, glancing down the garden with its vista of perfect lawns, sand dunes and sunlit sea. A single white dove flew out of the dovecot, over the tree-tops towards St. Thrif's Well – reminding me of the story of Noah - of the dove that had returned across the limitless waters bearing an olive branch, which was to become a sign of peace.

At first, Patrick didn't notice me standing in the doorway. He sat with his head in his hands. Seeing the feathers of fine dark hair lying against the soft skin of his neck, I longed to touch him, but didn't dare. The newspaper lay folded on the table in front of him, his glasses and a tumbler of water beside it. Around the summerhouse were signs of the family's occupation, crisp packets and coke bottles – an empty cup had been left on the table -

'Sorry to disturb you,' I said - my voice barely above a whisper, fear taking a tight grip on my stomach as I spoke.

He sat up, startled, and I couldn't read the expression in his eyes. His face was drawn - his skin sallow. He had lost so much weight, his clothes hung loosely on him and I could glimpse the old man he would become, gaunt like his father. None of the Pirans were handsome in a classic way – with Patrick it was the warmth and intensity of his energy which brought him alive, which was the source of his vitality and which was now missing.

'I didn't hear from you,' I said.

'I've been unwell, I only arrived back yesterday - but you can sit down, my malaise isn't contagious between humans - you'd have to encounter the right mosquito...' a flicker of humour played across his face.

I pulled up a chair beside him. 'Is Ursula with you?'

'She's in London with Margaret, who's been very good to us. We had to cut short our trip to the Lakes. I'd been on a bit of a mission and unfortunately, nobody – including me – had checked my jabs were up to date.'

The whine of the chain-saw started again – Nicholas was trimming logs, adding them to a pile he'd made at the side of the house.

'How is Ursula?'

'She had questions which needed answers and she has those answers now, though I'm not sure they've helped. Honor left Ursula in no doubt that she blames me for our break up...'

Seeing his vulnerability, his weakness, I searched for the right words of consolation, but felt inadequate, as insubstantial as the "little shadow" I'd been as a small child. When we'd become friends again in the spring, I'd longed for the Patrick of my childhood – hadn't bargained for a complex man with his own crises of heart and conscience – a man, as Verena had put it, in his own crucible.

'Until I began to get my strength back,' he said, 'I felt I had nothing to offer you or anyone else. I didn't think I should stay at Lyncross - Beatrix couldn't be expected to deal with two invalids. I hope you can understand.'

He was studying me, I had his attention - yet I couldn't gauge his mood or even my own.

'How were things in London..?' he asked.

I described all that had happened – David's marriage – the reading – my visit to Silvie - Flora's strange behaviour - and how difficult it had been for Minette leaving Yuuka. He reached out and took my hand. His thumb explored the place where I'd worn David's ring for so many years that the skin had sunk into a deep channel on my finger.

'David really hurt you,' he said, 'and so have I.'

'And I hurt you - but we both came back...' In his absence, I'd become as diffident as when he had arrived unexpectedly at the door of Marisands.

Patrick didn't reply and I didn't move. I hardly dared breathe as we remained in silence, the sea breeze flowing over us in gentle, cooling waves.

'Perhaps I shouldn't have come,' I said at last. I had perhaps been mistaken, had imagined the powerful feeling of inevitability which had brought me here, the sense that if I didn't take the risk of approaching him, I would regret it for the rest of my life. When he didn't disagree, I asked, 'Would you like me to leave?'

'Would you like to leave?' His eyes were fixed intently on my face, and mine on his trying to detect a glimmer of affection – not daring to expect love.

'I want to understand what changed – to understand what happened between us after Honor's phone call.'

Patrick pushed his hands through his hair in that gesture he used when he was upset or worried.

'Honor had been arrested and I thought she was in danger. Until then, I'd believed I was clear about my feelings, but it seems I wasn't. I needed to see her - to grasp the truth - it isn't that we stop loving, but sometimes we have to accept we can't be with a person because however hard we try, we just don't get on.'

'And now..?'

'Honor's one of the most courageous people I know, but I made a serious mistake, right at the start – confusing a passionate affair with something that could be lasting. It's been humbling, but I realise that having loved Honor doesn't preclude me from loving you.'

'Do you love me? You didn't ever say so...'

'Perhaps I should have done, might it have made a difference?'

'I was upset seeing my mother's things in James's house and not having an explanation. Hearing you speak to Honor, I panicked - it seemed all over between us, as if there was nothing and had been nothing of significance. I didn't know what to do.'

'We were both tired and distracted...'

'...But when you said I should have my distance...'

Patrick smiled. '...I meant it literally – not in anger. I meant if you need distance, have it and I'll wait until you're ready. But then I wasn't sure if you would like me to make contact...'

'You sounded angry...'

'...But not with you – the second call from the hospital reported a serious incident. I was involved because I'd given someone advice which unfortunately they'd ignored...'

'You said you'd noticed a few things at the hospital..?'

'I'd noticed a particular person, but they've gone now and there's no reason not to make a fresh start.' His eyes searched mine as he said, 'If we make a fresh start, will you run away every time I'm in a bad mood?'

'I can't promise not to...'

'Shall we start again?' he asked.

'You mean that literally too? I'll need to know what you want from me.'

'I want things to be clear between us – for us to have commitment - a shared sense of direction - that would pull everything else into place...' Patrick had struck at the truth like a homing device finding its target – we had both been in our own ways undecided, tentative.

'Nothing that happened in London has changed anything here,' I said.

'And nothing that happened in Kenya...'

The newspaper he'd been reading was left open at the *Overseas News* page. He talked about the difficult conditions in which he'd worked, under-staffed and under-resourced and the tension between us began to relax.

He suggested we walk to Coyle Sands. As Quirk seemed content with the other dogs, we left him behind.

The tide was out as we clambered over the rocks at the foot of the pier, hanging onto each other, making our way round to the deserted beach, sheltered by the walls of The Retreat and the mounds of steeply folded dunes.

The sea sparkled, sending out spangles of yellow light - our footsteps were soundless as we crossed the soft white sand to the place we'd sat, the day we had walked to the tower together.

'While I was in London, I'd almost forgotten how lovely the island is, wild and romantic,' I said.

'When I was in hospital, I couldn't wait to get back.'

'I've missed you and Ursula. When I first found Ursula hiding by the oratory, I was lonely - she made a difference, connecting me to life on Littern.'

'Perhaps we should think of everyone like that, making and re-making connections...'

I lay back and closed my eyes against the dazzling sunlight.

'I shouldn't have left you as brutally as I did...' Patrick said, smoothing my hair from my forehead.

'...And I should have waited - realised you're irretrievably tied to this place...' I said turning towards him.

'How long were you sitting outside in the car today?' he asked, his dark eyes shining, his smile giving away the fact he was teasing.

'I don't know.'

'I'd estimate it was over an hour,' he said, 'it was driving Nick mad.'

I laughed. Patrick seemed to prefer a universe with precise laws of time, space and human relationships. 'You'd like to inhabit a world in which you could analyse and divide things up neatly into categories,' I said.

'Would I? How exasperating - you on the other hand like to chase the spirits of the dead and converse with them. You're not the only one who needs to be long-suffering.'

I smiled and said, 'But - I didn't disappear for weeks on a mission to become a saint - and then feel surprised when things went wrong...'

'No-one's trying to become a saint...' he said, 'though it could happen...'

'What will happen now?' I asked, hoping our future could be something new and exciting.

'Have you ever felt terrified, as if you were about to be made intensely happy or devastatingly sad?'

'That's what exactly I feel...'

'How would you choose for our life to unfold?' he asked.

I felt the roughness of his thumb caressing my face and prayed this time we would understand each other – that we could find the understanding on which our happiness seemed to depend.

'We could live out our love on the island, among fragile but unequalled beauty, protected by the sea and sheltered by the hills...'

'But what about the real world?' he asked and kissed me.

I slipped my arms round his neck - needing not to draw on his strength, but to impart my life and strength to him. If we faltered again, there would be no going back - if we couldn't find a way to be content in each other, our lives on Littern Island would of necessity need to be torn up by the roots.

# Chapter 42

Minette returned to the island on a day that was warm and still, the garden overlaid with a pale honey light so that the statues, trees and flowers of the oratory garden appeared tinted gold. Beyond the garden, the whispering sea spoke of tranquillity and Quirk lay stretched out, his belly and chin pressed against the coolness of the grass.

In Safford Bridge, Minette was waiting outside the station manager's office, perched on a metal bench with her blue holdall and suitcases beside her. Her face was solemn, only her eyes giving away a glimmer of anticipation – but she looked well - her holiday in Brittany had done her good.

'You're very late,' she said, bouncing to her feet. 'I've lost five minutes and forty-seven seconds of my life,' she added, checking her new wrist watch.

'I'll try to make it up to you,' I promised.

The traffic in town was sluggish - the last of the summer holidaymakers had yet to make their way home and it was forty minutes, before we reached Narescombe and could speed along the peninsula towards the causeway.

'You did check the tide?' Minette asked.

She seemed much more positive towards Littern and I wondered if Rose had been working on her while they were in France, 'It should be just right,' I said.

The fine grey-blue line of the sea lay well back from the road. I took the crossing carefully, each day more chunks of the surface split away leaving deep potholes and sharp-edged lumps of cement, ruinous to the car's tyres. We bumped our way onto the island.

'If the tide closed behind us now...' Minette said, 'it would be like the Israelites crossing the Red Sea.'

I smiled at her – sympathetic to sense that the sea offered protection from the rest of the world.

In a few minutes, Minette cried out, 'There it is!' as the oak tree by the gate of Marisands came into sight.

I stopped the car to let her run up to the house. Before she'd reached the door, Eve had appeared from the porch with Quirk dancing round her feet and Ursula had leapt out of the tree house and down onto the lawn, her feet landing with a thud on the ground.

Ursula wore a coronet of daisies in her hair - she looked elfin, full of mischief.

'Dad told me Minette would be home,' she said.

Minette wanted to go straight to her bedroom, fold her clothes and put them away neatly in her drawers. Since she'd been boarding at school, she'd become such a tidy child, I'd wondered if it was normal.

'Where's your dad?' I asked Ursula before they disappeared.

Ursula shrugged.

'Tell me the truth,' I said. Ursula seemed to me no longer guileless – her trip to Africa had changed her - yet three nights ago, I'd heard the Pirans out in the woods shouting for her, and knew she must have run away again.

Ursula sighed, 'He's moving our stuff to Aspen Terrace – he drives over there, drops off one load and then comes back to Lyncross to pick up another. Aunt Beatrix hopes he hurries up and finishes because he's upsetting granddad.'

Eve had put the conservatory table outside in the oratory garden so we could have lunch there. In the kitchen were plates of food she'd prepared, set out carefully and covered with clean cloths. She'd acted in innocence, but it was close to the anniversary of Juliet's death and the scene she had created stirred up unhappy memories. That morning, I'd gathered my mother's things together, the black glass rosary and the figure of the White Virgin – I'd read the newspaper cuttings about Juliet's drowning and discovered that, even now, they carried a painful emotional charge.

Ursula interrupted my thoughts, 'May I have lunch with you?

When I agreed, she and Minette pursued Eve into the garden, where Boa and Brio were scrapping on the lawn rolling over one another so that their brindled coats were covered in stalks and seeds.

As always on the island, a sea breeze was blowing, ruffling our hair and clothes, tossing the grass, flowers and leaves. I poured iced lemonade and the girls sipped their drinks, the ice cubes making a soft clicking sound against their glasses. I leant against the honeysuckle hedge and breathed in its sweet perfume, wanting to savour the peace, to dismiss any restive thoughts which insinuated themselves into my mind. Thoughts of that other party, in the garden of Marisands, which had an atmosphere so very different from the good-will I felt around me that afternoon.

Eve had spread the table with a checked cloth and weighted the corners with pebbles just as Juliet used to do.

She carried out piles of plates and cutlery, 'I don't know about anyone else, but I'm starving,' she said.

While she set the table, Minette and Ursula fetched bowls of salad, cold meat, eggs, and fresh bread, Quirk dogging their heels, hoping they would drop something at his feet.

'Everyone's going to Morrow Bay, later, they'll want to see Minette,' Ursula said.

'Please, please let her come...'

Though Ursula and Minette might be quiet when alone, together they could become a pair of impulsive, excitable little demons.

'I could go with the girls,' Eve offered.

'You could bring a picnic later,' Minette suggested, her eyes shining, 'the last picnic of summer.'

When we'd eaten, the girls played - Ursula running about on the grass teasing Quirk with a ball. I wondered how she would react when it was time for them to return to school.

'Don't frown like that...' Eve said, touching my arm.

'Ursula's a worry for Patrick...'

'Perhaps you both need to lighten up...'

She meant to be kind, but things were still awkward. Patrick and I had made slow progress, rebuilding our relationship. His illness had affected him physically and mentally and his health remained tenuous. It was hard not to be anxious, afraid of where the experience might lead him – and us – and impossible for him not to be impatient as he struggled to recuperate.

When I'd helped Eve put the food away, I fetched my notes on the latest *Kenholme Mystery* and returned to the oratory garden to sit on the bench. During a rainy day on holiday in France, Minette had made me a folder, covered in sun-dried flowers – she'd glued more flowers onto a bookmark, to keep my place among the confusing jumble that was Laurence's idea of a list of instructions.

I'd barely begun to unwind the intricacies of Laurence's latest plot, when Patrick appeared - in the soft afternoon light, dressed in layers of holey t-shirts, he appeared especially endearing.

'Eve's taken the girls down to the beach,' I said.

Though the sunlight burnished his hands and face, he looked tired, his posture slack, as if exhaustion had seeped into every fibre of his being. I put the folder down on the grass and slid along the bench to make room for him. He kissed me, a brief tender kiss - after weeks of heartache, our love needed to be warmed back into life.

'I thought you wouldn't mind if I interrupted you...'

'You were right,' I said and smiled at him. 'We had lunch here – it was as if Eve had unconsciously recreated another day from another time – the day of Juliet's death.'

'Perhaps we all unknowingly recreate scenes from the past and déjà vu is like watching the process on a screen - don't you wonder about the nature of time?'

'Not often,' I admitted, 'but it gave me the creeps...'

'As many things do...' he said, teasing.

I leant against his shoulder. Patrick was easy to love - his dark eyes intelligent and perceptive - his character shaped by discipline and understanding. His clarity, the quality which most characterised him, I hoped would mean our future could be uncomplicated - our relationship something that would steal back into our lives, almost unheeded, like the diffident guest of my mother's favourite quote by Arnaud Brisbois.

'Shall we join the others at the beach? Pa and Beatrix will be there. I've been peacemaking – so could you overlook some of the stupid, unkind things they've said and done? Will you do that for me?'

I packed a picnic from the leftovers of lunch as Minette had asked. I could imagine her at Morrow Bay, checking her watch impatiently, counting the minutes, calculating how long she had been made to wait – though I hoped she was playing on the beach, swimming and laughing, able to forget the many painful things she'd recently experienced.

While Patrick loaded the car, I changed into cotton slacks and a tee-shirt, dabbed Juliet's tuberose perfume on my wrists and throat. Before we left, I locked the house, though it was scarcely necessary – in a couple of hours, the tide would have sealed us onto the island - "inhabitants only," as Edgar used to say.

Dust rose from the lane as we drove through the woods to the bay. Nicholas, Beatrix and Edgar were reclining on deckchairs, amid an untidy array of rugs and towels. Ursula and Minette were in the water, floating lazily - Rowena had stretched out on a towel, and was sunbathing, propped on her elbows, half watching them. Near the old quay, Dominic and Benedict kicked a ball around on the sand, so like Patrick and Nicholas as boys, intelligent and active, content within their private world.

As soon as Minette spotted us, she swam with flailing strokes for the shore and ran up the beach with Ursula behind her. She flung herself at me.

'I thought you'd never come, my watch says you've been almost an hour.'

'I suppose I have,' I agreed – the new watch, a holiday gift from Rose and Neil, was waterproof, she'd been testing it in the sea.

'Eve was so fed up of waiting - she went for a walk on the marshes...'

'And Ursula's been beside herself,' Nicholas remarked, '...thank God you're here.'

Ursula grinned knowingly, and skipped out of the way, 'Shall we go back in the sea now?' she asked and took Minette's hand.

Patrick's peacemaking meant no-one took much notice of me. Nicholas was discussing with Edgar the choice of a suitable expert on coastal erosion. He wanted someone who could suggest how things might be improved at The Retreat, without adding an unsightly barricade of rocks and stones that threatened to spoil the appearance of his garden. Their conversation became heated; Edgar thought each storm did such irreversible damage, that the gabions were an inconvenience which might have to be tolerated. If Nicholas wanted his dream life on the island to continue, he would need to be practical -

Rowena was listening to music through earphones, her foot tapping in the air as if she couldn't resist the rhythm - every now and then she silently mouthed a few lyrics - before settling down again, her face impassive. I watched as Minette and Ursula splashed each other, laughing and screaming, falling over and helping each other back onto their feet.

After a while, Minette shouted, 'My watch tells me I haven't eaten for over three hours.'

'See if the others are hungry...' I said.

Beatrix woke Edgar, who had fallen asleep while Nicholas was talking - he tipped back his sun-hat and seemed surprised both to be on the beach and to find his family around him. When I glanced over my shoulder towards the tower, Eve could be seen moving along the pathway, with the open expanse of the marshlands behind her, reeds and grasses waving in the wind.

By the time she reached us, everyone was scavenging from the picnic – the twins were sparring like cubs, pushing and trying to trip each other, finally collapsing on the sand near their father's feet.

'It's just like the old days - isn't it?' Edgar said, but no one was really listening to him.

After tea, the children set up a game of French cricket, with Nicholas, Eve and Beatrix. The sun spread a deep red-gold across the sky, tinting the clouds - the weather was changing.

I sipped my tea and let the salt-laden breeze wash over me, cool and cleansing.

Patrick stroked my back, and whispered, 'If Eve would baby-sit we could go to James's house. How would that be?'

'Good – but I wanted to ask, could we row out to the rocks? I've always wanted to go...'

Concern flickered in Patrick's eyes and I thought for a moment he would refuse. 'It's too far in *The Silver Arrow*,' he said, getting to his feet, 'the boat isn't up to it and neither am I, but I'll ask the boys to help fetch Nick's dinghy, it's got an outboard – but promise me, no morbid introspection, please.'

The twins wheeled the dinghy onto the beach on its trailer. Patrick started the motor and we made a wide curve west towards the pier to avoid being caught in the dangerous whirl of currents that met in the centre of the bay. The distance between the shore and the rocks was deceptive, it was much further than it looked and when we reached the rocks, we had to circle behind them to locate the rusty mooring ring where we could tie up the boat.

We held hands as we scrambled up a rough crevice to the plateau at the top of the rocks, resting while we caught our breath. Into my mind, flashed the image of the arc of Patrick's body as he had dived off the rocks to rescue me and with it came the sensation of cold fear, as I remembered how Juliet had been snatched away and had disappeared beneath the waves.

The view of the coastline was spectacular. The twins had taken their surf boards round to Coyle Sands and were riding the shallow, running waves. The curve of Morrow Bay made a crescent moon shape – the tip of the crescent ending at the finger of rock - the place where Juliet had stretched out on her towel, eyes closed and in pain.

We could look straight across to the marshes, Hagdon Hills and the tower and I asked, 'You and Nick didn't see what happened at the tower that day?'

'Your father and his friends were on the roof together. Antony had been watching Juliet – he watched her running back towards the beach, crossing the dunes – he pitched Beatrix out of the boat when your mother drew near, and went to her.'

I leant forward, resting my chin on my knees. My memory was that Antony and Beatrix had stayed in *The Silver Arrow*, almost until the end. 'I don't remember Antony speaking to my mother, you're sure..?'

'You were wading in the sea, waiting for us to come back from the rocks. Juliet refused to stop for Antony, she pushed him aside and he tried to hold on to her – that struck me as unlike him - I think he must have been very afraid for her, afraid of what might have been said or done at the tower...'

Though I'd kept looking to see where Juliet was - I'd missed their encounter, concerned only with how close she was to the bay.

'You were very intent on what you were doing,' Patrick reminded me, 'a bit cross with everybody and their meeting was over in the blink of an eye - Juliet wouldn't stop or acknowledge Antony...'

'I've always assumed we witnessed the same things that day.'

'We did - but everyone will remember what happened slightly differently. We notice what we expect to see, miss things that are important to someone else. But there was sufficient agreement for the coroner to be satisfied it was an accidental death. Without being callous, drowning is hardly unknown on this part of the coast...'

He wanted me to take a rational view. I gazed at the family, relaxing on the beach and thought about what he had said, wondering what conclusion the Coroner might have reached, had he been present at the incident that afternoon.

'James and Antony were both in love with my mother...' I said.

'...And that caused enmity in the family.'

'What could Antony have wanted to say to Juliet?'

Patrick rested his hand on my back, stroking my shoulder. 'I imagine something along the lines that he would look after her and her children whatever happened with James or William. I really think he would have given up everything to marry her – Antony never lost sight of his humanity or hers, he saw her many flaws and loved her anyway.'

I moved closer to him, feeling cold, trying to resist the morbid introspection he had warned against, yet wanting to ask more questions.

'Kelda's going to the tower bothers me. She'd been with James at Lyncross, we saw them on our way to the beach and my mother was angry. Enmity or not - she was deeply in love with James, as Kelda must have known. '

'...And she must have wanted to say anything which would cause trouble. James and your mother seemed to satisfy one another – but Kelda was insecure, a jealous teenager.'

'Meanwhile, my father was also jealous and Antony distressed...'

Patrick drew me into his arms. 'You know, my brother wasn't quite the saint he was reputed to be – he was every bit a man and found Juliet very desirable. The temptation is to mourn for what we think might have been - for an ideal rather than the real person. Do you think you might do that with your mother?'

'Perhaps...' I said.

He tugged gently at my plaited hair as he had used to when I was a girl. 'I think you do, Iris - but we'd better go back, it's going to rain.'

As he helped me to my feet, I said, 'I'd like to understand what James is really like...'

'Not to demonise him?' he said laughing. 'He's very different from the young man you knew – or the outward appearance anyway. He's learnt from his mistakes and no-one can do more than that...'

'You speak well of everyone,' I said, 'I'm so glad I disturbed you in Nick's summerhouse...'

'Isn't the nature of love to be disturbing?'

We climbed down the side of the rocks, holding tightly onto each other – I didn't dare look down as I struggled to keep a foothold. When we reached the bottom, waves broke over our legs, soaking us up to the thighs. The dinghy swayed wildly, tugging hard against its painter and Patrick stumbled as he jumped in so that the boat took on water. I hesitated, clinging to the rough outcrop of rock while he scooped the water out with child's plastic bucket. The noise of the sea drummed in my ears.

'Jump and I'll catch you...' Patrick shouted and reached out with his arms.

I stared down at the boat rocking wildly on a choppy sea and couldn't move.

He smiled in encouragement, 'Come on – I can't leave you here - it's perishing cold...'

Finally, I closed my eyes and made a leap for it, landing awkwardly, almost knocking him overboard.

'Why the hell did you do that?' he said, exasperated. 'I thought you enjoyed looking death in the face...'

'Perhaps I did and realised I didn't want to go there.'

The journey back to the shore was more turbulent than when we'd set out, and I was relieved to land back on the beach, on solid ground. Patrick asked Eve if she would mind taking care of Minette - if we were going to leave the island, we would have to hurry to beat the tide.

Ursula didn't want to stay at The Retreat and I heard Beatrix call her a cry- baby, when she started to whine.

As I gathered my bags together, Minette clung to me, 'Promise you'll be back tonight – low tide is at half past ten o'clock, I'll check on my watch...'

'You'll be all right, Eve's here,' I said, giving her a hug.

'Eve isn't my Mum, is she?' Minette objected and I thought she was close to tears.

'You'll be fine,' I assured her,' afraid that Ursula's insecurity might spread like a contagious disease.

Patrick suggested we went to The Crown and Anchor on the way to Aspen Terrace. It was where we'd had drinks with Richard and

Margaret, before he'd left for Nairobi. From the shelter of the terrace, we watched the last moments of sundown, Patrick's head and shoulders outlined against the burnt-orange sky. A cool wind wound its way up the estuary and rustled the trees – leaves blew about our feet, scratching at the paving stones. The church bells rang from the nearby village, Little Reeding, their tumbling notes tolling across the clear air of the evening.

We spoke about the events of the day, and I thought how David's gift to me had been his poetry and our children, yet being with Patrick was something I had unknowingly yearned for throughout my life. It seemed possible to harbour a deep longing for someone or something that couldn't be named or defined, until they appeared in your life and transformed it.

Since we'd returned to Littern, we hadn't been to Aspen Terrace together and Patrick warned, 'The house has a more relaxed, if not scruffy feel with my possessions in it – I'm sorry - I know how much you enjoyed all that timeless elegance...'

I asked what had become of Juliet's drawings, of her diary – had they been returned to James's house in London?

'James said you should have the diary, if it means something to you.'

I was glad not to have to ask – but wondered if Juliet's things had become a matter of indifference to James – didn't he care anymore?

James and Beth were in Johannesburg; Patrick told me James had become involved in a theatre project among the poor.

'You still miss working in Africa?'

'Am I so transparent?' he asked with a smile.

'I know you're restless sometimes...'

'But not dangerously so, though I've been asked to write a report about my experiences there, which I suppose will bring it all back...'

The conversation turned to Margaret and Richard – Richard was as enthusiastic about his many good causes as ever - Margaret was now considering buying a cottage in Devon, instead of Cornwall, and retaining a pied a terre in London.

When it was too chilly to sit out any longer, we drove to Aspen Terrace. If Clave Valley had been James and Juliet's trysting place, James's house was ours.

Leaving the town square, I sighted Kelda. She was crouching in the shadows, propped against the railings of small public garden, wrapped in a blanket like an Indian squaw – my dark angel - black hat on her head, her flute in its case on the ground beside her.

'Thank God she's alive,' I said, 'could you stop and let me out?'

Patrick pulled sharply over to the kerb. 'I'll walk down and meet you if you're not back in a few minutes,' he said.

As I approached her, Kelda began shouting. 'God, what the hell do you want?' she asked - her speech slurred.

'I wanted to see you again – where have you been..?'

'Hanging out with friends, having a drink or two - perhaps I should go with you and Patrick Piran to James's house,' she said sarcastically.

I ignored her taunting, though it was tempting to say *come on then* – to see what she would do. 'Are you going to sleep here tonight?'

'Will you join me?' she said as if enjoying her own joke.

She'd been sick down the front of her coat – pieces of half-digested food had dried out and stuck to the black cloth – the stench was terrible.

'You've been ill...'

'What is it to you?' she asked, but with less than her usual venom.

'You think nobody cares for you, but that isn't true.'

'Why not just give me some bloody money and fuck off?' she said - her mouth twisting into a heart-rending smile.

I took a twenty pound note out of my purse and dropped it into her lap. Kelda was surviving – she had the energy to be hostile - but I knew Patrick, seeing the state of her, would be drawn in, want to get involved and that Kelda might react aggressively.

'Edgar Piran's a flood-clear bastard,' she whispered, 'you want to watch out.'

Patrick was already walking down the hill - he would soon reach us - I moved away quickly to avoid him and Kelda getting into a confrontation.

As I hurried towards him, Kelda laughed, calling after me. 'Patrick's little shadow...' she jeered.

# Chapter 43

I drove Minette to St Mary's to begin her school life in Fernley, her smart appearance in her new royal blue uniform, spoiled only by her insistence on wearing last year's scuffed shoes.

She had been fractious that morning and we had left the house after a long stand-off over breakfast, barely speaking and both close to tears. When she did finally talk to me in the car, she told me grumpily that she hated the idea of school without Yuuka. Her form teacher, Sister Elisabeth, was a bad tempered old dragon and Ursula had suggested they both run away.

Minette still wrote to Yuuka most days and Verena had kept in touch about her progress at St. Catherine's. Over the summer, Sister Gabriel had suggested Yuuka should adopt a nickname, as her own name had been the cause of so much teasing. As an alternative, the nuns had come up with Sachiko, "happiness child", but Minette said crossly, 'she doesn't want to change her name - she'll always be Yuuka and I don't care what anyone says.'

Once I'd seen Minette safely into school, I returned to Narescombe for appointment at Mopheads, walking through the town square, alert as always for any sign of Kelda hanging about the steps and doorways of the shops. I couldn't see or hear her, but noticed in the window of Tippetts' clothes store, a midnight blue coat with a black velvet collar, cut so that it flared slightly from the waist, just as the blue coat I'd had worn as a child had done. It seemed perfect, and as I still had the money Alice and Flora had given me for my birthday, went into the shop and tried it on.

I was on my way to Petra Galleries and when I'd deposited the coat in the car, walked to Quay 11 for a coffee. Delia's favourite table in the corner was already taken, so I found a window seat, facing onto Napier Street. Shirley's gallery had a *To Let* sign nailed to the wall above the door and I wondered how long it would before she left Narescombe.

When I had last been to James's house with Patrick, I had borrowed Juliet's diary. In a similar way to the notebook from Wren House, she had written in two different places – starting from both the front and the back.

In the diary section, little was expressed explicitly – Juliet had abandoned the direct style of accounts of the early years of her marriage. The impression was of a web of secrets, so complex and entangled, it was impossible to decipher who was protecting whom.

There was no sign of anyone at the gallery, but the gate to the courtyard leading to Shirley's workshop had been left open. The double row of wooden tubs contained a display of nicotiana - masses of creamy white, pink and purple flowers. A selection of armatures, tall and narrow like totem poles, had been placed among the pots, their frames partially covered, like bodies with the flesh peeled back.

Shirley was talking on the phone. She caught sight of me and beckoned with her hand that I should go in to the workshop. The untidiness around her suggested she was in the process of dismantling the studio.

The phone clicked down and Shirley turned to me, her brassy blonde hair flared out wildly, like a burr around her head.

'You're moving away?' I asked.

'If you know anyone who might be interested in renting a gallery...' she said. 'I've been sorting the place out. I have something that might interest you.'

She opened a wooden cupboard and produced a thick cardboard file, pulled out the contents and spread them across her workbench – a sheaf of drawings Juliet had made of the sculptures in the oratory garden.

'You can take those, William gave them to me. I don't know why I've kept them all these years – except that I'd forgotten I had them.'

From the sketches, I could see the forms of the white statues when they were new and complete - as they had been when Juliet had first had them moved into the oratory garden. They appeared like a succession of nuns standing or kneeling, dressed in white, their veils and habits tossed and twisted in the wind. Were they intended to be nuns from the convent that had once been on the island? Or could they represent one figure in a succession of poses, St. Thrif..?

'I wouldn't take them too seriously,' Shirley said, 'to your mother, people and things were whatever she wanted them to be. Using a type of stone she knew wouldn't survive outside and then putting it outside anyway - maybe she was making a point – the ephemeral nature of life - and in the case of her work – the ephemeral nature of art.'

Shirley's tone was unmistakeably sardonic, but even if she was right, I believed my mother would have acted with conviction.

I watched as she filled the coffee percolator, switched it on and set out a mug by the sink, I was trying to find the courage to ask her what I really wanted to know.

'Geraldine thought Juliet made the statues because of the stillbirth of her child - she was pregnant again when she died...'

'...And so..?' Shirley's dismissive question signalled I'd better get to the point. 'Juliet conceived so easily – William thought she got pregnant just to annoy him. With him, she was frigid. He'd begun to think of divorce, even though it would have meant giving up Marisands and his life on Littern, something he was reluctant to do.'

'What did Kelda Sullivan say to my father? She must have said something that made Juliet feel particularly vulnerable...'

Shirley filled her mug with coffee, pulled a stool up to the workbench and sat down. 'We were all feeling vulnerable. William was in love with me, Geraldine was in love with William, and Juliet was in love with James. It was a tangle of resentments and suspicions. Nobody was happy. We were having a three way affair – William, Geraldine and I – homosexuality was illegal in those days – we thought we were sophisticated, anarchic, but also safe on the island. It made life interesting.'

'Did it make life interesting for my mother?' Her off-hand manner had upset me, 'The lunch party – agreeing to invite you to Marisands - Juliet wanted to please my father?'

'Juliet meant to shame him and us – though she was hardly in a position to take the moral high-ground.'

'So - when you went to the tower, what happened?' I persisted.

Shirley sipped her coffee, turning away from me, 'None of us wants to talk about that. Your mother had stolen William's freedom, for the sake of protecting her reputation. Do that to someone and you kill their spirit, unless they're prepared to rebel and that's what William did. The collapse of their marriage had gone too far - it hardly mattered what Kelda said, because William no longer had a scrap of sympathy or respect for Juliet.'

I wasn't sure for how much longer she would tolerate my presence in her workshop, so before she could dismiss me, I spoke out, 'Kelda Sullivan followed you to the tower - she was talking to my father. You and Geraldine were both there - you must have heard what she was saying...'

'Isn't it enough to know William didn't like what he heard?'

'Would you say that my mother disliked what *she* saw and heard enough to commit suicide?'

I had expected some kind of recoil from Shirley, but she got up and set about washing her mug then drying it on a rag, before replacing it carefully in a cardboard box containing odds and ends of china.

'Juliet was always inclined to dramatic gestures – when she ran into the sea, she might have been trying to upset James, attract his attention - your guess is as good as mine. When people fight, we usually ask who

530

started it – the answer in this case, according to Kelda, would have to be Juliet. She'd found a tinder box and she lit a match...'

'And when the tinder box exploded, my mother turned tail and ran? Juliet's hair was her beauty, why would she cut it off or allow someone else to disfigure her...?'

Shirley began to empty the cupboard from which she had taken the file containing Juliet's drawings. She shut the door and rifled through a collection of old chisels, discarding some and putting others in a box by the sink. I was afraid she wasn't going to answer me, but without stopping what she was doing, she spoke at last, 'William insisted Juliet would be all right. He said she'd go back to the Pirans or James and take solace there, he was certain she'd go back to the bay because of you.'

'No-one thought to go after her?'

'William needed to cool his temper. We were all shaken - he'd reacted so violently to what Kelda had said...'

What had Kelda said?' I repeated my question, 'And was she telling the truth?'

'You'll need to ask her that.'

'Kelda tells me nothing.'

Shirley said evenly, 'She probably feels guilty.'

'And you don't? While William was cooling his temper, my mother walked into the sea, dragging me with her and drowned...'

The woman I'd met previously, managing the gallery shop came into the studio bringing a pile of paintings balanced on a porter's trolley – as it turned out they were Geraldine's.

'Perfect timing,' Shirley said, 'Iris could take those to Geraldine – sale or return – they haven't sold.'

I glanced from one smug face to another, they eyed each other and from the intimacy of their look, it was obvious they were lovers. Wherever Shirley was going, her friend would be going with her and in the company of an ally she had become impenetrable to me.

Leaving them, I put my mother's sketches on the passenger seat and packed Geraldine's paintings into the boot of the car. All the way back to Marisands, I could feel a headache coming on – time seemed to be running out in so many different ways - soon I would run out of opportunities to harangue the same people with the same questions...

As soon as I reached Marisands, I took a headache pill and went to the study to write a brief letter to Silvie bringing her up to date. I needed to work - Laurence was edgy about his latest books and was only kept from constantly pestering me by the distraction of plans for televising a series of *The Kenholme Mysteries,* next year.

But instead of getting out Laurence's script, I spread Juliet's drawings of the white statues across the desk. Quirk flattened himself against the floor, his expressive eyebrows rising and falling as I fidgeted in the chair. When we'd spoken this time, Shirley seemed to have forgotten that she'd once suggested the statues represented nature spirits – as someone had once said - if you're going to lie you need to have to have a good memory.

I traced the lines of my mother's drawings with my index finger. The flowing, mobile shapes made me think of Isadora Duncan, who Juliet with her childhood longing to be a dancer had greatly admired and whose movements were free and graceful. Yet I knew, in my imagination, I might produce a thousand theories about my mother's work and they might all be wrong.

My conversation with Shirley had achieved little, except to make me feel I was losing sight of Juliet still further. With that uncertainty was a sense of not knowing how I should view myself as her daughter when all I had to rely on was my instinct that the stories people were telling me were flawed, though I couldn't pinpoint where the fault-line lay.

Eve offered to collect Minette from St. Mary's and I was grateful not to have to go out again. Patrick conducted his life along straight, though not rigid, lines, he had made the habit of calling in after work and I looked forward each day to seeing him. I heard his car turn into the drive – the doors slamming – the sound of his voice as he sent Ursula to play with Minette.

In a few minutes, he brought mugs of tea upstairs and settled into the study armchair.

'You're particularly enigmatic and writerly today,' he said, greeting me with his lovely smile.

'I'm drowning in enigma,' I told him and tidied away Laurence's notes, wanting to show him the drawings Shirley had given me.

I switched on the desk lamp and lay out the drawings in a pool of light. Patrick put on his glasses.

'The statues remind me of the story of *Echo*, she could only speak as a response to someone else's words – she had no voice of her own - any sound she made faded away to nothing. It's said her skeleton desiccated into stone...'

I put my hand to my head, the vestiges of a headache still bothering me – his proposal was no more or less valid than others which had been made, and perhaps expressed a truth about my mother. Was there something she had wanted to voice and couldn't? Had she lost her voice? In what sense were her actions merely a result of the actions of others?

Patrick touched my face gently with the back of his hand, 'Are you sure all these questions are helping you?'

'I don't know - sometimes I can't bear to think there could be more to discover – or to imagine what that might be...'

'I think you may need to decide which bothers you most, knowing or not knowing what happened. Beatrix has told me what she said to my mother, that you lured Juliet into the sea - but I've always assumed your mother was rescuing you. Isn't that more likely to be true than a spiteful remark made by my sister?'

'My mother ran from the tower as if the devil was after her and perhaps he was in the form of gossip or cruelty. This isn't about exonerating me or pleasing Silvie – not any longer. I need to know who my mother was - I need the truth about who my father was and time to reflect on the meaning of my identity...'

He patted the arm of the chair, indicating I should sit beside him, while he drank his tea. I told him how William had sent the carved box to Wren House and the promise I'd made to carry Juliet's life inside me, to live the life she would never have, to keep her spirit vital - *to be my mother*.

'I think you need to let that go,' he said quietly.

'I want to - but I don't know how...'

He took my hand and pulled me to my feet, 'Let's start by going for a walk. Are you ready to be torn away from your desk?'

Through the window, I could see it was a perfect September afternoon, the sun filtering through the trees, a pale blue sky softened by drifting wisps of white cloud.

'The children are beside themselves wanting to go to the beach - I told them we could, if I persuaded you to come. They're waiting for me to bring you down.'

'Sometimes I think Ursula should move in here,' I said and then apologised quickly, realising what my suggestion implied.

'It's all right, I frequently think the same,' he said.

Before shutting down the computer, I clicked onto e-mails. There was a message from Cameron to say he was back in Edinburgh, on his own, and had no news of Zoë. I tapped out a quick reply, asking him to let me know if he should hear anything.

I could hear the girls growing restive in the hall – every now and then one of them would clatter up a few stairs and jump down again, landing with a thump on the hall floor.

'If Zoë came back - everything would feel better,' I said.

Patrick circled me with his arms, 'Have you noticed when Ursula runs away, she only runs where we'll find her? Thank God so far, she's been unerring in her judgement of what and who might be safe.'

'Are you saying Zoë wants to be found?'

'Why else would she have kept in touch at all – however infrequent or cryptic her messages?'

'To torture me - you don't know Zoë.'

'But she obviously knows you,' he said and kissed me.

Ursula shouted hooray as we appeared on the landing. There had been jealousy between her and Minette, vying for Patrick's attention and for mine.

We wandered through the garden, Ursula skipping ahead calling to Quirk. In the orchard, the mature trees were hung with apples, pears and plums. The flower beds in the garden of Thrift Cottage were a mass of colour, the pink, blue and white of summer giving way to the yellow and red of autumn. Eve and I had been working on the vegetable patch, which now appeared like an illustration from a horticultural book, with its neat rows of beans and cabbages shining in the afternoon sun.

The remnants of Juliet's statues gleamed in the low sunlight - an outgrowth of my mother's need to find shape for her feelings and fears – to give them voice..? I'd begun to research the idea of the Mary Garden, which legend had been suggested St. Thrif had made in honour of the White Virgin. I'd compiled a list of plants I would like to grow around Thrif's gravestone under the silver birches. There were many flowers associated with Mary - columbines, lavender, Madonna lilies, marigolds and violets - some could be found in white forms and might survive in the shade of the trees.

In the studio, Eve's figure leant over her work, too intent on what she was doing to notice us passing by. I'd mentioned to Silvie, the idea of enclosing the garden of Thrift Cottage to give Eve privacy, something that might be lacking as Ursula and Patrick's presence at Marisands became an everyday occurrence. I slipped my arm through his - we were creating our own world - a world in which I hoped he might one day become my permanent companion.

The girls raced towards the gate with Quirk at their heels. Ursula's feyness had become a vehicle for Minette's imagination and Minette kept Ursula's feet on the ground. I wished Patrick would agree to the girls going to school together. I thought Ursula needed to be free from her many anxieties – free to move confidently between school and the homes of her family and feel secure in any of them.

We ambled along the beach as far as the oratory steps, the news from Cameron had been bothering me and I asked Patrick, 'Would you mind if I catch you up in a few minutes?'

'Communing with the spirits - *again*?' he asked.

He watched my progress as I clambered up the broken steps and then opened the oratory door. Each time I went there, my fear of falling seemed to grow and as I stepped inside, my heart was pounding fiercely.

Patrick's thoughts about Zoë had lodged in my mind - his suggestion that she might want to come home had given me hope. I lit candles and arranged shells and fronds of brightly coloured sea-weed on the stone altar – olive, rust and blue-green – Zoë's colours. I kept incense in the chapel and a jug of holy water from the well, which I poured into a shallow bowl laying them out deftly, like an acolyte at the celebration of Mass.

Sitting on the blanket with my back resting against the bench, in the quietness and dim light, I allowed images of Zoë to rise in my mind. Zoë had gone wandering in search of a home. Her many experiences – experiences I hadn't shared – would have shaped her in ways which I might struggle to understand.

The rhythmical sound of the sea was soothing - I wrapped the blanket around my shoulders and lulled by the waves, watched the flickering candles as their yellow light trembled against the shell-covered walls. Only when the candles guttered and burnt out, did I stand up, my feet and legs tingling. Knowing I would come back and repeat the ritual, I folded the blanket neatly onto the bench ready for my return.

I made my way down to the beach again, careful not to look at the sea churning on the rocks below. Descending the steps, my legs trembled as I grasped at the scrubby plants which had rooted on the rocky face of the cliff to steady myself against a fall.

Patrick was far ahead, almost at the stream, with the girls chasing round him, and Quirk pouncing on waves as they rose and then crashed, dissolving into a shower of white foam. I cupped my hands and called for him to wait – but it was Quirk who heard and bolted towards me.

When I caught up with them, Ursula was chatting, not pausing for breath. She'd had become attached to the *Seabright Island Adventures* - though they were meant for younger children, she read a different one each day.

'*Is* Jack my dad?' she kept saying.

'You must ask him...'

'*Agnes* is definitely my mum,' Minette said and smiled at me. She was still devoted to Yuuka, still reserved where Ursula was concerned.

We arrived at the stream and sat on a rock while the girls paddled for a while. When Patrick told them it was time to go home, as everyone was growing hungry - there was a chorus of complaints.

'Do we have to go *now*?' Ursula asked, pink-cheeked and over-excited.

Patrick didn't respond at once and she began repeating her question over and over again, a new habit since she had come back from seeing her mother.

I put my finger to my lips as a warning. Ursula pulled a grumpy face when Minette took her hand and swung her round towards Marisands. 'If you're good,' she said, '*they* may say we can have a sleep-over, soon.'

'At Marisands..? That sounds a good idea,' Patrick said, 'I don't know when I last had peace and quiet for an entire evening.'

After dinner, I went to the oratory garden and stood among Juliet's statues, spectral as the white bark of the birch trees beneath the rising moon – *a convention of ghosts* – my mother had called them and like supernatural beings, perhaps they would remain beyond my understanding.

When I returned to the house, Boa and Brio were like two pieces of darkness moving in the twilight. Quirk barked softly as I entered the porch and padded to the door to meet me.

From the music room, came the sound of Patrick playing the piano, a piece by Schumann that echoed Beethoven's *To the Distant Beloved...*

As I made coffee, I rested in the knowledge that I was no longer alone, no longer afraid that if I stayed on the island I would become detached from reality, an anchoress like St. Thrif, shunning company. Slowly, subtly and seemingly of its own volition, Marisands was becoming home and I wanted nothing to disturb or upset our newfound serenity.

# Chapter 44

Delia had invited Eve to visit her at Hintham Ridge and she was eager to show me the room where she and a group of community members were using music, art and craft as a means of self-expression for those who struggled to tell their stories in words.

On the way, we dropped off food at Whitcroft for Geraldine and as she seemed willing to deal with Eve, I left her to negotiate the return of the paintings, given to me by Shirley.

'Going to Hintham Ridge makes me think about Kos,' Eve said, chatting as we drove out of Narescombe, 'I really miss him at the soup kitchen – he was good with people – even Kelda talked to him, at least about music.'

'Kos seems to be a lost cause...' I said. I'd concluded if he was going to come back to Littern, he would have done so by now.

'That's what he felt about himself - he told me about his past and I reacted badly. He said he was advising me, in case I was thinking of falling in love with him...'

'And were you?'

'I don't fall in love very easily – love makes life complicated doesn't it..?'

Her credo evidently hadn't changed *I want to live simply and do my work.*

'I probably shouldn't tell you - but in a way you ought to know,' she went on...

She then related Kos's history. He'd been a music professor. He had a clever student who was also lazy and one day he'd lost his temper and hit him, while they were preparing for an important exam. Kos had never hit anyone before, but the boy wasn't trying and fate decreed Kos's slap would make the boy deaf in one ear.

Eve said, 'Kos was threatened with going to prison for assault, but he didn't care about that. What he cared about was that he'd ruined the student's career. When he was older, the boy took to the streets - busking, living rough. In the summer, Kos goes looking for him, tries to make sure he's all right.'

Her account made sense of Kos's reticence about his past, his self-effacing attitude to his accomplishments and though I pitied the student, I also felt sorry for him – a man who felt things deeply and was by temperament mild and compassionate.

Eve said, 'Kos wanted to prove he was a good man, but I no longer felt sure. I thought about Dad and how angry he used to get and when Kos opened his heart, I closed mine. I think in the end he hated me...'

'He couldn't hate you – he doesn't,' I assured her. 'Kos is hurt by his own failure - he's very proud.'

'I want him to come back, so I can say how sorry I am – if he does, do you promise not to let on what you know?'

We parked in the centre of Safford Bridge. There was sharpness in the air and as we walked through the main square, street people huddled together in groups as if to keep warm. I was going to Juliet's grave and chose flowers from the street vendor's cart, parked in its usual place, opposite the Priory. While I walked to the graveyard, Eve went to the art shop near Bridge House Books to choose materials for the community project.

I bought white alstroemeria, a few chrysanthemums in pale lemon and pink and roses for Juliet. As I laid them by the headstone of the grave, a slight movement ahead of me caught my attention. Kelda's figure was slumped against the hedge, her face almost hidden by her black hat. I approached cautiously as if she were a frightened animal. Her flute case, beside her in the grass, was dented and scratched and when I drew close the stench of alcohol, stale sweat and vomit were nauseating.

Kelda muttered something I couldn't hear and spitting the words out made her cough. Where her hair was visible beneath her hat, it was thickly matted. Her hands and face were encrusted with dirt, the black coat she wore was more stained and smeared with sick than the evening I had seen her near Aspen Terrace. She was one carrier down on her usual collection – her sleeping bag was missing.

'I'm going to Hintham Ridge, why don't I take you there?' I suggested.

Kelda wouldn't meet my eyes. 'More bloody questions..?' she said and spat on the ground.

'Half the time, no-one knows if you're dead or alive...'

She smiled her crooked smile, 'What do you think?'

'I'd say you were neither one nor the other...' I told her, shocked by her poor condition.

Kelda coughed again, this time so hard I thought she was going to throw up. I reached out and offered my hand. If she would stand up, I might persuade her to have a coffee, maybe something hot to eat from a take away, but she swatted my arm away.

'Fuck off...' she yelled, 'I can't move, I'm covered in fucking shit and I don't want you bloody stalking me.'

'Most of us are covered in shit, in various ways,' I said. 'But I only wanted to question you because I think you know what happened the day my mother died – you were out at the tower...'

'Chinese whispers...' Kelda murmured, making a hissing sound under her breath.

'Shirley Fredericks said the atmosphere was like a tinder box...'

'I only dropped the spark – the tinder box was waiting to explode...' She was echoing Shirley's words.

'Was it your own idea to drop the spark?'

Kelda fumbled in her great-coat pocket, took out a roll-up and lit it with a cheap yellow lighter.

'What difference does it make?'

'I thought it might make a difference to you,' I said and she glowered at me with her sly, dark eyes.

'Why don't you get up?' I asked.

She made a clumsy attempt to clamber to her feet and the smell of faeces filled the air. Where her trousers had been torn above the ankle, she had a deep gash on her leg which looked infected. She swayed violently on her feet and was about to fall - I stepped forward to catch her - but her dead weight was too much for me and she collapsed, almost dragging me to the ground.

'How long have you been lying here?' I asked.

Kelda looked dazed, '...No fucking idea.'

I couldn't move her but was unwilling to walk away. 'How can I help you..?' I said in desperation.

'So you can cross-examine me like fucking Delia? Move one step closer and I'll bloody deck you.'

I retreated to the Priory yard and called 999 on my mobile phone, then let Eve know where I was and what had happened. We waited, at a distance, keeping an eye on Kelda and looking out for the ambulance to arrive. By the time it came, siren blaring, Kelda had manoeuvred onto her knees and crawled towards the shelter of some yew trees before sinking to the ground in her filthy, stinking clothes.

There was a war of words, but she was too weak to protest as she was carried away on a stretcher. We could hear her cursing from inside the ambulance - Kelda's anger was her way of telling the world she was distressed. I made sure she had her hat, her bags and her flute, but she refused my efforts to persuade me to allow me to go to the hospital with her.

'Fuck off,' she kept saying if I moved in her direction, repeating the phrase like a mantra, until the ambulance doors were slammed closed and they took her away.

Eve and Delia tried to reassure me, I had done the right thing. Delia told me Kelda's condition had been going downhill and she had thought she might not survive another winter on the streets. She and other members of the community had gone out searching for her, 'One night, we drove round Safford Bridge, for hours,' she said. 'The back of the town is a rabbit warren. We trawled the pubs, but eventually someone found her in Narescombe, dead to the world on the steps of the Town Hall.'

The more Delia said, the worse I felt, but she couldn't seem to stop.

'People like Kelda die unnoticed,' she said, 'no-one bothers until it's too late, then they're discovered dead, huddled under a bridge or in a miserable squat, where everyone is too drunk or drugged to care what happens...'

I shut out her words. Though Kelda's accusations had been correct - I did want information from her - I also felt loyalty, sympathy for my "auntie", for the nuns' favourite pupil, who had turned her back on them and rebelled. If Delia was right, Kelda had got into bad company and allowed her life to slide off the scale. But whatever the community believed, I didn't want her uncontrolled descent to end with a lonely death in the gutter.

Eve showed me the art room where she worked. It was sparsely furnished, with four Formica-topped tables pushed together into the centre and a selection of old chairs arranged around them. I thought it unpromising, lacking character or anything to inspire, but Eve was cheerful as she stashed away the paints, paper and brushes she'd bought in town, into one of the many cupboards.

In an adjacent room was the potter's wheel and kiln she had spoken of and on the bench, her first attempts at making pottery, simple pots and bowls in clean shapes but with intense colours – they were striking, beautiful – redolent of Bernard's designs for Parfit China.

'We love having Eve here,' Delia said, 'when she walks in, she lights up the room.'

Eve's face turned a deep red.

'She's been a great help to me at Marisands.'

'With Patrick working for the community, we'll soon have the whole family,' Delia said, 'we were becoming smug and complacent – but Patrick's shaken us up.'

I didn't doubt that – it was Patrick's way – if he noticed something was wrong he set out to put it right and his methods could be ruthless. Unable to think what contribution I might make, I told Delia there were unopened art materials in the studio at Marisands and if Eve didn't want them, they could be brought here and put to good use.

We left Eve to discussions with two other members of the community and went to the kitchens where Delia was on duty making bread. While she measured out flour and yeast, I perched on a stool and watched her.

'Last time we met, you were unsettled, full of questions...' she began.

'I still am - Kelda feels I only bother with her because I want information - she made me feel guilty. I don't mean to use people, but no one will give a straight answer and I just want the simple truth.'

Delia plunged her hands deep into the bowl and began to mix the ingredients into dough. 'The truth is often more complex than we think,' she said. 'And our relationship with our parents is always complex, deeper than love or hatred. Our parents are in our blood and bones - they can nourish or act like a toxin. Kelda was involved with the events of your mother's death, I'm sure of that - and we do all have a responsibility towards each other - but I suspect Kelda's afraid of you finding out whatever it is she's done.'

Delia dropped the ball of smooth brown dough onto a wooden board. 'Terry Hart has been asking after you,' she said as she begun the rocking motion of kneading the bread.

She always seemed to prick my conscience in areas where it was most sensitive. I wondered if he'd told her that I'd completely and deliberately ignored his invitation to share what we both knew about William.

I tried to move the conversation on. I explained how Patrick believed either pride or fear was holding Zoë back from making contact – I spoke about Flora and my hopes of bringing her to Fernley.

'Flora always had one foot in this world and one in the next,' she said and smiled. She covered the bread and left it to prove, then suggested, 'Come and see what we've done with the caravans...'

I borrowed a pair of galoshes from the boot room and we walked through the farmyard to where one of the nearby fields had been grassed over and the caravans, parked in a tidy row. A few community members were working on one of the vans - the old interior had been torn out and lay scattered on the ground, beside a heap of new timber and tins of paint.

'You'll be amazed at the transformation,' Delia said, laughing at my lack of enthusiasm. 'It doesn't do to judge harshly – either caravans or people. Those people who you say won't speak to you – could you be pushing them into telling what you believe to be true?'

'It's possible – but also possible that I'm right...'

'...And equally possible you're wrong, we might all be wrong.'

'You implied James Millford loved women then let them down – Geraldine Ottley thinks I might be one of the consequences - and it's important for me to know. If Kelda had a child by James they would be my half-brother or sister. James has two children with Beth - and if Geraldine's right, they're related to me - I can hardly make sense of it.'

Delia patted my arm, 'I'd wait until you have your truth, simple or otherwise, don't jump to conclusions...'

I felt impatient. 'What can James think when he sees how Kelda is?'

'She blames herself for her way of life, not James and it might be better if you did the same...'

We looked over the few caravans that were finished – and I had to admit, however reluctantly, that they were greatly improved - comfortable, water-tight and fitted with new gas heaters.

I asked Delia, if when she was well, Kelda might come to the community and be cared for until she was strong enough to resume her usual way of life.

Delia promised to phone Safford Bridge Hospital and make enquiries about her. As Eve and I left, I suggested she shouldn't leave it too long, I had a strong suspicion Kelda would waste no time before discharging herself.

*

Wrapped up against the cold, Patrick and I took our afternoon tea out to the bench by the honeysuckle. I'd been studying my mother's watercolour of the garden again and thinking of new ideas - replanting some of the beds by Thrift Cottage with flowers in their palest forms, so the white beds near the oratory seemed a natural extension, not a separate area with a distinct entity of its own.

My thoughts amounted to not much more than a reverie, without Kos, there was no-one to do the work involved and Patrick disagreed with my suggestion in principle, 'Shouldn't the oratory garden be a sacred circle of protection? Then the nature spirits can make themselves at home and so can we...'

'Here come two dryads...' I replied. Minette and Ursula, in their school uniforms were standing under the pergola, deciding whether to join us.

Eve had uncovered a hedgehog living in the undergrowth behind the pond and the girls came each day to check on him and leave food.

'We wanted to go in the studio, but Eve isn't there,' Minette said, 'can we knock at the door of Thrift Cottage?'

Ursula hopped from one foot to another while they waited for my answer.

Eve spent a lot of time amusing and feeding the girls when they were home from school, 'Perhaps you should leave Eve alone,' I suggested.

Minette scowled and Ursula scowled back at her. Ursula had been subdued recently - she had exams coming up in November and had been taking extra lessons, though Patrick claimed they were to no great effect.

'Do as Iris asks,' Patrick said mildly, 'go to the house and change and we'll have a short walk on the beach together.'

Minette grabbed her hand and Ursula did as Patrick had told her - I heard the thud of their feet running across the lawn.

Patrick said, 'I called at Lyncross on the way here, Pa was quite voluble. He told me how towards the end of her life, Juliet had confided less in him and not at all in my mother. They knew Antony was in love with her and that she'd rejected him for James. It upset them both – in many ways, Juliet was the daughter Pa wished he'd had.'

'If my mother had loved Antony, we wouldn't be together,' I said.

Patrick laughed. 'In that sense, it was a fortunate instance of unrequited love, though Antony took it hard.'

'Shirley and Geraldine have implied Juliet's perceptions were skewed - but it could be that on the day she died, she saw things clearly. The situation wasn't working either with James or William - perhaps she regretted Antony, she must have known he really cared for her.'

'Pa said something else I thought was important, that he didn't believe Juliet would have done anything towards you that didn't grow from an impulse of love, however irrational her actions might have seemed...'

I slipped my arm through his - resting my head on his shoulder. Patrick did nothing that wasn't born of an impulse of love, understanding came easily to him. He didn't need to carve his beliefs out of stone like Juliet - or out of words like me.

'Delia thinks I need to be patient and forgiving.'

'More dilemmas then, confronted with the bunch of renegades you've been dealing with...' he said, the familiar note of teasing in his voice.

'Whatever you tell me about him, I can't seem to imagine James...'

'He's a good person - surely that's all that matters?'

But I'd said the same about Kos, who as it turned out, harboured his own dark secrets.

I told him then about my encounter with Kelda in Safford Bridge, and how unsure I felt that I had done the best for her.

As always, he was practical, 'It's no good hoping Kelda will change of her own accord, you have to deal with what's possible - provide food, rest, good hygiene, medication.'

'I acted in good faith...'

'But you're worried because you can't foresee the outcome? Whatever the outcome, I imagine it's going to be better than it would have been if you'd left her sick and unattended in the graveyard.'

'It must be so restful – being sensible,' I said.

'Restful for whom..? What else are you worrying about?'

'I was uncomfortable at Hintham Ridge with Eve. Her work on Juliet's paintings is exceptional - I don't want her distracted by another one of Delia's projects and surely they don't need Eve to help people dabble with paint, just when she might be finding her own direction...'

'You keep looking for trouble', he said.

'But if I don't look for it – it comes and finds me...'

We went to fetch the girls for their walk. I shouted up the stairs for them, but they didn't answer my calls. We searched the house, and then checked the studio. I knocked on the door of Thrift Cottage, but Eve didn't answer, so I looked through the house again, in case they were hiding and this time noticed the figure of the White Virgin and Juliet's rosary had been taken from their places on the landing and in the hall. I kept the key to the padlock on the gate in an old tea caddy in the kitchen and Minette would almost certainly have noticed me putting it there – when I lifted the lid, the key was missing.

'They must have gone to the oratory,' I said.

We ran down the footpath to the deserted shore. The tide was almost in, leaving a narrow strip of rocks to walk on. Slipping on the damp seaweed - I trailed Patrick across to the steps and up to the oratory door, crawling on my hands and knees past the area where the foot of the cliff had fallen away in the last storm.

Patrick reached the oratory first and pushed open the door. The girls were standing on the wooden bench, which they had pushed right up to the altar.

I was furious with them, 'What are you doing? You've been told not to come here alone,' I directed my reproaches towards Minette, who had given me her word.

'I cut my hand in the tree house...' Ursula said, 'Minette told me if I prayed it might be healed by the White Virgin.'

Patrick took Ursula's hand - there was a long scratch across her palm. 'You needn't have bothered the White Virgin with that - you can give it a good wash when we get home.'

My mother's figure of the White Virgin and her rosary were laid out on the altar.

'You took my things,' I said angrily. Turning to speak to Minette, I saw some of the shells had been pulled from the walls, leaving ugly gaps in the patterns, like missing teeth, 'Have you two been down here before?' I asked.

Minette nodded, 'Lots of times. There was a box of candles and matches, but we've used them all up.'

Ursula said, 'You told us candles were like living prayers, so I lit them all...' I admired her cold-bloodedness in the face of two irate adults.

I started to bundle them towards the door, 'You frightened us - you've taken things which don't belong to you.'

'I prayed Zoë might come back,' Minette assured me, as if that made everything all right. Until then, I'd just been glad they were safe, now I was unsure if she was being genuine or deliberately artful.

'You can pray anywhere,' Patrick said, 'you don't have to be disobedient, set the oratory on fire, or put yourselves in danger...' I could hear the faintest intimation of humour returning to his voice.

'We didn't mean to be naughty...' Minette said.

But Ursula rounded on me '...You come here on your own – often - Minette told me - you're a hypocrite.'

'Ursula!' Patrick said sharply, 'firstly you're being appallingly rude and secondly, Iris is allowed to come here, she's an adult and the oratory is her responsibility.'

Privately, I began to wonder if I shouldn't block off the oratory steps. Though the building was meant to be open to pilgrims – who went there except for the family?

'You're never to come here again unaccompanied. Do you promise?' I said.

'I promise,' Minette agreed. Ursula merely nodded her head.

I was tempted to leave the figure of the White Virgin and the rosary on the altar – without meaning to the girls had found their rightful place, the proper context in which they gained significance and power. Perhaps they could fend off whatever was causing the feeling of dread that had swept over me, threatening to destroy the fragile sense of home and belonging I had begun to enjoy – dread like the fear which had haunted Flora with her belief that the building of Marisands had desecrated holy ground and that Littern might one day exact its revenge.

I asked Minette to return the key and we stepped out onto the rocky plateau meaning to climb the steps to the garden – instead, Ursula suddenly darted downwards, her long dark hair flying out behind her.

'Don't!' I yelled and grabbed Minette's hand in case she followed.

The sea was breaking over the lower steps – the tide flowing in fast. Patrick clambered down as rapidly as he could, 'Stop now, Ursula!' he shouted.

But Ursula only came to a halt when she was poised on the lowest step and could see the beach was impassable. She turned to look up at Patrick and a large wave slapped across her side, almost knocking her off her feet - she lost her balance, teetering on one foot, until Patrick lunged forward and caught her.

She was soaked through, her clothes dripping as Patrick pulled her to safety.

As they climbed towards us, Ursula was weeping, 'I'm sorry, I'm sorry, sorry, sorry, sorry, sorry...'

She continued keening, all the way across the garden and I remembered what Patrick had once told me - never make Ursula cry.

When we reached the house, he said, 'I should take Ursula home – we need to talk...'

'It wasn't only Ursula,' I reminded him, not wanting him to leave. 'Maybe Minette needs to hear what you have to say. I'll find some dry clothes – please, let's try to salvage the rest of the evening.'

I was shaken, but they were children and children took risks without realising the consequences. I pointed out how Patrick and his brothers had done dangerous things – swimming to the rocks, diving from the pier, disobeying his parents the moment they turned their backs...

But there were times when I feared difficulties with Ursula might drive us apart, when I understood exactly why Honor had struggled to cope with her daughter. There were times when I wondered, would Ursula never loosen her grip on Honor? But then I realised that was hypocritical - I hadn't yet relinquished my connection with Juliet and I was both older and supposedly wiser.

When I'd made a hot drink for the girls, I handed Ursula a plastic bag for her wet clothes and sent her upstairs with Minette to change.

'I suppose this is about school,' I said – Ursula became less and less settled as the prospect of exams loomed closer.

'I know what you think, Iris,' Patrick told me. The incident had put everyone in a bad mood. 'Let's not argue – St. Mary's, Fernley isn't convenient for me and there's nothing more to be said about it...'

'At least it has a reputation for being kind...' I said, tired of his obstinacy.

'And for making little girls obsessed with the idea of becoming nuns - which is probably why they went to the oratory...'

'No - that's my fault,' I said. 'I've been going there at night because of Zoë – I knew it was risky...'

'But the suggestion Zoë might want to come home was mine – so I'm equally to blame, though looking for blame is generally a waste of time.'

Ursula and Minette crept back into the kitchen - they must have heard our raised voices.

'I wanted to say sorry,' Ursula whispered, wiping away a milky moustache from her upper lip with the back of her hand; she could be very engaging.

'Apology accepted,' I said, hoping to fend off a tirade from Patrick on the subject of her manners.

'You're cross though you're smiling,' she said, 'that's wrong – it's pretending.'

'We're both angry,' Patrick said, 'you put each other – and us - in danger.'

'You put Mum and me in danger,' she replied, 'It was your choice to...'

'I know what happened, Ursula,' Patrick said and the tension in the room increased again.

Before she could say any more, I interrupted, 'You girls are grounded for a week, and there'll be no going to the beach after school. Now, stay upstairs in Minette's room and keep out of our way.'

Minette shut the door behind them and I listened carefully, wanting to be sure they'd gone upstairs, not escaped through the front door or the conservatory.

Patrick ran his fingers through his hair, 'Ursula has every right to blame me – I insisted she came with us to Africa and having meningitis almost killed her...'

I stopped him, he'd told me the story of how when Ursula was a baby, Honor had wanted to return to Africa and he'd agreed, on condition they went as a family.

'... You did what you believed in all conscience to be right – keeping your family together.' I said and rested my arm round his shoulders, 'Ursula shouldn't reproach you, or use the past to excuse her bad behaviour now. And it wouldn't be possible to reach our stage of life without having regrets...'

'Thankfully, not all regrets are equally powerful.' He held onto my hands, 'Sometimes I struggle to believe in myself or my judgment...'

'But I believe in you – I love you,' I said and the words came as effortlessly as the autumn leaves falling from the trees, speckling the lawns with red and gold.

# Chapter 45

Edgar's party had to be postponed several times because of illness and finally reduced in scale to what Patrick referred to as one of the family's *terrible teas*.

Patrick had recently been to London and had stayed with Margaret for a few days, while he gave a talk on his work abroad to potential volunteers for the charity he supported. He had met James briefly on a stopover at his London house, and James had told him that with the change of date, he could no longer come to Littern. Now, he and Beth had already flown back to Johannesburg, but he'd thought his children, Danielle and Oliver, might drive down to the island if they could be persuaded away from their busy lives.

On the morning of the celebration, Patrick left early for Tom's house in Safford Bridge, taking Ursula and Minette with him. He was going to help Tom and Nina prepare for their guests and promised to pick me up in the afternoon.

While Marisands was quiet, I worked for a few hours, and then took a bath, using the tuberose scent that had once been Juliet's and which I had now adopted as my own. As a birthday present for Edgar, I'd chosen a small oil painting of the woods near Lyncross, carpeted with bluebells. I'd cut garden flowers – in bronze, lemon and cream for Nina - and Eve had made a cake.

I was doing my make-up when Eve knocked on my bedroom door. 'I've come to supervise - *please* don't have that horrible plait you wear every day...'

I sat patiently while she put my hair up in a loose knot – her blue-green tunic showed off her eyes and gleaming fair hair.

'Verena would say, you look *stunning*,' she said, as I slipped on my new blue coat.

'So do you,' I said and kissed her cheek.

The weather had become stormy with heavy showers of rain, a capricious wind howled through the trees. While we waited for Patrick, I went through the house and closed all the windows, wedging newspaper into those which rattled the most. The wind built in strength and I switched on the radio to hear the weather forecast, which threatened a series of gales over the next few days. Eve put out lamps and candles in case the electricity went down and I shut Quirk in the kitchen with plenty of water and food, concerned we might not get home that night.

By the time Patrick returned, rain was falling in steady torrents. Eve and I huddled under a huge black umbrella as we ran to the car, but in seconds the wind had whipped round the corner of the house and blown the umbrella inside out.

Ursula was in the back seat of the car, smart in a red dress with a white collar. She said hello - but seemed quiet and Patrick sent me a look, which suggested it would be better not to make enquiries about her state of mind.

At the causeway, water was lapping over the surface - waves crashed against the piles of rocks that formed the island's sea defences. We took the crossing slowly, but the wind struck the side of the car with such strength, it threatened to force us off the road. Palk's Reach was streaming with mud, littered with twigs and branches which had been blown down. Driving through the woods in bad weather always made me nervous and I was relieved to reach Narescombe, where there was no danger of a tree crashing down onto the roof of the car and crushing us.

Tom and Nina's house was near the Public Park in Safford Bridge, in a broad, tree-lined avenue. We ran the short distance from the car to the front door beneath a sky that had turned black, as if night had arrived in the middle of the afternoon.

Of all the Pirans, Tom was most like his father in temperament and his home reminded me of Lyncross - with its solid comfortable furnishings and feeling of durability and permanence. I deposited Nina's flowers in the kitchen sink - their petals battered and torn by the gale and then followed Patrick into the drawing room. He held my hand and for a few seconds I felt his thumb gently circling my wrist, stroking the sensitive inner skin.

Edgar was holding court among his family and friends. Above his chair, pinned to the wall, was a hand-written Happy 90th Birthday banner made by Ursula and Minette. As I handed him his present - he seemed frailer than when we'd last met at Lyncross, as if his grip on life was now so light it could be broken in a moment.

He kissed my hand with the old-fashioned, formal courtesy which had never left him. Patrick smiled at me in reassurance, a smile that felt private, special - as his father propped the painting up on a side table. Edgar asked after Silvie, Alice and Flora and I explained how they were all in residential care, though Flora had managed at Wren House with help, until recently.

'I seem to need endless help, what a bloody nuisance it is getting old...'

'But better than the alternative,' Nicholas reminded him.

'You think that because you're young and strong – wait until you're a useless old codger like me...'

Eve had spotted Mike Acworth as soon as we arrived and tried to avoid him as he advanced towards her, glass in hand, undaunted by her obvious reluctance to talk. Mike was full of himself – his ash blonde hair was styled boyishly, spiked with gel. He was extremely good-looking and knew it. Though his admiration for Eve was obvious from his eyes and the gestures of his hands, I couldn't bring myself to like a man who would think nothing of breaking her heart.

Eleanor, Antony's widow, was talking to Beatrix and I felt them looking at me. Beatrix's voice was the sort that carried and I overheard her say, 'I don't understand why Patrick wants all that again - he had enough trouble with Honor not to mention the trouble he still has with Ursula...'

Ursula must have overheard too, she crept up and took my hand. 'You smell like a lovely flower,' she whispered.

'And you look like a lovely flower. What have you done with Minette?'

'She's helping Uncle Tom find things,' she said vaguely and began to nibble on her thumb nail - the party was making her – like me - feel anxious.

I glanced round the room, hoping for a refuge, but Mike had cornered Eve and was holding forth, his posture suggesting his unshakeable faith in his own innate superiority. The Pirans, with all their individual quirks and oddities were like any family, arguing, chewing over the latest gossip, expressing concern for each other in ways that sometimes helped but as often stirred up aggravation – the trouble was, I wasn't yet a part of them.

I moved from group to group, trying not to appear as if I was waiting for an opportunity to bolt. Ursula stayed by my side, still holding my hand. When I asked why she didn't find Minette, she twirled her way from the drawing room in a blur of red and white, before returning to report that Minette was too busy helping to take any notice of her.

Sarah Almond, Nick's wife was there, her black hair and striking features, unmistakeable from the photograph I'd seen at The Retreat; she was talking to Eleanor and Nina. When Sarah moved away, I joined them and took the opportunity to say how sorry I was about Antony.

I found Eleanor quite outspoken, but I liked her openness, the same quality I enjoyed in Margaret, Patrick's friend. 'Beatrix tells me you're the one reputed to have been the cause of his accident,' she said.

Ursula, fidgeting at my side, stared at me as a wave of heat flooded across my face – I was embarrassed that Beatrix had made sure my reputation preceded me.

Nina spoke up quickly, 'Iris was six and at worst made a childish error of judgement. I was supposed to be watching her - if you want to blame someone, blame me.'

Our eyes met briefly and I hoped she read gratitude in mine – and that she perhaps felt relieved to have said something she had wanted to say since the day Juliet had died.

Unaware of our exchange, Eleanor went on, 'Actually, I'm not blaming anyone. If Antony hadn't injured his back, I doubt we'd have ever met – and though I miss him terribly, he and I had twenty very happy, successful years.'

A little later, Tom refilled my glass, 'Surviving?' he asked. 'Nina says it's a shame we can't divorce our families, but I think after all this time, she's adjusted to the fact that if she wanted to marry one of the Piran's sons, she had no choice but to tolerate mine.'

He told me he had recently retired. 'Nina and I were meant to be going on a cruise before deciding whether to move house – but almost without noticing, I find I've put off our holiday and allowed myself to be roped into the plans of the Hintham Ridge Community - Patrick can be surprisingly forceful.'

'Would you think of moving to the island?' I asked.

'I don't think so.' He began to expound on how unsuitable it was for older people to live on Littern - they might be taken seriously ill at a time when the tide made the causeway impassable...

Edgar had perhaps been intended to hear. 'Bloody nonsense,' he muttered, 'my health is better than most of my children.'

'Five minutes ago you were saying you were exhausted and wanted to go home...' Beatrix interrupted.

I observed the way Patrick moved quietly round the room chatting here and there, putting people at ease and envied him. After discussing the awful weather with Tom's neighbours, I slipped my hand out of Ursula's and escaped into the kitchen, as I had so often done at David's parties. Through the open door, I could see Eve chatting to Nina, Mike at her side, hovering protectively. I stood by the sink and looked out of the window as rain struck the pavement and a flash of forked lightning lit the dark sky, followed by a deep rumble of thunder.

Nina came to fetch Edgar's birthday cake. She lit the candles and the house lights flickered, dimmed and went out as a violent clap of thunder over the roof drowned out conversation. Laughter sounded round the room as people realised it wasn't a deliberately engineered dramatic effect, but a power cut due to the weather.

There was a scramble while candles were found and then Sarah played *Happy Birthday* on the piano and we all sang and clapped as Edgar blew out his candles. We were invited to go through to the dining room for tea, but I hung back as people flocked into the hall.

'The party seems a success,' I said to Beatrix.

'Really..? Pa's been lecturing me on how we've all gone to the devil after the considerable bother it took to instil right principles into us. When it comes to our misdemeanours, his memory is infallible...'

'I always assumed he meant well - when I was a child...' I said.

'Perhaps he did mean well - when you were a child - but I'm not certain he does now.' Two or three glasses of wine seemed to have loosened Beatrix's tongue, she said, 'I miss living in Oxford, my friends, my work – I've been jarred out of a life I understood and knocked into one I can't comprehend. And when Pa passes on, my brothers will descend on Lyncross like a flock of vultures and no doubt *won't* require my services as a housekeeper, at which point I'll find myself redundant and homeless...'

'They wouldn't do that to you...'

Beatrix said. 'I'd do it to myself - I have no intention of waiting hand and foot on any of them.'

I edged my way towards the queue of people waiting for the buffet tea. Eve slipped in beside me - she had finally managed to shake off Mike's dogged presence. Ursula and Minette clutched hold of Eve's hands, one on each side, as if they too had been aware of her discomfort. Minette helped herself to a well loaded plate of food from the table, but Ursula hung back, as jumpy as the first day I had met her by the oratory.

'Aren't you going to eat?' I asked, but she shook her head. 'I want to go home.'

The tell-tale whine in her voice spoke of tiredness and tension and I knew if something wasn't done to soothe her, the complaints would rapidly escalate.

'I'm ravenous,' I said, 'come and help me choose...'

Eve said, 'I've hardly spoken to anyone but Mike - thank God, he's latched onto someone else now, I think it's James Millford's daughter, Danielle - she looks as if she can handle herself.'

I glanced over my shoulder and saw Mike talking to a woman in her thirties, with auburn hair and a creamy complexion, the image of her father. Delia had said our parents were in our blood and bones - did Danielle and I share that commonality – was she of the same blood and bones as me? I couldn't feel any connection - didn't feel much beyond curiosity.

The buzz of conversation had quietened as people enjoyed the food. There was a sofa at one end of the dining room, so I settled down there with the girls, Minette eating as if she was starving while Ursula picked at morsels of food on my plate, like a little bird.

Eve and I chatted to Nick. 'It's lovely Sarah could be here,' Eve said to him.

'The children are pleased...' he remarked and I wondered how the reunion was going.

He mentioned a booklet he'd started writing about Littern – Eve had shown him *The Legends and History* and he thought it might be good to have something more up-to-date and scientifically based. He asked if Eve would be interested in doing the illustrations, but she side-stepped the question –

'Why don't you ask Iris?' she said, 'she has plenty of drawings of the island done by her mother...'

When Nicholas didn't respond to her suggestion, I thought perhaps he too felt only antipathy towards Juliet. He mentioned that he had plans to open access to Clave Valley – it was an aspect of the island's natural history which made it unique. In the spring, he would form a work party from the conservation group and see how a pathway could be created without damaging local environment and habitats.

'That'll need some sensitivity...' I said, thinking aloud.

'Do you think I lack the necessary sensitivity?' he asked seeming to take offence where none had been intended.

The phone rang and Oliver Millford clapped his hands and asked for quiet – it was James phoning from South Africa to speak to Edgar. The phone was passed round from one member of the family to another.

When he'd rung off, Edgar addressed the room, 'James is extraordinarily kind - just because someone's an actor - it doesn't mean they're negligent or difficult...'

'So you've said *ad nauseum*...' Nicholas replied.

Patrick intervened, 'It takes an exceptional man like my father to have the foresight to see that, after all, James would end up being as conscientious in his filial duty as any of his sons...'

'More conscientious...' Edgar grumbled.

There followed a few informal speeches, tributes from the family to Edgar, then Eve told me Beatrix had agreed to drive her home as she and her father would be leaving soon.

Nicholas had persuaded Tom and Nina to allow his children to stay for the night, but when Ursula was asked if she would like to join them, she shook her head and seemed close to tears. The weather had worsened and people were beginning to drift away. I found Patrick in the kitchen, wrapping plates of unwanted food and stacking them in the fridge.

'Ursula's overtired,' I said.

He nodded, 'We'll go as soon as we can.'

Nicholas was pouring himself a scotch. 'Sarah was going straight back to London, but I've persuaded her to stay,' he said.

'Then perhaps you should make sure you're in a fit state to talk to her,' Patrick warned him.

'Bloody nerve...' he said, his voice flat and humourless.

He wasn't drunk but he'd consumed a fair amount of wine, while we'd been talking earlier and was becoming slightly belligerent.

'I'll make some strong coffee,' Patrick said.

I left them, remembering what Beatrix had told me on the night of the Clootie Well ceremony, about the close bond between twins, a bond which should never be broken.

Rowena was sitting at the bottom of the stairs, with Oliver. She had a book open on her lap, but she was listening to them talking in the kitchen and I thought how I had once tried to make sense of my parents' life, by piecing together snatches of overheard conversation.

'My dad's really embarrassing,' she was saying.

'Like the rest of us oldies..?' Oliver asked.

Rowena grimaced. 'Crap - you read my mind,' she said, it was the kind of dry wit Zoë would have employed at the same age.

Oliver stood up, he was tall and rangy, tawny haired - from the photographs I had seen at Aspen Terrace, I thought he was like his mother, Beth.

'You must be Iris,' he said, 'I'm James's son – my father's looking forward to meeting you again, when he gets back to the U.K.'

'Is he?' I asked, trying to keep the edge out of my voice.

'We've been hearing about you and your family. We'll be in Devon for Christmas, persuade Patrick to arrange something – a reunion.'

I wasn't sure what to make of him – his sense of humour was evident in his eyes and the curve of his mouth – humour which I couldn't read - was it intended to be good-natured, or practised at my expense?

'I'll speak to Patrick,' I said, distracted by Ursula who had slipped past me into the kitchen and was becoming increasingly wound up about wanting to go home.

Finally, Patrick snapped and told her to be quiet. When Oliver raised his eyebrows and laughed, I excused myself - Patrick had been busy all day - he was tired and normally his patience with Ursula was without limits.

Retrieving our coats from the cloakroom, I thanked Tom and Nina for the party, and then stood waiting for Patrick in the hallway. Rowena and Oliver had gone upstairs with her twin brothers and a babble of excited chatter and laughter floated down, followed by the sound of loud music.

Minette had worn herself out; she was quiet and clung to my hand, head resting against my arm. I was thinking how relieved I felt to have been accepted by Nina and Eleanor, two sensitive and intelligent women - how grateful I was to have survived the afternoon -

Beatrix still hadn't left and I could hear her talking to Patrick, 'don't you think Iris's presence is upsetting Ursula? She doesn't want a substitute mother...'

I smoothed Minette's hair, as she looked up at me, listening for Patrick's reply, he said, 'Like other children – I'm sure Ursula can make the necessary adjustment...'

'But Ursula isn't like other children,' Beatrix said, 'isn't that always your argument?'

I didn't hear his answer, but knew him well enough to perceive the prickly atmosphere, Beatrix's words had been administered like drops of poison and though he hadn't raised his voice, I sensed he was extremely angry.

I tried to move away, but Minette clung tightly to me, refusing to shift as if her feet were fixed to the floor.

Beatrix had spoken again and Patrick's voice was raised now, 'I thought I'd made myself clear. I don't expect to find myself put in a position where my loyalties are divided between Iris and the family.'

'Then choose someone different,' Beatrix said her voice harsh, 'you could have anybody...'

'Except that whether it suits you or not, I've already made my choice - if subject to your malicious meddling, Iris will still have me...'

Minette had a worried frown on her face. 'It's all right - just a family squabble,' I assured her.

Patrick had recently raised the subject of marriage, but I wasn't ready to formalise our relationship - something that seemed to me unnecessary and premature – at least, until I had cleared up my questions about Juliet and James.

We were ready to leave - and stepping out into Park Avenue, were confronted by a blast of cold rain and wind. In the streets of Safford Bridge, the shop windows were dark and blank - the power cut had affected most of the town. Ursula pushed her way between Patrick and me, holding our hands, while Minette ran on ahead. In the gale, my coat flapped so hard it stung my legs as I walked. The wind blustered round street corners in unpredictable, violent gusts and thunder boomed overhead as a spear of lightning struck at a row of trees in the park.

Danielle and Oliver weren't planning to stay in Devon, and Patrick wanted to spend the night at Aspen Terrace, but Ursula was crying noisily at the prospect of being off the island. The weekend as far as she was concerned, was Littern time -

Patrick had allowed himself to be persuaded, but it took over an hour to reach Osford and when we arrived at the causeway, the sea, a churning mass of inky water, was still flowing so fast into the gully that we couldn't cross safely.

'I want to go to Marisands,' Ursula sobbed from the back seat.

Patrick got out of the car, slamming the door and walked down to the water, bending hard into the wind and heavy rain, hoping to gauge how long we might have to wait to get home. I followed him to the edge of the shore, where he stood, the tail of his coat snapping in the wind, as he contemplated the waves as they dashed down over the road, while above us, towering clouds covered the metallic, grey sky.

Shouting to make himself heard, he said, 'We could be sitting here for hours - I'm not going to risk it.'

I nodded, agreeing with him.

'You'll get soaked,' he said, his annoyance evident in his face, 'you'll ruin your clothes.'

I gestured that we might move over to the stone shelter, where we would at least be able to hear each other speak.

The shelter had stones missing from the walls, leaving open cavities that caused the wind to whistle as it blew in sharp little draughts round our heads - rain dripped through the roof - we huddled together but Patrick seemed no calmer.

'Something needs to happen with Ursula – our being stuck here, in the middle of bloody nowhere, is a symbol of the power she has over all of us.'

'She probably can't help it - none of us can help it,' I said.

'Help what?' he asked irritably.

'Our eccentricities or defence mechanisms, whatever it is we use when we're lost and don't know how else to act.'

'Is one of your eccentricities philosophising in this kind of situation?' he asked. 'Why not get back to the car? There's nothing heroic about a cold in the head.'

'Come with me then,' I coaxed, but he refused.

Across the water, the trees on the island shook like dancers in a frenzy as the wind hurled them this way and that.

I wasn't sure what to say, Ursula did upset people - frequently I found I was trying to protect her, to encourage her not to draw attention to herself in a negative way.

Patrick said, 'the family are no doubt sitting in the warmth and comfort of Tom's house, holding a party post-mortem over a few drinks - deciding who looked okay - who didn't look okay - who said what to offend whom...'

'Not really my scene,' I said.

'But an improvement on this...'

'At least we're together.'

'God preserve me from optimists,' he said and at last there was a trace of a smile on his face.

I leaned towards him, stroking away raindrops from his cheeks as he brushed my lips gently with the tips of his fingers.

'We're going to Aspen Terrace.'

Back at the car, he told the girls we were going to Safford Bridge and there should be no further argument.

Ursula began the high pitched chant which usually preceded an outburst, 'No, no, no,' she said, 'no, no, no.'

Minette put her hands over her ears.

Patrick started to explain, 'if the car was blown off the causeway into the sea...'

Ursula started to cry.

He spoke to her again, keeping his voice steady, 'It's all right...'

But I could hear her, 'No, no,' repeated softly under her breath.

The car which had been rocking, buffeted by the wind, swayed more violently as the storm renewed its strength. A flash of lightning from between the clouds lit up the gorse, bracken and boulders that bordered the road.

'I want to go to Marisands,' Ursula whined.

I shushed her - I could feel Patrick's tension, as a fresh blast of rain lashed against the car windows. He tried to reverse onto Osford Lane. It took ten minutes, as the car slipped and slid, going deeper and deeper into mud, before finally he could turn it round, away from the island.

The engine stalled and then wouldn't start. I put my hand out to touch the damp sleeve of his sweater - his hair was ruffled and I longed to smooth it –

Ursula had fallen silent. Minette with the simple common sense of a child had given her a sweet to suck and it seemed it wasn't possible to suck and whine at the same time.

We sat, rain thundering down on the roof of the car until, after a several attempts, Patrick managed to start the car.

'Are you absolutely sure you two girls wouldn't like to stay at Tom's tonight?' he asked.

They had linked arms and shook their heads together – whatever we said, they were staying with us.

'What a shame,' Patrick murmured, 'Iris is looking particularly lovely this evening in her blue coat and I had something special in mind.'

# Chapter 46

The storm had cleared the air and for a few days, the sun picked out the vibrant reds and yellows of autumn - it caught the pale feathers beneath gulls' wings and tinted them gold.

But then mid-October brought blowy days and the bright, burnished leaves swirled down and patterned the ground like torn fragments of cloth, blowing into the house and carpeting the hall. In the lane, leaves whirled up and skittered across the road and in the evenings, it was cold enough to light the first fire of the season.

With the promise of Verena bringing Yuuka to visit at half term, Minette had resigned herself to life at St. Mary's with only a few grumbles, but St. Safan's had only been back two weeks before Ursula was found by Eve hiding in the studio. Since the start of school her mood had been subdued and volatile, by turns. The exams she was taking in November, would decide her future and Patrick was anxious that if she performed badly, she would be forced to leave.

Ursula had been on the loose, out in the rain, since before nine o'clock. She told Eve that Patrick had left her at Tom's house on his way to work and Nina had watched her in through the school gates - but then she'd escaped from the playground, caught a bus from Safford Bridge to Narescombe and walked along Palk's Reach, crossing the causeway on foot.

Cold, hungry and wet, she stood in the kitchen sucking the fingers of her left hand through her woolly mitten. I handed her a warm towel to dry herself. When she'd changed, I hung her clothes in the airing cupboard, smoothing them with my hand, and heard a clanking sound from her blazer pockets – she had a collection of shells with fragments of plaster attached – obviously pulled off the oratory walls.

I phoned the school to let them know Ursula had been found and left a message for Patrick at the hospital. Ursula seemed to make little progress at St. Safan's and now sat at the kitchen table in Minette's clothes, with a pile of text books, pretending to do revision – every now and then, sighing and frowning in a self-conscious, irritating way. Unsure what Patrick would want me to do, I decided to attempt a different approach – as soon as her clothes had aired and we'd had lunch, I would take her back to school.

Ursula was crushed when I announced my intentions. I struggled to persuade her back into her school blouse and cardigan. She refused to put on her skirt or coat – we were engaged in the task for almost twenty minutes without any result. Though she looked slight with her thin legs and arms, she had a core of determination and considerable physical strength. Opting for a more psychological approach, I picked up her satchel and asked her to come to the car, ignoring the fact she was only half dressed.

She slumped down at the kitchen table and wound her legs tightly round the chair. Her face took on a stubborn expression, 'I'm not going – I'm sorry,' she said, squinting up at me from beneath her thick fringe.

Ursula had the ability of all the Pirans to descend from arrogance to humility in one graceful movement and my sympathy flowed out to her.

'Your Dad would be pleased if you went back...' I said. But since they'd returned from Nairobi, Ursula's devotion to Patrick had been replaced by rebellion. Whatever Honor had said, for the moment, had turned her against him.

Losing patience, I clutched at her wrist and pulled her to her feet, her shoes scraping along the terracotta tiles of the kitchen floor as I dragged her towards the hall. It was useless and driven to physical force, I was certain Patrick would think that the end, however desirable, didn't justify the means.

Ursula began sniffling. 'I don't like that school,' she said, tears welling in her eyes.

'Isn't it like any other school, both good and bad?' I suggested.

Darkness like a storm wave passed across Ursula's blue eyes. 'My legs are hurting,' she said.

I was still clinging to her - if I let go she would lose her balance and fall to the floor - so I lowered her carefully back onto the chair and released my grip on her hands.

She put her head down on her arms and sobbed.

'I'm sorry,' I said wearily.

But there was no pause in Ursula's crying - it began to rise to a crescendo. I took off my coat and hung it in the hall. My head throbbed to the orchestration of her weeping, as I sat down beside her at the table.

'I'm never leaving the island again,' she said, her peat-black eyelashes spangled with tears.

'I'm sure that isn't true,' I told her, 'you stay at Aspen Terrace with your dad, don't you like it there?'

Ursula ignored me, 'I like it on the island when we go for walks by the sea. I pretend Mum is with us...'

I passed her a tissue from a box on the window sill. She dried her eyes and scrubbed at her face, until a fresh bout of tears overtook her.

'At Uncle Tom's, he keeps telling me to hurry up – they don't understand children because they haven't got any. I don't like being hurried. Do you know why Uncle Nick has a beard?' she demanded, 'It's because it's such a rush in the morning to get Rowena and the twins to school he doesn't have time to shave.'

'I'm glad I don't have to shave,' I said, but didn't manage to raise a smile.

'I don't like it at Lyncross either. Granddad sits in his chair all day phoning people and sounding cross. He isn't allowed to go out in his car anymore because he knocked a man off his bicycle in Narescombe and his leg was broken, it was a compound fracture - Dad told me...

'...And Aunt Beatrix talks for hours about compost, seaweed and dung. I don't want to help with gardening and running the vegetable stall. Granddad says it's a bloody eyesore and I agree with him.

'...I tell Dad I want to stay here, I say it over and over, but he doesn't listen. When I repeat things, he says "you don't need to do that, Ursula", but I do, because no-one is listening - Rowena tells me to shut up, the twins say rude words and Uncle Nick says, "Stop that chanting, you're getting on my nerves". He shouts like the man who sells cauliflowers in Narescombe market.'

She rubbed her swollen red eyes as a further flood of tears coursed down her cheeks. And then as if spent by her outburst, became like a rag doll, flopping her head on her arms again, as if she hadn't the strength to hold herself upright.

'I only had a mum for little while,' she said.

I remembered how desolate I'd felt after Juliet had died, utterly abandoned. She dabbed at her damp cheeks with a sodden tissue and Quirk ambled towards us and sank down by her feet.

'My mum has hair like a big curly mop. When she was angry, my head whirled like a washing machine. Dad talked to her calmly, because that's the proper thing to do, but she wouldn't stop screaming at him.'

'That was difficult,' I said.

'I like Quirk,' she went, 'he doesn't say "shouldn't you be at school?" or "aren't you lonely and sad being at home all day?"'

'Dogs are good like that...'

'Geraldine used to say, "Shoo shoo, go away bloody dog" she made him live in a cave.'

'Perhaps she was afraid of him...'

Sounding brighter, Ursula sniffed loudly, 'I've decided - I don't need to know more things than I know already - so there isn't any point in going to school.'

As I passed her a clean tissue, I recalled how I had once shared her philosophy.

'I'm glad Geraldine doesn't come here anymore, she used to peer at me like an old owl, though owls can see very well and I don't think she sees well at all. I must have been a blur in the corner of her eye - she said I "loomed up" at the door of the studio. I used to run to Thrift Cottage. Why is Thrift Cottage so tiny?'

I explained how the cottage had been built for Alice, who had never married - how she'd described it as being like a doll's house.

'Does that mean Eve will never get married?'

'I don't know,' I said.

'Why is that painting in the studio all broken?' she asked, I guessed she meant William's canvas – his contribution to *The Stations* series.

'Because that's how some people think of life, made up of bits and pieces – dreams and secrets and being afraid. All the pieces are needed to make a complete picture. Just as all the shells are needed in the oratory to complete the patterns - you've been told not to go to there, Ursula.'

Ursula blew her nose, 'You won't tell Dad about the shells? That would be unkind.'

'Why don't you talk to your dad?' I asked.

'Because it would make him sad to know I'm unhappy.'

Ursula slipped off her chair and came for a hug. I glanced over her shoulder at the kitchen clock, it had taken so long to quieten her - it would be pointless to do anything now, other than keep her with me.

St. Mary's was holding an Autumn Fayre that afternoon and I had agreed with Minette I would go into school early and meet her there. When I explained my plan, Ursula showed no hesitation in putting on her clothes and jumping into the car, though we would be leaving the island, something she had vowed, only minutes earlier, she would never do again.

At the school, Minette was in the foyer, her bulging back pack trailing on the floor, her sports holdall, bursting open. I took them from her, she seemed unsurprised to see Ursula and I began to feel uncomfortable. I'd noticed how often Ursula was playing a part – *had I been taken in?* What I disliked most was my inability to tell.

Minette's pocket money was in an envelope, I handed it to her and gave Ursula some small change so she could buy something for herself and they ran off into the assembly hall where the Fayre was being held.

I searched the stalls for old clothes, bead necklaces, scarves and hats - including an enormous fur "Cossack" hat - to make up a dressing-up box at Marisands. The girls had soon joined a group making Christmas cards, with pictures cut from magazines, glitter, ribbon, fabric and feathers. Ursula seemed happy and at ease, looking up from her activities every now and then, taking in all the colour and busyness of the Fayre - then holding up her handiwork for me to admire. When she'd confided in me earlier, I'd been struck by her perceptive observations of people – it was her particular kind of intelligence – a gift which had perhaps been used on this occasion to dupe me.

While the girls were happily occupied, I collected Minette's coat from the cloakroom and phoned Patrick. His kindness and understanding touched me deeply and I couldn't bear the unpleasant feeling that Ursula might also be taking advantage of him -

Before we left the school, Patrick had appeared in the hallway. Ursula ran to him and Minette followed more diffidently, waiting expectantly until he drew her to his side.

Seeing Minette craving his love and attention made me wary, protective - they shared the virtue of being without guile - a quality which perhaps blinded them to the convoluted actions of people who were less straightforward than they were themselves.

*

Patrick often played Yvette's piano in the evenings as a way to unwind from the stresses of work, to satisfy what he called, *the urgent need for tranquillity*. Though he was a sensitive and proficient musician, nothing could match the many haunting moods that had marked both Kos's playing and his original compositions.

One morning, when I took out Quirk, I noticed a thin trail of smoke rising into the sky from the woods in the area of Kos's encampment and my heart lifted. I planned to drive along the lane later in the day and see if Kos was all right - but before I could do so, he had come to Marisands, arriving as quietly as the shadow of a bird passing across a window - behaving as if he had never been away - standing on the drive with his bicycle and the trailer full of gardening tools.

When I went to greet him, Kos pushed back his curtain of black hair to reveal his pale face and dark-rimmed eyes.

We'd been in the kitchen having lunch. 'Will you join us?' I asked. Patrick and Eve were still at the table.

'I shall keep a low profile,' Kos said. 'Sometimes the unbidden guest is one too many – that's a saying from the old country.'

I could have argued that I had just "bidden" him, but his attention was focussed on the overgrown rose bush on the trellis. He rummaged in his tool bag and moving away from me, began to clip it with the secateurs, making a heap of thorny branches on the ground.

'I'll save you some food...' I said.

He glanced up, 'Thank you, but I have no appetite.'

Noting his difficult mood, I went back indoors. When he had finished pruning the rose, I saw through the window he had started digging the flowerbeds, pulling out coarse grasses, collecting piles of weeds.

Eve left for the studio and Patrick went up to the study to work. I invited Kos again to come in and have a mug of tea. The weather was changing, becoming unpleasant, a mist had descended and settled on our clothes and skin like cold, damp flannel.

'Wouldn't you like to play the piano?' I asked when he refused, but he shook his head.

I fetched a sandwich and tea for him anyway. I'd noticed how he'd been reticent with Eve – despite his long absence, they had exchanged only a few words as she passed him, crossing the garden. Many things had changed since Kos had gone travelling - Minette had come home, and Patrick and Ursula were often at Marisands -

'Don't allow all the comings and goings put you off,' I said.

Kos didn't reply but began to clean and oil his tools with a rag. When he'd finished, he scraped a thick cake of mud off his leather boots and kicked it into the kitchen flower bed.

'We've all been hoping you'd come back - everybody here likes you,' I said, wanting to put him at ease.

'...Liking is a luxury, but loving is a privilege...' he said moodily.

'Is that a saying from the old country?'

'No, it is a saying of Kos...'

'Do you remember, how when you first came here to work, you made me feel it was possible to stay in this house? You were the only friend I had on the island...'

Kos pulled a face, his mouth turned down at the corners, 'For a while, this is true, I am your only friend, but now you have many friends and Eve too has many friends...'

'You're still in love with Eve?'

He shrugged, 'I am not afraid of love, love comes and goes...' he said.

'But we want it to stay – Eve was sorry - she's very fond of you...'

Kos frowned, 'This word *fond* - it is for children or old women - you English don't understand that there is no comfort in the word *fond*,' he paused, 'but it doesn't matter - I left in search of freedom not comfort...'

'Did you find what you were looking for?' I asked – thinking of the story Eve had told me about Kos and his student.

'If I find it, I'll let you know,' he said.

His pallor was unhealthy, sallow, like a plant that had been buried under a stone.

I said, 'I suppose you've been sleeping rough...'

'I leave my van for a while - I sleep on benches, under bridges, on the beach, in the woods...'

'Kelda went missing too – she's been in hospital.'

Kos nodded knowingly, 'We desire the freedom from guilt – that's what we share. We're all running away - but not you, perhaps now – this is your home.'

'And in a way, yours too...'

Kos nodded his head once, with that gesture of his that was almost a bow.

'Mending the steps to the oratory – that's become quite urgent...' I said. 'And we should finish the oratory garden...'

'Next time - I see what can be done - for St. Thrif and the White Virgin, I will do anything.'

It was a gracious thought, but something about his manner was unsettling, he was being evasive, as if he while he'd been away, he had retreated more deeply into his private world.

'Eve, she is happy with her boring doctor from Narescombe?' he asked.

'I believe not,' I told him, impatient with his sour mood - I wanted Marisands to be a place of peace and contentment – no more secrets, trouble or darkness. 'What's happened Kos?'

'A person dear to me has died, I am in mourning, he was like my son.'

'I'm sorry.'

'But I see from your face that Eve has told you what I've done?'

I studied the ground, not sure which would be the greatest travesty, to betray Eve's confidence or to lie to him. 'Eve told me something about your life – isn't it better we know each other as we really are.'

'I felt like a miscreant,' Kos said, 'now I feel like a murderer.'

'But you're not...' I insisted, though I understood his feelings - knowing how Beatrix's words, blaming me for Juliet's death, had also made me feel like a murderer.

'Perhaps one day I will believe this,' Kos said sounding full of doubt.

I nodded, hoping that one day, I might believe it too.

# Chapter 47

Verena and Yuuka had already arrived at Safford Bridge station as we rushed across the concourse. Yuuka was emerging from the train, seeking out Minette, who let go of my hand as soon as she spied her friend and raced along the platform to greet her.

A cold wind cut straight through the station, Verena shivered, 'Thank God you warned me about this place out of season - I've bought a suitcase full of warm jumpers for Yuuka and almost as many for myself.'

We took refuge in The Pilgrims' Inn for lunch and managed to find a window seat facing onto the town square. It was a blustery day. Shaken hard by the wind, the beech trees that lined the square sent their yellowing leaves fluttering down to the pavement.

As we ate, I watched a young girl with gold-red hair chasing her long woollen scarf. It blew along the ground by the iron railings of the narrow garden at the front of the Inn. The scarf was russet brown and kingfisher blue, colours which had suited Zoë. She ran a few steps, then reached out awkwardly, until she caught its tail and wound and knotted it securely round her neck.

The vignette was over in seconds and as the girl hurried on through the square, down towards the bridge, I convinced myself that had I managed to see her face, she would have borne no resemblance to Zoë. Zoë's pale red hair was unusual, but not unique - it was just that since her phone conversation with Eve suggesting she might be back in the country, I had found her silence yet more torturing.

Yuuka was eager to get to Littern after Minette had told her we had only a short time before the tide would cut off the island, so we didn't linger.

As we made the sharp descent into Narescombe, Yuuka said, 'This place is like a postcard,' she wrinkled her nose, 'London smells bad. Here the wind is like a good spirit that blows all the badness away...'

I could feel the girls' excitement, when we crossed the causeway, 'Look out for a giant oak tree...' Minette told her.

When we reached the gate, I stopped the car so they could run to the house and before they had reached the porch, Eve had appeared with Quirk's dark presence behind her.

'Yuuka's been looking forward to this so much...' Verena said.

'The school was all right about her coming?'

'Every concession is rather grudging – things take forever if they consult the grandmother - but they've given in and I suppose the arrangement doesn't have to be perfect...'

While Eve helped the girls settle - Verena and I talked over coffee.

'You seem quite balanced now,' Verena said archly. 'You had me worried in London.'

'I've heard nothing more from David and I'm glad...'

'...Because Patrick has swept you off your feet?'

'Probably not the words he would choose,' I said and smiled at her, 'and not exactly how it feels – there's a sense of being poised, waiting for something more...'

'...But for what?'

'For our love to deepen or mature – in the meantime - I enjoy his company and he enjoys mine...'

Verena studied me intently, 'Is there's something you're not telling me?'

'There are lots of things I'm not telling you.'

She eyed me expectantly, but I chose my words with care, my negotiations with Patrick on the subject of marriage were intensely personal, something I needed to resolve on my own. Patrick still missed Kenya - I could hear it in his voice when he talked to Richard on the phone, though he tried – lovingly – to disguise it.

'Patrick's considering working for the McGenis Charity, in London, just a few days a month, but I need to be sure he's content with that...' I said.

'He suffers from wanderlust..?'

'More than that, Patrick needs a sense of vocation – he told me the first time we met. And I need resolution where my family's concerned – I'm still making do with hints, suspicions and innuendoes, when what I need is facts...'

We decided to have a walk on the marshes. We would leave once Tom had dropped Ursula off at Marisands – he was on his way to visit Edgar. I was concerned there might be competition between Yuuka and Ursula for Minette's company, but when Verena placed the three of them in charge of Quirk for the afternoon, they worked well together.

Eve followed us along the lane in William's old car, with the girls and Quirk in the back and when we reached The Retreat, they set off along the footpath together. Verena asked how things were with Nicholas and I explained there were signs he and Sarah might get back together. Since Edgar's party, Sarah had been returning to the island whenever she was free to see him and the children.

Verena sighed. 'You were right to discourage me, Nicholas Piran and I needed to be kept apart.'

I took her arm, 'Don't be disappointed, managing Nicholas's children would have taken a woman of steel...'

'I could have been a woman of steel - I've had years of practice in school.'

'It needn't affect your ideas of moving to Safford Bridge, if that's still on your mind...'

'I'd given up, thanks to your obviously ambivalent reaction...' she teased.

As we approached the tower, I heard Eve call the children and Quirk, a flock of carrion crows were circling overhead, there was probably a dead animal nearby and the effect as they darkened the sky was menacing.

Eve wanted to climb the tower for an overall view of the island which she could include in her paintings of St. Thrif. I had tried to discourage her, but though I'd warned that the tower was dangerously unstable, when she mentioned it, Verena offered, if I would look after the girls, to climb up with her.

We waited while Eve and Verena picked their way across the rubble on the ground floor of the tower and climbed the steps, waving to them as they peered down over the parapet. Then I led the girls away over the sand dunes so they could have a run with the dog on Coyle Sands. The north wind was driving the sea ashore, in a steady stream of curling, waves, laced with spume. From a distance, the children - their long dark hair streaming behind them - could have been the offspring of one family.

Ursula was shouting and racing about – the lively breeze made the children and Quirk frisky. I glanced back at the tower, where Verena was looking out to sea and Eve sat perched on the parapet, making a sketch of Littern.

'Someone should campaign to have the tower made safe,' Verena said when they joined me, 'it makes a wonderful vantage point.'

Eve, her cheeks reddened by the cold wind showed me her drawing. The Hagdon Hills sloped gently like a woman's breasts and the whole of Littern appeared to form the outline of a female body. Holtleigh Hill made the figure large bellied as if she carried a child - the promontory of Beckhead Cliffs created a neck, with the small island as a severed head. At the causeway, the legs appeared cut off at the thigh and formed a horned crescent where the island, centuries ago, had broken away from Palk's Reach.

'I wonder who it is - St. Thrif, the White Virgin or the moon goddess..?' I asked.

'What a mysterious place...' Verena remarked, 'how suitable - the island as an image of rebirth...'

'It's spooky,' Yuuka said studying Eve's sketch and Ursula agreed.

'It's just an island shaped like a woman,' Minette said in her down to earth way, 'can we go somewhere else now?'

Eve was animated by her discovery and decided to go back to Thrift Cottage to work on her painting.

I sent the girls ahead on the path towards Beckhead Cliffs with Quirk, so Verena and I could talk.

Verena linked arms with me, 'Rose and I wanted to ask how you would feel about Yuuka staying with you - she could change school to St. Mary's. Rose says her greatest need is to have a family and I'm sure Patrick would take to her...'

'I'm sure he would - and I'm sure Rose is right, but I don't think I could manage, not now.'

'Why ever not..?' Verena said, pulling away from me, 'After all the work *we've* done to secure Yuuka's future – because *you* were concerned – you've decided to withdraw from the situation?'

She'd caught me unprepared and I wasn't sure how to defend myself, 'The house is already bursting at the seams.'

'If it's the practicalities, you'd be paid for Yuuka's upkeep and as you already have to juggle Minette and Ursula's needs, I can hardly see how one more would make any difference.'

I stared ahead at the girls, bright in their poster-coloured waterproofs hurrying along the path, Quirk trotting beside them. When Patrick had spoken of marriage, we'd also spoken of trying for a child of our own.

'Yuuka needs someone to take care of her - look at her - she's having a wonderful time,' Verena persisted, 'they're all getting along, she'll never want to go back to London and Rose and I have really stuck our necks out...'

I knew Verena was right - everyone needed to belong - to believe they had a refuge among a particular group of people in a particular place. I'd said as much to Sister Gabriel - and thought it about Kos, when he'd returned.

The rest of the walk was marred by Verena's bad mood. When she spoke to me, her voice was like the tail of a kite snapping in the breeze. She kept reminding me of all she and Rose had done; she told me how she had used every means of persuasion – fair and foul – to convince the nuns to help Yuuka – not to send her to Nottingham.

'My father said you had no real understanding of the importance of family,' Verena accused, 'Patrick will understand, he comes from a vast family...'

'And doesn't necessarily want another...'

In the end, we didn't make it all the way to Beckhead Cliffs, Yuuka wasn't used to walking so far and after an hour, all three girls complained they were hungry.

I had tried placating Verena, saying Yuuka would be welcome to stay in the holidays – *every holiday* - but when we arrived back at Marisands, she swept into the house like an icy gust of wind and went straight upstairs to her room.

Tired and tousle-headed the girls sat at the kitchen table devouring the scones Eve had made, while Quirk lay under their feet hoovering up the crumbs.

When Eve joined us for supper, she whispered, 'What's wrong? There's a terrible atmosphere...'

The meal had been so awkward and uncomfortable I'd sent the girls to eat in front of the TV. Verena chatted to Eve, but when she addressed me, she was distant and cold.

Later, Patrick dropped in to collect Ursula, he was on call and she would be staying at Tom's house. Yuuka was shy and easily over-awed, but he was a natural father and told the girls a bed-time story about smugglers and how they had hidden caskets of booty in the caves below Marisands. His visit passed too quickly and in no time, he was leaving me with a hasty kiss, encouraging Ursula into the car and departing for the evening.

That night I slept badly as the problem of Yuuka's future, raised by Verena, coursed through my mind and it seemed I had just fallen into a light doze, when she woke me, tapping on my bedroom door, early the next morning.

She'd brought mugs of tea and sat on the end of my bed, a cardigan over her nightdress and woolly socks protecting her feet from the coolness of the house.

'I've come to say sorry – about yesterday...' she said. 'We just thought that now you were established - Patrick's rooted here, you love each other – having Yuuka seemed a simple way in which you could play your part...'

'Patrick and I struggle to find time together - you've seen how it is...'

Verena shrugged, 'Isn't that the nature of love in maturity – complicated and overrun with other people's children?'

'We'd like our own child...' I told her, 'but I'm nearly forty and if it's going to happen, it will have to happen soon. Maybe it was presumptuous, but I'd thought caring for Yuuka was something that might bring comfort and pleasure to you...'

Verena sipped her tea, 'It might do, but I've heard from the boring engineer, he wrote to me from Geneva.'

'Does he have a name?' My heart sank at the prospect of Verena becoming embroiled once again with someone she had already declared unsatisfactory.

'Dieter – Dieter Schwegler - he's coming to London and wants to see me.'

'Perhaps he likes children – perhaps he'll take to Yuuka...' I said, teasing her.

She laughed. 'I don't intend to give him the chance – Yuuka would be much more content living on Iris's ark.'

Eve had offered to look after Minette and Yuuka for the morning. We would meet in Safford Bridge for lunch, collect Ursula from Tom's house and then Eve would take all three girls to the cinema.

Despite her denials, Verena's interest in the town hadn't waned. There was a hair salon that offered on-the-spot consultations and she tried to persuade me to make an appointment to have my hair cut and coloured, but I'd got into the routine of having it trimmed at Mopheads in Narescombe and didn't want to make a change.

'What a shame. It would give you such a lift...' she said, 'take years off you, especially now you're nearly forty...'

'Something you obviously feel is necessary...'

'Desirable...' she said.

The Bridge House Bookshop had undergone a reprieve of sorts and had re-opened selling remaindered books. When we crossed the square, I glanced around and listened out for the sound of Kelda's flute - Delia had let me know that Kelda was out of hospital and had been living at Hintham Ridge while she convalesced.

Just as we reached the river walk, I saw a pulse of colour as someone came out of the bookshop - Chinese turquoise and russet – the colours of a kingfisher - Zoë's colours.

'Did you see that girl?' I asked - she was hurrying towards the market.

'Which girl..?' Verena twisted round to follow my gaze.

'I keep thinking I've seen Zoë,' I admitted, knowing I'd never find her now among the crowds.

'This has happened before?'

'When she first left Pimlico, I thought I saw her all the time - but only once before here - recently.'

Verena tactfully withheld any comment about my state of mind and offered to take the photograph I kept of the girls in my handbag and ask the shop assistant if she had seen Zoë.

'She was probably a figment of my imagination,' I said feeling foolish and wishing I'd kept my thoughts to myself.

'It'll make up to for yesterday's fit of pique, a sort of apology,' she said - insisting I open my bag and retrieve the photograph so she could take it into the bookshop.

She came out a few minutes later, a coffee-table book on European history tucked under her arm, she looked pleased with herself.

'The assistant said she's seen the girl before – though she wasn't sure if she matched the picture of Zoë. The girl goes into the shop to warm up by the radiator and then vanishes – she never buys anything. The woman thought she might run a stall in the market - she's been going into the shop since the weather's turned cold.'

Verena's suggested we should wander round the market, but we found no-one resembling the girl in the turquoise coat and no sign of Zoë - and in an irrational way I was relieved, afraid if Zoë saw me first, pursuing her, she might turn tail and run.

We gave up searching and made our way to The Pilgrims' Inn to have coffee while we waited for the others to arrive. We sat at the large table I'd reserved for lunch, set out with a vase of holly with deep red berries and a spray of winter jasmine.

Verena said, '...Poor Yuuka... You must think I'm being selfish about Dieter - but I'm running out of opportunities...'

'I assumed you'd sort of adopted Yuuka – and I thought it was good for you.'

I'd imagined Yuuka softening her, wearing down her sharp edges, creating a brighter and more loving future for them both.

'I won't ask what you meant by that, and I suppose - unlike you - it may be my only chance of becoming a mother.'

We talked then about what I had learned of Juliet – her many secrets - and how difficult it had been to persuade people to talk – to break the circle of silence.

'Perhaps they believe you're like Juliet - someone who reacts strongly..?'

'Something happened when my mother went to the tower – it's always been a place for lover's trysts or illicit meetings. Juliet must have had some idea what she was going to discover...'

'Something monstrous and gothic..?' she suggested with a smile. 'Perhaps you should write a new monstrous and gothic series of the *Seabright Island Adventures*...'

I laughed at her. 'People seem to like them as they are, traditional and nostalgic, that's their charm. I'd only re-write them if I could be sure of a happy ending...'

'Do you doubt it?' Verena asked.

Her question caused a shiver to run down my spine but before I could think of a suitable answer, Eve had arrived with Minette and Yuuka – both pink-cheeked from the cold air outside. Eve's blond hair, ruffled by the wind, fell softly round her face and Minette and Yuuka were bright-eyed, bursting with energy and life.

'Are you okay?' Eve asked.

I nodded, but I wasn't sure what had unnerved me most – my strange "sightings" of Zoë - the need to persist in discovering the truth about Juliet and the identity of my father – or a superstitious dread of the future.

# Chapter 48

Verena and Yuuka returned to London at the end of half term and the year descended rapidly towards a chilly, damp winter – a sea mist settled over Littern and refused to shift for days.

While the fog remained, Patrick couldn't get to the island and I couldn't get to the mainland. I slept badly and if I managed to drift off, the Narescombe foghorn boomed in the distance and woke me or I dreamed about Zoë and about the oratory garden, which in my subconscious had become an impenetrable thicket of silver birch trees, whose trunks and branches had been eaten into lace by enormous moths and butterflies.

When I couldn't settle, I went down to the kitchen, switched on the heating, made coffee and sat hunched by the radiator wearing an old wool dressing gown. I moved round the house quietly, but the heating system clanked as it started up and Eve, who had been sleeping at Marisands because of the coldness of the cottage, appeared at the kitchen door to join me.

'Looks like we won't be able to leave Littern again today,' she said, pulling back the curtain and peering out at the grey morning.

'Minette will be pleased,' I'd been keeping her at home and knew she would be glad of another day off school – she was missing Yuuka.

After breakfast, I dressed and put on a warm jacket and took Quirk onto the beach. All along the footpath, the trees were encircled by mist; it curled round them like an endless translucent white scarf. As I walked, drops of moisture settled on my skin leaving it cool and clammy. My hair fell into damp strands that clung to my cheeks and forehead, and Quirk looked like a sugar-frosted dog, with silver beads of moisture all over his black coat.

I'd almost reached the end of the footpath when a shape reared up at me out of the gloom. I was so startled I screamed. The shape screamed back and I realised it was Ursula, but fear had knocked the wind out of me.

'Why did you do that?' I demanded, 'Please don't ever do that again!'

'Sorry...' Ursula said, and from her voice I knew she was going to cry if I didn't act quickly.

'All right,' I said catching my breath, 'you can keep an eye on Quirk - I don't want to lose him in the fog.' I picked up a stick to throw for the dog and handed it to her, 'just don't throw it too far.'

Ursula did as I'd asked and a storm of tears seemed to have been averted. I let her play with the dog, though even when he had moved only a few yards away, he disappeared into the haze, and all I could hear was the sound of his paws - a soft padding on the sand - or him splashing about through the indolent waves.

'How did you get to the island in this awful weather?' I asked.

'Uncle Nicholas fetched me last night – for a little while, the sky was clear, full of twinkly stars – but then the fog came again. Uncle Tom and Nina have gone down with flu, so he told Dad I could have breakfast with Rowena and the twins and he'd take me to school if we could get off the island.'

We didn't stay long on the beach before I suggested we went back to the house, it was a miserable day for being outside, though Quirk, sniffing round the rocks didn't seem to mind.

I phoned The Retreat and Nicholas said he'd prefer to leave Ursula with me, if she was content at Marisands. Minette was having breakfast and Eve seemed happy to amuse the children, so I went to the study and tried to get on with Laurence's work.

Some days, I could find little inspiration; I paced round the room, stared out of the window at the blank foggy garden and sat again, thinking of David, who'd worn the carpet threadbare at Hurst Row with his endless walking up and down.

I'd grown to like Peter Kenholme, Laurence's ingenuous detective - the plots Laurence put forward were convoluted and intriguing, so I lectured myself against the temptation to abandon writing for the day and tried once more to resolve the latest Kenholme Mystery.

When I went downstairs for lunch, Ursula was lying on the sofa feeling unwell. Patrick had said recently he wasn't sure if she was genuinely ill or malingering. Seeing her white-faced, with violet rings under her eyes, I wondered if she was suffering those pangs and mood swings that can be a prelude to the onset of a first period. Eve had given her a blanket and a hot water bottle and was trying to reassure her - Minette meanwhile was curled up in an armchair, drawing pictures of the house and the island - half in and half out of the fog - ready to send to Yuuka.

I lit the fire in the sitting room to keep Ursula warm, and we sat together eating - Ursula nibbling at her food and moaning between nibbles that she wanted her dad *now*. But by late afternoon, the fog hadn't dispersed, and I phoned Patrick to say Ursula could stay with us and advised him not to try to get to Marisands.

The murky weather was followed by rain and gales, and though I could drive Minette to school, I had to proceed at a snail's pace - Osford Lane was running with water and I couldn't see the deep cracks and pot holes clearly enough to avoid them. My worries about living on the island and the viability for Minette, who needed to get to Fernley every day, seemed to be justified - conditions were worse than I'd imagined.

A few days later, while working in the kitchen - I'd put on the radio as I started to make supper – listening to warnings of severe gales, blowing in across the West Country overnight. I switched to a music station, thinking it was annoying how the media hyped up even the weather forecast – they seemed to have been threatening storms every day since the end of summer.

The trees enclosing the garden swayed violently, bending low towards the house and whipping back to an upright position between squalls. When I heard a loud cracking noise from the woodlands, I ran across the garden to the studio to check on Eve. I hoped Kos would have the sense to drive his van out of the woods and park it somewhere safe.

Quirk, who had followed me, shook his head as his fur streamed back from his face, showing the shape of his delicate, pointed nose and exposing his eyes to the full force of the rain and bitterly cold wind. I brought plenty of wood to the house and laid out candles, matches and torches where we could find them easily.

Eve had offered to collect Ursula and Minette from school and would stop in Narescombe to stock up with milk and bread and a few tins of food that we could heat on the camping stove, if the power on the island went down.

By the time she returned, it was only half past four but the sky was black. Ursula had half an hour to play with Minette before Eve took her to Lyncross for tea – it was Beatrix's birthday and Patrick would be joining the party later.

Minette and I took Quirk for a quick run on the beach, where the cove was being pounded and pummelled by waves smashing against the rocks with such relentless power that Minette was frightened and I felt darkness - something more than a physical darkness - had descended over Littern.

Back at the house, I checked the garden to ensure there was nothing liable to blow about and cause damage, I put the dustbins in an outhouse, closed the windows and locked the studio door. As I made my last foray from the wood shed with a load of logs, the rain started to fall in sheets, thunder boomed overhead and lightning forked down as if it would split the island in half.

Eve, Minette and I settled down for a lazy evening, we put on a cartoon film and while the electricity stayed on, sat watching the television with mugs of tea and the remnants of a chocolate cake.

Minette dozed by the fire, as the second film we watched was a long, slow evocation of love breaking into the everyday life of a mature woman. Her anguished thoughts and questions seemed in tune with my own struggles and Eve squeezed my arm playfully, when I reached for a tissue and wiped my eyes.

The wind rose and began to shake the windows and beat against the walls of the house until Quirk grew restless, refusing to stop whining. I let him jump up on the sofa with Eve who smoothed his head to quieten him down. With the house shuddering and creaking, we were all beginning to feel on edge. We'd turned up the volume on the television while the storm was overhead, but then suddenly the lights and the TV went off.

'Damn!' Eve said laughing - the film had almost reached its climax.

I lit candles and carried them through to the living room and fed more logs onto the fire.

'What now?' Minette asked sleepily, 'I suppose we could play Ludo or Chinese Chequers.'

I'd brought a few of the children's games from Hurst Row, but they weren't unpacked. I took a candle and went upstairs to find the boxes, which I had pushed out of the way under Minette's bed.

When the telephone rang, Eve jumped up and went to answer.

'That was Nick,' she said, 'Patrick was late getting to Lyncross and nobody had noticed Ursula had gone missing.'

'...In this weather..?' I asked thinking no-one should be outside on such a rough night – especially not a child.

'Patrick's searching with Nick. Rowena and the twins are still at Lyncross - Nick didn't manage to get there for Beatrix's tea, there's a tree down across the road near The Retreat.'

'What can we do?' Minette asked.

I didn't want her to see I was ruffled – I was worried not only for Ursula, but for Patrick and his family out scouring the island.

'We could begin by looking in the garden,' Eve said, 'maybe Quirk heard something outside earlier when he was barking.'

Minette was instructed to stay in the house and not move. I shut Quirk in the sitting room with her for company.

Rain slashed down, soaking us in minutes. Using torches, their faint light eerie, we hunted among the trees and bushes - up in The Robin's

Nest - constantly calling out for Ursula. I went through the sheds and outhouses, which I had opened earlier to stow things away, and Eve checked the studio and Thrift Cottage. When we'd failed to track Ursula down, I searched the house again, in case somehow she had slipped inside while we were out in the garden looking for her.

I returned to the garden, the sky had turned a threatening greeny blue. Everything around us had become no more than a black silhouette against a dark sky – except when the clouds parted and moonlight flashed out like the intermittent beam from a lighthouse.

'I'm going down to the beach,' I told Eve when we met in the shelter of the porch.

'Not on your own, it isn't safe.'

'Can't I go?' Minette said. She had been listening for us and had come to the door - she was afraid in the house alone.

'Go back indoors with Eve.'

Eve, I thought, shouldn't be out in the wet weather or she'd be ill again as she had been the previous winter.

Blinded by rain, I fought against the wind to walk down the narrow path to the cove, the hedges acted as a funnel, increasing the wind's strength and the path was running like a stream with rainwater.

It was useless to call out for Ursula as my voice was carried off across the rain-sodden island. I had hoped I might find her crouched down, sheltering under the hedge as she had done before during the foggy weather, but there was no sign of her.

The tide raced in and there was little more than a narrow ledge of beach, barely enough to stand on, and with the waves breaking so violently, it wasn't safe to risk clambering along the bottom of the cliff, over the rocks. If there was a pause in the rain, sand was whisked up in the air and into my face, stinging my eyes. At the foot of the oratory steps, where the cliff had collapsed, mud and rubble were being washed down into the sea by a fast flowing runnel of water and battering waves had slashed away so hard at the bottom few feet of earth, that the last few steps now hung precariously in the air.

I made my way back to the house and the wind wailed as it forced its way through the trees. I thought of searching the oratory, but when I opened the gate from the garden, I couldn't stand on the cliff top without someone to hold me steady. The cliff seemed to be disintegrating into a stream laden with stones and branches that had fallen from overhanging trees. I turned back - surely Ursula couldn't have tried to get down to the oratory in such perilous conditions.

At Marisands, I checked the phone in case there was a message, the lines hadn't gone down, but there were no news from Lyncross or The Retreat.

'I don't know what to do,' I said to Eve.

'Stay here in case Ursula turns up, someone needs to be with Minette...'

'You're not going out on your own,' I said to her, just as she had warned me.

'It's my turn, we all have to do what we can - you need to get dry...'

Minette burst into tears and while we were arguing, the phone rang. Shivering, trembling with anxiety, I listened while Eve spoke to Beatrix.

'Okay,' Eve said and when she'd replaced the receiver explained, 'Nick's called the police - he's hunting in the area around The Retreat and the marshes as far as the tower. Patrick's heading this way, walking along the lane. He's going to comb the woods up to Marisands – enlist Kos's help. Why don't I go out into the lane and meet him...'

I insisted on going myself - the wind had dropped slightly and I could take Quirk with me, he might pick up the scent, if Ursula was somewhere nearby.

Pieces of broken branches and twigs cracked and crunched underfoot, the lane was covered with them. Just before we had reached Lyncross, Quirk tugged on the lead and I saw Patrick's torch moving towards us in the distance.

'You shouldn't be out here,' he said when he reached me. He told me he'd checked Thrifswell Woods and spoken to Kos, who was walking the edge of the bay from his campsite towards The Retreat.

We made our way down to the causeway, taking one side of the lane each, shining our torches far into the undergrowth, calling out Ursula's name against the screaming force of the wind.

It took almost an hour to reach Osford - Patrick signalled we should go into the shelter on the island side of the causeway and have a few moments respite from the rain and the incessant noise of the wind in the trees.

Water dripped from our clothes and made puddles on the stone floor. Patrick's face was ghostly white in the beam of his torch.

'Ursula doesn't usually escape *after* school,' I said to him, raising my voice to be heard.

Patrick explained how the twins and Rowena had walked to Lyncross for Beatrix's tea-party. Nicholas had stayed at The Retreat, afraid the sea might encroach on the garden putting the house at risk. Ursula had last been seen in the dining room with Rowena, listening to music, but she'd wandered off to the kitchen, saying she was hungry and in the terrible weather no-one had dreamt she would venture outside.

Patrick was exhausted. Wanting to reassure him, I said, 'She'll be all right - think of all the times we've been worried before. Is it worth looking up by the chapel?' I had once discovered Ursula hiding in the bushes there.

The road to Osford Chapel was little more than a track that zigzagged its way to the hilltop, where a graveyard surrounded the chapel building. We battled up the hill, leaning into the land as the wind blasted its way from the west and threatened to sweep us back down onto the lane.

Before we were half way to the top, slipping and sliding in the mud, the rain started to beat down again and we ran the last hundred yards until we reached the chapel porch.

Patrick shone his torch round the porch. In the beam of light we saw a heavy padlock and chain had been used to keep the door firmly closed. I was ready to turn back, but first circled the perimeter and checked if there were any other doors or openings. I found a small window that had been left ajar. An adult would never have got through, but Ursula might, if she reached the sill by climbing onto a nearby tomb.

When I told him, Patrick began frantically fiddling with the padlock, hurling it back against the wooden door - until he found a narrow stone, levered the rusty chain away from its metal ring and forced it until it snapped and fell to the ground.

We burst into the blackness of the chapel. I called Ursula's name, and began to hunt for her under the pews and beneath a pile of old curtains. Inside, there was no movement - not so much as a bird, bat or church mouse.

'I'm going back to the woods,' Patrick said, grimly, 'but I think you should go home.'

'Let's stop at Marisands first and phone round,' I said and we left at once - there was no time to be wasted on discussion.

At Marisands, the lights were weak and flickering, but the electricity had come back on. There was no fresh news, except that so far the Police were unable to get onto the island. Patrick set off alone.

Eve hung my wet clothes in front of the stove, she'd made toast for Minette who was feeling hungry – but I couldn't face anything more than a cup of tea.

'Nick's been to The Retreat again,' Eve told me, 'to check Ursula didn't slip in, but there's no sign. She must have taken cover - let's hope somewhere safe - there are more trees down in the woods.'

Fighting images of Ursula being swept out to sea or crushed under a fallen tree, I gulped down my scalding hot tea and said, 'I'm going out again,' it was hopeless sitting there worrying.

I half-ran – half-walked along the lane to the place where Kos had broken through the wall with his van, hoping to catch up with Patrick, following the track of the van's tyres, now little more than a dissolving stream of mud.

Shining my torch all around – I grew increasingly edgy as there was no response - beyond the glade, in the dripping darkness, the trees looked impenetrable. I yelled "Ursula" at the top of my voice, but there was no answering call. In the centre of the glade, a young birch tree had fallen across the stone circle where Kos made his fire, pieces of litter had blown about and become caught in the bushes. I shivered wondering how Kos could bear to camp in such a cheerless place. Feeling nervous in the woods, I called once more but hearing only the sound of rustling and creaking trees hurried back to the road.

Somehow, I must have missed Patrick and stood paralysed with indecision – which way should I go? I could see lights at Lyncross but didn't want to disturb Edgar and Beatrix. I was tired and knew I couldn't walk as far as The Retreat. I trudged back down the hill to Marisands and again searched the garden, the pathway and the beach before retreating inside.

I heard Patrick's voice in the kitchen, talking to Eve. His face stark white, his eyes dull, sunk within shadowy hollows.

'Ursula has to stop this,' I said.

'I don't think she can stop,' Patrick said, 'not until she's settled what she's looking for and with our adult insensitivity we haven't yet worked out what that is.'

My mind was jumping from one thought to another. 'We didn't look under the altar when we went to the chapel,' I said.

Patrick was on his feet at once.

'We'll take my car,' I said, 'there were no trees down on that part of the road...'

I grabbed the keys from the hook but before I got any further, Eve said, 'Let me go, you need a break.'

Patrick agreed, and I gave in, anxious thoughts tumbling through my head - Eve driving through the debris on the road – the fact I should have warned her not to try to get the car up the hill below the chapel - the tyres were worn and would have no grip on the slippery surface - I imagined them sliding helplessly back down towards the lane.

It was unbearable doing nothing, so I persuaded Minette to stay indoors and mind the phone, while I went out onto the footpath and checked the beach, just once more. Quirk bounded onto the path with his usual enthusiasm, but soon had to slow down as he struggled to keep his footing in the flow of water. I shone my torch all around the cove, but the sea had reached the foot of the cliff and to think of looking there anymore was pointless.

As soon as we were back in the garden, Quirk raced over to the gate that led from the garden to the oratory steps and started whining. My heart pounding, I prayed Ursula might be standing, hanging onto the gate, so I could grab her and haul her to back to the safety of the house.

In the oratory garden, the statues glimmered damply in the moonlight. Beyond the gate, water was pouring down the cliff in deep, narrow streams, cascading down the steps to the sea below.

I tied Quirk's lead to a tree and when I was sure he was secure, opened the lock on the gate. Lightning flashed, the sea thrashed and splintered on the rocks below as the moon broke through the clouds in fragmentary bursts of cold white light.

Struck by a blast of wind, I rocked on my feet and had to catch at the gatepost to keep my balance, but through the squall of rain I was sure I could see a dim light at the oratory window and began to make my way slowly down the steps, clutching at the gorse and the remnants of the handrail to stop being hurled down into the raging sea.

The wind whirled round me and I struggled to keep my footing on the slippery steps, but as I drew nearer, I grew certain the glimmer of light I'd seen was real - not a trick of the moon. Behind me, falling stones made a scrabbling noise too loud to be drowned out by the wind and rain - a violent grating sound - rock grinding against rock.

Easing my way down the last few steps towards the oratory, I reached the plateau where I clung to the strong iron handle of the door. Bracing my body against it, I pushed the door open and stepped inside, my wet shoes squeaking on the stone floor.

Several candles had been lit on the altar.

'I know you're hiding, Ursula.' I tried not to sound angry, recriminations could wait until later. I called again, encouraging her, 'You must be cold and fed-up - we'd all like to go home and get warm.'

There was no answer.

'I'll count to ten,' I said, 'then if you haven't appeared I'll come and get you.'

I counted, taking my time and had reached seven before a damp, bedraggled Ursula crawled out of the cavern-like back of the oratory. She was wearing the fur hat from the dressing up box in the house - it was draped with cobwebs and sat askew on her head. She had put on a white dress over her clothes – she and Minette often enacted the story of St. Thrif.

I didn't move, just watched. In different circumstances I might have been amused by the theatricality of her emergence into the room, where she stood facing me as if centre stage.

'Is this where you've been all the time?' I asked, having to shout above the scream of the wind as it swirled round the building.

Taking her by the shoulders, I pulled her closer.

'I wanted to come to see you,' she said. 'Then I was frightened to go up the steps and the tide had come in, so I couldn't go down either.' She shook her head as she spoke, so that the hat slipped to a rakish angle over her left eye.

I could have put my arms round her, but I held back, distressed with her for causing so much anguish – especially to her father.

'We've all been out looking for you, getting tired, cold and wet. Your uncle phoned the Police.'

'I prayed for the storm to stop, I asked the White Virgin,' she cried.

'You didn't have to risk your neck and everyone else's to get God's attention.'

'That's what Granddad told Dad when he went to Africa.'

'I'm sure he did,' I said. 'We'd better get back to the house and let the others know you're all right.'

Ursula looked anxiously down at the oratory floor, 'Couldn't we stay here until the storm's blown over...'

I was disconcerted - what I was hearing wasn't the fear or panic I felt, but the straight talking of a self-possessed young person.

'Leave the hat and the dress here, or you'll take off in the wind.' I said.

Removing my scarf, I wrapped it round her head, tying it in a firm knot under her chin.

As I forced opened the door, a gust of wind grabbed it, buffeting so hard against the building, it almost knocked me off my feet. I retreated back into the shelter of the oratory and tried to think how to manage things safely. We could stay there until the storm had died down, but given the condition of the cliff, I wasn't sure the building was stable.

I took Ursula's hand as we grappled our way outside, then sent her in front of me up the steps, both of us bowed down - almost bowed in half - crawling up the cliff-side – if she slipped, I hoped I would be strong enough to break her fall.

I'd warned Ursula to focus her attention on Quirk who was barking furiously – I ordered her to hang onto the bushes as hard as she could. When we were almost at the top, where the wind whirled round like a small tornado, I shouted to her to go ahead and watched her, creeping on her hands and knees towards the gate and the sanctuary of the garden.

As soon as she was through the gate and had Quirk's lead in her hand, I signalled that she should run up the garden to Marisands, while I began the last few feet of ascent, my muscles shaking and my teeth chattering with fear and cold.

I imagined getting back to the warmth of the house, Ursula could stay the night. I pictured the relief flooding through Patrick's face, which had been grey with exhaustion and if there had been no other reason to be both incensed with Ursula and to save her - that would have been enough – he could spend the night too.

When we had stepped out onto the plateau, I must not have quite closed the oratory door - hearing it slam shut, I turned and stared down at the churning, convulsive sea and the pinnacle of rocks – and then - hunched against the cliff, no amount of willpower would make my legs or arms move.

The storm now had a violent irritability. I was stiff, aching, deathly tired and terrified as the torrent of water rushing down the cliff, threatened to pitch me off my feet. Nothing was quite real - huddled on the steps, I stayed there unmoving until I heard voices - Patrick and Nicholas were at the gate of the oratory garden. I saw Patrick come through onto the cliff top – I saw him pushed back by the wind, until with Nicholas grasping his arm, he reached out for my hand, 'Come on Iris...' he shouted.

I wanted to shout back, but no words would come, I wanted to signal to Patrick not to risk the steps but I couldn't raise my arms.

Patrick beckoned - he cupped his hands and roared his encouragement, 'Come on. Ursula's safely back at the house...'

Quirk was with them, barking so loudly, I could hear him clearly above the howling wind. And then there was a different sound, earth, stones and water slipping and falling down the bank. I heard Nicholas bellow a warning and saw him jerk Patrick back from the cliff-top, before water, rubble and earth struck me and sent me tumbling down the steps. I threw out my hands trying to grab onto gorse or ferns, but I couldn't stop myself falling.

I heard Patrick's shout, 'God! ...My God.' His voice was barely distinguishable from the raging of the wind.

The words, *I was born here and I'm going to die here* flashed through my mind, as the sound of his fear mingled with the waves booming against the foot of the cliff. But then instead of hurtling down into the sea, I saw a brilliant white light – a woman in a long dress and veil - and my head smashed against the oratory wall.

# Chapter 49

At first, my family feared I would die, but I had fallen into a deep sleep and while I slept, I dreamed the story of my life - the past interjected itself as if a crack in my mind had opened releasing a flood of memories. I heard Juliet whispering "come with me..." but then became confused as we hung on a rock, where water poured down from a hill above, threatening to sweep us over the cliffs and into the bay. I saw the white statues in the oratory garden moving – a sequence of round-bellied women, like the pregnant woman's body represented by the island of Littern.

For weeks, the dream repeated itself like a stuck record and waking involved the slow emergence from a vivid, colourful, world into the neutral blur of a hospital room.

My memory was patchy, like a landscape where paint and varnish had dried, cracked and peeled off to reveal blank grey spaces – a picture of incompleteness. People spoke and their voices came from nowhere. People appeared, vaguely familiar, but even when I could put a name to their face - I had no recollection of how we had arrived in this moment or this place together. Bewildered and disorientated, I spent the greater part of those days in a state of panic.

Almost two months passed before I woke fully, remembering nothing of my rescue from the oratory steps, only learning what had taken place as other people related their stories. Patrick described how difficult it had been for him not only then, with all the drama, but afterwards in the hospital, where he had been unable to do anything except act as an onlooker, though he understood the risks of my treatment and the danger I was in. Distraught, he had called on Margaret for support and she had stayed for several days at the house in Aspen Terrace – encouraging everyone to believe I would get better.

Minette kept saying, 'You missed your birthday, Christmas *and* the New Year!'

Patrick said that forgetting my ordeal was one of the gifts of Morpheus. And life had carried on without me as if I was entirely dispensable. While I was in hospital, Eve had moved back into Marisands to look after her sister. Minette described, eyes shining, how the Christmas tree had stood in the hall and the house had been filled with candles and coloured lights. Eve said Patrick had taken care of them like a loving father.

Later, it would become a family joke that when I first came round and a nurse had offered to call Patrick, I had asked in a way that was anything but friendly, "Call whom?"

Eve read to me from the local newspaper, reports of how much damage had been caused by the storm, along the coast: part of the roof of the North Star pub had blown off and there were trees down in the Market Square in Narescombe and Safford Bridge, many of the roads in the area had been closed. A Bailey bridge had been constructed over the causeway and for days, tractors and trucks had trundled along Osford Lane, clearing away debris, as workmen repaired the banks and walling where the water had breached them - causing stones and thick mud to flow across the road.

At The Retreat, the tide had been so high during that evening the house had become marooned on a small island of garden, surrounded by the wild sea. Soon after my fall, the front wall of the oratory had collapsed and if Ursula hadn't been rescued, she almost certainly would have been washed down the cliffs by the stream of mud and rocks or have been blown into the sea,

My moods changed quickly and without warning, alternating between weepiness and irritability. Terry Hart asked to visit me and I refused to see him. There was no news of Zoë and that depressed me; my low spirits made me a misery to be around, but I couldn't control my emotions any more than I could control the severe headache that troubled me constantly, fracturing my vision, so that the world looked as fragmented as one of Juliet's paintings.

In a while, a nurse had brought me a mirror. I'd gashed my forehead on the oratory wall. The arms of a red scar, like an inverted Y, reached down my temple to below my left eyebrow, obliterating the scar I had from my quarrel with David - it was likely to show, even when my hair grew back. A section of my hair had been shaved off and the rest lopped at shoulder level so that my reflection appeared alien and unfamiliar, that of a stranger. Eve had kept my long braid of hair, but as fast as I could grasp at my old identity, it slithered away until in despair I simply let it go.

Tiredness overwhelmed me. I slept a lot – too much - often waking to find Patrick by my bed watching and waiting. Confused by sleep, I would stretch out my hand to touch his arm, to see if he was real.

I'd wanted to be the one who broke the news that we were expecting a baby, something that had been discovered while I was in hospital. Anxiously, I fixed my gaze on him, knowing I couldn't bear a flicker of doubt or displeasure to cross his face – couldn't bear the thought of hearing the same recriminations from his lips as I had heard from David's...

Patrick was often serious in those days, but a smile had risen to the surface before I had finished speaking, 'How marvellous,' he said.

'You're not shocked?' I asked. '*You knew already..?*' I was suddenly suspicious.

He laughed, '...*Officially*, I didn't know – though there are few secrets in a hospital. I thought I'd see how long it would take you to tell me – it's the best news I've had since you regained consciousness.'

One afternoon when I was resting, he brought an arrangement of white and gold flowers, including hellebores from beside the holy well, and set them down on a cupboard, where I could see them easily from the bed.

'Those are from Ursula - she'd like to talk to you.'

'She's here?'

'In the corridor, with Nina - Ursula and I hope very much this hasn't changed how you feel about our life together.'

'I'm not sure...' I said nervously. At that time the future had no meaning and uncertainty was the answer which seemed to fit every aspect of my life.

'Perhaps you'll know better when you get home to Marisands...' he suggested and I understood my wavering must be painful for him. Patrick was so gentle, so endearing, I loved him for his willingness to overlook the difficult person I had become.

'Eve's told me all you've done,' I said hoping to console him.

'I haven't done much – just tried to maintain a level of normality. What happened woke me up, I thought I'd understood Ursula and her problems, but I'd overlooked her sense of powerlessness. In the face of Honor's leaving and my intractability, she felt completely helpless to influence what happened to her...'

I sympathised, feeling the same helplessness, the same inability to influence what happened to me. I had been asking my doctor each day when I might be allowed to go back to the island - a reward for the hard work needed to regain physical strength - to restore my damaged sense of balance and relearn the ability to walk.

'When can I go home?' I asked, plaintive like a child.

'Soon – you'll be able to go home soon, I promise,' Patrick said. 'You were daring, courageous rescuing Ursula – but now you need patience...'

I found it difficult to feel courageous about actions of which I had no recall and even more difficult to be patient with a body which refused to function normally. His words reminded me of Sister Miriam, who when

I had left school, had made her prognosis for my life – it was to be one of endurance.

When I didn't speak, he told me Ursula would be going to St. Mary's with Minette after half term. She hadn't achieved sufficiently high marks in her exams to stay at St. Safan's and he felt it would be misguided to do as the headmistress had advised and send her away to boarding school.

'Minette will be excited,' I said, though I felt remote from the small, domestic problems which had once commanded so much of my attention.

'I've rearranged things at work, so we can spend more time together – Pa's helping with Ursula's school fees – so I feel less anxious about supporting us all.'

I squeezed his hand. He had already raised the question of marriage again – as he had put it, *while we had his family's attention, in a positive way, wasn't the time ripe for us to make a formal commitment?*

Patrick stood up to fetch Ursula from the corridor.

'Do I look frightening?' I asked suddenly unsure, remembering how Juliet had alarmed me with her hair shorn, dragging me into the sea. The details of my life had begun to return, sometimes seeping back slowly and steadily or often as if the spark from one memory lit another and another until they leapt and crackled through my mind like a series of firecrackers.

'Ursula's been warned,' he said with a smile. 'But I'm afraid for a while each time she looks at you it will remind her of how nearly she caused a tragedy.'

Ursula appeared at the door holding her father's hand, dragging a little behind him. However I felt about what she had done, I'd resolved not to burden her with the kind of guilt I had suffered throughout my life, believing I was the cause of Juliet's death.

'Thank you for the flowers,' I said.

Ursula kissed my cheek, an almost imperceptible touch, like a butterfly landing.

'I want to say sorry,' she whispered, 'sorry, sorry, sorry, sorry...'

Putting my fingers to my lips, I said, 'Sometimes we want to change, but we find we're stuck, afraid of behaving differently.'

Ursula stared at the blue and white bedcover, her fingers plucking the edge where it had frayed.

'None of us can escape who or what we are or the things that have happened to us, that's why I came to Littern – but only when several people had pointed out that I needed to do so if I wanted to feel better about my life.'

Ursula fidgeted, but I didn't doubt she understood. As I'd learned, the moment of knowing and being known can be an uncomfortable one.

'Uncle Nicholas said I'm worse than a bloody nuisance,' Ursula confided and we couldn't help laughing.

'Sometimes your Uncle Nicholas thinks everyone's worse than a bloody nuisance,' I said.

'That just makes you part of the family,' Patrick assured her.

I patted the bed beside me to indicate Ursula should sit down. 'Why did you run away that night?' I asked.

'Aunt Beatrix wouldn't let me phone Dad - I hated her and wanted to make her angry.'

'But you don't hate the rest of us - or do you?'

Ursula shook her head.

'You'll be going to St. Mary's soon?' I asked and her face lit up.

'I can sit with Minette. Miss Grieves said so.'

'That's good,' I said lying back against my pillows.

I was soon exhausted and with tiredness came depression. Patrick sent Ursula out into the corridor to find Nina.

When she'd gone, I said, 'I used to believe that love could heal everything, but sometimes love doesn't seem to be enough - it seems I'm not yet ready for forgiveness...'

'But I know you – you will be, one day soon. When I think of the risk you took on Ursula's and my behalf I'm convinced that even if loving can't provide all the answers – it eases the harshness of the world.'

Patrick stroked my forehead, his hands cool - my mind was ready to drift away from his words, drift back into sleep, but there was something I needed to say, while we were alone.

'...I don't expect anything – not because of the accident - not because I'm pregnant. You spoke of marriage – but I won't hold you to it...'

'You're overtired,' Patrick soothed, 'marriage is more important to me now than before – since the news of our baby, perhaps essential. Do you remember how Pa cherished and cared for my mother, even when she was seriously ill? Why would I behave differently?'

'Because in a matter of weeks, I've aged by about twenty years and I'm soon to add to your many responsibilities...'

Patrick leant down and kissed me. 'You above anyone should have faith in recovery, you've defied death twice, that's more than most of us have the opportunity to do. You've seen the White Virgin – that must be a sure sign you're going to get well...'

I returned his kiss, not ready to admit how I was struggling not only with believing I could regain health but with acceptance of what had happened on the night of my accident. Ursula had unnerved me - as much with her cold self-possession as with her hiding in the oratory, when anyone else would have been terrified.

His family, with the possible exception of Beatrix, had been kind and attentive but I wasn't yet sure if I could handle the complex web of connections and interconnections that comprised both our lives. While in hospital, I'd perhaps had had too much time to think and the possibility that I might discover James Millford to be my father had played repeatedly and disturbingly on my mind.

*

When I was well enough to go home, Patrick drove me through Safford Bridge, so I could admire the swathes of yellow and purple crocuses lining the river banks – the first sign of spring.

Returning to Marisands, I tried to behave as if everything was normal, though I struggled to articulate my thoughts, couldn't walk far or drive and with the loss of independence, developed a persistent fear of being trapped on the island. Being ill for so long, I'd defaulted on the contract for *Minor Lights* and the latest *Kenholme Mystery* and could no longer resort to the distraction of work. It was only thanks to Neil's tactful intervention that Laurence hadn't pressed for a financial penalty, agreeing reluctantly that I'd been the victim of "a unique act of God" and so might possibly work for him again, at some time in the future.

Patrick had thought I might like to live with Minette at Aspen Terrace for a few weeks, but I was determined to prove I could take care of myself and didn't want Eve to be left alone to manage Marisands. She was now impatient to complete the *St. Thrif* paintings.

Eve had described the state of the garden and cliffs after the storm. The seaward side of the oratory had fallen away - the cliff was raw with the exposure of earth, broken stones and shells. Kos and Nicholas had plans to restore it - once the cliff face had been stabilised and reinforced, they would repair the steps, "as if nothing had happened," Kos had said optimistically – but I couldn't imagine I would ever have the nerve to risk that descent towards the jagged rocks and toiling sea again.

I'd received many cards and letters. Silvie sent an almost constant stream of flowers – usually including a spray of irises, which were in season. They were delicate and ephemeral, but Silvie wrote, *you've lived up to your name, which means faith, valour and wisdom - your parents chose well. The three petals of the iris are a symbol of divine protection – a sign of healing.* Only after a while, did she begin to remind me gently of my search for the truth about Juliet and my father, a search which I'd been forced to lay aside.

In the afternoons, I rested in a chair by the window of my childhood bedroom, the texts of my past spread before me as I collected memories from the journals and notebooks, brooded over the secrets, hearsay and lies - the many inventions in which I had hoped to find my mother and in finding her, to discover my own identity.

Reading wasn't easy in those days. And however plausible my sources, all their words and meanings could be reinterpreted endlessly; I tried to pin them down but they remained fickle, mutable.

Once, I swept the whole lot to the floor – *did I want to delve among those fragments - to disturb the past again?* I asked Eve to write to Silvie to explain that I could no longer remain in conversation with the dead – a few days later, she replied that neither could I remain haunted by the mysteries of the living. Without her prompting me to recall the promises I had made to uncover the truth for her and for Flora, I might have let those mysteries go, unable to perceive how my willingness to resume that search would exert a powerful influence on my recovery.

When I'd first returned to the island, it had felt as if a confluence of stars, aligning in a particular configuration had made it impossible to resist the urge to change and grow. Whatever had happened since – I knew a force, either divine or of my own making - had urged me towards a new existence.

With little else to do but observe the natural transformations in the garden, I identified with the plants, birds and insects of Littern and measured my recovery against their progress, as winter became spring. The light failed early each afternoon and as the sun sunk onto the horizon, a watery green luminescence flowed into the room. The cherry trees in the oratory garden showed tight, unfurled blooms, naked against a pale turquoise sky. As night fell, through the half-light of dusk, life in the garden faded from sight and everything, including me, seemed in a state of transition.

I'd begun to adjust to my altered appearance – Minette said with my scar, I looked like a pirate. We welcomed visitors at Marisands, Patrick was insistent, "There are ways of isolating yourself that don't involve living on an island," he warned. Among our visitors was Margaret, who having purchased a cottage in Devon looked forward to her move, in the summer, to Little Reeding, near where I had first met her at The Crown and Anchor.

Eve had told David of my accident and he had asked John to write. With his usual earnestness, John had addressed me as if I was dying, but in his letter confided he'd always felt it was an inverted form of pride which had prevented David from coming to terms with himself or his illness, despite the love and stability I had tried to offer.

His letter was timely – too often I felt in need of assurances that I was of some use, capable of love – I'd found no trace of affection or joy between Juliet and William and their loveless relationship sometimes seemed to condemn me also. Enclosed in one of Juliet's many diaries was a folded paper, it fell out on my lap one day as I was reading. On it was a childish drawing I'd made of my mother, her brown hair spread wide across a green background, the soft blue-green of her dress crudely portrayed. Inside, she had pressed an iris flower – the juice from the petals staining the page. *What did it mean – however touching - did it reveal anything of her true feelings?* Unsure - I had hidden it, replaced it where it had remained out of sight for so many years.

In late February, the weather grew wild and the wind whistling round the house made me uneasy - as if the real business of the last big storm had not yet been concluded.

I was anxious to be more active and determined to begin by walking Quirk and though no-one agreed with me, persisted until Patrick gave in and offered to help me down the footpath to the cove. As we stepped out from the porch, the cold wind sliced through me - I'd lost my resilience to Littern and its brutal weather. It wasn't long since I'd abandoned the walking sticks I'd been using for support and my legs trembled uncontrollably, though Patrick supported me. Crossing the uneven grass, I felt sea-sick as I inched forward, placing one foot slowly and unevenly in front of the other.

When we finally reached the shore, I took a few paces unaided to where I could see the steps to the oratory had been blocked off with boards and netted with razor wire. I stared up at the shell of the stone hut which had broken my fall, saved me from plummeting down onto the rocks or into the sea. The bitter wind stung my eyes, making them water as I clung to Patrick, knowing that if he and Nicholas hadn't found courage and ingenuity that night, I would almost certainly have died.

Icy rain drove through the air and after a few minutes I capitulated and asked to go home. We stopped, so I could rest, when we drew level with the oratory garden, bleak with its wind-blown white blossom and tiny narcissi shuddering beneath the birch trees. The white statues rose from the lawn without definition in the dull grey light - the amorphous images seem to symbolise my condition - one of the figures had collapsed, split and fractured into an unidentifiable heap of white stone. Soon, their meaning would be rendered unintelligible – ending our speculation - the guessing game that had no answers.

*

Patrick drove me to Safford Bridge for an appointment at the hospital, while I saw my doctor and then the midwife, he would shop in town - we'd arranged to meet at Aspen Terrace for lunch.

I let myself into James's house, slipped off my coat and hung it in the hall.

'I hope you're hungry,' Patrick called from the kitchen, 'I've bought steaks...'

'Man food?' I asked teasing him. But he'd gone to a lot of trouble; there were flowers on the dining table, crisp linen napkins, his best plates and cutlery. We had discovered we were having twins and there was some logic in his feeding me as if I was eating for three.

'You look particularly pretty, today,' he told me.

I'd borrowed a baggy blue sweater from Eve, which I was wearing with soft denim jeans that didn't cut in to my developing bump.

Patrick smiled. 'You're looking *very* serious...' he said, 'was everything was all right?'

'Fine – they said everything was fine. I can start driving again – if I take things carefully...' Since my accident, Patrick had been over-protective, anxious I should come to no further harm.

While he began to make sauce for the steaks, he said, 'I don't think I ever told you that I *really* fell in love with you at Pa's party, it was your wonderful blue coat – didn't you have something similar as a child?'

'You have a prodigious memory...' I said.

He was engrossed in his cooking, but glanced up at me. 'Whenever you use long words, I know something's up, I measure the severity by the number of syllables and you have that particular look - are you going to tell me?'

'The midwife was all doom and gloom - the babies are likely to be premature – she said it will take all manner of medical hocus pocus to ensure a safe delivery - I had Tristan and Minette naturally...'

Patrick laughed. 'All manner of medical hocus pocus recently saved your life,' he drew me into his arms. 'Let's enjoy the situation – think together about creating a home in which our love and our children can grow happily - if the twins are both girls, how do you think I'll survive in a house overrun with small females?'

'I keep wondering what our children will be like...' Tristan had been so fragile, he had demanded all my attention and energy through his brief life, yet Minette was solidly of the earth, a survivor from the start. I said, 'Before my accident, Verena asked if Yuuka could live with us...'

'Iris's ark might capsize...'

'It's listing to starboard already,' I said.

He switched off the hob and took my hands between his, 'I'm wondering again if you thought you might like to marry me.'

I smiled at him – so tentative – Patrick believed love to be a reasoned and conscious choice - and what his approach lacked in sentiment, it gained in steadfastness and reliability.

Looking away, I said, 'Until I find out about James, you don't know quite who you're asking to marry you and I don't quite know who's answering – I'm not even sure of my name – Muys – Armsted – Millford..?'

'If you said yes, it would be Piran, wouldn't that simplify everything?'

'Or complicate it still further..?'

'So I have to wait?' he said, 'I'm prepared to - though not necessarily patiently. Shall I speak to James and my father again – tell them we deserve to know the truth and quickly..?'

I leaned across and kissed his cheek, his persistent kindliness had moved our love across the divide from an affair to a relationship which might have the strength to endure.

'What a beautiful, solemn, enigmatic smile...' he said, 'but my God, you're impossible.'

'And you're endlessly tolerant, I suppose - though love shouldn't rest on self sacrifice...'

'Nor on any of the other single facets which make it up,' Patrick replied. 'You may not remember, but when you'd just come round, you asked, "Am I dead?" and the nurse said, "Not according to your vital signs..." Love is the same - if the vital signs are there – however it looks - you learn to accept it must be alive and kicking.'

594

# Chapter 50

Kelda was in hospital again. When Delia rang to tell me the news, she suggested we meet before I visited her - Kelda had been unstable and sometimes violent.

I waited for Delia by the doors of the hospital cafe – a small, bright room near the main entrance.

Delia held out her arms, 'You've faced death – survived and came back to us,' she said kissing my cheek. 'I heard you saw the White Virgin – lucky you - has that provided you with a fresh sense of vision?'

'Perhaps a fresh sense of vision will come later,' I suggested. I'd been feeling I'd like to start work again, if I could only think clearly...

I ordered coffee for us both and we settled into a corner table. 'Tell me about Kelda...' I said.

'She'd been staying at Hintham Ridge in one of the renovated caravans – we were hoping to persuade her she isn't up to living rough any more. She's in her fifties, but she could be seventy or eighty, physically...'

'I can't imagine her accepting it...'

'Kelda argues the greatest kindness would be to leave her alone. I've explained to her, that's something God and the Hintham Ridge Community are reluctant to do and a member of the community has been encouraging her to develop her gifts, she's a fine musician and a poet...

'There's a commonly held stereotype of street people and of drunks, but Kelda isn't mindless or dissolute, if anything, she's a penitent.'

'She's running away from her past and yet has a terrible fascination with it..?'

Delia nodded. 'She wants to speak to you - Terry Hart exerted some influence - told her she might feel better if things were out in the open...'

I hoped he hadn't exerted too much pressure – I'd wanted Kelda to reach the decision to talk to me on her own. The bonds of the school auntie system were known to be strong, it wasn't unusual for them to last a lifetime - and in some ways I felt that relationship with Kelda.

Delia said, 'Kelda's sobered up and clean, but she's also heavily sedated – you need to understand that she may be unable to share her confidences – but also to know that she has done wrong.'

I thought Delia looked worried, as if she didn't trust me to receive Kelda's story without anger or hatred – perhaps Terry Hart had endorsed William's view that I had an unforgiving nature.

We walked together to where Kelda had been admitted to the small psychiatric unit, situated in a converted Edwardian cottage behind the main hospital, overlooking an area of lawns and trees. When we went in, I was relieved Delia had accompanied me, as we passed along the corridors, doors fell locked behind us making me ill at ease.

In the communal sitting room, some people sat with glazed eyes in front of the TV, while others shuffled round in their slippers as if they had nowhere to go, no purpose in their lives. One woman met my gaze with a dark-eyed stare so sinister and calculating, I turned away both frightened and ashamed.

Delia had suggested she should go into Kelda's room first to tell her I had come to visit. I waited outside, expecting an outburst, but I could hear Kelda's voice, slightly slurred but calm.

When she beckoned me to go in, I pulled up the plastic chair by Kelda's bed and Delia promised she would be in the entrance hall by Reception when I'd finished.

I said hello and Kelda closed her eyes. Though she was free of the usual stench of sweat and alcohol, her dark hair was matted and dull against the pillow, a strange, sweet unhealthy odour lingered about her and she seemed unresponsive - hardly aware that I was there.

All the walls in the Unit were painted white, but there were colourful prints hung on the walls, including one of a vase of vivid carmine poppies outside Kelda's door – somehow strangely inappropriate. Her bedspread and curtains were of a checked pattern in the same warm bright colours, though the room was otherwise bare. I opened her bedside locker, but there was no sign of her personal possessions and I hoped her flute, hat and collection of bags were safe somewhere.

Not sure how to begin, I reached out and touched the back of Kelda's hand and felt her rough skin. Her eyes flickered open, startling me.

I said, 'I know other people have acted badly towards you...'

'Do you?' she said - her voice thick with whatever medication was coursing through her veins. Tears dripped down her cheeks and onto the orange bedspread, where they made dark stains the colour of bitter chocolate. 'My head's messed up, they've brought me to a place of zombies and I've become one of them...'

'You'll never be that...' I assured her, searching the lines and hollows of her face to discern what she was feeling – panic or terror? That would have been an accurate description of my own emotions –

horror, compassion, recoil and a sense of failure, all made up the turbulent state in which I found myself.

'It's a lifetime since I made my last confession...' she said in self-mockery, but I was glad of a vestige of her old humour. 'If I don't say sorry, I suppose I'm damned...'

As she began to speak, I lifted her hand from the bedspread and held it between mine. She told me how her family had been rigid and unforgiving, her father especially. Despite her talent for music, in her teens she was awkward and immature and couldn't leave James alone. James as a young man had represented everything her family feared and despised - she had believed she was in love with him, but knew he was in love with my mother.

She was desperately jealous of Juliet and my mother had been jealous of her. Kelda had been afraid James and Juliet would run away together, she'd heard them talking. James was always bragging about the career he'd have in London and she imagined the big city as a place where two lovers could easily disappear.

The day she died, Juliet had gone to Lyncross and spoken to James, perhaps afraid he and Kelda were sleeping together. While they were talking at the front door and Geraldine and I were in the garden, she had told him, in front of Kelda, she was pregnant with his child.

As if in retribution, when Kelda left James at Morrow Bay, she had walked to the tower and informed William in front of his friends that his wife was carrying James's child, but that James didn't want her. In one brief sentence, she had confirmed William's suspicions, humiliated him and exposed Juliet, so that when she turned up not long after, a violent row had ensued.

Shirley and Geraldine had remained – perhaps unwilling witnesses - at the top of the tower while William and Juliet hurled abuse at each other. William had grabbed Juliet's hair and dragged her over to the parapet - shouting that he wanted nothing more to do with her.

Geraldine tried to pull him away, afraid of what he might do - his unrelenting fury had terrified her. Juliet had dropped her basket and when the contents – her sewing - had spilt out – she had wrenched her head down and with her free arm grabbed the scissors and hacked off her plait so that William reeled back, almost losing his balance at the edge of the roof.

Juliet had run away and Kelda had followed her at a distance - when Juliet had cut off her hair - that had frightened Kelda more than anything - more than the intensity of William's anger. As they headed back to the beach – Kelda had shouted after her and Juliet had stopped on the path. Kelda told her she was pregnant too and that James was also the father of her child. Shocked, Juliet had slapped her face and called her a liar and Kelda had waited, letting her go, until she could make her way off the island alone and unseen.

'I've always been a bloody loud-mouth,' she said, 'who do you think spread rumours about you at school...'

'You hold yourself responsible for what happened?'

She looked uncomfortable and didn't reply.

After a while, I asked, 'Was it true? Was James the father of your child?'

'I wish...' Kelda said. 'I thought of saying it was Antony Piran's, that was a great temptation, to destroy "the sainted brother" - but I liked James and liked the idea of him fathering my bastard.'

I understood many things now – but what Kelda couldn't tell me and I couldn't imagine was what my mother had been thinking as she ran from the tower towards the beach believing James had betrayed her in every possible way. The twenty minutes or so of that journey surely held the key to whether Juliet had killed herself and yet her thoughts would always remain unknown.

James had kept out of the situation - and that troubled me too. He must have known what Kelda intended to say at the tower – was he so cowardly that he wouldn't do anything to protect Juliet and his unborn child? He hadn't gone to her, even when she had returned to the beach in a state of distress. It was Antony who had spoken to her and James's inaction, more than anything, must have informed her that there was insufficient between them to believe he would ever fulfil her hopes or dreams.

In the warm stuffiness of the room, Kelda drifted in and out of sleep. She didn't speak again and when a nurse came, she told me it might be hours before she awoke.

Delia was in the small lobby off the entrance hall as she had promised. There was a grubby table covered with crumbs and rings of spilt tea and coffee. Discarded plastic cups overflowed onto the floor from the waste-paper bin.

'Kelda hates herself...' I said. 'I should probably feel angry - but I didn't want to leave her...'

Delia said, 'You'll see her again? I think that's essential for you both. When anger does hit you - and it will – remember Kelda has nobody - you have Patrick and your family.' She laid down the dog-eared copy of The Sun newspaper she had found among the heap of old magazines and papers, 'I think I'll ask someone to track Patrick down – he should take you home.'

While we waited, I felt a new despondency - Kelda's trouble-making had been a disaster for my mother and also for her own life – she was a victim of jealousy, immaturity and the failure of other people to live up to her expectations – not only James - but her parents who had rejected her and her unborn child.

But what was striking me forcefully and repeatedly was that no-one but God could know what had been on Juliet's mind – whatever Silvie or Flora hoped, whatever I had hoped – however much evidence I gathered, we might never uncover the truth behind her drowning.

*

It was raining hard as I turned towards the artists' quarter of Narescombe and parked in a side road off Napier Street, hoping to find Shirley still at Petra - no-one seemed to have heard if she had yet moved on. I passed the rows of terraced cottages, in their vivid shades of green, turquoise, orange and yellow and my arm brushed against their windowsills as I hurried along the narrow pavement.

At Petra Galleries, the window display had been rearranged - the grey stone shapes moved to the periphery and two large seascapes placed centrally in the window, though the shop was unlit and appeared closed. The wide wooden door of the courtyard was open, the path to Shirley's workshop, lined with tubs of acid yellow daffodils. The columnar shapes, like totem poles, which had previously forested the yard had been dismantled and lay on the ground.

I approached the studio door and Shirley appeared, wearing a faded blue overall over her jeans and sweater and a pair of protective glasses, which she had pushed up on her forehead so they rested against the brassy curls of her hair.

'I didn't expect to see you again...'

'May I come in?'

She moved aside and I stepped into the gloomy interior of her workshop. There was a squarish block of stone on the bench, the shape of a face beginning to emerge from one side. Chisels, in different sizes, were set out around it, but the rest of the place had been cleared out and was almost empty.

'What brings you back?' she asked.

'Eve's almost completed Juliet's paintings...'

'*The Stations of the Cross*..?'

'Her original work had been used as a palimpsest – these are paintings of the legend of St. Thrif – they relate closely to the island. I wondered if they might be hung in the Arts Centre – perhaps a small exhibition with other things from Marisands...'

Shirley removed the glasses from her head and laid them on the bench. 'I'm no longer involved with the Arts Centre,' she said. 'You'd have to ask someone else – in fact there's a vacancy on the committee, if you're interested, why don't you get involved..?'

'You're leaving Devon?'

'I wanted to go back to the south of France years ago – I suggested it to William - even if we had to take Geraldine in tow. But as he'd already decamped from Holland, he didn't want to go to another country where he couldn't speak the language and had to come to terms with a different culture – it was a pity.'

'I wanted you tell you that I know what Kelda said at the tower, the day my mother died. You and Geraldine both suggested Juliet was depressed - but I was sure something else had happened - that Kelda's presence had an influence...'

Shirley found a stool for me, dusted it off and we sat at the workbench on opposite sides, facing each other.

'I vowed to William I'd never tell anyone what happened,' she sighed heavily and I was afraid she wouldn't continue, 'but I suppose it doesn't matter now that William and Juliet are both dead.'

She drew in a deep breath, studying the face she was carving out of stone. 'We'd had a bit to drink at lunchtime, things became overheated. William wanted to draw us at the top of the tower with the island as a background – he had in his mind an image of a woman's naked body against the obviously female features of the landscape of Littern. We were talking and laughing and didn't hear Kelda coming up the stairway. Geraldine was posing and I suppose it must have looked as if the three of us had been caught *in flagrante*.

'William wanted to take Kelda out of the tower – though she wanted to be sophisticated, she was only a schoolgirl. Geraldine and I got dressed as William tried to send Kelda away, but she was determined to get out what she'd come to say. She was full of venom - and though what she told him was no more than we'd all suspected, when Juliet turned up, somehow the scene disintegrated - into an emotional hell. To Kelda, it was probably just a malicious game, but she dealt Juliet a fatal blow by saying James wanted nothing more to do with her.'

I waited, scarcely breathing, as Shirley's hand, coarse and reddened with work, caressed the block of stone, the forehead and nose of the face she'd been shaping. She stared into the eyes, still no more than a few vague chiselled lines, as if she might find the words she needed to speak engraved there.

She went on, 'We hadn't really sobered up, we'd been in high spirits and to us there was something ridiculous about the situation – it was bizarre. Afterwards, I kept remembering Golding's *Lord of the Flies* - it was as if we saw Juliet's weakness and became inhuman - taunting her like savage children.

'William's temper was violent, he dragged Juliet to the parapet and they were grappling each other towards the edge - she took out the scissors and I was afraid she meant to stab him.

'When Juliet cut off her hair, it made a stunning impact, but when she ran away, we were relieved. The trouble was James had broken her heart, and we'd used her pain against her – used it to destroy her.'

As she spoke, I recalled William's question, *have you never done something really bad?*

Shirley flinched, 'You must think we were animals. In a sense, we were like animals and Juliet hacked at her hair like a madwoman...

'For us and for William, decadence had become an art form – we relished anarchy, we had uncontrolled appetites for sex and the freedom to indulge our particular tastes without hindrance. What took place at the tower was a piece of theatre, powerful, macabre, an event for which we had an aesthetic appreciation...'

'Is there anything else?' I asked, fighting my contempt as I stood up to leave.

Shirley didn't move. 'What more do you want? We've suffered years of guilt and remorse - after that everything fell apart - William remained at war with himself until the day he died...'

I picked up my bag from the bench and walked out, allowing the studio door to slam behind me. I hurried along Napier Street towards *Quay Eleven*, not with the intention of going in, but needing a landmark, feeling I could walk endlessly, straying into unfamiliar places with no intention of coming back. I felt if I could walk far enough, I might disappear and carry my mother's anguish with me, the anguish which she must have felt as she ran into the sea at Morrow Bay. Whatever Antony Piran had said to her, it must have been too late – insufficient - the only person who could have saved her was James - and he did nothing.

Scarcely aware of my steps, I climbed the western hill of Narescombe, through the narrow back streets until I came in sight of the sea. I stood on the hillside, shivering and staring at the toiling grey water reaching far out to the curve of a distant horizon. My thoughts circled the understanding that William, Geraldine and Shirley had remained close, not because they had been lovers, but because they had been complicit in my mother's suffering and determined no-one should ever know of their cruelty.

Shirley had described their behaviour like that of animals, but animals weren't heartless and bullying – that was left to the worst sort of humans.

When we'd met in London, William had asked for forgiveness and in ignorance of the facts I might easily have agreed to what would have been a gross betrayal of my mother.

Now, Kelda, Geraldine and Shirley offered the same temptation, with their explanations and justifications – the implied, unspoken requests for atonement. I'd found it difficult to forgive Ursula and didn't know any more whether forgiveness would be possible when Juliet's story was finally told.

*

When I arrived home, Quirk was in his usual place under the kitchen table - I leaned down and scratched his head. Eve was observing every move, trying to gauge what was wrong as I gazed at my plate, barely touching the lunch she'd prepared.

'You were ages, I was worried about you,' she said at last.

'I went to see Shirley Fredericks. And now instead of being full of questions, I'm full of anger and hatred – sometimes, I feel so sickened, I'm not sure I'll be able to stay on the island.'

Eve didn't ask what had passed between Shirley and me, but I wanted to tell her how Juliet had been manipulated and bullied, how she had become utterly distraught, overwhelmed by Kelda's gossip, Shirley and Geraldine's taunting, James's betrayals and William's rage. More than enough to lead anyone to take their own life –

'Why don't you speak to Rose?' Eve asked.

'I'm all right.'

But when we'd cleared the kitchen and she'd gone back to the studio, I dialled Rose's number and repeated the story, 'I'll never forgive them for their heartlessness,' I wept. 'Wouldn't their callousness be enough to push someone over the edge?'

'...But to take the lives of their children? A mother's love would make her *save* her child – that's the over-powering instinct – Juliet was pregnant by a man she loved - she loved you – can you imagine yourself deliberately drowning Minette?'

'No...' I said – her question was vile, shocking.

'And apart from her natural instincts, Juliet was brought up on the same moral diet we were fed. Service and Sacrifice – in my mind that precludes a premeditated decision to kill yourself or to murder your children, there must be something else, something still missing.'

I couldn't bear to think she was right, but in another way I hoped to God she was. When I put down the phone, the house was silent and I ran Shirley's story through my mind, trying to break it down, recall anything I might have missed. When the taunting had stopped, had an awful silence occurred, a silence which seemed to contain all Juliet's disappointment and fear? Had that silence terrified her into acting in ways that went against normal human instincts?

Against all the odds, I wanted to hang onto my own instinct that after all that had been said, there was a rationale to Juliet's behaviour, some influence or causative factor I hadn't yet identified. What was certain was that if I lost courage and didn't pursue my quest to the end, I would never know.

I grabbed my coat from the hall. My legs and back aching from my walk in Narescombe, I set out in the car for Osford, freewheeling down the hill towards the causeway. As I crossed the gully, I could see beneath the Bailey bridge what was left of the cracked and pock-marked surface of the road. The encroaching sea was already flowing round the foot of the cliffs in Whitcroft Cove - I had about half an hour before Littern would be cut off from the mainland.

The light at Whitcroft shone across the garden of the cottage - Geraldine must be working in the front room. I hadn't seen her since my accident, though Eve had continued to ensure she had sufficient to eat, taking cooked meals to her door.

Geraldine let me in without comment - she was bundled up in an old tweed coat and wool hat with a chequered scarf. I picked my way through the muddle of books, journals and canvases to where she was painting a picture of the tower – for me now, a symbol of the guilt and remorse of which Shirley had spoken.

She picked up her paintbrush and I took that as my invitation to speak. 'I've seen Shirley again - she told me how you, she and William mistreated Juliet at the tower, taunted her until she ran away...'

'Is that what she said?' Geraldine lit up a cigarette and carried on working.

'You disagree..?' I asked.

'After Kelda had said what she came to say, Juliet began to shout and accuse William. In the face of her affair with James Millford, he said her behaviour was beyond hypocritical - it was insane. She had in the past accused him of madness, something she claimed was demonstrated through the chaotic nature of his art. He told her the white statues in the oratory garden were all the evidence anyone would need to have her locked away.

'Recriminations were bandied back and forth, I hadn't seen William so furious before and Juliet lost all perspective. What was said struck at the core of her personality, her fears about her moral and mental state and her ungovernable affection for James...'

'She'd tried to control her feelings...' I objected.

'William and Juliet were as ill-matched as a couple could be – how could things end, other than badly? No-one was planning for her to die. There was no scheme or plot, though for William it might have provided a convenient solution to their problems...' Her bead-like eyes glimmered, small, narrow and buried in loose folds of skin...'You've been trying to find meaning in Juliet's life, to find the connective tissue to her story? William would have called that pretentious bloody twaddle - people do and say more foolish things than wise – we all end up mired with each other's messes, isn't that the essence of being human?'

'At the end of his life, did William *want* to die?' I asked - unwilling to let her get away with generalised theories, her personal philosophy of negativity and alienation. 'Was his death a gesture of despair?'

'You won't find answers, by trying to force conclusions.'

'Then help me. My mother's life will only make sense if I can find meaning in her death.' It was a dangerous plea to a woman who I disliked and who disliked me. 'William died believing he was morally culpable, didn't he?

Geraldine's turned her eyes fully onto mine, her expression one of both scorn and capitulation. 'William was a risk-taker - he had an appetite for young women. Juliet wasn't the first of his students he'd become involved with – he was bound to meet his match one day - it just happened to be your mother - and fool that he was, he couldn't see it coming.

'When Shirley arrived on Littern, we formed an intimate group which excluded Juliet, but then she had the Pirans and James, she had you. William had never wanted to create a domestic paradise - but whatever he did Juliet troubled him in the most powerful way. From the time of her death he was scarred, as if she had incised an indelible mark on his conscience – he forgot, as did Juliet, that you can't regain your innocence once it's lost, any more than you can regain your virginity. When he knew he was dying, William tried to complete her paintings as he believed she would want. A useless gesture of self-redemption - encouraged by that fool, Terry Hart.'

'Surely he realised he couldn't undo Juliet's death with a *gesture*? Did he expect God - or anyone else - to be placated so easily?'

'Did Juliet expect she could placate God so easily? Don't forget the artful trick she had played on William, backed up by her family...'

I saw Geraldine then as a disappointed, embittered old woman, who couldn't stop defending and protecting the man she loved, she had no interest in justice or reason.

'Why were you faithful to William? He didn't treat you well - you were jealous - you could never kindle the spark of love in him.'

'But I was always there. William was my friend and I was his – we understood the subtleties of companionship. You're Juliet's daughter - you think in terms of good and evil – but William didn't believe life was so simple and neither do I.'

Her words made me ashamed, all too often I forgot Silvie's injunction not to resort to moral judgements, like Alice.

'Are you satisfied now?' Geraldine asked. 'William wasn't just a libertine, he was a man who looked for inspiration but failed to find it. If you could understand that, you might comprehend that *his life* also ended in tragedy.'

The sting of sarcasm was there, but Geraldine had taught me something about love, that her persistence with William through many hurts and betrayals had a bleak kind of beauty. She could hardly be blamed if experience had hardened her when years of loyalty hadn't brought the desire of her heart.

I left the house. It had begun to sleet and the wind drove icy raindrops into my face as I climbed back into the car. The sea lapped the edges of the Bailey bridge as I crossed the gully - as the car crawled along the lane, muddy water from the pot-holes and puddles splashed up against the windows.

At Marisands, Patrick was working in the garden, staking the new fruit trees Kos had planted. Ursula and Minette were running about - supposedly helping - but Quirk had caught their excitement and rushed in circles round the lawn as if infected with spring fever.

Minette and Ursula must have been set the task of scarifying the lawn as they twirled, dancing with the springbok rake, among the whirling flakes of snow. Quirk chased the rake, barking softly and Patrick warned him off with that delicious combination of perfect humour and perfect seriousness I had grown to love.

He called to the girls to put away the garden tools in the outhouse – the snow was falling in thick flakes, resting on their clothes, catching the children's hats and forming a crust on their eyebrows, so they began to look like a pair of miniature yeti.

Patrick tapped on the car window, 'Are you coming in?'

The day had been painful and demanding – the stories I'd heard full of emotion and brutality - I felt the loneliness and emptiness of my search and longed for his company to fill the painful places that Shirley and Geraldine had hollowed out.

Minette fresh faced and full of fun threw a snowball at my shoulder as I walked towards the house. Before I could retaliate, Patrick had thrown one back in my defence and then Ursula threw one at him...

'Geraldine's told you what you wanted to know?' Patrick asked when he came indoors.

'I can't be sure until I've spoken to your father and James - I'm tired of speculating.'

'Then you've probably speculated sufficiently for one day.'

Minette and Ursula came into the hall, dropping their wellingtons on the floor, creating two damp puddles of melting snow.

'Isn't it tea time yet?' Minette said, checking her watch, 'We're all starving hungry.'

After tea, we retired to the sitting room, Patrick in the fireside chair, his legs stretched out towards the hearth. I was glad to put my feet up on the sofa.

Beside me, Minette was embroidering a tiny piece of white cloth – something for the altar in the school chapel - while Ursula read to her, 'Just like the nuns do when they're working and eating...' she said.

Patrick had informed me recently he was growing a little tired of "nun mania", but I knew he was relieved to see Ursula happy.

When it was bedtime for the children, I made hot chocolate, enjoying the air of contentment, the four of us watching as embers burned low in the grate, relishing a peaceful evening together. Patrick read the paper and I fetched him a glass of wine and made a mug of tea for myself.

Once we were alone, I said, 'I wish I understood why my mother painted over *St. Thrif* - can you think of any reason why James would have persuaded her..? Eve's tried to uncover what was underneath, but she says the small amount she's managed to reveal isn't that helpful.'

Patrick folded the paper and laid it aside. 'I'm still concerned that revealing the truth about your mother and the identity of your father won't help much either, just create a lot of bad feeling.'

'I can't abdicate responsibility - that's how I feel.'

'...Because it's how Silvie has made you feel – how she wants you to feel.'

'You think I'm unreasonable?'

'Yes – but I always have faith you'll see sense in the end,' he said with a smile.

I sighed, 'Do you think people who've had faith ever really lose it?'

'You ask such difficult questions, especially at night - but I prefer to think faith endures - once you've believed, everything else is just a different shade of response to that belief – even disbelief...'

Eve's sense that St. Thrif had the ability to inspire had kept alive my hope that Juliet had continued in a relationship of faith, despite her failings and the unhappy things which had comprised her life at the end. Had the concept of Christ's death and resurrection been something she clung to? Why else would she have painted *The Stations*? Surely it didn't matter if her interpretation was unconventional. James seemed to have broken most of the rules of the church he belonged to – yet Delia said he had been the force within Juliet's life which had drawn her to God – or at least to his religion.

Patrick said, 'James is coming to Devon in a week or two – you could talk to him then.'

Weary at the thought of talking to anyone else, I covered my face with my hands, rubbing my eyes with my fingers.

I asked, 'what must Beth think, or James's children? If I persuade him to talk they'll hate me - *he's* going to hate me – perhaps he already hates me for stirring things up - and I don't know how I'm going to feel. If he says he's my father – I'll be angry because he's been no better than William, if he says he's not, I'm stuck with William anyway...'

'Don't cry...' Patrick said, 'there really is no need...'

'I'm not crying...'

'I think you are, Iris,' he said reaching out and taking my hand. 'James might hate you - though it's unlikely. But even if he does, it won't matter, hate is nothing, just one of the uglier faces of love. And if he could be persuaded to tell you the truth freely – without compulsion - mightn't that bring relief, possibly joy?'

# Chapter 51

The snow lasted almost a week. Since my conversation with Geraldine I'd felt a sense of urgency about speaking to Edgar. I wanted to hear what he had to say before seeing James - and understanding my distress, Patrick had insisted his father agree a time when I could visit Lyncross.

Like a fortress, the house stood firm against the icy wind - my great-grandfather, Bernard's, stronghold against the world - his love-nest, a place of protection for Yvette whose constitution had in the end become so sensitive, she had trembled like quaking grass and seemed to have passed on her tremulousness to Flora.

Patrick had offered to come with me to see his father, but I preferred to go alone - I needed to be open, free to allow Edgar's words to act on me – act like saltwater, astringent and cleansing.

The porch smelt of damp stone, moss, spiders, dogs and leather boots. I lifted the rough metal knocker and dropped it hard against the door, grey and weathered, but strong enough to withstand Littern's worst storms.

Inside, on a dreary afternoon, the house seemed shrouded in velvet darkness, the scent of polish ingrained in the oak panelling, which gleamed softly in the dim light.

By the drawing room fire, Edgar sat with his hand to his head, as if wounded, his arms long and thin like a scarecrow's.

Looking up, he said, 'Iris – come here, sit beside me.'

I slipped off my coat and pulled an armchair close to the fire, where he could hear and see me comfortably. Beatrix brought in the tea things with unusual grace and ceremony, as if a sacrament was about to be performed - for the time being, she had laid down her hostility.

'What can I tell you?' Edgar asked.

'...Everything you know about my mother's death...'

Edgar groaned - his long-fingers working against his face, the shape of the gesture familiar from Patrick, who did the same when distressed.

'Your mother's death wasn't caused by a single person, or act or word.'

In the quiet of the room, I could hear my own soft breathing and Edgar's more laboured breaths.

'Is that true?'

Edgar raised his hand - a sign of helplessness, 'Antony spoke to me of what had taken place, not long after your mother died. And I have

608

James's affirmation of his part in the whole disastrous affair - there's little cause now for him or any of us to lie.'

'I haven't been certain – did James love my mother?'

'The story is complex – it's difficult to fit the pieces together – but I believe he did love her – as best as he could at that stage in his life – though his love turned out to be woefully inadequate.'

'When Juliet had an abortion, I wondered, did you help her arrange it...'

'Dear God no,' he said, 'apart from my religious point of view, there was my professional position. Abortion was illegal at that time, if Juliet had asked for my help – which she didn't - I could only have provided support in other ways. Women had so few choices then - when things went wrong, they were forced to resort to subterfuge.'

'But my mother acted against her deeply held beliefs and instincts – was her mind sound?'

'She'd lost her heart, not her mind, Iris. For a while, I think Juliet really believed she could change things by being a good wife to William – but that proved a thankless task. He was proud, possessive, cynical - an insecure, troubled man. His sport, particularly when he realised he had been duped by the Armsteds, was to break down Juliet's fragile armour, aided and abetted by Geraldine Ottley and Shirley Fredericks. To be just, the fault was by no means all on William's side, any more than it was on your mother's.

'When we first moved to the island with the family, Juliet was bored and lonely, she was growing up fast, her father had deserted her and Flora, as you know, has her little ways.

'After Alice joined Bernard in London - Juliet and Antony became friends and through him she befriended James. He opened up a whole new world to her - firstly exploring the island - then later he introduced her to the pleasures of the clandestine, sensual - and to a young girl, I suppose, romantic. James perhaps underestimated his power over her - his charisma – girls seemed to throw themselves at him and it went to his head.'

'You've always protected James...'

'And he has protected himself – you must forgive our pride, the weakness of men. Antony knew what was going on, Juliet was frightened, her conscience was troublesome and he tried to guide her – but he loved her and would never have broken her confidence, not at the time. I needed to shelter Kathleen and my family from scandal. As a family doctor, in a small place like Narescombe, I couldn't afford to have muck sticking to me and I could see how I might become implicated - James was as good as my son - Juliet had been like my daughter.'

Edgar reached out and cradled my hands in his.

'Do you think we can put the past aside? How many times in the course of our lives do we have to do that? Let go of hatred, fear and sometimes of love - we always recoil, believe it will be too much to bear...'

He fell silent and I listened to the clock ticking in the background, not sure how to respond, not sure how I could answer him, honestly. I struggled to make peace with these confused, disappointed and disappointing people – to make peace with myself.

When he went on, he said, 'James was distraught at Juliet's death. If it's any comfort, I don't believe he's forgiven himself yet for what happened to your mother. The precepts of the church prohibited their marriage, though in a sense it didn't matter, marriage doesn't necessarily lead to happiness, only to respectability. James and Juliet were young and inexperienced – you could say if you wanted to be charitable - that their only sin was to fall in love with the right person at the wrong time.'

'For Juliet there must have been a moment when all hope and light were eclipsed by self-doubt and fear...'

'And the darkness was so unbearable she took her own life..?' he asked.

'Yes...'

'Juliet had become depressed, quite unlike the warm, passionate girl we'd loved, when we first met. Antony was devoted, he saw the lost person within, who desperately needed someone to love and cherish her - she missed her father and then James had let her down, terribly. She had told Antony once, she believed it would be better if she was out of everyone's way - she was sensitive - finely tuned. It's difficult to write a prescription for suffering of her type, but when Juliet swam towards you, she intended to pull you to safety – I'm convinced of that now. Then in a trice – she was caught in a rip tide and suddenly, you were both at risk of drowning.' He leant back in the chair. 'Who knows why these things happen, the sudden and inexplicable arrangement of circumstances?'

Edgar was drained by our conversation, re-living so many painful emotions. He released my hands so they lay on my lap and I waited until he was ready to continue.

'I was unjustly angry with you the day your mother died, too ready to believe Beatrix's story. You were a small child and I spoke harshly before I was in possession of the facts. I've been unjust since your return – hardened my heart - an old man who couldn't bear to face the truth about those he loved - can you forgive my vanity, my foolishness..?'

'Perhaps when I know everything – when I know who I am...'

Edgar shook his head. 'Who we are depends on our memories and on what we make of them, how we use them to create a future for ourselves and others. You're like Juliet, though she lacked your strength and constancy. That's a gift, Iris,' and for the first time that afternoon, he smiled. 'You've become an anchor for Patrick and Ursula.'

'I think it's Patrick who has anchored me.'

'Really..?' he asked. 'Patrick may be the best of my sons, but can be bloody exasperating, wouldn't you agree..? I'm hoping he'll make an honest woman of you soon, but sometimes he needs a bomb under him...'

I shook my head, 'It isn't him - it's my fault...'

'Marriage offends your liberal principles?' he asked, eyes twinkling. 'That's understandable, saving each other from our weaknesses takes a great deal of time, sometimes years, but in your case, I shouldn't leave it too long,' he said glancing at my pregnant belly. 'Besides, for Patrick to be foot-loose is rather a waste of a good man. If you tie the knot, I could make reparation to you - become the father I should always have been...'

I didn't move, too tired to think about what might have been, still grappling with the dissonance between what I'd thought I knew, the conclusions I'd reached and what seemed to be the truth. As Edgar had said at the beginning, Juliet's death hadn't been caused by any single person, act or word.

I deliberately hadn't asked if James was my father – I wanted to hear that from James himself. The place I had reached in Juliet's story seemed not so very far from where I had begun – I had little need to go further – except, with James's help, to fit in the final piece - and that could wait.

Edgar had closed his eyes. I waited now, listening to his gentle snores, until Patrick appeared at the drawing room door and I went to him, needing to be held. He fingered the ragged fringe of my hair, he put his hand to my bump and there was a gentle fluttering movement, like a butterfly opening and closing its wings, as his children were moved to meet his touch.

*

I'd been meaning to go to Mopheads to have my hair re-styled for weeks. While I was pregnant, my hair would be easier to manage kept shorter and it had grown enough at the front for me to have a proper fringe cut, which would partially cover the pink scar over my eyebrow.

When I'd finished at the hairdressers I drove to Safford Bridge, leaving my car parked in Aspen Terrace - I would collect it when I came back from

611

Esterlea and my visit to Silvie. When we had parted in the summer, we hadn't been on easy terms. I had discovered though the truth can be liberating, it can also be painful - but Silvie believed that knowing the truth would heal the wounds of the past and I needed her guidance.

Patrick was impatient with my plans – there were times when my pregnancy seemed to draw the last bit of strength from me - but we negotiated until he agreed that provided I didn't drive to Sussex, and promised to contact Margaret in London if I was unwell, angry or unhappy, he would help Eve to take care of the children.

I arrived in Esterlea on a cold, bright March afternoon and having left my luggage at the Guest House where I was staying, walked to Castle Rise. In the garden, the cherry trees were a mass of pale pink blossom. I rang the bell and waited on the front step until a nurse in a wine coloured tunic answered the door.

'You must be Miss Armsted's niece,' she said, 'you're very alike.'

'How is she?' I asked.

'As sharp as ever in her mind, but she's growing weak physically, the doctor says her heart has had enough – every movement seems a strain.'

Silvie's room had been re-arranged - she had recently become bed-ridden and her wheelchair had been removed from its place - but the important things, familiar from my previous visits remained. Silvie's watercolours of Littern, Bernard's painting, *The Wild Irises*, the view through the window of the formal garden, where tulips now stood in ranks within neat box hedging and the fountain soared towards a cloudless sky, fanning out, before tumbling down into the circular stone basin.

Silvie lay deeply asleep, propped against the pillows, her white hair coiled in a neat bun – she was undisturbed by my entering the room. The bookcase with its leather bound volumes on art, history, literature, mythology and religion – looked dusty, untouched. On the dressing table and chest of drawers were figures in faience pottery – something new - perhaps Flora had sent them when she moved to The Maples.

I pulled up the chair beside her bed. Her rosary beads of olive wood and silver were laced round her gnarled fingers. I leant down to kiss her cool cheek and then kissed her hand, but she didn't stir. I stroked her face - she had once been a beautiful woman – the eldest, the adopted sister of Flora and Alice and the loveliest of what she had called *the unholy trinity of Armsted sisters*.

'I came as soon as I could,' I whispered touching the dry transparent skin of her arm, through which every vein seemed visible.

At last, Silvie's eyes flickered open and met mine, eyes that were a misty violet-grey, 'You're not too late, not quite,' she said and in a few moments reached out and rang the bell for tea.

'It's good to see you...'

'Still alive..? Silvie said and laughed - a soft murmuring sound deep in her chest.

A young assistant brought a tray. I poured two cups of tea and placed them on the bedside table.

''We need to talk,' she said.

I lifted her so she could sit upright to drink. As I slipped my arms round her, I felt the bird bones of her ribs, so fragile I was afraid she might break. When she was comfortable, I plumped the pillows, wrapping her thin shoulders with a woollen shawl.

Her gaze, strong and direct, observed my face and swept down over my body, I pulled my cardigan round me, folding my arms across my non-existent waist.

'How are things at home?' she asked.

Tears welled in my eyes - Silvie had asked the very question I wanted to avoid – I was afraid Patrick's patience over my refusal to marry had begun to run out.

She passed me a clean handkerchief from her bedside drawer. 'You can't fool me Iris - I was there only minutes after you were born.'

I smiled – she'd said something similar before.

'Now, is the story complete?' she asked.

'Not quite,' I admitted, 'I'm still not clear what happened between Juliet and William before they were married.'

'Alice happened...' Silvie said. 'I'd always smelt a rat. Bernard asked Alice to take care of things when Juliet's pregnancy became evident – she told Juliet if the father of the child wouldn't marry her, she'd better find someone who would – and she did, William Muys. William wanted Juliet and she kept him wanting, not giving into his desires until it became expedient...'

'She sounds callous – calculating...' I said, disappointed.

'On the contrary, Alice was domineering and Juliet more like Flora than she and most other people realised. You might say she was easily led, easily pressured. She tried to hide her more tender side, afraid she might break, like her mother and grandmother, who Alice had always insisted were weak.'

'I wanted Juliet to be blameless,' I said, 'I wanted that for myself.'

'Our flaws make us human - no one is blameless, not in this world. Somehow we have to forgive them and ourselves - for all the mistakes and injustices- and in the case of the Armsteds - the deliberate concealments...'

'I can see why William wanted nothing to do with me – I was a sore reminder and not just of my mother...'

'We have that in common - being a sore reminder,' Silvie said, 'I was the daughter – the sister – that no-one except my father would own.' She pressed her fingers to her mouth as if her memories were hard to capture, as if they might escape before she could frame them in the right words. 'I was Bernard and Yvette's natural daughter, you know. The adoption was nothing more than an elaborate charade, intended to protect Yvette from gossip or criticism. People used to believe that to have a child who was physically or mentally deficient was a moral judgement by God. Add to that the fact I was conceived out of wedlock, and I was an impossible inconvenience for my parents - so began their machinations – putting me in children's homes in Sussex and on the island – then rescuing me – like you, I was the cause of layers of secrecy.'

'No–one else knew?'

'Juliet never knew – she passed on the story she'd been told and which she believed to be true. Flora and Alice found out when our father died – Alice had contested Bernard's will and the only way to resolve the impasse was for the facts to be revealed. My father had confided in me years before, when he took me to Clave Valley as a child – I'd promised never to tell – inheriting Marisands was a bribe, a sop to keep me quiet. But then as death came in sight, I found I couldn't forgive myself, for agreeing to the falsehood – I needed to share it with someone – to speak the truth – and I chose you.'

'But you loved Bernard – you said so...'

'He was a loving man. Once he'd found a way to draw me into the family he devoted his life to making me content, but he couldn't control what happened after Yvette died and he had moved to Dulwich. Alice was supposed to support Flora and take care of me, but she was bitter, resentful, and quite cruel. Life, I suppose, had been cruel to her – Flora was our mother's favourite and I was my father's – there was no special place for Alice. She would have been better living quietly with Edith somewhere...'

'You've been through so much...'

'And survived because I was loved – my father loved me - I discovered him to be generous, kind-hearted and I adored him – you would have liked him too, if you had known him better. And dear Flora accepted me – whether we were related by blood or not made little difference to her - that was the way in which she cared for everyone and everything.'

Silvie's complexion had become an unhealthy grey, I wondered if I should call the nurse.

'Are you all right?' I asked.

'I've warned you – I'm not for this world much longer.'

'I feel I've barely had a chance to know you...'

'Then we feel the same,' she said.

614

'Juliet described the thought of having William's baby as carrying *an alien presence* – if William was my father – would she have felt that about me?'

Silvie held my hand, 'She might - I can only speak the truth, Iris, isn't that what we've been about? Take the house now, Marisands should be yours - share it with Patrick and your children. And now you know the truth about me, perhaps you can find a way of weaving my story into the story of our family - then take comfort because you've helped to make someone happy.'

I visited Silvie every day until her death. On the last evening, she asked me to leave, not to sit up with her, 'You have new life growing within you,' she said, 'you need to rest not watch an old woman dying.' But though I missed Patrick and the children and it was true I was tired - I couldn't leave her.

Patrick and I spoke on the phone, he told me how people can change when they know death is near – sometimes their most tender feelings fade away. But I wanted to stay until Silvie, whose life had been one of hiddeness, who had been imprisoned in a useless body, had left the world – glad when she departed without fear or protest – whatever turbulence she had had suffered in her life, she passed away peacefully.

We had discussed many things. Silvie described the White Virgin as a messenger from the divine, but also from within us – that part of our selves capable of bringing healing, as water springing from the earth had once healed St. Thrif. We spoke too of forgiveness, Silvie had asked for a priest and before the end, she told me she had forgiven them all – the Armsteds and William, those who had been cruel to her because of her disability - and she too had been forgiven.

She had wanted me to have her possessions, instructed me to go home, not wait to attend her funeral - her ashes would be sent to me at Marisands. When I contacted Margaret, she offered to drive me to Littern - she had plans to decorate her cottage, before moving in – so the arrangement, she said, suited her perfectly.

I paid a brief visit to Flora and Alice at The Maples. Silvie had suggested I should leave them – Flora to her inner world and Alice to her new life with Edith, but my conscience wouldn't allow me to just slip away without seeing them.

Flora was resting – she'd been knitting *angel tops* for the babies – 'they simply flew off her needles,' the assistant said – a powerful, if slightly surreal image. Flora lay resting on her bed, propped against the pillows – surrounded by her pictures and collection of Yvette's faience china. A few favourite books were piled on a table and the lovely clear mirror from her bedroom hung over the dresser. The faint smell of mothballs escaped from the wardrobe, seeping into the room, mixing strangely with her lily of the valley soap and cologne, arranged on her bedside cabinet.

I took her hand and kissed her soft cheek.

'How lovely to see you,' she said.

I helped her drink her coffee, holding the cup to her lips, as she trembled all over, her hands shaking visibly.

She reached out to rest her hand on my bump. 'Was it one of the Piran boys?' she asked.

'I'm afraid so – they're Patrick's babies – I'm having twins,' I reminded her.

'Do you love him, really love him?'

'I think I do...'

'Juliet was so hasty...' she said, but I didn't want to dwell on the subject of my mother and was glad when her thoughts quickly moved on, 'Mrs. Stuart visits us each week,' she said.

'She keeps an eye on you...'

'Which is just as well, I don't see much of Alice, Edith has taken her over,' she confided with a wavering smile.

I explained about Silvie's death. 'Silvie told me the truth about her identity – it was one of the Armsted's best kept secrets.'

'How sad to lose a sister,' Flora said and for a moment, she faltered.

'She'd made peace with her life.'

'She was a good woman.'

When Flora had fallen asleep, I went to speak to the manageress. No place had yet become vacant at Hartbury Court – I wanted to know, was Flora still unsettled? She hadn't mentioned Marisands or Littern during the course of our conversation and I had begun to wonder if it would be wise to move old bones - would she recover?

Soon after, I took the opportunity to leave - gathering the bag of angel tops - dropping a kiss on Flora's forehead. When she woke, my visit would seem to her no more real than a dream.

Alice and Edith were strolling in the gardens, Edith leading Alice by the arm.

Edith and I hadn't met - she seemed embarrassed when I introduced myself and I was sure they must have been talking about me.

While we admired the roses, I broke the news of Silvie's death and Alice's face tightened. 'I hope you didn't believe everything she told you,' she said, 'with Silvie there was always a need to practice discernment.'

# Chapter 52

Silvie hadn't wanted me to mourn. Margaret collected me from Castle Rise and after visiting Tristan's grave we drove straight to Aspen Terrace, where Patrick was waiting.

During our journey, she told me how while I was in hospital, Patrick had found fulfilment in caring for me and for the family, his yearning for Africa, she believed, had gone.

'He loves you as deeply as one human being can love another, don't ever doubt that. Couldn't you put the man out of his misery and agree to get married?'

When we reached Aspen Terrace, Margaret had coffee and then as soon as we'd unloaded the car, she set off for Little Reeding and her cottage. She was a generous, warm person, who had come into my life at the perfect time – in the future I felt she would help to fill the emptiness left by Silvie, with her wisdom and good humour.

We were alone and Patrick took me into his arms, 'I'm sorry about Silvie,' he said, 'I hope you aren't too sad.'

'...And I'm sorry...'

'For what..?'

'Making the pull of the past more important than the needs of the present...'

'Oh that...' he said teasing, 'I've grown quite used to it.'

'Margaret says you don't want to go to Kenya anymore – but if you did...'

'Too late...' he said, 'But I do think we should get back to the island – the girls are anxious to see you.'

We pulled into the drive at Marisands, and I sensed immediately something was different. As usual, Quirk barked joyfully, eager to round up his tribe, but boxes and bags were strewn all over the hall – and when I turned into the kitchen, Zoë was there - chatting to Minette, Ursula and Eve.

I caught my breath in disbelief. Zoë was standing by the kitchen table, dressed in Chinese turquoise and russet, the colours of a kingfisher. The girl I had seen in Safford Bridge, chasing her scarf - the girl I had seen in the bookshop, her hair flowing down her back, a pale gingery blonde mane - had been my daughter after all.

'You might have been here when I arrived home, Iris,' she complained. She wore her coat partly undone. Her hands rested against the radiator as if she needed to get warm, her pale complexion made her wraith-like, wan.

Her eyes travelled over my body taking in my pregnancy. 'What a surprise...' she said sarcastically and seemed let down.

Slowly, she opened her coat and there in a canvas sling was a baby asleep, lying against her breast. 'Snap...' she said. Zoë with her penchant for drama had created a pantomime out of her return.

'Who's this?' I asked.

'Zackary...'

I stepped forward, wanting to give her a hug, to see the baby, but she recoiled and feeling Patrick squeeze my hand as a warning, I pretended to be shrugging off my jacket and hanging it over the back of a chair. I felt if I made one false move, Zoë would take off through the door in a fit of temper.

'Have they made up a room for you..?' I asked.

'I'm staying in the van, I parked in the woods near your friend, Kos,' she said. 'I heard about you falling down a cliff.'

Zoë settled into the corner seat of the table – shifting Zackary in her arms as if she struggled to carry the weight of her child.

'You are all right?' I asked.

She glanced up at me. 'Let's not all start blubbing, I can't cope with it.'

I sat next to her, Minette on my lap, there was something of the cornered animal about Zoë - she wasn't to be rushed or crowded.

'You didn't need to do all that worrying,' she said.

'I didn't know where you'd gone...'

Zoë grinned. 'We went to France for a bit and to Spain and Greece, it was all right in the summer, there was work and we could camp, but then we headed east, I wanted to be on the move and Cameron was moaning all the time. I suppose it's a bit of a shock,' Zoë yawned. 'Cam said I should tell you about the baby. But I thought that would spoil things.'

Minette rested her head against my shoulder. Being at Marisands had grounded her like a tree whose roots went down deep into the earth – I thought, if Zoë would only stay for a while, Littern might do the same for her.

Ursula was standing by Patrick, he smiled at me, irredeemably soft-hearted and I smiled back in a way I hoped told him I was glad he was there, part of my family.

Zoë began to describe her adventures, the difficulties of her travels, but soon Zack's cries could be heard from beneath her coat - he needed changing. Patrick asked Minette and Ursula to help bring in wood for the sitting room fire - even momentous days, it seemed, ended up revolving around mundane things, the need to keep warm and well-fed, to sleep in safety and comfort.

That evening, Eve made a huge bowl of pasta for supper and we ate in the sitting room from bowls on our laps. Zoë fed Zack in front of the fire, but when the baby had fallen asleep - Patrick drove them along the lane and walked with her through the woods to Kos's camp, where she'd parked the van.

'I thought Zoë might stay in the house,' I said when he came back.

'Zoë's tetchy, it might be best to do things her way...'

'The trouble is things have always been done Zoë's way,' Eve said.

'She's okay - she's given her word - she won't take off again unexpectedly - provided we respect her need to work out how she can slip back into the stream. Rule number one - is there are to be no questions...'

I let the subject drop. Patrick was beginning to sound edgy. Managing the family, his hours at the hospital and working for the Hintham Ridge Community amounted to more than a full-time job and he told me, Tom had been lecturing him "like a dose of nasty medicine," about taking life more easily.

Zoë didn't turn up at Marisands in the morning, so after lunch I went out to the van with Eve. The clearing was alight with sunshine filtering through the leaves, the blue of the sea visible through the trees. Zoë had parked her van well away from Kos - the dilapidated vehicle in which she had left Pimlico had taken a battering – its once black roof was crazed and peeling, the green paint faded to an unhealthy bruise-blue.

I knocked tentatively – I'd been knocking nervously on Zoë's door since she was a child. The windows of the van were hung with pieces of madras cloth, so it was impossible to tell if anyone was inside and there was no smoke rising from the chimney, but eventually, Zoë opened the door with the baby cradled in her arms - crying softly - a thin trail of a whimper.

'If it's a bad time...' I began.

'It's okay,' she said and let us in.

The dim orange light from the windows revealed the state of the van. I wondered how she could bear the uncomfortable, cramped conditions, especially now, with a baby. She placed Zack in a wooden cradle. I parted the blanket, gently touching his cheek, his skin was soft and smooth, his pale eyelashes rested against his cheeks, curved like twin moons.

Wearing a black leather jacket, which had once been Cameron's, Zoë's pale red hair flowed out from underneath a brown woollen cap. Crumpled and ungainly in a long cotton skirt, her expression fierce - the warrior woman, Boudicca, came to mind.

'Does David know he's a grandfather?' I asked.

'Why would you want to know?'

I'd broken the rules - no questions. 'I just wondered if you'd seen your dad,' I said backing down.

'I didn't expect you to get into trouble,' she said, indicating my belly. 'When we left London, I thought if much more went wrong in your life, people would start to laugh. Don't you think it's grossly weird – Zack your sort of grandson is going to be older than your kid..? We're like some totally dysfunctional family.'

I smiled at her wry sense of humour, the way she missed the thrust of her own irony.

'Actually, I did go and see Dad,' she said. 'He told me about your accident. You should see their place at Hurst Row. Helen's chucked out Gran's kitsch, and tarted the place up like a miniature palace. Dad daren't sit on the delicate chairs – the coffee machine could perform a surgical operation...'

'David's well and Helen..?'

She shrugged. 'Helen's opening a new shop, and is as spoilt and pretentious as ever. Dad's more paranoid, a total hypochondriac....'

Zoë meant well. Freckle-cheeked, red hair falling askew, her black leather jacket with its greenish tint, as if it was beginning to go off – spoke of her vulnerability and I felt only tenderness towards her. She told me how she'd been earning money, making things for a market stall which sold t-shirts, cotton bags and skirts, she'd hand-sewed from fabric bought in India. She'd come back to England not long after Zack was born.

'You've got plans..?' I said.

Zoë frowned in the fierce way she had. Head hung, gazing at Zack, she said, 'I want to go back to college. Now I've got a child, I can't go bumming around forever.'

'People do, until they're ready to settle down.'

'Maybe I'm ready to see how settling down feels.'

Zoë seemed chilled; she pulled her jacket closely round her. She passed Zack to Eve, where he lay in her arms murmuring, crooning softly. There was a camp cooker in the van so Zoë made tea and we ate ginger cake which Eve had brought from Marisands.

'Why don't you spend the evening with us,' I suggested.

Zoë pulled a face, 'I didn't want to get into the whole family thing.' Then contradicting herself she asked, 'Do I need a formal invitation these days?'

'You know what I meant, Zoë. You and Zack are welcome whenever you like.'

'Let's not argue.' Eve had been quiet and I wondered what she was thinking, if she was comparing her own way of life with her sister's.

If we'd been alone, I would have apologised to Zoë, said how sorry I was if I'd driven her away from London. In the wake of David's departure, I'd been unsympathetic - but I wanted to understand her now.

'Ssshhhh,' Zoë said as Zack whimpered and she lifted her baby from her sister's lap. The movement disturbed him and he began to cry loudly, 'This is where hippy meets maternity,' Zoë said and unbuttoned her tunic to feed him. Smiling down at her baby as he suckled, her face was beautiful, kind-hearted and full of love.

Wrapped in many blankets, Zack looked like fat little sausage with a tuft of red hair peeking out – he had soon fallen asleep and Eve cradled him again, resting her cheek on his forehead, rocking him gently.

'You're so steady, Eve...'

'An illusion,' Eve said and smiled at Zoë. But it seemed now that in any circumstances Eve could be comfortable just being Eve, 'Don't you find it too gloomy here in the woods, like being buried?' she asked.

'I need space to get my head together.'

Studying her as she lounged in a broken armchair, I read Zoë's posture, her tense expression. Zack's frailty would be a barrier to her independence and beneath her bravado, she was afraid for herself and for her child.

'Zack feels really hot,' Eve said.

Zoë laid the baby in his crib and peeled off the top layers of his clothes. 'He was cold in the van last night...'

The baby hardly stirred as Zoë bathed his face. A new life could be ephemeral, as fragile as Tristan's had been, as fragile as the cherry blossom blown from the trees in the oratory garden, where bruised petals lay scattered across the grass.

'Why don't you stay with us at Marisands?' I asked.

Zoë wouldn't look at me. 'I want to stay here...'

'Zack might be ill,' I suggested, 'and so might you...'

For a few moments, there was nothing but silence, but then I saw the fight leave her, she was exhausted and when we'd gathered their things together, Eve drove us home.

Zoë and Zack rested on the sofa. I boiled a cup of water, cooled it and gave it to Zoë to see if the baby would drink – she sat defensively, Zack clutched tightly against her breast and I thought it better to leave them.

The sight of her things in the hall, her leather jacket, her scarf, her sandy shoes dumped in a corner, touched me – there was no need for questions – it was likely that Zoë had no rational explanation for her need to wander, any more than I could account for what had brought me to a place I'd thought I hated and feared.

I sat in the kitchen with Minette and Ursula – Eve had given them soup for tea, when they'd complained of hunger.

'You have a really worried face,' Minette said.

'You're not supposed to worry when you're pregnant,' Ursula added, 'Dad told me - it's very, very bad for you.'

'I must try not to then,' I assured her.

But when Patrick came home from work, I asked him to speak to Zoë. Relieved to find them talking together, I was confident he could persuade her to take the baby to see a doctor.

Mike Acworth decided Zack should spend a few days in Safford Bridge Hospital as he had a chest infection. Patrick lent Zoë a set of keys to the house in Aspen Terrace, so she could choose either to stay at the hospital or take a break if she needed to get away.

When I'd dropped Minette and Ursula off at school the next morning, I went straight into Safford Bridge. The children's ward was bright with stickers of ducks and rabbits decorating the walls. Zoë, standing by Zack's cot, nursing a plastic cup half-full of cold coffee, was as colourful as her surroundings in a shocking-pink wrap that clashed violently with her red hair and the long orange tunic of Indian cotton which she wore with white jeans and a pair of jewelled slippers.

Zack was resting peacefully, but he looked tiny tucked up beneath a thin blanket. His tuft of bright ginger hair stood up at the front of his head above the full round cheeks he had inherited from his father, though his clear grey eyes had a touch of green that came from Zoë.

'Have you eaten?'

Zoë nodded, 'Patrick bought me a sandwich. He says Zack's okay, he just needs special care because he's a baby.'

I leaned over and tickled Zack's plump, pink hand, 'He's a lovely baby.'

'Patrick's been really good,' she said, 'he doesn't make a fuss about everything...' and though she didn't say it, I could hear her unspoken, *like you*.

There was a vending machine in the corridor, so I bought us both a hot drink.

'When you wrote that you were ill, was that when you were pregnant?' I asked.

Zoë sipped her coffee, blowing on it to cool it down, 'We'd almost reached India - Cameron went off because he couldn't stick the heat and was scared about the baby. I nearly lost Zack, I started bleeding and the pain was terrible.'

'How did you manage?'

'I just had to...' Zoë's account of how she had procured help from strangers was graphic and alarming. 'I realised when Zack was born, we all need somebody. I wanted you there when I was having my baby – you, not Sleesy - how pathetic is that?'

'Not pathetic at all...'

While she had been away, she'd become a woman and I loved her for it – she'd changed, but not as I'd feared become someone I didn't know and couldn't relate or talk to.

'I've realised Cam runs away from things even more than I do.'

Her transparency made me smile. Now Zack was all right, there was a newfound serenity about her – I hoped there was a truce between us.

'Patrick's offered to speak to him – he says Cam has to face his responsibilities.'

I agreed.

Zoë grinned. 'He said how much I'd upset and worried everyone – he's made me promise not to devastate you. I reminded him how much you'd upset me, but then I realised that was only half true – it was Dad – Dad and Helen – I couldn't stick what they were doing...'

'Would Cameron come here to see you?'

'I'm going to ask – if he says no, I'll set your boyfriend on him. Don't expect much, we're hardly likely to get married just because of Zack.'

'Cam's out of his depth, perhaps...' I said thoughtfully.

'Like drowning - I was really pissed off with him. We set off heading south with no idea where we were going, no map. I thought the van wouldn't last more than a few weeks and we'd hardly any money. Cam's so open - he made friends and tagged along with other travellers we met, though half the time they stole his stuff. When the van broke down, he wanted to dump it, but I earned money doing street theatre – a living statue all painted white, like Cam used to – and I managed to get the van repaired.'

'You were very brave.'

I'd seen Zoë as unstable and Cameron as stolid, but she had held herself together through a series of crises. The ability to be both volatile and fragile was her essential nature – and with all my being, I felt the desire to be part of her future and for her to be part of mine.

Zoë stretched her arms and legs like a cat putting itself at ease. 'Maybe I'll stick around on the island for a bit, see what happens...' she said.

I hoped the strength of my yearning that she would, was as good as a prayer.

'You'll be very welcome – Cam too, if he wants...'

'God,' she said. 'Pregnancy has softened your brain.'

# Chapter 53

Shirley had written to say she'd persuaded the committee of All Soul's to agree to the showing of the *St. Thrif* panels – but it would be up to Eve and me to make arrangements. The decision marked the end of her involvement with the Arts Centre as she and her shop manager, Diana, were soon moving to Ceret, where as Shirley put it, 'No-one will give a damn who I am or what I do.'

When she had seen Eve's work and Juliet's sketches for the panels, Shirley had suggested Juliet had probably painted over St. Thrif because she'd lost her nerve. Studied carefully, it was clear that the faces in the background were of people she'd known on Littern, placed in roles from Thrif's legend, not entirely flattering to their characters.

A few days earlier, I had driven out to Hintham Ridge to see Kelda, who was living there in the caravans. The renovations were finished and the caravans had been moved into their final position, sheltered by the community building and a row of beech trees growing from a mossy bank – a place less exposed and desolate than the deep valley where Delia had taken me, when I'd first visited her at the community.

In the sunshine, the new leaves on the beech trees were a fresh lime green - there was pussy willow and in the grass, massed clusters of primroses.

The front door of Kelda's van was open and by the step was a bowl full of dirty clothes, soaking in soapsuds.

'What the hell are you doing here?' Kelda said when she saw me, but she sounded reasonably friendly. 'If I could only behave myself, I could move into the main building...' she added, mimicking Delia, a mischievous glint in her eyes.

Kelda lifted the heavy bowl of washing, slopping soapy water on the ground and walked towards a piece of rope strung up as a washing line between two trees. She rinsed the clothes in a barrel of rainwater, wrung them and hung them out to dry, struggling to make clothes and washing line meet, while I stood beside her, holding the broken basket she used for pegs.

'Coming in?' she asked me when she'd finished - her darting look towards Delia suggested she wasn't invited.

Inside the van, there was little light, but the room was free of the unpleasant, rancid smell that had seemed to accompany Kelda everywhere, even in hospital. There was a pot of stew on the stove and a sink full of peeled potatoes.

Kelda was living out of her tattered bags, her black hat hung on a hook on the wall - she had decorated the van with a few postcards – reproductions of Munch and of Adolf Wolfli - *Art Brut* - the art form associated with madness, neo-paganism and nudism. Though the connection was probably accidental, I remembered the accusations of the gossips levelled at my parents, when I'd been at school – *they danced naked in the rain,* gossip which Kelda claimed she had begun.

We sat on the sofa and Kelda wrapped herself in a torn quilt, beside her were two or three books with worn, broken covers and her flute which lay on the rug that she used to cover the seat.

'Are you well now?' I asked.

Kelda scowled, as if the frailty of her body was an insult to her independence. She retained a strange dignity, even now, when the shadows cast across her face accentuated the darkness of her eyes and made her face appear skeletal.

'When you first came here you seemed to think we might be friends...' she laughed dismissively, 'now I suppose you've come to forgive me...' she indicated Delia with a jerk of her head, 'was that her idea?'

'All I wanted to do was to tell you your actions were only part of my mother's story. I thought you deserved to know your sense of responsibility for Juliet's death was in some ways justified, but probably overstated...'

Kelda adopted an expression which was one of complete lack of interest.

'I've had a long talk with Edgar Piran,' I went on, 'he said there is no sense in which blame for Juliet's death could be said to lie with any one person and I believe him – I need to believe him.'

'...Really..?' Kelda asked with contempt in her voice.

'The relationship between my parents, the Pirans and William's friends – between Juliet and James was impossibly complex – you were only seventeen and however sophisticated you believed yourself to be, you walked into a situation you didn't fully understand. You and I have lived out our penance in different ways, but it's time to stop - no more poisonous secrets – no more paralysing guilt...'

Kelda reached out down the side of the sofa and produced a crumpled cigarette and her lighter. 'Maybe I don't want to forgive myself. Isn't it fucking cowardly? I could say when I spoke to William it was okay because "*I was only telling the truth...*"' she spoke in mockery of her own voice, '*I was only young,*' she added for my benefit.

Her lighter must have run out. She stumbled to her feet, found a taper and lit her cigarette from the stove, hand trembling. In the orange glow from the flames I could see her skin was shiny, moist, as if she had a fever, her hennaed hair was limp and clinging to her head.

'There's something wrong?'

'What's that to do with you?' Kelda asked.

But in a few minutes she stubbed out her cigarette and disappeared into the darkness behind a beaded curtain, pulling it across behind her. I heard her as she vomited violently.

I waited until she'd finished clearing up her mess. She reappeared, streaks of kohl running down her cheeks, and sunk back onto the sofa, 'What were we saying?' she asked in a perfect parody of good manners. Her mood had shifted from honest anger to flippancy

'I can't understand why you wouldn't want to be free - something good should come of all this...' I said, echoing Silvie's words.

Kelda laughed. 'What did you have in mind? You're set up...' she said and her eyes rested on the curve of my pregnant belly.

'I could have come full of recriminations...'

Kelda jerked her face away from me and I thought perhaps she would get up to be sick again, she was holding herself stiffly, taking shallow breaths.

'...You were young, you were in a fix - you'd been badly mistreated by James,' I said. But Kelda was hostile to any expression of fellow-feeling, immune to any sympathy from me.

The van had an air of desolation - the other vans appeared empty, Kelda had no neighbours as if she had been abandoned.

'Did you know they rewrote the Ten Commandments here – break any of their rules and you commit the unforgiveable sin?'

'I think everyone here has good intentions...' I said, perhaps stupidly.

'Aren't good intentions the path to hell?' she sneered, 'which is where I'm going for certain - maybe I'll see you there...'

'I brought you this...' I handed her a copy of David's book, *Indigo.* Written at the height of his career and of his depression – it had been hailed as having unusual understanding and insight. 'It's a gift from one poet to another.'

Kelda flicked through the pages without reading.

As I let myself out of the caravan – I could see that the connection I had felt to her, in the end seemed to mean nothing – we remained worlds apart.

Outside, the cool, fresh air was a relief, I breathed in deeply. Delia was waiting across the farmyard, by the door of the community building. I didn't look back at the van, though Kelda shouted after me – if I stayed, it seemed likely Kelda would get into serious trouble. If the rule was, as she'd said, that people could earn a place in the community building, I had a strong feeling Kelda was never going to make the transition.

When Zack had been in hospital, everyone had said it had been a particularly hard winter – there'd been several epidemics of flu and they still lingered on.

'Kelda's ill,' I told Delia, 'she shouldn't be out in the van.'

'She knows the rules.'

'She needs help - isn't that more important than rules?'

'The sort of help Kelda needs requires resources which as a community we can't provide, even if she would agree to it...'

Delia had been kind to me; I didn't want to imply that her judgment had been blinded by the rigidity of the community, or to let her see I had preferred her company when she had been a member of the Sisters of St. Stephen.

'Perhaps one day I'll speak to James about Kelda,' I said, 'he could afford to help.'

Delia looked confused, 'I thought you said James *wasn't* the father of Kelda's baby...'

'But it seems he was my father,' I said, and it was the first time I had spoken those words out aloud.

*

Silvie's ashes arrived at Marisands in a flat green box decorated with gold. Among her things had been Bernard's sketch map of the route to Clave Valley and the notes he had made to his painting of the irises. The map was no longer needed, as Nicholas and his group of conservationists had opened a way through the dense copse that blocked the way, but it had given me the idea of retracing Bernard's walk, timing it exactly, to be a hundred years from the day he had first stumbled across Littern Island.

It was a beautiful morning, and as I walked the lane alone, I tried to notice the things that had attracted Bernard's attention – the wayside flowers – the insects humming – the distant sound of the sea in the background.

With Silvie's ashes, I carried her copy of Messenger's *English Poetry*, given to me as a child, I thought I should find something significant to say and would read Shelley's poem, which included his description of the purple iris flower. To mark the place in the book, I'd used Silvie's little painting of a dragonfly, which had once symbolised for me the hope that it was possible to make a new life.

On the way to the valley, I turned off the lane following the narrow path bordered with the hellebores, towards St. Thrif's Well, where I tied a white lace mantilla of Silvie's to an ash tree. My body had become ungainly, clumsy, but I knelt down and washed my face with water from the spring. Drinking the healing water, I thought how the beginning of Silvie's story had become the beginning of mine – how our stories had become inseparable, entwined through Juliet, who we had both loved.

Silvie had left a letter with the solicitor for me to read after her death – explaining how much the island had meant to her – how she was certain that the place in which I was to scatter her ashes would become of special significance to me too – and not just because it had been Juliet and James's trysting place. She wrote - *The island is where your roots are literally, it's your home – don't allow bad memories to blot out that important truth - the pain of Juliet's life and death should be over now – think of her as a creature of nature - remember how hard it is to take something wild and tame it...*

When I neared Morrow Bay, I took the footpath that led towards the marshes and walked along the gentle slopes at the foot of the Hagdon Hills until I reached the steep knoll of scrubby trees, Clave Copse. The way into the valley hadn't been cut as a clear path, more as a thinning out of the undergrowth, through which it was possible to take a zig-zag route towards the tight fold in the land. Stepping into the valley remained a revelation - dusky blue irises flowed down the hillside, in a broad stream -

Above the river of flowers, I sat on the grass and for the first time wept for Silvie's death. It had taken over a year to unravel the truth about my mother and the process had involved more difficulties and twists and turns than Silvie or I could ever have imagined. I had known Silvie in depth for not much more than that year, though she had set me on a journey which had changed my life for the better.

When I had read Shelley's poem, I lifted the lid of the green box and cast the ashes up into the air. The gentle west wind caught them and skimmed them over the petals of the irises, where they seemed to float, as if on water.

At the end, Silvie and I had talked a great deal about trust and forgiveness - of our own failings as well as those of others – but even now, I found it difficult to cease sifting pieces of information, to stop turning them this way and that – examining them to see of what my past had been made.

The sun was almost at its height and I moved into the shade of the willow tree, the place where Silvie's father had told her the truth about her relationship to the family. I thought of Juliet and her many rambles across the island hunting wild flowers, butterflies and birds, of her coming to this place to be with her lover. I lay back on the warm, soft carpet of grass and closed my eyes.

Then, a shadow falling over my face disturbed me – someone was there.

'You've chosen to sleep in the precise place where your life was conceived...' James said.

I clambered awkwardly to my feet and brushed myself down.

His appearance was distinguished – as I'd imagined – his hair auburn, with a swathe of silver hair at the front that fell across his forehead – I put up my hand to my fringe.

'Sometimes words aren't necessary,' he said, 'we simply need to open our eyes and see what's in front of us.'

'Did Patrick tell you I was here?' I asked angrily. When I met James, I had wanted to be prepared, able to meet him with equanimity.

'It was that gardener of yours – Kos – I called at Marisands to see you. You're looking very lovely – *blooming* – isn't that the word for someone in your condition? I should also tell you how much my children enjoyed the *Seabright Island Adventures* when they were young. Those books were full of clear seas and bright light, rather like today.'

'I'm afraid I misinterpreted our life on Littern,' I said.

I kept looking at him, I couldn't help it. He had the polished, slightly self-important manner and perfect clipped speech of an actor. I wanted to know – *was he genuine?*

'My philosophy has been to put the past firmly behind me – move on...' he said.

'Mine has been to try to understand it...'

'When we were lounging about at Morrow Bay, who would have thought how we'd all end up?' he said.

Given the tragic circumstances the last time he had lounged around at Morrow Bay, his remark seemed insensitive. 'What did you think when you saw me as a child – did it mean nothing?' I demanded. 'Why didn't you acknowledge me in any way?' I felt a hard nut of anger, deep inside.

'To acknowledge you, would have made trouble for your mother – Juliet and I had agreed – it was better if everyone thought William was your father.'

'You felt nothing then?' I asked scornfully.

'I didn't say that, Iris.'

'You betrayed Juliet – when she came back to island, having covered for you with a disastrous marriage – you simply went off and left her – carried on with your own precious life ...'

'The real betrayal was long before then...'

'And continued until her death – it continues for me – you've refused to own me as your child...' I protested.

But then I thought of Silvie – of the long years of her concealment – conscious that her suffering had been far greater than mine, yet she had counselled forgiveness.

James said, 'I can't change the past and even if what you say is true – all I can do is encourage you to believe I would be proud to own you as my daughter now.'

'What about your wife and children?' I asked – but added less bitterly - 'Don't do anything to distress them...'

'I've been honest with Beth – Oliver and Danielle are robust, they've been told the truth and they're anxious we should put things right.'

I was wary – I didn't know what qualities I might find in my father – but I knew something within me needed to change. I wasn't seeking common ground, I was struggling against finding evidence of any further resemblance between us – I didn't want to recognise a gesture or expression as mine – or discover the hint of a shared thought or belief.

I started to make my way down the slope, the grass was sappy and moist, slippery underfoot, and James caught my arm as I almost fell. He kept a grip on my elbow as we traced the path back through the thick clump of trees.

'It's difficult to believe everyone didn't know – the Pirans..?' I said.

'The twins and Beatrix were regarded as children – Antony, Tom and I as adults, distant from the others – you have nothing with which to reproach Patrick, if that's what you mean...'

'Do you reproach yourself? Juliet gave up her career as a dancer, she was pregnant with your child and you didn't support her. She bore your children again and again and you - I assume, ignored all of them. I thought you'd fathered Kelda's child...'

'That I'm afraid was one of Kelda's many fantasies...' he began.

But I interrupted giving him no chance to answer my other accusations, 'Did you seduce Juliet or was she willing? I doubt very much Flora thought it important to inform her of the ways of men...'

James's grip on my arm tightened. He pulled me round roughly, forcing me to face him. 'What do you want me to say? I was callow, ambitious and utterly selfish and my remorse is beyond words, but don't imply that I didn't love your mother...'

I stepped away from him, my limbs trembling. An invisible threshold had been crossed, the foundations of my rage and resentment had been knocked away and in their place I found a well of longing, for which I had no words.

My anger faded and with it my energy. Uncomfortably hot and having missed lunch, I was feeling light headed. James offered his arm - I took it, allowing him to support me, until we came in sight of the tower.

'That night, when I found you at the tower, what were you doing?' I asked remembering the encounter we'd had over thirty years ago.

'Thinking of your mother – I missed her terribly – though I love Beth, Juliet was my soul mate. Sometimes love acts like an irresistible force – it sweeps away all sense and principle, destroys all other loyalties. It's a pity I lost that love because I had no instinct for honour or self-sacrifice.'

We'd almost reached the lane - Morrow Bay and Coyle Sands spread out before us their broad white curves, stark against a vivid blue sea.

'Do you think Juliet killed herself?' I asked.

'She was about to be accepted into the Catholic faith - one of the tenets is that suicide can only result in condemnation...'

'I don't believe that...'

'Nor me. I spoke about the tenets of the church not a personal belief in them – casuistry perhaps – but it allows us to hear the voice of compassion. The only honest answer is that I don't know – I don't think any of us know. William was convinced she had taken her own life, but his inner world was a dark one, controlling, ungenerous and ambivalent towards women. Juliet attracted and repelled him – her opposing moods of movement and stillness fascinated and maddened him.'

I recalled the row in the kitchen at Marisands, when Juliet had been anything but still, hurling a plate across the kitchen at William's head – both must have known the other was playing a double game.

'Patrick said Antony spoke to Juliet on the beach – only minutes before she drowned...'

'He offered to take her away – he would have done anything – and to hell with the consequences.'

'When Juliet cut off her hair, William should have seen she was dangerously unstable – and you – when she came back to the beach, you didn't stir, not until it was too late...'

He seemed wrung out and I thought I saw the real man and his feelings – hoped that the wounded expression on his face told the truth.

'Things had already gone too far - I had no idea how to drag them back – but you're right, I should have tried...'

I stopped to catch my breath as we stood in the shadow of the tower.

'Do you think we can progress beyond blame?' he asked. 'Could you see those of us who remain, as what we are now – not what we were - or what we threatened to become? Don't things become better with time?'

I nodded and repeated what Edgar had said, that no one person or circumstance was to blame.

'Thank you,' he said.

'Will you help Kelda?' I asked meeting his gaze directly.

'If I can...'

'Then speak to Patrick - he'll tell you how.'

'I've brought the car, could I drive you to Marisands, or do you have to replicate Bernard's walk all the way home?'

I managed a smile, 'Bernard was cut off by the tide and spent the night sleeping on the bench in the oratory. I'd prefer a lift and a comfortable bed for the night.'

'I suppose all those daughters of yours are in a sense my grandchildren, it's quite an adjustment. Do you know what you're having this time?'

'Patrick's hoping for one of each.'

'That's typical Patrick - fair minded, even handed,' James said and helped me into the car.

And those were the qualities which gave Patrick his faith in people – in James – who he believed to be capable of change, of becoming a good man.

'Perhaps you'll come to Eve's exhibition? Without Juliet's work – there would be no paintings,' I said.

'I've made plans to come down from London again, as soon as possible.'

'Did you ask Juliet to paint *The Stations*?'

'She wanted to tell the story - the ultimate story of love – she was one of life's lovers.'

I leant back in my seat and closed my eyes – as Zoë had put it so pithily, when she turned up at Marisands – *let's not all start blubbing.* But James's words were sufficient – enough for now – enough to redeem my trust in my mother.

*

Eve had fetched the girls from school in William's car, which stood on the drive looking more battered than ever for its treatment over the last year.

I nibbled at the children's food, as my pregnancy progressed I always seemed to be hungry.

'If Zoë wanted to live here, I've worked out how to fit everyone in...' I said.

Eve laughed. 'Helped by the fact Patrick and I would move out?'

We left the girls at the kitchen table doing their homework and took mugs of tea through into the oratory garden.

'Kos told me about James, he called at the house,' she said.

'It's difficult to resist putting him to the test...'

'And no-one could blame you. I keep thanking God that Patrick's better than Dad, he's come at the right time for Minette and for you - before you both lost all faith in men...'

I smiled at her, Patrick had stepped willingly and easily into the role of father and had been accepted by the girls – but with James and me, it was going to be different – perhaps painful. I needed time – I seemed always to be asking for more time – and knew how fortunate I had been that Patrick had remained steadfastly good-humoured over my procrastination regarding our marriage.

'The weather's changing,' Eve said, and on the horizon, the blue sky was rapidly disappearing beneath threatening black clouds.

Another storm would shake us all out like leaves - blow us together into our corner of the island and then perhaps disperse us again. What was taking place at Marisands was a fragile gathering and whatever my dreams or plans, it was likely there would be partings soon – Zoë might leave with Zack - Eve might persist with her idea of joining the Hintham Ridge Community.

Eve squeezed my hand, 'Patrick's here...'

She left us, making her way across the garden to the studio – her easy, fluid movements suggesting the lightness of her spirit.

Patrick sat beside me and I rested my head on his shoulder, his loving, concerned face brought me close to tears.

'Things went all right with James?'

633

I nodded. 'But when things are uncertain it helps - having someone to hang onto...'

'I met James in the lane - I think he was feeling uncertain too,' he said and I relished the play of light in his eyes.

'Will you cope when the house is *absolutely* full..?' I asked.

'Will you? I can't imagine a love that doesn't encompass other people - lovers belong with each other, not to each other, isn't that what they say?'

Minette appeared at the pergola, 'What are you two up to?' she asked, echoing the question I so often asked her and Ursula.

'Nothing,' I said, just as they would have done.

Ursula's face appeared behind Minette, 'We were wondering,' she said, 'is there a *Seabright Island* story about Clave Valley?'

'I don't believe there is...' I said.

'You could write one and put us in it,' Ursula suggested, 'Minette can be the sensible one, and I'll be the adventurer - Jack and Agnes are really old fashioned.'

'I like them as they are,' Minette said loyally.

'And isn't their quaintness the secret of their charm?' Patrick countered.

We sent the girls back inside, bribing them with the prospect of supper in the sitting room by the fire, followed by a game of their choice.

Patrick took my hand, 'Look at the sky, it's going to be a wonderful night – full of contrast and drama.'

As the wind got up, the black clouds raced high above the canopy of the trees, across a twilight sky in which we could already see a clear moon and a sprinkling of crystal stars. The white trees and flowers looked spectral, shining silver in the flashes of light as the whispering of the trees and the breaking waves in the distance melted into single sound.

We huddled together, wrapped in each other's arms, 'Do you mind that we haven't done all the usual things, dinner, theatre, concerts?'

'Could anything be better than being here?' I asked... 'I wouldn't mind writing more *Seabright Island Adventures...*'

'What would Jack and Agnes do now?' he asked.

'Make a blood pact, lifelong friendship.'

'I hoped we'd already done that...' Patrick said, drawing me closer, 'you know how much I love you?'

I touched my head against his, 'I suppose we're too old for casual relationships.'

'That's right...'

'I know what I would like - and we seem to want the same thing...'

'To be together..?'

'To enjoy a love which is something new, something neither of us has experienced before...'

'Some deeper truth beyond outward show or desire, beyond simple understanding...'

'...Something both ordinary and extraordinary...' I said.

Each day we spent together, my love for him grew – he was a kind man, who spread his kindness generously, a rare sort of selfless kindness. His gentleness and faithfulness while I'd been ill had, more than anything, convinced me of his enduring love.

'What have you in mind?' he asked and smiled at me.

'What your father would call a sort of hole in the corner affair, with hardly any people apart from you, me and a few suitable witnesses...'

'My family will be devastated - they'll blame you for years to come...'

We sat out in the garden until rain began to fall steadily and drove us inside. We had left them for so long - Ursula and Minette hadn't bothered to wait – they'd eaten, tidied their games away and changed for bed.

The living room looked warm and welcoming in the lamp light. The girls had settled on cushions, in front of the hearth. Minette like a little goddess with her perfect posture and rounded figure and Ursula cocooned in a sleeping bag, a fire wraith with the orange of the flames burnishing her pale face. As Quirk lay across her feet, she fed him crusts of cinnamon toast, sharing her supper.

While no-one was paying attention, I slipped upstairs to the study and put David's note – the one that had been with the poem *Laocoon* - into an envelope with a brief letter and addressed it to Hurst Row. For Helen's sake, he needed to remember the way in which his feelings could be genuine, he needed to remember who he was when he was being real, not playing the role of rogue or melancholy poet.

In the bedroom, I took out my braid of hair from the drawer, wrapped it in tissue paper and put it into the small, carved wooden box - William's gift to me when I was nine. The figure of St. Thrif and Juliet's rosary, I would keep out, but my mother's photograph and the newspaper clippings relating to her drowning were no longer necessary I needed no memorial of her death.

I carried the box to the music room and removing the filet of wood that held the wedding chest open, lifted the lid and pushed the box into the cavity where it fitted perfectly. I touched my mother's pink dress, breathed in her scent – one last time - and then allowed the lid of the chest to drop. When I'd replaced the piles of art books, I joined the others in the living room, threw the scrap of wood onto the glowing embers of the fire and watched it burn.

# Chapter 54

With Richard's help, Patrick had arranged for our marriage to take place in the small chapel of an Anglican religious community in Safford Bridge, behind the Priory. Zoë and Zack would remain at Marisands until the wedding, so we could be together as a family. I resisted the many efforts of the Pirans to turn our modest arrangements into a grand occasion, with the promise of a gathering at Marisands afterwards, which would be open to the entire family and all our friends.

Cam had agreed to come to Littern and made his way to the island from Edinburgh, over a few days, on the small motor-bike he had recently acquired. Only as he had approached the tip of Palk's Reach had the dense sea fog begun to blow away and he had turned up at the door, cold and miserable, hugging his jacket tightly round him, his face protected by a purple silk scarf patterned with black skulls.

Zoë had been pushing Zack in his pram in the garden, trying to rock him to sleep. When she saw Cameron, she didn't wave or smile.

'It's great to see you,' Cameron said, when I went out to meet him.

But if his insouciant manner hadn't altered, his appearance was improved by a new firmness and leanness which he'd lacked when I'd last seen him in London.

'How's Zoë?' he asked nervously, glancing over his shoulder. 'Is she doing the whole baby-angst thing?'

'Zoë's feeling a bit sensitive.'

Cameron stood as if frozen to the spot, staring at Zoë as she moved to and fro with Zack's pram. Quirk bounced out through the front door, Minette behind him, but they slowed down, sensing Cameron's uncertain mood.

'Don't you like it here?' Minette asked him.

'The island's great – like a magic world...' Cameron said.

'Go and say hello,' I told him wondering how many magic worlds Cameron was familiar with, 'meet your son.'

Through the kitchen window, I watched briefly as Zoë and Cam spoke in the garden - the diffused apricot sunshine catching the light in her hair - Zack wrapped in a thick blanket, was cradled in her arms.

Eve said, 'It's like a French painting with people planted decoratively here and there to give meaning to the landscape.'

'But I'm not yet sure what the meaning is...'

I waited until, at last, Zoë brought Cam into the kitchen, made coffee and found a packet of almond biscuits in the larder to keep him going until lunchtime. I tried not to get under Eve's feet while she finished the cooking; my bump had grown to such a size, Patrick said I was a liability, especially in confined spaces.

Minette and Ursula stir fried vegetables and I prepared salad and cut bread, while Eve made pancakes. I laid the table, spread the cloth, arranged a few roses in a pottery jug and put them on the window sill.

'Cameron's family are *really* old-fashioned,' Zoë said, her eyes widening as if in disbelief, 'but they're being okay about everything. If I want to go to Edinburgh with Zack, we can sell the van and they'll find us somewhere to live.'

It hadn't crossed my mind that Zoë might go to Scotland permanently and I felt her eyes searching mine.

'Cam and I have to try for Zack's sake, isn't that what you did with Dad?' she asked.

'I want what you want, Zoë,' I said resorting to sophistry.

'My parents would like to see the baby,' Cameron told us. 'My dad said he'll make things right for me at the College – he knows the head of the music department. I'll get a proper job – not busking – until September and then work in my spare time.'

When I'd had a rest, I changed into a dress, put on a dash of scent and combed my hair carefully to hide the pink branches of the scar on my forehead. Then we sat in the living room chatting, Minette and Ursula on the floor, cuddling up to Quirk. Zack sleeping soundly on Cam's shoulder, while Zoë and Eve stretched out on the sofa – feet to feet.

When Patrick arrived home, I poured him a drink and we went to the music room, taking a few quiet moments together.

'When I first came here, I couldn't imagine how I would ever be happy - now I can't imagine why I wanted to run back to London...'

'I never did know why you wanted to run back to London,' he teased. 'And speaking of London, I've had a request from James – could he come to the wedding?'

*

The day of our marriage was arranged for the middle of June and rather than suffering wedding nerves, I felt ridiculous. I would have liked to have worn the cream lace dress in which Flora and then my mother had been married, but I was eight months pregnant, enormous, and elegance was out of the question, as I had developed a distinct waddle.

We had made endless lists - Cam, Zoë and Zack could move into Thrift Cottage, while Eve returned to Marisands, allowing Flora, Verena and Yuuka to stay on the island for a few days. Despite my misgivings, Verena had collected Flora from The Maples, claiming she would take responsibility for the consequences. A place had come vacant at Hartbury Court and Flora, she was convinced, was quite strong enough to move to Fernley.

There seemed to be endless comings and goings, Yuuka kept asking, "Can I stay here forever?" and despite my words to Patrick, I was tempted once more to run away.

Verena had brought me a loose jacket in midnight blue, studded with seed pearls, something to add glamour to my maternity dress and Flora's straw hat – I would wear the lapis earrings she had given me, for my last Christmas in Pimlico.

'When I saw the jacket, I thought of you, she said. 'Anyway, you've fulfilled your ambition, all your chicks are more or less under one roof.'

'For the moment...'

Verena rolled her eyes.

'It's the truth...' I said smiling at her.

Patrick arrived bringing arms-full of foliage from Lyncross, sent by Beatrix, who had been engaged in long and heated conversations with Kos on the subject of flowers for the house, their disputes heightened by interjections from Verena who, however polite, was cast in quite a different mould from Patrick's sister and was determined she should make a contribution.

Eve spent her time in the studio and I retreated there to escape the chaos in the house and garden. The paintings of St. Thrif were to be on display - straight and true as a flame, Eve stood at the easel, checking her work, sunlight catching the tiny filaments of her sweater as if there was a nimbus surrounding her.

Eve's work was precise, accurate but also sensuous, full of organic shapes that curved and twisted like pieces of sandstone, shaped and moulded by the sea.

'I've loved painting St. Thrif,' she said, 'it is probably blasphemous, but she's more interesting than the White Virgin – she's so human.'

Nicholas and Eve had made a video in which the ordinary figures of men and women morphed through a cycle in which they became St. Thrif - the White Virgin - then Jesus – then themselves again.

Eve said, 'I asked Richard about it, he said it's either the perfect expression of incarnation or it might become *The Littern Island Heresy*.'

'Kos is in love with you, still,' I said, he'd been tireless setting up her work in the studio as she would like it – he had promised to help set up the exhibition in Narescombe and in Safford Bridge, where it was now planned the paintings should be shown in the Priory.

Eve shrugged. 'Sometimes, I envy Zoë, having a baby to love and care for, but I want to enjoy my freedom - for a bit longer.'

I'd thought it strange how Zoë with her wild, ginger-marmalade hair, passionate and impulsive, inclined to noisiness and fuss was ready to try to settle down, while Eve calmer and more reflective appeared reluctant to take the risk of relationship. With quiet determination, she could lay love down – as if she didn't need to be lit by another, she was lit from inside.

Eve began tidying the studio, though it was perfectly tidy already.

'Will you and Patrick stay on the island now?'

I hesitated, 'I've been digging around in the past all these months, stirring up unhappiness – can sadness cling to a place..?'

'What about the good times, the times that created *Seabright Island* and the good times now, aren't they as real? Nobody could doubt that you and Patrick are Agnes and Jack.'

I laughed and didn't deny it, 'But you can't expect me to behave like Agnes.'

'With her "unquenchable spirit"..?' Eve said. 'Can't your passion for this place lie in undoing the harm done to you and to your mother? Patrick's mellow and comforting – just what you need...'

Eve was ready to lock up and return to the house, 'I'd like to stay here for a while,' I said.

The intricate, mysterious paintings of St. Thrif intrigued me - their truth would continue to unfold and to inspire. I had once hoped for a simple revelation, a miracle of insight, but comprehension might take years – perhaps a lifetime. Though the legend was a spiritual story, it was full of earthiness and humanity – Eve's figures of shepherds and woodsmen, their wives and children were delightfully real - she had painted a companion for Thrif, a black dog that bore a remarkable likeness to Quirk. And Thrif seemed not just a legendary figure, but a woman before her time, self-determining and intent on following her calling – her creativity expressed through the garden she had made.

I considered what had been Juliet's essential qualities as an artist and a woman. Transience - changeability like the moon – strangely coupled with a single-minded and faithful search for meaning. And there had

639

been honour in her love, a deeper current running beneath her disappointment, outrage and frustration – she had understood the paradoxical nature of feelings and however painfully, had in the end accepted and expressed their complexity in her work.

God, I believed, had begun to shape me to become a fitting companion for Patrick as I hoped my experiences of *being my mother* had prepared me for a compassionate understanding of her story. I'd come to the island needing to discover who I was *apart from Juliet* and had made peace with her, by seeing her accurately and objectively, not only by loving her.

Ursula, when we had first met, had talked of finding people in their things - and I had, thanks to Eve - found the image of Juliet in her work - while I had discovered myself in Patrick's love – that extraordinary yet ordinary love of which we had recently spoken.

Silvie's version of St. Thrif's legend was to be displayed with the paintings –something of hers woven into our story - made visible – it was a good way of expressing her sense of belonging to the island - lush, burgeoning, wild and unpredictable -

I locked up the studio. Ahead of me were the tender spears and shoots of leaves that would grow into the summer flowers in the new Mary Garden. The glass of the studio windows gleamed - Kos kept them spotless for Eve. This summer, would he disappear again or had the pattern been broken by the death of his student?

I thought how the lover whose love is not returned is depicted as a fool – love without satisfaction a matter for derision - was that how it had been for Geraldine and her lifetime of desiring my father?

When I entered the house, I could hear Cameron playing his guitar upstairs and Patrick the piano in the music room. Eve was in the kitchen, and through the open door of the living room I could see Zoë, Ursula, Yuuka and Minette who had formed a circle round Zack, asleep in his crib.

I crept into the music room and sat next to Patrick on the stool, by the end of the following day, his tribe would have become mine and mine his – another paradox - the island's families irrevocably joined, if not undivided.

*

The marriage ceremony was simple, dignified and quiet, just as we had wished. We left the chapel and I heard the sound of a flute playing and turned, looking into the doorways and shadowy places of the town square, until I saw Kelda, my dark angel, hiding there.

Marisands teemed with people – the garden had altered from the place it had been in my childhood. With the Mary Garden complete - a gift for our marriage from Kos - the final effect was informal, less structured and somehow right for our family.

'A little disorder allows love to breathe and grow...' Kos said.

'A saying from the old country..?'

'Another saying of Kos...'

I saw how his eyes followed Eve's figure, her hair gold against the navy blue of her knitted top as she carried a tray of drinks, agile and confident, among our guests.

Flora sat by the pool in a cane chair, protected by a colourful array of cushions and a huge sunshade. I wondered what memories must play through her mind – her quaint origins, as if her life was part of a fiction – the sprinkling of artists and literati – the blindness and foolishness of middle-class liberalism.

'Juliet was highly strung,' she said, her gaze resting on the tiny cairns of alabaster that remained on the lawn, the last remnants of the white statues.

'Wasn't that the source of her intuition?' I asked. Flora herself was an example of sensitivity, self-sacrifice and self-effacement - qualities without which it was impossible to be an artist.

Flora smiled her wavering smile as if glad I had understood.

'I was sorry Alice couldn't be here,' I said.

'Alice never liked weddings.'

Rose joined us in the oratory garden - she had been studying the photographs of Juliet's white statues on display in the studio, showing their steady decline over the years. Eve now maintained that they were almost certainly related to St. Thrif's legend -

'They're like frozen emotions that have melted and broken apart,' Rose said.

And I smiled, thinking Shirley had been right – the figures were whatever you wanted them to be.

'Coming to the island, I can see why you've become as you are,' she said, 'I suppose we're all dyed by the tincture of where we've come from.'

When Neil joined us, we discussed the idea of more *Seabright Island Adventures,* he was willing to promote them, convinced that with the right treatment, they would sell. 'Perhaps you could ask Laurence to write an endorsement,' he said wickedly.

'Would that be fact or fiction?'

Neil laughed. 'That's understandably waspish. I don't think Laurence has quite made up his mind about you and your provenance, he talks about you as if you were a work of art.'

'Hardly that at the moment...' I said caressing my bump.

'You and everything here looks very well,' he said.

'I'm overwhelmed.'

'I noticed you were hiding – I know you, Iris...'

'I'm wondering if I'll ever work again,' I said.

'Why not..? You've been under Laurence's domination for far too long – it's time to find your own voice – do as you suggest, write about the island.'

Neil's son, Simon, Yuuka, Minette and Ursula ran up to us, 'We wanted to show Simon the pond again – we're looking for frogs...' Yuuka said - her cheeks flushed pink with excitement.

'Don't fall in,' I warned, recalling David's wedding, 'this time, I have no intention of rescuing anyone.'

'No-one will fall in,' Ursula promised earnestly, she had begun to adopt the role of responsible older sister and I was growing to trust her.

There were to be no speeches, we had wanted a relaxed summer party, but there was a cake to cut and as I was growing tired from standing, I took Flora's arm; we supported each other as we walked towards the house.

'The image of this place has never left my mind,' Flora said. 'We can never lose those things and those people we have loved and treasured most.'

Patrick, handsome in a dark suit, was waiting for me, where the long table had been set out on the lawn, draped in a white damask cloth. Beatrix had drunk too much champagne and had become morose, she said, 'I envy you – all I ever had in my armoury was my mind...'

She was interrupted as her brothers shouted down Nicholas, who insisted on saying a few words – assurance of Patrick's love, assurance that his brother's infuriating habits were no reflection on the family - and that I'd have their sympathy in the trials of living with him.

When the ritual of slicing the cake was over, Nina approached me.

'Your husband says I'm to take you inside and encourage you to rest,' she said.

We went together into the music room, where I settled in an armchair, grateful to slip off my shoes and sit down.

Nina talked about her life with Tom and the fact they had been unable to have children. But our conversation was curtailed as James had come to find me and before I could protest, Nina had tactfully disappeared.

James took her place in the easy chair, clasping a parcel in his hand.

'You and Patrick must continue to have the use of the house in Safford Bridge. And I have more of your mother's work in London – you must come and see - but I thought the drawings of you as an infant, from Aspen Terrace, might make a suitable wedding present.'

I lay the drawings out across the lid of the wooden chest, 'I didn't recognise myself,' I told him and laughed.

'Whatever you think – I didn't forget you – I'd wondered often if our paths would ever cross and what would we make of each other.'

'Patrick tells me you're a good man and I trust his judgement.'

'That's more than I deserve - more than I hoped for...'

'Your family are delightful,' I said, Beth and Danielle I knew had decorated the chapel, Oliver had helped Kos in setting up the party in the garden.

'What else can we do?' James asked.

I didn't need to think, the answer seemed to come from nowhere, 'I'd like Juliet's headstone engraved - *She was one of life's lovers...* your words.'

And I hoped if that was true of Juliet, perhaps, one day, it might also be true of me.

*

A honeymoon had seemed inappropriate. But as the Bailey bridge would be underwater at the point of high tide, our guests would be forced to leave Littern in the late afternoon and the family would leave soon after - for a few hours, the island was to be entirely our own.

Verena, Flora and Yuuka were staying at the Seamark in Safford Bridge that night - Verena would return Flora to The Maples the following day. Before she left, I asked if she would drive me to Morrow Bay, it would only take a few minutes and I was sure no-one would miss me.

The tide was flowing in, but we could still make our way across the sand and round to the foot of the quay. I threw a few white roses from my bouquet into the waves for Juliet and watched as they were tossed about on the clear water.

'How fragile and heroic...' Verena said. 'I hate to admit it, but you were courageous coming here.'

'I'd be very afraid if I had to re-establish my life again,' I admitted. I linked my arm through hers. 'I'm shocked each time I see my face in the mirror,' I ran my fingers over the Y shaped contours of the scar on my face.

'Your hair's growing back,' she said, 'and we're all hoping your hideous plait has gone forever.'

I couldn't help smiling at her bluntness - we were friends again, bantering, at ease. Things with Dieter hadn't worked out but I hoped that with Yuuka to care for, Verena might undergo an emotional awakening – one that brought her contentment.

She told me then that David's latest work – a chapbook of new poems - had received a round of blisteringly bad reviews attacking his reputation – she'd heard he was drinking again.

'That's London for you,' she said, 'it can be heartless.' She hesitated, 'now you and Patrick are married, you won't exclude me from your life, will you?'

I shook my head, 'Of course not...'

'You've found a decent man – how unexciting and yet how desirable that is as one grows older. For the first time in fifty years, I've discovered that I'm really rather afraid...'

'Don't be,' I said. 'When I decided to come here, Flora reminded me of the advice she had given me as a child - the things you believe will overwhelm you are nothing but tricks of the mind.'

When we returned to the house, Beatrix and Nicholas had cleared the debris of food, glasses and crockery and Kos had tidied the garden. They were ready to leave Littern for the night, taking Edgar, the children, Quirk and the Piran's three dogs with them.

Ursula found Patrick and gave him a bear-hug and I was glad to see him taking comfort in his daughter, glad to see that he had rediscovered his tenderness where Ursula was concerned.

Zoë told me she'd, 'had enough of the whole bosom of the family thing,' and advised me to 'stay chilled', it was the only way to cope with pregnancy.

Minette reminded me they would be coming back first thing tomorrow.

Taking her aside, I thanked Eve for all she had done - her work had been enjoyed by many people. 'You used your skill and your sensitivity to make something satisfying of Juliet's ideas.'

'St. Thrif inspired me – she followed her calling.'

'But her calling may not be yours...' I said. 'Please, don't do anything hasty.' I meant like joining the Hintham Ridge Community.

Eve kissed my cheek, 'You gave so much to make Dad happy – but he couldn't be happy, perhaps I'm like that. I see how things are with you and Patrick and I'm not sure I could love anyone in that way - not now, not ever.'

At last everyone had gone. I imagined them leaving the island, still scarred by last autumn's storm - the ravaged woods by the lane - the old trees that had fallen down and been sawn into mountainous piles of logs by the side of the road.

It could be cool in the evenings and Kos had lit the sitting room fire, a stream of smoke spiralled up into the sky from the chimneys of Marisands, scenting the air with the pungent aroma of burning wood.

'Such peace,' Patrick said.

We had gone to sit in the oratory garden, in our favourite place by the honeysuckle. The evening was dry, bright and warm - the late cherry trees were swathed with pure white blooms.

The water in the pool was perfectly clear, reflecting the flowers and remnants of the white statues on its still surface. I had begun to think of the fragments as pieces which could be designed into some form of memorial for Juliet - Eve had thought of a collage of white stones.

Beneath the cherry trees, white irises, like butterflies, swirled across the dark earth in a series of curves - everything was intensified, including my feelings which ebbed and flowed like waves on the surface of the sea with their continuous rise and fall.

'We were both afraid we would never love again, but here we are,' I said.

'And on difficult days, when we might feel otherwise – the love of two people can hold the world steady...'

'I'd like to cling to those words for the rest of my life,' I said and took his hand.

'People were full of praise for Eve's paintings...'

'I was afraid I might feel defensive about Juliet – compelled to argue for her spiritual integrity. But belief doesn't have to be explicit, does it? Juliet's faith in natural patterns revealed an awareness of the sacredness of life.'

Patrick kissed my fingers. 'What a chaotic stream of thoughts fill your head.'

'I didn't like the idea she'd lost faith in goodness or in the truth that life should always have meaning.'

'If she had, I think for Juliet it would only have been momentary – a state of mind or an emotional reaction that had, temporarily, got the better of her.'

'Delia told me that all Terry Hart had wanted to say was that I shouldn't judge William harshly, not until I'd heard his story. Richard's sworn he won't ever ask you to go to Africa again...'

'Really..? He suggested to me we might go together - he thought if you saw the work in action you might change your mind...'

I groaned.

'...But I told him, *no* – and I meant no forever. Sometimes the shadow of a thing is more frightening than the thing itself - but now you know there is no shadow.'

The atmosphere of peace and quietness descended again, as he leaned over to kiss me. Against a turquoise sky, the cherry trees were a froth of exuberant white blossoms. I had looked forward to this night in which we would be held in the safety and warmth of Marisands and of each other.

Patrick said, 'If the house and garden are to become a sanctuary, they have to hold all our grief, worries and joys – all the pain and the ecstasy. I've grown to enjoy our nomadic existence, half in the real world and half in the world of fantasy - it reminds me of you.'

Since Silvie's death, I'd begun to understand how William and Juliet in their subversive way had become an integral part of the history of Littern – perhaps we and our children would too, and with that thought came a sense of responsibility. Silvie had left me money, as well as the house, with which I could contribute to the development and protection of the island – renovating St. Thrif's Well – rebuilding the oratory - repaying some of my father's debts to ensure the causeway and the road were kept sound.

'The outside world will inevitably intrude,' Patrick said as if reading my mind.

'I think it's intruding already.' A wave of pain had swept through me. I stood up and rubbed my back.

Watching me, Patrick combed his hair with his fingers. 'For heaven's sake, Iris, you can't go into labour, now. We won't be able to leave the island for hours.'

'You could time my contractions...' I offered, thinking he would be less worried and cross if he had something useful to do.

'We should have had the party at Aspen Terrace.'

'I wanted it at home – our home.'

We went indoors, where I had imagined a romantic evening, listening to music, relaxing by the fire Kos had lit for us - a night of passion being out of the question. Now I wanted nothing more than to lie down – to contain my fears, my memories of Tristan – to control the powerful force taking over my body, until we could get to Safford Bridge and the security of the hospital.

All evening, the white cherry blossom fizzed and frothed in the westerly wind – blithe, ephemeral, cool, soft and translucent – a blackbird sang - light hung suspended by an invisible force at the very tips of leaves. Warmed by low evening sunlight the branches were tossed in the sea-breeze, but the blossom didn't fly away or fall to the ground, it clung to the source of life, jostled, uncertain, waving, shuddering, trembling and then settling again, against a twilight sky.

As my pains increased and became more frequent, the imprint of the bright trees became fixed in my mind, visible on my closed eyes, like an after-image. The mystery of a half glimpsed world filled my imagination, until I could have recalled those gently moving branches, as clearly as I might recall a loved one in their absence.

The pains came and went and in the brief, quiescent phases, I thought how the people who enter our lives, and the circumstances that come our way, are sometimes fleeting, sometimes enduring - how each has its value, whether it floats on the surface of our existence or enters to the very heart.

All those who made up my life were me and I was them, indivisible, just as poets and mystics have claimed to have union with the rhythmic whisper of the sea and its roar, with the trees, grass and sand.

I thought of the alabaster statues, as rough and pitted as the surface of the moon, now broken into pieces of dust. They would endure another year of rain and sun and then perhaps disappear - it wasn't our place to say when the work of a creation was done.

Soft as a breath, Patrick was there beside me. I felt his steadiness, his warmth, though he didn't speak or touch me. He knew I had gone to an unreachable place, Flora's world, Juliet's world, poised between the temporal and the spiritual - only to be brought down to earth by searing pain and the breaking of my waters.

For me, he had become all earthly comfort. His grace and intelligence had authority, yet he was a sensitive lover, a gentle man, playful, caring and honourable. His spirit, held in perfect balance, fulfilled the peace of the island. His silence conveyed all I needed to know – we had no need of words – we could share the silence – share fear and wonder.

The miracle that was the gift of new life would soon appear, in the form of our son, Aidan, and daughter, Lucy – fire and light – each entering the world with a strong cry - disturbing the night.

A month later, we walked with our family, from Lyncross to Thrifswell Woods where we tied white muslin to the trees in the clearing and the two children were blessed by Richard with spring water from the well - water at its most healing and efficacious - on the feast day of St. Thrif.

# Acknowledgments

Particular thanks are due to:

Denise Hill, my friend, writing companion and long-term support

Jonathan Lockett, for his insight and skills in producing the concept for the cover

E. Ann McIntyre, fellow writer, for much needed technical advice and help

Rebecca Emin for her guidance, wisdom and technical support

Jacqui Flint, Graham Howell and Jenny Jackson for reading an early version of the book

And many others who have offered encouragement in the long writing process:

Keith and Lynn Emslie, Barry Jackson, Sue Maines, Richard Murphy, Therese & Nigel Spencer, Christine Watt and Kate Wilkinson

# About the Author

**S.J. Richfield** gained a degree in English Literature in the 1970's before post-graduate training and working in London for a religious book publishing company.

After several years, she moved to the West Country where she took a diploma in Counselling, studied poetry and worked as a private tutor in English and Study Skills.

She now lives in Devon with her family and draws inspiration for her spirituality and writing from the local landscape, especially the sea.

For more information, visit her website at www.thewildirises.com

Email: thewildirises@hotmail.co.uk